Ardath

Ardath

The Story of a Dead Self

Marie Corelli

MINT EDITIONS

Ardath: The Story of a Dead Self was first published in 1889.

This edition published by Mint Editions 2021.

ISBN 9781513281551 | E-ISBN 9781513286570

Published by Mint Editions®

 MINT
EDITIONS

minteditionbooks.com

Publishing Director: Jennifer Newens
Design & Production: Rachel Lopez Metzger
Project Manager: Micaela Clark
Typesetting: Westchester Publishing Services

Contents

PART I
SAINT AND SCEPTIC

"What merest whim
Seems all this poor endeavor after Fame
To one who keeps within his steadfast aim
A love immortal, an Immortal too!
Look not so 'wildered, for these things are true
And never can be borne of atomics
That buzz about our slumbers like brain-flies
Leaving us fancy-sick. No, I am sure
My restless spirit never could endure
To brood so long upon one luxury.
Unless it did, though fearfully, espy
A Hope Beyond The Shadow Of A Dream!"

—Keats

I

The Monastery

Deep in the heart of the Caucasus mountains a wild storm was gathering. Drear shadows drooped and thickened above the Pass of Dariel,—that terrific gorge which like a mere thread seems to hang between the toppling frost-bound heights above and the black abysmal depths below,—clouds, fringed ominously with lurid green and white, drifted heavily yet swiftly across the jagged peaks where, looming largely out of the mist, the snow-capped crest of Mount Kazbek rose coldly white against the darkness of the threatening sky. Night was approaching, though away to the west a road gash of crimson, a seeming wound in the breast of heaven, showed where the sun had set an hour since. Now and again the rising wind moaned sobbingly through the tall and spectral pines that, with knotted roots fast clenched in the reluctant earth, clung tenaciously to their stony vantageground; and mingling with its wailing murmur, there came a distant hoarse roaring as of tumbling torrents, while at far-off intervals could be heard the sweeping thud of an avalanche slipping from point to point on its disastrous downward way. Through the wreathing vapors the steep, bare sides of the near mountains were pallidly visible, their icy pinnacles, like uplifted daggers, piercing with sharp glitter the density of the low-hanging haze, from which large drops of moisture began presently to ooze rather than fall. Gradually the wind increased, and soon with sudden fierce gusts shook the pine-trees into shuddering anxiety,—the red slit in the sky closed, and a gleam of forked lightning leaped athwart the driving darkness. An appalling crash of thunder followed almost instantaneously, its deep boom vibrating in sullenly grand echoes on all sides of the Pass, and then—with a swirling, hissing rush of rain—the unbound hurricane burst forth alive and furious. On, on! splitting huge boughs and flinging them aside like straws, swelling the rivers into riotous floods that swept hither and thither, carrying with them masses of rock and stone and tons of loosened snow—on, on! with pitiless force and destructive haste, the tempest rolled, thundered, and shrieked its way through Dariel. As the night darkened and the clamor of the conflicting elements grew more sustained and violent, a sudden sweet sound floated softly through the turbulent air—the slow, measured tolling of a bell. To and fro, to and fro, the silvery chime swung with mild distinctness—it was the vesper-bell ringing in the Monastery of Lars far up among the crags crowning the ravine. There the wind roared and blustered its loudest; it whirled round and round the quaint castellated building, battering the gates and moving their heavy iron hinges to a most dolorous groaning; it flung rattling hailstones at the narrow windows, and raged and howled at every corner and through every crevice; while snaky twists of lightning played threateningly over the tall iron Cross that surmounted the roof, as though bent on striking it down and splitting open the firm old walls it guarded. All was war and tumult without:—but within, a tranquil peace prevailed, enhanced by the grave murmur of organ music; men's voices mingling together in mellow unison chanted the Magnificat, and the uplifted steady harmony of the grand old anthem rose triumphantly above the noise of the storm. The monks who inhabited this mountain eyrie, once a fortress, now a religious refuge, were assembled in their little chapel—a sort of grotto roughly hewn out of the natural rock. Fifteen in number, they stood in rows of three abreast, their white woollen robes touching the ground, their white cowls thrown back, and their dark faces and flashing eyes turned devoutly toward the altar whereon blazed in strange and solitary brilliancy a Cross of Fire. At the first glance it was easy to see that they were a peculiar Community devoted to some peculiar form of worship, for their costume was totally different in character and detail from any such as are worn by the various religious fraternities of the Greek, Roman, or Armenian faith, and one especial feature of their outward appearance served as a distinctly marked sign of their severance from all known monastic orders—this was the absence of the disfiguring tonsure. They were all fine-looking men seemingly in the prime of life, and they intoned the Magnificat not drowsily or droningly, but with a rich tunefulness and warmth of utterance that stirred to a faint surprise and contempt the jaded spirit of one reluctant listener present among them. This was a stranger who had arrived that evening at the monastery, and who intended remaining there for the night—a man of distinguished and somewhat haughty bearing, with a dark, sorrowful, poetic face, chiefly remarkable for its mingled expression of dreamy ardor and cold scorn, an expression such as the unknown sculptor of Hadrian's era caught and fixed in the marble of his ivy-crowned Bacchus-Antinous, whose half-sweet, half-cruel smile suggests a perpetual doubt of all things and all men. He was clad in the rough-and-ready garb of the travelling Englishman, and his athletic figure in its plain-cut modern attire looked curiously out of place in that mysterious grotto which, with its rocky walls and flaming symbol of salvation, seem suited only to the picturesque prophet-like forms of the white-gowned brethren whom he now surveyed, as he stood behind their ranks, with a gleam of something like mockery in his proud, weary eyes.

"What sort of fellows are these?" he mused—"fools or knaves? They must be one or the other,—else they would not thus chant praises to a Deity of whose existence there is, and can be, no proof. It is either sheer ignorance or hypocrisy,—or both combined. I can pardon ignorance, but not hypocrisy; for however dreary the results of Truth, yet Truth alone prevails; its killing bolt destroys the illusive beauty of the Universe, but what then? Is it not better so than that the Universe should continue to seem beautiful only through the medium of a lie?"

His straight brows drew together in a puzzled, frowning line as he asked himself this question, and he moved restlessly. He was becoming impatient; the chanting of the monks grew monotonous to his ears; the lighted cross on the altar dazzled him with its glare. Moreover he disliked all forms of religious service, though as a lover of classic lore it is probable he would have witnessed a celebration in honor of Apollo or Diana with the liveliest interest. But the very name of Christianity was obnoxious to him. Like Shelley, he considered that creed a vulgar and barbarous superstition. Like Shelley, he inquired, "If God has spoken, why is the world not convinced?" He began to wish he had never set foot inside this abode of what he deemed a pretended sanctity, although as a matter of fact he had a special purpose of his own in visiting the place-a purpose so utterly at variance with the professed tenets of his present life and character that the mere thought of it secretly irritated him, even while he was determined to accomplish it. As yet he had only made acquaintance with two of the monks, courteous, good-humored personages, who had received him on his arrival with the customary hospitality which it was the rule of the monastery to afford to all belated wayfarers journeying across the perilous Pass of Dariel. They had asked him no questions as to his name or nation, they had simply seen in him a stranger overtaken by the storm and in need of shelter, and had entertained him accordingly. They had conducted him to the refectory, where a well-piled log fire was cheerfully blazing, and there had set before him an excellent supper, flavored with equally excellent wine. He had, however, scarcely begun to converse with them when the vesper-bell had rung, and, obedient to its summons, they had hurried away, leaving him to enjoy his repast in solitude. When he had finished it, he had sat for a while dreamily listening to the solemn strains of the organ, which penetrated to every part of the building, and then moved by a vague curiosity to see how many men there were dwelling thus together in this lonely retreat, perched like an eagle's nest among the frozen heights of Caucasus, he had managed to find his way, guided by the sound of the music, through various long corridors and narrow twisting passages, into the cavernous grot where he now stood, feeling infinitely bored and listlessly dissatisfied. His primary object in entering the chapel had been to get a good full view of the monks, and of their faces especially,—but at present this was impossible, as from the position he was obliged to occupy behind them their backs alone were visible.

"And who knows," he thought moodily, "how long they will go on intoning their dreary Latin doggerel? Priestcraft and Sham! There's no escape from it anywhere, not even in the wilds of Caucasus! I wonder if the man I seek is really here, or whether after all I have been misled? There are so many contradictory stories told about him that one doesn't know what to believe. It seems incredible that he should be a monk; it is such an altogether foolish ending to an intellectual career. For whatever may be the form of faith professed by this particular fraternity, the absurdity of the whole system of religion remains the same. Religion's day is done; the very sense of worship is a mere coward instinct—a relic of barbarism which is being gradually eradicated from our natures by the progress of civilization. The world knows by this time that creation is an empty jest; we are all beginning to understand its bathos! And if we must grant that there is some mischievous supreme Farceur who, safely shrouded in invisibility, continues to perpetrate so poor and purposeless a joke for his own amusement and our torture, we need not, for that matter, admire his wit or flatter his ingenuity! For life is nothing but vexation and suffering; are we dogs that we should lick the hand that crushes us?"

At that moment, the chanting suddenly ceased. The organ went on, as though musically meditating to itself in minor cords, through which soft upper notes, like touches of light on a dark landscape, flickered ripplingly,—one monk separated himself from the clustered group, and stepping slowly up to the altar, confronted the rest of his brethren. The fiery Cross shone radiantly behind him, its beams seeming to gather in a lustrous halo round his tall, majestic figure,—his countenance, fully illumined and clearly visible, was one never to be forgotten for the striking force, sweetness, and dignity expressed in its every feature. The veriest scoffer that ever made mock of fine beliefs and fair virtues must have been momentarily awed and silenced in the presence of such a man as this,—a man upon whom the grace of a perfect life seemed to have fallen like a royal robe, investing even his outward appearance with spiritual authority and grandeur. At sight of him, the stranger's indifferent air rapidly changed to one of eager interest,—leaning forward, he regarded him intently with a look of mingled astonishment and unwilling admiration,—the monk meanwhile extended his hands as though in blessing and spoke aloud, his Latin words echoing through the rocky temple with the measured utterance of poetical rhythm. Translated they ran thus:

"Glory to God, the Most High, the Supreme and Eternal!"

And with one harmonious murmur of accord the brethren responded:

"GLORY FOR EVER AND EVER! AMEN!"
"Glory to God, the Ruler of Spirits and Master of Angels!"
"GLORY FOR EVER AND EVER! AMEN!"
"Glory to God who in love never wearies of loving!"
"GLORY FOR EVER AND EVER! AMEN!"
"Glory to God in the Name of His Christ our Redeemer!"
"GLORY FOR EVER AND EVER! AMEN!"
"Glory to God for the joys of the Past, the Present and Future!"
"GLORY FOR EVER AND EVER! AMEN!"
"Glory to God for the Power of Will and the working of Wisdom!"
"GLORY FOR EVER AND EVER! AMEN!"
"Glory to God for the briefness of life, the gladness of death, and the promised Immortal Hereafter!"
"GLORY FOR EVER AND EVER! AMEN!"

Then came a pause, during which the thunder outside added a tumultuous Gloria of its own to those already recited,—the organ music died away into silence, and the monk now turning so that he faced the altar, sank reverently on his knees. All present followed his example, with the exception of the stranger, who, as if in deliberate defiance, drew himself resolutely up to his full height, and, folding his arms, gazed at the scene before him with a perfectly unmoved demeanor,—he expected to hear some long prayer, but none came. There was an absolute stillness, unbroken save by the rattle of the rain-drops against the high oriel window, and the whistling rush of the wind. And as he looked, the fiery Cross began to grow dim and pale,—little by little, its scintillating lustre decreased, till at last it disappeared altogether, leaving no trace of its former brilliancy but a small bright flame that gradually took the shape of a seven-pointed Star which sparkled through the gloom like a suspended ruby. The chapel was left almost in complete darkness—he could scarcely discern even the white figures of the kneeling worshippers,—a haunting sense of the Supernatural seemed to permeate that deep hush and dense shadow,—and notwithstanding his habitual tendency to despise all religious ceremonies, there was something novel and strange about this one which exercised a peculiar influence upon his imagination. A sudden odd fancy possessed him that there were others present besides himself and the brethren,—but who these "others" were, he could not determine. It was an altogether uncanny, uncomfortable impression—yet it was very strong upon him—and he breathed a sigh of intense relief when he heard the soft melody of the organ once more, and saw the oaken doors of the grotto swing wide open to admit a flood of cheerful light from the outer passage. The vespers were over,—the monks rose and paced forth two by two, not with bent heads and downcast eyes as though affecting an abased humility, but with the free and stately bearing of kings returning from some high conquest. Drawing a little further back into his retired corner, he watched them pass, and was forced to admit to himself that he had seldom or never seen finer types of splendid, healthful, and vigorous manhood at its best and brightest. As noble specimens of the human race alone they were well worth looking at,—they might have been warriors, princes, emperors, he thought—anything but monks. Yet monks they were, and followers of that Christian creed he so specially condemned,—for each one wore on his breast a massive golden crucifix, hung to a chain and fastened with a jewelled star.

"Cross and Star!" he mused, as he noticed this brilliant and singular decoration, "an emblem of the fraternity, I suppose, meaning. . . what? Salvation and Immortality? Alas, they are poor, witless builders on shifting sand if they place any hope or reliance on those two empty words, signifying nothing! Do they, can they honestly believe in God, I

MARIE CORELLI

wonder? or are they only acting the usual worn-out comedy of a feigned faith?"

And he eyed them somewhat wistfully as their white apparelled figures went by—ten had already left the chapel. Two more passed, then other two, and last of all came one alone—one who walked slowly, with a dreamy, meditative air, as though he were deeply absorbed in thought. The light from the open door streamed fully upon him as he advanced—it was the monk who had recited the Seven Glorias. The stranger no sooner beheld him than he instantly stepped forward and touched him on the arm.

"Pardon!" he said hastily in English, "I think I am not mistaken—your name is, or used to be Heliobas?"

The monk bent his handsome head in a slight yet graceful salutation, and smiled.

"I have not changed it," he replied, "I am Heliobas still." And his keen, steadfast, blue eyes rested half inquiringly, half compassionately, on the dark, weary, troubled face of his questioner who, avoiding his direct gaze, continued:

"I should like to speak to you in private. Can I do so now—to-night—at once?"

"By all means!" assented the monk, showing no surprise at the request. "Follow me to the library, we shall be quite alone there."

He led the way immediately out of the chapel, and through a stone-paved vestibule, where they were met by the two brethren who had first received and entertained the unknown guest, and who, not finding him in the refectory where they had left him, were now coming in search of him. On seeing in whose company he was, however, they drew aside with a deep and reverential obeisance to the personage called Heliobas—he, silently acknowledging it, passed on, closely attended by the stranger, till he reached a spacious, well-lighted apartment, the walls of which were entirely lined with books. Here, entering and closing the door, he turned and confronted his visitor—his tall, imposing figure in its trailing white garments calling to mind the picture of some saint or evangelist—and with grave yet kindly courtesy, said:

"Now, my friend, I am at your disposal! In what way can Heliobas, who is dead to the world, serve one for whom surely as yet the world is everything?"

II

CONFESSION

H is question was not very promptly answered. The stranger stood still, regarding him intently for two of three minutes with a look of peculiar pensiveness and abstraction, the heavy double fringe of his long dark lashes giving an almost drowsy pathos to his proud and earnest eyes. Soon, however, this absorbed expression changed to one of sombre scorn.

"The world!" he said slowly and bitterly. "You think *I* care for the world? Then you read me wrongly at the very outset of our interview, and your once reputed skill as a Seer goes for naught! To me the world is a graveyard full of dead, worm-eaten things, and its supposititious Creator, whom you have so be praised in your orisons to-night, is the Sexton who entombs, and the Ghoul who devours his own hapless Creation! I myself am one of the tortured and dying, and I have sought you simply that you may trick me into a brief oblivion of my doom, and mock me with the mirage of a life that is not and can never be! How can you serve me? Give me a few hours' respite from wretchedness! that is all I ask!"

As he spoke his face grew blanched and haggard, as though he suffered from some painfully repressed inward agony. The monk Heliobas heard him with an air of attentive patience, but said nothing; he therefore, after waiting for a reply and receiving none, went on in colder and more even tones:

"I dare say my words seem strange to you—though they should not do so if, as reported, you have studied all the varying phases of that purely intellectual despair which, in this age of excessive over-culture, crushes men who learn too much and think too deeply. But before going further I had better introduce myself. My name is Alwyn. . ."

"Theos Alwyn, the English author, I presume?" interposed the monk interrogatively.

"Why, yes!" this in accents of extreme surprise—"how did you know that!"

"Your celebrity," politely suggested Heliobas, with a wave of the hand and an enigmatical smile that might have meant anything or nothing.

Alwyn colored a little. "Your mistake," he said indifferently, "I have no celebrity. The celebrities of my country are few, and among them those most admired are jockeys and divorced women. I merely follow in the rear-line of the art or profession of literature—I am that always unluckiest and most undesirable kind of an author, a writer of verse—I lay no claim, not now at any rate, to the title of poet. While recently staying in Paris I chanced to hear of you. . ."

The monk bowed ever so slightly—there was a dawning gleam of satire in his brilliant eyes.

"You won special distinction and renown there, I believe, before you adopted this monastic life?" pursued Alwyn, glancing at him curiously.

"Did I?" and Heliobas looked cheerfully interested. "Really I was not aware of it, I assure you! Possibly my ways and doings may have occasionally furnished the Parisians with something to talk about instead of the weather, and I know I made some few friends and an astonishing number of enemies, if that is what you mean by distinction and renown!"

Alwyn smiled—his smile was always reluctant, and had in it more of sadness than sweetness, yet it gave his features a singular softness and beauty, just as a ray of sunlight falling on a dark picture will brighten the tints into a momentary warmth of seeming life.

"All reputation means that, I think," he said, "unless it be mediocre—then one is safe; one has scores of friends, and scarce a foe. Mediocrity succeeds wonderfully well nowadays—nobody hates it, because every one feels how easily they themselves can attain to it. Exceptional talent is aggressive—actual genius is offensive; people are insulted to have a thing held up for their admiration which is entirely out of their reach. They become like bears climbing a greased pole; they see a great name above them—a tempting sugary morsel which they would fain snatch and devour—and when their uncouth efforts fail, they huddle together on the ground beneath, look up with dull, peering eyes, and impotently snarl! But you,"—and here his gazed rested doubtfully, yet questioningly, on his companion's open, serene countenance—"you, if rumor speaks truly, should have been able to tame Your bears and turn them into dogs, humble and couchant! Your marvellous achievements as a mesmerist—"

"Excuse me!" returned Heliobas quietly, "I never was a mesmerist."

"Well-as a spiritualist then; though I cannot admit the existence of any such thing as spiritualism."

"Neither can I," returned Heliobas, with perfect good-humor, "according to the generally accepted meaning of the term. Pray go on, Mr. Alwyn!"

Alwyn looked at him, a little puzzled and uncertain how to proceed. A curious sense of irritation was growing up in his mind against this monk with the grand head and flashing eyes—eyes that seemed to strip bare his innermost thoughts, as lightning strips bark from a tree.

"I was told," he continued after a pause, during which he had apparently considered and prepared his words, "that you were chiefly known in Paris as being the possessor of some mysterious internal force—call it magnetic, hypnotic, or spiritual, as you please—which, though perfectly inexplicable, was yet plainly manifested and evident to all who placed themselves under your influence. Moreover, that by this force you were able to deal scientifically and practically with the active principle of intelligence in man, to such an extent that you could, in some miraculous way, disentangle the knots of toil and perplexity in an over-taxed brain, and restore to it its pristine vitality and vigor. Is this true? If so, exert your power upon me,—for something, I know not what, has of late frozen up the once overflowing fountain of my thoughts, and I have lost all working ability. When a man can no longer work, it were best he should die, only unfortunately I cannot die unless I kill myself,—which it is possible I may do ere long. But in the meantime,"— he hesitated a moment, then went on, "in the meantime, I have a strong wish to be deluded—I use the word advisedly, and repeat it—Deluded into an imaginary happiness, though I am aware that as an agnostic and searcher after truth—truth absolute, truth positive—such a desire on my part seems even to myself inconsistent and unreasonable. Still I confess to having it; and therein, I know, I betray the weakness of my nature. It may be that I am tired"—and he passed his hand across his brow with a troubled gesture—"or puzzled by the infinite, incurable distress of all living things. Perhaps I am growing mad!—who knows!— but whatever my condition, you,—if report be correct,—have the magic skill to ravish the mind away from its troubles and transport it to a radiant Elysium of sweet illusions and ethereal ecstasies. Do this for me, as you have done it for others, and whatever payment you demand, whether in gold or gratitude, shall be yours."

He ceased; the wind howled furiously outside, flinging gusty dashes of rain against the one window of the room, a tall arched casement that clattered noisily with every blow inflicted upon it by the storm. Heliobas gave him a swift, searching glance, half pitying, half disdainful.

"Haschisch or opium should serve your turn," he said curtly. "I know of no other means whereby to temporarily still the clamorings of conscience."

Alwyn flushed darkly. "Conscience!" he began in rather a resentful tone,

"Aye, conscience!" repeated Heliobas firmly. "There is such a thing. Do you profess to be wholly without it?"

Alwyn deigned no reply—the ironical bluntness of the question annoyed him.

"You have formed a very unjust opinion of me, Mr. Alwyn," continued Heliobas, "an opinion which neither honors your courtesy nor your intellect—pardon me for saying so. You ask me to 'mock' and 'delude' you as if it were my custom and delight to make dupes of my suffering fellow-creatures! You come to me as though I were a mesmerist or magnetizer such as you can hire for a few guineas in any civilized city in Europe—nay, I doubt not but that you consider me that kind of so-called 'spiritualist' whose enlightened intelligence and heaven-aspiring aims are demonstrated in the turning of tables and general furniture-gyration. I am, however, hopelessly deficient in such knowledge. I should make a most unsatisfactory conjurer! Moreover, whatever you may have heard concerning me in Paris, you must remember I am in Paris no longer. I am a monk, as you see, devoted to my vocation; I am completely severed from the world, and my duties and occupations in the present are widely different to those which employed me in the past. Then I gave what aid I could to those who honestly needed it and sought it without prejudice or personal distrust; but now my work among men is finished, and I practice my science, such as it is, on others no more, except in very rare and special cases."

Alwyn heard, and the lines of his face hardened into an expression of frigid hauteur.

"I suppose I am to understand by this that you will do nothing for me?" he said stiffly.

"Why, what CAN I do?" returned Heliobas, smiling a little. "All you want—so you say—is a brief forgetfulness of your troubles. Well, that is easily obtainable through certain narcotics, if you choose to employ them and take the risk of their injurious action on your bodily system. You can drug your brain and thereby fill it with drowsy suggestions of ideas—of course they would only he SUGGESTIONS, and very vague and indefinite ones too, still they might be pleasant enough to absorb and repress bitter memories for a time. As for me, my poor skill would scarcely avail you, as I could promise you neither self-oblivion nor visionary joy. I have a certain internal force, it is true—a spiritual force which when strongly exercised overpowers and subdues the material—and by exerting this I could, if I thought it well to do so, release your SOUL—that is, the Inner Intelligent Spirit which is the actual You—from its house of clay, and allow it an interval of freedom. But what its experience might be in that unfettered condition, whether glad or sorrowful, I am totally unable to predict."

Alwyn looked at him steadfastly.

"You believe in the Soul?" he asked.

"Most certainly!"

"As a separate Personality that continues to live on when the body perishes?"

"Assuredly."

"And you profess to be able to liberate it for a time from its mortal habitation—"

"I do not profess," interposed Heliobas quietly. "I CAN do so."

"But with the success of the experiment your power ceases?—you cannot foretell whether the unimprisoned creature will take its course to an inferno of suffering or a heaven of delight?—is this what you mean?"

Heliobas bent his head in grave assent.

Alwyn broke into a harsh laugh—"Come then!" he exclaimed with a reckless air,—"Begin your incantations at once! Send me hence, no matter where, so long as I am for a while escaped from this den of a world, this dungeon with one small window through which, with the death rattle in our throats, we stare vacantly at the blank unmeaning honor of the Universe! Prove to me that the Soul exists—ye gods! Prove it! and if mine can find its way straight to the mainspring of this revolving Creation, it shall cling to the accused wheels and stop them, that they may grind out the tortures of Life no more!"

He flung up his hand with a wild gesture: his countenance, darkly threatening and defiant, was yet beautiful with the evil beauty of a rebellious and fallen angel. His breath came and went quickly,—he seemed to challenge some invisible opponent. Heliobas meanwhile watched him much as a physician might watch in his patient the workings of a new disease, then he said in purposely cold and tranquil tones:

"A bold idea! singularly blasphemous, arrogant, and—fortunately for us all—impracticable! Allow me to remark that you are overexcited, Mr. Alwyn; you talk as madmen may, but as reasonable men should not. Come," and he smiled,—a smile that was both grave and sweet, "come and sit down—you are worn out with the force of your own desperate emotions—rest a few minutes and recover your self."

His voice thouqh gentle was distinctly authoritative, and Alwyn meeting the full gaze of his calm eyes felt bound to obey the implied command. He therefore sank listlessly into an easy chair near the table, pushing back the short, thick curls from his brow with a wearied movement; he was very pale,—an uneasy sense of shame was upon him, and he sighed,—a quick sigh of exhausted passion. Heliobas seated himself opposite and looked at him earnestly; he studied with sympathetic attention the lines of dejection and fatigue which marred the attractiveness of features otherwise frank, poetic, and noble. He had seen many such men. Men in their prime who had begun life full of high faith, hope, and lofty aspiration, yet whose fair ideals once bruised in the mortar of modern atheistical opinion had perished forever, while they themselves, like golden eagles suddenly and cruelly shot while flying in mid-air, had fallen helplessly, broken-winged among the dust-heaps of the world, never to rise and soar sunwards again. Thinking this, his accents were touched with a certain compassion when after a pause he said softly:

"Poor boy!—poor, puzzled, tired brain that would fain judge Infinity by merely finite perception! You were a far truer poet, Theos Alwyn, when as a world-foolish, heaven-inspired lad you believed in God, and therefore, in godlike gladness, found all things good!"

Alwyn looked up—his lips quivered.

"Poet—poet!" he murmured—"why taunt me with the name?" He started upright in his chair—"Let me tell you all," he said suddenly; "you may as well know what has made me the useless wreck I am; though perhaps I shall only weary you."

"Far from it," answered Heliobas gently. "Speak freely—but remember I do not compel your confidence."

"On the contrary, I think you do!" and again that faint, half-mournful smile shone for an instant in his deep, dark eyes, "though you may not be conscious of it. Anyhow I feel impelled to unburden my heart to you: I have kept silence so long! You know what it is in the world, . . . one must always keep silence, always shut in one's grief and force a smile, in company with the rest of the tormented, forced-smiling crowd. We can never be ourselves—our veritable selves—for, if we were, the air would resound with our ceaseless lamentations! It is HORRIBLE to think of all the pent-up sufferings of humanity—all the inconceivably hideous agonies that remain forever dumb and unrevealed! When I was young,—how long ago that seems! yes, though my actual years are taut thirty, I feel an alder-elde of accumulated centuries upon me—when I was young, the dream of my life was Poesy. Perhaps I inherited the fatal love of it from my mother—she was a Greek-and she had a subtle music in her that nothing could quell, not even my father's English coldness. She named me Theos, little guessing what a dreary sarcasm that name would prove! It was well, I think, that she died early."

"Well for her, but perhaps not so well for you," said Heliobas with a keen, kindly glance at him.

Alwyn sighed. "Nay, well, for us both,—for I should have chafed at her loving restraint, and she would unquestionably have been disappointed in me. My father was a conscientious, methodical business man, who spent all his days up to almost the last moment of his life in amassing money, though it never gave him any joy so far as I could see, and when at his death I became sole possessor of his hardly-earned fortune, I felt far more sorrow than satisfaction. I wished he had spent his gold on himself and left me poor, for it seemed to me I had need of nothing save the little I earned by my pen—I was content to live an anchorite and dine off a crust for the sake of the divine Muse I worshipped. Fate, however, willed it otherwise,—and though I scarcely cared for the wealth I inherited, it gave me at least one blessing—that of perfect independence. I was free to follow my own chosen vocation, and for a brief wondering while I deemed myself happy, . . . happy as Keats must have been when the fragment of 'Hyperion' broke from his frail life as thunder breaks from a summer-cloud. I was as a monarch swaying a sceptre that commanded both earth and heaven; a kingdom was mine-a kingdom of golden ether, peopled with shining shapes Protean,—alas! its gates are shut upon me now, and I shall enter it no more!"

"'No more' is a long time, my friend!" interposed Heliobas gently. "You are too despondent,—perchance too diffident, concerning your own ability."

"Ability!" and he laughed wearily. "I have none,—I am as weak and inapt as an untaught child—the music of my heart is silenced!

Yet there is nothing I would not do to regain the ravishment of the past—when the sight of the sunset across the hills, or the moon's silver transfiguration of the sea filled me with deep and indescribable ecstasy—when the thought of Love, like a full chord struck from a magic harp, set my pulses throbbing with delirious delight—fancies thick as leaves in summer crowded my brain—Earth was a round charm hung on the breast of a smiling Divinity—men were gods—women were angels'—the world seemed but a wide scroll for the signatures of poets, and mine, I swore, should be clearly written!"

He paused, as though ashamed of his own fervor, and glanced at Heliobas, who, leaning a little forward in his chair was regaling him with friendly, attentive interest; then he continued more calmly:

"Enough! I think I had something in me then,—something that was new and wild and, though it may seem self praise to say so, full of that witching glamour we name Inspiration; but whatever that something was, call it genius, a trick of song, what you will,—it was soon crushed out of me. The world is fond of slaying its singing buds and devouring them for daily fare—one rough pressure of finger and thumb on the little melodious throats, and they are mute forever. So I found, when at last in mingled pride, hope, and fear I published my poems, seeking for them no other recompense save fair hearing and justice. They obtained neither—they were tossed carelessly by a few critics from hand to hand, jeered at for a while, and finally flung back to me as lies—lies all! The finely spun web of any fancy,—the delicate interwoven intricacies of thought,—these were torn to shreds with as little compunction as idle children feel when destroying for their own cruel sport the velvety wonder of a moth's wing, or the radiant rose and emerald pinions of a dragon-fly. I was a fool—so I was told with many a languid sneer and stale jest—to talk of hidden mysteries in the whisper of the wind and the dash of the waves—such sounds were but common cause and effect. The stars were merely conglomerated masses of heated vapor condensed by the work of ages into meteorites and from meteorites into worlds—and these went on rolling in their appointed orbits, for what reason nobody knew, but then nobody cared! And Love—the key-note of the theme to which I had set my mistaken life in tune—Love was only a graceful word used to politely define the low but very general sentiment of coarse animal attraction—in short, poetry such as mine was altogether absurd and out of date when confronted with the facts of every-day existence—facts which plainly taught us that man's chief business here below was simply to live, breed, and die—the life of a silk-worm or caterpillar on a slightly higher platform of ability; beyond this—nothing!"

"Nothing?" murmured Heliobas, in a tone of suggestive inquiry—"really nothing?"

"Nothing!" repeated Alwyn, with an air of resigned hopelessness; "for I learned that, according to the results arrived at by the most advanced thinkers of the day, there was no God, no Soul, no Hereafter—the loftiest efforts of the highest heaven—aspiring minds were doomed to end in non-fruition, failure, and annihilation. Among all the desperately hard truths that came rattling down upon me like a shower of stones, I think this was the crowning one that killed whatever genius I had. I use the word 'genius' foolishly—though, after all, genius itself is nothing to boast of, since it is only a morbid and unhealthy condition of the intellectual faculties, or at least was demonstrated to me as such by a scientific friend of my own who, seeing I was miserable, took great pains to make me more so if possible. He proved,—to his own satisfaction if not altogether to mine,—that the abnormal position of certain molecules in the brain produced an eccentricity or peculiar bias in one direction which, practically viewed, might be described as an intelligent form of monomania, but which most people chose to term 'genius,' and that from a purely scientific standpoint it was evident that the poets, painters, musicians, sculptors, and all the widely renowned 'great ones' of the earth should be classified as so many brains more or less affected by abnormal molecular formation, which strictly speaking amounted to brain-deformity. He assured me, that to the properly balanced, healthily organized brain of the human animal, genius was an impossibility—it was a malady as unnatural as rare. 'And it is singular, very singular,' he added with a complacent smile, 'that the world should owe all its finest art and literature merely to a few varieties of molecular disease!' I thought it singular enough, too,—however, I did not care to argue with him; I only felt that if the illness of genius had at any time affected Me, it was pretty well certain I should now suffer no more from its delicious pangs and honey-sweet fever. I was cured! The probing-knife of the world's cynicism had found its way to the musically throbbing centre of divine disquietude in my brain, and had there cut down the growth of fair imaginations for ever. I thrust aside the bright illusions that had once been my gladness; I forced myself to look with unflinching eyes at the wide waste of universal Nothingness revealed to me by the rigid positivists and iconoclasts of the century; but my heart died within me; my whole being froze as it were into an icy apathy,—I wrote no more; I doubt whether I shall ever write again. Of a truth, there is nothing to write about. All has been said. The days of the Troubadours are past,— one cannot string canticles of love for men and women whose ruling passion is the greed of gold. Yet I have sometimes thought life would be drearier even than it is, were the voices of poets altogether silent; and I wish—yes! I wish I had it in my power to brand my sign-manual on the brazen face of this coldly callous age-brand it deep in those letters of living lire called Fame!"

A look of baffled longing and un gratified ambition came into his musing eyes,-his strong, shapely white hand clenched nervously, as though it grasped some unseen yet perfectly tangible substance. Just then the storm without, which had partially lulled during the last few minutes, began its wrath anew: a glare of lightning blazed against the uncurtained window, and a heavy clap of thunder burst overhead with the sudden crash of an exploding bomb.

"You care for Fame?" asked Ileliobas abruptly, as soon as the terrific uproar had subsided into a distant, dull rumbling mingled with the pattering dash of hail.

"I care for it—yes!" replied Alwyn, and his voice was very low and dreamy. "For though the world is a graveyard, as I have said, full of unmarked tombs, still here and there we find graves, such as Shelley's or Byron's, whereon pale flowers, like sweet suggestions of ever-silenced music, break into continuous bloom. And shall I not win my own death-garland of asphodel?"

There was an indescribable, almost heart-rending pathos in his manner of uttering these last words—a hopelessness of effort and a despairing sense of failure which he himself seemed conscious of, for, meeting the fixed and earnest gaze of Ileliobas, he quickly relapsed into his usual tone of indolent indifference.

"You see," he said, with a forced smile, "my story is not very interesting! No hairbreadth escapes, no thrilling adventures, no love intrigues—nothing but mental misery, for which few people have any sympathy. A child with a cut finger gets more universal commiseration than a man with a tortured brain and breaking heart, yet there can be no quotion as to which is the most intense duel long enduring anguish of the two. However, such as my troubles are I have told you all I have laid bare my 'wound of living'—a wound that throbs and burns, and aches, more intolerably with every pissing hour and day—it is not unnatural, I think, that I should seek for a little cessation of suffering; a brief dreaming space in which to rest for a while, and escape from the deathful Truth—Truth, that like the flaming sword placed east of the fabled garden of Eden, turns ruthlessly every way, keeping us out of the forfeited paradise of imaginative aspiration, which made the men of old time great because they deemed themselves immortal. It was a glorious faith! that strong consciousness, that in the change and upheaval of whole universes the soul of man should forever over-ride disaster! But now that we know ourselves to be of no more importance, relatively speaking, than the animalculae in a drop of stagnant water, what great works can be done, what noble deeds accomplished, in the face of the declared and proved futility of everything? Still, if you can, as you say, liberate me from this fleshly prison, and give me new sensations and different experiences, why then let me depart with all possible speed, for I am certain I shall find in the storm-swept areas of space nothing worse than life as lived in this present world. Remember, I am quite incredulous as to your professed power—" he paused and glanced at the white-robed, priestly figure opposite, then added, lightly, "but I am curious to test it all the same. Are you ready to being your spells?—and shall I say the Nunc Dimittis?"

III

Departure

Heliobas was silent—he seemed engaged in deep and anxious thought,—and he kept his steadfast eyes fixed on Alwyn's countenance, as though he sought there the clew to some difficult problem.

"What do you know of the Nunc Dimittis?" he asked at last, with a half-smile. "You might as well say PATER NOSTER,—both canticle and prayer would be equally unmeaning to you! For poet as you are,—or let me say as you WERE,—inasmuch as no atheist was ever a poet at the same time—"

"You are wrong," interrupted Alwyn quickly. "Shelley was an atheist."

"Shelley, my good friend, was NOT an atheist*. He strove to be one,—nay, he made pretence to be one,—but throughout his poems we hear the voice of his inner and better self appealing to that Divinity and Eternity which, in spite of the material part of him, he instinctively felt existent in his own being. I repeat, poet as your WERE, and poet as you will be again when the clouds on your mind are cleared,—you present the strange, but not uncommon spectacle of an Immortal Spirit fighting to disprove its own Immortality. In a word, you will not believe in the Soul."

"I cannot!" said Alwyn, with a hopeless gesture.

"Why?"

"Science can give us no positive proof of its existence; it cannot be defined."

"What do you mean by Science?" demanded Heliobas. "The foot of the mountain, at which men now stand, grovelling and uncertain how to climb? or the glittering summit itself which touches God's throne?"

Alwyn made no answer.

"Tell me," pursued Heliobas, "how do you define the vital principle? What mysterious agency sets the heart beating and the blood flowing? By the small porter's lantern of to-day's so-called Science, will you fling

---

* See the last two verses of Adonais.

a light on the dark riddle of an apparently purposeless Universe, and explain to me why we live at all?"

"Evolution," responded Alwyn shortly, "and Necessity."

"Evolution from what?" persisted Heliobas. "From one atom? WHAT atom? And FROM WHENCE came the atom? And why the NECESSITY of any atom?"

"The human brain reels at such questions!" said Alwyn, vexedly and with impatience. "I cannot answer them—no one can!"

"No one?" Heliobas smiled very tranquilly. "Do not be too sure of that! And why should the human brain 'reel'?—the sagacious, calculating, clear human brain that never gets tired, or puzzled, or perplexed!—that settles everything in the most practical and common-sense manner, and disposes of God altogether as an extraneous sort of bargain not wanted in the general economy of our little solar system! Aye, the human brain is a wonderful thing!—and yet by a sharp, well-directed knock with this"—and he took up from the table a paper-knife with a massive, silver-mounted, weighty horn-handle—"I could deaden it in such wise that the SOUL could no more hold any communication with it, and it would lie an inert mass in the cranium, of no more use to its owner than a paralyzed limb."

"You mean to infer that the brain cannot act without the influence of the soul?"

"Precisely! If the hands on the telegraph dial will not respond to the electric battery, the telegram cannot be deciphered. But it would be foolish to deny the existence of the electric battery because the dial is unsatisfactory! In like manner, when, by physical incapacity, or inherited disease, the brain can no longer receive the impressions or electric messages of the Spirit, it is practically useless. Yet the Spirit is there all the same, dumbly waiting for release and another chance of expansion."

"Is this the way you account for idiocy and mania?" asked Alwyn incredulously.

"Most certainly; idiocy and mania always come from man's interference with the laws of health and of nature—never otherwise. The Soul placed within us by the Creator is meant to be fostered by man's unfettered Will; if man chooses to employ that unfettered Will in wrong directions, he has only himself to blame for the disastrous results that follow. You may perhaps ask why God has thus left our wills unfettered: the answer is simple—that we may serve Him by CHOICE and not by COMPULSION. Among the myriad million worlds that acknowledge His goodness gladly and undoubtingly, why should He seek to force unwilling obedience from us castaways!"

"As we are on this subject," said Alwyn, with a tinge of satire in his tone, "if you grant a God, and make Him out to be supreme Love, why in the name of His supposed inexhaustible beneficence should we be castaways at all?"

"Because in our overweening pride and egotism we have ELECTED to be such," replied Heliobas. "As angels have fallen, so have we. But we are not altogether castaways now, since this signal," and he touched the cross on his breast, "shone in heaven."

Alwyn shrugged his shoulders disdainfully.

"Pardon me," he murmured coldly, "with every desire to respect your religious scruples, I really cannot, personally speaking, accept the tenets of a worn-out faith, which all the most intellectual minds of the day reject as mere ignorant superstition. The carpenter's son of Judea was no doubt a very estimable person,—a socialist teacher whose doctrines were very excellent in theory but impossible of practice. That there was anything divine about Him I utterly deny; and I confess I am surprised that you, a man of evident culture, do not seem to see the hollow absurdity of Christianity as a system of morals and civilization. It is an ever-sprouting seed of discord and hatred between nations; it has served as a casus belli of the most fanatical and merciless character; it is answerable for whole seas of cruel and unnecessary bloodshed. . ."

"Have you nothing NEW to say on the subject?" interposed Heliobas, with a slight smile. "I have heard all this so often before, from divers kinds of men both educated and ignorant, who have a willful habit of forgetting all that Christ Himself prophesied concerning His creed of Self-renunciation, so difficult to selfish humanity: 'Think not that I come to send peace on the earth. I come, not to send peace, but a sword.' Again 'Ye shall be hated of all men for my name's sake.' . . . 'all ye shall be offended because of me.' Such plain words as these seem utterly thrown away upon this present generation. And do you know I find a curious lack of originality among so-called 'freethinkers'; in fact their thoughts can hardly be designated as 'free' when they all run in such extremely narrow grooves of similitude—a flock of sheep mildly trotting under the guidance of the butcher to the slaughterhouse could not be more tamely alike in their bleating ignorance as to where they are going. Your opinions, for instance, differ scarce a whit from those of the common boor who, reading his penny Radical paper, thinks he can dispense with God, and talks of the 'carpenter's son of Judea' with the same easy flippancy and scant reverence as yourself. The 'intellectual minds of the day' to which you allude, are extraordinarily limited of comprehension, and none of them, literary or otherwise, have such a grasp of knowledge as any of these dead and gone authors," and he waved his hand toward the surrounding loaded bookshelves, "who lived centuries ago, and are now, as far as the general public is concerned, forgotten. All the volumes you see here are vellum manuscripts copied from the original slabs of baked clay, stone tablets, and engraved sheets of ivory, and among them is an ingenious treatise by one Remeni Adranos, chief astronomer to the then king of Babylonia, setting forth the Atom and Evolution theory with far more clearness and precision than any of your modern professors. All such propositions are old—old as the hills, I assure you; and these days in which you live are more suggestive of the second childhood of the world than its progressive prime. Especially in your own country the general dotage seems to have reached a sort of climax, for there you have the people actually forgetting, deriding, or denying their greatest men who form the only lasting glories of their history; they have even done their futile best to tarnish the unsoilable fame of Shakespeare. In that land you,—who, according to your own showing, started for the race of life full of high hopes and inspiration to still higher endeavor—you have been, poisoned by the tainted atmosphere of Atheism which is slowly and insidiously spreading itself through all ranks, particularly among the upper classes, who, while becoming every day more lax in their morals and more dissolute of behavior, consider themselves far too wise and 'highly cultured' to believe in anything. It is a most unwholesome atmosphere, charged with the morbidities and microbes of national disease and downfall; it is difficult to breathe it without becoming fever-smitten; and in your denial of the divinity of Christ, I do not blame you any more than I would blame a poor creature struck down by a plague. You have caught the negative, agnostic, and atheistical infection from others,—it is not the natural, healthy condition of your temperament."

"On the contrary it Is, so far as that point goes," said Alwyn with sudden heat—"I tell you I am amazed,—utterly amazed, that you, with your intelligence, should uphold such a barbaric idea as the Divinity of Christ! Human reason revolts at it,—and after all, make as light of it as you will, reason is the only thing that exalts us a little above the level of the beasts."

"Nay—the beasts share the gift of reason in common with us," replied Heliobas, "and Man only proves his ignorance if he denies the fact. Often indeed the very insects show superior reasoning ability to ourselves, any thoroughly capable naturalist would bear me out in this assertion."

"Well, well!" and Alwyn grew impatient—"reason or no reason, I again repeat that the legend on which Christianity is founded is absurd and preposterous,—why, if there were a grain of truth in it, Judas Iscariot instead of being universally condemned, ought to be honored and canonized as the first of saints!"

"Must I remind you of your early lesson days?" asked Heliobas mildly. "You will find it written in a Book you appear to have forgotten, that Christ expressly prophesied, 'Woe to that man' by whom He was betrayed. I tell, you, little as you credit it, there is not a word that the Sinless One uttered while on this earth, that has not been or shall not be in time fulfilled. But I do not wish to enter into any controversies with you; you have told me your story,—I have heard it with interest,—and I may add with sympathy. You are a poet, struck dumb by Materialism because you lacked strength to resist the shock,—you would fain recover your singing-speech—and this is in truth the reason why you have come to me. You think that if you could gain some of the strange experiences which others have had while under my influence, you might win back your lost inspiration—though you do not know WHY you think this— neither do I—I can only guess."

"And your guess is. . . ?" demanded Alwyn with an air of affected indifference.

"That some higher influence is working for your rescue and safety," replied Heliobas. "What influence I dare not presume to imagine, but— there are always angels near!"

"Angels!" Alwyn laughed aloud. "How many more fairy tales are you going to weave for me out of your fertile Oriental imagination? Angels! . . . See here, my good Heliobas, I am perfectly willing to grant that you may be a very clever man with an odd prejudice in favor of Christianity,—but I must request that you will not talk to me of angels and spirits or any such nonsense, as if I were a child waiting to be amused, instead of a full-grown man with. . ."

"With so full-grown an intellect that it has out-grown God!" finished Heliobas serenely. "Quite so! Yet angels, after all, are only immortal Souls such as yours or mine when set free of their earthly tenements.

For instance, when I look at you thus," and he raised his eyes with a lustrous, piercing glance—"I see the proud, strong, and rebellious Angel in you far more distinctly than your outward shape of man. . . and you. . . when you look at me—"

He broke off, for Alwyn at that moment sprang from his chair, and, staring fixedly at him, uttered a quick, fierce exclamation.

"Ah! I know you now!" he cried in sudden and extraordinary excitement—"I know you well! We have met before!—Why,—after all that has passed,—do we meet again?"

This singular speech was accompanied by a still more singular transfiguration of countenance—a dark, fiery glory burned in his eyes, and, in the stern, frowning wonder and defiance of his expression and attitude, there was something grand yet terrible,—menacing yet supernaturally sublime. He stood so for an instant's space, majestically sombre, like some haughty, discrowned emperor confronting his conqueror,—a rumbling, long-continued roll of thunder outside seemed to recall him to himself, and he pressed his hand tightly down over his eyelids, as though to shut out some overwhelming vision. After a pause he looked up again,—wildly, confusedly,—almost beseechingly,—and Heliobas, observing this, rose and advanced toward him.

"Peace!" he said, in low, impressive tones,—"we have recognized each other,—but on earth such recognitions are brief and soon forgotten!" He waited for a few seconds,—then resumed lightly, "Come, look at me now! . . . what do you see?"

"Nothing. . . but yourself!" he replied, sighing deeply as he spoke—"yet. . . oddly enough, a moment ago I fancied you had altogether a different appearance,—and I thought I saw. . . no matter what! . . . I cannot describe it!" His brows contracted in a puzzled line. "It was a curious phenomenon—very curious. . . and it affected me strangely. . ." he stopped abruptly,—then added, with a slight flush of annoyance on his face, "I perceive you are an adept in the art of optical illusion!"

Heliobas laughed softly. "Of course! What else can you expect of a charlatan, a trickster, and a monk to boot! Deception, deception throughout, my dear sir! . . . and have you not ASKED to be deceived?"

There was a fine, scarcely perceptible satire in his manner; he glanced at the tall oaken clock that stood in one corner of the room—its hands pointed to eleven. "Now, Mr. Alwyn," he went on, "I think we have talked quite enough for this evening, and my advice is, that you retire to rest, and think over what I have said to you. I am willing to help you if I can,—but with your beliefs, or rather your non-beliefs, I do not hesitate to tell you frankly that the exertion of My internal force upon Yours in your present condition might be fraught with extreme danger and suffering. You have spoken of Truth, 'the deathful Truth'; this being, however, nothing but Truth according to the world's opinion, which changes with every passing generation, and therefore is not Truth at all. There is another Truth—the everlasting Truth—the pivot of all life, which never changes; and it is with this alone that my science deals. Were I to set you at liberty as you desire,—were your intelligence too suddenly awakened to the blinding awfulness of your mistaken notions of life, death, and futurity, the result might be more overpowering than either you or I can imagine! I have told you what I can do,—your incredulity does not alter the fact of my capacity. I can sever you,—that is, your Soul, which you cannot define, but which nevertheless exists,— from your body, like a moth from its chrysalis; but I dare not even picture to myself what scorching flame the moth might not heedlessly fly into! You might in your temporary state of release find that new impetus to your thoughts you so ardently desire, or you might not,—in short, it is impossible to form a guess as to whether your experience might be one of supernal ecstasy or inconceivable horror." He paused a moment,—Alwyn was watching him with a close intentness that bordered on fascination and presently he continued, "It is best from all points of view, that you should consider the matter more thoroughly than you have yet done; think it over well and carefully until this time to-morrow—then, if you are quite resolved—"

"I am resolved Now!" said Alwyn slowly and determinately. "If you are so certain of your influence, come! . . . unbar my chains! . . . open the prison-door! Let me go hence to-night; there is no time like the present!"

"To night!" and Heliobas turned his keen, bright eyes full upon him, with a look of amazement and reproach—"Tonight without faith, preparation or prayer, you are willing to be tossed through the realms of space like a grain of dust in a whirling tempest? Beyond the glittering gyration of unnumbered stars—through the sword-like flash of streaming comets—through darkness—through light—through depths of profoundest silence—over heights of vibrating sound—you—You will dare to wander in these God-invested regions—you a blasphemer and a doubter of God!"

His voice thrilled with passion,—his aspect was so solemn, and earnest, and imposing that Alwyn, awed and startled, remained for a moment mute—then, lifting his head proudly, answered—

"Yes, I Dare! If I am immortal I will test my immortality! I will face God and find these angels you talk about! What shall prevent me?"

"Find the angels!" Heliobas surveyed him sadly as he spoke. "Nay! . . . pray rather that they may find Thee!" He looked long and steadfastly at Alwyn's countenance, on which there was just then the faint glimmer of a rather mocking smile,—and as he looked, his own face darkened suddenly into an expression of vague trouble and uneasiness—and a strange quiver passed visibly through him from head to foot.

"You are bold, Mr. Alwyn,"—he said at last, moving a little away from his guest and speaking with some apparent effort—"bold to a fault, but at the same time you are ignorant of all that lies behind the veil of the Unseen. I should be much to blame if I sent you hence to-night, utterly unguided—utterly uninstructed. I myself must think—and pray—before I venture to incur so terrible a responsibility. To-morrow perhaps—to-night, no! I cannot—moreover I will not!"

Alwyn flushed hotly with anger. "Trickster!" he thought. "He feels he has no power over me, and he fears to run the risk of failure!"

"Did I hear you aright?" he said aloud in cold determined accents. "You cannot? you will not? . . . By Heaven!"—and his voice rose, "I say you Shall!" As he uttered these words a rush of indescribable sensations overcame him,—he seemed all at once invested with some mysterious, invincible, supreme authority,—he felt twice a man and more than half a god, and moved by an irresistible impulse which he could neither explain nor control, he made two or three hasty steps forward,—when Heliobas, swiftly retreating, waved him off with an eloquent gesture of mingled appeal and menace.

"Back! back!" he cried warningly. "If you come one inch nearer to me I cannot answer for your safety—back, I say! Good God! you do not know your Own power!"

Alwyn scarcely heeded him,—some fatal attraction drew him on, and he still advanced, when all suddenly he paused, trembling violently. His nerves began to throb acutely,—the blood in his veins was like fire,—there was a curious strangling tightness in his throat that interrupted and oppressed his breathing,—he stared straight before him with large, luminous, impassioned eyes. What—WHAT was that dazzling something in the air that flashed and whirled and shone like

MARIE CORELLI

glittering wheels of golden flame? His lips parted. . . he stretched out his hands in the uncertain manner of a blind man feeling his way. . . "Oh God! . . . God!" . . . he muttered as though stricken by some sudden amazement,—then, with a smothered, gasping cry, he staggered and fell heavily forward on the floor—insensible!

At the self-same instant the window blew open, with a loud crash— it swung backward and forward on its hinges, and a torrent of rain poured through it slantwise into the room. A remarkable change had taken place in the aspect and bearing of Heliobas,—he stood as though rooted to the spot, trembling from head to foot,—he had lost all his usual composure,—he was deathly pale, and breathed with difficulty. Presently recovering himself a little he strove to shut the swinging casement, but the wind was so boisterous, that he had to pause a moment to gain strength for the effort, and instinctively he glanced out at the tempestuous night. The clouds were scurrying over the sky like great black vessels on a foaming sea,—the lightning flashed incessantly, and the thunder reverberated Over the mountains in tremendous volleys as of besieging cannon. Stinging drops of icy sleet dashed his face and the front of his white garb as he inhaled the stormy freshness of the strong, upward-sweeping blast for a few seconds—and then, with the air of one gathering together all his scattered forces, he shut to the window firmly and barred it across. Turning now to the unconscious Alwyn, he lifted him from the floor to a low couch near at hand, and there laid him gently down. This done, he stood looking at him with an expression of the deepest anxiety, but made no attempt to rouse him from his death-like swoon. His own habitual serenity was completely broken through,—he had all the appearance of having received some unexpected and overwhelming shock,—his very lips were blanched and quivered nervously.

He waited for several minutes, attentively watching the recumbent figure before him, till gradually,—very gradually,—that figure took upon itself the pale, stern beauty of a corpse from which life has but recently and painlessly departed. The limbs grew stiff and rigid—the features smoothed into that mysteriously wise placidity which is so often seen in the faces of the dead,—the closed eyelids looked purple and livid as though bruised. . . there was not a breath, not a tremor, to offer any outward suggestion of returning animation,—and when, after some little time, Heliobas bent down and listened, there was no pulsation of the heart. . . it had ceased to beat! To all appearances

Alwyn was DEAD—any physician would have certified the fact, though how he had come by his death there was no evidence to show. And in that condition, . . . stirless, breathless. . . white as marble, cold and inanimate as stone, Heliobas left him. Not in indifference, but in sure knowledge—knowledge far beyond all mere medical science—that the senseless clay would in due time again arise to life and motion; that the casket was but temporarily bereft of its jewel,—and that the jewel itself, the Soul of the Poet, had by a superhuman access of will, managed to break its bonds and escape elsewhere. But whither? . . . Into what vast realms of translucent light or drear shadow? . . . This was a question to which the mystic monk, gifted as he was with a powerful spiritual insight into "things unseen and eternal," could find no satisfactory answer, and in his anxious perplexity he betook himself to the chapel, and there, by the red glimmer of the crimson star that shone dimly above the altar, he knelt alone and prayed in silence till the heavy night had passed, and the storm had slain itself with the sword of its own fury on the dark slopes of the Pass of Dariel.

IV

"ANGELUS DOMINE"

The next morning dawned pallidly over a sea of gray mist—not a glimpse of the landscape was visible—nothing but a shadowy vastness of floating vapor that moved slowly fold upon fold, wave upon wave, as though bent on blotting out the world. A very faint, chill light peered through the narrow arched window of the room where Alwyn lay, still wrapped in that profound repose, so like the last long sleep from which some of our modern scientists tell us there can be no awakening. His condition was unchanged,—the wan beams of the early clay falling cross his features intensified their waxen stillness and pallor,—the awful majesty of death was on him,—the pathetic helplessness and perishableness of Body without Spirit. Presently the monastery bell began to ring for matins, and as its clear chime struck through the deep silence, the door opened, and Heliobas, accompanied by another monk, whose gentle countenance and fine, soft eyes betokened the serenity of his disposition, entered the apartment. Together they approached the couch, and gazed long and earnestly at the supernaturally slumbering man.

"He is still far away!" said Heliobas at last, sighing as he spoke. "So far away that my mind misgives me. . . Alas, Hilarion! how limited is our knowledge! . . . even with all the spiritual aids of spiritual life how little can be accomplished! We learn one thing, and another presents itself—we conquer one difficulty, and another instantly springs up to obstruct our path. Now if I had only had the innate perception required to foresee the possible flight of this released Immortal creature, might I not have saved it from some incalculable misery and suffering?"

"I think not," answered in rather musing accents the monk called Hilarion—"I think not. Such protection can never be exercised by mere human intelligence, if this soul is to be saved or shielded in its invisible journeying it will be by some means that not all the marvels of our science can calculate. You say he was without faith?"

"Entirely"

"What was his leading principle?"

"A desire for what he called Truth," replied Heliobas.

"He, like many others of his class, never took the trouble to consider very deeply the inner meaning of Pilate's famous question, 'What Is Truth?' We know what it is, as generally accepted—a few so called facts which in a thousand years will all be contradicted, mixed up with a few finite opinions propounded by unstable minded men. In brief, Truth, according to the world, is simply whatever the world is pleased to consider as Truth for the time being. 'Tis a somewhat slight thing to stake one's immortal destinies upon!"

Hilarion raised one of Alwyn's cold, pulseless hands—it was stiff, and white as marble.

"I suppose," he said, "there is no doubt of his returning hither?"

"None whatever," answered Heliobas decisively. "His life on earth is assured for many years yet,—inasmuch as his penance is not finished, his recompense not won. Thus far my knowledge of his fate is certain."

"Then you will bring him back to-day?" pursued Hilarion.

"Bring him back? I? I cannot!" said Heliobas, with a touch of sad humility in his tone. "And for this very reason I feared to send him hence,—and would not have done so,—not without preparation at any rate,—could I have had my way. His departure was more strange than any I have ever known—moreover, it was his own doing, not mine. I had positively refused to exert my influence upon him, because I felt he was not in my sphere, and that therefore neither I nor any of those higher intelligences with which I am in communication could control or guide his wanderings. He, however, was as positively determined that I Should exert it—and to this end he suddenly concentrated all the pent up fire of his nature in one rapid effort of Will, and advanced upon me. . . I warned him, but in vain! quick as lightning flash meets lightning flash, the two invisible Immortal Forces within us sprang into instant opposition,—with this difference, that while he was ignorant and unconscious of His power, I was cognizant and fully conscious of Mine. Mine was focused, as it were, upon him,—his was untrained and scattered,—the result was that mine won the victory: yet understand me well, Hilarion,—if I could have held myself in, I would have done so. It was he,—he who Drew my force out of me as one would draw a sword out of its scabbard—the sword may be ever so stiffly fixed in its sheath, but the strong hand will wrench it forth somehow, and use it for battle when needed."

"Then," said Hilarion wonderingly, "you admit this man possesses a power greater than your own?"

"Aye, if he knew it!" returned Heliobas, quietly. "But he does not know. Only an angel could teach him—and in angels he does not believe."

"He may believe now. . . !"

"He may. He will—he must, . . . if he has gone where I would have him go."

"A poet, is he not!" queried Hilarion softly, bending down to look more attentively at the beautiful Antinous-like face colorless and cold as sculptured alabaster.

"An uncrowned monarch of a world of song!" responded Heliobas, with a tender inflection in his rich voice. "A genius such as the earth sees but once in a century! But he has been smitten with the disease of unbelief and deprived of hope,—and where there is no hope there is no lasting accomplishment." He paused, and with a touch as gentle as a woman's, rearranged the cushions under Alwyn's heavy head, and laid his hand in grave benediction on the broad white brow shaded by its clustering waves of dark hair. "May the Infinite Love bring him out of danger into peace and safety!" he said solemnly,—then turning away, he took his companion by the arm, and they both left the room, closing the door quietly behind them. The chapel bell went on tolling slowly, slowly, sending muffled echoes through the fog for some minutes— then it ceased, and profound stillness reigned.

The monastery was always a very silent habitation,—situated as it was on so lofty and barren a crag, it was far beyond the singing-reach of the smaller sweet-throated birds—now and then an eagle clove the mist with a whirr of wings and a discordant scream on his way toward some distant mountain eyrie—but no other sound of awakening life broke the hush of the slowly widening dawn. An hour passed—and Alwyn still remained in the same position,—as pallidly quiescent as a corpse stretched out for burial. By and by a change begin to thrill mysteriously through the atmosphere, like the flowing of amber wine through crystal—the heavy vapors shuddered together as though suddenly lashed by a whip of flame,—they rose, swayed to and fro, and parted asunder. . . then, dissolving into thin, milk-white veils of fleecy film, they floated away, disclosing as they vanished, the giant summits of the encircling mountains, that lifted themselves to the light, one above another, in the form of frozen billows. Over these a delicate pink flush flitted in tremulous wavy lines—long arrows of gold began to pierce the tender shimmering blue of the sky—soft puffs of cloud tinged with vivid crimson and pale green were strewn along the eastern horizon like flowers in the path of an advancing hero,—and then all at once there was a slight cessation of movement in the heavens—an attentive pause as though the whole universe waited for some great splendor as yet unrevealed. That splendor came, in a red blaze of triumph the Sun rose, pouring a shower of beamy brilliancy over the white vastness of the heights covered with perpetual snow,—jagged peaks, sharp as scimetars and sparkling with ice, caught fire, and seemed to melt away in an absorbing sea of radiance, ... the waiting clouds moved on, redecked in deeper hues of royal purple—and the full Morning glory was declared. As the dazzling effulgence streamed through the window and flooded the couch where Alwyn lay, a faint tinge of color returned to his face,—his lips moved,—his broad chest heaved with struggling sighs,—his eyelids quivered,—and his before rigid hands relaxed and folded themselves together in an attitude of peace and prayer. Like a statue becoming slowly and magically flushed with life, the warm hues of the naturally flowing blood deepened through the whiteness of his skin,—his breathing grew more and more easy and regular,—his features gradually assumed their wonted appearance, and presently. . . without any violent start or exclamation. . . he awoke! But was it a real awakening? or rather a continuation of some strange impression received in slumber?

He rose to his feet, pushing back the hair from his brow with an entranced look of listening wonderment—his eyes were humid yet brilliant—his whole aspect was that of one inspired. He paced once or twice up and down the room, but he was evidently unconscious of his surroundings—he seemed possessed by thoughts which absorbed his whole being. Presently he seated himself at the table, and absently fingering the writing materials that were upon it, he appeared meditatively to question their use and meaning. Then, drawing several sheets of paper toward him, he began to write with extraordinary rapidity and eagerness—his pen travelled on smoothly, uninterrupted by blot or erasure. Sometimes he paused—but when he did it was always with an upraised, attentively listening expression. Once he murmured aloud "ARDATH! Nay, I shall not forget!—we will meet at ARDATH!" and again he resumed his occupation. Page after page he covered with close writing-no weak, uncertain scrawl, but a firm bold, neat caligraphy,—his own peculiar, characteristic hand. The sun mounted higher and higher in the heavens, ... hour after hour passed, and still lie wrote on, apparently unaware of the flitting time. At mid-day the

MARIE CORELLI

bell, which had not rung since early dawn, began to swing quickly to and fro in the chapel turret,—the deep bass of the organ breathed on the silence a thunderous monotone, and a bee-like murmur of distant voices proclaimed the words: "Angelas Domine nuntiavit Mariae."

At the first sound of this chant, the spell that enchained Alwyn's mind was broken; drawing a quick dashing line under what he had written, he sprang up erect and dropped his pen.

"Heliobas!" he cried loudly, "Heliobas! WHERE IS THE FIELD OF ARDATH?"

His voice seemed strange and unfamiliar to his own ears,—he waited, listening, and the chant went on—"Et Verbo caro factus est, et habitavit in nobis."

Suddenly, as if he could endure his solitude no longer, he rushed to the door and threw it open, thereby nearly flinging himself against Heliobas, who was entering the room at the same moment. He drew back, . . . stared wildly, and passing his hand across his forehead confusedly, forced a laugh.

"I have been dreaming!" he said, . . . then with a passionate gesture he added, "God! if the dream were true!"

He was strongly excited, and Heliobas, slipping one arm round him in a friendly manner, led him back to the chair he had vacated, observing him closely as he did so.

"You call THIS dreaming," he inquired with a slight smile, pointing to the table strewn with manuscript on which the ink was not yet dry. "Then dreams are more productive than active exertion! Here is goodly matter for printers! . . . a fair result it seems of one morning's labor!"

Alwyn started up, seized the written sheets, and scanned them eagerly.

"It is my handwriting!" he muttered in a tone of stupefied amazement.

"Of course! Whose handwriting should it be?" returned Heliobas, watching him with scientifically keen, yet kindly interest.

"Then it Is true!" he exclaimed. "True—by the sweetness of her eyes,—true, by the love-lit radiance of her smile!—true, O thou God whom I dared to doubt! true by the marvels of Thy matchless, wisdom!"

And with this strange outburst, he began to read in feverish haste what he had written. His breath came and went quickly,—his cheeks flushed, his eyes dilated,—line after line he perused with apparent wonder and rapture,—when suddenly interrupting himself he raised his head and recited in a half whisper:

"With thundering notes of song sublime I cast my sins away from me—On stairs of sound I mount—I climb! The angels wait and pray for me!

"I heard that stanza somewhere when I was a boy. . . why do I think of it now? SHE has waited,—so she said,—these many thousand days!"

He paused meditatively,—and then resumed his reading, Heliobas touched his arm.

"It will take you some time to read that, Mr. Alwyn," he gently observed. "You have written more than you know."

Alwyn roused himself and looked straight at the speaker. Putting down his manuscript and resting one hand upon it, he gazed with an air of solemn inquiry into the noble face turned steadfastly toward his own.

"Tell me," he said wistfully, "how has it happened? This composition is mine and yet not mine. For it is a grand and perfect poem of which I dare not call myself the author! I might as well snatch HER crown of starry flowers and call myself an Angel!"

He spoke with mingled fervor and humility. To any ordinary observer he would have seemed to be laboring under home strange hallucination,—but Heliobas was more deeply instructed.

"Come, come! . . . your thoughts are wide of this world," he said kindly. "Try to recall them! I can tell you nothing, for I know nothing. . . you have been absent many hours."

"Absent? yes!" and Alwyn's voice thrilled with an infinite regret. "Absent from earth. . . ah! would to God I might hive stayed with her, in Heaven! My love, my love! where shal I find her if not in the FIELD OF ARDATH?"

V

A Mystic Tryst

As he uttered the last words, his eyes darkened into a soft expression of musing tenderness, and he remained silent for many minutes, during which the entranced, almost unearthly beauty of his face underwent a gradual change. . . the mystic light that had for a time transfigured it, faded and died away—and by degrees he recovered all his ordinary self possession. Presently glancing at Heliobas, who stood patiently waiting till he should have overcome whatever emotions were at work in his mind, he smiled.

"You must think me mad!" he said. "Perhaps I am,—but if so, it is the madness of love that has seized me. Love! . . . it is a passion I have never known before. I have used it as a mere thread whereon to string madrigals, a background of uncertain tint serving to show off the brighter lines of Poesy—but now! . . . now I am enslaved and bound, conquered and utterly subdued by love! . . . love for the sweetest, queenliest, most radiant creature that ever captured or commanded the worship of man! I may SEEM mad—but I know I am sane—I realize the actual things of this world about me mind is—my clear, my thoughts are collected, and yet I repeat, I LOVE! . . . aye! with all the force and fervor of this strongly beating human heart of mine;"—and he touched his breast as he spoke. "And it comes to this, most wise and worthy Heliobas,—if your spells have conjured up this vision of immortal youth and grace and purity that has suddenly assumed such sovereignty over my life—then you must do something further, . . . you must find, or teach me how to find, the living Reality of my Dream!"

Heliobas surveyed him with some wonder and commiseration.

"A moment ago and you yourself declared your DREAM was true!" he observed. "This," and he pointed to the manuscript on the table, "seemed to you sufficient to prove it. Now you have altered you opinion: Why? I have worked no spells upon you, and I am entirely ignorant as to what your recent experience has been. Moreover, what do you mean by a 'living Reality'? The flesh and blood, bone and substance that perishes in a brief seventy years or so and crumbles into indistinguishable dust? Surely, . . . if, as I conjecture from your words, you have seen one of the fair inhabitants of higher spheres than ours, . . . you would not drag her spiritual and death unconscious brightness down to the level of the reality of a merely human life? Nay, if you would, you could not!"

Alwyn looked at him inquiringly and with a perplexed air.

"You speak in enigmas," he said somewhat vexedly. "However, the whole thing is an enigma and would puzzle the most sagacious head. That the physicial workings of the brain, in a site of trance, should arouse in me a passion of love for an imaginary being, and, at the same time, enable to write a poem such as must make the fame of any man, is certainly a remarkable and noteworthy result of scientific mesmerism!"

"Now, my dear sir," interrupted Heliobas in a tone of good-natured remonstrance,—"do not—if you have any respect for science at all— do not, I beg of you, talk to me of the 'physical workings' of a DEAD BRAIN?"

"A dead brain!" echoed Alwyn. "What do you mean?"

"What I say," returned Heliobas, composedly. "'Physical workings' of any kind are impossible unless the motive power of physical life be in action. You, regarded as a HUMAN creature merely, had during seven hours practically CEASED TO BE,—the vital principle no longer existed in your body, having taken its departure together with its inseparable companion, the Soul. When it returned, it set the clockwork of your material mechanism in motion again, obeying the sovereignty of the Spirit that sought to express by material means, the utterance of heaven-inspired thought. Thus your hand mechanically found its way to the pen—thus you wrote, unconscious of what you were writing, yielding yourself entirely to the guidance of the spiritual part of your nature, which AT THAT PARTICULAR JUNCTURE was absolutely predominant, though now weighted anew by earthy influences it has partially relaxed its supernal sway. All this I readily perceive and understand. . . but what you did, and where you were conducted during the time of your complete severance from the tenement of clay in which you are again imprisoned, . . . this I have yet to learn."

While Heliobas was speaking, Alwyn's countenance had grown vaguely troubled, and now into his deep poetic eyes there came a look of sudden penitence.

"True!" he said softly, almost humbly, "I will tell you everything while I remember it,—though it is not likely I shall ever forget! I believe there must be some truth after all in what you say concerning the Soul, . . . at any rate, I do not at present feel inclined to call your theories in question. To begin with, I find myself unable altogether to explain what it was that happened to me during my conversation with you last night. It was a very strange sensation! I recollect that I had expressed a wish to be placed under your magnetic or electric influence, and that you had refused my request. Then an odd idea suggested itself to me—namely, that I could if I chose COMPEL your assent,—and, filled with this notion, I think I addressed you, or was about to address you, in a rather peremptory manner, when—all at once—a flash of blinding light struck me fiercely across the eyes like a scourge! Stung with the hot pain, and dazzled by the glare, I turned away from you and fled. . . or so it seemed—fled on my own instinctive impulse. . . into DARKNESS!"

He paused and drew a long, shuddering breath, like one who has narrowly escaped imminent destruction.

"Darkness!" he went on in low accents that thrilled with the memory of a past feat—"dense, horrible, frightful darkness!—darkness that palpitated heavily with the labored motion of unseen things!—darkness that clung and closed about me in masses of clammy, tangible thickness,—its advancing and resistless weight rolled over me like a huge waveless ocean—and, absorbed within it, I was drawn down—down—down toward some hidden, impalpable but All Supreme Agony, the dull unceasing throbs of which I felt, yet could not name. 'O GOD!' I cried aloud, abandoning myself to wild despair, 'O GOD! WHERE ARE THOU?' Then I heard a great rushing sound as of a strong wind beaten through with wings, and a Voice, grand and sweet as a golden trumpet blown suddenly in the silence of night, answered: 'HERE! . . . AND EVERYWHERE!' With that, a slanting stream of opaline radiance cleft the gloom with the sweep of a sword-blade, and I was caught up quickly. . . I know not how. . . for I saw nothing!"

Again he pushed and looked wistfully at Heliobas, who in turn regarded him with gentle steadfastness.

"It was wonderful—terrible!" . . . he continued slowly—"yet beautiful! . . . that Invisible Strength that rescued, surrounded, and uplifted me; and—" here he hesitated, and a faint flush colored his cheeks and stole up to the roots of his clustering hair—"dream or no dream, I feel I cannot now altogether reject the idea of an existing Divinity. In brief. . . I believe in God!"

"Why?" asked Heliobas quietly.

Alwyn met his gaze frankly and with a soft brightening of his handsome features.

"I cannot give you any logical reasons," he said. "Moreover, logical reasoning would not now affect me in a matter which seems to me more full of conviction than any logic. I believe, . . . simply because I believe!"

Heliobas smiled—a very warm and kindly smile—but said nothing, and Alwyn resumed his narrative.

"As I tell you, I was caught up,—snatched out of that black profundity with inconceivable swiftness,—and when the ascending movement ceased, I found myself floating lightly like a wind-blown leaf through twining arches of amber mist, colored here and there with rays of living flame. . . I heard whispers, and fragments of song and speech, all sweeter than the sweetest of our known music, . . . and still I saw nothing. Presently some one called me by name—'THEOS! . . . THEOS!' I strove to answer, but I had no words wherewith to match that silver-toned, far-reaching utterance; and once again the rich vibrating notes pealed through the vaporous fire-tinted air—'THEOS, MY BELOVED! HIGHER! . . . HIGHER! . . . All my being thrilled and quivered to that call. I yearned to obey, . . . I struggled to rise—my efforts were in vain; when, to my joy and wonder, a small, invisible hand, delicate yet strong, clasped mine, and I was borne aloft with breathless, indescribable, lightning-like rapidity—on. . . on. . . and ever upward, till at last, alighting on a smooth, fair turf, thick-grown with fragrant blossoms of strange loveliness and soft hues, I beheld Her! . . . and she bade me welcome."

"And who," questioned Heliobas, in tones of hushed reverence, "Who was this Being that thus enchants your memory?"

"I know not!" replied Alwyn, with a dreamy smile of rapture on his lips and in his eyes. "And yet her face. . . oh! the entrancing beauty of that face! . . . was not altogether unfamiliar. I felt that I must have loved and lost her ages upon ages ago! Crowned with white flowers, and robed in a garb that seemed spun from midsummer moonbeams, she stood. . . a smiling Maiden-Sweetness in a paradise of glad sights and sounds, . . . ah! Eve, with the first sunrise radiance on her brows, was not more divinely fair! . . . Venus, new-springing from the silver sea-foam, was not more queenly glorious! 'I WILL REMIND THEE OF ALL THOU HAST FORGOTTEN,' she said, and I understood her soft, half-reproachful accents. 'IT IS NOT YET TOO LATE! THOU HAST LOST MUCH AND SUFFERED MUCH, AND THOU HAST BLINDLY ERRED, BUT NOTWITHSTANDING ALL THESE THINGS, THOU ART MY BELOVED SINCE THESE MANY THOUSAND DAYS!'"

"Days—which the world counts as years!" murmured Heliobas. "You saw no one but her?"

"No one—we were alone together. A vast woodland stretched before us, she took my hand and led me beneath broad-arching trees to where a lake, silvered by some strange radiance, glittered diamond-like in the stirring of a balmy wind. Here she bade me rest—and sank gently on the flowery bank beside me. Then viewing her more closely I greatly feared her beauty—for I saw a wondrous halo wide and dazzling—a golden aureole that spread itself around her in scintillating points of light—light that reflected itself also on me and bathed me in its luminous splendor. And as I gazed at her in speechless awe, she leaned toward me nearer and nearer, her deep, pure eyes burning softly into mine. . . her hands touched me—her arms closed round me. . . her bright head lay in all its shining loveliness on my breast! A tremulous ecstasy thrilled me as with fire. . . I gazed upon her as one might gaze on some fluttering, rare-plumaged bird. . . I dare not move or speak. . . I drank her sweetness down into my soul! Now and then a sound as of distant harps playing broke the love-weighted silence. . . and thus we remained together a heavenly breathing-space of wordless rapture; till suddenly and swiftly, as though she had received an invisible summons, she arose, her looks expressing a saintly patience, and laying her two hands upon my brows—'Write,' she said, 'WRITE AND PROCLAIM A MESSAGE OF HOPE TO THE SORROWFUL STAR! WRITE AND LET THINE UTTERANCE BE A TRUE ECHO OF THE ETERNAL MUSIC WITH WHICH THESE SPHERES ARE FILLED! WRITE TO THE RHYTHMIC BEAT OF THE HARMONIES WITHIN THEE. . . FOR LO! ONCE MORE AS IN AFORETIME MY CHANGELESS LOVE RENEWS IN THEE THE POWER OF PERFECT SONG!' With that she moved away serenely and beckoned me to follow. . . I obeyed in haste and trembling. . . long rays of rosy light swept after her like trailing wings, and as she walked, the golden nimbus round her form glowed with a thousand brilliant and changeful hues like the rainbows seen in the spray of falling water! Through lush green grass thick with blossom,—under groves heavy with fragrant leaves and laden with the songs of birds. . . over meadows cool and mountain-sheltered, on we went—she, like the goddess of advancing Spring, I eagerly treading in her radiant footsteps. . . and presently we came to a place where two paths met, . . . one all overgrown with azure and white flowers, that ascended away and away into undiscerned distance, . . . the other sloping deeply downward, and full of shadows, yet dimly illumined by a pale, mysterious splendor like frosty moonlight streaming on sad-colored seas. Here she turned and faced me, and I saw her divine eyes droop with the moisture of unshed tears. 'THEOS! . . . THEOS!' . . . she cried, and the passionate cadence of her voice was as the singing of a nightingale in lonely woodlands. . . 'AGAIN . . . AGAIN WE MUST PART! . . . PART! . . . OH, MY BELOVED! . . . MY BELOVED! HOW LONG WILT THOU SEVER ME FROM THY SOUL AND LEAVE ME ALONE AND SORROWFUL AMID THE JOYS OF HEAVEN?' As she thus spoke a sense of utter shame and loss and failure overwhelmed me, . . . pierced to the very core of my being by an unexplained yet most bitter remorse, I cast myself down in deep abasement before her, . . . I caught her glittering robe. . . I strove to say 'Forgive!' but I was speechless as a convicted traitor in the presence of a wronged queen! All at once the air about us was rent by a great noise of thunder intermingled with triumphal music,—she drew her sheeny garment from my touch in haste, and stooping to me where I knelt, she kissed my forehead. . . 'THY ROAD LIES THERE'—she murmured in quick, soft tones, pointing to the vista of varying light and shadow,—'MINE, YONDER!' and she looked toward the flower-garlanded avenue—'HASTEN! . . . IT IS TIME THOU WERT FAR HENCE! . . . RETURN TO THINE OWN STAR LEST ITS PORTALS BE CLOSED ON THEE FOREVER AND THOU BE PLUNGED INTO DEEPER DARKNESS! SEEK THOU THE FIELD OF ARDATH!—AS CHRIST LIVES, I WILL MEET THEE THERE! FAREWELL!' With these words she left me, passing away, arrayed in glory, treading on flowers, and ever ascending till she disappeared! . . . while I, stricken with a great repentance, went slowly, as she bade me, down into the shadow, and a rippling breeze-like melody, as of harps and lutes most tenderly attuned, followed me as I descended. And now," said Alwyn, interrupting his narrative and speaking with emphatic decision, "surely there remains but one thing for me to do—that is, to find the 'Field of Ardath.'"

Heliobas smiled gravely. "Nay, if you consider the whole episode a dream," he observed, "why trouble yourself? Dreams are seldom realized, . . . and as to the name of Ardath, have you ever heard it before?"

"Never!" replied Alwyn. "Still—if there is such a place on this planet I will most certainly journey thither! Maybe You know something of its whereabouts?"

"Finish your story," said Heliobas, quietly evading the question. "I am curious to hear the end of your strange adventure."

　　　　　　　　　　　　　　　　　　　　　　　　MARIE CORELLI

"There is not much more to tell," and Alwyn sighed a little as he spoke. "I wandered further and further into the gloom, oppressed by many thoughts and troubled by vague fears, till presently it grew so dark that I could scarcely see where I was going, though I was able to guide myself in the path that stretched before me by means of the pale luminous rays that frequently pierced the deepening obscurity, and these rays I now noticed fell ever downwards in the form of a cross. As I went on I was pursued as it were by the sound of those delicate harmonies played on invisible, sweet strings; and after a while I perceived at the extreme end of the long, dim vista a door standing open, through which I entered and found myself alone in a quiet room. Here I sat down to rest,—the melody of the distant harps and lutes still floated in soft echoes on the silence. . . and presently words came breaking through the music, like buds breaking from their surrounding leaves. . . words that I was compelled to write down as quickly as I heard them. . . and I wrote on and on, obeying that symphonious and rhythmical dictation with a sense of growing ease and pleasure, . . . when all suddenly a dense darkness overcame me, followed by a gradual dawning gray and golden light. . . the words dispersed into fragmentary half-syllables. . . the music died away, . . . I started up amazed. . . to find myself here! . . . here in this monastery of Lars, listening to the chanting of the Angelus!"

He ceased, and looked wistfully out through the window at the white encircling rim of the opposite snow-mountains, now bathed in the full splendor of noon. Heliobas advanced and laid one hand kindly on his shoulder. . .

"And do not forget," he said, "that you have brought with you from the higher regions a Poem that will in all probability make your fame! 'Fame! fame! next grandest word to God!' . . . so wrote one of your craft, and no doubt you echo the sentiment! Have you not desired to blazon your name on the open scroll of the world? Well! . . . now you can have your wish—the world waits to receive your signature!"

"That is all very well!" and Alwyn smiled rather dubiously as he glanced at the manuscript on the table beside him. "But the question is,—considering how it was written,—can I, dare I call this poem MINE?"

"Most assuredly you can," returned Heliobas. "Though your hesitation is a worthy one, and as rare as it is worthy. Well would it be for all poets and artists were they to pause thus, and consider before rashly calling their work their own! Self-appreciation is the death-blow of genius. The poem is as much yours as your life is yours—no more and no less. In brief, you have recovered your lost inspiration; the lately dumb oracle speaks again:—and are you not satisfied?"

"No!" said Alwyn quickly, with a sudden brightening of his eyes as he met the keenly searching glance that accompanied this question. "No! for I love! . . . and the desire of love burns in me as ardently as the desire of fame!" He paused, and in quieter tones continued, "You see I speak freely and frankly to you as though—," and he laughed a little, "as though I were a good Catholic, and you my father-confessor! Good heavens! if some of the men I know in London were to hear me, they would think me utterly crazed! But craze or no craze, I feel I shall never be satisfied now till I find out whether there Is anywhere is the world a place called Ardath. Can you, will you help me in the search? I am almost ashamed to ask you, for you have already done so much for me, and I really owe to your wonderful power my trance or soul-liberty, or whatever it may be called. . ."

"You owe me nothing," interposed Heliobas calmly, "not even thanks. Your own will accomplished your freedom, and I am not responsible for either your departure or your return. It was a predestined occurrence, yet perfectly scientific and easy of explanation. Your inward force attracted mine down upon you in one strong current, with the result that your Spirit instantly parted asunder from your body, and in that released condition you experienced what you have described. But *I* had no, more to do with that experience than I shall have with your journey to the 'field of Ardath,' should you decide to go there."

"There Is an Ardath then!" cried Alwyn excitedly.

Heliobas eyed him with something of scorn. "Naturally! Are you still so much of a sceptic that you think an ANGEL would have bidden you seek a place that had no existence? Oh, yes! I see you are inclined to treat your ethereal adventure as a mere dream,—but *I* know it was a reality, more real than anything in this present world." And turning to the loaded bookshelves he took down a large volume, and spread it open on the table.

"You know this book?" he asked.

Alwyn glanced at it. "The Bible! Of course!" he replied indifferently. "Everybody knows it!"

"Pardon!" and Heliobas smiled. "It would be more correct to say nobody knows it. To read is not always to understand. There are meanings and mysteries in it which have never yet been penetrated, and which only the highest and most spiritually gifted intellects can ever hope to unravel. Now" . . . and he turned over the pages carefully till he came to the one he sought, "I think there is something here that will interest you—listen!" and he read aloud, "'The Angel Uriel came unto me and said: Go into a field of flowers where no house is builded and eat only the flowers of the field—taste no flesh, drink no wine, but eat flowers only. And pray unto the Highest continually, and then will I come and talk to thee. So I went my way into the field which is called ARDATH, . . .'"

"The very place!" exclaimed Alwyn, eagerly bending over the sacred book; then drawing back with a gesture of disappointment he added, "But you are reading from Esdras, the Apocrypha! an utterly unreliable source of information!"

"On the contrary, as reliable as any history ever written," rejoined Heliobas calmly. "Study it for yourself, . . . you will see that the prophet was at that time resident in Babylon; the field he mentions was near the city. . ."

"Yes—WAS!" interrupted Alwyn incredulously.

"Was and Is," continued Heliobas. "No earthquake has crumbled it, no sea has invaded it, and no house has been 'builded' thereon. It is, as it was then, a waste field, lying about four miles west of the Babylonian ruins, and there is nothing whatever to hinder you from journeying thither when you please."

Alwyn's expression as he heard this was one of stupefied amazement. Part of his so-called "dream" had already proved itself true—a "field of Ardath" actually existed!

"You are certain of what you say?" he demanded.

"Positively certain!" returned Heliobas.

There was a silence, during which a little tinkling bell resounded in the outer corridor, followed by the tread of sandaled feet on the stone pavement. Heliobas closed the Bible and returned it to its shelf.

"That was the dinner-bell," he announced cheerfully. "Will you accompany me to the refectory, Mr. Alwyn? . . . we can talk further of this matter afterwards." Alwyn roused himself from the fit of abstraction into which he had fallen, and gathering together the loose sheets of his so strangely written manuscript, he arranged them all in an orderly heap without speaking. Then he looked up and met the earnest eyes of Heliobas with an expression of settled resolve in his own.

"I shall set out for Babylon to-morrow," he said quietly. "As well go there as anywhere! . . . and on the result of my journey I shall stake my future! In the mean time—" He hesitated, then suddenly extending his hand with a frank grace that became him well, "In spite of my brusquerie last night, I trust we are friends?"

"Why, most assuredly we are!" returned Heliobas, heartily pressing the proffered palm. "You had your doubts of me and you have them still; but what of that! I take no offence at unbelief. I pity those who suffer from its destroying influence too profoundly to find room in my heart for anger. Moreover, I never try to convert anybody. . . it is so much more satisfactory when sceptics convert themselves, as you are unconsciously doing! Come, . . . shall we join the brethren?"

Over Alwyn's face flitted a transient shade of uneasiness and hauteur.

"I would rather they knew nothing about all this," he began.

"Make your mind quite easy on that score," rejoined Heliobas. "None of my companions here are aware of your recent departure, except my very old personal friend Hilarion, who, with myself, saw your body while in its state of temporary death. But he is one of those remarkably rare wise men who know when it is best to be silent; then again, he is ignorant as to the results of your soul-transmigration, and will, as far as I am concerned, remain in ignorance. Your confidence I assure you is perfectly safe with me—as safe as though it had been received under the sacred seal of confession."

With this understanding Alwyn seemed relieved and satisfied, and thereupon they left the apartment together.

VI

"Nourhalma" and the Original Esdras

Later on in the afternoon of the same day, when the sun, poised above the western mountain-range, appeared to be lazily looking about him with a drowsy, golden smile of farewell before descending to his rest, Alwyn was once more alone in the library. Twilight shadows were already gathering in the corners of the long, low room, but he had moved the writing-table to the window, in order to enjoy the magnificence of the surrounding scenery, and sat where the light fell full upon his face as he leaned back in his chair, with his hands clasped behind his head, in an attitude of pleased, half-meditative indolence. He had just finished reading from beginning to end the poem he had composed in his trance... there was not a line in it he could have wished altered,—not a word that would have been better omitted,— the only thing it lacked was a title, and this was the question on which he now pondered. The subject of the poem itself was not new to him— it was a story he had known from boyhood, ... an old Eastern love-legend, fantastically beautiful as many such legends are, full of grace and passionate fervor—a theme fitted for the nightingale-utterance of a singer like the Persian Hafiz—though even Hafiz would have found it difficult to match the exquisitely choice language and delicately ringing rhythm in which this quaint idyll of long past ages was now most perfectly set like a jewel in fine gold. Alwyn himself entirely realized the splendid literary value of the composition—he knew that nothing more artistic in conception or more finished in treatment had appeared since the St. Agnes Eve of Keats—and as he thought of this, he yielded to a growing sense of self-complacent satisfaction which gradually destroyed all the deeply devout humility he had at first felt concerning the high and mysterious origin of his inspiration. The old inherent pride of his nature reasserted itself—he reviewed all the circumstances of his "trance" in the most practical manner—and calling to mind how the poet Coleridge had improvised the delicious fragment of Kubla Khan in a dream, he began to see nothing so very remarkable in his own unconscious production of a complete poem while under mesmeric or magnetic influences.

"After all," he mused, "the matter is simple enough when one reasons it out. I have been unable to write anything worth writing for a long time, and I told Heliobas as much. He, knowing my apathetic condition of brain, employed his force accordingly, though he denies having done so, . . . and this poem is evidently the result of my long pent-up thoughts that struggled for utterance yet could not before find vent in words. The only mysterious part of the affair is this 'Field of Ardath,' . . . how its name haunts me! . . . and how HER face shines before the eyes of my memory! That SHE should be a phantom of my own creation seems impossible—for when have I, even in my wildest freaks of fancy, ever imagined a creature half so fair!"

His gaze rested dreamily on the opposite snow-clad peaks, above which large fleecy clouds, themselves like moving mountains, were slowly passing, their edges glowing with purple and gold as they neared the sinking sun. Presently rousing himself, he took up a pen and first of all addressing an envelope to

"THE HONBLE. FRANCIS VILLIERS,
"Constitutional Club,
"LONDON"

he rapidly wrote off the following letter:

MONASTERY OF LARS,
PASS OF DARIEL, CAUCASUS

"MY DEAR VILLIERS:
Start not at the above address! I am not yet vowed to perpetual seclusion, silence or celibacy! That I of all men in the world should be in a Monastery will seem to you, who know my prejudices, in the last degree absurd—nevertheless here I am,—though here I do not remain, as it is my fixed intention to-morrow at daybreak to depart straightway from hence en route for the supposed site and ruins of Babylon. Yes,—Babylon! why not? Perished greatness has always been a more interesting subject of contemplation to me than existing littleness—and I dare say I shall wander among the tumuli of the ancient fallen city with more satisfaction than in the hot, humanity-packed streets of London, Paris, or Vienna—all destined to become tumuli in their turn.

Moreover. I am on the track of an adventure,—on the search for a new sensation, having tried nearly all the old ones and found them NIL. You know my nomadic and restless disposition. . . perhaps there is something of the Greek gipsy about me—a craving for constant change of scene and surroundings,—however, as my absence from you and England is likely to be somewhat prolonged, I send you in the mean time a Poem—there! 'Season your admiration for a while,' and hear me out patiently. I am perfectly aware of all you would say concerning the utter folly and uselessness of writing poetry at all in this present age of milk-and-watery-literature, shilling sensationals, and lascivious society dramas,—and I have a very keen recollection too of the way in which my last book was maltreated by the entire press—good heavens! how the critics yelped like dogs about my heels, snapping, sniffing, and snarling! I could have wept then like the sensitive fool I was. . . I can laugh now! In brief, my friend—for you ARE my friend and the best of all possible good fellows—I have made up my mind to conquer those that have risen against me—to break through the ranks of pedantic and pre-conceived opinions—and to climb the heights of fame, regardless of the little popular pipers of tame verso that obstruct my path and blow their tin whistles in the public ears to drown, if possible, my song. I WILL be heard! . . . and to this end I pin my faith on the work I now transmit to your care. Have it published immediately and in the best style—I will cover all expenses. Advertise sufficiently, yet with becoming modesty, for 'puffery' is a thing I heartily despise,—and were the whole press to turn round and applaud me as much as it has hitherto abused and ridiculed me, I would not have one of its penny lines of condescendingly ignorant approval quoted in connection with what must be a perfectly unostentatious and simple announcement of this new production from my pen. The manuscript is exceptionally clear, even for me who do not as a male write a very bad scrawl—so that you can scarcely have much bother with the proof-correcting—though even were this the case, and the printers turned out to be incorrigible blockheads and blunderers, I know you would grudge neither time nor trouble expended in my service. Good Frank Villiers! how much I owe you!—and yet I willingly incur another debt of gratitude by placing this matter in your hands, and am content to borrow more of your friendship, but only believe me, in order to repay it again with the truest interest! By the way, do you remember when we visited the last Paris Salon together, how fascinated we were by one picture—the head of a monk whose eyes looked out like a veritable illumination from under the folds of a drooping white cowl? . . . and on referring to our catalogues we found it described as the portrait of one 'Heliobas,' an Eastern mystic, a psychist formerly well known in Paris, but since retired into monastic life? Well! I have discovered him here; he is apparently the Superior or chief of this Order—though what Order it is and when founded is more than I can tell. There are fifteen monks altogether, living contentedly in this old, half-ruined habitation among the barren steeps of the frozen Caucasus,—splendid, princely looking fellows all of them, Heliobas himself being an exceptionally fine specimen of his race. I have just dined with the whole community, and have been fairly astonished by the fluent brilliancy and wit of their conversation. They speak all languages. English included, and no subject comes amiss to them, for they are familiar with the latest political situations in all countries,— they know all about the newest scientific discoveries (which, by-the-by, they smile at blandly, as though these last were mere child's play), and they discuss our modern social problems and theories with a Socratic-like incisiveness and composure such as our parliamentary howlers would do well to imitate. Their doctrine is. . . but I will not bore you by a theological disquisition,—enough to say it is founded on Christianity, and that at present I don't quite know what to make of it! And now, my dear Villiers, farewell! An answer to this is unnecessary; besides I can give you no address, as it is uncertain where I shall be for the next two or three months. If I don't get as much pleasure as I anticipate from the contemplation of the Babylonian ruins, I shall probably take up my abode in Bagdad for a time and try to fancy myself back in the days of 'good Haroun Alrascheed'. At any rate, whatever becomes of me, I know I have entrusted my Poem to safe hands—and all I ask of you is that it may be brought out with the least possible delay,—for its IMMEDIATE PUBLICATION seems to me just now the most vitally important thing in the world, except. . . except the adventure on which I am at present engaged, of which more hereafter, . . . when we meet. Until then think as well of me as you can, and believe me

Ever and most truly your friend,
THEOS ALWYN

This letter finished, folded, and sealed, Alwyn once more took up his manuscript and meditated anew concerning its title. Stay! . . . why not call it by the name of the ideal heroine whose heart-passion and sorrow formed the nucleus of the legend? . . . a name that he in very truth was all unconscious of having chosen, but which occurred frequently with musical persistence throughout the entire poem. "NOURHALMA!" . . . it had a soft sound. . . it seemed to breathe of Eastern languor and love-singing,—it was surely the best title he could have. Straightway deciding thereon, he wrote it clearly at the top of the first page, thus: "Nourhalma; A Love Legend of the Past," . . . then turning to the end, he signed his own name with a bold flourish, thus attesting his indisputable right to the authorship of what was not only destined to be the most famous poetical masterpiece of the day, but was also to prove the most astonishing, complex, and humiliating problem ever suggested to his brain. Carefully numbering the pages, he folded them in a neat packet, which he tied strongly and sealed—then addressing it to his friend, he put letter and packet together, and eyed them both somewhat wistfully, feeling that with them went his great chance of immortal Fame. Immortal Fame!—what a grand vista of fair possibilities those words unveiled to his imagination! Lost in pleasant musings, he looked out again on the landscape. The sun had sunk behind the mountains so far, that nothing was left of his glowing presence but a golden rim from which great glittering rays spread upward, like lifted lances poised against the purple and roseate clouds. A slight click caused by the opening of the door disturbed his reverie,—he turned round in his chair, and half rose from it as Heliobas entered, carrying a small richly chased silver casket.

"Ah, good Heliobas! here you are at last," he said with a smile. "I began to think you were never coming. My correspondence is finished,—and, as you see, my poem is addressed to England—where I pray it may meet with a better fate than has hitherto attended my efforts!"

"You PRAY?" queried Heliobas, meaningly, "or you HOPE? There is a difference between the two."

"I suppose there is," he returned nonchalantly. "And certainly—to be correct—I should have said I HOPE, for I never pray. What have you there?"—this as Heliobas set the casket he carried down on the table before him. "A reliquary? And is it supposed to contain a fragment of the true cross? Alas! I cannot believe in these fragments,—there are too many of them!"

Heliobas laughed gently.

"You are right! Moreover, not a single splinter of the true cross is in existence. It was, like other crosses then in general use, thrown aside as lumber,—and had rotted away into the earth long before the Empress Helena started on her piously crazed wanderings. No, I have nothing of that sort in here,"—and taking a key from a small chain that hung at his girdle he unlocked the casket. "This has been in the possession of the various members of our Order for ages,—it is our chief treasure, and is seldom, I may say never, shown to strangers,—but the mystic mandate you have received concerning the 'field of Ardath' entitles you to see what I think must needs prove interesting to you under the circumstances." And opening the box he lifted out a small square volume bound in massive silver and double-clasped. "This," he went on, "is the original text of a portion of the 'Visions of Esdras,' and dates from the thirteenth year after the downfall of Babylon's commercial prosperity."

Alwyn uttered an exclamation of incredulous amazement. "Not possible!" he cried. . . then he added eagerly, "May I look at it?"

Silently Heliobas placed it in his outstretched hand. As he undid the clasps a faint odor like that of long dead rose-leaves came like a breath on the air, . . . he opened it, and saw that its pages consisted of twelve moderately thick sheets of ivory, which were covered all over with curious small characters finely engraved thereon by some evidently sharp and well-pointed instrument. These letters were utterly unknown to Alwyn: he had seen nothing like them in any of the ancient tongues, and he examined them perplexedly.

"What language is this?" he asked at last, looking up. "It is not Hebrew—nor yet Sanskrit—nor does it resemble any of the discovered forms of hieroglyphic writing. Can YOU understand it?"

"Perfectly!" returned Heliobas. "If I could not, then much of the wisdom and science of past ages would be closed to my researches. It is the language once commonly spoken by certain great nations which existed long before the foundations of Babylon were laid. Little by little it fell into disuse, till it was only kept up among scholars and sages, and in time became known only as 'the language of prophecy.' When Esdras wrote his Visions they were originally divided into two hundred and four books,—and, as you will see by referring to what is now called the Apocrypha,* he was commanded to publish them all openly to the 'worthy and unworthy' all except the 'seventy last,' which were to be delivered solely to such as were 'wise among the people.' Thus one hundred and thirty-four were written in the vulgar tongue,—the remaining seventy in the 'language of prophecy,' for the use of deeply learned and scientific men alone. The volume you hold is one of those seventy."

"How did you come by it?" asked Alwyn, curiously turning the book over and over.

"How did our Order come by it, you mean," said Heliobas. "Very simply. Chaldean fraternities existed in the time of Esdras, and to the supreme Chief of these, Esdras himself delivered it. You look dubious, but I assure you it is quite authentic,—we have its entire history up to date."

"Then are you all Chaldeans here?"

"Not all—but most of us. Three of the brethren are Egyptians, and two are natives of Damascus. The rest are, like myself, descendants of a race supposed to have perished from off the face of the earth, yet still powerful to a degree undreamed of by the men of this puny age."

Alwyn gave an upward glance at the speaker's regal form—a glance of genuine admiration.

"As far as that goes," he said, with a frank laugh, "I'm quite willing to believe you and your companions are kings in disguise,—you all have that appearance! But regarding this book,"—and again he turned over the silver-bound relic—"if its authenticity can be proved, as you say, why, the British Museum would give, ah! . . . let me see!—it would give. . ."

"Nothing!" declared Heliobas quietly, "believe me, nothing! The British Government would no doubt accept it as a gift, just as it would

---

* Vide 2 Esdras xiv.44–48.

with equal alacrity accept the veritable signature of Homer, which we also possess in another retreat of ours on the Isle of Lemnos. But our treasures are neither for giving nor selling, and with respect to this original 'Esdras,' it will certainly never pass out of our hands."

"And what of the other missing sixty-nine books?" asked Alwyn.

"They may possibly be somewhere in the world,—two of them, I know, were buried in the coffin of one of the last princes of Chaldea,—perhaps they will be unearthed some day. There is also a rumor to the effect that Esdras engraved his 'Last Prophecy' on a small oval tablet of pure jasper, which he himself secreted, no one knows where. But to come to the point of immediate issue, . . . shall I find out and translate for you the allusions to the 'field of Ardath' contained in this present volume?"

"Do!" said Alwyn, eagerly, at once returning the book to Heliobas, who, seating himself at the table, began carefully looking over its ivory pages—"I am all impatience! Even without the vision I have had, I should still feel a desire to see this mysterious Field for its own sake,—it must have some very strange associations to be worth specifying in such a particular manner!"

Heliobas answered nothing—he was entirely occupied in examining the small, closely engraved characters in which the ancient record was written; the crimson afterglow of the now descended sun flared through the window and sent a straight, rosy ray on his bent head and white robes, lighting to a more lustrous brilliancy the golden cross and jeweled star on his breast, and flashing round the silver clasps of the time-honored relic before him. Presently he looked up. . .

"Here we have it!" and he placed his finger on one especial passage—it reads as follows:

"'And the Angel bade me enter a waste field, and the field was barren and dry save of herbs, and the name of the field was ARDATH.

"'And I wandered therein through the hours of the long night, and the silver eyes of the field did open before me and I saw signs and wonders:

"'And I heard a voice crying aloud, Esdras, Esdras.

"'And I arose and stood on my feet and listened and refrained not till I heard the voice again.

"'Which said unto me, Behold the field thou thoughtest barren, how great a glory hath the moon unveiled!

"'And I beheld and was sore amazed: for I was no longer myself but another.

"'And the sword of death was in that other's soul, and yet that other was but myself in pain;

"'And I knew not those things that were once familiar,—and my heart failed within me for very fear.

"'And the voice cried aloud again saying: Hide thee from the perils of the past and the perils of the future, for a great and terrible thing is come upon thee, against which thy strength is as a reed in the wind and thy thoughts as flying sand. . .

"'*And, lo, I lay as one that had been dead and mine understanding was taken from me. And he (the Angel) took me by the right hand and comforted me and set me upon my feet and said unto me:

"'What aileth thee? and why art thou so disquieted? and why is thine understanding troubled and the thoughts of thine heart?

"'And I said, Because thou hast forsaken me and yet I did according to thy words, and I went into the field and lo! I have seen and yet see that I am not able to express.'"

Here Heliobas paused, having read the last sentence with peculiarly impressive emphasis.

"That is all"—he said—"I see no more allusions to the name of Ardath. The last three verses are the same as those in the accepted Apocrypha."

---

* See 2 Esdras x. 30–32.

VII

An Undesired Blessing

Alwyn had listened with an absorbed yet somewhat mystified air of attention.

"The venerable Esdras was certainly a poet in his own way!" he remarked lightly. "There is something very fascinating about the rhythm of his lines, though I confess I don't grasp their meaning. Still, I should like to have them all the same,—will you let me write them out just as you have translated them?"

Willingly assenting to this, Heliobas read the extract over again, Alwyn taking down the words from his dictation.

"Perhaps," he then added musingly, "perhaps it would be as well to copy a few passages from the Apocrypha also."

Whereupon the Bible was brought into requisition, and the desired quotations made, consisting of verses xxiv to xxvi in the* ninth chapter of the Second Book of Esdras, and verses xxv to xxvi in the tenth chapter of the same. This done, Heliobas closed and clasped the original text of the Prophet's work and returned it to its casket; then addressing his guest in a kindly, yet serious tone, he said: "You are quite resolved to undertake this journey, Mr. Alwyn?"

Alwyn looked dreamily out of the window at the flame of the sunset hues reflected from the glowing sky on the white summit of the mountains.

"Yes, . . . I . . . I think so!" The answer had a touch of indecision in it.

"In that case," resumed Heliobas, "I have prepared a letter of introduction for you to one of our Order known as Elzear of Melyana,— he is a recluse, and his hermitage is situated close to the Babylonian ruins. You will find rest and shelter there after the fatigues of travel. I have also traced out a map of the district, and the exact position of the field you seek, . . . here it is," and he laid a square piece of parchment on the table; "you can easily perceive at a glance how the land lies. There are a few directions written at the back, so I think you will have

---

* The reader is requested to refer to the parts of "Esdras" here indicated.

MARIE CORELLI

no difficulty. This is the letter to Elzear,"—here he held out a folded paper—"will you take it now?"

Alwyn received it with a dubious smile, and eyed the donor as if he rather suspected the sincerity of his intentions.

"Thanks very much!" he murmured listlessly. "You are exceedingly good to make it all such plain sailing for me,—and yet. . . to be quite frank with you, I can't help thinking I am going on a fool's errand!"

"If that is your opinion, why go at all?" queried Heliobas, with a slight disdain in his accents. "Return to England instead—forget the name of 'Ardath,' and forget also the one who bade you meet her there, and who has waited for you 'these many thousand days!'"

Alwyn started as if he had been stung.

"Ah!" he exclaimed. "If I could be certain of seeing her again! . . . if. . . good God! the idea seems absurd! . . . if that Flower-Crowned Wonder of my dream should actually fulfill her promise and keep her tryst. . ."

"Well!" demanded Heliobas—"If so, what then?"

"Well then I will believe in anything!" he cried—"No miracle will seem miraculous. . . no impossibility impossible!"

Heliobas sighed, and regarded him thoughtfully.

"You THINK you will believe!" he said somewhat sadly—"But doubts such as yours are not easily dispelled. Angels have ere now descended to men, men have neither received nor recognized them. Angels walk by our side through crowded cities and lonely woodlands,—they watch us when we sleep, they hear us when we pray, . . . and yet the human eye sees nothing save the material objects within reach of its vision, and is not very sure of those, while it can no more discern the spiritual presences than it can without a microscope discern the lovely living creatures contained in a drop of dew or a ray of sunshine. Our earthly sight is very limited—it can neither perceive the infinitely little nor the infinitely great. And it is possible,—nay, it is most probable, that even as Peter of old denied his Divine Master, so you, if brought face to face with the Angel of your last night's experience, would deny and endeavor to disprove her identity."

"Never!" declared Alwyn, with a passionate gesture—"I should know her among a thousand!"

For one instant Heliobas bent upon him a sudden, searching, almost pitiful glance, then withdrawing his gaze he said gently:

"Well, well! let us hope for the best—God's ways are inscrutable—and you tell me that now—now after your strange so-called 'vision'—you believe in God?"

"I did say so, certainly. . ." and Alwyn's face flushed a little. . . "but. . ."

"Ah! . . . you hesitate! there is a 'but' in the case!" and Heliobas turned upon him with a grand reproach in his brilliant eyes. "Already stepping backward on the road! . . . already rushing once again into the darkness! . . ." He paused, then laying one hand on the young man's shoulder, continued in mild yet impressive accents: "My friend, remember that the doubter and opposer of God, is also the doubter and opposer of his own well-being. Let this unnatural and useless combat of Human Reason, against Divine Instinct cease within you—you, who as a poet are bound to EQUALIZE your nature that it may the more harmoniously fulfil its high commission. You know what one of your modern writers says of life? . . . that it is a 'Dream in which we clutch at shadows as though they were substances, and sleep deepest when fancying ourselves most awake.'* Believe me, You have slept long enough—it is time you awoke to the full realization of your destinies."

Alwyn heard in silence, feeling inwardly rebuked and half ashamed—the earnestly spoken words moved him more than he cared to show—his head drooped—he made no reply. After all, he thought, he had really no more substantial foundation for his unbelief than others had for their faith. With all his studies in the modern schools of science, he was not a whit more advanced in learning than Democritus of old—Democritus who based his system of morals on the severest mathematical lines, taking as his starting-point a vacuum and atoms, and who after stretching his intellect on a constant rack of searching inquiry for years, came at last to the unhappy conclusion that man is absolutely incapable of positive knowledge, and that even if truth is in his possession he can never be certain of it. Was he, Theos Alwyn, wiser than Democritus? . . . or was this stately Chaldean monk, with the clear, pathetic eyes and tender smile, and the symbol of Christ on his breast, wiser than both? . . . wiser in the wisdom of eternal things than any of the subtle-minded ancient Greek philosophers or modern imitators of their theories? Was there, COULD there be something not yet altogether understood or fathomed in the Christian creed? . . . as

---

* Carlyle's Sartor Resartus.

this idea occurred to him he looked up and met his companion's calm gaze fixed upon him with a watchful gentleness and patience.

"Are you reading my thoughts, Heliobas?" he asked, with a forced laugh. "I assure you they are not worth the trouble."

Heliobas smiled, but made no answer. Just then one of the monks entered the room with a large lighted lamp, which he set on the table, and the conversation thus interrupted was not again resumed.

The evening shadows were now closing in rapidly, and already above the furthest visible snow-peak the first risen star sparkled faintly in the darkening sky. Soon the vesper bell began ringing as it had rung on the previous night when Alwyn, newly arrived, had sat alone in the refectory, listlessly wondering what manner of men he had come amongst, and what would be the final result of his adventure into the wilds of Caucasus. His feelings had certainly undergone some change since then, inasmuch as he was no longer disposed to ridicule or condemn religious sentiment, though he was nearly as far from actually believing in Religion itself as ever. The attitude of his mind was still distinctly skeptical—the immutable pride of what he considered his own firmly rooted convictions was only very slightly shaken—and he now even viewed the prospect of his journey to the "field of Ardath" as a mere fantastic whim—a caprice of his own fancy which he chose to gratify just for the sake of curiosity.

But notwithstanding the stubbornness of the materialistic principles with which he had become imbued, his higher instincts were, unconsciously to himself, beginning to be aroused—his memory involuntarily wandered back to the sweet, fresh days of his earliest manhood before the poison of Doubt had filtered through his soul—his character, naturally of the lofty, imaginative, and ardent cast, re-asserted its native force over the blighting blow of blank Atheism which had for a time paralyzed its efforts—and as he unwittingly yielded more and more to the mild persuasions of these genial influences, so the former Timon-like bitterness of his humor gradually softened. There was no trace in him now of the dark, ironic, and reckless scorn that, before his recent visionary experience, had distinguished his whole manner and bearing—the smile came more readily to his lips—and he seemed content for the present to display the sunny side of his nature—a nature impassioned, frank, generous, and noble, in spite of the taint of overweening, ambitious egotism which somewhat warped its true quality and narrowed the range of its sympathies. In his then frame of mind, a curious, vague sense of half-pleasurable penitence was upon him,—delicate, undefined, almost devotional suggestions stirred his thoughts with the refreshment that a cool wind brings to parched and drooping flowers,—so that when Heliobas, taking up the silver "Esdras" reliquary and preparing to leave the apartment in response to the vesper summons, said gently, "Will you attend our service, Mr. Alwyn?" he assented at once, with a pleased alacrity which somewhat astonished himself as he remembered how, on the previous evening, he had despised and inwardly resented all forms of religious observance.

However, he did not stop to consider the reason of his altered mood, . . . he followed the monks into chapel with an air of manly grace and quiet reverence that became him much better than the offensive and defensive demeanor he had erewhile chosen to assume in the same prayer-hallowed place,—he listened to the impressive ceremonial from beginning to end without the least fatigue or impatience,—and though when the brethren knelt, he could not humble himself so far as to kneel also, he still made a slight concession to appearances by sitting down and keeping his head in a bent posture—"out of respect for the good intentions of these worthy men," as he told himself, to silence the inner conflict of his own opposing and contradictory sensations. The service concluded, he waited as before to see the monks pass out, and was smitten with a sudden surprise, compunction, and regret, when Heliobas, who walked last as usual, paused where he stood, and confronted him, saying:

"I will bid you farewell here, my friend! . . . I have many things to do this evening, and it is best I should see you no more before your departure."

"Why?" asked Alwyn astonished—"I had hoped for another conversation with you."

"To what purpose!" inquired Heliobas mildly. "That I should assert. . . and you deny. . . facts that God Himself will prove in His own way and at His own appointed time? Nay, we should do no good by further arguments."

"But," stammered Alwyn hastily, flushing hotly as he spoke, "you give me no chance to thank you. . . to express my gratitude."

"Gratitude?" questioned Heliobas almost mournfully, with a tinge of reproach in his soft, mellow voice. "Are you grateful for being, as you think, deluded by a trance? . . . cheated, as it were, into a sort of semi-belief in the life to come by means of mesmerism? Your first request to me, I know, was that you might be deceived by my influence into a state of imaginary happiness,—and now you fancy your last night's experience was merely the result of that pre-eminently foolish desire. You are wrong! . . . and, as matters stand, no thanks are needed. If I had indeed mesmerized or hypnotized you, I might perhaps have deserved some reward for the exertion of my purely professional skill, but. . . as I have told you already. . . I have done absolutely nothing. Your fate is, as it has always been, in your own hands. You sought me of your own accord. . . you used me as an instrument, an unwilling instrument, remember! . . . whereby to break open the prison doors of your chafed, and fretting spirit,—and the end of it all is that you depart from hence tomorrow of your own free-will and choice, to fulfill the appointed tryst made with you, as you believe, by a phantom in a vision. In brief"—here he spoke more slowly and with marked emphasis—"you go to the field of Ardath to solve a puzzling problem. . . namely, as to whether what we call life is not a Dream—and whether a Dream may not perchance be proved Reality! In this enterprise of yours I have no share—nor will I say more than this. . . God speed you on your errand!"

He held out his hand—Alwyn grasped it, looking earnestly meanwhile at the fine intellectual face, the clear pathetic eyes, the firm yet sensitive mouth, on which there just then rested a serious yet kindly smile.

"What a strange man you are, Heliobas!" he said impulsively. . . "I wish I knew more about you!"

Heliobas gave him a friendly glance.

"Wish rather that you knew more about yourself"—he answered simply—"Fathom your own mystery of being—you shall find none deeper, greater, or more difficult of comprehension!"

Alwyn still held his hand, reluctant to let it go. Finally releasing it with a slight sigh, he said:

"Well, at any rate, though we part now it will not be for long. We Must meet again!"

"Why, if we must, we shall!" rejoined Heliobas cheerily. "Must cannot be prevented! In the mean time. . . farewell!"

"Farewell!" and as this word was spoken their eyes met. Instinctively and on a sudden impulse, Alwyn bowed his head in the lowest and most reverential salutation he had perhaps ever made to any creature of mortal mold, and as he did so Heliobas paused in the act of turning away.

"Do you care for a blessing, gentle Skeptic!" he asked in a soft tone that thrilled tenderly through the silence of the dimly-lit chapel,—then, receiving no reply, he laid one hand gently on the young man's dark, clustering curls, and with the other slowly traced the sign of the cross upon the smooth, broad fairness of his forehead.—"Take it, my son! . . . the only blessing I can give thee,—the blessing of the Cross of Christ, which in spite of thy desertion claims thee, redeems thee, and will yet possess thee for its own!"

And before Alwyn could recover from his astonishment sufficiently to interrupt and repudiate this, to him, undesired form of benediction, Heliobas had gone, and he was left alone. Lifting his head he stared out into the further corridor, down which he just perceived a distant glimmer of vanishing white robes,—and for a moment he was filled with speechless indignation. It seemed to him that the sign thus traced on his brow must be actually visible like a red brand burnt into his flesh,—and all his old and violent prejudices against Christianity rushed back upon him with the resentful speed of once baffled foes returning anew to storm a citadel. Almost as rapidly, however, his anger cooled,—he remembered that in his vision of the previous night, the light that had guided him through the long, shadowy vista had always preceded him in the form of a Cross,—and in a softer mood he glanced at the ruby Star shining steadily above the otherwise darkened altar. Involuntarily the words "We have seen His Star in the East and have come to worship Him"—occurred to his memory, but he dismissed them as instantly as they suggested themselves, and finding his own thoughts growing perplexing and troublesome he hastily left the chapel.

Joining some of the monks who were gathered in a picturesque group round the fire in the refectory he sat chatting with them for about half an hour or so, hoping to elicit from them in the course of conversation some particulars concerning the daily life, character, and professing aims of their superior,—but in this attempt he failed. They spoke of Heliobas as believing men may speak of saints, with hushed reverence and admiring tenderness—but on any point connected with his faith, or the spiritual nature of his theories, they held their peace, evidently deeming the subject too sacred for discussion. Baffled in all his inquiries Alwyn at last said good-night, and retired to rest in the small sleeping-apartment prepared for his accommodation, where he enjoyed a sound, refreshing, and dreamless slumber.

The next morning he was up at daybreak, and long before the sun had risen above the highest peak of Caucasus, he had departed from the Lars Monastery, leaving a handsome donation in the poor-box toward the various charitable works in which the brethren were engaged, such as the rescue of travellers lost in the snow, or the burial of the many victims murdered on or near the Pass of Dariel by the bands of fierce mountain robbers and assassins, that at certain seasons infest that solitary region. Making the best of his way to the fortress of Passanaur, he there joined a party of adventurous Russian climbers who had just successfully accomplished the assent of Mount Kazbek, and in their company proceeded through the rugged Aragua valley to Tiflis, which he reached that same evening. From this dark and dismal-looking town, shadowed on all sides by barren and cavernous hills, he dispatched the manuscript of his mysteriously composed poem, together with the letter concerning it, to his friend Villiers in England,—and then, yielding to a burning sense of impatience within himself,—impatience that would brook no delay,—he set out resolutely, and at once, on his long pilgrimage to the "land of sand and ruin and gold"—the land of terrific prophecy and stern fulfilment,—the land of mighty and mournful memories, where the slow river Euphrates clasps in its dusky yellow ring the ashes of great kingdoms fallen to rise no more.

VIII

BY THE WATERS OF BABYLON

It was no light or easy journey he had thus rashly undertaken on the faith of a dream,—for dream he still believed it to be. Many weary days and nights were consumed in the comfortless tedium of travel, . . . and though he constantly told himself what unheard-of folly it was to pursue an illusive chimera of his own imagination,—a mere phantasm which had somehow or other taken possession of his brain at a time when that brain must have been acted upon (so he continued to think) by strong mesmeric or magnetic influence, he went on his way all the same with a sort of dogged obstinacy which no fatigue could daunt or lessen. He never lay down to rest without the faint hope of seeing once again, if only in sleep, the radiant Being whose haunting words had sent him on this quest of "Ardath,"—but herein his expectations were not realized. No more flower-crowned angels floated before him—no sweet whisper of love, encouragement, or promise came mysteriously on his ears in the midnight silences,—his slumbers were always profound and placid as those of a child and utterly dreamless.

One consolation he had however, . . . he could write. Not a day passed without his finding some new inspiration. . . some fresh, quaint, and lovely thought, that flowed of itself into most perfect and rhythmical utterance,—glorious lines of verse glowing with fervor and beauty seemed to fall from his pencil without any effort on his part,— and if he had had reason in former times to doubt the strength of his poetical faculty, it was now very certain he could do so longer. His mind was as a fine harp newly strung, attuned, and quivering with the consciousness of the music pent-up within it,—and as he remembered the masterpiece of poesy he had written in his seeming trance, the manuscript of which would soon be in the hands of the London publishers, his heart swelled with a growing and irrepressible sense of pride. For he knew and felt—with an undefinable yet positive certainty— that however much the public or the critics might gainsay him, his fame as a poet of the very highest order would ere long be asserted and assured. A deep tranquillity was in his soul. . . a tranquillity that seemed to increase the further he went onward,—the restless weariness that had once possessed him was past, and a vaguely sweet content pervade his being like the odor of early roses pervading warm air. . . he felt, he hoped, he loved! . . . and yet his feelings, hopes, and longings turned to something altogether undeclared and indefinite, as softly dim and distant as the first faint white cloud-signal wafted from the moon in heaven, when, on the point of rising, she makes her queenly purpose known to her waiting star-attendants.

Practically considered, his journey was tedious and for the most part dull and uninteresting. In these Satan-like days of "going to and fro in the earth and walking up and down in it" travelling has lost much of its old romantic charm, . . . the idea of traversing long distances no more fills the expectant adventurer with a pleasurable sense of uncertainty and mystery—he knows exactly what to anticipate. . . it is all laid out for him plainly on the level lines of the commonplace, and nothing is left to his imagination. The Continent of Europe has been ransacked from end to end by tourists who have turned it into a sort of exhausted pleasure-garden, whereof the various entertainments are too familiarly known to arouse any fresh curiosity,—the East is nearly in the same condition,—hordes of British and American sight-seers scamper over the empire-strewn soil of Persia and Syria with the unconcerned indifference of beings to whom not only a portion of the world's territory, but the whole world itself, belongs,—and soon there will not be an inch of ground left on the narrow extent of our poor planet that has not been trodden by the hasty, scrambling, irreverent footsteps of some one or other of the ever-prolific, all-spreading English-speaking race.

On his way Alwyn met many of his countrymen,—travellers who, like himself, had visited the Caucasus and Armenia and were now en route, some for Damascus, some for Jerusalem and the Holy Land—others again for Cairo and Alexandria, to depart from thence homeward by the usual Mediterranean line, . . . but among these birds-of-passage acquaintance he chanced upon none who were going to the Ruins of Babylon. He was glad of this—for the peculiar nature of his enterprise rendered a companion altogether undesirable,—and though on one occasion he encountered a gentleman-novelist with a note-book, who was exceedingly anxious to fraternize with him and discover whither he vas bound, he succeeded in shaking off this would-be incubus at Mosul, by taking him to a wonderful old library in that city where there were a number of French translations of Turkish and Syriac romances. Here the gentleman-novelist straightway ascended to the seventh heaven of plagiarism, and began to copy energetically whole scenes and descriptive passages from dead-and-gone authors, unknown to English critics, for the purpose of inserting them hereafter into his own "original" work of fiction—and in this congenial occupation he forgot all about the "dark handsome man, with the wide brows of a Marc Antony and the lips of a Catullus," as he had already described Alwyn in the note-book before-mentioned. While in Mosul, Alwyn himself picked up a curiosity in the way of literature,—a small quaint volume entitled "The Final Philosophy Of Algazzali The Arabian." It was printed in two languages—the original Arabic on one page, and, facing it, the translation in very old French. The author, born A.D. 1058, described himself as "a poor student striving to discern the truth of things"—and his work was a serious, incisive, patiently exhaustive inquiry into the workings of nature, the capabilities of human intelligence, and the deceptive results of human reason. Reading it, Alwyn was astonished to find that nearly all the ethical propositions offered for the world's consideration to-day by the most learned and cultured minds, had been already advanced and thoroughly discussed by this same Algazzali. One passage in particular arrested his attention as being singularly applicable to his own immediate condition, . . . it ran as follows,—

"I began to examine the objects of sensation and speculation to see if they could possibly admit of doubt. Then, doubts crowded upon me in such numbers that my incertitude became complete. Whence results the confidence I have in sensible things? The strongest of all our senses is sight,—yet if we look at the stars they seem to be as small as money-pieces—but mathematical proofs convince us that they are larger than the earth. These and other things are judged by the Senses, but rejected by Reason as false. I abandoned the senses therefore, having seen my confidence in their Absolute Truth shaken. Perhaps, said I, there is no assurance but in the notions of reason? . . . that is to say, first principles, as that ten is more than three? Upon this the Senses replied: What assurance have you that your confidence in Reason is not of the same nature as your confidence in Us? When you relied on us, reason stepped in and gave us the lie,—had not reason been there you would have continued to rely on us. Well, nay there not exist some other judge Superior to reason who, if he appeared, would refute the judgments of reason in the same way that reason refuted us? The non-appearance of such a judge is no proof of his non-existence. . . I strove to answer this objection, and my difficulties increased when I came to reflect on sleep. I said to myself: During sleep you give to visions a reality and consistence, and on awakening you are made aware that they were nothing but visions. What assurance have you that all you feel and know does actually exist? It is all true as respects your condition at the moment,—but it is nevertheless possible that another condition should present itself which should be to your awakened state, that which your awakened state is now to your sleep,—So That, As Respects This Higher Condition Your Waking Is But Sleep."

Over and over again Alwyn read these words and pondered on the deep and difficult problems they suggested, and he was touched to an odd sense of shamed compunction, when at the close of the book he came upon Algazzali's confession of utter vanquishment and humility thus simply recorded:

"I examined my actions and found the best were those relating to instruction and education, and even there I saw myself given up to unimportant sciences all useless in another world. Reflecting on the aim of my teaching, I found it was not pure in the sight of the Lord. And that all my efforts were directed toward the acquisition of glory to myself. Having therefore distributed my wealth I left Bagdad and retired into Syria, where I remained in solitary struggle with my soul, combating my passions and exercising myself in the purification of my heart and in preparation for the other world."

This ancient philosophical treatise, together with the mystical passage from the original text of Esdras and the selected verses from the Apocrypha, formed all Alwyn's stock of reading for the rest of his journey,—the rhapsodical lines of the Prophet he knew by heart, as one knows a favorite poem, and he often caught himself unconsciously repeating the strange words: "Behold the field thou thoughtest barren: how great a glory hath the moon unveiled!"

"And I beheld, and was sore amazed, for I was no longer myself but another.

"And the sword of death was in that other's soul: and yet that other was but myself, in pain.

"And I knew not the things that were once familiar and my heart failed within me for very fear. . ."

What did they mean, he wondered? or had they any meaning at all beyond the faint, far-off suggestions of thought that may occasionally and with difficulty be discerned through obscure and reckless ecstasies of language which, "full of sound and fury, signify nothing"? Was there, could there, be anything mysterious or sacred in this "wiste field" anciently known as "Ardath"? These questions flitted hazily from time to time through his brain, but he made no attempt to answer them either by refutation or reason, . . . indeed sober, matter-of-fact reason, he was well aware, played no part in his present undertaking.

It was late in the afternoon of a sultry parching day when he at last arrived at Hillah. This dull little town, built at the beginning of the twelfth century out of the then plentifully scattered fragments of Babylon, has nothing to offer to the modern traveller save various annoyances in the shape of excessive heat, dust, or rather fine blown sand,—dirt, flies, bad food, and general discomfort; and finding the aspect of the place not only untempting, but positively depressing, Alwyn left his surplus luggage at a small and unpretentious hostelry kept by a Frenchman, who catered specially for archaeological tourists and explorers, and after an hour's rest, set out alone and on foot for the "eastern quarter" of the ruins,—namely those which are considered by investigators to begin about two miles above Hillah. A little beyond them and close to the river-bank, according to the deductions he had received, dwelt the religious recluse for whom he brought the letter of introduction from Heliobas,—a letter bearing on its cover a superscription in Latin which translated ran thus:—"To the venerable and much esteemed Elzear of Melyana, at the Hermitage, near Hillah. In faith, peace, and good-will. Greeting." Anxious to reach Elzear's abode before nightfall, he walked on as briskly as the heat and heaviness of the sandy soil would allow, keeping to the indistinctly traced path that crossed and re-crossed at intervals the various ridges of earth strewn with pulverized fragments of brick, bitumen, and pottery, which are now the sole remains of stately buildings once famous in Babylon.

A low red sun was sinking slowly on the edge of the horizon, when, pausing to look about him, he perceived in the near distance, the dark outline of the great mound known as Birs-Nimroud, and realized with a sort of shock that he was actually surrounded on all sides by the crumbled and almost indistinguishable ruins of the formerly superb all-dominant Assyrian city that had been "as a golden cup in the Lord's hand," and was now no more in very truth than a "broken and an empty vessel." For the words, "And Babylon shall become heaps," have certainly been verified with startling exactitude—"heaps" indeed it has become,—nothing BUT heaps,—heaps of dull earth with here and there a few faded green tufts of wild tamarisk, which while faintly relieveing the blankness of the ground, at the same time intensify its monotonous dreaminess. Alwyn, beholding the mournful desolation of the scene, felt a strong sense of disappointment,—he had expected something different,—his imagination had pictured these historical ruins as being of larger extent and more imposing character. His eyes rested rather wearily on the slow, dull gleam of the Euphrates, as it wound past the deserted spaces where "the mighty city the astonishment of nations" had once stood, . . . and poet though he was to the very core of his nature, he could see nothing poetical in these spectral mounds and stone heaps, save in the significant remembrance they offered of the old Scriptural prophecy—"Babylon is fallen—is fallen! Her princes, her wise men, her captains, her rulers, and her mighty men shall sleep a perpetual sleep and not wake, saith the King who is the Lord of Hosts." And truly it seemed as if the curse which had blighted the city's bygone splendor had doomed even its ruins to appear contemptible.

Just then the glow of the disappearing sun touched the upper edge of Birs-Nimroud, giving it for one instant a weird effect, as though the ghost of some Babylonian watchman were waving a lit torch from its summit,—but the lurid glare soon faded and a dead gray twilight settled solemnly down over the melancholy landscape. With a sudden feeling of dejection and lassitude upon him, Alwyn, heaving a deep sigh, went onward, and soon perceived, lying a little to the north of the river, a small, roughly erected tenement with a wooden cross on its roof. Rightly concluding that this must be Elzear of Melyana's hermitage, he quickly made his way thither and knocked at the door.

It was opened to him at once by a white-haired, picturesque old man, who received him with a mute sign of welcome, and who at the same time laid one hand lightly but expressively on his own lips to signify that he was dumb. This was Elzear himself. He was attired in the same sort of flowing garb as that worn by the monks of Dariel, and with his tall, spare figure, long, silvery beard and deep-sunken yet still brilliant dark eyes, he might have served as a perfect model for one of the inspired prophets of bygone ancient days. Though Nature had deprived him of speech, his serene countenance spoke eloquently in his favor, its mild benevolent expression betokening that inward peace of the heart which so often renders old age more beautiful than youth. He perused with careful slowness the letter Alwyn presented to him,—and then, inclining his head gravely, he made a courteous and comprehensive gesture, to intimate that himself and all that his house contained were at the service of the newcomer. He proceeded to testify the sincerity of this assurance at once by setting a plentiful supply of food and wine before his guest, waiting upon him, moreover, while he ate and drank, with a respectful humility which somewhat embarrassed Alwyn, who wished to spare him the trouble of such attendance and told him so many times with much earnestness. But all to no purpose—Elzear only smiled gently and continued to perform the duties of hospitality in his own way. . . it was evidently no use interfering with him. Later on he showed his visitor a small cell-like apartment containing a neat bed, together with a table, a chair, and a large Crucifix, which latter object was suspended against the wall, . . . and indicating by eloquent signs that here the weariest traveller might find good repose, he made a low salutation and departed altogether for the night.

What a still place the "Hermitage" was, thought Alwyn, as soon as Elzear's retreating steps had died away into silence. There was not a sound to be heard anywhere, . . . not even the faint rustle of leaves stirred by the wind. And what a haunting, grave, wistfully tender expression filled the face of that sculptured Image on the Cross, which in intimate companionship with himself seemed to possess the little room! He could not bear the down-drooping appealing, penetrating look in those heavenly-kind yet piteous Eyes, . . . turning abruptly away he opened the narrow window, and folding his arms on the sill surveyed the scene before him. The full moon was rising slowly, . . . round and large, she hung like a yellow shield on the dark, dense wall of the sky. The Rums of Babylon were plainly visible. . . the river shone like a golden ribbon,—the outline of Birs-Nimoud was faintly rimmed with light, and had little streaks of amber radiance wandering softly up and down its shadowy slopes.

"'AND I WENT INTO THE FIELD CALLED ARDATH AND THERE I SAT AMONG THE FLOWERS!'" mused Alwyn half aloud, his dreamy gaze fixed on the gradually brightening heavens. . . "Why not go there at once. . . Now!"

IX

THE FIELD OF FLOWERS

This idea had no sooner entered his mind than he prepared to act upon it,—though only a short while previously, feeling thoroughly overcome by fatigue, he had resolved to wait till next day before setting out for the chief goal of his long pilgrimage. But now, strangely enough, all sense of weariness had suddenly left him,—a keen impatience burned in his veins,—and a compelling influence stronger than himself seemed to urge him on to the instant fulfillment of his purpose. The more he thought about it the more restless he became, and the more eagerly desirous to prove, with the least possible delay, the truth or the falsity of his mystic vision at Danel. By the light of the small lamp left on the table he consulted his map,—the map Heliobas had traced,—and also the written directions that accompanied it—though these he had read so often over and over again that he knew them by heart. They were simply and concisely worded thus: "On the east bank of the Euphrates, nearly opposite the 'Hermitage,' there is the sunken fragment of a bronze Gate, formerly belonging to the Palace of the Babylonian Kings. Three miles and a half to the southwest of this fragment and in a direct line with it, straight across country, will be found a fallen pillar of red granite half buried in the earth. The square tract of land extending beyond this broken column is the field known to the Prophet Esdras as the 'FIELD OF ARDATH.'"

He was on the east bank of the Euphrates already,—and a walk of three miles and a half could surely be accomplished in an hour or very little over that time. Hesitating no longer he made his way out of the house, deciding that if he met Elzear he would say he was going for a moonlight stroll before retiring to rest. That venerable recluse, however, was nowhere to be seen,—and as the door of the "Hermitage" was only fastened with a light latch he had no difficulty in effecting a noiseless exit. Once in the open air he stopped, . . . startled by the sound of full, fresh, youthful voices singing in clear and harmonious unison. . . "KYRIE ELEISON! CHRISTE ELEISON! KYRIE ELEISON!" He listened, . . . looking everywhere about him in utter amazement. There was no habitation in sight save Elzear's,—and the chorus certainly did not proceed from thence, but rather seemed to rise upward through the earth, floating in released sweet echoes to and fro upon the hushed air. "KYRIE ELEISON! . . . CHRISTE ELEISON!" How it swayed about him like a close chime of bells!

He stood motionless, perplexed and wondering, . . . was there a subterranean grotto near at hand where devotional chants were sung?—or, . . . and a slight tremor ran through him at the thought, . . . was there something supernatural in the music, notwithstanding its human-seeming speech and sound? Just then it ceased, . . . all was again silent as before, . . . and angry with himself for his own foolish fancies, he set about the task of discovering the "sunken fragment" Heliobas had mentioned. Very soon he found it, driven deep into the soil and so blackened and defaced by time that it was impossible to trace any of the elaborate carvings that must have once adorned it. In fact it would not have been recognizable as a portion of a gate at all, had it not still possessed an enormous hinge which partly clung to it by means of one huge thickly rusted nail, dose beside it, grew a tree of weird and melancholy appearance—its trunk was split asunder and one half of it was withered. The other half leaning mournfully on one side bent down its branches to the ground, trailing a wealth of long, glossy green leaves in the dust of the ruined city. This was the famous tree called by the natives Athel, of which old legends say that it used to be a favorite evergreen much cultivated and prized by the Babylonian nobility, who loving its pleasant shade, spared no pains to make it grow in their hanging gardens and spacious courts, though its nature was altogether foreign to the soil. And now, with none to tend it or care whether it flourishes or decays, it faithfully clings to the deserted spot where it was once so tenderly fostered, showing its sympathy with the surrounding desolation, by growing always in split halves, one withered and one green—a broken-hearted creature, yet loyal to the memory of past love and joy. Alwyn stood under its dark boughs, knowing nothing of its name or history,—every now and then a wailing whisper seemed to shudder through it, though there was no wind,—and he heard the eerie lamenting sigh with an involuntary sense of awe. The whole scene was far more impressive by night than by day,—the great earth mounds of Babylon looked like giant graves inclosing a glittering ring of winding waters. Again he examined the imbedded fragment of the ancient gate,—and then feeling quite certain of his starting-point he set his face steadily toward the southwest,—there the landscape before him lay flat and bare in the beamy lustre of the moon. The soil was sandy and heavy to the tread,—moreover it was an excessively hot night,—too hot to walk fast. He glanced at his watch,—it was a few minutes past ten o'clock. Keeping up the moderate pace the heat enforced, it was possible he might reach the mysterious field about half-past eleven, . . . perhaps earlier. And now his nerves began to quiver with strong excitement, . . . had he yielded to the promptings of his own feverish impatience, he would most probably have run all the way in spite of the sultriness of the air,—but he restrained this impulse, and walked leisurely on purpose, reproaching himself as he went along for the utter absurdity of his expectations.

"Was ever madman more mad than I!" he murmured with some self-contempt—"What logical human being in his right mind would be guilty of such egregious folly! But am I logical? Certainly not! Am I in my right mind? I think I am,—yet I may be wrong. The question remains, . . . what Is logic? . . . and what Is being in one's right mind? No one can absolutely decide! Let me see if I can review calmly my ridiculous position. It comes to this,—I insist on being mesmerized. . . I have a dream, . . . and I see a woman in the dream"—here he suddenly corrected himself. . . "a woman did I say? No! . . . she was something far more than that! A lovely phantom—a dazzling creature of my own imagination. . . an exquisite ideal whom I will one day immortalize. . . yes!—IMMORTALIZE in song!"

He raised his eyes as he spoke to the dusky firmament thickly studded with stars, and just then caught sight of a fleecy silver-rimmed cloud passing swiftly beneath the moon and floating downwards toward the earth,—it was shaped like a white-winged bird, and was here and there tenderly streaked with pink, as though it had just travelled from some distant land where the sun was rising. It was the only cloud in the sky,—and it had a peculiar, almost phenomenal effect by reason of its rapid motion, there being not the faintest breeze stirring. Alwyn watched it gliding down the heavens till it had entirely disappeared, and then began his meditations anew.

"Any one,—even without magnetic influence being brought to bear upon him, might have visions such as mine! Take an opium-eater, for instance, whose life is one long confused vista of visions,—suppose he were to accept all the wild suggestions offered to his drugged brain, and persist in following them out to some sort of definite conclusion,—the only place for that man would be a lunatic asylum. Even the most ordinary persons, whose minds are never excited in any abnormal way, are subject to very curious and inexplicable dreams,—but for all that, they are not such fools as to believe in them. True, there is my poem,—I don't know how I wrote it, yet written it is, and complete from beginning to end—an actual tangible result of my vision, and strange enough in its way, to say the least of it. But what is stranger still is that I LOVE the radiant phantom that I saw. . . yes, actually love her with a love no mere woman, were she fair as Troy's Helen, could ever arouse in me! Of course,—in spite of the contrary assertions made by that remarkably interesting Chaldean monk Heliobas,—I feel I am the victim of a brain-delusion,—therefore it is just as well I should see this 'field of Ardath' and satisfy myself that nothing comes of it—in which case I shall be cured of my craze."

He walked on for some time, and presently stopped a moment to examine his map by the light of the moon. As he did so, he became aware of the extraordinary, almost terrible, stillness surrounding him. He had thought the "Hermitage" silent as a closed tomb—but it was nothing to the silence here. He felt it inclosing him like a thick wall on all sides,—he heard the regular pulsations of his own heart—even the rushing of his own blood—but no other sound was audible. Earth and the air seemed breathless, as though with some pent-up mysterious excitement,—the stars were like so many large living eyes eagerly gazing down on the solitary human being who thus wandered at night in the land of the prophets of old—the moon itself appeared to stare at him in open wonderment. He grew uncomfortably conscious of this speechless watchfulness of nature,—he strained his ears to listen, as it were to the deepening dumbness of all existing things,—and to conquer the strange sensations that were overcoming him, he proceeded at a more rapid pace,—but in two or three minutes came again to an abrupt halt. For there in front of him, right across his path, lay the fallen pillar which, according to Heliobas, marked the boundary to the field he sought! Another glance at his map decided the position. . . he had reached his journey's end at last! What was the time? He looked—it was just twenty minutes past eleven.

A curious, unnatural calmness suddenly possessed him, . . . he surveyed with a quiet, almost cold, unconcern the prospect before him,—a wide level square of land covered with tufts of coarse grass and clumps of wild tamarisk, . . . nothing more. This was the Field of Ardath. . . this bare, unlovely wilderness without so much as a tree to grace its outline! From where he stood he could view its whole extent,—and as he beheld its complete desolation he smiled,—a faint, half-bitter smile. He thought of the words in the ancient book of "Esdras:" "And the Angel bade me enter a waste field, and the field was barren and dry save of herbs, and the name of the field was Ardath. And I wandered therein through the hours of the long night, and the silver eyes of the field did open before me and therein I saw signs and wonders."

"Yes,—the field is 'barren and dry' enough in all conscience!" he murmured listlessly—"But as for the 'silver eyes' and the 'signs and wonders,' they must have existed only in the venerable Prophet's imagination, just as my flower-crowned Angel-maiden exists in mine. Well! . . . now, Theos Alwyn" . . . he continued, apostrophizing himself aloud,—"Are you contented? Are you quite convinced of your folly? . . . and do you acknowledge that a fair Dream is as much of a lie and a cheat as all the other fair-seeming things that puzzle and torture poor human nature? Return to your former condition of reasoning and reasonable skepticism,—aye, even atheism if you will, for the materialists are right, . . . you cannot prove a God or the possibility of any purely spiritual life. Why thus hanker after a phantom loveliness? Fame—fame! Win fame! . . . that is enough for you in this world, . . . and as for a next world, who believes in it?—and who, believing, cares?"

Soliloquizing in this fashion, he set his foot on Ardath itself, determining to walk across and around it from end to end. The grass was long and dry, yet it made no rustle beneath his tread. . . he seemed to be shod with the magic shoes of silence. He walked on till he reached about the middle of the field, where perceiving a broad flat stone near him, he sat down to rest. There was a light mist rising,—a thin moonlit-colored vapor that crept slowly upward from the ground and remained hovering like a wide, suddenly-spun gossamer web, some two or three inches above it, thus giving a cool, luminous, watery effect to the hot and arid soil.

"According to the Apocrypha, Esdras 'sat among the flowers,'" he idly mused—"Well! . . . perhaps there were flowers in those days,—but it is very evident there are none now. A more dreary, utterly desolate place than this famous 'Ardath' I have never seen!"

At that moment a subtle fragrance scented the still air, . . . a fragrance deliciously sweet, as of violets mingled with myrtle. He inhaled the delicate odor, surprised and confounded.

"Flowers after all!" he exclaimed. . . "Or maybe some aromatic herb. . ." and he bent down to examine the turf at his feet. To his amazement he perceived a thick cluster of white blossoms, star-shaped and glossy-leaved, with deep golden centres, wherein bright drops of dew sparkled like brilliants, and from whence puffs of perfume rose like incense swung at unseen altars! He looked at them in doubt that was almost dread, . . . were they real? . . . were these the "silver eyes" in which Esdras had seen "signs and wonders"? . . . or was he hopelessly brain-sick with delusions, and dreaming again?

He touched them hesitatingly. . . they were actual living things, with creamy petals soft as velvet,—he was about to gather one of them,— when all at once his attention was caught and riveted by something like a faint shadow gliding across the plain. A smothered cry escaped his lips, . . . he sprang erect and gazed eagerly forward, half in hope,—half in fear. What slight Figure was that, pacing slowly, serenely, and all alone in the moonlight? . . . Without another instant's pause he rushed impetuously toward it,—heedless that as he went, he trod on thousands of those strange starry blossoms, which now, with sudden growth, covered and whitened every inch of the ground, thus marvellously fulfilling the words spoken of old: . . . "Behold the field thou thoughest barren; how great a glory hath the moon unveiled!"

X

God's Maiden Edris

He ran on swiftly for a few paces,—then coming more closely in view of the misty Shape he pursued, he checked himself abruptly and stood still, his heart sinking with a bitter and irrepressible sense of disappointment. Here surely was no Angel wanderer from unseen spheres! . . . only a girl, clad in floating gray draperies that clung softly to her slim figure, and trailed behind her as she moved sedately along through the snow-white blossoms that bent beneath her noiseless tread. He had no eyes for the strange flower-transfiguration of the lately barren land,—all his interest was centered on the slender, graceful form of the mysterious Maiden. She, meanwhile, went on her way, till she reached the western boundary of the field,—there she turned, . . . hesitated a moment, . . . and then came back straight toward him. He watched her approach as though she were some invisible fate,—and a tremor shook his limbs as she drew nearer. . . still nearer! He could see her distinctly now, all but her face,—that was in shadow, for her head was bent and her eyes were downcast. Her long, fair hair flowed in a loose rippling mass over her shoulders. . . she wore a wreath of the Ardath flowers, and carried a cluster of them clasped between her small, daintily shaped hands. A few steps more, and she was close beside him—she stopped as if in expectation of some word or sign. . . but he stood mute and motionless, not daring to speak or stir. Then—without raising her eyes—she passed, . . . passed like a flitting vapor,—and he remained as though rooted to the spot, in a sort of vague, dumb bewilderment! His stupefaction was brief however—rousing himself to swift resolution, he hastened, after her.

"Stay! stay!" he cried aloud.

Obedient to his call she paused, but did not turn. He came up with her. . . he caught at her robe, soft to the touch as silken gauze, and overwhelmed by a sudden emotion of awe and reverence, he sank on his knees.

"Who, and what are you?" he murmured in trembling tones—"Tell me! If you are mortal maid I will not harm you, I swear! . . . See! . . . I am only a poor crazed fool that loves a Dream, . . . that stakes his life upon a chance of Heaven, . . . pity me as you are gentle! . . . but do not fear me. . . only speak!"

No answer came. He looked up—and now in the rich radiance of the moon beheld her face. . . how like, and yet how altogether unlike it was to the face of the Angel in his vision! For that ethereal Being had seemed dazzlingly, supremely beautiful beyond all mortal power of description,—whereas this girl was simply fair, small, and delicate, with something wistful and pathetic in the lines of her sweet mouth, and shadows as of remembered sorrows slumbering in the depths of her serene, dove-like eyes. Her fragile figure drooped wearily as though she were exhausted by some long fatigue, . . . yet, . . . gazing down upon him, she smiled, . . . and in that smile, the faint resemblance she bore to his Spirit-ideal flashed out like a beam of sunlight, though it vanished again as quickly as it had shone. He waited eagerly to hear her voice, . . . waited in a sort of breathless suspense,—but as she still kept silence, he sprang up from his kneeling attitude and seized her hands. . . how soft they were and warm!—he folded them in his own and drew her closer to himself. . . the flowers she held fell from her grasp, and lay in a tumbled fragrant heap between them. His brain was in a whirl—the Past and the Future—the Real and the Unreal—the Finite and the Infinite—seemed all merging into one another without any shade of difference or division!

"We have met very strangely, you and I!"—he said, scarcely conscious of the words he uttered—"Will you not tell me your name?"

A faint sigh escaped her.

"My name is Edris," she answered, in low musical accents, that carried to his sense of hearing a suggestion, of something sweet and familiar.

"Edris!" he repeated—"Edris!" and gazing at her dreamily he raised her hands to his lips and kissed them gently—"My fairest Edris! From whence do you come?"

She met his eyes with a mild look of reproach and wonderment.

"From a far, far country, Theos!" and he started as she thus addressed him—"A land where no love is wasted and no promise forgotten!"

Again that mystic light passed over her pale face—the blossom-coronal she wore seemed for a moment to glitter like a circlet of stars. His heart beat quickly—could he believe her? . . . was she in very truth that shining Peri whose aerial loveliness had so long haunted his imagination? Nay!—it was impossible! . . . for if she were, why should she veil her native glory in such simple maiden guise?

Searchingly he studied every feature of her countenance, and as he did so his doubts concerning her spirit-origin became more and more confirmed. She was a living, breathing woman—an actual creature of flesh and blood,—yet how account for her appearance on the field of Ardath? This puzzled him. . . till all at once a logical explanation of the whole mystery dawned upon his mind. Heliobas had sent her hither on purpose to meet him! Of course! how dense he had been not to see through so transparent a scheme before! The clever Chaldean had resolved that he, Theos Alwyn, should somehow be brought to accept his trance as a real experience, so that henceforth his faith in "things unseen and eternal" might be assured. Many psychological theorists would uphold such a deceit as not only permissible, but even praise-worthy, if practiced for the furtherance of a good cause. Even the venerable hermit Elzear might have shared in the conspiracy, and this "Edris," as she called herself, was no doubt perfectly trained in the part she had to play! A plot for his conversion! . . . well! . . . he would enter into it himself, he resolved! . . . why not? The girl was exquisitely fair,—a veritable Psyche of soft charms!—and a little lovemaking by moonlight would do no harm, . . . here he suddenly became aware that while these thoughts were passing through his brain he had unconsciously allowed her hands to slip from his hold, and she now stood apart at some little distance, her eyes fixed full upon him with an expression of most plaintive piteousness. He made a hasty step or two toward her,—and as he did so, his pulses began to throb with an extraordinary sensation of pleasure,—pleasure so keen as to be almost pain.

"Edris!" . . . he whispered,—"Edris. . ." and stopped irresolutely.

She looked up at him with the appealing wistfulness of a lost and suffering child, and a slight shudder ran through all her delicate frame.

"I am cold, Theos!" she murmured half beseechingly, stretching out her hands to him once more,—hands as fine and fair as lily-leaves,—little white hands which he gazed at wonderingly, yet did not take. "Cold and very weary! The way has been long, and the earth is dark!"

"Dark?" repeated Alwyn mechanically, still absorbed in the dubious contemplation of her lovely yielding form, her sweet upturned face and gold-glistening hair—"Dark? . . . here? . . . beneath the brightness of the moon? Nay,—I have seen many a full day look less radiant than this night of stars!"

Her eyes dwelt upon him with a certain pathetic bewilderment,—she let her extended arms drop wearily at her sides, and a shadow of pained recollection crossed the fairness of her features.

"Ah, I forgot! . . ." and she sighed deeply—"This is that strange, sad world where Darkness is called Light."

At these words uttered with so much sorrowful meaning, a quick thrill stirred Alwyn's blood, an inexplicable sharp thrill, that was like the touch of scorching flame. He gazed at her perplexedly. . . his pride resented what he imagined to be the deception practiced upon him, but at the same time he was not insensible to the weird romance of the situation.

He began to consider that as this fair girl, trained so admirably in mystical speech and manner, had evidently been sent on purpose to meet him, he could scarcely be blamed for taking her as she presented herself, and enjoying to the full a thoroughly novel and picturesque adventure.

His eyes flashed as he surveyed her standing there before him, utterly unprotected and at his mercy—his old, languid, skeptical smile played on his proud lips,—that smile of the marble Antinous which says "Bring me face to face with Truth itself and I shall still doubt!" An expression of reluctant admiration and awakening passion dawned on his countenance, . . . he was about to speak,—when she whose looks were fastened on him with intense, powerful, watchful, anxious entreaty, suddenly wrung her hands together as though in despair, and gave vent to a desolate sobbing cry that smote him to the very heart.

"Theos! Theos!" and her voice pealed out on the breathless air in sweet, melodious, broken echoes. "Oh, my unfaithful Beloved, what can I do for thee! A love unseen thou wilt not understand,—a love made manifest thou wilt not recognize! Alas!—my journey is in vain. . . my errand hopeless! For while thine unbelief resists my pleading, how can I lead thee from danger into safety? . . . how bridge the depths between our parted souls? . . . how win for thee pardon and blessing from Christ the King!"

Bright tears filled her eyes and fell fast and thick through her long, drooping lashes, and Alwyn, smitten with remorse at the sight of such grief, sprang to her side overcome by shame, love, and penitence.

"Weeping? . . . and for me?"—he exclaimed—"Sweet Edris! . . . Gentlest of maidens! . . . Weep not for one unworthy, . . . but rather smile and speak again of love! . . ." and now his words pouring forth impetuously, seemed to utter themselves independently of any previous thought,—"Yes! speak only of love,—and the discourse of those tuneful lips shall be my gospel, . . . the glance of those, soft eyes my creed, . . .

and as for pardon and blessing I crave none but thine! I sought a Dream. I have found a fair Reality. . . a living proof of Love's divine omnipotence! Love is the only god—who would doubt his sovereignty, or grudge him his full measure of worship? . . . Not I, believe me!"—and carried away by the force of a resistless inward fervor, he threw himself once more at her feet—"See!—here do I pay my vows at Love's high altar!—heart's desire shall be the prayer—heart's ecstasy the praise! . . . together we will celebrate our glad service of love, and heaven itself shall sanctify this Eve of St. Edris and All Angels!"

She listened,—looking down upon him with grave, half timid tenderness,—her tears dried, and a sudden hope irradiated her fair face with a soft, bright flush, as lovely as the light of morning falling on newly opened flowers. When he ceased, she spoke—her accents breaking through the silence like clear notes of music sweetly sung.

"So be it!" she said. . . "May Heaven truly sanctify all pure thoughts, and free the soul of my Beloved from sin!"

And slowly bending forward, as a delicate iris-blossom bends to the sway of the wind, she laid her hands about his neck, and touched his lips with her own. . .

Ah! . . . what divine ecstasy,—what wild and fiery transport filled him then! . . . Her kiss, like a penetrating lighting-flash, pierced to the very centre of his being,—the moonbeams swam round him in eddying circles of gold—the white field heaved to and fro, . . . he caught her waist and clung to her, and in the burning marvel of that moment he forget everything, save that, whether spirit or mortal, she was in woman's witching shape, and that all the glamour of her beauty was his for this one night at least, . . . this night which now in the speechless, glorious delirium of love that overwhelmed him, seemed like the Mahometan's night of Al-Kadr, "better than a thousand months!"

Drawn to her by some subtle mysterious attraction which he could neither explain nor control, and absorbed in a rapture beyond all that his highest and most daring flights of poetical fancy had ever conceived, he felt as though his very life were ebbing out of him to become part of hers, and this thought was strangely sweet,—a perfect consummation of all his best desires! . . .

All at once a cold shudder ran freezingly through his veins,—a something chill and impalpable appeared to pass between him and her caressing arms—his limbs grew numb and heavy—his sight began to fail him. . . he was sinking. . . sinking, he knew not where, when suddenly she withdrew herself from his embrace. Instantly his strength came back to him with a rush—he sprang to his feet and stood erect, breathless, dizzy, and confused—his pulses beating like hammer-strokes and every fiber in his frame quivering with excitement.

Entranced, impassioned, elated,—filled with unutterable incomprehensible joy, he would have clasped her again to his heart,—but she retreated swiftly from him, and standing several paces off, motioned him not to approach her more nearly. He scarcely heeded her warning gesture, . . . plunging recklessly through the flowers he had almost reached her side, when to his amazement and fear, his eager progress was stopped!

Stopped by some invisible, intangible barrier, which despite all his efforts, forcibly prevented him from advancing one step further,—she was close within an arm's length of him—and yet he could not touch her! . . . Nothing apparently divided them, save a small breadth of the Ardath blossoms gleaming ivory-soft in the moonlight. . . nevertheless that invincible influence thrust him back and held him fast, as though he were chained to the ground with weights of iron!

"Edris!" he cried loudly, his former transport of delight changed into agony. "Edris! . . . Come to me! I cannot come to you! What is this that parts us?"

"Death!" she answered. . . and the solemn word seemed to toll slowly through the still air like a knell.

He stood bewildered and dismayed. Death! What could she mean? What in the name of all her beautiful, delicate, glowing youth, had she to do with death? Gazing at her in mute wonder, he saw her stoop and gather one flower from the clusters growing thickly around her—she held it shieldwise against her breast, where it shone like a large white jewel, and regarded him with sweet, wistful eyes full of a mournful longing.

"Death lies between us, my Beloved!" she continued—"One line of shadow. . . only one little line! But thou mayest not pass it, save when God commands,—and I—I cannot! For I know naught of death, . . . save that it is a heavy dreamless sleep allotted to over-wearied mortals, wherein they gain brief rest 'twixt many lives,—lives that, like recurring dawns, rouse them anew to labor. How often hast thou slept thus, my Theos, and forgotten me!"

She paused, . . . and Alwyn met her clear, steadfast looks with a swift glance of something like defiance. For as she spoke, his previous idea concerning her came back upon him with redoubled force. He was keenly conscious of the vehement fever of love into which her presence had thrown him,—but all the same he was unable to dispossess himself of the notion that she was a pupil and an accomplice of Heliobas, thoroughly trained and practiced in his mysterious doctrine, and that therefore she most probably had some magnetic power in herself that at her pleasure not only attracted him To her, but also held him thus motionless at a distance, FROM her.

She talked, of course, in an indefinite mystic way either to intimidate or convince him. . . but, . . . and he smiled a little. . . in any case it only rested with himself to unmask this graceful pretender to angelic honors! And while he thought thus, her soft tones trembled on the silence again, . . . he listened as a dreaming mariner might listen to the fancied singing of the sea-fairies.

"Through long bright aeons of endless glory," she said—"I have waited and prayed for thee! I have pleaded thy cause before the blinding splendors of God's Throne, I have sung the songs of thy native paradise, but thou, grown dull of hearing, hast caught but the echo of the music! Life after life hast thou lived, and given no thought to me—yet I remember and am faithful! Heaven is not all Heaven to me without thee, my Beloved, . . . and now in this time of thy last probation, . . . now, if thou lovest me indeed. . ."

"Love thee?" suddenly exclaimed Theos, half beside himself with the strange passion of yearning her words awakened in him—"Love thee, Edris?—Aye! . . . as the gods loved when earth was young! . . . with the fullness of the heart and the vigor of glad life even so I love thee! What sayest thou of Heaven? . . . Heaven is here—here on this bridal field of Ardath, o'er-canopied with stars! Come, sweet one, . . . cease to play this mystic midnight fantasy—I have done with dreams! . . . Edris, be thyself! . . . for them art Woman, not Angel—thy kiss was warm as wine! Nay, why shrink from me?" this, as she retreated still further away, her eyes flashing with unearthly brilliancy, . . . "I will make thee a queen, fair Edris, as poets ever make queens of the women they love,—my fame shall be a crown for thee to wear,—a crown that the whole world, gazing on, shall envy!"

And in the heat and ardor of the moment, forgetful of the unseen barrier that divided her from him, he made a violent effort to spring forward—when lo! a wave of rippling light appeared to break from beneath her feet, . . . it rolled toward him, and completely flooded the space between them like a glittering pool,—and in it the flowers of Ardath swayed to and fro as water-lilies on a woodland lake sway to the measured dash of passing oars! Starting back with a cry of terror, he gazed wildly on this miracle,—a voice richer than all music rang silvery clear across the liquid radiance.

"Fame!" said the voice. . . "Wouldst thou crown Me, Theos, with so perishable a diadem?"

Paralyzed and speechless, he lifted his straining, dazzled eyes—was THAT Edris?—that lustrous figure, delicate as a sea-mist with the sun shining through? He stared upon her as a dying man might stare for the last time on the face of his nearest and dearest, . . . he saw her soft gray garments change to glistening white, . . . the wreath she wore sparkled as with a million dewdrops. . . a roseate halo streamed above her and around her,—long streaks of crimson flared down the sky like threads of fire swung from the stars,—and in the deepening glory, her countenance, divinely beautiful, yet intensely sad, expressed the touching hope and fear of one who makes a final farewell appeal. Ah God! . . . he knew her now! . . . too late, too late he knew her! . . . the Angel of his vision stood before him! . . . and humbled to the very dust and ashes of despair he loathed himself for his unworthiness and lack of faith!

"O doubting and unhappy one!" she went on, in accents sweeter than a chime of golden bells—"Thou art lost in the gloom of the Sorrowful Star where naught is known of life save its shadow! Lost. . . and as yet I cannot rescue thee—ah! forlorn Edris that I am, left lonely up in Heaven! But prayers are heard, and God's great patience never tires,—learn therefore 'FROM THE PERILS OF THE PAST, THE PERILS OF THE FUTURE'—and weigh against an immortal destiny of love the worth of fame!"

Wider and more dazzling grew the brilliancy surrounding her—raising her eyes, she clasped her hands in an attitude of impassioned supplication. . .

"O fair King Christ!" she cried, and her voice seemed to strike a melodious passage through the air. "THOU canst prevail!" A burst of music answered her, . . . music that rushed wind-like downwards and swept in strong vibrating chords over the land,—again the "KYRIE ELEISON! CHRISTE ELEISON! KYRIE ELEISON!" pealed forth in the same full youthful-toned chorus that had before sounded so mysteriously outside Elzear's hermitage—and the separate crimson rays glittering aurora-wise about her radiant figure, suddenly melted all together in the form of a great cross, which, absorbing moon and stars in its fiery redness, blazed from end to end of the eastern horizon!

Then, like a fair white dove or delicate butterfly she rose. . . she poised herself above the bowing Ardath bloom. . . anon, soaring aloft, she floated higher. . . higher! . . . and ever higher, serenely and with aerial slow ease,—till drawn into the glory of that wondrous flaming cross whose outstretched beams seemed waiting to receive her,—she drifted straight upwards through its very centre. . . and so vanished! . . .

Theos stared aghast at the glowing sky. . . whither had she gone? Her words still rang in his ears,—the warmth of her kiss still lingered on his lips,—he loved her! . . . he worshipped her! . . . why, why had she left him "lost" as she herself had said, in a world that was mere emptiness without her? He struggled for utterance. . .

"Edris. . . !" he whispered hoarsely—"Edris! . . . My Angel-love! . . . come back! Come back. . . pity me! . . . forgive! . . . Edris!"

His voice died in a hard sob of imploring agony,—smitten to the very soul by a remorse greater than he could bear, his strength failed him, and he fell senseless, face forward among the flowers of the Prophet's field; . . . flowers that, circling snowily around his dark and prostrate form, looked like fairy garlands bordering a Poet's Grave!

PART II
IN AL-KYRIS

"That which hath been, is now: and that which is to be, hath already been: . . . and God requireth that which is past."

—Ecclesiastes

XI

THE MARVELLOUS CITY

Profound silence,—profound unconsciousness,—oblivious rest! Such are the soothing ministrations of kindly Nature to the overburdened spirit; Nature, who in her tender wisdom and maternal solicitude will not permit us to suffer beyond a certain limit. Excessive pain, whether it be physical or mental, cannot last long,—and human anguish wound up to its utmost quivering-pitch finds at the very height of desolation, a strange hushing, Lethean calm. Even so it was with Theos Alwyn,—drowned in the deep stillness of a merciful swoon, he had sunk, as it were, out of life,—far out of the furthest reach or sense of time, in some vast unsounded gulf of shadows where earth and heaven were alike forgotten! . . .

How long he lay thus he never knew,—but he was roused at last. . . roused by the pressure of something cold and sharp against his throat, . . . and on languidly opening his eyes he found himself surrounded by a small body of men in armor, who, leaning on tall pikes which glistened brilliantly in the full sunlight, surveyed him with looks of derisive amusement. One of these, closer to him than the rest, and who seemed from his dress and bearing to be some officer in authority, held instead of a pike a short sword, the touch of whose pointed steel blade had been the effectual means of awakening him from his lethargy.

"How now!" said this personage in a rough voice as he withdrew his weapon—"What idle fellow art thou? . . . Traitor or spy? Fool thou must be, and breaker of the King's law, else thou hadst never dared to bask in such swine-like ease outside the gates of Al-Kyris the Magnificent!"

Al-Kyris the Magnificent! What was the man talking about? Uttering a hasty exclamation, Alwyn staggered to his feet with an effort, and shading his eyes from the hot glare of the sun, stared bewilderedly at his interlocutor.

"What. . . what is this?" he stammered dreamily—"I do not understand you! . . . I. . . I have slept on the field of Ardath!"

The soldiers burst into a loud laugh, in which their leader joined.

"Thou hast drunk deep, my friend!" he observed, putting up his sword with a sharp clatter into its shining sheath,—"What name sayst thou? . . . ARDATH? We know it not, nor dost thou, I warrant, when sober! Go to—make for thy home speedily! Aye, aye! the flavor of good wine clings to thy mouth still,—'tis a pleasant sweetness that I myself am partial to, and I can pardon those who, like thee, love it somewhat too well! Away!—and thank the gods thou hast fallen into the hands of the King's guard, rather then Lysia's priestly patrol! See! the gates are open,—in with thee! and cool thy head at the first fountain?"

"The gates?" . . . What gates? Removing his hand from his eyes Alwyn gazed around confusedly. He was standing on an open stretch of level road, dustily-white, and dry, with long-continued heat,—and right in front of him was an enormously high wall, topped with rows of bristling iron spikes, and guarded by the gates alluded to,—huge massive portals seemingly made of finely molded brass, and embellished on either side by thick, round, stone watch towers, from whose summits scarlet pennons drooped idly in the windless air. Amazed, and full of a vague, trembling terror, he fixed his wondering looks once more upon his strange companions, who in their turn regarded him with cool military indifference."

"I must be mad or dreaming," he thought,—then growing suddenly desperate he stretched out his hands with a wild appealing gesture:

"I swear to you I know nothing of this place!" he cried—"I never saw it before! Some trick has been played on me. . . who brought me here? Where is Elzear the hermit? . . . the Ruins of Babylon? . . . where is, . . . Good God! . . . what fearful freak of fate is this!"

The soldiers laughed again,—their commander looked at him a little curiously.

"Nay, art THOU one of the escaped of Lysia's lovers?" he asked, suspiciously—"And has the Silver Nectar failed of its usual action, and driven thy senses to the winds, that thou ravest thus? For if thou art a stranger and knowest naught of us, how speakest thou our language? . . . Why wearest thou the garb of our citizens?"

Alwyn shrank and shivered as though he had received a deadening blow,—an awful, inexplicable chill horror froze his blood. It was true! . . . he understood the language spoken! . . . it was perfectly familiar to him,—more so than his own native tongue,—stop! what WAS his native tongue?

He tried to think—and, the sick fear at his heart grew stronger,—he could not remember a word of it! And his dress! . . . he glanced at it dismayed and appalled,—he had not noticed it till now. It bore some resemblance to the costume of ancient Greece, and consisted of a white linen tunic and loose upper vest, both garments being kept in place by a belt of silver. From this belt depended a sheathed dagger, a square writing tablet, and a pencil-shaped implement which he immediately recognized as the antique form of stylus. His feet were shod with sandals—his arms were bare to the shoulder, and clasped at the upper part by two broad silver armlets richly chased.

Noting all these details, the fantastic awfulness of his position smote him with redoubled force,—and he felt as a madman may feel when his impending doom has not entirely asserted itself,—when only grotesque and leering suggestions of madness cloud his brain,—when hideous faces, dimly discerned, loom out of the chaos of his nightly visions,— and when all the air seems solid darkness, with one white line of fire cracking it asunder in the midst, and that the fire of his own approaching frenzy. Such a delirium of agony possessed Alwyn at that moment,—he could have shrieked, laughed, groaned, wept, and fallen down in the dust before these bearded armed men, praying them to slay him with their weapons there where he stood, and put him mercifully and at once out of his mysterious misery. But an invisible influence stronger than himself, prevented him from becoming altogether the victim of his own torturing emotions, and he remained erect and still as a marble figure, with a wondering, white piteous face of such unutterable affliction that the officer who watched him seemed touched, and, advancing, clapped his shoulder in a friendly manner.

"Come, come!" he said—"Thou need'st fear nothing,—we are not the men to blab of thy trespass against the city's edict,—for, of a truth, there is too much whispering away of young and goodly lives nowadays. What!—thou art not the first gay gallant, nor wilt thou be the last, that has seen the world turn upside down in a haze of love and late feasting! If thou hast not slept long enough, why sleep again an thou wilt,—but not here. . ."

He broke off abruptly,—a distant clatter of horses' hoofs was heard, as of one galloping at full speed. The soldiers started, and assumed an attitude of attention,—their leader muttered something like an oath, and seizing Alwyn by the arm, hurried him to the brass gates which, as he had said, stood open, and literally thrust him through.

"In, in, my lad!" he urged with rough kindliness,—"Thou hast a face fairer than that of the King's own minstrel, and why wouldst thou die for sake of an extra cup of wine? If Lysia is to blame for this scattering of thy wits, take heed thou do not venture near her more—it is ill jesting with the Serpent's sting! Get thee hence quickly, and be glad of thy life,—thou hast many years before thee yet in which to play the lover and fool!"

With this enigmatical speech he signed to his men to follow him,—they all filed through the gates, which closed after them with a jarring clang, . . . a dark bearded face peered out of a narrow loophole in one of the watch-towers, and a deep voice called:

"What of the hour?"

The officer raised his gauntleted hand, and answered promptly:

"Peace and safety!"

"Salutation!" cried the voice again.

"Salutation!" responded the officer, and with a reassuring nod and smile to the bewildered Alwyn, he gathered his little band around him, and they all marched off, the measured clink-clank of their footsteps making metallic music, as they wheeled round a corner and disappeared from sight.

Left to himself Alwyn's first idea was to sit down in some quiet corner, and endeavor calmly to realize what strange and cruel thing had chanced to him. But happening to look up, he saw the bearded face in the watchtower observing him suspiciously,—he therefore roused himself sufficiently to walk away, on and on, scarce heeding whither he went, till he had completely lost sight of those great gold-glittering portals which had shut him, against his will, within the walls of a large, splendid, and populous City. Yes! . . . hopelessly perplexing and maddening as it was, there could be no doubt of this fact,—and though he again and again tried to convince himself that he was laboring under some wild and exceptional hallucination, his senses all gave evidence of the actual reality of his situation,—he felt, he moved, he heard, he saw, . . . he was even beginning to be conscious of hunger, thirst, and fatigue.

The further he went, the more gorgeous grew the surroundings, . . . his unguided steps wandered as it seemed, of their own accord, into wide streets, paved entirely with mosaics, and lined on both sides with lofty, picturesque, and palace-like buildings,—he crossed and recrossed broad avenues, shaded by tall feathery palms, and masses of graceful flowering foliage,—he passed rows upon rows of brilliant shops, whose frontages glittered with the most costly and beautiful wares of every description,—and as he strolled about aimlessly, uncertain whither to go, he was constantly jostled by the pressing throngs of people that crowded the thoroughfares, all more or less apparently bent on pleasure, to judge from their animated countenances and frequent bursts of gay laughter.

The men were for the most part arrayed like himself,—though here and there he met some few whose garments were of soft silk instead of linen, who wore gold belts in place of silver, and who carried their daggers in sheaths that were literally encrusted all over with flashing jewels.

As he advanced more into the city's centre, the crowds increased,—so much so that the noise of traffic and clatter of tongues became quite deafening to his ears. Richly ornamented chariots drawn by spirited horses, and driven by personages whose attire seemed to be a positive blaze of gold and gems, rolled past in a continuous procession,—fruit-sellers, carrying their lovely luscious merchandise in huge gilded moss-wreathed baskets, stood at almost every corner,—flower-girls, fair as flowers, bore aloft in their gracefully upraised arms wide wicker trays, overflowing with odorous blossoms tied into clusters and wreaths,—and there were countless numbers of curious little open square carts to which mules, wearing collars of bells, were harnessed, the tinkle-tinkle of their constant passage through the throng making incessant merry music. These vehicles bore the names of traders,—purveyors in wine and dealers in all sorts of provisions,—but with the exception of such necessary business caterers, the streets were full of elegant loungers of both sexes, who seemed to have nothing whatever to do but amuse themselves.

The women were especially noticeable for their lazy grace of manner,—they glided to and fro with an indolent floating ease that was indescribably bewitching,—the more so as many of them were endowed with exquisite beauty of form and feature,—beauty greatly enhanced by the artistic simplicity of their costume.

This was composed of a straight clinging gown, slightly gathered at the throat, and bound about the waist with a twisted girdle of silver, gold, and, in some cases, jewels,—their arms, like those of the men, were bare, and their small, delicate feet were protected by sandals fastened with crossed bands of ribbon coquettishly knotted. The arrangement of their hair was evidently a matter of personal taste, and not the slavish copying of any set fashion,—some allowed it to hang in loosely flowing abundance over their shoulders,—others had it closely braided, or coiled carelessly in a thick soft mass at the top of the head,—but all without exception wore white veils,—veils, long, transparent, and filmy as gossamer, which they flung back or draped about them at their pleasure. . . and presently, after watching several of these fairy creatures pass by and listening to their low laughter and dulcet speech, a sudden memory leaped into Alwyn's confused brain,—an old, old memory that seemed to have lain hidden among his thoughts for centuries,—the memory of a story called "Lamia" told in verse as delicious as music aptly played. Who wrote the story? . . . He could not tell,—but he recollected that it was about a snake in the guise of a beautiful woman. And these women in this strange city looked as if they also had a snake-like origin,—there was something so soft and lithe and undulating about their movements and gestures. Weary of walking, distracted by the ever-increasing clamor, and feeling lost among the crowd, he at last perceived a wide and splendid square, surrounded wild stately houses, and having in its centre a huge, white granite obelisk which towered like a pillar of snow against the dense blue of the sky. Below it a massively sculptured lion, also of white granite, lay couchant, holding a shield between its paws,—and on either side two fine fountains were in full play, the delicate spiral columns of water being dashed up beyond the extreme point of the obelisk, so that its stone face was wet and glistening with the tossing rainbow shower.

Here he turned aside out of the main thoroughfare,—there were tall, shady trees all about, and fantastically carved benches underneath them, . . . he determined to sit down and rest, and steadily THINK OUT his involved and peculiar condition of mind.

As he passed the sculptured lion, he saw certain words engraved on the shield it held,—they were. . . "THROUGH THE LION AND THE SERPENT SHALL AL-KYRIS FLOURISH."

There was no disorder in his intelligence concerning this sentence,— he was able to read it clearly and comprehensively, . . . and yet. . . WHAT was the language in which it was written, and how did he come to know it so thoroughly? . . . With a sigh that was almost a groan, he sank listlessly on a seat, and burying his head in his hands to shut out all the strange sights which so direfully perplexed his reason, he began to subject himself to a patient, serious cross-examination.

In the first place. . . WHO WAS HE? Part of the required answer came readily,—THEOS. Theos what? His brain refused to clear up this point,— it repeated THEOS—THEOS,—over and over again, but no more!

Shuddering with a vague dread, he asked himself the next question, . . . From Whence Had He Come? The reply was direct and decisive—From Ardath.

But what was Ardath? It was neither a country nor a city—it was a "waste field," where he had seen. . . ah! Whom had he seen? He struggled furiously with himself for some response to this, . . . none came! Total dumb blankness was the sole result of the inward rack to which he subjected his thoughts!

And where had he been before he ever saw Ardath? . . . had he No recollection of any other place, any other surroundings?—Absolutely None!—torture his wits as he would,—Absolutely None! . . . This was frightful. . . incredible! . . . Surely, surely, he mused piteously, there must have been something in his life before the name of "Ardath" had swamped his intelligence! . . .

He lifted his head, . . . his face had grown ashen gray and rigid in the deep extremity of his speechless trouble and terror,—there was a sick faintness at his heart, and rising, he moved unsteadily to one of the great fountains, and there dipping his hands in the spray, he dashed some drops on his brow and eyes. Then, making a cup of the hollowed palms, he drank thirstily several draughts of the cool, sweet water,—it seemed to allay the fever in his blood. . .

He looked around him with a wild, vague smile,—Al-Kyris! . . . of course! . . . he was in Al-Kyris!—why was he so distressed about it? It was a pleasant city,—there was much to see,—and also much to learn! . . . At that instant a loud blast of silver-toned trumpets split the air, followed by a storm-roar of distant acclamation surging up from thousands of throats,—crowds of men and women suddenly flocked into the Square, across it, and out of it again, all pressing impetuously in one direction,—and urged forward by the general rush as well as by a corresponding impulse within himself, he flung all meditation to the winds, and plunged recklessly into the shouting, onsweeping throng. He was borne swiftly with it down a broad avenue lined with grand old trees and decked with flying flags and streamers, to the margin of a noble river, as still as liquid amber in the wide sheen and heat of the noonday sun. A splendid marble embankment, adorned with colossal statues, girdled it on both sides,—and here, under silken awnings of every color, pattern and design, an enormous multitude was assembled,—its white attired, closely packed ranks stretching far away into the blue distance on either hand.

All the attention of this vast concourse appeared to be centered on the slow approach of a strange, gilded vessel, that with great curved prow and scarlet sails flapping idly in the faint breeze, was gliding leisurely yet majestically over the azure blaze of the smooth water. Huge oars like golden fins projected from her sides and dipped lazily every now and then, apparently wielded by the hands of invisible rowers, whose united voices supplied the lack of the needful wind,—and as he caught sight of this cumbrously quaint galley, Theos, moved by sudden interest, elbowed his way resolutely though the dense crowd till he gained the edge of the embankment, where leaning against the marble balustrade, he watched with a curious fascination its gradual advance.

Nearer and nearer it came, . . . brighter and brighter glowed the vivid scarlet of its sails, . . . a solemn sound of stringed music rippled enchantingly over the glassy river, mingling itself with the wild shouting of the populace,—shouting that seemed to rend the hollow vault of heaven! . . . Nearer. . . nearer. . . and now the vessel slid round and curtsied forward, . . . its propelling fins moved more rapidly. . . another graceful sweep,—and lo! it fronted the surging throng like a glittering, fantastic Apparition drawn out of dreamland! . . .

Theos stared at it, dazzled and stricken with a half-blind breathless wonder,—was ever a ship like this he thought?—a ship that sparkled all over as though it were carven out of one great burning jewel? . . . Golden hangings, falling in rich, loose folds, draped it gorgeously from stem to stern,—gold cordage looped the sails,—on the deck a band of young gals clad in white, and crowned with flowers, knelt, playing softly on quaintly shaped instruments,—and a cluster of tiny, semi-nude boys, fair as young cupids, were grouped in pretty reposeful attitudes along the edge of the gilded prow holding garlands of red and yellow blossoms which trailed down to the surface of the water beneath.

As a half-slumbering man may note a sudden brilliant glare of sunshine flashing on the wall of his sleeping-chamber, so Theos at first viewed this floating pageant in confused, uncomprehending bewilderment, . . . when all at once his stupefied senses were roused to hot life and pulsing action,—with a smothered cry of ecstasy he fixed his straining, eager gaze on one supreme, fair Figure,—the central Glory of the marvellous picture! . . .

A Woman or a Goddess?—a rainbow Flame in mortal shape?—a spirit of earth, air, fire, water? . . . or a Thought of Beauty embodied into human sweetness and made perfect? . . . Clothed in gold attire,

MARIE CORELLI

and girdled with gems, she stood, leaning indolently against the middle mast of the vessel, her great, sombre, dusky eyes resting drowsily on the swarming masses of people, whose frenzied roar of rapture and admiration sounded like the breaking of billows.

Presently, with a slow, solemn smile on her haughtily curved lips, she extended one hand and arm, snow-white and glittering with jewels, and made an imperious gesture to command silence. Instantly a profound hush ensued. Lifting a long, slender, white wand, at the end of which could be plainly seen the gleaming silver head of a Serpent, she described three circles in the air with a perfectly even, majestic motion, and as she did this, her marvellous eyes turned toward Theos, and dwelt steadily upon him.

He met her gaze fully, absorbing into his inmost soul the mesmeric spell of her matchless loveliness,—he saw, without actually realizing the circumstance, that the whole vast multitude around him had fallen prostrate in an attitude of worship,—and still he stood erect, drinking in the warmth of those dark, witching, sleepy orbs that flashed at him half-resentfully, half-mockingly, . . . and then, . . . the beauty-burdened ship began to sway gently, and move onwards,—she, that wondrous Siren-Queen was vanishing,—vanishing!—she and her kneeling maidens, and music, and flowers,—vanishing. . . Where?

With a start he sprang from his post of observation,—he felt he must go after her at all risks,—he must find out her place of abode,— her rank,—her title,—her name! . . . All at once he was roughly seized by a dozen or more of hands,—loud, angry voices shouted on all sides. "A traitor! . . . a traitor!" . . . "An infidel!"

"A spy!" "A malcontent!"

"Into the river with him!"

"He refuses worship!" "He denies the gods!"

"Bear him to the Tribunal!" . . . And in a trice of time, he was completely surrounded and hemmed in by an exasperated, gesticulating crowd, whose ominous looks and indignant mutterings were plainly significant of prompt hostility. With a few agile movements he succeeded in wrenching himself free from the grasp of his assailants, and standing among them like a stag at bay he cried:

"What have I done? How have I offended? Speak! Or is it the fashion of Al-Kyris to condemn a man unheard?"

No one answered this appeal,—the very directness of it seemed to increase the irritation of the mob, that pressing closer and closer, began to jostle and hustle him in a threatening manner that boded ill for his safety,—he was again taken prisoner, and struggling in the grasp of his captors, he was preparing to fight for his life as best he could, against the general fury, when the sound of musical strings, swept carelessly upwards in the ascending scale, struck sweetly through the clamor. A youth, arrayed in crimson, and carrying a small golden harp, marched sedately between the serried ranks that parted right and left at his approach,—thus clearing the way for another personage who followed him,—a graceful, Adonis-like personage in glistening white attire, who wore a myrtle-wreath on his dark, abundant locks, and whom the populace—forgetting for a moment the cause of their recent disturbance—greeted with a ringing and ecstatic shout of "HAIL! SAH-LUMA!"

Again and again this cry was uplifted, till far away on the extreme outskirts of the throng the joyous echo of it was repeated faintly yet distinctly. . . "HAIL! HAIL, SAH-LUMA!"

XII

SAH-LUMA

The new-comer thus enthusiastically welcomed bowed right and left, with a condescending air, in response to the general acclamation, and advancing to the spot where Theos stood, an enforced prisoner in the close grip of three or four able-bodied citizens, he said:

"What turbulence is here? By my faith! . . . when I heard the noise of quarrelsome contention jarring the sweetness of this nectarous noon, methought I was no longer in Al-Kyris, but rather in some western city of barbarians where music is but an unvalued name!"

And he smiled—a dazzling, child-like smile, half petulant, half-pleased—a smile of supreme self-consciousness as of one who knew his own resistless power to charm away all discord.

Several voices answered him in clamorous unison:

"A traitor, Sah-luma!" "A profane rebel!" . . . "An unbeliever!" . . . "A most insolent knave!"—"He refused homage to the High Priestess!" . . . "A renegade from the faith!"

"Now, by the Sacred Veil!" cried Sah-luma impatiently—"Think ye I can distinguish your jargon, when like ignorant boors ye talk all at once, tearing my ears to shreds with such unmelodious tongue-clatter! Whom have ye seized thus roughly? . . . Let him stand forth!"

At this command, the men who held Theos relaxed their grasp, and he, breathless and burning with indignation at the treatment he had received, shook himself quickly free of all restraint, and sprang forward, confronting his rescuer. There was a brief pause, during which the two surveyed each other with looks of mutual amazement. What mysterious indication of affinity did they read in one another's faces? . . . Why did they stand motionless, spell-bound and dumb for a while, eying half-admiringly, half-enviously, each other's personal appearance and bearing? . . .

Undoubtedly a curious, far-off resemblance existed between them,— yet it was a resemblance that had nothing whatever to do with the actual figure, mien, or countenance. It was that peculiar and often undefinable similarity of expression, which when noticed between two brothers who are otherwise totally unlike, instantly proclaims their relationship.

Theos realized his own superior height and superior muscular development,—but what were these physical advantages compared to the classic perfection of Sah-luma's beauty?—beauty combining the delicate with the vigorous, such as is shadowed forth in the artist-conceptions of the god Apollo. His features, faultlessly regular, were redeemed from all effeminacy by the ennobling impress of high thought and inward inspiration,—his eyes were dark, with a brilliant under-reflection of steel-gray in them, that at times flashed out like the soft glitter of summer-lightning in the dense purple of an August heaven,—his olive-tinted complexion was flushed warmly with the glow of health,—and he had broad, bold, intellectual brows over which the rich hair clustered in luxuriant waves,—hair that was almost black, with here and there a curious fleck of reddish gold brightening its curling masses, as though a stray sunbeam or two had been caught and entangled therein. He was arrayed in a costume of the finest silk,—his armlets, belt, and daggersheath were all of jewels,—and the general brilliancy of his attire was furthermore increased by a finely worked flexible collar of gold, set with diamonds. The first exchange of wondering glances over, he viewed Theos with a critical, half supercilious air.

"What art thou?" he demanded. . . "What is thy calling?"

Theos hesitated,—then spoke out boldly and unthinkingly—

"I am a Poet!" he said.

A murmur of irrepressible laughter and derision ran through the listening crowd. Sah-luma's lip curled haughtily—

"A Poet!" and his fingers played idly with the dagger at his belt—"Nay, not so! There is but one Poet in Al-Kyris, and I am he!"

Theos looked at him steadily,—a subtle sympathy attracted him toward this charming boaster,—involuntarily he smiled, and bent his head courteously.

"I do not seek to figure as your rival. . ." he began.

"Rival!" echoed Sah-luma—"I have no rivals!"

A burst of applause from those nearest to them in the throng declared the popular approval of this assertion, and the boy bearing the harp, who had loitered to listen to the conversation, swept the strings of his instrument with a triumphant force and fervor that showed how thoroughly his feelings were in harmony with the expression of his master's sentiments. Sah-luma conquered, with an effort, his momentary irritation, and resumed coldly:

MARIE CORELLI

"From whence do you come, fair sir? We should know your name,—
POETS are not so common!" This with an accent of irony.

Taken aback by the question, Theos stood irresolute, and uncertain what to say. For he was afflicted with a strange and terrible malady such as he dimly remembered having heard of, but never expected to suffer from,—a malady in which his memory had become almost a blank as regarded the past events of his life—though every now and then shadowy images of by-gone things flitted across his brain, like the transient reflections of wind-swept clouds on still, translucent water. Presently in the midst of his painful indecision, an answer suggested itself like a whispered hint from some invisible prompter:

"Poets like Sah-luma are no doubt as rare as nightingales in snow!" he said with a soft deference, and an increasing sense of tenderness for his haughty, handsome interlocutor—"As for me, I am a singer of sad songs that are not worth the hearing! My name is Theos,—I come from far beyond the seas, and am a stranger in Al-Kyris,—therefore if I have erred in aught, I must be blamed for ignorance, not malice!"

As he spoke Sah-luma regarded him intently,—Theos met his gaze frankly and unflinchingly. Surely there was some singular power of attraction between the two! . . . for as their flashing eyes again dwelt earnestly on one another, they both smiled, and Sah-luma, advancing, proffered his hand. Theos at once accepted it, a curious sensation of pleasure tingling through his frame, as he pressed those slender blown fingers in his own cordial clasp.

"A stranger in Al-Kyris?—and from beyond the seas? Then by my life and honor, I insure thy safety and bid thee welcome! A singer of sad songs? . . . Sad or merry, that thou are a singer at all makes thee the guest of the King's Laureate!" A look of conscious vanity illumined his face as he thus announced with proud emphasis his own title and claim to distinction. "The brotherhood of poets," he continued laughingly—"is a mystic and doubtful tie that hath oft been questioned,—but provided they do not, like ill-conditioned wolves, fight each other out of the arena, there should be joy in the relationship". Here, turning full upon the crowd, he lifted his rich, melodious voice to higher and more ringing tones:

"It is like you, O hasty and misjudging Kyrisians, that finding a harmless wanderer from far off lands, present at the pageant of the Midsummer Benediction, ye should pounce upon him, even as kites on a straying sea-bird, and maul him with your ruthless talons! Has he broken the law of worship! Ye have broken the law of hospitality! Has he failed to kneel to the passing Ship of the Sun? So have ye failed to handle him with due courtesy! What report shall he bear hence of your gentleness and culture to those dim and unjoyous shores beyond the gray green wall of ocean-billows, where the very name of Al-Kyris serves as a symbol for all that is great and wise and wondrous in the whole round circle of the world? Moreover ye know full well that foreigners and sojourners in the city are exempt from worship,—and the King's command is that all such should be well and nobly entertained, to the end that when they depart they may carry with them a full store of pleasant memories. Hence, scatterbrains, to your homes!—No festival can ye enjoy without a gust of contention!—ye are ill-made instruments all, whose jarring strings even I, crowned Minstrel of the King, can scarce keep one day in happy tune! Look you now! . . . this stranger is my guest!—. Is there a man in Al-Kyris who will treat as an enemy one whom Sah-luma calls friend?"

A storm of applause followed this little extempore speech,—applause accompanied by an odorous rain of flowers. There were many women in the crowd, and these had pressed eagerly forward to catch every word that dropped from the Poet-Laureate's mellifluous lips,—now, moved by one common impulse, they hastily snatched off their posies and garlands, and flung them in lavish abundance at his feet. Some of the blossoms chancing to fall on Theos and cling to his garments, he quickly shook them off, and gathering them together, presented them to the personage for whom they were intended. He, however, gayly rejected them, moving his small sandalled foot playfully among the thick wealth of red and white roses that lay waiting to be crushed beneath his tread.

"Keep thy share!" he said, with an amused flash of his glorious eyes. "Such offerings are my daily lot! . . . I can spare thee one handful from the overflowing harvest of my song!"

It was impossible to be offended with such charming self-complacency,—the naive conceit of the man was as harmless as the delight of a fair girl who has made her first conquest, and Theos smiling, kept the flowers. By this time the surrounding throng had broken up into little knots and groups,—all ill-humor on the part of the populace had completely vanished,—and large numbers were now leaving the embankment and dispersing in different directions to their several homes. All those who had been within hearing distance of Sah-luma's voice appeared highly elated, as though they had enjoyed some special privilege and pleasure, . . . to be reproved by the Laureate was evidently considered better than being praised by any one else. Many persons pressed up to Theos, and shaking hands with him, offered their eager excuses and apologies for the misunderstanding that had lately taken place, explaining with much animation both of look and gesture, that the fact of his wearing the same style of dress as themselves had induced them to take it for granted that he must be one of their fellow-citizens, and therefore subject to the laws of the realm. Theos was just beginning to feel somewhat embarrassed by the excessive politeness and cordiality, of his recent antagonists, when Sah-luma, again interposing, cut all explanations short.

"Come, come! cease this useless prating!" he said imperatively yet good-naturedly—"In everything ye showed your dullard ignorance and lack of discernment. For, concerning the matter of attire, are not the fashions of Al-Kyris copied more or less badly in every quarter of the habitable globe?—even as our language and literature form the chief study and delight of all scholars and educated gentlemen? A truce to your discussions!—Let us get hence and home;" here he turned to Theos with a graceful salutation—"You, my good friend, will doubtless be glad to rest and recover from my countrymen's ungentle treatment of your person."

Thus saying, he made a slight commanding sign,—the clustering people drew back on either side,—and he, taking Theos by the arm, passed through their ranks, talking, laughing, and nodding graciously here and there as he went, with the half-kindly, half-indifferent ease of an affable monarch who occasionally bows to some of his poorest subjects. As he trod over the flowers that lay heaped about his path, several girls rushed impetuously forward, struggling with each other for possession of those particularly favored blossoms that had received the pressure of his foot, and kissing them, they tied them in little knots, and pinned them proudly on the bosoms of their white gowns.

One or two, more daring, stretched out their hands to touch the golden frame of the harp as it was carried past them by the youth in crimson,—a pretty fellow enough, who looked extremely haughty, and almost indignant at this effrontery on the part of the fair poet-worshippers, but he made no remonstrance, and merely held his head a little higher and walked with a more consequential air, as he followed his master at a respectful distance. Another long ecstatic shout of "Hail Sah-luma!" arose on all sides, rippling away,—away,—down, as it seemed, to the very furthest edge of echoing resonance,—and then the remainder of the crowd quickly scattered right and left, leaving the spacious embankment almost deserted, save for the presence of several copper-colored, blue-shirted individuals who were commencing the work of taking down and rolling up the silken awnings, accompanying their labors by a sort of monotonous chant that, mingling with the slow, gliding plash of the river, sounded as weird and mournful as the sough of the wind through leafless trees.

Meanwhile Theos, in the company of his new friend, began to express his thanks for the timely rescue he had received,—but Sah-luma waived all such acknowledgments aside.

"Nay, I have only served thee as a crowned Laureate should ever serve a lesser minstrel,"—he said, with that indescribably delicious air of self-flattery which was so whimsical, and yet so winning,—"And I tell thee in all good faith that, for a newly arrived visitor in Al-Kyris, thy first venture was a reckless one! To omit to kneel in the presence of the High Priestess during her Benediction, was a violation of our customs and ceremonies dangerous to life and limb! A religiously excited mob is merciless,—and if I had not chanced upon the scene of action, . . ."

"I should have been no longer the man I am!" smiled Theos, looking down on his companion's light, lithe, elegant form as it moved gracefully by his side—"But that I failed in homage to the High Priestess was a most unintentional lack of wit on my part,—for if THAT was the High Priestess,—that dazzling wonder of beauty who lately passed in a glittering ship, on her triumphant way down the river, like a priceless pearl in a cup of gold. . ."

"Aye, aye!" and Sah-luma's dark brows contracted in a slight frown—"Not so many fine words, I pray thee! Thou couldst not well mistake her,—there is only one Lysia!"

"Lysia!" murmured Theos dreamily, and the musical name slid off his lips with a soft, sibilant sound,—"Lysia! And I forgot to kneel to that enchanting, that adorable being! Oh unwise, benighted fool!—where were my thoughts? Next time I see her I will atone!—no matter what creed she represents,—I will kiss the dust at her feet, and so make reparation for my sin!"

Sah-luma glanced at him with a somewhat dubious expression.

"What!—art thou already persuaded?" he queried lightly, "and wilt thou also be one of us? Well, thou wilt need to kiss the dust in very truth, if thou servest Lysia, . . . no half-measures will suit where she, the Untouched and Immaculate, is concerned,"—and here there was a faint inflection of mingled mockery and sadness in his tone—"To love her is, for many men, an absolute necessity,—but the Virgin Priestess of the Sun and the Serpent receives love, as statues may receive it,—moving all others to frenzy, she is herself unmoved!"

Theos listened, scarcely hearing. He was studying every line in Sah-luma's face and figure with fixed and wistful attention. Almost unconsciously he pressed the arm he held, and Sah-luma looked up at him with a half-smile.

"I fancy we shall like each other!" he said—"Thou art a western singing bird-of-passage, and I a nested nightingale amid the roses of the East,—our ways of making melody are different,—we shall not quarrel!"

"Quarrel!" echoed Theos amazedly—"Nay! . . . I might quarrel with my nearest and dearest, but never with thee, Sah-luma! For I know thee for a very prince of poets! . . . and would as soon profane the sanctity of the Muse herself, as violate thy proffered friendship!"

"Why, so!" returned Sah-luma, his brilliant eyes flashing with undisguised pleasure,—"An' thou thinkest thus of me we shall be firm and fast companions! Thou hast spoken well and not without good instruction—I perceive my fame hath reached thee in thine own ocean-girdled lands, where music is as rare as sunshine. Right glad am I that chance has thrown us together, for now thou wilt be better able to judge of my unrivalled master-skill in sweet word-weaving! Thou must abide with me for all the days of thy sojourn here. . . Art willing?"

"Willing? . . . Aye! more than willing!" exclaimed Theos enthusiastically—"But,—if I burden hospitality. . ."

"Burden!" and Sah-luma laughed—"Talk not of burdens to me!—I, who have feasted kings, and made light of their entertaining! Here," he added as he led the way through a broad alley, lined with magnificent palms—"here is the entrance to my poor dwelling!" and a sparkling, mischievous smile brightened his features.—"There is room enough in it, methinks to hold thee, even if thou hadst brought a retinue of slaves!"

He pointed before him as he spoke, and Theos stood for a moment stock-still and overcome with astonishment, at the size and splendor of the palace whose gates they were just approaching. It was a dome-shaped building of the purest white marble, surrounded on all sides by long, fluted colonnades, and fronted by spacious court paved with mosaics, where eight flower-bordered fountains dashed up to the hot, blue sky, incessant showers of refreshing spray.

Into this court and across it, Sah-luma led his wondering guest, . . . ascending a wide flight of steps, they entered a vast open hall, where the light poured in through rose-colored and pale blue glass, that gave a strange yet lovely effect of mingled sunset and moonlight to the scene. Here—reclining about on cushions of silk and velvet—were several beautiful girls in various attitudes of indolence and ease,—one laughing, black-haired houri was amusing herself with a tame bird which flew to and from her uplifted finger,—another in a half-sitting posture, played cup-and-ball with much active and graceful dexterity,—some were working at gold and silver embroidery,—others, clustered in a semicircle round a large osier basket filled with myrtle, were busy weaving garlands of the fragrant leaves,—and one maiden, seemingly younger than the rest, and of lighter and more delicate complexion, leaned somewhat pensively against an ebony-framed harp, as though she were considering what sad or suggestive chords she should next awaken from its responsive strings. As Sah-luma and Theos appeared, these nymphs all rose from their different occupations and amusements, and stood with bent heads and folded hands in statuesque silence and humility.

"These are my human rosebuds!" said Sah-luma softly and gayly, as holding the dazzled Theos by the arm he escorted him past these radiant and exquisite forms—"They bloom, and fade, and die, like the flowers thrown by the populace,—proud and happy to feel that their perishable loveliness has, even, for a brief while, been made more lasting by contact with my deathless poet-fame! Ah, Niphrata!" and he paused at the side of the girl standing by the harp—"Hast thou sung many of my songs to-day? . . . or is thy voice too weak for such impassioned cadence? Thou art pale, . . . I miss thy soft blush and dimpling smile,—what ails thee, my honey-throated oriole?"

"Nothing, my lord"—answered Niphrata in a low tone, raising a pair of lovely, dusky, violet eyes, fringed with long black lashes,—"Nothing,—save that my heart is always sad in thine absence!"

Sah-luma smiled, well pleased.

"Let it be sad no longer then!" he said, caressing her cheek with his hand,—and Theos saw a wave of rich color mounting swiftly to her fair brows at his touch, as though she were a white poppy warming to crimson in the ardent heat of the sun—"I love to see thee merry,—mirth suits a young and beauteous face like thine! Look you, Sweet!—I bring with me here a stranger from far-off lands,—one to whom

Sah-luma's name is as a star in the desert!—I must needs have thy voice in all its full lusciousness of tune to warble for his pleasure those heart-entangling ditties of mine which thou hast learned to render with such matchless tenderness! . . . Thanks, Gisenya," . . . this as another maiden advanced, and, gently removing the myrtle-wreath he wore, placed one just freshly woven on his clustering curls, . . . then, turning to Theos, he inquired—"Wilt thou also wear a minstrel-garland, my friend? Niphrata or Gisenya will crown thee!"

"I am not worthy"—answered Theos, bending his head in low salutation to the two lovely girls, who stood eying him with a certain wistful wonder—"One spray from Sah-luma's discarded wreath will best suffice me!"

Sah-luma broke into a laugh of absolute delight.

"I swear thou speakest well and like a true man!" he said joyously. "Unfamous as thou art, thou deservest honor for the frank confession of thy lack of merit! Believe me, there are some boastful rhymers in Al-Kyris who would benefit much by a share of thy becoming modesty! Give him his wish, Gisenya—" and Gisenya, obediently detaching a sprig of myrtle from the wreath Sah-luma had worn all day, handed it to Theos with a graceful obeisance—"For who knows but the leaves may contain a certain witchery we wot not of, that shall endow him with a touch of the divine inspiration!"

At that moment, a curious figure came shuffling across the splendid hall,—that of a little old man somewhat shabbily attired, upon whose wrinkled countenance there seemed to be a fixed, malign smile, like the smile of a mocking Greek mask. He had small, bright, beady black eyes placed very near the bridge of his large hooked nose,—his thin, wispy gray locks streamed scantily over his bent shoulders, and he carried a tall staff to support his awkward steps,—a staff with which he made a most disagreeable tapping noise on the marble pavement as he came along.

"Ah, Sir Gad-about!" he exclaimed in a harsh, squeaky voice as he perceived Sah-luma—"Back again from your self-advertising in the city! Is there any poor soul left in Al-Kyris whose ears have not been deafened by the parrot-cry of the name of Sah-luma?—If there is,—at him, at him, my dainty warbler of tiresome trills!—at him, and storm his senses with a rhodomontade of rhymes without reason!—at him, Immortal of the Immortals!—Bard of Bards!—stuff him with quatrains and sextains!—beat him with blank verse, blank of all meaning!—lash him with ballad and sonnet-scourges, till the tortured wretch, howling for mercy, shall swear that no poet save Sah-luma, ever lived before, or will ever live again, on the face of the shuddering and astonished earth!"

And breathless with this extraordinary outburst, he struck his staff loudly on the floor, and straightway fell into such a violent fit of coughing that his whole lean body shook with the paroxysm.

Sah-luma laughed heartily,—laughter in which he was joined by all the assembled maidens, including the gentle, pensive-eyed Niphrata. Standing erect in his glistening princely attire, with one hand resting familiarly on Theos's arm, and the sparkle of mirth lighting up his handsome features, he formed the greatest contrast imaginable to the little shrunken old personage, who, clinging convulsively to his staff, was entirely absorbed in his efforts to control and overcome his sudden and unpleasant attack of threatened suffocation.

"Theos, my friend,"—he said, still laughing—"Thou must know the admirable Zabastes,—a man of vast importance in his own opinion! Have done with thy wheezing,"—he continued, vehemently thumping the struggling old gentleman on the back—"Here is another one of the minstrel craft thou hatest,—hast aught of bitterness in thy barbed tongue wherewith to welcome him as guest to mine abode?"

Thus adjured, the old man peered up at Theos inquisitively, wiping away the tears that coughing had brought into his eyes, and after a minute or two began also to laugh in a smothered, chuckling way,—a laugh that resembled the croaking of frogs in a marshy pool.

"Another one of the minstrel-craft," he echoed derisively—"Aye, aye! . . . Like meets like, and fools consorts with fool. The guest of Sah-luma, . . . Hearken, young man,—" and he drew closer, the malign grin widening on his furrowed face,—"Thou shalt learn enough trash here to stock thee with idiot-songs for a century. Thou shalt gather up such fragments of stupidity, as shall provide thee with food for all the puling love-sick girls of a nation! Dost thou write follies also? . . . thou shalt not write them here, thou shalt not even think them!—for here Sah-luma,—the great, the unrivalled Sah-luma,—is sole Lord of the land of Poesy. Poesy,—by all the gods!—I would the accursed art had never been invented. . . so might the world have been spared many long-drawn nothings, enwoofed in obscure and distracting phraseology! . . . Thou a would-be Poet?—go to!—make brick, mend sandals, dig entrenchments, fight for thy country,—and leave the idle stringing of words, and the tinkling of rhyme, to children like Sah-luma, who play with life instead of living it."

And with this, he hobbled off uneasily, grunting and grumbling as he went, and waving his staff magisterially right and left to warn the smiling maidens out of his way,—and once more Sah-luma's laughter, clear and joyous, pealed through the vaulted vestibule.

"Poor Zabastes!" he said in a tone of good-humored tolerance—"He has the most caustic wit of any man in Al-Kyris! He is a positive marvel of perverseness and ill-humor, well worth the four hundred golden pieces I pay him yearly for his task of being my scribe and critic. Like all of us he must live, eat and wear decent clothing,—and that his only literary skill lies in the abuse of better men than himself is his misfortune, rather than his fault. Yes! . . . he is my paid Critic, paid to rail against me on all occasions public or private, for the merriment of those who care to listen to the mutterings of his discontent,—and, by the Sacred Veil! . . . I cannot choose but laugh myself whenever I think of him. He deems his words carry weight with the people,—alas, poor soul! his scorn but adds to my glory,—his derision to my fame! Nay, of a truth I need him,—even as the King needs the court fool,—to make mirth for me in vacant moments,—for there is something grotesque in the contemplation of his cankered clownishness, that sees nought in life but the eating, the sleeping, the building, and the bargaining. Such men as he can never bear to know that there are others, gifted by heaven, for whom all common things take radiant shape and meaning,—for whom the flowers reveal their fragrant secrets,—for whom birds not only sing, but speak in most melodious utterance—for whose dreaming eyes, the very sunbeams spin bright fantasies in mid-air more lasting than the kingdoms of the world! Blind and unhappy Zabastes! . . . he is ignorant as a stone, and for him the mysteries of Nature are forever veiled. The triumphal hero-march of the stars,—the brief, bright rhyme of the flashing comet,—the canticle of the rose as she bears her crimson heart to the smile of the sun,—the chorus of green leaves chanting orisons to the wind—the never completed epic of heaven's lofty solitudes where the white moon paces, wandering like a maiden in search of love,—all these and other unnumbered joys he has lost—joys that Sah-luma, child of the high gods and favorite of Destiny drinks in with the light and the air."

His eyes softened with a dreamy, intense lustre that gave them a new and almost pathetic beauty, while Theos, listening to each word he uttered, wondered whether there were ever any sounds sweeter than the rise and fall of his exquisite voice,—a voice as deliciously clear and mellow as a golden flute tenderly played.

"Yes!—though we must laugh at Zabastes we should also pity him,"—he resumed in gayer accents—"His fate is not enviable. He is nothing but a Critic—he could not well be a lesser man,—one who, unable himself to do any great work, takes refuge in finding fault with the works of others. And those who abhor true Poesy are in time themselves abhorred,—the balance of Justice never errs in these things. The Poet wins the whole world's love, and immortal fame,—his adverse Critic, brief contempt, and measureless oblivion. Come,"—he added, addressing Theos—"we will leave these maidens to their duties and pastimes,—Niphrata!" here his dazzling smile flashed like a beam of sunlight over his face—"thou wilt bring us fruit and wine yonder,—we shall pass the afternoon together within doors. Bid my steward prepare the Rose Chamber for my guest, and let Athazel and Zimra attend there to wait upon him."

All the maidens saluted, touching their heads with their hands in token of obedience, and Sah-luma leading the way, courteously beckoned Theos to follow. He did so, conscious as he went of two distinct impressions,—first, that the mysterious mental agitation he had suffered from when he had found himself so unexpectedly in a strange city, was not completely dispelled,—and secondly, that he felt as though he must have known Sah-luma all his life! His memory still remained a blank as regarded his past career,—but this fact had ceased to trouble him, and he was perfectly tranquil, and altogether satisfied with his present surroundings. In short, to be in Al-Kyris, seemed to him quite in keeping with the necessary course of events,—while to be the friend and companion of Sah-luma was more natural and familiar to his mind, than all once natural and familiar things.

MARIE CORELLI

XIII

A POET'S PALACE

Gliding along with that graceful, almost phantom-like swiftness of movement that was so much a part of his manner, Sah-luma escorted his visitor to the further end of the great hall. There,—throwing aside a curtain of rich azure silk which partially draped two large folding-doors,—he ushered him into a magnificent apartment opening out upon the terrace and garden beyond,—a garden filled with such a marvellous profusion of foliage and flowers, that looking at it from between the glistening marble columns surrounding the palace, it seemed as though the very sky above rested edge-wise on towering pyramids of red and white bloom. Awnings of pale blue stretched from the windows across the entire width of the spacious outer colonnade, and here two small boys, half nude, and black as polished ebony, were huddled together on the mosaic pavement, watching the arrogant deportment of a superb peacock that strutted majestically to and fro with boastfully spreading tail and glittering crest as brilliant as the gleam of the hot sun on the silver fringe of the azure canopies.

"Up, lazy rascals!" cried Sah-luma imperiously, as with the extreme point of his sandaled foot he touched the dimpled, shiny back of the nearest boy—"Up, and away! . . . Fetch rose-water and sweet perfumes hither! By the gods! ye have let the incense in yonder burner smoulder!"—and he pointed to a massive brazen vessel, gorgeously ornamented, from whence rose but the very faintest blue whiff of fragrant smoke—"Off with ye both, ye basking blackamoors! bring fresh frankincense,—and palm-leaves wherewith to stir this heated air—hence and back again like a lightning-flash! . . . or out of my sight forever!"

While he spoke, the little fellows stood trembling and ducking their woolly heads, as though they half expected to be seized by their irate master and flung, like black balls, out into the wilderness of flowers, but glancing timidly up and perceiving that even in the midst of his petulance he smiled, they took courage, and as soon as he had ceased they darted off with the swiftness of flying arrows, each striving to outstrip the other in a race across the terrace and garden. Sah-luma laughed as he watched them disappear,—and then stepping back into the interior of the apartment he turned to Theos and bade him be seated. Theos sank unresistingly into a low, velvet-cushioned chair richly carved and inlaid with ivory, and stretching his limbs indolently therein, surveyed with new and ever-growing admiration the supple, elegant figure of his host, who, throwing himself full length on a couch covered with leopard-skins, folded his arms behind his head, and eyed his guest with a complacent smile of vanity and self-approval.

"'Tis not an altogether unfitting retreat for a poet's musings"—he said, assuming an air of indifference, as he glanced round his luxurious, almost royally appointed room—"I have heard of worse!—But truly it needs the highest art of all known nations to worthily deck a habitation wherein the divine Muse may daily dwell, . . . nevertheless, air, light, and flowers are not lacking, and on these methinks I could subsist, were I deprived of all other things!"

Theos sat silent, looking about him wistfully. Was ever poet, king, or even emperor, housed more sumptuously than this, he thought? . . . as his eyes wandered to the domed ceiling, wreathed with carved clusters of grapes and pomegranates,—the walls, frescoed with glowing scenes of love and song-tournament,—the groups of superb statuary that gleamed whitely out of dusky, velvet-draped corners,—the quaintly shaped book-cases, overflowing with books, and made so as to revolve round and round at a touch, or move to and fro on noiseless wheels,— the grand busts, both in bronze and marble, that stood on tall pedestals or projecting bracket; and,—while he dimly noted all these splendid evidences of unlimited wealth and luxury,—the perfume and lustre of the place, the glitter of gold and azure, silver and scarlet, the oriental languor pervading the very air, and above all the rich amber and azure-tinted light that bathed every object in a dream-like and fairy radiance, plunged his senses into a delicious confusion,—a throbbing fever of delight to which he could give no name, but which permeated every fibre of his being.

He felt half blinded with the brilliancy of the scene,—the dazzling glow of color,—the sheen of deep and delicate hues cunningly intermixed and contrasted,—the gorgeous lavishness of waving blossoms that seemed to surge up like a sea to the very windows,—and though many thoughts flitted hazily through his brain, he could not shape them into utterance. He stared vaguely at the floor,—it was paved with variegated mosaic and strewn with the soft, dark, furry skins of wild animals,— at a little distance from where he sat there was a huge bronze lectern supported by a sculptured griffin with horns,—horns which curving over at the top, turned upward again in the form of candelabra,—the harp-bearer had brought in the harp, and it now stood in a conspicuous position decked with myrtle, some of the garlands woven by the maidens being no doubt used for this purpose.

Yet there was something mirage-like and fantastic in the splendor that everywhere surrounded him,—he felt as though he were one of the spectators in a vast auditorium where the curtain had just risen on the first scene of the play He was dubiously considering in his own perplexed mind, whether such princely living were the privilege, or right, or custom of poets in general, when Sah-luma spoke again, waving his hand toward one of the busts near him—a massive, frowning head, magnificently sculptured.

"There is the glorious Orazel!" he said—"The father, as we all must own, of the Art of Poesy, and indeed of all true literature! Yet there be some who swear he never lived at all—aye! though his poems have come down to us,—and many are the arguments I have had with so-called wise men like Zabastes, concerning his style and method of versification. Everything he has written bears the impress of the same master-touch,—nevertheless garrulous controversialists hold that his famous work the 'Ruva-Kalama' descended by oral tradition from mouth to mouth till it came to us in its 'improved' present condition. 'Improved!'" and Sah-luma laughed disdainfully,—"As if the mumbling of an epic poem from grandsire to grandson could possibly improve it! . . . it would rather be deteriorated, if not altogether changed into the merest doggerel! Nay, nay!—the 'Ruva-Kalama,' is the achievement of one great mind,—not twenty Oruzels were born in succession to write it,—there was, there could be only one, and he, by right supreme, is chief of the Bards Immortal! As well might fools hereafter wrangle together and say there were many Sah-lumas! . . . only I have taken good heed posterity shall know there was only ONE,—unmatched for love-impassioned singing throughout the length and breadth of the world!"

He sprang up from his recumbent posture and attracted Theos's attention to another bust even finer than the last,—it was placed on a pedestal wreathed at the summit and at the base with laurel.

"The divine Hyspiros!" he exclaimed pointing to it in a sort of ecstasy—"The Master from whom it may be I have caught the perfect entrancement of my own verse-melody! His fame, as thou knowest, is unrivalled and universal—yet—canst thou believe it! . . . there has been of late an ass found in Al-Kyris who hath chosen him as a subject for his braying—and other asses join in the uneuphonius chorus. The marvellous Plays of Hyspiros! . . . the grandest tragedies, the airiest comedies, the tenderest fantasies, ever created by human brain, have been called in question by these thistle-eating animals!—and one most untractable mule-head hath made pretence to discover therein a passage of secret writing which shall, so the fool thinks, prove that Hyspiros was not the author of his own works, but only a literary cheat, and forger of another and lesser man's inspiration! By the gods!—one's sides would split with laughter at the silly brute, were he not altogether too contemptible to provoke even derision! Hyspiros a traitor to the art he served and glorified? . . . Hyspiros a literary juggler and trickster? . . . By the Serpent's Head! they may as well seek to prove the fiery Sun in Heaven a common oil-lamp, as strive to lessen by one iota the transcendent glory of the noblest poet the centuries have ever seen!"

Warmed by enthusiasm, with his eyes flashing and the impetuous words coursing from his lips, his head thrown back, his hand uplifted, Sah-luma looked magnificent,—and Theos, to whose misty brain the names of Oruzel and Hyspiros carried no positively distinct meaning, was nevertheless struck by a certain suggestiveness in his remarks that seemed to bear on some discussion in the literary world that had taken place quite recently. He was puzzled and tried to fix the precise point round which his thoughts strayed so hesitatingly, but he could arrive at no definite conclusion. The brilliant, meteor-like Sah-luma meantime flashed hither and thither about the room, selecting certain volumes from his loaded book-stands, and bringing them in a pile, he set them on a small table by his visitor's side.

"These are some of the earliest editions of the plays of Hyspiros"—he went on, talking in that rapid, fluent way of his that was as musical as a bird's song—"They are rare and curious. See you!—the names of the scribes and the dates of issue are all distinct. Ah!—the treasures of poetry enshrined within these pages! . . . was ever papyrus so gemmed with pearls of thought and wisdom?—If there were a next world, my friend,"—and here he placed his hand familiarly on his guest's shoulder, while the bright, steel-gray under-gleam sparkled in his splendid eyes— "'twould be worth dwelling in for the sake of Hyspiros,—as grand a god as any of the Thunderers in the empyrean!"

"Surely there is a next world"—murmured Theos, scarcely knowing what he said—"A world where thou and I, Sah-luma, and all the masters and servants of song shall meet and hold high festival!"

Sah-luma laughed again, a little sadly this time, and shrugged his shoulders.

"Believe it not!" he said, and there was a touch of melancholy in his rich voice—"We are midges in a sunbeam,—emmets on a sand-hill. . . no more! Is there a next world, thinkest thou, for the bees who die of surfeit in the nilica-cups?—for the whirling drift of brilliant butterflies that sleepily float with the wind unknowing whither, till met by the icy blast of the north, they fall like broken and colorless leaves in the dust of the high-road? Is there a next world for this?"—and he took from a tall vase near at hand a delicate flower, lily-shaped and deliciously odorous, . . . "The expression of its soul or mind is in its fragrance,— even as the expression of ours finds vent in thought and aspiration,— have we more right to live again than this most innocently fair blossom, unsmirched by deeds of evil? Nay!—I would more easily believe in a heaven for birds and flowers, than for women and men!"

A shadow of pain darkened his handsome face as he spoke, . . . and Theos, gazing full at him, became suddenly filled with pity and anxiety,—he passionately longed to assure him that there was in very truth a future higher and happier existence,—he, Theos, would vouch for the fact! But how? . . . and why? . . . What could he say? . . . what could he prove? . . .

His throat ached,—his eyeballs burned, he was, as it were, forbidden to speak, notwithstanding the yearning desire he felt to impart to the soul of his new-found friend something of that indescribable sense of EVERLASTINGNESS which he himself was now conscious of, even as one set free of prison is conscious of liberty. Mute, and with a feeling as of hot, unshed tears welling up from his very heart, he turned over the volumes of Hyspiros almost mechanically,—they were formed of sheets of papyrus artistically bound in loose leather coverings and tied together with gold-colored ribbon.

The Kyrisian language was, as has been before stated, perfectly familiar to him, though he could not tell how he had acquired the knowledge of it,—and he was able to see at a glance that Sah-luma had good cause to be enthusiastic in his praise of the author whose genius he so fervently admired. There was a ringing richness in the rush of the verse,—a wealth of simile combined with a simplicity and directness of utterance that charmed the ear while influencing the mind, and he was beginning to read in sotto-voce the opening lines of a spirited battle-challenge running thus:

> *"I tell thee, O thou pride enthroned King*
> *That from these peaceful fields, these harvest lands,*
> *Strange crops shall spring, not sown by thee or thine!*
> *Arm'd millions, bristling weapons, helmed men*
> *Dreadfully plum'd and eager for the fray,*
> *Steel crested myrmidons, toss'd spears, wild steeds,*
> *Uplifted flags and pennons, horrid swords,*
> *Death gleaming eyes, stern hands to grasp and tear*
> *Life from beseeching life, till all the heavens*
> *Strike havoc to the terror-trembling stars"* . . .

when the two small, black pages lately dispatched in such haste by Sah-luma returned, each one bearing a huge gilded bowl filled with rose water, together with fine cloths, lace-fringed, and soft as satin.

Kneeling humbly down, one before Theos, the other before Sah-luma, they lifted these great, shining bowls on their heads, and remained motionless. Sah-luma dipped his face and hands in the cool, fragrant fluid,—Theos followed his example,—and when these light ablutions were completed, the pages disappeared, coming back almost immediately with baskets of loose rose-leaves, white and red, which they scattered profusely about the room. A delightful odor subtly sweet, and yet not faint, began to freshen the already perfumed air,—and Sah-luma, flinging himself again on his couch, motioned Theos to take a similar resting-place opposite.

He at once obeyed, yielding anew to the sense of indolent luxury and voluptuous ease his surroundings engendered,—and presently the aroma of rising incense mingled itself with the scent of the strewn rose-petals,—the pages had replenished the incense-burner, and now, these duties done so far, they brought each a broad, long stalked palm-leaf, and placing themselves in proper position, began to fan the two young men slowly and with measured gentleness, standing as mute as little black statues, the only movement about them being the occasional rolling of their white eyeballs and the swaying to and fro of their shiny arms as they wielded the graceful, bending leaves.

"This is the way a poet should ever live!" murmured Theos, glancing up from the soft cushions among which he reclined, to Sah-luma, who lay

MARIE CORELLI

with his eyes half-closed and a musing smile on his beautiful mouth—"Self centered in a circle of beauty,—with naught but fair suggestions and sweet thoughts to break the charm of solitude. A kingdom of happy fancies should be his, with gates shut last against unwelcome intruders,—gates that should never open save to the conquering touch of woman's kiss! . . . for the master-key of love must unlock all doors, even the doors of a minstrel's dreaming!"

"Thinkest thou so?" said Sah-luma lazily, turning his dark, delicate head slightly round on his glistening, pale-rose satin pillow—"Nay, of a truth there are times when I could bar out women from my thoughts as mere disturbers of the translucent element of poesy in which my spirit bathes. There is fatigue in love, . . . whose pretty human butterflies too oft weary the flower whose honey they seek to drain. Nevertheless the passion of love hath a certain tingling pleasure in it, . . . I yield to it when it touches me, even as I yield to all other pleasant things,—but there are some who unwisely carry desire too far, and make of love a misery instead of a pastime. Many will die for love,—fools are they all! To die for fame, . . . for glory, . . . that I can understand, . . . but for love! . . ." he laughed, and taking up a crushed rose-petal he flipped it into the air with his finger and thumb—"I would as soon die for sake of that perished leaf as for sake of a woman's transient beauty!"

As he uttered these words Niphrata entered, carrying a golden salver on which were placed a tall flagon, two goblets, and a basket of fruit. She approached Theos first, and he, raising himself on his elbow, surveyed her with fresh admiration and interest while he poured out the wine from the flagon into one of those glistening cups, which he noticed were rough with the quantity of small gems used in their outer ornamentation.

He was struck by her fair and melancholy style of loveliness, and as she stood before him with lowered eyes, the color alternately flushing and paling on her cheeks, and her bosom heaving restlessly beneath the loosely drawn folds of her prim rose-hued gown, an inexplicable emotion of pity smote him, as if he had suddenly been made aware of some inward sorrow of hers which he was utterly powerless to console. He would have spoken, but just then could find nothing appropriate to say, . . . and when he had selected a fine peach from the heaped-up dainties offered for his choice, he still watched her as she turned to Sah-luma, who smiled, and bade her set down her salver on a low, bronze stand at his side. She did so, and then with the warm blood burning in her cheeks, stood waiting and silent. Sah-luma, with a lithe movement of his supple form, lifted himself into a half-sitting posture, and throwing one arm round her waist, drew her close to his breast and kissed her.

"My fairest moonbeam!" he said gayly—"Thou art as noiseless and placid as thy yet unembodied sisters that stream through heaven and dance on the river when the world is sleeping! Myrtle! . . ." and he detached a spray from the bosom of her dress—"What hast thou to do with the poet's garland? By my faith, thou art like Theos yonder, and hast chosen to wear a sprig of my faded crown for thine adornment—is't not so?" A hot and painful blush crimsoned Niphrata's face,—a softness as of suppressed tears glistened in her eyes,—she made no answer, but looked beseechingly at the little twig Sah-luma held. "Silly child!" he went on laughingly, replacing it himself against her bosom, where the breath seemed to struggle with such panting haste and fear—"Thou art welcome to the dead leaves sanctified by song, if thou thinkest them of value, but I would rather see the rosebud of love nestled in that pretty white breast of thine, than the cast-off ornaments of fame!"

And filling himself a cup of wine he raised it aloft, looking at Theos smilingly as he did so.

"To your health, my noble friend!" he cried, "and to the joys of the passing hour!"

"A wise toast!" answered Theos, placing his lips to his own goblet's rim,—"For the past is past,—'twill never return,—the future we know not,—and only the present can be called our own! To the health of the divine Sah-luma, whose fame is my glory!—whose friendship is dear to me as life!"

And with this, he drained off the wine to the last drop. Scarcely had he done so, when the most curious sensation overcame him—a sensation of bewildering ecstasy as though he had drunk of some ambrosian nectar or magic drug which had suddenly wound up his nerves to an acute tension of indescribable delight. The blood coursed more swiftly through his veins,—he felt his face flush with the impulsive heat and ardor of the moment,—he laughed as he set the cup down empty, and throwing himself back on his luxurious couch, his eyes flashed on Sah-luma's with a bright, comprehensive glance of complete confidence and affection. It was strange to note how quickly Sah-luma returned that glance,—how thoroughly, in so short a space of time, their friendship had cemented itself into a more than fraternal bond of union! Niphrata, meanwhile, stood a little aside, her wistful looks wandering from one to the other as though in something of doubt or wonder. Presently she spoke, inclining her fair head toward Sah-luma.

"My lord goes to the Palace to-night to make his valued voice heard in the presence of the King?" she inquired timidly.

"Even so, Niphrata!" responded the Laureate, passing his hand carelessly through his clustering curls—"I have been summoned thither by the Royal command. But what of that, little one? Thou knowest 'tis a common occurrence,—and that the Court is bereft of all pleasure and sweetness when Sah-luma is silent."

"My lord's guest goes with him?" pursued Niphrata gently.

"Aye, most assuredly?" and Sah-luma smiled at Theos as he spoke— "Thou wilt accompany me to the King, my friend?" he went on—"He will give thee a welcome for my sake, and though of a truth His Majesty is most potently ignorant of all things save the arts of love and warfare, nevertheless he is man as well as monarch, and thou wilt find him noble in his greeting and generous of hospitality."

"I will go with thee, Sah-luma, anywhere!" replied Theos quickly— "For in following such a guide, I follow my own most perfect pleasure."

Niphrata looked at him meditatively, with a melancholy expression in her lovely eyes.

"My lord Sah-luma's presence indeed brings joy!" she said softly and tremulously—"But the joy is too sweet and brief—for when he departs, none can fill the place he leaves vacant!"

She paused,—Sah-luma's gaze rested on her intently, a half-amused, half-tender light leaping from under the drooping shade of his long, silky black lashes,—she caught the look, and a little shiver ran through her delicate frame,—she pressed one hand on her heart, and resumed in steadier and more even tones,—"My lord has perhaps not heard of the disturbances of the early morning in the city?"—she asked— "The riotous crowd in the marketplace—the ravings of the Prophet Khosrul? . . . the sudden arrest and imprisonment of many,—and the consequent wrath of the King?"

"No, by my faith!" returned Sah-luma, yawning slightly and settling his head more comfortably on his pillows—"Nor do I care to heed the turbulence of a mob that cannot guide itself and yet resists all guidance. Arrests? . . . imprisonments? . . . they are common,—but why in the name of the Sacred Veil do they not arrest and imprison the actual disturbers of the peace,—the Mystics and Philosophers whose street orations filter through the mind of the disaffected, rousing them to foolish frenzy and disordered action?—Why, above all men, do they not seize Khosrul?—a veritable madman, for all his many years and seeming wisdom! Hath he not denounced the faith of Nagaya and foretold the destruction of the city times out of number? . . . and are we not all weary to death of his bombastic mouthing? If the King deemed a poet's counsel worth the taking, he would long ago have shut this bearded ranter within the four walls of a dungeon, where only rats and spiders would attend his lectures on approaching Doom!"

"Nay, but my lord—" Niphrata ventured to say timidly—"The King dare not lay hands on Khosrul. . ."

"Dare not!" laughed Sah-luma lazily stretching out his hand and helping himself to a luscious nectarine from the basket at his side— "Sweet Niphrata! . . . settest thou a limit to the power of the King? As well draw a boundary-line for the imagination of the poet! Khosrul may be loved and feared by a certain number of superstitious malcontents who look upon a madman as a sort of sacred wild animal,—but the actual population of Al-Kyris,—the people who are the blood, bone, and sinew of the city,—these are not in favor of change either in religion, laws, manners, or customs. But Khosrul is old,—and that the King humors his vagaries is simply out of pity for his age and infirmity, Niphrata,—not because of fear! Our Monarch knows no fear."

"Khosrul prophesies terrible things!" . . . murmured the girl hesitatingly—"I have often thought. . . if they should come true. . ."

"Thou timid dove!" and Sah-luma, rising from his couch, kissed her neck lightly, thus causing a delicate flush of crimson to ripple through the whiteness of her skin—"Think no more of such folly—thou wilt anger me. That a doting graybeard like Khosrul should trouble the peace of Al-Kyris the Magnificent, . . . by the gods—the whole thing is absurd! Let me hear no more of mobs or riots, or road-rhetoric,—my soul abhors even the suggestion of discord. Tranquillity! . . . Divinest calm, disturbed only by the flutterings of winged thoughts hovering over the cloudless heaven of fancy! . . . this, this alone is the sum and centre of my desires.—and to-day I find that even thou, Niphrata—" here his voice took upon itself an injured tone,—"thou, who art usually so gentle, hast somewhat troubled the placidity of my mind by thy foolish talk concerning common and unpleasant circumstances, . . ." He stopped short and a line of vexation and annoyance made its appearance between his broad, beautiful brows, while Niphrata seeing this expression of almost baby-petulance in the face she adored threw herself suddenly at his feet, and raising her lovely eyes swimming in tears, she exclaimed:

"My lord! Sah-luma! Singing-angel of Niphrata's soul!—Forgive me! It is true, . . . thou shouldst never hear of strife or contention among the coarser tribe of men,—and I, . . . I, poor Niphrata, would give my life to shield thee from the faintest shadow of annoy! I would have thy path all woven sunbeams,—thou shouldst live like a fairy monarch embowered 'mid roses, sheltered from rough winds, and folded in loving arms, fairer maybe, but not more fond than mine!" . . . Her voice broke,—stooping, she kissed the silver fastening of his sandal, and springing up, rushed from the room before a word could be uttered to bid her stay.

Sah-luma looked after her with a pretty, half-pleased perplexity.

"She is often thus!" he said in a tone of playful resignation,—"As I told thee, Theos,—women are butterflies, hovering hither and thither on uneasy pinions, uncertain of their own desires. Niphrata is a woman-riddle,—sometimes she angers me,—sometimes she soothes, . . . now she prattles of things that concern me not,—and anon converses with such high and lofty earnestness of speech, that I listen amazed, and wonder where she hath gathered up her store of seeming wisdom."

"Love teaches her all she knows!" interrupted Theos quickly and with a meaning glance.

Sah-luma laughed languidly, a faint color warming the clear olive pallor of his complexion.

"Aye,—poor tender little soul, she loves me," . . . he said carelessly— "That is no secret! But then all women love me,—I am more like to die of a surfeit of love than of anything else" He moved towards the open window "Come!—" he added—"It is the hour of sunset,—there is a green hillock in my garden yonder from whence we can behold the pomp and panoply of the golden god's departure. 'Tis a sight I never miss,—I would have thee share its glory with me."

"But art thou then indifferent to woman's tenderness?" asked Theos half banteringly, as he took his arm—"Dost thou love no one?"

"My friend"—replied Sah-luma seriously—"I love Myself! I see naught that contents me more than my own Personality,—and with all my heart I admire the miracle and beauty of my own existence! There is nothing even in the completest fairness of womanhood that satisfies me so much as the contemplation of my own genius,—realizing as I do its wondrous power and perfect charm! The life of a poet such as I am is a perpetual marvel!—the whole Universe ministers to my needs,—Humanity becomes the merest bound slave to the caprice of my imperial imagination,—with a thought I scale the stars,—with a wish I float in highest ether among spheres undiscovered yet familiar to my fancy—I converse with the spirits of flowers and fountains,—and the love of women is a mere drop in the deep ocean of my unfathomed delight! Yes,—I adore my own Identity! . . . and of a truth Self-worship is the only Creed the world has ever followed faithfully to the end!"

He glanced up with a bright, assured smile,—Theos met his gaze wonderingly, doubtfully,—but made no reply,—and together they paced slowly across the marble terrace, and out into the glorious garden, rich with the riotous roses that clambered and clustered everywhere, their hues deepening to flame-like vividness in the burning radiance of the sinking sun.

XIV

The Summons of the Signet

They walked side by side for some little time without speaking, through winding paths of alternate light and shade, sheltered by the latticework of crossed and twisted green boughs where only the amorous chant of charming birds now and then broke the silence with fitful and tender sweetness. All the air about them was fragrant and delicate,—tiny rainbow-winged midges whirled round and danced in the warm sunset-glow like flecks of gold in amber wine,—while here and there the distant glimmer of tossing fountains, or the soft emerald sheen of a prattling brook that wound in and out the grounds, amongst banks of moss and drooping fern, gave a pleasant touch of coolness and refreshment to the brilliant verdure of the luxuriant landscape.

"Speaking of creeds, Sah-luma"—said Theos at last, looking down with a curious sense of compassion and protection at his companion's slight, graceful form—"What religion is it that dominates this city and people? To-day, through want of knowledge, it seems I committed a nearly unpardonable offence by gazing at the beauty of the Virgin Priestess when I should have knelt face-hidden to her benediction,— thou must tell me something of the common laws of worship, that I err not thus blindly again."

Sah-luma smiled.

"The common laws of worship are the common laws of custom,"— he replied—"No more,—no less. And in this we are much like other nations. We believe in no actual Creed,—who does? We accept a certain given definition of a supposititious Divinity, together with the suitable maxims and code of morals accompanying that definition, . . . we call this Religion, . . . and we wear it as we wear our clothing for the sake of necessity and decency, though truly we are not half so concerned about it as about the far more interesting details of taste in attire. Still, we have grown used to our doctrine, and some of us will fight with each other for the difference of a word respecting it,—and as it contains within itself many seeds of discord and contradiction, such dissensions are frequent, especially among the priests, who, were they but true to their professed vocation, should be able to find ways of smoothing over all apparent inconsistencies and maintaining peace and order. Of course we, in union with all civilized communities, worship the Sun, even as thou must do,—in this one leading principle at least, our faith is universal!"

Theos bent his head in assent. He was scarcely conscious of the action, but at that moment he felt, with Sah-luma, that there was no other form of Divinity acknowledged in the world than the refulgent Orb that gladdens and illumines earth, and visibly controls the seasons.

"And yet—" went on Sah-luma thoughtfully,—"the well-instructed know through our scientists and astronomers (many of whom are now languishing in prison for the boldness of their researches and discoveries) that the Sun is no divinity at all, but simply a huge planet,—a dense body surrounded by a luminous, flame-darting atmosphere,—neither self-acting nor omnipotent, but only one of many similar orbs moving in strict obedience to fixed mathematical laws. Nevertheless this knowledge is wisely kept back as much as possible from the multitude,— for, were science to unveil her marvels too openly to semi-educated and vulgarly constituted minds, the result would be, first Atheism, next Republicanism, and finally Anarchy and Ruin. If these evils,—which like birds of prey continually hover about all great kingdoms,—are to be averted, we must, for the welfare of the country and people, hold fast to some stated form and outward observance of religious belief."

He paused. Theos gave him a quick, searching glance.

"Even if such a belief should have no shadow of a true foundation?" he inquired—"Can it be well for men to cling superstitiously to a false doctrine?"

Sah-luma appeared to consider this question in his own mind for some minutes before replying.

"My friend, it is difficult to decide what is false and what is true—"he said at last with a little shrug of his shoulders—"But I think that even a false religion is better for the masses than none at all. Men are closely allied to brutes, . . . if the moral sense ceases to restrain them they at once leap the boundary line and give as much rein to their desires and appetites as the hyenas and tigers. And in some natures the moral sense is only kept alive by fear,—fear of offending some despotic, invisible Force that pervades the Universe, and whose chief and most terrible attribute is not so much creative as destructive power. To propitiate and pacify an unseen Supreme Destroyer is the aim of all religions,—and it is for this reason we add to our worship of the Sun that of the White Serpent,

Nagaya the Mediator. Nagaya is the favorite object of the people's adoration,—they may forget to pay their vows to the Sun, but never to Nagaya, who is looked upon as the emblem of Eternal Wisdom, the only pleader whose persuasions avail to soften the tyrannic humor of the Invincible Devourer of all things. We know how men hate Wisdom and cannot endure to be instructed, and yet they prostrate themselves in abject crowds before Wisdom's symbol every day in the Sacred Temple yonder,—though I much doubt whether such constant devotional attendance is not more for the sake of Lysia than the Deified Worm!"

He laughed with a little undercurrent of scorn in his laughter,—and Theos saw as it were, the lightning of an angry or disdainful thought flashing through the sombre splendor of his eyes.

"And Lysia is. . . —?" began Theos suggestively.

"The High Priestess of Nagaya," responded Sah-luma slowly— "Charmer of the god, as well as of the hearts of men! The hot passion of love is to her a toy, clasped and unclasped so! in the pink hollow of her hand. . ." and as he spoke he closed his fingers softly on the air and unclosed them again with an expressive gesture—"And so long as she retains the magic of her beauty, so long will Nagaya worship hold Al-Kyris in check. Otherwise. . . who knows!—there have been many disturbances of late,—the teachings of the Philosophers have aroused a certain discontent,—and there are those who are weary of perpetual sacrifices and the shedding of innocent blood. Moreover this mad Khosrul of whom Niphrata spoke lately, thunders angry denunciations of Lysia and Nagaya in the open streets, with so much fervid eloquence that they who pass by cannot choose but hear, . . . he hath a strange craze,—a doctrine of the future which he most furiously proclaims in the language prophets use. He holds that far away in the centre of a Circle of pure Light, the true God exists,—a vast all glorious Being who with exceeding marvellous love controls and guides Creation toward some majestic end—even as a musician doth melodize his thought from small sweet notes to perfect chord-woven harmonies. Furthermore, that thousands of years hence, this God will embody a portion of his own Existence in human form and will send hither a wondrous creature, half-God, half-Man, to live our life, die our death, and teach us by precept and example, the surest way to eternal happiness. 'Tis a theory both strange and wild!—hast ever heard of it before?"

He put the question indifferently, but Theos was mute. That horrible sense of a straining desire to speak when speech was forbidden again oppressed him,—he felt as though he were being strangled with his own unfalling tears. What a crushing weight of unutterable thoughts burdened his brain!—he gazed up at the serenely glowing sky in aching, dumb despair,—till slowly. . . very slowly, words came at last like dull throbs of pain beating between his lips. . .

"I think. . . I fancy. . . I have heard a rumor of such doctrine. . . but I know as little of it as. . . as Thou, Sah-luma! . . . I can tell thee no more. . . than Thou hast said! . . ." He paused and gaining more firmness of tone went on—"It seems to me a not altogether impossible conception of Divine Benevolence,—for if God lives at all, He must be capable of manifesting Himself in many ways both small and great, common and miraculous, though of a truth there are no miracles beyond what Appear as such to our limited sight and restricted intelligence. But tell me"—and here his voice had a ring of suppressed anxiety within it—"tell me, Sah-luma, thine own thought concerning it!"

"I?—I think naught of it!" replied Sah-luma with airy contempt—"Such a creed may find followers in time to come,—but now, of what avail to warn us of things that do not concern our present modes of life? Moreover in the face of all religion, my own opinion should not alter,—I have studied science sufficiently well to know that there is No God!—and I am too honest to worship an unproved and merely supposititious identity!"

A shudder, as of extreme cold, ran through Theos's veins, and as if impelled on by some invisible monitor he said almost mournfully:

"Art thou sure, Sah-luma, thou dost not instinctively feel that there is a Higher Power hidden behind the veil of visible Nature?—and that in the Far Beyond there may be an Eternity of Joy where thou shalt find all thy grandest aspirations at last fulfilled?"

Sah-luma laughed,—a clear, vibrating laugh as mellow as the note of a thrush in spring-time.

"Thou solemn soul!" he exclaimed mirthfully—"My aspirations Are fulfilled!—I aspire to no more than fame,—and that I hold,—that I shall keep so long as this world is lighted by the sun!"

"And what use is Fame to thee in Death!" demanded Theos with sudden and emphatic earnestness.

Sah-luma stood still,—over his beautiful face came a shadow of intense melancholy,—he raised his brilliant eyes full of wistful pathos and pleading.

"I pray thee do not make me sad, my friend!" he murmured

tremulously—"These thoughts are like muttering thunder in my heaven! Death!" . . . and a quick sigh escaped him—"'Twill be the breaking of my harp and heart! . . . the last note of my failing voice and eversilenced song!"

A moisture as of tears glistened on the silky fringe of his eyelids,— his lips quivered,—he had the look of a Narcissus regretfully bewailing his own perishable loveliness. On a swift impulse of affection Theos threw one arm round, his neck in the fashion of a confiding school-boy walking with his favorite companion.

"Nay, thou shalt never die, Sah-luma!" he said with a sort of passionate eagerness,—"Thy bright soul shall live forever in a sunshine sweeter than that of earth's fairest midsummer noon! Thy song can never be silenced while heaven pulsates with the unwritten music of the spheres,—and even were the crown of immortality denied to lesser men, it is, it must be the heritage of the poet! For to him all crowns belong, all kingdoms are thrown open, all barriers broken down,—even those that divide us from the Unseen,—and God Himself has surely a smile to spare for His Singers who have made the sad world joyful if only for an hour!"

Sah-luma looked up with a pleased yet wondering glance.

"Thou hast a silvery and persuasive tongue!" he said gently—"And thou speakest of God as if thou knewest one akin to Him. Would I could believe all thou sayest! . . . but alas!—I cannot. We have progressed too far in knowledge, my friend, for faith. . . yet. . ." He hesitated a moment, then with a touch of caressing entreaty in his tone went on. . . "Thinkest thou in very truth that I shall live again? For I confess to thee, it seems beyond all things strange and terrible to feel that this genius of mine,—this spirit of melody which inhabits my frame, should perish utterly without further scope for its abilities. There have been moments when my soul, ravished by inspiration, has, as it were, seized Earth like a full goblet of wine, and quaffed its beauties, its pleasures, its loves, its glories all in one burning draught of song! . . . when I have stood in thought on the shadowy peaks of time, waiting for other worlds to string like beads on my thread of poesy,—when wondrous creatures habited in light and wreathed with stars have floated round and round me in rosy circles of fire,—and once, methought. . .'twas long ago now—I heard a Voice distinct and sweet that called me upward, onward and away, I know not where,—save that a hidden Love awaited me!" He broke off with a rapt almost angelic expression in his eyes, then sighing a little he resumed: "All dreams of course! . . . vague phantoms,—creations of my own imaginative brain,—yet fair enough to fill my heart with speechless longings for ethereal raptures unseen, unknown! Thou hast, methinks, a certain faith in the unsolved mysteries,—but I have none,—for sweet as the promise of a future life may seem, there is no proof that it shall ever be. If one died and rose again from the dead, then might we all believe and hope. . . but otherwise. . ."

Oh, miserable Theos!—What would he not have given to utter aloud the burning knowledge that ate into his mind like slow-devouring fire! Again mute! . . . again oppressed by that strange swelling at the heart that threatened to break forth in stormy sobs of penitence and prayer! Instinctively he drew Sah-luma closer to his side—his breath came thick and fast. . . he struggled with all his might to speak the words. . . "One HAS died and risen from the dead!"—but not a syllable could he form of the desired sentence!

"Thou shalt live again, Sah-luma!" was all he could say in low, half-smothered accents—"Thou hast within thee a flame that cannot perish!"

Again Sah-luma's eyes dwelt upon him with a curious, appealing tenderness.

"Thy words savor of sweet consolation! . . ." he said half gayly, half sadly. "May they be fulfilled! And if indeed there is a brighter world than this beyond the skies, I fancy thou and I will know each other, there as here, and be somewhat close companions! See!"—and he pointed to a small green hillock that rose up like a shining emerald from the darker foliage of the surrounding trees—"Yonder is my point of vantage whence we shall behold the sun go down like a warrior sinking on the red field of battle, the chimes are ringing even now for his departure,—listen!"

They stood still for a space, while the measured, swinging cadence of bells came pealing through the stillness,—bells of every tone, that smote the air with soft or loud resonance as the faint wind wafted the sounds toward them,—and then they began to climb the little hill, Sah-luma walking somewhat in advance, with a tread as light and elastic as that of a young fawn.

Theos, following, watched his movements with a strange affection,—every turn of his head, every gesture of his hand seemed fraught with meanings as yet inexplicable. The grass beneath their feet was soft as velvet and dotted with a myriad wild flowers,—the ascent was gradual and easy, and in a few minutes they had reached the summit, where

Sah-luma, throwing himself indolently on the smooth turf, pulled Theos gently down by his side. There they rested in silence, gazing at the magnificent panorama laid out before them,—a panorama as lovely as a delicately pictured scene of fairy-land. Above, the sky was of a dense yet misty rose-color,—the sun, low on the western horizon appeared to rest in a vast, deep, purple hollow, rifted here and there with broad gashes of gold,—long shafts of light streamed upwards in order like the waving pennons of an angel-army marching,—and beyond, far away from this blaze of splendid color, the wide ethereal expanse paled into tender blue, whereon light clouds of pink and white drifted like the fluttering blossoms that fall from apple-trees in spring.

Below, and seen through a haze of rose and amber, lay the city of Al-Kyris,—its white domes, towers and pinnacled palaces rising out of the mist like a glorious mirage afloat on the borders of a burning desert. Al-Kyris the Magnificent!—it deserves its name, Theos thought, as shading his eyes from the red glare he took a wondering and gradually comprehensive view of the enormous extent of the place. He soon perceived that it was defended by six strongly fortified walls, each placed within the other at long equal distances apart, so that it might have been justly described as six cities all merged together in one,—and from where he sat he could plainly discern the great square where he had rested in the morning, by reason of the white granite obelisk that lifted itself sheer up against the sky, undwarfed by any of the surrounding buildings.

This gigantic monument was the most prominent object in sight, with the exception of the sacred temple, which Sah-luma presently pointed out,—a round, fortress-like piece of architecture ornamented with twelve gilded towers from which bells were now clashing and jangling in a storm of melodious persistency. The hum of the city's traffic and pleasure surged on the air like the noise made by swarming bees, while every now and then the sweet, shrill tones of some more than usually clear girl's voice, crying out the sale of fruit or flowers, soared up song-wise through the luminous, semi-transparent vapor that half-veiled the clustering house-tops, tapering spires and cupolas in a delicate, nebulous film.

Completely fascinated by the wizard-like beauty of the scene, Theos felt as though he could never look upon it long enough to master all its charms, but his eyes ached with the radiance in which everything seemed drenched as with flame, and turning his gaze once more toward the sun, he saw that it had nearly disappeared. Only a blood-red rim peered spectrally above the gold and green horizon-and immediately overhead, a silver rift in the sky had widened slowly in the centre and narrowed at its end, thus taking the shape of a great outstretched sword that pointed directly downward at the busy, murmuring, glittering city beneath. It was a strange effect, and made on the mind of Theos a strange impression,—he was about to call Sah-luma's attention to it, when an uncomfortable consciousness that they were no longer alone came over him,—instinctively he turned round, uttered a hasty exclamation, and springing erect, found himself face to face with a huge black,—a man of some six feet in height and muscular in proportion, who, clad, in a vest and tunic of the most vivid scarlet hue, leered confidentially upon him as their eyes met. Sah-luma rising also, but with less precipitation, surveyed the intruder languidly and with a certain haughtiness.

"What now, Gazra? Always art thou like a worm in the grass, crawling on thine errand with less noise than the wind makes in summer, . . . I would thy mistress kept a fairer messenger!"

The black smiled,—if so hideous a contortion of his repulsive countenance might be called a smile, and slowly raising his jetty arms hung all over with strings of coral and amber, made a curious gesture, half of salutation, half of command. As he did this, the clear, olive cheek of Sah-luma flushed darkly red,—his chest heaved, and linking his arm through that of Theos, he bent his head slightly and stood like one in an enforced attitude of attention. Then Gazra spoke, his harsh, strong voice seeming to come from some devil in the ground rather than from a human throat.

"The Virgin Priestess of the Sun and the Divine Nagaya hath need of thee to-night, Sah-luma!" he said, with a sort of suppressed derision underlying his words,—and taking from his breast a ring that glittered like a star, he held it out in the palm of one hand—"And also"—he added—"of thy friend the stranger, to whom she desires to accord a welcome. Behold her signet!"

Theos, impelled by curiosity, would have taken the ring up to examine it, had not Sah-luma restrained him by a warning pressure of his arm,—he was only just able to see that it was in the shape of a coiled-up serpent with ruby eyes, and a darting tongue tipped with small diamonds. What chiefly concerned him however was the peculiar change in Sah-luma's demeanor,—something in the aspect or speech of Gazra had surely exercised a remarkable influence upon him. His frame trembled through and through with scarcely controlled excitement, . . . his eyes shot forth an almost evil fire, . . . and a cold, calm, somewhat cruel smile played on the perfect outline of his delicate month. Taking the signet from Gazra's palm, he kissed it with a kind of angry tenderness, . . . then replied.

"Tell thy mistress we shall obey her behest! Doubtless she knows, as she knows all things, that to-night. I am summoned by express command, to the Palace of our sovereign lord the King. . . I am bound thither first as is my duty, but afterwards. . ." He broke off as if he found it impossible to say more, and waved his hand in a light sign of dismissal. But Gazra did not at once depart. He again smiled that lowering smile of his which resembled nothing so much as a hung criminal's death-grin, and returned the jewelled signet to his breast.

"Afterwards! . . . yes. . . afterwards!" he said in emphatic yet mock solemn tones. "Even so!" Advancing a little he laid his heavy, muscular hand on Theos's chest, and appeared mentally to measure his height and breadth—"Strong nerves! . . . iron sinews! . . . goodly flesh and blood! . . . 'twill serve!"—and his great, protruding eyes gleamed maliciously as he spoke,—then bowing profoundly he added, addressing both Sah-luma and Theos. "Noble sirs, to-night out of all men in Al-Kyris shall you be the most envied! Farewell!"—and once more making that curious salutation which had in it so much imperiousness and so little obeisance, he walked backward a few paces in the full lustre of the set sun's after-glow, which intensified the vivid red of his costume and lit up all the ornaments of clear-cut amber that glittered against his swarthy skin,—then turning, he descended the hillock so swiftly that he seemed to have melted out of sight as utterly as a dark mist dissolving in air.

"By my word, a most sooty and repellent bearer of a lady's greeting!" laughed Theos lightly, as he sauntered arm in arm with his host on the downward path leading to the garden and palace—"And I have yet to learn the true meaning of his message!"

"'Tis plain enough!" replied Sah-luma somewhat sulkily, with the deep flush still coming and going on his face—"It means that we are summoned, . . . thou as well as I, . . . to one of Lysia's midnight banquets,—an honor that falls to few,—a mandate none dare disobey! She must have spied thee out this morning—the only unkneeling soul in all the abject multitude-hence, perhaps, her present desire for thy company."

There was a touch of vexation in his voice, but Theos heeded it not. His heart gave a great bound against his ribs as though pricked by a fire-tipped arrow,—something swift and ardent stirred in his blood like the flowing of quicksilver, . . . the picture of the dusky-eyed, witchingly beautiful woman he had seen that morning in her gold-adorned ship, seemed to float between him and the light,—her face shone out like a growing glory-flower in the tangled wilderness of his thoughts, and his lips trembled a little as he replied:

"She must be gracious and forgiving then, even as she is fair! For in my neglect of reverence due, I merited her scorn, . . . not her courtesy. But tell me, Sah-luma, how could she know I was a guest of thine?"

Sah-luma glanced at him half-pityingly, half disdainfully.

"How could she know? Easily!—inasmuch as she knows all things. 'Twould have been strange indeed had she NOT known!" and he caught at a down-drooping rose and crushed its fragrant head in his hand with a sort of wanton petulance—"The King himself is less acquainted with his people's doings than the wearer of the All-Reflecting Eye! Thou hast not yet seen that weird mirror and potent dazzler of human sight, . . . no,—but thou WILT see it ere long,—the glittering Fiend-guarding of the whitest breast that ever shut in passion!" His voice shook, and he paused,—then with some effort continued—"Yes,—Lysia has her secret commissioners everywhere throughout the length and breadth of the city, who report to her each circumstance that happens, no matter how trifling,—and doubtless we were followed home,—tracked step by step as we walked together, by one of her stealthy-footed servitors,—in this there would be naught unusual."

"Then there is no freedom in Al-Kyris,—" said Theos wonderingly— "if the whole city thus lies under the circumspection of a woman?"

Sah-luma laughed rather harshly.

"Freedom! By the gods, 'tis a delusive word embodying a vain idea! Where is there any freedom in life? All of us are bound in chains and restricted in one way or the other,—the man who deems himself politically free is a slave to the multitude and his own ambition—while he who shakes himself loose from the trammels of custom and creed, becomes the tortured bondsman of desire, tied fast with bruising cords to the rack of his own unbridled sense and appetite. There is no such thing as freedom, my friend, unless haply it may be found in death! Come,—let us in to supper,—the hour grows late, and my heart aches with an unsought heaviness,—I must cheer me with a cup of wine, or my songs to-night will sadden rather than rouse the King. Come,—and thou shalt speak to me again of the life that is to be lived hereafter,"—

and he smiled with certain pathos in his smile,—"for there are times, believe me, when in spite of all my fame and the sweetness of existence, I weary of earth's days and nights, and find them far too brief and mean to satisfy my longings. Not the world,—but worlds—should be the Poet's heritage."

Theos looked at him, with a feeling of unutterable yearning affection, and regret, but said nothing, . . . and together they ascended the steps of the stately marble terrace and paced slowly across it, keeping as near to each other as shadow to substance, and thus reentered the palace, where the sound of a distant harp alone penetrated the perfumed stillness. It must be Niphrata who was playing, thought Theos, . . . and what strange and plaintive chords she swept from the vibrating strings! . . . They seemed laden with the tears of broken-hearted women dead and buried ages upon ages ago!

XV

SAH-LUMA SINGS

As they left the garden the night fell, or appeared to fall, with almost startling suddenness, and at the same time, in swift defiance of the darkness, Sah-luma's palace was illuminated from end to end by thousands of colored lamps, all apparently lit at once by a single flash of electricity. A magnificent repast was spread for the Laureate and his guest, in a lofty, richly frescoed banqueting-hall,—a repast voluptuous enough to satisfy the most ardent votary that ever followed the doctrines of Epicurus. Wonderful dainties and still more wonderful wines were served in princely profusion—and while the strangely met and sympathetically united friends ate and drank, delicious music was played on stringed instruments by unseen performers. When, at intervals, these pleasing sounds ceased, Sah-luma's conversation, brilliant, witty, refined, and sparkling with light anecdote and lighter jest, replaced with admirable sufficiency, the left-off harmonies,—and Theos, keenly alive to the sensuous enemy of his own emotions, felt that he had never before enjoyed such an astonishing, delightful, and altogether fairy-like feast. Its only fault was that it came to an end too soon, he thought, when, the last course of fruit and sweet comfits being removed, he rose reluctantly from the glittering board, and prepared to accompany his host, as agreed, to the presence of the King.

In a very short time, so bewilderingly short as to seem a mere breathing-space,—he found himself passing through the broad avenues and crowded thoroughfares of Al-Kyris on his way to the Royal abode. He occupied a place in Sah-luma's chariot,—a gilded car, shaped somewhat like the curved half of a shell, deeply hollowed, and set on two high wheels that as they rolled made scarcely any sound; there was no seat, and both he and Sah-luma stood erect, the latter using all the force of his slender brown hands to control the spirited prancing of the pair of jet-black steeds which, harnessed tandem-wise to the light-vehicle, seemed more than once disposed to break loose into furious gallop regardless of their master's curbing rein.

The full moon was rising gradually in a sky as densely violet as purple pansy-leaves—but her mellow lustre was almost put to shame by the brilliancy of the streets, which were lit up on both sides by vari-colored lamps that diffused a peculiar, intense yet soft radiance, produced, as Sah-luma explained, from stored-up electricity. On the twelve tall Towers of the Sacred Temple shone twelve large, revolving stars, that as they turned emitted vivid flashes of blue, green, and amber flame like light-house signals seen from ships veering shorewards,—and the reflections thus cast on the mosaic pavement, mingling with the paler beams of the moon, gave a weird and most fantastic effect to the scene. Straight ahead, a blazing arch raised like a bent bow against heaven, and having in its centre the word

ZEPHORANIM,

written in scintillating letters of fire, indicated to all beholders the name and abode of the powerful Monarch under whose dominion, according to Sah-luma, Al-Kyris had reached its present height of wealth and prosperity.

Theos looked everywhere about him, seeing yet scarcely realizing the wonders on which he gazed,—leaning one arm on the burnished edge of the car, he glanced now and then up at the dusky skies growing thick with swarming worlds, and meditated dreamily whether it might not be within the range of possibility to be lifted with Sah-luma, chariot, steeds and all into that beautiful, fathomless empyrean, and drive among planets as though they were flowers, reining in at last before some great golden gate, which unbarred should open into a lustrous Glory-Land fairer than all fair regions ever pictured!

How like a god Sah-luma looked, he mused! . . . his eyes resting tenderly on the light, glittering form he was never weary of contemplating. Could there be a more perfect head than that dark one crowned with myrtle? . . . could there be a more dazzling existence than that enjoyed by this child of happy fortune, this royal Laureate of a mighty King? How many poets starving in garrets and waiting for a hearing, would not curse their unlucky destinies when comparing themselves with such a Prince of Poesy, each word of whose utterance was treasured and enshrined in the hearts of a grateful and admiring people!

This was Fame indeed, . . . Fame at its utmost best,—and Theos sighed once or twice restlessly as he inwardly reflected how poor and unsatisfying were his own poetical powers, and how totally unfitted he was to cope with a rival so vastly his superior. Not that he by any means desired to cross swords with Sah-luma in a duel of song,-that was an idea that never entered his mind; he was simply conscious of a certain humiliated feeling,—an impression that it' he would be a poet at all, he must go back to the very first beginning of the art and re-learn all he had ever known, or thought he knew.

Many strange and complex emotions were at work within him, . . . emotions which he could neither control nor analyze,—and though he felt himself fully alive,—alive to his very finger-tips, he was ever and anon aware of a curious sensation like that experienced by a suddenly startled somnambulist, who, just on the point of awaking, hesitates reluctantly on the threshold of dreamland, unwilling to leave one realm of shadows for another more seeming true, yet equally transient. Entangled in perplexed reveries he scarcely noticed the brilliant crowds of people that were flocking hither and thither through the streets, many of whom recognizing Sah-luma waved their hands or shouted some gay word of greeting,—he saw, as it were without seeing. The whirling pageant around him was both real and unreal,—there was always a deep sense of mystery that hung like a cloud over his mind,—a cloud that no resolution of his could lift,—and often he caught himself dimly speculating as to what lay BEHIND that cloud. Something, he felt sure,—something that like the clew to an intricate problem, would explain much that was now altogether incomprehensible,—moreover he remorsefully realized that he had formerly known that clew and had foolishly lost it, but how he could not tell.

His gaze wandered from the figure of Sah-luma to that of the attendant harp-bearer who, perched on a narrow foothold on the back of the chariot, held his master's golden instrument aloft as though it were a flag of song,—the signal of a poet's triumph, destined to float above the world forever!

Just then the equipage—arrived at the Kings palace. Turning the horses' heads with a sharp jerk so that the mettlesome creatures almost sprang erect on their haunches, Sah-luma drove them swiftly into a spacious courtyard, lined with soldiers in full armor, and brilliantly illuminated, where two gigantic stone Sphinxes, with lit stars ablaze between their enormous brows, guarded a flight of steps that led up to what seemed to be an endless avenue of white marble columns. Here slaves in gorgeous attire rushed forward, and seizing the prancing coursers by the bridle rein, held them fast while the Laureate and his companion alighted. As they did so, a mighty and resounding clash of weapons struck the tesselated pavement,—every soldier flung his drawn sword on the ground and doffed his helmet, and the cry of

"HAIL, SAH-LUMA!"

rose in one brief, mellow, manly shout that echoed vibratingly through the heated air. Sah-luma meanwhile ascended half-way up the steps, and there turning round, smiled and bowed with an exquisite grace and infinite condescension,—and again Theos gazed at him yearningly, lovingly, and somewhat enviously too. What a picture he made standing between the great frowning sculptured Sphinxes! . . . contrasted with those cold and solemn visages of stone he looked like a dazzling butterfly or stray bird of paradise. His white garb glistened at every point with gems, and from his shoulders, where it was fastened with large sapphire clasps, depended a long mantle of cloth of gold, bordered thickly with swansdown,—this he held up negligently in one hand as he remained for a moment in full view of the assembled soldiery, graciously acknowledging their enthusiastic greetings, . . . then with easy and unhasting tread he mounted the rest of the stairway, followed by Theos and his harp-bearer, and passed into the immense outer entrance hall of the Royal Palace, known, as he explained to his guest, as the Hall of the Two Thousand Columns.

Here among the massively carved pillars which looked like straight, tall, frosted trunks of trees, were assembled hundreds of men young and old,—evident aristocrats and nobles of high degree, to judge from the magnificence of their costumes, while in and out their brilliant ranks glided little pages in crimson and blue,—black slaves, semi-nude or clothed in vivid colors,—court officials with jewelled badges and insignias of authority,—military guards clad in steel armor and carrying short, drawn scimetars,—all talking, laughing, gesticulating and elbowing one another as they moved to and fro,—and so thickly were they pressed together that at first sight it seemed impossible to penetrate through so dense a crowd: but no sooner did Sah-luma appear, than they all fell back in orderly rows, thus making an open avenue-like space for his admittance.

He walked slowly, with proudly-assured mien and a confident smile,—bowing right and left in response to the respectful salutations he received from all assembled,—many persons glanced inquisitively at Theos, but as he was the Laureate's companion he was saluted with nearly equal courtesy. The old critic Zabastes, squeezing his lean, bent body from out the throng, hobbled after Sah-luma at some little distance behind the harp-bearer, muttering to himself as he went, and bestowing many a side-leer and malicious grin on those among his acquaintance whom he here and there recognized. Theos noted his behavior with a vague sense of amusement,—the man took such evident delight in his own ill-humor, and seemed to be so thoroughly convinced that his opinion on all affairs was the only one worth having.

"Thou must check thy tongue today, Zabastes!" said a handsome youth in dazzling blue and silver, who, just then detaching himself from the crowd, laid a hand on the Critic's arm and laughed as he spoke—"I doubt me much whether the King is in humor for thy grim fooling! His Majesty hath been seriously discomposed since his return from the royal tiger-hunt this morning, notwithstanding that his unerring spear slew two goodly and most furious animals. He is wondrous sullen,-and only the divine Sah-luma is skilled in the art of soothing his troubled spirit. Therefore,—if thou hast aught of crabbed or cantankerous to urge against thy master's genius, thou hadst best reserve it for another time, lest thy withered head roll on the market-place with as little reverence as a dried gourd flung from a fruiterer's stall!"

"I thank thee for thy warning, young jackanapes!" retorted Zabastes, pausing in his walk and leaning on his staff while he peered with his small, black, bad-tempered eyes at the speaker-"Thou art methinks somewhat over well-informed for a little lacquey! What knowest thou of His Majesty's humors? Hast been his fly-i'-the-ear or cast-off sandal-string? I pray thee extend not thy range of learning beyond the proper temperature of the bath, and the choice of rare unguents for thy skin-greater knowledge than this would injure the tender texture of thy fragile brain! Pah!"—and Zabastes sniffed the air in disgust—"Thou hast a most vile odor of jessamine about thee! . . . I would thou wert clean of perfumes and less tawdry in attire!"

Chuckling hoarsely he ambled onward, and chancing to, catch the wondering backward glance of Pheos, he made expressive signs with his fingers in derision of Sah-luma's sweeping mantle, which now, allowed to fall to its full length, trailed along the marble floor with a rich, rustling sound, the varied light sparkling on it at every point and making it look like a veritable shower of gold.

On through the seemingly endless colonnades they passed, till they

MARIE CORELLI

came to a huge double door formed of two glittering, colossed winged figures holding enormous uplifted shields. Here stood a personage clad in a silver coat-of-mail, so motionless that at first he appeared to be part of the door, . . . but at the approach of Sah-luma he stirred into life and action, and touching a spring beside him, the arms of the twin colossi moved, the great double shields were slowly lowered, and the portals slid asunder noiselessly, thus displaying the sumptuous splendor of the Royal Presence-Chamber.

It was a spacious and lofty saloon, completely lined with gilded columns, between which hung numerous golden lamps having long, pointed, amber pendants, that flashed down a million sparkles as of sunlight on the magnificent mosaic floor beneath. On the walls were rich tapestries storied with voluptuous scenes of love as well as ghastly glimpses of warfare, . . . and languishing beauties reposing in the arms of their lovers, or listening to the songs of passion, were depicted side by side with warriors dead on the field of battle, or struggling hand to hand in grim and bleeding conflict. The corners of this wonderful apartment were decked with all sorts of flags and weapons, and in the middle of the painted ceiling was suspended a huge bird with the spread wings of an eagle and the head of an owl, that held in its curved talons a superb girandole formed of a hundred extended swords, each bare blade having at its point a bright lamp in the shape of a star, while the clustered hilts composed the centre.

Officers in full uniform were ranged on both sides of the room, and a number of other men richly attired stood about, conversing with each other in low tones, . . . but though Theos took in all these details rapidly at a glance, his gaze soon became fixed on the glittering Pavilion that occupied the furthest end of the saloon, where on a massive throne of ivory and silver sat the chief object of attraction, . . . Zephoranim the King. The steps of the royal dais were strewn ankle-deep with flowers, . . . on either hand a bronze lion lay couchant, . . . and four gigantic black statues of men supported the monarch's gold-fringed canopy, their uplifted arms being decked with innumerable rows of large and small pearls. The King's features were not just then visible—he was leaning back in an indolent attitude, resting on his elbow, and half covering his face with one hand. The individual in the silver coat-of-mail whispered something in Sah-luma's ear either by way of warning or advice, and then advanced, prostrating himself before the dais and touching the ground humbly with his forehead and hands. The King stirred slightly, but did not alter his position, . . . he was evidently wrapped in a deep and seemingly unpleasant reverie.

"Dread my lord. . . !" began the Herald-in-Waiting. A movement of decided impatience on the part of the monarch caused him to stop short.

"By my soul!" said a rich, strong voice that made itself distinctly audible throughout the spacious hall—"Thou art ever shivering on the edge of thy duty when thou shouldst plunge boldly into the midst thereof! How long wilt mouth thy words? . . . Canst never speak plain?"

"Most potent sovereign!" went on the stammering herald—"Sah-luma waits thy royal pleasure!"

"Sah-luma!" and the monarch sprang erect, his eyes flashing fire— "Nay, that HE should wait, bodes ill for thee, thou knave! How darest thou bid him wait?—Entreat him hither with all gentleness, as befits mine equal in the realm!"

As he thus spoke, Theos was able to observe him more attentively; indeed it seemed as though a sudden and impressive pause had occurred in the action of a drama in order to allow him as spectator, to thoroughly master the meaning of one special scene. Therefore he took the opportunity offered, and, looking full at Zephoranim, thought he had never beheld so magnificent a man. Of stately height and herculean build, he was most truly royal in outward bearing,—though a physiognomist judging him from the expression of his countenance would at once have given him all the worst vices of a reckless voluptuary and utterly selfish sensualist. His straight, low brows indicated brute force rather than intellect,—his eyes, full, dark, and brilliant, had in them a suggestion of something sinister and cruel, despite their fine clearness and lustre, while the heavy lines of his mouth, only partly concealed by a short, thick black beard, plainly betokened that the monarch's tendencies were by no means toward the strict and narrow paths of virtue.

Nevertheless he was a splendid specimen of the human animal at its best physical development, and his attire, which was a mixture of the civilized and savage, suited him as it certainly would not have suited any less stalwart frame. His tunic was of the deepest purple broidered with gold,—his vest of pale amber silk was thrown open so as to display to the greatest advantage his broad muscular chest and throat glittering all over with gems,—and he wore, flung loosely across his left shoulder, a superb leopard skin, just kept in place by a clasp of diamonds. His

MARIE CORELLI

feet were shod with gold-colored sandals,—his arms were bare and lavishly decked with jewelled armlets,—his rough, dark hair was tossed carelessly about his brow, whereon a circlet of gold studded with large rubies glittered in the light,—from his belt hung a great sheathed sword, together with all manner of hunting implements,—and beside him, on a velvet-covered stand, lay a short sceptre, having at its tip one huge egg-shaped pearl set in sapphires.

Noting the grand poise of his figure, and the statuesque grace of his attitude, a strange, hazy, far-off memory began to urge itself on Theos's mind,—a memory that with every second grew more painfully distinct, . . . HE HAD SEEN ZEPHORANIM BEFORE! Where, he could not tell,—but he was as positive of it as that he himself lived! . . . and this inward conviction was accompanied by a certain undefinable dread,—a vague terror and foreboding, though he knew no actual cause for fear.

He had however no time to analyze his emotion,—for just then the Herald-in-Waiting, having performed a backward evolution from the throne to the threshold of the audience-chamber, beckoned impatiently to Sah-luma, who at once stepped forward, bidding Theos keep close behind him. The harp-bearer followed, . . . and thus all three approached the dais where the King still stood erect, awaiting them. Zabastes the Critic glided in also, almost unnoticed, and joined a group of courtiers at the furthest end of the long, gorgeously lighted room, while at sight of the Laureate the assembled officers saluted, and all conversation ceased. At the foot of the throne Sah-luma paused, but made no obeisance,—raising his glorious eyes to the monarch's face he smiled,—and Theos beheld with amazement, that here it was not the Poet who reverenced the King, but the King who reverenced the Poet!

What a strange state of things! he thought,—especially when the mighty Zephoranim actually descended three steps of his flower-strewn dais, and grasping Sah-luma's hands raised them to his lips with all the humility of a splendid savage paying homage to his intellectual conqueror! It was a scene Theos was destined never to forget, and he gazed upon it as one gazes on a magnificently painted picture, wherein two central figures fascinate and most profoundly impress the beholder's imagination. He heard, with a vague sense of mingled pleasure and sadness, the deep, mellow tones of the monarch's voice vibrating through the silence, . . .

"Welcome, my Sah-luma!—Welcome at all times, but chiefly welcome when the heart is weighted by care! I have thought of thee all day, believe me! . . . aye, since early dawn, when on my way to the chase I heard in the depths of the forest a happy nightingale singing, and deemed thy voice had taken bird-shape and followed me! And that I sent for thee in haste, blame me not!—as well blame the desert athirst for rain, or the hungry heart agape for love to come and fill it!" Here his restless eye flashed on Theos, who stood quietly behind Sah-luma, passive, yet expectant of he knew not what.

"Whom hast thou there? . . . A friend?" This as Sah-luma apparently explained something in a low tone, . . . "He is welcome also for thy sake"—and he extended one hand, on which a great ruby signet burned like a red star, to Theos, who, bending over it, kissed it with the grave courtesy he fancied due to kings. Zephoranim appeared good-naturedly surprised at this action, and eyed him somewhat scrutinizingly as he said: "Thou art not of Sah-luma's divine calling assuredly, fair sir, else thou wouldst hardly stoop to a mere crowned head like mine! Soldiers and statesmen may bend the knee to their chosen rulers, but to whom shall poets bend? They, who with arrowy lines cause thrones to totter and fall,—they, who with deathless utterance brand with infamy or hallow with honor the most potent names of kings and emperors,— they by whom alone a nation lives in the annals of the future,—what homage do such elect gods owe to the passing holders of one or more earthly sceptres? Thou art too humble, methinks, for the minstrel-vocation,—dost call thyself a Minstrel? or a student of the art of song?"

Theos looked up, his eyes resting full on the monarch's countenance, as he replied in low, clear tones:

"Most noble Zephoranim, I am no minstrel! . . . nor do I deserve to be called even a student of that high, sweet music-wisdom in which Sah-luma alone excels! All I dare hope for is that I may learn of him in some small degree the lessons he has mastered, that at some future time I may approach as nearly to his genius as a common flower on earth can approach to a fixed star in the furthest blue of heaven!"

Sah-luma smiled and gave him a pleased, appreciative glance,— Zephoranim regarded him somewhat curiously.

"By my faith, thou'rt a modest and gentle disciple of Poesy!" he said—"We receive thee gladly to our court as suits Sah-luma's pleasure and our own! Stand thee near thy friend and master, and listen to the melody of his matchless voice,—thou shalt hear therein the mysteries of many things unravelled, and chiefly the mystery of love, in which all other passions centre and have power."

MARIE CORELLI

Re-ascending the steps of the dais, he flung himself indolently back in his throne,—whereupon two pages brought a magnificent chair of inlaid ivory and placed it near the foot of the dais at his right hand. In this Sah-luma seated himself, the pages arranging his golden mantle around him in shining, picturesque folds,—while Theos, withdrawing slightly into the background, stood leaning against a piece of tapestry on which the dead figure of a man was depicted lying prone on the sward with a great wound in his heart, and a bird of prey hovering above him expectant of its grim repast. Kneeling on one knee close to Sah-luma, the harp-bearer put the harp in tune, and swept his fingers lightly over the strings,—then came a pause. A clear, small bell chimed sweetly on the stillness, and the King, raising himself a little, signed to a black slave who carried a tall silver wand emblematic of some office.

"Let the women enter!" he commanded—"Speak but Sah-luma's name and they will gather like waves rising to the moon,—but bid them be silent as they come, lest they disturb thoughts more lasting than their loveliness."

This with a significant glance toward the Laureate, who, sunk in his ivory chair, seemed rapt in meditation.

His beautiful face had grown grave, . . . even sad, . . . he played idly with the ornaments at his belt, . . . and his eyes had a drowsy yet ardent light within them, as they flashed now and then from under the shade of his long curling lashes. The slave departed on his errand. . . and Zabastes edging himself out from the hushed and attentive throng of nobles stood as it were in the foreground of the picture, his thin lips twisted into a sneer, and his lean hands grasping his staff viciously as though he longed to strike somebody down with it.

A moment or so passed, and then the slave returned, his silver rod uplifted, marshalling in a lovely double procession of white-veiled female figures that came gliding along as noiselessly as fair ghosts from forgotten tombs, each one carrying a garland of flowers. They floated, rather than walked, up to the royal dais, and there prostrated themselves two by two before the King, whose fiery glance rested upon them more carelessly than tenderly,—and as they rose, they threw back their veils, displaying to full view such exquisite faces, such languishing, brilliant eyes, such snow-white necks and arms, such graceful voluptuous forms, that Theos caught at the tapestry near him in reeling dazzlement of sight and sense, and wondered how Sah-luma seated tranquilly in the reflective attitude he had assumed, could maintain so unmoved and indifferent a demeanor.

Indifferent he was, however, even when the unveiled fair ones, turning from the King to the Poet, laid all their garlands at his feet,—he scarcely noticed the piled-up flowers, and still less the lovely donors, who, retiring modestly backwards, took their places on low silken divans, provided for their accommodation, in a semicircle round the throne. Again a silence ensued,—Sah-luma was evidently centred like a spider in a web of his own thought-weaving,—and his attendant gently swept the strings of the harp again to recall his wandering fancies. Suddenly he looked up, . . . his eyes were sombre, and a musing trouble shadowed the brightness of his face.

"Strange it is, O King"—he said in low, suppressed tones that had in them a quiver of pathetic sweetness,—"Strange it is that to-night the soul of my singing dwells on sorrow! Like a stray bird flying 'mid falling leaves, or a ship drifting out from sunlight to storm, so does my fancy soar among drear, flitting images evolved from the downfall of kingdoms,—and I seem to behold in the distance the far-off shadow of Death. . ."

"Talk not of death!" interrupted the King loudly and in haste,—"'Tis a raven note that hath been croaked in mine ears too often and too harshly already! What! . . . hast thou been met by the mad Khosrul who lately sprang on me, even as a famished wolf on prey, and grasping my bridle-rein bade me prepare to die! 'Twas an ill jest, and one not to be lightly forgiven! 'Prepare to die, O Zephoranim?' he cried—'For thy time of reckoning is come!' By my soul!" and the monarch broke into a boisterous laugh—"Had he bade me prepare live 'twould have been more to the purpose! But yon frantic graybeard prates of naught but death, . . .'twere well he should be silenced." And as he spoke, he frowned, his hand involuntarily playing with the jewelled hilt of his sword.

"Aye,—death is an unpleasing suggestion!" suddenly said Zabastes, who had gradually moved up nearer and nearer till he made one of the group immediately round Sah-luma—"'Tis a word that should never be mentioned in the presence of Kings! Yet, . . . notwithstanding the incivility of the statement, . . . it is most certain that His Most Potent Majesty as well as His Majesty's Most Potent Laureate, MUST. . . DIE. . . !" And he accompanied the words "must. . . die. . ." with two decisive taps of his staff, smacking his withered lips meanwhile as though he tasted something peculiarly savory.

MARIE CORELLI

"And thou also, Zabastes!" retorted the King with a dark smile, jestingly drawing his sword and pointing it full at him,—then, as the old Critic shrank slightly at the gleam of the bare steel, replacing it dashingly in its sheath,—"Thou also! . . . and thine ashes shall be cast to the four winds of heaven as suits thy vocation, while those of thy master and thy master's King lie honorably urned in porphyry and gold!"

Zabastes bowed with a sort of mock humility.

"It may be so, most mighty Zephoranim," he returned composedly— "Nevertheless ashes are always ashes,—and the scattering of them is but a question of time! For urns of gold and porphyry do but excite the cupidity of the vulgar-minded, and the ashes therein sealed, whether of King or Poet, stand as little chance of reverent handling by future generations as those of many lesser men. And 'tis doubtful whether the winds will know any difference in the scent or quality of the various pinches of human dust tossed on their sweeping circles,—for the substance of a man reduced to earth-atoms is always the same,—and not a grain of him can prove whether he was once a Monarch crowned, a Minstrel pampered, or a Critic contemned!"

And he chuckled, as one having the best of the argument. The King deigned no answer, but turned his eyes again on Sah-luma, who still sat pensively silent.

"How long wilt thou be mute, my singing-emperor?" he demanded gently—"Canst thou not improvise a canticle of love even in the midst of thy soul's sudden sadness?"

At this, Sah-luma roused himself,—signing to his attendant he took the harp from him, and resting it lightly on one knee, passed his hands over it once or twice, half musingly, half doubtfully. A ripple of music answered his delicate touch,—music as soft as the evening wind murmuring among willows. Another instant and his voice thrilled on the silence,—a voice wonderful, far-reaching, mellow, and luscious as with suppressed tears, containing within it a passion that pierced to the heart of the listener, and a divine fullness such as surely was never before heard in human tones!

Theos leaned forward breathlessly, his pulses beating with unwonted rapidity, . . . what. . . WHAT was it that Sah-luma sang? . . . A Love-song! in those caressing vowel-sounds which composed the language of Al-Kyris, . . . a love-song, burning as strong wine, tender as the murmur of the sea on mellow, moon-entranced evenings,—an arrowy shaft of rhyme tipped with fire and meant to strike home to the core of feeling and there inflict delicious wounds! . . . but, as each well-chosen word echoed harmoniously on his ears, Theos shrank back shuddering in every limb, . . . a black, frozen numbness seemed to pervade his being, an awful, maddening terror possessed his brain and he felt as though he were suddenly thrown into a vast, dark chaos where no light should ever shine! For Sah-luma's song was HIS song! . . . HIS OWN, HIS VERY OWN! . . . He knew it well? He had written it long ago in the hey-day of his youth when he had fancied all the world was waiting to be set to the music of his inspiration, . . . he recognized every fancy, . . . every couplet. . . every rhyme! . . . The delicate glowing ballad was HIS, . . . HIS ALONE! . . . and Sah-luma had no right to it! He, Theos, was the Poet, . . . not this royally favored Laureate who had stolen his deas and filched his jewels of thought. . . aye! and he would tell him so to his face! . . . he would speak! . . . he would cry aloud his claims in the presence of the King and demand instant justice! . . .

He strove for utterance,—his voice was gone! . . . his lips were moveless as the lips of a stone image! Stricken absolutely mute, but with his sense of hearing quickened to an almost painful acuteness, he stood erect and motionless,—rage and fear contending in his heart, enduring the torture of a truly terrific mystery of mind-despair, . . . forced, in spite of himself, to listen passively to the love-thoughts of his own dead Past revived anew in his Rival's singing!

XVI

THE PROPHET OF DOOM

A few slow, dreadful minutes elapsed, . . . and then,—then the first sharpness of his strange mental agony subsided. The strained tension of his nerves gave way, and a dull apathy of grief inconsolable settled upon him. He felt himself to be a man mysteriously accurst,—banished as it were out of life, and stripped of all he had once held dear and valuable. How HAD IT HAPPENED? Why was he set apart thus, solitary, poor, and empty of all worth, WHILE ANOTHER REAPED THE FRUITS OF HIS GENIUS? . . . He heard the loud plaudits of the assembled court shaking the vast hall as the Laureate ended his song—and, drooping his head, some stinging tears welled up in his eyes and fell scorchingly on his clasped hands—tears wrung from the very depth of his secretly tortured soul. At that moment the beautiful Sah-luma turned toward him smiling, as one who looked for more sympathetic approbation than that offered by a mixed throng,—and meeting that happy self-conscious, bland, half-inquiring gaze, he strove his best to return the smile. Just then Zephoranim's fiery glance swept over him with a curious expression of wonder and commiseration.

"By the gods, yon stranger weeps!" said the monarch in a half-bantering tone. . . then with more gentleness he added. "Yet 'tis not the first time Sah-luma's voice hath unsealed a fountain of tears! No greater triumph can minstrel have than this,—to move the strong man's heart to woman's tenderness! We have heard tell of poets, who singing of death have persuaded many straightway to die,—but when they sing of sweeter themes, of lover's vows, of passion-frenzies, and languorous desires, cold is the blood that will not warm and thrill to their divinely eloquent allurements. Come hither, fair sir!" and he beckoned to Theos, who mechanically advanced in obedience to the command—"Thou hast thoughts of thine own, doubtless, concerning Love, and Love's fervor of delight, . . . hast aught new to tell us of its bewildering spells whereby the most dauntless heroes in every age have been caught, conquered, and bound by no stronger chain than a tress of hair, or a kiss more luscious than all the honey hidden in lotus-flowers?"

Theos looked up dreamily. . . his eyes wandered from the King to Sah-luma as though in wistful search for some missing thing, . . . his lips were parched and burning and his brows ached with a heavy weight of pain, . . . but he made an effort to speak and succeeded, though his words came slowly and without any previous reflection on his own part.

"Alas, most potent Sovereign!" he murmured. "I am a man of sad memories, whose soul is like the desert, barren of all beauty! I may have sung of love in my time, but my songs were never new,—never worthy to last one little hour! And whatsoever of faith, passion, or heart-ecstasy my fancy could with devious dreams devise, Sah-luma knows, . . . and in Sah-luma's song all my best thoughts are said!"

There was a ring of intense pathos in his voice as he spoke,—and the King eyed him compassionately.

"Of a truth thou seemest to have suffered!" he observed in gentle accents. "Thou hast a look as of one bereft of joy. Hast lost some maiden love of thine? . . . and dost thou mourn her still?"

A pang bitter as death shot through Theos's heart, . . . had the monarch suddenly pierced him with his great sword he could scarcely have endured more anguish! For the knowledge rushed upon him that he had indeed lost a love so faithful, so unfathomable, so pure and perfect, that all the world weighed in the balance against it would have seemed but a grain of dust compared to its inestimable value! . . . but what that love was, and from whom it emanated, he could no more tell than the tide can tell in syllabled language the secret of its attraction to the moon. Therefore he made no answer, . . . only a deep, half-smothered sigh broke from him, and Zephoranim apparently touched by his dejection continued good-naturedly:

"Nay, nay!—we will not seek to pry into the cause of thy spirit's heaviness. . . Enough! think no more of our thoughtless question,—there is a sacredness in sorrow! Nevertheless we shall strive to make thee in part forget thy grief ere thou leavest our court and city, . . . meanwhile sit thou there"—and he pointed to the lower step of the dais, . . . "And thou, Sah-luma, sing again, and this time let thy song he set to a less plaintive key."

He leaned hack in his throne, and Theos sat wearily down among the flowers at the foot of the dais as commanded. He was possessed by a strange, inward dread,—the dread of altogether losing the consciousness of his own identity,—and while he strove to keep a firm grasp on his mental faculties he at the same time abandoned all hope

MARIE CORELLI

of ever extricating himself from the perplexing enigma in which he was so darkly involved. Forcing himself by degrees into comparative calmness, he determined to resign himself to his fate,—and the idea he had just had of boldly claiming the ballad sung by Sah-luma as his own, completely passed out of his mind.

How could he speak against this friend whom he loved, . . . aye!—more than he had ever loved any living thing!—besides what could he prove? To begin with, in his present condition ho could give no satisfactory account of himself,—if he were asked questions concerning his nation or birth-place he could not answer them, . . . he did not even know where he had come from, save that his memory persistently furnished him with the name of a place called "ARDATH." But what was this "Ardath" to him, he mused?—What did it signify? . . . what had it to do with his immediate position? Nothing, so far as he could tell! His intellect seemed to be divided into two parts—one a total blank, . . . the other filled with crowding images that while novel were yet curiously familiar. And how could he accuse Sah-luma of literary theft, when he had none of his own dated manuscripts to bear out his case? Of course he could easily repeat his boyhood's verses word for word, . . . but what of that? He, a stranger in the city, befriended and protected by the Laureate, would certainly be considered by the people of Al-Kyris as far more likely to steal Sah-luma's thoughts than that Sah-luma should steal his!

No!—there was no help for it,—as matters stood he could say nothing,—he could only feel as though he were the sorrowful ghost of some long-ago dead author returned to earth to hear others claiming his works and passing them off as original compositions. And thus he was scarcely moved to any fresh surprise when Sah-luma, giving back the harp to his attendant, rose up, and standing erect in an attitude unequalled for grace and dignity, began to recite a poem he remembered to have written when he was about twenty years of age,—a poem daringly planned, which when published had aroused the bitterest animosity of the press critics on account of what they called its "forced sublimity." The sublimity was by no means "forced"—it was the spontaneous outcome of a fresh and ardent nature full of enthusiasm and high-soaring aspiration, but the critics cared nothing for this, . . . all they saw was a young man presuming to be original, and down they came upon him accordingly.

He recollected all the heart-sore sufferings he had endured through that ill-fated and cruelly condemned composition,—and now he was listlessly amazed at the breathless rapture and excitement it evoked here in this marvellous city of Al-Kyris, where everything seemed more strange and weird than the strangest dream! It was a story of the gods before the world was made,—of love deep buried in far eternities of light, . . . of vast celestial shapes whose wanderings through the blue deep of space were tracked by the birth of stars and suns and wonder-spheres of beauty, . . . a fanciful legend of transcendent heavenly passion, telling how all created worlds throbbed amorously in the purple seas of pure ether, and how Love and Love alone was the dominant cloud of the triumphal march of the Universe. . . And with what matchless eloquence Sah-luma spoke the glowing lines! . . . with what clear and rounded tenderness of accent! . . . how exquisitely his voice rose and fell in a rhythmic rush like the wind surging through many leaves, . . . while ever and anon in the very midst of the divinely entrancing joy that chiefly characterized the poem, his musicianly art infused a touch of minor pathos,—a suggestion of the eternal complaint of Nature which even in the happiest moments asserts itself in mournful under-tones. The effect of his splendid declamation was heightened by a few soft, running passages dexterously played on the harp by his attendant harpist and introduced just at the right moments; and Theos, notwithstanding the peculiar position in which he was placed, listened to every well-remembered word of his own work thus recited with a gradually deepening sense of peace,—he knew not why, for the verses, in themselves, were strangely passionate and wild. The various impressions produced on the hearers were curious to witness—the King moved restlessly, his bronzed cheeks alternately flushing and paling, his hand now grasping his sword, now toying with the innumerable jewels that blazed on his breast—the women's eyes at one moment sparkled with delight and at the next grew humid with tears,—the assembled courtiers pressed forward, awed, eager, and attentive,—the very soldiers on guard seemed entranced, and not even a small side-whisper disturbed the harmonious fall and flow of dulcet speech that rippled from the Laureate's lips.

When he ceased, there broke forth such a tremendous uproar of applause that the amber pendents of the lamps swung to and fro in the strong vibration of so many uplifted voices,—shouts of frenzied rapture echoed again and again through the vaulted roof like thuds of thunder,—shouts in which Theos joined,—as why should he not? He had as good a right as any one to applaud his own poem! It had been sufficiently abused heretofore,—he was glad to find it now so well appreciated, at least in Al-Kyris,—though he had no intention of putting forward any claim to its authorship. No,—for it was evident he had in some inscrutable way been made an outcast from all literary honor,—and a sort of wild recklessness grew up within him,—a bitter mirth, arising from curiously mingled feelings of scorn for himself and tenderness for Sah-luma,—and it was in this spirit that he loudly cheered the triumphant robber of his stores of poesy, and even kept up the plaudits long after they might possibly have been discontinued. Never perhaps did any poet receive a grander ovation, . . . but the exquisitely tranquil vanity of the Laureate was not a whit moved by it, . . . his dazzling smile dawned like a gleam of sunshine all over his beautiful face, but, save for this, he gave no sign of even hearing the deafening acclamations that resounded about him on all sides.

"A new Ilyspiros!" cried the King enthusiastically, and, detaching a magnificently cut ruby from among the gems he wore, he flung it toward his favored minstrel. It flashed through the air like a bright spark of flame and fell, glistening redly, on the pavement just half-way between Theos and Sah-luma. . . Theos eyed it with faintly amused indifference, . . . the Laureate bowed gracefully, but did not stoop to raise it,—he left that task to his harp-bearer, who, taking it up, presented it to his master humbly on one knee. Then, and only then Sah-luma received it, kissed it lightly and placed it negligently among his other ornaments, smiling at the King as he did so with the air of one who graciously condescends to accept a gift out of kindly feeling for the donor. Zabastes meanwhile had witnessed the scene with an expression of mingled impatience, malignity, and disgust written plainly on his furrowed features, and as soon as the hubbub of applause had subsided, he struck his staff on the ground with an angry clang, and exclaimed irritably:

"Now may the god shield us from a plague of fools! What means this throaty clamor? Ye praise what ye do not understand, like all the rest of the discerning public! Many is the time, as the weariness of my spirit witnesseth, that I have heard Sah-luma rehearse,—but never in all my experience of his prolix multiloquence, hath he given utterance to such a senseless jingle-jangle of verse-jargon as to-night! Strange it is that the so-called 'poetical' trick of confusedly heaping words together regardless of meaning, should so bewilder men and deprive them of all wise and sober judgment! By my faith! . . . I would as soon listen to the gabble of geese in a farmyard as to the silly glibness of such inflated twaddle, such mawkish sentiment, such turgid garrulity, such ranting verbosity. . ."

A burst of laughter interrupted and drowned his harsh voice,—laughter in which no one joined more heartily than Sah-luma himself. He had resumed his seat in his ivory chair, and leaning back lazily, he surveyed his Critic with tolerant good-humor and complete amusement, while the King's stentorian "Ha, ha, ha!" resounded in ringing peals through the great audience-chamber.

"Thou droll knave!" cried Zephoranim at last, dashing away the drops his merriment had brought into his eyes—"Wilt kill me with thy bitter-mouthed jests? . . . of a truth my sides ache at thee! What ails thee now? . . . Come,—we will have patience, if so be our mirth can be restrained,—speak!—what flaw canst thou find in our Sah-luma's pearl of poesy?—what spots on the sun of his divine inspiration? As the Serpent lives, thou art an excellent mountebank and well deservest thy master's pay!"

He laughed again,—but Zabastes seemed in nowise disconcerted. His withered countenance appeared to harden itself into lines of impenetrable obstinacy,—tucking his long staff under his arm he put his fingers together in the manner of one who inwardly counts up certain numbers, and with a preparatory smack of his lips he began: "Free speech being permitted to me, O most mighty Zephoranim, I would in the first place say that the poem so greatly admired by your Majesty, is totally devoid of common sense. It is purely a caprice of the imagination,—and what is imagination? A mere aberration of the cerebral nerves,—a morbidity of brain in which the thoughts brood on the impossible,—on things that have never been, and never will be. Thus, Sah-luma's verse resembles the incoherent ravings of a moon-struck madman,—moreover, it hath a prevailing tone of FORCED SUBLIMITY. . ." here Theos gave an involuntary start,—then, recollecting where he was, resumed his passive attitude—"which is in every way distasteful to the ears that love plain language. For instance, what warrant is there for this most foolish line:

"'*The solemn chanting of the midnight stars.*'

'Tis vile, 'tis vile! for who ever heard the midnight stars or any other stars chant? . . . who can prove that the heavenly bodies are given to the

MARIE CORELLI

study of music? Hath Sah-luma been present at their singing lesson?" Here the old critic chuckled, and warming with his subject, advanced a step nearer to the throne as he went on: "Hear yet another jarring simile:

> "'*The wild winds moan for pity of the world.*'

Was ever a more indiscreet lie? A brazen lie!—for the tales of shipwreck sufficiently prove the pitilessness of winds,—and however much a verse-weaver may pretend to be in the confidence of Nature, he is after all but the dupe of his own frenetic dreams. One couplet hath most discordantly annoyed my senses—'tis the veriest doggerel:

> "'*The sun with amorous clutch*
> *Tears off the emerald girdle of the rose!*'

O monstrous piece of extravagance!—for how can the Sun (his Deity set apart) 'clutch' without hands?—and as for 'the emerald girdle of the rose'—I know not what it means, unless Sah-luma considers the green calyx of the flower a 'girdle,' in which case his wits must be far gone, for no shape of girdle can any sane man descry in the common natural protection of a bud before it blooms! There was a phrase too concerning nightingales,—and the gods know we have heard enough and too much of those over-praised birds! . . ." Here he was interrupted by one of his frequent attacks of coughing, and again the laughter of the whole court broke forth in joyous echoes.

"Laugh—laugh!" said Zabastes, recovering himself and eying the throng with a derisive smile—"Laugh, ye witless bantlings born of folly!—and cling as you will to the unsubstantial dreams your Laureate blows for you in the air like a child playing with soap-bubbles! Empty and perishable are they all,—they shine for a moment, then break and vanish,—and the colors wherewith they sparkled, colors deemed immortal in their beauty, shall pass away like a breath and be renewed no more!"

"Not so!" interposed Theos suddenly, unknowing why he spoke, but feeling inwardly compelled to take up Sah-luma's defence—"for the colors ARE immortal, and permeate the Universe, whether seen in the soap-bubble or the rainbow! Seven tones of light exist, co-equal with the seven tones in music, and much of what we call Art and Poesy is but the constant reflex of these never-dying tints and sounds. Can a Critic enter more closely into the secrets of Nature than a Poet? . . . nay!—for he would undo all creation were he able, and find fault with its fairest productions! The critical mind dwells too persistently on the mere surface of things, ever to comprehend or probe the central deeps and well-springs of thought. Will a Zabastes move us to tears and passion? . . . Will he make our pulses beat with any happier thrill, or stir our blood into a warmer glow? He may be able to sever the petals of a lily and name its different sections, its way of growth and habitude,—but can he raise it from the ground alive and fair, a perfect flower, full of sweet odors and still sweeter suggestions? No!—but Sah-luma with entrancing art can make us see, not one lily but a thousand lilies, all waving in the light wind of his fancy,—not one world but a thousand worlds, circling through the empyrean of his rhythmic splendor,— not one joy but a thousand joys, all quivering song-wise through the radiance of his clear illumined inspiration. The heart,—the human heart alone is the final touchstone of a poet's genius,—and when that responds, who shall deny his deathless fame!"

Loud applause followed these words, and the King, leaning forward, clapped Theos familiarly on the shoulder:

"Bravely spoken, sir stranger!" he exclaimed—"Thou hast well vindicated thy friend's honor! And by my soul!—thou hast a musical tongue of thine own!—who knows but that thou also may be a poet yet in time to come!—And thou, Zabastes—" here he turned upon the old Critic, who, while Theos spoke, had surveyed him with much cynical disdain—"get thee hence! Thine arguments are all at fault, as usual! Thou art thyself a disappointed author—hence thy spleen! Thou art blind and deaf, selfish and obstinate,—for thee the very sun is a blot rather than a brightness,—thou couldst, in thine own opinion, have created a fairer luminary doubtless had the matter been left to thee! Aye, aye!—we know thee for a beauty hating fool,—and though we laugh at thee, we find thee wearisome! Stand thou aside and be straightway forgotten!—we will entreat Sah-luma for another song."

The discomfited Zabastes retired, grumbling to himself in an undertone,—and the Laureate, whose dreamy eyes had till now rested on Theos, his self constituted advocate, with an appreciative and almost tender regard, once more took up his harp, and striking a few rich, soft chords was about to sing again, when a great noise as of clanking armor was heard outside, mingled with a steadily increasing, sonorous hum of many voices and the increased tramp, tramp of marching feet. The doors were flung open,—the Herald-in-Waiting entered in hot haste and excitement, and prostrating himself before the throne exclaimed:

"O great King, may thy name live forever! Khosrul is taken!"

Zephoranim's black brows drew together in a dark scowl and he set his lips hard.

"So! For once thou art quick tongued in the utterance of news!" he said half-scornfully—"Bring hither the captive,—an he chafes at his bonds we will ourselves release him. . ." and he touched his sword significantly—"to a wider freedom than is found on earth!"

A thrill, ran through the courtly throng at these words, and the women shuddered and grew pale. Sah-luma, irritated at the sudden interruption that had thus distracted the general attention from his own fair and flattered self, gave an expressively petulant glance toward Theos, who smiled back at him soothingly as one who seeks to coax a spoilt child out of its ill-humor, and then all eyes were turned expectantly toward the entrance of the audience-chamber.

A band of soldiers clad from head to foot in glittering steel armor, and carrying short drawn swords, appeared, and marched with quick, ringing steps, across the hall toward the throne—arrived at the dais, they halted, wheeled about, saluted, and parted asunder in two compact lines, thus displaying in their midst the bound and manacled figure of a tall, gaunt, wild-looking old man, with eyes that burned like bright flames beneath the cavernous shadow of his bent and shelving brows,—a man whose aspect was so grand, and withal so terrible, that an involuntary murmur of mingled admiration and affright broke from the lips of all assembled, like a low wind surging among leaf-laden branches. This was Khosrul,—the Prophet of a creed that was to revolutionize the world,—the fanatic for a faith as yet unrevealed to men,—the dauntless foreteller of the downfall of Al-Kyris and its King!

Theos stared wonderingly at him. . . at his funereal, black garments which clung to him with the closeness of a shroud,—at his long, untrimmed beard and snow-white hair that fell in disordered, matted locks below his shoulders,—at his majestic form which in spite of cords and feathers he held firmly erect in an attitude of fearless and composed dignity. There was something supernaturally grand and awe-inspiring about him, . . . something commanding as well as defiant in the straight and steady look with which he confronted the King,—and for a moment or so a deep silence reigned,—silence apparently born of superstitious dread inspired by the mere fact of his presence. Zephoranim's glance rested upon him with cold and supercilious indifference,—seated haughtily upright in his throne, with one hand resting on the hilt of his sword, he showed no sign of anger against, or interest in, his prisoner, save that, to the observant eye of Theos, the veins in his forehead seemed to become suddenly knotted and swollen, while the jewels on his bare chest heaved restlessly up and down with the unquiet panting of his quickened breath.

"We give thee greeting, Khosrul!" he said slowly and with a sinister smile—"The Lion's paw has struck thee down at last! Too long hast thou trifled with our patience,—thou must abjure thy heresies, or die! What sayest thou now of doom,—of judgment,—of the waning of glory? Wilt prophesy? . . . wilt denounce the Faith? . . . Wilt mislead the people? . . . Wilt curse the King? . . . Thou mad sorcerer!—devil bewitched and blasphemous! . . . What shall hinder me from at once slaying thee?" And he half drew his formidable sword from its sheath.

Khosrul met his threatening gaze unflinchingly.

"Nothing shall hinder thee, Zephoranim," he replied, and his voice, deeply musical and resonant, struck to Theos's heart with a strange, foreboding chill—"Nothing—save thine own scorn of cowardice!"

The monarch's hand fell from his sword-hilt,—a flush of shame reddened his dark face. He bent his fiery eyes full on the captive—and there was something in the sorrowful grandeur of the old man's bearing, coupled with his enfeebled and defenceless condition, that seemed to touch him with a sense of compassion, for, turning suddenly to the armed guard, he raised his hand with a gesture of authority. . .

"Unloose his fetters!" he commanded.

The men hesitated, apparently doubting whether they had heard aright.

Zephoranim stamped his foot impatiently.

"Unloose him, I say! . . . By the gods! must I repeat the same thing twice? Since when have soldiers grown deaf to the voice of their sovereign? . . . And why have ye bound this aged fool with such many and tight bonds? His veins and sinews are not of iron,—methinks ye might have tied him with thread and met with small resistance! I have known many a muscular deserter from the army fastened less securely when captured! Unloose him—and quickly too!—Our pleasure is that, ere he dies, he shall speak an he will, in his own defence as a free man."

In trembling haste and eagerness the guards at once set to work

MARIE CORELLI

to obey this order. The twisted cords were untied, the heavy iron fetters wrenched asunder,—and in a very short space Khosrul stood at comparative liberty. At first he did not seem to understand the King's generosity toward him in this respect, for he made no attempt to move,—his limbs were rigidly composed as though they were still bound,—and so stiff and motionless was his weird, attenuated figure that Theos beholding him, began to wonder whether he were made of actual flesh and blood, or whether he might not more possibly be some gaunt spectre, forced back by mystic art from another world in order to testify, of things unknown, to living men. Zephoranim meanwhile called for his cup-bearer, a beautiful youth radiant as Ganymede, who at a sign from his royal master approached the Prophet, and pouring wine from a jewelled flagon into a goblet of gold, offered it to him with a courteous salute and smile. Khosrul started violently like one suddenly wakened from a deep dream,—shading his eyes with his lean and wrinkled hand he stared dubiously at the young and gayly attired servitor,—then pushed the goblet aside with a shuddering gesture of aversion.

"Away. . . Away!" he muttered in a thrilling whisper that penetrated to every part of the vast hall—"Wilt force me to drink blood?" He paused,—and in the same low, horror-stricken tone, continued. "Blood. . . Blood! It stains the earth and sky! . . . its red, red waves swallow up the land! . . . The heavens grow pale and tremble,—the silver stars blacken and decay, and the winds of the desert make lament for that which shall come to pass ere ever the grapes be pressed or the harvest gathered! Blood. . . blood! The blood of the innocent! . . .'tis a scarlet sea, wherein, like a broken and empty ship, Al-Kyris founders. . . founders. . . never to rise again!"

These words, uttered with such hushed yet passionate intensity produced a most profound impression. Several courtiers exchanged uneasy glances, and the women half rose from their seats, looking toward the King as though silently requesting permission to retire. But an imperious negative sign from Zephoranim obliged them to resume their places, though they did so with obvious nervous reluctance.

"Thou art mad, Khosrul"—then said the monarch in calmly measured accents—"And for thy madness, as also for thine age, we have till now retarded justice, out of pity. Nevertheless, excess of pity in great Kings too oft degenerates into weakness—and this we cannot suffer to be said of us, not even for the sake of sparing thy few poor remaining years. Thou hast overstepped the limit of our leniency,—and madman as thou art, thou showest a madman's cunning,—thou dost break the laws and art dangerous to the realm,—thou art proved a traitor, and must straightway die. Thou art accused. . ."

"Of honesty!" interrupt Khosrul suddenly, with a touch of melancholy satire in his tone. "I have spoken Truth in an age of lies! 'Tis a most death-worthy deed!"

He ceased, and again seemed to retire within himself as though he were a Voice entering at will into the carven image of man. Zephoranim frowned angrily, yet answered nothing—and a brief pause ensued. Theos grew more and more painfully interested in the scene,—there was something in it that to his mind seemed fatefully suggestive and fraught with impending evil. Suddenly Sah-luma looked up, his bright face alit with laughter.

"Now by the Sacred Veil,"—he said gayly, addressing himself to the King—"Your Majesty considers this venerable gentleman with too much gravity! I recognize in him one of my craft,—a poet, tragic and taciturn of humor, and with a taste for melodramatic simile, . . . marked you not the mixing of his word-colors in the picture he drew of Al-Kyris, foundering like a wrecked ship in a blood-red sea, whilst overhead trembled a white sky set thick with blackening stars? As I live, 'twas not ill-devised for a madman's brain! . . . and so solemn a ranter should serve your Majesty to make merriment withal, in place of my poor Zabastes, whose peevish jests grow somewhat stale owing to the Critic's chronic want of originality! Nay, I myself shall be willing to enter into a rhyming joust with so disconsolately morose a contemporary, and who knows whether, betwixt us twain, the chords of the major and minor may not be harmonized in some new and altogether marvellous fashion of music such as we wot not of!" And turning to Khosrul he added—"Wilt break a lance of song with me, sir gray-beard? Thou shalt croak of death, and I will chant of love,—and the King shall pronounce judgment as to which melody hath the most potent and lasting sweetness!"

Khosrul lifted his head and met the Laureate's half-mirthful, half-mocking smile with a look of infinite compassion in his own deep, solemnly penetrating eyes.

"Thou poor deluded singer of a perishable day!" he said mournfully—"Alas for thee, that thou must die so, soon, and be so soon forgotten! Thy fame is worthless as a grain of sand blown by the breath of the sea! . . . thy pride and thy triumph evanescent as the mists of the morning that vanish in the heat of the sun! Great has been the measure of thine inspiration,—yet thou hast missed its true teaching,—and of all the golden threads of poesy placed freely in thy hands thou hast not woven one clew whereby thou shouldst find God! Alas, Sah-lum! Bright soul unconscious of thy fate! . . . Thou shalt be suddenly and roughly slain, and THERE sits thy destroyer!"

And as he spoke he raised his shrunken, skeleton-like hand and pointed steadfastly to—the King! There was a momentary hush. . . a stillness as of stupefied amazement and horror, . . . then, to the apparent relief of all present, Zephoranim burst out laughing.

"By all the virtues of Nagaya!" he cried—"This is most excellent fooling! I, Zephoranim, the destroyer of my friend and first favorite in the realm? . . . Old man, thy frenzy exceeds belief and exhausts patience,—though of a truth I am sorry for the shattering of thy wits,—'tis sad that reason should be lacking to one so revered and grave of aspect. Dear to me as my royal crown is the life of Sah-luma, through whose inspired writings alone my name shall live in the annals of future history—for the glory of a great poet must ever surpass the renown of the greatest King. Were Al-Kyris besieged by a thousand enemies, and these strong palace-walls razed to the ground by the engines of warfare, we would ourselves defend Sah-luma!—aye, even cry aloud in the heat of combat that he, the Chief Minstrel of our land, should be sheltered from fury and spared from death, as the only one capable of chronicling our vanquishment of victory!"

Sah-luma smiled and bowed gracefully in response to this enthusiastic assurance of his sovereign's friendship,—but nevertheless there was a slight shadow of uneasiness on his bold, beautiful brows. He had evidently been uncomfortably impressed by Khosrul's words, and the restless anxiety reflected in his face communicated itself by a sort of electric thrill to Theos, whose heart began to beat heavily with a sense of vague alarm. "What is this Khosrul?" he thought half resentfully—"and how dares he predict for the adored, the admired Sah-luma so dark and unmerited an end? . . ." Hark! . . . what was that low, far-off rumbling as of underground wheels rolling at full speed? . . . He listened,—then glanced at those persons who stood nearest to him, . . . no one seemed to hear anything unusual. Moreover all eyes were fixed fearfully on Khosrul, whose before rigidly sombre demeanor had suddenly changed, and who now with raised head, tossed hair, outstretched arms, and wild gestures looked like a flaming Terror personified.

"Victory. . . Victory!" he cried, catching at the King's last word. . . "There shall be no more victory for thee, Zephoranim! . . . Thy conquests are ended, and the flag of thy glory shall cease to wave on the towers of thy strong citadels! Death stands behind thee! . . . Destruction clamors at thy palace-gates! . . . and the enemy that cometh upon thee unawares is an enemy that none shall vanquish or subdue, not even they who are mightiest among the mighty! Thy strong men of war shall be trodden down as wheat,—thy captains and rulers shall tremble and wail as children bewildered with fear:—thy great engines of battle shall be to thee as naught,—and the arrows of thy skilled archers shall be useless as straws in the gathering tempest of fire and fury! Zephoranim! Zephoranim! . . ." and his voice shrilled with terrific emphasis through the vaulted chamber. . . "The days of recompense are come upon thee,— swift and terrible as the desert-wind! . . . The doom of Al-Kyris is spoken, and who shall avert its fulfilment! Al-Kyris the Magnificent shall fall. . . shall fall! . . . its beauty, its greatness, its pleasantness, its power, shall be utterly destroyed. . . and ere the waning of the midsummer moon not one stone of its glorious buildings shall be left to prove that here was once a city? Fire! . . . Fire! . . ." and here he ran abruptly to the foot of the royal dais, his dark garments brushing against Theos as he passed,— and springing on the first step, stood boldly within hand-reach of the King, who, taken aback by the suddenness of his action, stared at him with a sort of amazed and angry fascination. "To arms, Zephoranim! . . . To arms! . . . take up thy sword and shield. . . get thee forth and fight with fire! Fire! . . . How shall the King quench it? . . . how shall the mighty monarch defend his people against it? See you not how it fills the air with red devouring tongues of flame! . . . the thick smoke reeks of blood! . . . Al-Kyris the Magnificent, the pleasant city of sin, the idolatrous city, is broken in pieces and is become a waste of ashes! Who will join with me in a lament for Al-Kyris? I will call upon the desert of the sea to hear my voice, . . . I will pour forth my sorrows on the wind, and it shall carry the burden of grief to the four quarters of the earth,—all nations shall shudder and be astonished at the direful end of Al-Kyris, the city beautiful, the empress of kingdoms! Woe unto Al-Kyris, for she hath suffered herself to be led astray by her rulers! . . . she hath drunken deep of the innocent blood and hath followed after idols, . . . her abominations are manifold and the hearts of her young men and maidens are full of evil! Therefore because Al-Kyris delighteth in pride and despiseth repentance, so shall destruction descend furiously

MARIE CORELLI

upon her, even as a sudden tempest in the mid-watches of the night,—she shall be swept away from the surface of the earth, ... wolves shall make their lair in her pleasant gardens, and the generations of men shall remember her no more! Oh ye kings, princes, and warriors!—Weep, weep for the doom of Al-Kyris!" and now his wild voice sank by degrees into a piteous plaintiveness—"Weep!—for never again on earth shall be found a fairer dwelling-place for the lovers of joy! ... never again shall be builded a grander city for the glory and wealth of a people! Al-Kyris! Al-Kyris! Thou that boastest of ancient days and long lineage! ... thou art become a forgotten heap of ruin! ... the sands of the desert shall cover thy temples and palaces, and none hereafter shall inquire concerning thee! None shall bemoan thee, ... none shall shed tears for the grievous manner of thy death, ... none shall know the names of thy mighty heroes and men of fame,—for thou shalt vanish utterly and be lost far out of memory even as though thou hadst never been!"

Here he stopped abruptly and caught his breath hard,—his blazing eyes preternaturally large and brilliant fixed themselves steadfastly on the sculptured ivory shield that surmounted the back of the King's throne, and over his drawn and wrinkled features came an expression of such ghastly horror that instinctively every one present turned their looks in the same direction. Suddenly a shriek, piercing and terrible, broke from his lips,—a shriek that like a swiftly descending knife seemed to saw the air discordantly asunder.

"See. . . See!" he cried in fierce haste and eagerness. . . "See how the crested head gleams! . . . How the soft, shiny throat curves and glistens! . . . how the lithe body twists and twines! . . . Hence!—Hence, accursed Snake! . . . thou poisoner of peace! . . . thou quivering sting in the flesh!—thou destroyer of the strength of manhood! What hast thou to do with Zephoranim, that thou dost wind thy many coils about his heart? . . . Lysia. . . Lysia! . . ." here the King started violently, his face flushing darkly red, "Thou delicate abomination! . . . Thou tyrannous treachery. . . what shall be done unto thee in the hour of darkness! Put off, put off the ornaments of gold and the jewels wherewith thou adornest thy beauty, and crown thyself with the crown of an endless affliction! . . . for thou shalt be girdled round about with flame, and fire shall be thy garment! . . . thy lips that have drunken sweet wine shall be steeped in bitterness!—vainly shalt thou make thyself fair and call aloud on thy legion of lovers, . . . they shall be as dead men, deaf to thine entreaties, and none shall answer thee,—no, not one! None shall hide thee from shame or offer thee comfort,—in the midst of thy lascivious delights shalt thou suddenly perish! . . . and my soul shall be avenged on thy sins, thou unvirgined Virgin!—thou Queen-Courtesan!"

Scarcely had he uttered the last word, when the King with a furious oath sprang upon him, grasped him by the throat, and thrusting him fiercely down on the steps of the dais, placed one foot on his prostrate body. Then drawing his gigantic sword he lifted it on high, . . . the blight blade glittered in air. . . an audible gasp of terror broke from the throng of spectators, . . . another second and Khosrul's life would have paid the forfeit for his temerity. . . when crash! . . . a sudden and tremendous clap of thunder shook the hall, and every lamp was extinguished! Impenetrable darkness reigned, . . . thick, close, suffocating darkness, . . . the thunder rolled away in sullen, vibrating echoes, and there was a short, impressive silence. Then piercing through the profound gloom came the clamorous cries and shrieks of frightened women, . . . the horrible, selfish scrambling, pushing and struggling of a bewildered, panic-stricken crowd, . . . the helpless, nerveless, unreasoning distraction that human beings exhibit when striving together for escape from some imminent deadly peril,—and though the King's stentorian voice could be heard above all the tumult loudly commanding order, his alternate threats and persuasions were of no avail to calm the frenzy of fear into which the whole court was thrown. Groans and sobs, . . . wild entreaties to Nagaya and the Sun-God. . . curses from the soldiery, who intent on saving themselves were brutally trying to force a passage to the door regardless of the wailing women, whose frantic appeals for rescue and assistance were heart-rending to hear, . . . all these sounds increased the horror of the situation,—and Theos, blind, giddy, and confused, listened to the uproar around him with something of the affrighted compassion that a stranger in Hell might be supposed to feel when hearkening to the ceaseless plaints of the self-tortured wicked. He endeavored to grope his way to Sah-luma's side,—and just then lights appeared, . . . lights that were not of earth's kindling, . . . strange, wandering flames that danced and flitted along the tapestried walls like will-o'-the-wisps on a dark morass, and flung a ghastly blue glare on the pale, uneasy faces of the scared people, till gathering in a sort of lurid ring round the throne, they outlined in strong relief the enraged, Titanesque figure of Zephoranim whose upraised sword looked in itself like an arrested flash of lightning. Brighter and brighter grew the weird lustre, illumining the whole scene. . . the vast length of the splendid hall, . . . the shining armor of the soldiers. . . the white robes of the women. . . the flags and pennons that hung from the roof and swayed to and fro as though blown by a gust of wind. . . every object near and distant was soon as visible as in broad day,—and then. . . a terrible cry of rage burst from the King,—the cry of a maddened wild beast.

"Death and fury!" he shouted, striking his sword with a fierce clang against the silver pedestal of the throne, . . . "Where is Khosrul?"

The silence of an absolute dismay answered him, . . . Khosrul had fled! Like a cloud melting in air, or a ghost vanishing into the nether-world, he had mysteriously disappeared! . . . he had escaped, no one knew how, from under the very feet and out of the very grasp of the irate monarch, whose baffled wrath now knew no bounds.

"Dolts, idiots, cowards!" . . . and he hurled these epithets at the timorous crowd with all the ferocity of a giant hurling stones at a swarm of pigmies. "Babes that are frighted by a summer thunder-storm! . . . Ye have let yon accursed heretic slip from my hands ere I had choked him with his own lie! O ye fools! Ye puny villains! . . . I take shame to myself that I am King of such a race of weaklings! Lights! . . . Bring lights hither, ye whimpering slaves,—ye shivering poltroons! . . . What! call yourselves men! Nay, ye are feeble girls prankt out in men's attire, and your steel corselets cover the faintest hearts that ever failed for dastard fear! Shut fast the palace-gates! . . . close every barrier! . . . search every court and corner, lest haply this base false Prophet be still here in hiding,—he that blasphemed with ribald tongue the High Priestess of our Faith, the holy Virgin Lysia! . . . Are ye all turned renegades and traitors that ye will suffer him to go free and triumph in his lawless heresy? Ye shameless knaves! Ye milk-veined rascals! . . . What abject terror makes ye thus quiver like aspen-leaves in a storm? . . . this darkness is but a conjurer's trick to scare women, and Khosrul's followers can so play with the strings of electricity that ye are duped into accepting the witch-glamour as Heaven's own cloud-flame! By the gods! If Al-Kyris falls, as yon dotard pronounceth, her ruins shall bury but few heroes! O superstitious and degraded souls! . . . I would ye were even as I am—a man dauntless,—a soldier unafraid."

His powerful and indignant voice had the effect of partially checking the panic and restoring something like order,—the pushing and struggling for an immediate exit ceased,—the armed guards in shamed silence began to marshal themselves together in readiness to start on the search for the fugitive,—and several pages rushed in with flaring torches, which cast a wondrous fire-glow on the surging throng of eager and timid faces, the brilliant costumes, the flash of jewels, the glimmer of swords and the dark outlines of the fluttering tapestry,—all forming together a curious chiaroscuro, from which the massive figure of Zephoranim stood out in bold and striking prominence against the white and silver background of his throne. Vaguely bewildered and lost in a dim stupefaction of wonderment, Theos looked upon everything with an odd sense of strained calmness, . . . the glittering saloon whirled before his eyes like a passing picture in a magic glass. . . and then. . . an imperative knowledge forced itself upon his mind,—HE HAD WITNESSED THIS SELF-SAME SCENE BEFORE! Where? and when? . . . Impossible to say,—but he distinctly remembered each incident! This impression however left him as rapidly as it had come, before he had any time to puzzle himself about it, . . . and just at that moment Sah-luma's hand caught his own,—Sah-luma's voice whispered in his ear:

"Let us away, my friend,—there will be naught now but mounting of guards and dire confusion,—the King is as a lion roused, and will not cease growling till his vengeance be satisfied! A plague on this shatter-pated Prophet!—he hath broken through my music, and jarred poesy into discord!—By the Sacred Veil!—Didst ever hear such a hideous clamor of contradictory tongues! . . . all striving to explain what defies explanation, namely, Khosrul's flight, for which, after all, no one is to blame so much as Zephoranim himself,—but 'tis the privilege of monarchs to shift their own mistakes and follies on to the shoulders of their subjects! Come! Lysia awaits us, and will not easily pardon our tardy obedience to her summons,—let us hence ere the gates of the palace close."

Lysia! . . . The "unvirgined Virgin"—the "Queen Courtesan"! So had said Khosrul. Nevertheless her name, like a silver clarion, made the heart of Theos bound with indescribable gladness and feverish expectation, and without an instant's pause he readily yielded to Sah-luma's guidance through the gorgeously colored confusion of the swaying crowd. Arm-in-arm, the twain,—one a POET RENOWNED, the other a POET FORGOTTEN,—threaded their rapid way between the ranks of nobles, officers, slaves, and court-lacqueys, who were all excitedly discussing the recent scare, the Prophet's escape, and the dread wrath of the King,—and hurrying along the vast Hall of the Two Thousand Columns, they passed together out into the night.

XVII

A Virgin Unshrined

Under the cloudless, star-patterned sky, in the soft, warm air that brimmed with the fragrance of roses, they drove once more together through the spacious streets of Al-Kyris—streets that were now nearly deserted save for a few late passers-by whose figures were almost as indistinct and rapid in motion as pale, flitting shadows. There was not a sign of storm in the lovely heavens, though now and again a sullen roll as of a distant cannonade hinted of pent-up anger lurking somewhere behind that clear and exquisitely dark-blue ether, in which a million worlds blazed luminously like pendulous drops of white fire. Sah-luma's chariot whirled along with incredible swiftness, the hoofs of the galloping horses occasionally striking sparks of flame from the smooth mosaic-pictured pavement; but Theos now began to notice that there was a strange noiselessness in their movements—that the whole Cortege appeared to be environed by a magic circle of silence—and that the very night itself seemed breathlessly listening in entranced awe to some unlanguaged warning from the gods invisible.

Compared with the turbulence and terror just left behind at the King's palace, this weird hush was uncomfortably impressive, and gave a sense of fantastic unreality to the scene. The sleepy, mesmeric radiance of the full moon, shining on the delicate traceries of the quaintly sculptured houses on either hand, made them look brittle and evanescent; the great heavy, hanging orange-boughs and the feathery frondage of the tall palms seemed outlined in mere mist against the sky; and the glimpses caught from time to time of the broad and quietly flowing river were like so many flashes of light seen through a veil of cloud. Theos, standing beside his friend with one hand resting familiarly on his shoulder, dreamily admired the phantom-like beauty of the city thus transfigured in the moonbeams, and though he vaguely wondered a little at the deep, mysterious stillness that everywhere prevailed, he scarcely admitted to himself that there was or could be anything unusual in it. He took his position as he found it—indeed he could not well do otherwise, since he felt his fate was ruled by some resolute, unseen force, against which all resistance would be unavailing.

Moreover, his mind was now entirely possessed by the haunting vision of Lysia—a vision half-human, half-divine—a beautiful, magical, irresistible Sweetness that allured his soul, and roused within him a wordless passion of infinite desire.

He exchanged not a syllable with Sah-luma—an indefinable yet tacit understanding existed between them,—an intuitive foreknowledge and subtle perception of each other's character, intentions, and aims, that for the moment rendered speech unnecessary. And there was something, after all, in the profound silence of the night that, while strange, was also eloquent—eloquent of meanings, unutterable, such as lie hidden in the scented cups of flowers when lovers gather them on idle summer afternoons and weave them into posies for one another's wearing. How fleetly the gilded, shell-shaped car sped on its way!— trees, houses, bridges, domes, and cupolas, seemed to fly past in a varied whirl of glistening color! Now and again a cluster of fire-flies broke from some thicket of shade and danced drowsily by in sparkling tangles of gold and green; here and there from great open squares and branch-shadowed gardens gleamed the stone face of an obelisk, or the white column of a fountain; while over all things streamed the long prismatic rays flung forth from the revolving lights in the Twelve Towers of the Sacred Temple, like flaming spears ranged lengthwise against the limitless depth of the midnight horizon. With straining necks, tossed manes, and foam flying from their nostrils, Sah-luma's fiery coursers dashed onward at almost lightning speed, and the journey became a wild, headstrong rush through the dividing air—a rush toward some voluptuous end, dimly discerned, yet indefinite!

At last they stopped. Before them rose a lofty building, crested with fantastic pinnacles such as are formed by ice on the roof in times of intense cold; a great gate stood open, and pacing slowly up and down in front of it was a tall slave in white tunic and turban, who, turning his gleaming eyeballs on Sah-luma, nodded by way of salutation, and then uttered a sharp, peculiar whistle. This summons brought out two curious, dwarfish figures of men, whose awkward misshapen limbs resembled the contorted branches of wind-blown trees, and whose coarse and repulsive countenances betokened that malignant delight in evil-doing which only demons are supposed to know. These ungainly servitors possessed themselves of the Laureate's chafing steeds, and led them and the chariot away into some unseen courtyard; while the Laureate himself, still saying no word, kept fast hold of his companion's arm, and hurried him along a dark avenue overshadowed with thick boughs that drooped heavily downward to the ground—a solitary place where the intense quiet was disturbed only by the occasional drip, drip of dewy moisture trickling tearfully from the leaves, or the sweet, faint, gurgling sound of fountains playing somewhere in the distance.

On they went for several paces, till at a sharp bend in the moss-grown path, an amethystine light broke full between the arched green branches; directly in front of them glimmered a broad piece of water, and out of the purple-tinted depths rose the white, nude, lovely form of a woman, whose rounded, outstretched arms appeared to beckon them, . . . whose mouth smiled in mingled malice and sweetness, . . . and round whose looped-up tresses sparkled a diadem of sapphire flame. With a cry of astonishment and ecstacy Theos sprang forward: Sah-luma held him back in laughing remonstrance.

"Wilt drown for a statue's sake?" he inquired mirthfully. "By my soul, good Theos, if thy wits thus wander at sight of a witching, marble nymph illumed by electric glamours, what will become of thee when thou art face to face with living, breathing loveliness! Come, thou hotheaded neophyte! thou shalt not waste thy passion on images of stone, I warrant thee! Come!"

But Theos stood still. His eyes roved from Sah-luma to the glittering statue and from the statue back again to Sah-luma in mingled doubt and dread. A vague foreboding filled his mind, he fancied that a bevy of mocking devils peered at him from out the wooded labyrinth, . . . and that Sin was the name of the white siren yonder, whose delicate body seemed to palpitate with every slow ripple of the surrounding waters. He hesitated,—with that often saving hesitation a noble spirit may feel ere willfully yielding to what it instinctively knows to be wrong,—and for the briefest possible space an imperceptible line was drawn between his own self-consciousness and the fascinating personality of his lately found friend—a line that parted them asunder as though by a gulf of centuries.

"Sah-luma," he said, in a tremulous, low tone, "tell me truly,—is it good for us to be here?"

Sah-luma regarded him in wide-eyed amazement.

"Good? good?" he repeated with a sort of impatient disdain. "What dost thou mean by 'good'? What is good? What is evil? Canst thou tell? If so, thou art wiser than I! Good to be here? If it is good to drown remembrance of the world in draughts of pleasure; if it is good to love and be beloved; if it is good to Enjoy, aye! enjoy with burning zest every pulsation of the blood and every beat of the heart, and to feel that life is a fiery delight, an exquisite dream of drained-off rapture, then it is good to be here! If," and he caught Theos's hand in his own warm palm and pressed it, while his voice sank to a soft and infinitely caressing sweetness, "if it is good to climb the dizzy heights of joy and drowse in the deep sunshine of amorous eyes, . . . to slip away on elfin wings into the limitless freedom of Love's summerland, . . . to rifle rich kisses from warm lips even as rosebuds are rifled from the parent rose, and to forget! . . . —to forget all bitter things that are best forgotten—"

"Enough, enough!" cried Theos, fired with a reckless impulse of passionate ardor. "On, on, Sah-luma! I follow thee! On! let us delay no more!"

At that moment a far-off strain of music saluted his ears—music evidently played on stringed instruments. It was accompanied by a ringing clash of cymbals; he listened, and listening, saw a smile lighten Sah-luma's features—a smile sweet, yet full of delicate mockery. Their eyes met; a wanton impetuosity flashed like reflected flame from one face to the other, and then, without another instant's pause, they hurried on.

Across a broad, rose-marbled terrace garlanded with a golden wealth of orange-trees and odorous oleanders. . . under a trellis-work covered with magnolias whose half-shut, ivory-tinted buds glistened in the moonlight like large suspended pearls, . . . then through a low-roofed stone-corridor, close and dim, lit only by a few flickering oil-lamps placed at far intervals, . . . then on they went, till at last, ascending three red granite steps on which were carved some curious hieroglyphs, they plunged into what seemed to be a vast jungle enclosed in some dense tropical forest. What a strange, unsightly thicket of rank verdure was here, thought Theos! . . . it was as though Nature, grown tired of floral beauty, had, in a sudden malevolent mood, purposely torn and blurred the fair green frondage and twisted every bud awry! Great, jagged leaves covered with prickles and stained all over with blotches as of spilt poison, . . . thick brown stems glistening with slimy moisture and coiled up like the sleeping bodies of snakes, . . . masses of purple and blue fungi, . . . and blossoms seemingly of the orchid species, some like fleshy tongues, others like the waxen yellow fingers of a dead hand, protruded spectrally through the matted foliage,—while all manner of strange, overpowering odors increased the swooning oppressiveness of the sultry, languorous air.

This uncouth botanical garden was apparently roofed in by a lofty glass dome, decorated with hangings of watery-green silk, but the grotesque trees and plants grew to so enormous a height that it was impossible to tell which were the falling draperies and which the straggling leaves. Curious birds flew hither and thither, voiceless creatures, scarlet and amber winged; a huge gilded brazier stood in one corner from whence ascended the constant smoke of burning incense, and there were rose-shaded lamps all about, that shed a subdued mysterious lustre on the scene, and bestowed a pale glitter on a few fantastic clumps of arums and nodding lotus-flowers that lazily lifted themselves out of a greenish pool of stagnant water sunk deeply in on one side of the marble flooring. Theos, holding Sah-luma's arm, stepped eagerly across the threshold; he was brimful of expectation: . . . and what mattered it to him whether the weed-like things that grew in this strange pavilion were pure or poisonous, provided he might look once more upon the witching face that long ago had so sweetly enticed him to his ruin! . . . Stay! what was he thinking of? Long ago? Nay, that was impossible,—since he had only seen the Priestess Lysia for the first time that very morning! How piteously perplexing it was to be thus tormented with these indistinct ideas!—these half-formed notions of previous intimate acquaintance with persons and places he never could have known before!

All at once he drew back with a startled exclamation; an enormous tigress, sleek and jewel-eyed, bounded up from beneath a tangled mass of red and yellow creepers and advanced toward him with a low savage snarl.

"Peace, Aizif, peace;" said Sah-luma, carelessly patting the animal's head. "Thou art wont to be wiser in distinguishing 'twixt thy friends and foes." Then turning to Theos he added—"She is harmless as a kitten, this poor Aizif! Call her, good Theos, she will come to thy hand—see!" and he smiled, as Theos, not to be outdone by his companion in physical courage, bent forward and stroked the cruel-looking beast, who, while submitting to his caress, never for a moment ceased her smothered snarling. Presently, however, she was seized with a sudden fit of savage playfulness,—and throwing herself on the ground before him, she rolled her lithe body to and fro with brief thirsty roars of satisfaction, . . . roars that echoed through the whole pavilion with terrific resonance: then rising, she shook herself vigorously and commenced a stealthy, velvet-footed pacing up and down, lashing her tail from side to side, and keeping those sly, emerald-like eyes of hers watchfully fixed on

Sah-luma, who merely laughed at her fierce antics. Leaning against one of the dark, gnarled trees, he tapped his sandaled foot with some impatience on the marble pavement, while Theos, standing close beside him, wondered whether the mysterious Lysia knew of their arrival.

Sah-luma appeared to guess his thoughts, for he answered them as though they had been spoken aloud.

"Yes," he said, "she knows we are here—she knew the instant we entered her gates. Nothing is or can be hidden from her! He who would have secrets must depart out of Al-Kyris and find some other city to dwell in, . . . for here he shall be unable to keep even his own counsel. To Lysia all things are made manifest; she reads human nature as one reads an open scroll, and with merciless analysis she judges men as being very poor creatures, limited in their capabilities, disappointing and monotonous in their passions, unproductive and circumscribed in their destinies. To her ironical humor and icy wit the wisest sages seem fools; she probes them to the core, and discovers all their weaknesses; . . . she has no trust in virtue, no belief in honesty. And she is right! Who but a madman would be honest in these days of competition and greed of gain? And as for virtue, 'tis a pretty icicle that melts at the first touch of a hot temptation! Aye! the Virgin Priestess of Nagaya hath a most profound comprehension of mankind's immeasurable brute stupidity; and, strong in this knowledge, she governs the multitude with iron will, intellectual force, and dictative firmness: . . . when she dies I know not what will happen."

Here he interrupted himself, and a dark shadow crossed his brows. "By my soul!" he muttered, "how this thought of death haunts me like the unburied corpse of a slain foe! I would there were no such thing as Death; 'tis a cruel and wanton sport of the gods to give us life at all if life must end so utterly and so soon!"

He sighed deeply. Theos echoed the sigh, but answered nothing. At that moment the restless Aizif gave another appalling roar, and pounced swiftly toward the eastern side of the pavilion, where a large painted panel could be dimly discerned, the subject of the painting being a hideous idol, whose long, half-shut, inscrutable eyes leered through the surrounding foliage with an expression of hateful cunning and malevolence. In front of this panel the tigress lay down, licking the pavement thirstily from time to time and giving vent to short purring sounds of impatience: . . . then all suddenly she rose with ears pricked, in an attitude of attention. The panel slowly moved, it glided back,—

MARIE CORELLI

and the great brute leaped forward, flinging her two soft paws on the shoulders of the figure that appeared—the figure of a woman, who, clad in glistening gold from head to foot, shone in the dark aperture like a gilded image in a shrine of ebony. Theos beheld the brilliant apparition in some doubt and wonder. Was this Lysia? He could not see her face, as she wore a thick white veil through which only the faintest sparkle of dark eyes glimmered like flickering sunbeams; nor was he able to discern the actual outline of her form, as it was completely enveloped and lost in the wide, shapeless folds of her stiff, golden gown. Yet every nerve in his body thrilled at her presence! . . . every drop of blood seemed to rush from his heart to his brain in a swift, scorching torrent that for a second blinded his eyes with a red glare and made him faint and giddy.

Woman and tigress! They looked strangely alike, he thought, as they stood mutually caressing each other under the great drooping masses of fantastic leaves. Yet where was the resemblance? What possible similarity could there be between a tawny, treacherous brute of the forests, full of sly malice and voracious cruelty, and that dazzling, gold-garmented creature, whose small white hand, flashing with jewels, now tenderly smoothed the black, silken stripes on the sleek coat of her savage favorite?

"Down, sweet Aizif, down!" she said, in a grave, dulcet voice as softly languorous as the last note of a love-song. "Down, my gentle one! thou art too fond, down! so!" this as the tigress instantly removed its embracing paws from her neck, and, trembling in every limb, crouched on the ground in abjectly submissive obedience. Another moment, and she advanced leisurely into the pavilion, Aizif slinking stealthily along beside her and seeming to imitate her graceful gliding movements, till she stood within a few paces of Theos and Sah-luma, just near the spot where the lotus-flowers swayed over the grass-green, stagnant pool. There she paused, and apparently scrutinized her visitors intently through the folds of her snowy veil. Sah-luma bent his head before her in a half haughty, half humble salutation.

"The tardy Sah-luma!" she said, with an undercurrent of laughter in her musical tones, "the poet who loves the flattery of a foolish king, and the applause of a still more foolish court! And so Khosrul disturbed the flood of thine inspiration to-night, good minstrel? Nay, for that he should die, if for no other crime! And this," here she turned her veiled features toward Theos, whose heart beat furiously as he caught a luminous flash from those half-hidden, brilliant eyes, "this is the unwitting stranger who honored me by so daring a scrutiny this morning! Verily, thou hast a singularly venturesome spirit of thine own, fair sir! Still, we must honor courage, even though it border on rashness, and I rejoice to see that the wrathful mob of Al-Kyris hath yet left thee man enough to deserve my welcome! Nevertheless thou were guilty of most heinous presumption!" Here she extended her jewelled hand. "Art thou repentant? and wilt thou sue for pardon?"

Scarcely conscious of what he did, Theos approached her, and kneeling on one knee took that fair, soft hand in his own and kissed it with passionate fervor.

"Criminal as I am," he murmured tremulously, "I glory in my crime, nor will I seek forgiveness! Nay, rather will I plead, with thee that I may sin so sweet a sin again, and blind myself with beauty unreproved!"

Slowly she withdrew her fingers from his clasp.

"Thou art bold!" she said, with a touch of indolent amusement in her accents. "But in thy boldness there is something of the hero. Knowest thou not that I, Lysia, High Priestess of Nagaya, could have thee straightway slain for that unwise speech of thine?—unwise because over-hasty and somewhat over-familiar. Yes, I could have thee slain!" and she laughed,—a rippling little laugh like that of a pleased child. "Howbeit thou shalt not die this time for thy foolhardiness—thy looks are too much in thy favor! Thou art like Sah-luma in his noblest moods, when tired of verse-stringing and sonnet-chanting he condescends to remember that he is not quite divine! See how he chafes at that!" and plucking a lotus-bud she threw it playfully at the Laureate, whose handsome face flushed vexedly at her words. "And thou art prudent, Sir Theos—do I not pronounce thy name aptly?—thou wilt be less petulant than he, and less absorbed in self-adoration, for here men—even poets—are deemed no more than men, and their constant querulous claim to be considered as demi-gods meets with no acceptance! Wilt 'blind thyself with beauty' as thou say'st? Well then, lose thine eyes, but guard thy heart!"

And with a careless movement she loosened her veil; it fell from her like a soft cloud, and Theos, springing to his feet, gazed upon her with a sense of enraptured bewilderment and passionate pain. It was as though he saw the wraith of some fair, dead woman he had loved of old, risen anew to redemand from him his former allegiance. O, unfamiliar yet well-known face! . . . O, slumbrous, starry eyes that seemed to hold the memory of a thousand love-thoughts! . . . O, sweet curved lips whereon a delicious smile rested as softly as sunlight on young rose-petals! Where, . . . where, in God's name, had he seen all this marvelous, witching, maddening loveliness BEFORE? His heart beat with heavy, laboring thuds, . . . his brain reeled, . . . a dim, golden, suffused radiance seemed to hover like an aureole above that dazzling white brow, adorned with a clustering wealth of raven-black tresses, whose massive coils were crowned with the strangest sort of diadem—a wreath of small serpents' heads cunningly fashioned in rubies and rose brilliants, and set in such a manner that they appeared to lift themselves erect from out the dusky hair as though in darting readiness to sting. Full of a vague, wild longing, he instinctively stretched out his arms, . . . then on a sudden impulse turned swiftly away, in a dizzy effort to escape from the basilisk fire-gleam of those sombre, haunting eyes that plunged into his inmost soul, and there aroused such dark desires, such retrospective evil, such wild weakness as shamed the betterness of his nature! Sah-luma's clear, mocking laugh just then rang sharply through the perfumed stillness.

"Thou mad Theos! Whither art thou bound?" cried the Laureate mirthfully. "Wilt leave our noble hostess ere the entertainment has begun? Ungallant barbarian! What frenzy possesses thee?"

These words recalled him to himself. He came back slowly step by step, and with bowed head, to where Lysia stood—Lysia, whose penetrating gaze still rested upon him with strangely fixed intensity.

"Forgive me," he said, in a low, unsteady voice that to his own ears sounded full of suppressed yet passionate appeal. "Forgive me, lady, that for one moment I have seemed discourteous. I am not so, in very truth. Sad fancies fret my brain at times, and—and there is that within thine unveiled beauty which sword-like wounds my soul! I am not joyous natured: . . . unlike Sah-luma, chosen favorite of fortune, I have lost all, all that made my life once seem fair. I am dead to those that loved me, . . . forgotten by those that honored me, . . . a wanderer in strange lands, a solitary wayfarer perplexed with many griefs to which I cannot give a name! Nevertheless," and he drew a quick, hard breath, "if I may serve thee, fairest Lysia,—as Sah-luma serves thee,—subject to thy sovereign favor,—thou shalt not find me lacking in obedience! Command me as thou wilt; let me efface myself to worship thee! Let me, if it be possible, drown thought,—slay memory,—murder conscience,—so that I may once more, as in the old time, be glad with the gladness that only love can give and only death can take away!"

As he finished this unpremeditated, uncontrollable outburst his eyes wistfully sought hers. She met his look with a languid indifference and a half-disdainful smile.

"Enough! restrain thine ardor!" she said coldly, her dark dilating orbs shining like steel beneath the velvet softness of her long lashes. "Thou dost speak ignorantly, unknowing what thy words involve— words to which I well might bind thee, were I less forbearing to thine inconsiderate rashness. How like all men thou art! How keen to plunge into unfathomed deeps, merely to snatch the pearl of present pleasure! How martyr-seeming in thy fancied sufferings, as though THY little wave of personal sorrow swamped the world! O wondrous human Egotism! that sees but one great absolute 'I' scrawled on the face of Nature! 'I' am afflicted, let none dare to rejoice! 'I' would be glad, let none presume to grieve!" . . . She laughed, a little low laugh of icy satire, and then resumed: "I thank thee for thy proffered service, sir stranger, albeit I need it not,—nor do I care to claim it at thy hands. Thou art my guest—no more! Whether thou wilt hereafter deserve to be enrolled my bondsman depends upon thy prowess and—my humor!"

Her beautiful eyes flashed scornfully, and there was something cruel in her glance. Theos felt it sting him like a sharp blow. His nerves quivered,—his spirit rose in arms against the cynical hauteur of this woman whom he loved; yes,—LOVED, with a curious sense of revived passion—passion that seemed to have slept in a tomb for ages, and that now suddenly sprang into life and being, like a fire kindled anew on dead ashes!

Acting on a sudden proud impulse he raised his head and looked at her with a bold steadfastness,—a critical scrutiny,—a calmly discriminating valuation of her physical charms that for the moment certainly appeared to startle her self-possession, for a deep flush colored the fairness of her face and then faded, leaving her pale as marble. Her emotion, whatever it was, lasted but a second,—yet in that second he had measured his mental strength against hers, and had become aware of his own supremacy! This consciousness filled him with peculiar satisfaction. He drew a long breath like one narrowly escaped from close peril. He had now no fear of her—only a great, all-absorbing, all-evil love, and to that he was recklessly content to yield. Her eyes dwelt glitteringly first upon him and then on Sah-luma, as the eyes of a falcon dwell on its prey, and her smile was touched with a little malice, as she said, addressing them both:

MARIE CORELLI

"Come, fair sirs! we will not linger in this wilderness of wild flowers. A feast awaits us yonder—a feast prepared for those who, like yourselves obey the creed of sweet self indulgence, . . . the world-wide creed wherein men find no fault, no shadow of inconsistency! The truest wisdom is to enjoy,—the only philosophy that which teaches us how best to gratify our own desires! Delight cannot satiate the soul, nor mirth engender weariness! Follow me!—" and with a lithe movement she swept toward the door, her pet tigress creeping closely after her; then suddenly looking back she darted a lustiously caressing glance over her shoulder at Sah-luma and stretched out her hand. He at once caught it in his own and kissed it with an almost brusque eagerness.

"I thought you had forgotten me!" he murmured in a vexed, half-reproachful tone.

"Forgotten you? Forgotten Sah-luma? Impossible!" and her silvery laughter shook the air into little throbs of music. "When the greatest poet of the age is forgotten, then fall Al-Kyris! . . . for there shall be no more need of kingdoms!"

Laughing still and allowing her hand to remain in his, she passed out of the pavilion, and Theos followed them both as a man might follow the beckoning sylphs in a fairy dream.

A mellow, luminous, witch-like radiance seemed to surround them as they went—two dazzling figures gliding on before him with the slow, light grace of moonbeams flitting over a smooth ocean. They seemed made for each other, . . . he could not separate them in his thoughts; but the strangest part of the matter was the feeling he had, that he himself somehow belonged to them and they to him. His ideas on the subject, however, were very indefinite; he was in a condition of more or less absolute passiveness, save when strong shudders of grief, memory, remorse or roused passion shook him with sudden force like a storm blast shaking some melancholy cypress whose roots are in the grave. He mused on Lysia's scornful words with a perplexed pain. Was he then so selfish? "The one great absolute 'I' scrawled on the face of Nature!" Could that apply to him? Surely not! since in his present state of mind he could hardly lay claim to any distinct personality, seeing that that personality was forever merging itself and getting lost in the more clearly perfect identity of Sah-luma, whom he regarded with a species of profound hero-worship such as one man seldom feels for another. To call himself a Poet Now seemed the acme of absurdity; how should such an one as he attempt to conquer fame with a rival like Sah-luma already in the field and already supremely victorious?

Full of these fancies, he scarcely heeded the wonders through which he passed, as he followed his two radiant guides along. His eyes were tired, and rested almost indifferently on the magnificence that everywhere surrounded him, though here and there certain objects attracted his attention as being curiously familiar. These lofty corridors, gorgeously frescoed, . . . these splendid groups of statuary, . . . these palm-shaded nooks of verdure where imprisoned nightingales warbled plaintive songs that were all the sweeter for their sadness, . . . these spacious marble loggias cooled by the rising and falling spray of myriad fountains—did he not dimly recognize all these things? He thought so, yet was not sure,—for he had arrived at a pass when he could neither rely on his reason nor his memory. Naught of deeper humiliation could he have than this, to feel within himself that he was still AN INTELLECTUAL, THINKING, SENTIENT HUMAN BEING, and that yet at the same time, his INTELLIGENCE COULD DO NOTHING TO EXTRICATE HIM from the terrific mystery which had engulfed him like a huge flood, and wherein he was now tossed to and fro as helplessly as a floating straw.

On, still on he went, treading closely in Sah-luma's footsteps and wistfully noting how often the myrtle-garlanded head of his friend drooped caressingly toward Lysia's dusky perfumed locks, whence those jewelled serpents' fangs darted flashingly upward like light from darkness. On, still on, till at last he found himself in a grand vestibule, built entirely of sparkling red granite. Here were ten sphinxes, so huge in form that a dozen men might have lounged at ease on each one of their enormous paws; they were ranged in rows of five on each side, and their coldly meditative eyes appeared to dwell steadfastly on the polished face of a large black Disc placed conspicuously on a pedestal in the exact centre of the pavement. Strange letters shone from time to time on this ebony tablet, . . . letters that seemed to be written in quicksilver; they glittered for a second, then ran off like phosphorescent drops of water, and again reappeared, but the same signs were never repeated twice over. All were different, . . . all were rapid in their coming and going as flashes of lightning. Lysia, approaching the Disc, turned it slightly; at her touch it revolved like a flying wheel, and for a brief space was literally covered with mysterious characters, which the beautiful Priestess perused with an apparent air of satisfaction. All

MARIE CORELLI

at once the fiery writing vanished, the Disc was left black and bare,— and then a silver ball fell suddenly upon it, with a clang, from some unseen height, and rolling off again instantly disappeared. At the same moment a harsh voice, rising as it were from the deepest underground, chanted the following words in a monotonous recitative:

"Fall, O thou lost Hour, into the dreadful Past! Sink, O thou Pearl of Time, into the dark and fathomless abyss! Not all the glory of kings or the wealth of empires can purchase thee back again! Not all the strength of warriors or the wisdom of sages can draw thee forth from the Abode of Silence whither thou art fled! Farewell, lost Hour!—and may the gods defend us from thy reproach at the Day of Doom! In the name of the Sun and Nagaya, . . . Peace!"

The voice died away in a muffled echo, and the slow, solemn boom of a brazen-tongued bell struck midnight. Then Theos, raising his eyes, saw that all further progress was impeded by a great wall of solid rock that glistened at every point with flashes of pale and dark violet light—a wall composed entirely of adamantine spar, crusted thick with the rough growth of oriental amethyst. It rose sheer up from the ground to an altitude of about a hundred feet, and apparently closed in and completed the vestibule.

Surely there was no passing through such a barrier as this? . . . he thought wonderingly; nevertheless Lysia and Sah-luma still went on, and he—as perforce he was compelled—still followed. Arrived at the foot of the huge erection that towered above him like a steep cliff of molten gems, he fancied he heard a faint sound behind it as of clinking glasses and boisterous laughter, but before he had time to consider what this might mean, Lysia laid her hand lightly on a small, protruding knob of crystal, pressed it, and lo! . . . the whole massive structure yawned open suddenly without any noise, suspending itself as it were in sparkling festoons of purple stalactites over the voluptuously magnificent scene disclosed.

At first it was difficult to discern more than a gorgeous maze of swaying light and color as though a great field of tulips in full bloom should be seen waving to and fro in the breath of a soft wind; but gradually this bewildering dazzle of gold and green, violet and crimson, resolved itself into definite form and substance; and Theos, standing beside his two companions on the elevated threshold of the partition through which they had entered, was able to look down and survey with tolerable composure the wondrous details of the glittering picture—a picture that looked like a fairy-fantasy poised in a haze of jewel-like radiance as of vaporized sapphire.

He saw beneath him a vast circular hall or amphitheatre, roofed in by a lofty dome of richest malachite, from the centre of which was suspended a huge globe of fire, that revolved with incredible swiftness, flinging vivid, blood-red rays on the amber-colored silken carpets and embroideries that strewed the floor below. The dome was supported by rows upon rows of tall, tapering crystal columns, clear as translucent water and green as the grass in spring, . . . and between and beyond these columns on the left-hand side there were large, oval-shaped casements set wide open to the night, through which the gleam of a broad lake laden with water-lilies could be seen shimmering in the yellow moon. The middle of the hall was occupied by a round table covered with draperies of gold, white, and green, and heaped with all the costly accessories of a sumptuous banquet such as might have been spread before the gods of Olympus in the full height of their legendary prime. Here were the lovely hues of heaped-up fruit,—the tender bloom of scattered flowers,—the glisten of jewelled flagons and goblets, the flash of massive golden dishes carried aloft by black slaves attired in white and crimson,—the red glow of poured-out wine; and here, in the drowsy warmth, lounging on divans of velvet and embroidered satin, eating, drinking, idly gossiping, loudly laughing, and occasionally bursting into wild snatches of song, were a company of brilliant-looking personages,—all men, all young, all handsome, all richly clad, and all evidently bent on enjoying the pleasures offered by the immediate hour. Suddenly, however, their noisy voices ceased—with one accord, as though drawn by some magnetic spell, they all turned their heads toward the platform where Lysia had just silently made her appearance,—and springing from their seats they broke into a boisterous shout of acclamation and welcome. One young man whose flushed face had all the joyous, wanton, effeminate beauty of a pictured Dionysius, reeled forward, goblet in hand, and tossing the wine in air so that it splashed down again at his feet, staining his white garments as it fell with a stain as of blood, he cried, tipsily:

"All hail, Lysia! Where hast thou wandered so long, thou Goddess of Morn? We have been lost in the blackness of night, sunk in the depths of a hell-like gloom—but lo! now the clouds have broken in the east, and our hearts rejoice at the birth of day! Vanish, dull moon, and be ashamed! . . . for a fairer planet rules the sky! Hence, ye stars! . . .

puny glow-worms lazily crawling in the fields of ether! Lysia invests the heaven and earth, and in her smile we live! Ha! art thou there, Sah-luma? Come, praise me for my improvised love-lines; they are as good as thine, I warrant thee! Canst compose when thou art drunk, my dainty Laureate? Drain a cup then, and string me a stanza! Where is thy fool Zebastes? I would fain tickle his long ears with ribald rhyme, and hearken to the barbarous braying forth of his asinine reflections! Lysia! what, Lysia! . . . dost thou frown at me? Frown not, sweet queen, but rather laugh! . . . thy laughter kills, 'tis true, but thy frown doth torture spirits after death! Unbend thy brows! Night looms between them like a chaos! . . . we will have no more night, I say, but only noon! . . . a long, languorous, lovely noon, flower-girdled and sunbeam-clad!

"'With roses, roses, roses crown my head, For my days are few! And remember, sweet, when I am dead, That my heart was true!'"

Singing unsteadily, with the empty goblet upside-down in his hand, he looked up laughing,—his bright eyes flashing with a wild feverish fire, his fair hair tossed back from his brows and entangled in a half-crushed wreath of vine-leaves,—his rich garments disordered, his whole demeanor that of one possessed by a semi-delirium of sensuous pleasure. . . when all at once, meeting Lysia's keen glance, he started as though he had been suddenly stabbed,—the goblet fell from his clasp, and a visible shudder ran through his strong, supple frame. The low, cold, merciless laughter of the beautiful Priestess cut through the air hissingly like the sweep of a scimetar.

"Thou art wondrous merry, Nir-jalis," she said, in languid, lazily enunciated accents. "Knowest thou not that too much mirth engenders weeping, and that excessive rejoicing hath its fitting end in grievous lamentation? Nay, even now already thou lookest more sadly! What sombre cloud has crossed thy wine-hued heaven? Be happy while thou mayest, good fool! . . . I blame thee not! Sooner or later all things must end! . . . in the mean time, make thou the most of life while life remains; 'tis at its best an uncertain heritage, that once rashly squandered can never be restored,—either here or hereafter."

The words were gently, almost tenderly, spoken; but Nir-jalis hearing them, grew white as death—his smile faded, leaving his lips set and stern as the lips of a marble mask. Stooping, he raised his fallen goblet and held it out almost mechanically to a passing slave, who re-filled it with wine, which he drank off thirstily at a draught, though the generous liquid brought no color back to his drawn and ashy features.

Lysia paid no further heed to his evident discomfiture; bidding Sah-luma and Theos follow her, she descended the few steps that led from the raised platform into the body of the brilliant hall; the rocky screen of amethyst closed behind her as noiselessly as it had opened, and in another moment she stood among her assembled guests, who at once surrounded her with eager salutations and gracefully worded flatteries. Smiling on them all with that strange smile of hers that was more scornful than sweet, and yet so infinitely bewitching, she said little in answer to their greetings, . . . she moved as a queen moves through a crowd of courtiers, the varied light of crimson and green playing about her like so many sparkles of living flame, . . . her dark head, wreathed with those jewelled serpents, lifting itself proudly erect from her muffling golden mantle, and her eyes shining with that frosty gleam of mockery which made them look so lustrous yet so cold. And now Theos perceived that at one end of the splendid banquet table a dais was erected, draped richly in carnation-colored silk, and that on this dais a throne was placed—a throne composed entirely of BLACK crystals, whose needle-like points sparkled with a dark flash as of bayonets seen through the smoke of battle. It was cushioned in black velvet, and above it was a bent arch of ivory on which glittered a twisted snake of clustered emeralds.

With that slow, superb ease that distinguished all her actions, Lysia, attended closely by her tigress, mounted the dais,—and as she did so a loud clash of brazen bells rang out from some invisible turret beyond the summit of the great dome. At the sound of the jangling chime four negresses appeared—goblin creatures that looked as though they had suddenly sprung from some sooty, subterranean region of gnomes—and humbly prostrating themselves before Lysia, kissed the ground at her feet. This done, they rose, and began to undo the fastenings of her golden, domino-like garment; but either they were slow, or the fair priestess was impatient for she suddenly shook herself free of their hands, and, loosening the gorgeous mantle herself from its jewelled clasps, it fell slowly from her symmetrical form on the perfumed floor with a rustle as of falling leaves.

A sigh quivered audibly through the room—whether of grief, joy, hope, relief, or despair it was difficult to tell. The pride and peril of a matchless loveliness was revealed in all its fatal seductiveness and invincible strength—the irresistible perfection of woman's beauty was openly displayed to bewilder the sight and rouse the reckless passions

MARIE CORELLI

of man! Who could look on such delicate, dangerous, witching charms unmoved? Who could gaze on the exquisite outlines of a form fairer than that of any sculptured Venus and refuse to acknowledge its powerfully sweet attraction?

The Virgin Priestess of the Sun had stepped out of her shrine; . . . no longer a creature removed, impersonal, and sacred, she had become most absolutely human. Moreover, she might now have been taken for a bacchante, a dancer, or any other unsexed example of womanhood inasmuch as with her golden mantle she had thrown off all disguise of modesty. Her beautiful limbs, rounded and smooth as pearl, could be plainly discerned through the filmy garb of silvery tissue that clung like a pale mist about the voluptuous curves of her figure and floated behind her in shining gossamer folds; her dazzling white neck and arms were bare; and from slim wrist to snowy shoulder, little twining diamond snakes glistened in close coils against the velvety fairness of her flesh. A silver serpent with a head of sapphires girdled her waist, and just above the full wave of her bosom, that rose and fell visibly beneath the transparent gathers of her gauzy drapery, shone a large, fiery jewel, fashioned in the semblance of a human Eye. This singular ornament was so life-like as to be absolutely repulsive, and as it moved to and fro with its wearer's breathing it seemed now to stare aghast,—anon to flash wickedly as with a thought of evil,—while more often still it assumed a restlessly watchful expression as though it were the eye of a fiend-inquisitor intent on the detection of some secret treachery. Poised between those fair white breasts it glared forth a glittering Menace; . . . a warning of unimaginable horror; and Theos, gazing at it fixedly, felt a curious thrill run through him, as if, so to speak, a hook of steel had been suddenly thrust into his quivering veins to draw him steadily and securely on toward some pitfall of unknown tortures. Then he remembered what Sah-luma had said about the "all-reflecting Eye, the weird mirror and potent dazzler of human sight," and wondered whether its mystical properties were such as to compel men to involuntarily declare their inmost thoughts, for it seemed to him that its sinister glow penetrated into the very deepest recesses of his mind, and there discovered all the hidden weaknesses, follies, and passions of the worst side of his nature!

He trembled and grew faint,—his dazed eyes wandered over the dainty grace and marvel of Lysia's almost unclad loveliness with mingled emotions of allurement and repugnance. Fascinated, yet at the same time repelled, his soul yearned toward her as the soul of the knight in the Lore-lei legend yearned toward the singing Rhine-siren, whose embrace was destruction; and then. . . he became filled with a strange, sudden fear; fear, not for himself, but for Sah-luma, whose ardent glance burned into her dark, languid-lidded, amorous orbs with the lustre of flame meeting flame—Sah-luma, whose beautiful flushed face was as that of a god inspired, or lover triumphant. What could he do to shield and save this so idolized friend of his?—this dear familiar for whom he had such close and ever-increasing sympathy! Might he not possibly guard him in some way and ward off impending danger? But what danger? What spectral shadow of dread hovered above this brilliant scene of high feasting and voluptuous revelry? None that he could imagine or define, and yet he was conscious, of an ominous, unuttered premonition of peril in the very air—peril for Sah-luma, always for Sah-luma, never for himself, . . . Self seemed dead and entombed forever! Involuntarily lifting his eyes to the great green dome where the globe of fire twirled rapidly like a rolling star, he saw some words written round it in golden letters, they were large and distinct, and ran thus:

"Live in the Now, but question not the Afterwards!"

A wise axiom! . . . yet almost a platitude, for did not every one occupy themselves exclusively with the Now, regardless of future consequences? Of course! Who but sages—or fools—would stop to question the Afterwards!

Just then Lysia ascended her black crystal throne in all her statuesque majesty, and sinking indolently amid its sable cushions, where she shone in her wonderful whiteness like a glistening pearl set in ebony, she signed to her guests to resume their places at table. She was instantly obeyed. Sah-luma took what was evidently his accustomed post at her right hand, while Theos found a vacant corner on her left, next to the picturesque, lounging figure of the young man Nir jahs, who looked up at him with a half smile as he seated himself, and courteously made more room for him among the tumbled emerald silk diapers of the luxurious divan, they now shared together. Nir jahs was by no means sober, but he had recovered a little of his self-possession since Lysia's sleepy eyes had darted such cold contempt upon him, and he seemed for the present to be on his guard against giving any further possible cause of offence.

"Thou art a new comer,—a stranger, if I mistake not?" he inquired in a low, abrupt, yet kindly tone.

"Yes," replied Theos in the same soft sotto-voce. "I am a mere sojourner in Al-Kyris for a few days only, . . . the guest of the divine Sah-luma."

Nir-jahs raised his eyebrows with an expression of amused wonder.

"Divine!" he exclaimed "By my faith! what neophyte have we here!" and supporting himself on one elbow he stared at his companion as though he saw in him some singular human phenomenon. "Dost thou really believe," he went on jestingly, "in the divinity of poets? Dost thou think they write what they mean, or practice what they preach? Then art thou the veriest innocent that ever wore the muscular semblance of man! Poets, my friend, are the most absolute impostors, . . . they melodize their rhymed music on phases of emotion they have never experienced; as for instance our Lameate yonder will string a pretty sonnet on the despair of love, he knowing nothing of despair, . . . he will write of a broken heart, his own being unpricked by so much as a pin's point of trouble; and he will speak in his verso of dying for love when he would not let his little finger ache for the sake of a woman who worshipped him! Look not so vaguely! 'tis so, indeed! and as for the divine part of him, wait but a little, and thou shalt see thy poet-god become a satyr!"

He laughed maliciously, and Theos felt an angry flush rising to his brows. He could not bear to hear Sah-luma thus lightly maligned even by this half-drunken reveller, it stung him to the quick, as if he personally were included in the implied accusation of unworthiness. Nir-jalis perceived his annoyance, and added good naturedly:

"Tush, man! Vex not thy soul as to thy friend's virtues or vices—what are they to thee? And of truth Sah-luma is no worse than the rest of us. All I maintain is that he is certainly no better. I have known many poets in my day, and they are all more or less alike—petulant as babes, peevish as women, selfish as misers, and conceited as peacocks. They SHOULD be different? Oh, yes!—they SHOULD be the perpetual youth of mankind, the faithful singers of love idealized and made perfect. But then none of us are what we ought to be! Besides, if we were all virtuous, . . . by the gods! the world would become too dull a hole to live in! Enough! Wilt drink with me?" and beckoning a slave, he had his own goblet and that of Theos filled to the brim with wine.

"To our more intimate acquaintance!" he said smilingly, and Theos, somewhat captivated by the easy courtesy of his manner, could do no less than respond cordially to the proffered toast. At that moment a triumphant burst of music, like the sound of mingled flutes, hautboys, and harps, pushed through the dome like a strong wind sweeping in from the sea, and with it the hum and buzz of conversation began in good earnest. Theos, lifting his gaze toward Lysia's seat, saw that she was now surrounded by the four attendant negresses, who, standing two on each side of her throne, held large fans of peacock plumes, which, as they were waved slowly to and fro, emitted a thousand scintillations of jewel-like splendor. A slave, attired in scarlet, knelt on one knee before her, proffering a golden salver loaded with the choicest fruits and wines; a lazy smile played on her lips—lips that outrivaled the dewy tint of half-opening roses; the serpents in her hair and on her rounded arms quivered in the light like living things; the great Symbolic Eye glanced wickedly out from the white beauty of her heaving breast; and as he surveyed her, thus resplendent in all the startling seductiveness of her dangerous charms, her loveliness entranced and intoxicated him like the faint perfume of some rare and powerful exotic, . . . his senses seemed to sink drowningly in the whelming influence of her soft and dazzling grace; and though he still resented, he could not resist her mesmeric power. No wonder, he thought, that Sah-luma's eyes darkened with passions as they dwelt on her! . . . and no wonder that he, like Sah-luma, was content to be gently but surely drawn within the glittering web of her magic spell—a spell fatal, yet too bewilderingly sweet for human strength to fight against. The mysterious sense he had of danger lurking somewhere for Sah-luma applied, so he fancied, in no way to himself—it did not much matter what happened to HIM—HE was a mere nobody. He could be of no use anywhere; he was as one banished into strange exile; his brain—that brain he had once deemed so clear, so subtle, so eminently reasoning and all-comprehensive—was now nothing but a chaotic confusion of vague suggestions, and only served to very slightly guide him in the immediate present, giving him no practical clue at all as to the past through which he had lived, or the circumstances he most wished to remember. He was a fool—a dreamer—ungifted—unfamous! . . . were he to die, not a soul would regret his loss. His own fate therefore concerned him little—he could handle fire recklessly and not feel the flame; he could, so he believed, run any risk, and yet escape, comparatively free of harm.

But with Sah-luma it was different! Sah-luma must be guarded and cherished; his was a valuable life—the life of a genius such as the world sees but once in a century—and it should not, so Theos determined,—

MARIE CORELLI

be emperilled or wasted; no! not even for the sake of the sensuous, exquisite, conquering beauty of this dazzling Priestess of the Sun—the fairest sorceress that ever triumphed over the frail yet immortal Spirit of Man!

XVIII

The Love That Kills

How the time went he could not tell; in so gay and gorgeous a scene hours might easily pass with the swiftness of unmarked moments. Peals of laughter echoed now and again through the vaulted dome, and excited voices were frequently raised in clamorous disputations and contentious arguments that only just sheered off the boundary-line of an actual quarrel. All sorts of topics were discussed—the laws, the existing mode of government, the latest discoveries in science, and the military prowess of the King—but the conversation chiefly turned on the spread of disloyalty, atheism, and republicanism among the population of Al-Kyris,—and the influence of Khosrul on the minds of the lower classes. The episode of the Prophet's late capture and fresh escape seemed to be perfectly well known to all present, though it had occurred so recently; one would have thought the detailed account of it had been received through some private telephone, communicating with the King's palace.

As the banquet progressed and the wine flowed more lavishly, the assembled guests grew less and less circumspect in their general behavior; they flung themselves full length on their luxurious couches, in the laziest attitudes, now pulling out handfuls of flowers from the tall porcelain jars that stood near, and pelting one another with them for mere idle diversion, . . . now summoning the attendant slaves to refill their wine-cups while they lay lounging at ease among their heaped-up cushions of silk and embroidery; and yet with all the voluptuous freedom of their manners, the picturesque grace that distinguished them was never wholly destroyed. These young men were dissolute, but not coarse; bold, but not vulgar; they took their pleasure in a delicately wanton fashion that was infinitely more dangerous in its influence on the mind than would have been the gross mirth and broad jesting of a similar number of uneducated plebeians. The rude licentiousness of an uncultivated boor has its safety-valve in disgust and satiety, . . . but the soft, enervating sensualism of a trained and cultured epicurean aristocrat is a moral poison whose effects are so insidious as to be scarcely felt till all the native nobility of character has withered, and naught is left of a man but the shadow-wreck of his former self.

There was nothing repulsive in the half-ironical, half-mischievous merriment of these patrician revellers; their witticisms were brilliant and pointed, but never indelicate; and if their darker passions were roused, and ready to run riot, they showed as yet no sign of it. They ENJOYED—yes! with that selfish animal enjoyment and love of personal indulgence which all men, old and young without exception, take such delight in—unless indeed they be sworn and sorrowful anchorites, and even then you may be sure they are always regretting the easy license and libertinage of their bygone days of unbridled independence when they could foster their pet weaknesses, cherish their favorite vices, and laugh at all creeds and all morality as though Divine Justice were a mere empty name, and they themselves the super-essence of creation. Ah, what a ridiculous spectacle is Man! the two-legged pigmy of limited brain, and still more limited sympathies, that, standing arrogantly on his little grave the earth, coolly criticises the Universe, settles law, and measures his puny stature against that awful Unknown Force, deeply hidden, but majestically existent, which for want of ampler designation we call GOD—God, whom some of us will scarcely recognize, save with the mixture of doubt, levity, and general reluctance; God, whom we never obey unless obedience is enforced by calamity; God, whom we never truly love, because so many of us prefer to stake our chances of the future on the possibility of His non-existence!

Strangely enough, thoughts of this God, this despised and forgotten Creator, came wandering hazily over Theos's mind at the present moment when, glancing round the splendid banquet-table, he studied the different faces of all assembled, and saw Self, Self, Self, indelibly impressed on every one of them. Not a single countenance was there that did not openly betray the complacent hauteur and tranquil vanity of absolute Egotism, Sah-luma's especially. But then Sah-luma had something to be proud of—his genius; it was natural that he should be satisfied with himself—he was a great man! But was it well for even a great man to admire his own greatness? This was a pertinent question, and somewhat difficult to answer. A genius must surely be more or less conscious of his superiority to those who have no genius? Yet why? May it not happen, on occasions, that the so-called fool shall teach a lesson to the so-called wise man? Then where is the wise man's superiority if a fool can instruct him? Theos found these suggestions curiously puzzling; they seemed simple enough, and yet they opened up a vista of intricate disquisition which he was in no humor to follow.

To escape from his own reflections he began to pay close attention to the conversation going on around him, and listened with an eager, almost painful interest, whenever he heard Lysia's sweet, languid voice chiming through the clatter of men's tongues like the silver stroke of a small bell ringing in a storm at sea.

"And how hast thou left thy pale beauty Niphrata?" she was asking Sah-luma in half-cold, half-caressing accents. "Does her singing still charm thee as of yore? I understand thou hast given her her freedom. Is that prudent? Was she not safer as thy slave?"

Sah-luma glanced up quickly in surprise. "Safer? She is as safe as a rose in its green sheath," he replied. "What harm should come to her?"

"I spoke not of harm," said Lysia, with a lazy smile. "But the day may come, good minstrel, when thy sheathed rose may seek some newer sunshine than thy face! . . . when thy much poesy may pall upon her spirit, and thy love-songs grow stale! . . . and she may string her harp to a different tune than the perpetual adoration-hymn of Sah-luma!"

The handsome Laureate looked amused.

"Let her do so then!" he laughed carelessly. "Were she to leave me I should not miss her greatly; a thousand pieces of gold will purchase me another voice as sweet as hers,—another maid as fair! Meanwhile the child is free to shape her own fate,—her own future. I bind her no longer to my service; nevertheless, like the jessamine-flower, she clings,—and will not easily unwind the tendrils of her heart from mine."

"Poor jessamine-flower!" murmured Lysia negligently, with a touch of malice in her tone. "What a rock it doth embrace; how little vantage-ground it hath wherein to blossom!" And her drowsy eyes shot forth a fiery glance from under their heavily fringed drooping white lids.

Sah-luma met her look with one of mingled vexation and reproach; she smiled and raising a goblet of wine to her lips, kissed the brim, and gave it to him with an indescribably graceful, swaying gesture of her whole form that reminded one of a tall white lily bowing in the breeze. He seized the cup eagerly, drank from it and returned it,—his momentary annoyance, whatever it was, passed, and a joyous elation illumined his fine features. Then Lysia, refilling the cup, kissed it again and handed it to Theos with so much soft animation and tenderness in her face as she turned to him, that his enforced calmness nearly gave way, and he had much ado to restrain himself from falling at her feet in a transport of passion, and crying out! . . . "Love me, O thou sorceress-sovereign of beauty! . . . love me, if only for an hour, and then let me

MARIE CORELLI

die! . . . for I shall have lived out all the joys of life in one embrace of thine!" His hand trembled as he took the goblet, and he drank half its contents thirstily,—then imitating Sah-luma's example, he returned it to her with a profound salutation. Her eyes dwelt meditatively upon him.

"What a dark, still, melancholy countenance is thine, Sir Theos!" she said abruptly—"Thou art, for sure, a man of strongly repressed and concentrated passions, . . . 'tis a nature I love! I would there were more of thy proud and chilly temperament in Al-Kyris! . . . Our men are like velvet-winged butterflies, drinking honey all day and drowsing in sunshine—full to the brows of folly,—frail and delicate as the little dancing maidens of the King's seraglio, . . . nervous too, with weak heads, that art apt to ache on small provocation, and bodies that are apt to fail easily when but slightly fatigued. Aye!—thou art a man clothed complete in manliness,—moreover. . ."

She paused, and leaning forward so that the dark shower of her perfumed hair brushed his arm. . . "Hast ever heard travellers talk of volcanoes? . . . those marvellous mountains that oft wear crowns of ice on their summits and yet hold unquenchable fire in their depths? . . . Methinks thou dost resemble these,—and that at a touch, the flames would leap forth uncontrolled!"

Her magical low voice, more melodious in tone than the sound of harps played by moonlight on the water, thrilled in his ears and set his pulses beating madly,—with an effort he checked the torrent of love-words that rushed to his lips, and looked at her in a sort of wildly wondering appeal. Her laughter rang out in silvery sweet ripples, and throwing herself lazily back in her throne, she called.

"Aizif! . . . Aizif!"

The great tigress instantly bounded forward like an obedient hound, and placed its fore-paws on her knees, while she playfully held a sugared comfit high above its head.

"Up, Aizif! up!" she cried mirthfully. "Up! and be like a man for once! . . . snatch thy pleasure at all hazards!"

With a roar, the savage brute leaped and sprang, its sharp white teeth fully displayed, its sly green eyes glisteningly prominent,—and again Lysia's rich laughter pealed forth, mingling with the impatient snarls of her terrific favorite. Still she held the tempting morsel in her little snowy hand that glittered all over with rare gems,—and still the tigress continued to make impotent attempts to reach it, growing more and more ferocious with every fresh effort,—till all at once she shut her palm upon the dainty so that it could not be seen, and lightly catching the irritated beast by the throat brought its eyes on a level with her own. The effect was instantaneous, . . . a strong shudder passed through its frame—and it cowered and crouched lower and lower, in abject fear,—the sweat broke out, and stood in large drops on its sleek hide, and panting heavily, as the firm grasp its mistress slowly relaxed, it sank down prone, in trembling abasement on the second step of the dais, still looking up into those densely brilliant gazelle eyes that were full of such deadly fascination and merciless tyranny.

"Good Aizif!" said Lysia then, in that languid, soft voice, that while so sweet, suggested hidden treachery. "Gentle fondling! . . . Thou hast fairly earned thy reward! . . . Here! . . . take it!"—and unclosing her roseate palm, she showed the desired bonne-bouche, and offered it with a pretty coaxing air,—but the tigress now refused to touch it, and lay as still as an animal of painted stone.

"What a true philosopher she is, my sweet Aizif!" she went on amusedly stroking the creature's head,—"Her feminine wit teaches her what the dull brains of men can never grasp, . . . namely, that pleasures, no matter how sweet, turn to ashes and wormwood when once obtained,—and that the only happiness in this world is the charm of DESIRE! There is a subject for thee, Sah-luma! . . . write an immortal Ode on the mysteries, the delights, the never-ending ravishment of Desire! . . . but carry not thy fancy on to desire's fulfilment, for there thou shalt find infinite bitterness! The soul that wilfully gratifies its dearest wish, has stripped life of its supremest joy, and stands thereafter in an emptied sphere, sorrowful and alone,—with nothing left to hope for, nothing to look forward to, save death, the end of all ambition!"

"Nay, fair lady,"—said Theos suddenly,—"We who deem ourselves the children of the high gods, and the offspring of a Spirit Eternal, may surely aspire to something beyond this death, that, like a black seal, closes up the brief scroll of our merely human existence! And to us, therefore, ambition should be ceaseless,—for if we master the world, there are yet more worlds to win: and if we find one heaven, we do but accept it as a pledge of other heavens beyond it! The aspirations of Man are limitless,—hence his best assurance of immortality, . . . else why should he perpetually long for things that here are impossible of attainment? . . . things that like faint, floating clouds rimmed with light, suggest without declaring a glory unperceived?"

MARIE CORELLI

Lysia looked at him steadfastly, an under-gleam of malice shining in her slumbrous eyes.

"Why? . . . Because, good sir, the gods love mirth! . . . and the wanton Immortals are never more thoroughly diverted, than, when leaning downward from their clear empyrean, they behold Man, their Insect-Toy, arrogating to himself a share in their imperishable Essence! To keep up the Eternal Jest, they torture him with vain delusions, and prick him on with hopes never to be realized; aye! and the whole vast Heaven may well shake with thunderous laughter at the pride with which he doth put forth his puny claim to be elected to another and fairer state of existence! What hath he done? . . . what does he do, to merit a future life? . . . Are his deeds so noble? . . . is his wisdom so great? . . . is his mind so stainless? He, the oppressor of all Nature and of his brother man,—he, the insolent, self-opinionated tyrant, yet bound slave of the Earth on which he dwells. . . why should he live again and carry his ignoble presence into the splendors of an Eternity too vast for him to comprehend? . . . Nay, nay! . . . I perceive thou art one of the credulous, for whom a reasonless worship to an unproved Deity is, for the sake of state-policy, maintained, . . . I had thought thee wiser! . . . but no matter! thou shalt pay thy vows to the shrine of Nagaya to-morrow, and see with what glorious pomp and panoply we impose on the faithful, who like thee believe in their own deathless and divinely constituted natures, and enjoy to the full the grand Conceit that persuades them of their right to Immortality!"

Her words carried with them a certain practical positiveness of meaning, and Theos was somewhat impressed by their seeming truth. After all, it WAS a curious and unfounded conceit of a man to imagine himself the possessor of an immortal soul,—and yet. . . if all things were the outcome of a divine Creative Influence, was it not unjust of that Creative Influence to endow all humanity with such a belief if it had no foundation whatever? And could injustice be associated with divine law? . . .

He, Theos, for instance, was certain of his own immortality,—so certain that, surrounded as he was by this brilliant company of evident atheists, he felt himself to be the only real and positive existing Being among an assembly of Shadow-figures,—but it was not the time or the place to enter into a theological discussion, especially with Lysia, . . . and for the moment at least, he allowed her assertions to remain uncontradicted. He sat, however, in a somewhat stern silence, now and then glancing wistfully and anxiously at Sah-luma, on whom the potent wines were beginning to take effect, and who had just thrown himself down on the dais at Lysia's feet, close to the tigress that still lay couched there in immovable quiet. It was a picture worthy of the grandest painter's brush, . . . that glistening throne black as jet, with the fair form of Lysia shining within it, like a white sea-nymph at rest in a grotto of ocean-stalactites, . . . the fantastically attired negresses on each side, with their waving peacock-plumes,—the vivid carnation-color of the dais, against which the black and yellow stripes of the tigress showed up in strong and brilliant contrast, . . . and the graceful, jewel-decked figure of the Poet Laureate, who, half sitting, half reclining on a black velvet cushion, leaned his handsome head indolently against the silvery folds of Lysia's robe, and looked up at her with eyes in which burned the ardent admiration and scarcely restrained passion of a privileged lover.

Suddenly and quite involuntarily Theos thought of Niphrata, . . . alas, poor maiden! how utterly her devotion to Sah-luma was wasted! What did he care for her timid tenderness, . . . her unselfish worship? Nothing? . . . less than nothing! He was entirely absorbed by the sovereign-peerless beauty of this wonderful High Priestess,—this witch-like weaver of spells more potent than those of Circe; and musing thereon, Theos was sorry for Niphrata, he knew not why. He felt that she had somehow been wronged,—that she suffered, . . . and that he, as well as Sah-luma, was in some mysterious way to blame for this, though he could by no means account for his own share in the dimly suggested reproach. This peculiar, remorseful emotion was transitory, like all the vaguely incomplete ideas that travelled mistily through his perplexed brain, and he soon forgot it in the increasing animation and interest of the scene that immediately surrounded him.

The general conversation was becoming more and more noisy, and the laughter more and more boisterous,—several of the young men were now very much the worse for their frequent libations, and Nir-jalis, particularly, began again to show marked symptoms of an inclination to break loose from all the bonds of prudent reserve. He lay full length on his silk divan, his feet touching Theos, who sat upright,—and, singing little snatches of song to himself, he pulled the vine-wreath from his tumbled fair locks as though he found it too weighty, and flung it on the ground among the other debris of the feast. Then folding his arms lazily behind his head, he stared straight and fixedly before him at Lysia, seeming to note every jewel on her dress, every curve of her body, every slight gesture of her hand, every faint, cold smile that played on her lovely lips. One young man whom the others addressed as Ormaz, a haughty, handsome fellow enough, though with rather a sneering mouth just visible under his black mustache, was talking somewhat excitedly on the subject of Khosrul's cunningly devised flight, . . . for it seemed to be universally understood that the venerable Prophet was one of the Circle of Mystics,—persons whose knowledge of science, especially in matters connected with electricity, enabled them to perform astonishing juggleries, that were frequently accepted by the uninitiated vulgar as almost divine miracles. Not very long ago, according to Ormaz, who was animatedly recalling the circumstance for the benefit of the company, the words "FALL, AL-KYRIS!" had appeared emblazoned in letters of fire on the sky at midnight, and the phenomenon had been accompanied by two tremendous volleys of thunder, to the infinite consternation of the multitude, who received it as a supernatural manifestation. But a member of the King's Privy Council, a satirical skeptic and mistruster of everybody's word but his own, undertook to sift the matter,—and adopting the dress of the Mystics, managed to introduce himself into one of their secret assemblies, where with considerable astonishment, he saw them make use of a small wire, by means of which they wrote in characters of azure flame on the whiteness of a blank wall,—moreover, he discovered that they possessed a lofty turret, built secretly and securely in a deep, unfrequented grove of trees, from whence, with the aid of various curious instruments and reflectors, they could fling out any pattern or device they chose on the sky, so that it should seem to be written by the finger of Lightning. Having elucidated these mysteries, and become highly edified thereby, the learned Councillor returned to the King, and gave full information as to the result of his researches, whereupon forty Mystics were at once arrested and flung into prison for life, and their nefarious practices were made publicly known to all the inhabitants of the city. Since then, no so-called "spiritual" demonstrations had taken place till now, when on this very night Zephoranim's Presence-Chamber had been suddenly enveloped in the thunderous and terrifying darkness which had so successfully covered Khosrul's escape.

"The King should have slain him at once—" declared Ormaz emphatically, turning to Lysia as he spoke. . . "I am surprised that His Majesty permitted so flagrant an impostor and trespasser of the law to speak one word, or live one moment in his royal presence."

"Thou art surprised, Ormaz, at most things, especially those which savor of simple good-nature and forbearance. . ." responded Lysia coldly. "Thou art a wolfish, youth, and wouldst tear thine own brother to shreds if he thwarted thy pleasure! For myself I see little cause for astonishment, that a soldier-hero like Zephoranim should take some pity on so frail and aged a wreck of human wit as Khosrul. Khosrul blasphemes the Faith, . . . what then? . . . do ye not all blaspheme?"

"Not in the open streets!" said Ormaz hastily.

"No—ye have not the mettle for that!"—and Lysia smiled darkly, while the great eye on her breast flashed forth a sardonic lustre— "Strong as ye all are, and young, ye lack the bravery of the weak old man who, mad as he may be, has at least the courage of his opinions! Who is there here that believes in the Sun as a god, or in Nagaya as a mediator? Not one, . . . but ye are cultured hypocrites all, and careful to keep your heresies secret!"

"And thou, Lysia!" suddenly cried Nir-jalis, . . . "Why if thou canst so liberally admire the valor of thy sworn enemy Khosrul, why dost not Thou step boldly forth, and abjure the Faith thou art Priestess of, yet in thy heart deridest as a miserable superstition?"

She turned her splendid flashing orbs slowly upon him, . . . what an awful chill, steely glitter leaped forth from their velvet-soft depths!

"Prithee, be heedful of thy speech, good Nirjalis!" she said, with a quiver in her voice curiously like the suppressed snarl of her pet tigress. "The majority of men are fools, . . . like thee! . . . and need to be ruled according to their folly!"

Ormaz broke into a laugh. "And thou dost rule them, wise Virgin, with a rod of iron!" he said satirically. . . "The King himself is but a slave in thy hands!" "The King is a devout believer,"—remarked a dainty, effeminate-looking youth, arrayed in a wonderfully picturesque garb of glistening purple,—"He pays his vows to Nagaya three times a day, at sunrise, noon, and sunset,—and 'tis said he hath oft been seen of late in silent meditation alone before the Sacred Veil, even after midnight. Maybe he is there at this very moment, offering up a royal petition for those of his less pious subjects who, like ourselves, love good wine more than long prayers. Ah!—he is a most austere and noble monarch,—a very anchorite and pattern of strict religious discipline!" And he shook his head to and fro with an air of mock solemn fervor. Every one laughed, . . . and Ormaz playfully threw a cluster of half-crushed roses at the speaker.

MARIE CORELLI

"Hold thy foolish tongue, Pharnim,—" he said,—"The King doth but show a fitting example to his people, . . . there is a time to pray, and a time to feast, and our Zephoranim can do both as becomes a man. But of his midnight meditations I have heard naught, . . . since when hath he deserted his Court of Love for the colder chambers of the Sacred Temple?"

"Ask Lysia!" muttered Nir-jalis drowsily, under his breath—"She knows more of the King than she cares to confess!"

His words were spoken in a low voice, and yet they were distinct enough for all present to hear. A glance of absolute dismay went round the table, and a breathless silence followed like the ominous hush of a heated atmosphere before a thunder-clap. Nir-jalis, apparently struck by the sudden stillness, looked lazily round from among the tumbled cushions where he reclined,—a vacant, tipsy smile on his lips.

"What a company of mutes ye are!" he said thickly.

"Did ye not hear me? I bade ye ask Lysia, . . ." and all at once he sat bolt upright, his face crimsoning as with an access of passion. "Ask Lysia!" he repeated loudly. "Ask her why the mighty Zephoranim creeps in and out the Sacred Temple at midnight like a skulking slave instead of a King! . . . at midnight, when he should be shut within his palace walls, playing the fool among his women! I warrant 'tis not piety that persuades him to wander through the underground Passage of the Tombs alone and in disguise! Sah-luma! . . . pretty pampered hound as thou art! . . . thou art near enough to Our Lady of Witcheries,— ask her, . . . ask her! . . . she knows, . . ." and his voice sank into an incoherent murmur, . . . "she knows more than she cares to confess!"

Another deep and death like pause ensued, . . . and then Lysia's silvery cold tones smote the profound silence with calm, clear resonance.

"Friend Nir-jalis," she said, . . . how tuneful were her accents, . . . how chilly sweet her smile! . . . "Methinks thou art grown altogether too wise for this world! . . . 'tis pity thou shouldest continue to linger in so narrow and incomplete a sphere! . . . Depart hence therefore! . . . I shall frely excuse thine absence, since THY HOUR HAS COME! . . ."

And, taking from the table at her side a tall crystal chalice fashioned in the form of a lily set on a golden stem, she held it up toward him. Starting wildly from his couch he looked at her, as though doubting whether he had heard her words aright, . . . a strong shudder shook him from head to foot, . . . his hands clenched themselves convulsively together,—and then slowly, slowly, he staggered to his feet and stood upright. He was suddenly but effectually sobered—the flush of intoxication died off his cheeks—and his eyes grew strained and piteous. Theos, watching him in wonder and fear, saw his broad chest heave with the rapid-drawn gasping of his breath, . . . he advanced a step or two—then all at once stretched out his hands in imploring agony.

"Lysia!" he murmured huskily. "Lysia! . . . pardon! . . . spare me! . . . For the sake of past love have pity!"

At this Sah-luma sprang up from his lounging posture on the dais, his hand on the hilt of his dagger, his whole face flaming with wrath.

"By my soul!" he cried, "what doth this fellow prate of? . . . Past love? . . . Thou profane boaster! . . . how darest thou speak of love to the Priestess of the Faith?"

Nir-jalis heeded him not. His eyes were fixed on Lysia, like the eyes of a tortured animal who vainly seeks for mercy at the hand of its destroyer. Step by step he came hesitatingly to the foot of her throne, . . . and it was then that Theos perceived rear at hand a personage he immediately recognized,—the black scarlet-clad slave Gazia, who had brought Lysia's message to Sah-luma that same afternoon. He had made his appearance now so swiftly and silently, that it was impossible to tell where he had come from,—and he stood close to Nir-jalis, his muscular firms folded tightly across his chest, and his hideous mouth contorted into a grin of cruel amusement and expectancy. Absolute quiet reigned within the magnificent banquet hall, . . . the music had ceased,—and not a sound could be heard, save the delicate murmur of the wind outside swaying the water-lilies on the moonlit lake. Every one's attention was centred on the unhappy young man, who with lifted head and rigidly clasped hands, faced Lysia as a criminal faces a judge, . . . Lysia, whose dazzling smile beamed upon him with the brightness of summer sunbeams,—Lysia, whose exquisite voice lost none of its richness as she spoke his doom.

"By the vow which thou hast vowed to me, Nir-jalis—" she said slowly. . . "and by thine oath sworn on the Symbolic Eye of Raphon" . . . here she touched the dreadful Jewel on her breast—"which bound thy life to my keeping, and thy death to my day of choice, I herewith bestow on thee the Chalice of Oblivion—the Silver Nectar of Peace! Sleep, and wake no more!—drink and die! The gateways of the Kingdom of Silence stand open to receive thee! . . . thy service is finished! . . . fare-thee-well!"

With the utterance of the last word, she gave him the glittering cup she held. He took it mechanically,—and for one instant glared about him on all sides, scanning the faces of the attentive guests as though in the faint hope of some pity, some attempt at rescue. But not a single look of compassion was bestowed upon him save by Theos, who, full of struggling amazement and horror, would have broken out into indignant remonstrance, had not an imperative glance from Sah-luma warned him that any interference on his part would only make matters worse. He therefore, sorely against his will, and only for Sah-luma's sake, kept silence, watching Nir-jalis meanwhile in a sort of horrible fascination.

There was something truly awful in the radiant unquenchable laughter that lurked in Lysia's lovely eyes, ... something positively devilish in the grace of her manner, as with a negligent movement, she reseated herself in her crystal throne, and taking a knot of magnolia-flowers that lay beside her, idly toyed with their creamy buds, all the while keeping her basilisk gaze fixed immovably and relentlessly on her sentenced victim. He, grasping the lily-shaped chalice convulsively in his right hand, looked up despairingly to the polished dome of malachite, with its revolving globe of fire that shed a solemn blood-red glow upon his agonized young face, ... a smile was on his lips,—the dreadful smile of desperate, maddened misery.

"Oh, ye malignant gods!" he cried fiercely—"ye immortal Furies that made Woman for Man's torture, ... Bear witness to my death! ... bear witness to my parting spirit's malediction! Cursed be they who love unwisely and too well! ... cursed be all the wiles of desire and the haunts of dear passion!—cursed he all fair faces whose fairness lures men to destruction! ... cursed be the warmth of caresses, the beating of heart against heart, the kisses that color midnight with fire! Cursed be Love from birth unto death!—may its sweetness be brief, and its bitterness endless!—its delight a snare, and its promise treachery! O ye mad lovers!—fools all!" ... and he turned his splendid wild eyes round on the hushed assemblage,—"Despise me and my words as ye will, throughout ages to come, the curse of the dead Nir-jalis shall cling!"

He lifted the goblet to his lips, and just then his delirious glanced lighted on Sah-luma.

"I drink to thee, Sir Laureate!" he said hoarsely, and with a ghastly attempt at levity—"Sing as sweetly as thou wilt, thou must drain the same cup ere long!"

And without another second's hesitation he drank off the entire contents of the chalice at a draught. Scarcely had he done so, when with a savage scream he fell prone on the ground, his limbs twisted in acute agony,—his features hideously contorted,—his hands beating the air wildly, as though in contention with some invisible foe, . . . while in strange and terrible dissonance with his tortured cries, Lysia's laughter, musically mellow, broke out in little quick peals, like the laughter of a very young child.

"Ah, ah, Nir-jalis!" she exclaimed. "Thou dost suffer! That is well! . . . I do rejoice to see thee fighting for life in the very jaws of death! Fain would I have all men thus tortured out of their proud and tyrannous existence! . . . their strength made strengthless, their arrogance brought to naught, their egotism and vain-glory beaten to the dust! Ah, ah! thou that wert the complacent braggart of love,—the self-sufficient proclaimer of thine own prowess, where is thy boasted vigor now? . . . Writhe on, good fool! . . . thy little day is done! . . . All honor to the Silver Nectar whose venom never fails!"

Leaning forward eagerly, she clapped her hands in a sort of fierce ecstasy—and apparently startled by the sound, the tigress rose up from its couchant posture, and shaking itself with a snarling yawn, glared watchfully at the convulsed human wretch whose struggles became with each moment more and more frightful to witness. The impassive, cold-blooded calmness with which all the men present, even Sah-luma, looked on at the revolting spectacle of their late comrade's torture, filled Theos with shuddering abhorrence, . . . sick at heart, he strove to turn away his eyes from the straining throat and upturned face of the miserable Nir-jalis,—a face that had a moment or two before been beautiful, but was now so disfigured as to be almost beyond recognition. Presently as the anguish of the poisoned victim increased, shriek after shriek broke from his pallid lips, . . . rolling himself on the ground like a wild beast, he bit his hands and arms in his frenzy till he was covered with blood, . . . and again and yet again the dulcet laughter of the High Priestess echoed through the length and breadth of the splendid hall,—and even Sah-luma, the poet Sah-luma, condescended to smile! That smile, so cold, so cruel, so unpitying, made Theos for a moment hate him, . . . of what use, he thought, was it, to be a writer of soft and delicate verse, if the inner nature of the man was merciless, selfish, and utterly regardless of the woes of others? . . . The rest of the guests were profoundly indifferent,—they kept silence, it is true, . . . but they went on drinking their wine with perfectly unabated enjoyment. . . they were evidently accustomed to such scenes. The attendant slaves stood all mute and motionless, with the exception of Gazra, who surveyed the torments of Nir-jalis with an air of professional interest, and appeared to be waiting till they should have reached that pitch of excruciating agony when Nature, exhausted, gives up the conflict and welcomes death as a release from pain.

But this desirable end was not yet. Suddenly springing to his feet, Nir-jalis tore open his richly jewelled vest, and pressed his two hands hard upon his heart, . . . the veins in his flesh were swollen and blue,— his labored breath seemed as though it must break his ribs in its terrible, panting struggle,—his face, livid and lined with purple marks like heavy bruises, bore not a single trace of its former fairness, . . . and his eyes, rolled up and fixed glassily in their quivering sockets, seemed to be dreadfully filled with the speechless memory of his lately spoken curse. He staggered toward Theos, and dropped heavily on his knees, . . .

"Kill me!" he moaned piteously, feebly pointing to the sheathed dagger in the other's belt. "In mercy! . . . Kill me! . . . One thrust! . . . release me! . . . this agony is more than I can bear, . . . Kill. . . Kill. . . !"

His voice died away in an inarticulate, gasping cry,—and Theos stared down upon him in dizzy fear and horror! For. . . He Had Seen This Same Nir-jalis Dying Thus Cruelly Before! Oh God! . . . where,—where had this tragedy been previously enacted? Bewildered and overcome with unspeakable dread, he drew his dagger—he would at least, he thought, put the tortured sufferer out of his misery, . . . but scarcely had his weapon left the sheath, when Lysia's clear, cold voice exclaimed:

"Disarm him!" and with the silent rapidity of a lightning-flash, Gazra glided to his side, and the steel was snatched from his hand. Full of outraged pride and wrath, he sprang up, a torrent of words rushing to his lips, but before he could utter one, two slaves pounced upon him, and holding his arms, dexterously wound a silk scarf tight about his mouth.

"Be silent!" whispered some one in his ear,—"As you value your life and the life of Sah-luma,—be silent!"

But he cared nothing for this warning, . . . reckless of consequences, he tore the scarf away and breaking loose from the hands that held him, made a bound toward Lysia. . . here he paused. Her eyes met his languidly, shedding a sombre, mysterious light upon him through the black shower of her abundant hair, . . . the evil glitter of the great Symbolic Gem she wore fixed him with its stony yet mesmeric luster. . .

a delicious smile parted her roseate lips,—and breaking off a magnolia-bud from the cluster she held, she kissed and gave it to him. . .

"Be at peace, good Theos!" she said in a low, tender tone, . . . "Beware of taking up arms in the defence of the unworthy, . . . rather reserve thy courage for those who know how best to reward thy service!"

As one in a trance he took the flower she offered,—its fragrance, subtle and sweet, seemed to steal into his veins, and rob his manhood of all strength, . . . sinking submissively at her feet he gazed up at her in wondering wistfulness and ardent admiration, . . . never was there a woman so bewilderingly beautiful as she! What were the sufferings of Nir-jalis now? . . . what was anything compared to the strangely enervating ecstasy he felt in letting his eyes dwell fondly on the fairness of her face, the whiteness of her half-veiled bosom, the delicate, sheeny dazzle of her polished skin, the soft and supple curves of her whole exquisite form, . . . and spell-bound by the witchery of her loveliness, he almost forgot the very presence of her dying victim. Occasionally indeed, he glanced at the agonized creature where he lay huddled on the ground in the convulsive throes of his dreadful death-struggle,—but it was now with precisely the same quiet and disdainful smile as that for which he had momentarily hated Sah-luma! There was a sound of singing somewhere,—singing that had a mirthful under-throbbing in it, as though a thousand light-footed fairies were dancing to its sweet refrain! And Nir-jalis heard it! . . . dying inch by inch as he was, he heard it, and with a last superhuman effort forced himself up once more to his feet, . . . his arms stiffly outstretched, . . . his anguished eyes full of a softened, strangely piteous glory.

"To die!" he whispered in awed accents that penetrated the air with singular clearness—"To die! . . . nay. . . not so! . . . There is no death! . . . I see it all! . . . I know! . . . . To die is to live! . . .to live again. . . and to remember. . . to remember,—and repent, . . . the past!"

And with the last word he fell heavily, face forward, a corpse. At the same moment a terrific roar resounded through the dome, and the tigress Aizif sprang stealthily down from the dais, and pounced upon the warm, lifeless body, mounting guard over it in an ominously significant attitude, with glistening eyes, lashing tail and nervously quivering claws. A slight thrill of horror ran through the company, but not a man moved.

"Aizif!—Aizif!" called Lysia imperiously.

The animal looked round with an angry snarl, and seemed for once disposed to disobey the summons of its mistress. She therefore rose from her throne, and stepping forward with a swift, agile grace, caught the savage beast by the neck, and dragged it from its desired prey. Then, with the point of her little, silver-sandaled foot, she turned the fallen face of the dead man slightly round, so that she might observe it more attentively, and noting its livid disfigurement, smiled.

"So much for the beauty and dignity of manhood!" she said with a contemptuous shrug of her snowy shoulders,—"All perished in the space of a few brief moments! Look you, ye fair sirs that take pride in your strength and muscular attainments! . . . Ye shall not find in all Al-Kyris a fairer face or more nobly knit frame than was possessed by this dead fool, Nir-jalis, and yet, lo!—how the Silver Nectar doth make havoc on the sinews of adamant, the nerves of steel, the stalwart limbs! Tried by the touchstone of Death, ye are, with all your vaunted intelligence, your domineering audacity and self-love, no better than the slain dogs that serve vultures for carrion! . . . —moreover, ye are less than dogs in honesty, and vastly shamed by them in fidelity!"

She laughed scornfully as she spoke, still grasping the tigress by the neck in one slight hand,—and her glorious eyes flashed a mocking defiance on all the men assembled. Their countenances exhibited various expressions of uneasiness amounting to fear, . . . some few smiled forcedly, others feigned a careless indifference, . . . Sah-luma flushed an angry red, and Theos, though he knew not why, felt a sudden pricking sense of shame. She marked all these signs of disquietude with apparently increasing amusement, for her lovely face grew warm and radiant with suppressed, malicious mirth. She made a slight imperative gesture of command to Gazra, who at once approached, and, bending over the dead Nir-jalis, proceeded to strip off all the gold clasps and valuable jewels that had so lavishly adorned the ill-fated young man's attire,—then beckoning another slave nearly as tall and muscular as himself, they attached to the neck and feet of the corpse round, leaden, bullet-shaped weights, fastened by means of heavy iron chains. This done, they raised the body from the floor and carried it between them to the central and largest casement of all that stood open to the midnight air, and with a dexterous movement flung it out into the waters of the lake beneath. It fell with a sullen splash, the pale lilies on the surface rocking stormily to and fro as though blown by a gust of wind, while great circling ripples shone softly in the yellow gleam of the moonlight, as the dead man sank down, down, down like a stone into his crystal-quiet grave.

Lysia returned to her throne with a serene step and unruffled brow, followed by the sulky and disappointed Aizif, . . . smiling gently on Theos and Sah-luma she reseated herself, and touched a small bell at her side. It gave a sharp kling-klang like a suddenly struck cymbal—and lo! . . . the marble floor yawned asunder, and the banquet-table with all its costly fruits and flowers vanished underground with the swiftness of lightning! The floor closed again, . . . the broad, circular centre-space of the hall was now clear from all obstruction,—and the company of revellers roused themselves a little from their drowsy postures of half-inebriated languor. The singing voices that had stirred Nir-jalis to sudden animation even in his dying agony, sounded nearer and nearer, and the globe of fire overhead changed its hue from that of crimson to a delicate pink. At the extreme end of the glittering vista of pale-green, transparent columns, a door suddenly opened, and a flock of doves came speeding forth, their white, spread wings colored softly in the clear rose-radiance,—they circled round and round the dome three times, then fluttered in a palpitating arch over Lysia's head, and finally sped straight across the hall to the other end, where they streamed snowily through another aperture and disappeared. Still nearer rippled the sound of singing, . . . and all at once a troop of girls came dancing noiselessly as fire-flies into the full, quivering pinkness of the jewel-like light that floated about them, . . . girls as lovely, as delicate, as dainty as cyclamens that wave in the woods in the early days of an Italian spring. Their garments were so white, so transparent, so filmy and clinging, that they looked like elves robed in mountain-vapor rather than human creatures, . . . there were fifty of them in all, and as they tripped forward, they, like the doves that had heralded their approach, surrounded Lysia flutteringly, saluting her with gestures of exquisite grace and devout humility, while she, enthroned in supreme fairness, with her tigress crouched beside her, looked down on them like a goddess calmly surveying a crowd of vestal worshippers. Their salutations done, they rushed pell-mell, like a shower of white rose-leaves drifting before a gale, into the exact centre of the hall, and there poising bird-like, with their snowy arms upraised as though about to fly, they waited, . . . their lovely faces radiant with laughter, their eyes flashing dangerous allurement, their limbs glistening like polished alabaster through the gauzy attire that betrayed rather than concealed their exquisite forms. Then came the soft pizzicato of pulled strings, . . . and a tinkling jangle of silver bells beating out a measured, languorous

MARIE CORELLI

rhythm,—and with one accord, they all merged together in the voluptuous grace of a dance more ravishing, more wild and wondrous than ever poet pictured in his word-fantasies of fairy-land! Theos drank in the intoxicating delight of the scene with eager, dazzled eyes and heavily beating heart, . . . the mysterious passion of mingled love and hatred he felt for Lysia stole over him more strongly than ever in the sultry air of this strange night, . . . this night of sweet delirium, in which all that was most dangerous and erring in his nature woke into life and mastered his better will! A curious, instinctive knowledge swept across his mind,—namely THAT SAH-LUMA'S EMOTIONS WERE THE FAITHFUL REFLEX OF HIS OWN,—but as he had felt no anger against his rival in fame, so now he had no jealousy of his possible rival in love. Their sympathies were too closely united for distrust to mar the friendship so ardently begun, . . . nevertheless, as he fell resistlessly deeper and deeper into the glittering snares that were spread for his destruction, he was CONSCIOUS OF EVIL THOUGH HE LACKED FORCE TO OVERCOME IT. At any rate, he would save Sah-luma from harm, he resolved, if he could not save himself! Meantime he watched the bewildering evolutions and witching entanglements of the gliding maze of fair faces, snowy bosoms and twining limbs, that palpitated to and fro under the soft rose-light of the dome like white flowers colored by the sunset, and, glancing ever and again at Lysia's imperial sorceress-beauty, he thought dreamily. . . "Better the love that kills than no love at all!" And he thereupon gave himself up a voluntary captive to the sway of his own passions, determining to enjoy the immediate present, no matter what the future might have in store. Outside, the water-lilies nodded themselves to sleep in their shrouding, dark leaves, . . . and the unbroken smoothness of the lake spread itself out in the moon like a sheet of molten gold over the spot where Nir-jalis had found his chilly rest. "THE CURSE OF THE DEAD NIR-JALIS SHALL CLING!" Yes,—possibly!—in the hereafter! . . . but now his parting malison seemed but a foolish clamor against destiny, . . . he was gone! . . . none of his late companions missed him, . . . none regretted him—like all dead men, once dead he was soon forgotten!

XIX

A Strange Temptation

On went the dance, . . . faster, faster, and ever faster! Only the pen of some mirth-loving, rose-crowned Greek bard could adequately describe the dazzling, wild beauty and fantastic grace of those whirling fairy forms, that now inspired to a bacchante-like ardor, urged one another to fresh speed with brief soft cries of musical rapture! Now advancing,—now retreating. . . now intermingling all together in an undulating garland of living loveliness, . . . now parting asunder with an air of sweet coquettishness and caprice, . . . —anon meeting again, and winding arm within arm,—till bending forward in attitudes of the tenderest entreaty, they seemed, with their languid, praying eyes and clasped hands, to be waiting for Love to soothe the breathless sweetness of their parted lips with kisses! The light in the dome again changed its hue,—from pale rose-pink it flickered to delicate amber-green, flooding the floor with a radiance as of watery moonbeams, and softening the daintily draped outlines of that exquisite group of human blossoms, till they looked like the dimly imagined shapes of Nereids floating on the glistening width of the sea.

And now the extreme end of the vast hall began to waver to and fro as though shaken at its foundation by subterranean forces,—a flaring shaft of flame struck through it like the sweeping blade of a Titan's sword,—and presently with a thunderous noise the whole wall split asunder, and recoiling backwards on either side, disclosed a garden, golden with the sleepy glory of the late moon, and peacefully fair in all the dreamy attractiveness of drooping foliage, soft turf, and star-sprinkled, violet sky. In full view, and lit up by the reflected radiance flung out from the dome, a rushing waterfall made sonorous surgy music of its own as it tumbled headlong into a rocky recess overgrown with lotus-lilies and plumy fern,—here and there, small, white and gold tents or pavilions glimmered invitingly through the shadows cast by the great magnolia trees, from whose lovely half-shut buds balmy odors crept deliciously through the warm air. The sound of sweet pipes and faintly tinkling cymbals echoed from distant shady nooks, as though elfin shepherds were guarding their fairy flocks in some hidden corner

MARIE CORELLI

of this ambrosial pasturage, and ever by degrees the light grew warmer and more mellow in tint, till it resembled the deep hue of an autumn, yellow sunset, flecked through with emerald haze.

Another clash of cymbals! . . . this time stormily persistent and convincing! . . . another! . . . yet another! . . . and then, a chime of bells,—a steady ringing, persuasive chime, such as brings tears to the eyes of many a wanderer, who, hearing a similar sound when far away from home, straightway thinks of the village church of his earlier years, . . . those years of the best happiness we ever know on earth, because we enjoy in them the bliss of ignorance, the glory of youth! A curious stifling sensation began to oppress Theos's heart as he listened to those bells, . . . they reminded him of such strange things, . . . things to which he could not give a name,—things foolish, yet sweet, . . . odd suggestions of fair women who were wont to pray for those they loved, and who believed, . . . alas, the pity of it!—that their prayers would be heard. . . and granted! What was it that these dear, loving, credulous ones said, when in the silence of the night they offered up their patient supplications to an irresponsive Heaven? "LEAD US NOT INTO TEMPTATION, BUT DELIVER US FROM EVIL!" Yes! . . . he remembered,—those were the words,—the simple-wise words that for positive-practical minds had neither meaning nor reason,—and that yet were so infinitely pathetic in their perfect humility and absolute trust!

"LEAD US NOT INTO TEMPTATION!" . . . He murmured the phrase under his breath as he gazed with straining eyes out into the languorous beauty of that garden-scene that spread its dewy, emerald glamour before him,—and—"deliver us from evil!" broke from his lips in a half-sobbing sigh, as the peal of the chiming bells softened by degrees into a subdued tunefulness of indistinct and tremulous semitones, and the clarion-clearness of the cymbals again smote the still air with forceful and jarring clangor. Then. . . like a rainbow-garmented Peri floating easefully out of some far-off sphere of sky-wonders,—an aerial Maiden-Shape glided into the full lustre of the varying light,—a dancer, nude save for the pearly glistening veil that was carelessly cast about her dainty limbs, her white arms and delicate ankles being adorned with circlets of tiny, golden bells, which kept up a melodious jingle-jangle as she moved. And now began the strangest music,—music that seemed to hover capriciously between luscious melody and harsh discord,—a wild and curious medley of fantastic, minor suggestions in which the imaginative soul might discover hints of tears and folly, love and madness. To this uncertain yet voluptuous measure the glittering girl-dancer leaped forward with a startlingly beautiful abruptness,—and halting, as it were, on the boundary-line between the dome and the garden beyond, raised her rounded arms in a snowy arch above her head, and so for one brief instant, looked like an exquisite angel ready to soar upward to her native realm. Her pause was a mere breathing space in duration, . . . dropping her arms again with a swift decision that set all the little bells on them clashing stormily, she straightway hurled herself, so to speak, into the giddy paces of a dance that was more like an enigma than an exercise. Round and round she floated wildly, like an opal-winged butterfly in a net of sunbeams,—now seemingly shaken by delicate tremors as aspen leaves are shaken by the faintest wind, . . . now assuming the most voluptuous eccentricities of posture, . . . sometimes bending wistfully toward the velvet turf on which she trod, as though she listened to the chanting of demon voices underground, . . . and again, with her waving white hands, appearing to summon spirits downward from their wanderings in upper air. Her figure was in perfect harmony with the seductive grace of her gestures,—not only her twinkling feet, but her whole body danced,—her very features bespoke entire abandonment to the frenzy of rapid movement,—her large black eyes flashed with something of fierceness as well as languor; her raven hair streamed behind her like a dark spread wing, . . . her parted lips pouted and quivered with excitement and ardor while ever and anon she turned her beautiful head toward the eagerly attentive group of revelers who watched her performance, with an air of indescribable sweetness, malice, and mockery. Again and again she whirled,—she flew, she sprang,—and wild cries of "Hail, Nelida!" "Triumph to Nelida!" resounded uproariously through the dome. Suddenly the character of the music changed, . . . from an appealing murmurous complaint and persuasion, it rose to a martial and almost menacing fervor; the roll of drums and the shrill, reedy warbling of pipes and other fluty minstrelsy crossed the silvery thread of strung harps and viols, . . . the light from the fiery globe shot forth a new effulgence, this time in two broad rays, one a dazzling, pale azure, the other a clear, pearly white. Nelida's graceful movements grew slower and slower, till she merely seemed to sway indolently to and fro like a mermaid rocking herself to sleep on the summit of a wave, . . . and then,—from among the veiling shadows of the trees, there stepped forth a man,—beautiful as a sculptured god, of magnificently moulded form and noble stature, clothed from chest

MARIE CORELLI

to knee in a close fitting garb of what seemed to be a thick network of massively linked gold. His dark hair was crowned with ivy, and at his belt gleamed an unsheathed dagger. Slowly and with courtly grace he approached the panting Nelida, who now, with half-closed eyes and slackening steps, looked as though she were drowsily footing her way into dreamland. He touched her snowy shoulder,—she started with an inimitable gesture of surprise, . . . a smile, brilliant as morning, dawned on her face,—withdrawing herself slightly, she assumed an air of haughtily sweet disdain and refusal, . . . then capriciously relenting, she gave him her hand, and in another instant, to the sound of a joyous melody that seemed to tumble through the air as billows tumble on the beach, the dazzling pair whirled away in a giddy waltz like two bright flames blown suddenly together by the wind. No language could give an adequate idea of the marvelous bewitchment and beauty of their united movements, and as they flew over the dark smooth turf, with the flower-laden trees drooping dewily about them, and the yellow moonbeams like melted amber beneath their noiseless feet, . . . while the pale sapphire and white radiations from the dome, sparkling upon them aureole-wise, gave them the appearance of glittering birds circling through a limitless space of luminous and never-clouded ether. On, on! . . . and they scarcely touched the earth as they spun dizzily round and round, their gracefully entwined limbs shining like polished ivory in the light, . . . on, on!—with ever-increasing swiftness they sped, till their two forms seemed to merge into one, . . . when as though oppressed by their own abandonment of joy they paused hoveringly, their embracing arms closing round one another, their lips almost touching, . . . their eyes reflecting each other's ardent looks, . . . then, . . . their figures grew less and less distinct, . . . they appeared to melt mysteriously into the azure, pearly light that surrounded them, and finally, like faint clouds fading on the edge of a sea-horizon, they vanished! The effect of this brief voluptuous dance, and its equally voluptuous end, was simply indescribable,—the young men, who had watched it through in silence and flushed ecstasy, now sprang from their couches with shouts of rapture and unrestrained excitement, and seizing the other dancing-maidens who had till now remained in clustered, half-hidden groups behind the crystalline columns of the hall, whirled them off into the inviting pleasaunce beyond, where the little white and gold pavilions peeped through the heavy foliage,—and before Theos, in the picturesque hurry and confusion of the scene, could quite realize what had happened, the great globe in the dome was suddenly extinguished, . . . a firm hand closed imperiously on his own, and he was drawn along swiftly, he knew not whither!

A slight tremor shook him as he discovered that Sah-luma was no longer by his side. . . the friend whom he so ardently desired to protect had gone,—and he could not tell where. He glanced about him,—in the semi-obscurity he was able to discern the sheen of the lake with its white burden of water-lilies, and the branchy outlines of the moonlit garden, . . . and. . . yes! it was Lysia whose grasp lay so warmly on his arm, . . . Lysia whose lovely, tempting face was so perilously near his own,—Lysia whose smile colored the soft gloom with such alluring lustre! . . . His heart beat,—his blood burned,—he strove in vain to imagine what fate was now in store for him. He was conscious of the beauty of the night that spread its star-embroidered splendors about him,—conscious too of the vital youth and passion that throbbed amorously in his veins, endowing him with that keenly sweet, headstrong rapture which is said to come but once in a lifetime, and which in the very excess of its fond folly is too often apt to bring sorrow and endless remorse in its train. One moment more and he found himself in an exquisitely adorned pavilion of painted silk, faintly lit by one lamp of tenderest rose lustre, and carpeted with gold-spangled tissue. It was surrounded by a thicket of orange trees in full bloom, and the fragrance of the waxen-white flowers clung heavily to the air, breathing forth delicate suggestions of languor and sleep. The measured rush of the near waterfall alone disturbed the deep silence, with now and then the subdued and plaintive trill of a nightingale soothing itself to rest with its own song in some deep shadowed copse. Here, on a couch of heaped-up, stemless roses, such as might have been prepared for the repose of Titania, Lysia seated herself, while Theos stood gazing at her in fascinated wonderment and gradually increasing masterfulness of passion. She looked lovelier than ever in that dim, soft, mingled light of rosy lamp and silver moonbeams,—her smile was no longer cold but warmly sweet,—her eyes had lost their mocking glitter, and swam in a soft languor that was strangely bewitching,—even the Orbed Symbol on her white bosom seemed for once to drowse. Her lips parted in a faint sigh,—a glance like fire flashed from beneath her black, silken lashes, . . .

"Theos!" she said tremulously. "Theos!" and waited.

He, mute and oppressed by indistinct, hovering recollections, fed his gaze on her seductive fairness for one earnest moment longer,—then suddenly advancing he knelt before her, and took her unresisting hands in his.

"Lysia!"—and his voice, even to his own ears, had a solemn as well as passionate thrill,—"Lysia, what wouldst thou have with me? Speak! . . . for my heart aches with a burden of dark memories,—memories conjured up by the wizard spell of thine eyes,—those eyes so cruel-sweet that seem to lure me to my soul's ruin! Tell me—have we not met before? . . . loved before? . . . wronged each other and God before? . . . parted before? . . . Maybe 'tis but a brain sick fancy,—nevertheless my spirit knows thee,—feels thee,—clings to thee,—and yet recoils from thee as one whom I did love in by-gone days of old! My thoughts of thee are strange, fair Lysia!"—and he pressed her warm, delicate fingers with unconscious fierceness,—"I would have sworn that in the Past thou didst betray me!"

Her low laugh stirred the silence into a faint, tuneful echo.

"Thou foolish dreamer!" she murmured half mockingly, half tenderly. . . "Thou art dazed with wine, steeped in song, bewitched with beauty, and knowest nothing of what thou sayest! Methinks thou art a crazed poet, and more fervid than Sah-luma in the mystic nature of thine utterance,—thou shouldst be Laureate, not he! What if thou wert offered his place? . . . his fame?"

He looked at her, surprised and perplexed, and paused an instant before replying. Then he said slowly:

"So strange a thing could never be. . . for Sah-luma's place, once empty, could not again be filled! I grudge him not his glory-laurels,—moreover, . . . what is Fame compared to Love!" He uttered the last words in a low tone as though he spoke them to himself, . . . she heard,—and a flash of triumph brightened her beautiful face.

"Ah! . . ." and she drooped her head lower and lower till her dark, fragrant tresses touched his brow. . . "Then, . . . thou dost love me?"

He started. A dull pang ached in his heart,—a chill of vague uncertainty and dread. Love! . . . was it love indeed that he felt? . . . love, . . . or. . . base desire? Love. . . The word rang in his ears with the same sacred suggestiveness as that conveyed by the chime of bells,—surely, Love was a holy thing, . . . a passion pure, impersonal, divine, and deathless,—and it seemed to him that somewhere it had been written or said. . . "Wheresoever a man seeketh himself, there he falleth from Love" And he, . . . did he not seek himself, and the gratification of his own immediate pleasure? Painfully he considered, . . . it was a supreme moment with him,—a moment when he felt himself to be positively held within the grasp of some great Archangel, who, turning grandly reproachful eyes upon him, demanded. . .

"Art thou the Servant of Love or the Slave of Self?" And while he remained silent, the silken sweet voice of the fairest woman he had ever seen once more sent its musical cadence through his brain in that fateful question:

"Thou dost love me?"

A deep sigh broke from him, . . . he moved nearer to her, . . . he entwined her warm waist with his arms, and stared upon her as though he drank her beauty in with his eyes. Up to the crowning masses of her dusky hair where the little serpents' heads darted forth glisteningly,—over the dainty curve of her white shoulders and bosom where the symbolic Eye seemed to regard him with a sleepy weirdness,—down to the blue-veined, small feet in the silvery sandals, and up again to the red witchery of her mouth and black splendor of those twin fire-jewels that flashed beneath her heavy lashes—his gaze wandered hungrily, searchingly, passionately,—his heart beat with a loud, impatient eagerness like a wild thing struggling in its cage, but though his lips moved, he said no word,—she too was silent. So passed or seemed to pass some minutes,—minutes that were almost terrible in the weight of mysterious meaning they held unuttered. Then, with a half-smothered cry, he suddenly released her and sprang erect.

"Love!" he cried, . . . "Nay!—'tis a word for children and angels!—not for me! What have I to do with love? . . . what hast thou? . . . thou, Lysia, who dost make the lives of men thy sport and their torments thy mockery! There is no name for this fever that consumes me when I look upon thee, . . . no name for this unquiet ravishment that draws me to thee in mingled bliss and agony! If I must perish of mine own bitter-sweet frenzy, let me be slain now and most utterly, . . . but Love has no abiding-place 'twixt me and thee, Lysia! . . . Love! . . . ah, no, no! . . . speak no more of love. . . it hath a charmed sound, recalling to my soul some glory I have lost!"

He spoke wildly, incoherently, scarcely knowing what he said, and she, half lying on her couch of roses, looked at him curiously, with somber, meditative eyes. A smile of delicate derision parted her lips.

"Of a truth, our late feasting hath roused in thee a most singular delirium!" she murmured indolently with a touch of cold amusement

MARIE CORELLI

in her accents—"Thou dost seem to dwell in the Past rather than the Present! What ails thee? . . . Come hither—closer!"—and she stretched out her lovely arms on which the twisted diamond snakes glittered in such flashing coils,—"Come! . . . or is thy manful guise mere feigning, and dost thou fear me?"

"Fear thee!"—and stung to a sudden heat Theos made one bound to her side and seizing her slim wrists, held them in a vise-like grip—"So little do I fear thee, Lysia, so well do I know thee, that in my very caresses I would slay thee, couldst thou thus be slain! Thou art to me the living presence of an unforgotten Sin,—a sin most deadly sweet and unrepented of, . . . ah! why dost thou tempt me!"—and he bent over her more ardently—"must I not meet my death at thy hands? I must,—and more than death!—yet for thy kiss I will risk hell,—for one embrace of thine I will brave perdition! Ah, cruel enchantress!"— and winding his arms about her, he drew her close against his breast and looked down on the dreamy fairness of her face,—"Would there WERE such a thing as Death for souls like mine and thine! Would we might die most absolutely thus, heart against heart, never to wake again and loathe eathtypo or archaism? other! Who speaks of the cool sweetness of the grave,—the quiet ending of all strife,—the unbreaking seal of Fate, the deep and stirless rest? . . . These things are not, and never were, . . . for the grave gives up its dead,—the strife is forever and ever resumed,—the seal is broken, and in all the laboring Universe there shall be found no rest, and no forgetfulness, . . . ah, God! . . . no forgetfulness!" A shudder ran through his frame,—and clasping her almost roughly, he stooped toward her till his lips nearly touched hers, . . . "Thou art accursed, Lysia,—and I share thy curse! Speak— how shall we cheer each other in the shadow-realm of fiends? Thou shall be Queen there, and I thy servitor,—we will make us merry with the griefs of others,—our music shall be the dropping of lost women's tears, and the groans of betrayed and tortured men,—and the light around us shall be quenchless fire! Shall it not be so, Lysia? . . . and thinkest thou that we shall ever regret the loss of Heaven?"

The words rushed impetuously from his lips; he thought little and cared less what he said, so long as he could, by speech, no matter how incoherent, relieve in part, the terrible oppression of vague memories that burdened his brain. But she, listening, drew herself swiftly from his embrace and stood up,—her large eyes fixed full upon him with an expression of wondering scorn and fear.

"Thou art mad!" she said, a quiver of alarm in her voice. . . "Mad as Khosrul, and all his evil-croaking brethren! I offer thee Love,—and thou pratest of death,—life is here in all the fulness of the now, for thy delight, and thou ravest of an immortal Hereafter which is not, and can never be! Why talk thus wildly? . . . why gaze on me with so distraught a countenance? But an hour agone, thou wert the model of a cold discretion and quiet valor,—thus I had judged thee worthy of my favor—favor sought by many, and granted to few, . . . but an thou dost wander amid such chaotic and unreasoning fancies, thou canst not serve me,—nor therefore canst thou win the reward that would otherwise have awaited thee." . . .

Here she paused,—a questioning, keen under-glance flashed from beneath her dark lashes, . . . he, however, with pained, wistful eyes raised steadfastly to hers, gave no sign of apology or contrition for the disconnected strangeness of his recent outburst. Only he became gradually conscious of an inward, growing calm,—as though the Divine Voice that had once soothed the angry waves of Galilee were now hushing his turbulent emotions with a soft "Peace be still!" She watched him closely, . . . and all at once apparently rendered impatient by his impassive attitude, she came coaxingly toward him, and laid one soft hand on his shoulder.

"Canst thou not be happy, Theos?" she whispered gently—"Happy as other men are, when loved as thou art loved?"

His upturned gaze rested on the glittering serpents' heads that crowned her dusky tresses,—then on the great Eye that stared watchfully between her white breasts. A strong tremor shook him, and he sighed.

"Happy as other men are, when they love and are deceived in love!"— he said. "Yes, even so, Lysia,—I can be happy!"

She threw one arm about him. "Thou shalt not be deceived"—she murmured quickly,—"Thou shalt be honored above the noblest in the realm, . . . thy dearest hopes shall be fulfilled, . . . thy utmost desires shall be granted, . . . riches, power, fame,—all shall be thine,—If Thou Wilt Do My Bidding!"

She uttered the last words with slow and meaning emphasis. He met her eager, burning looks quietly, almost coldly,—the curious numb apathy of his spirit increased, and when he spoke, his voice was low and faint like the voice of one who speaks unconsciously in his sleep.

"What canst thou ask that I will not grant?" he said listlessly. "Is it

MARIE CORELLI

not as it was in the old time,—thou to command, and I to obey? . . . Speak, fair Queen!—how can I serve thee?"

Her answer came, swift and fierce as the hiss of a snake:

"KILL SAH-LUMA!"

The brief sentence leaped into his brain with the swift, fiery action of some burning drug,—a red mist rose to his eyes,—pushing her fiercely from him, he started to his feet in a bewildered, sick horror. KILL SAH-LUMA! . . . kill the gracious, smiling, happy creature whose every minute of existence was a joy,—kill the friend he loved,—the poet he worshipped! . . . Kill him! . . . ah God! . . . never! . . . never! . . . He staggered backward dizzily,—and Lysia with a sudden stealthy spring, like that of her favorite tigress, threw herself against his breast and looked up at him, her splendid eyes ablaze with passion, her black hair streaming, her lips curved in a cruel smile, and the hateful Jewel on her breast seeming to flash with ferocious vindictiveness.

"Kill him!" she repeated eagerly—"Now—in his sottish slumber,— now when he hath lost sight of his Poetmission in the hot fumes of wine,—now, when, despite his genius, he hath made of himself a thing lower than the beasts! Kill him! . . . —I will keep good council, and none shall ever know who did the deed! He loves me, and I weary of his love, . . . I would have him dead—dead as Nir-jalis! . . . but were he to drain the Silver Nectar, the whole city would cry out upon me for his loss,—therefore he may not perish so. But an thou wilt slay him, . . . see!" and she clung to Theos with the fierce tenacity of some wild animal—"All this beauty of mine, is thine!—thy days and nights shall be dreams of rapture,—thou shalt be second to none in Al-Kyris,— thou shalt rule with me over King and people,—and we will make the land a pleasure-garden for our love and joy! Here is thy weapon. . ."— and she thrust into his hand a dagger,—the very dagger her slave Gazra, had deprived him of, when by its prompt use he might have mercifully ended the cruel torments of Nir-jalis,—"Let thy stroke be strong and unfaltering, . . . stab him to the heart,—the cold, cold, selfish heart that has never ached with a throb of pity! . . . kill him!—'tis an easy task,— for lo! how fast he sleeps!"

And suddenly throwing back a rich gold curtain that depended from one side of the painted pavilion, she disclosed a small interior chamber hung with amber and crimson, where, on a low, much-tumbled couch covered with crumpled glistening draperies, lay the King's Chief Minstrel,—the dainty darling of women,—the Laureate of the realm, sunk in a heavy, drunken stupor, so deep as to be almost death-like. Theos stared upon him amazed and bewildered, . . . how came he there? Had he heard any of the conversation that had just passed between Lysia and himself? . . . Apparently not, . . . he seemed bound as by chains in a stirless lethargy. His posture was careless, yet uneasy,—his brilliant attire was torn and otherwise disordered,—and some of his priceless jewels had fallen on the couch, and gleamed here and there like big stray dewdrops. His face was deeply flushed, and his straight dark brows were knit frowningly, his breathing was hurried and irregular, . . . one arm was thrown above his head,—the other hung down nervelessly, the relaxed fingers hovering immediately above a costly jewelled cup that had dropped from his clasp,—two emptied wine flagons lay cast on the ground beside him, and he had evidently experienced the discomfort and feverous heat arising from intoxication, for his silken vest was loosened as though for greater ease and coolness, thus leaving the smooth breadth of his chest bare and fully exposed. To this Lysia pointed with a fiendish glee, as she pulled Theos forward.

"Strike now!" she whispered. "Quick. . . why dost thou hesitate?"

He looked at her fixedly, . . . the previous hot passion he had felt for her froze like ice within his veins, . . . her fairness seemed no longer so distinctly fair, . . . the witching radiance of her eyes had lost its charm, . . . and he motioned her from him with a silent gesture of stern repugnance. Catching sight of the sheeny glimmer of the lake through the curtained entrance of the tent, he made a sudden spring thither— dashed aside the draperies, and flung the dagger he held, far out towards the watery mirror. It whirled glittering through the air, and fell with a quick splash into the silver-rippled depths,—and, gravely contented, he turned upon her, dauntless and serene in the consciousness of power.

"Thus do I obey thee!" he said, in firm tones that thrilled through and through with scorn and indignation,—"Thou evil Beauty! . . . thou fallen Fairness! . . . Kill Sah-luma? . . . Nay, sooner would I kill myself. . . or thee! His life is a glory to the world, . . . his death shall never profit thee!" . . .

For one instant a lurid anger blazed in her face,—the next her features hardened themselves into a rigidly cold expression of disdain, though her eyes widened with wrathful wonder. A low laugh broke from her lips.

"Ah!" she cried—"Art thou angel or demon that thou darest defy me?

MARIE CORELLI

Thou shouldst be either or both, to array thyself in opposition against the High Priestess of Nagaya, whose relentless Will hath caused empires to totter and thrones to fall! His life a glory to the world? . . ." and she pointed to Sah-luma's recumbent figure with a gesture of loathing and contempt, . . . "His? . . . the life of a drunken voluptuary? . . . a sensual egotist? . . . a poet who sees no genius save his own, and who condemns all vice, save that which he himself indulges in! A laurelled swine! . . . a false god of art! . . . and for him thou dost reject Me! . . . ah, thou fool!" and her splendid eyes shot forth resentful fire. "Thou rash, unthinking, headstrong fool! thou knowest not what thou hast lost! Aye, guard thy friend as thou wilt,—thou dost guard him at thine own peril! . . . think not that he, . . . or thou, . . . shall escape my vengeance! What!—dost thou play the heroic with me? . . . thou who art Man, and therefore No hero? . . . For men are cowards all, except when in the heat of battle they follow the pursuit of their own brief glory! . . . poltroons and knaves in spirit, incapable of resisting their own passions! . . . and wilt Thou pretend to be stronger than the rest? . . . Wilt thou take up arms against thyself and Destiny? Thou madman!"—and her lithe form quivered with concentrated rage—"Thou puny wretch that dost first clutch at, and then refuse my love!—thou who dost oppose thy miserable force to the Fate that hunts thee down!—thou who dost gaze at me with such grave, child-foolish eyes! . . . Beware, . . . beware of me! I hate thee as I hate All men! . . . I will humble thee as I have humbled the proudest of thy sex! . . . —wheresoever thou goest I will track thee out and torture thee! . . . and thou shalt die—miserably, lingeringly, horribly,— as I would have every man die could I fulfil my utmost heart's desire! To-night, be free! . . . but to-morrow as thou livest, I will claim thee!"

Like an enraged Queen she stood,—one white, jewelled arm stretched forth menacingly,—her bosom heaving, and her face aflame with wrath, but Theos, leaning against Sah-luma's couch, heard her with as much impassiveness as though her threatening voice were but the sound of an idle wind. Only, when she ceased, he turned his untroubled gaze calmly and full upon her,—and then,—to his own infinite surprise she shivered and shrank backwards, while over her countenance flitted a vague, undefinable, almost spectral expression of terror. He saw it, and swift words came at once to his lips,—words that uttered themselves without premeditation.

"To-morrow, Lysia, thou shalt claim nothing!" he said in a still, composed voice that to himself had something strange and unearthly in its tone. . . "Not even a grave! Get thee hence! . . . pray to thy gods if thou hast any,—for truly there is need of prayer! Thou shalt not harm Sah-luma, . . . his love for thee may be his present curse,—but it shall not work his future ruin! As for me, . . . though canst not slay me, Lysia,—seeing that to myself I am dead already! . . . dead, yet alive in thought, . . . and thou dost now seem to my soul but the shadow of a past Crime, . . . the ghost of a temptation overcome and baffled! Ah, thou sweet Sin!" here he suddenly moved toward her and caught her hands hard, looking fearlessly the while at her flushed half-troubled face,—"I do confess that I have loved thee, . . . I do own that I have found thee fair! . . . but now—now that I see thee as thou art, in all the nameless horror of thy beauty, I do entreat," . . . and his accents sank to a low yet fervent supplication—"I do entreat the most high God that I may be released from thee forever!"

She gazed upon him with dilated, terrified eyes, . . . and he dimly wondered, as he looked, why she should seem to fear him?—Not a word did she utter in reply, . . . step by step she retreated from him, . . . her glittering, exquisite form grew paler and more indistinct in outline—and presently, catching at the gold curtain that divided the two pavilions, she paused. . . still regarding him steadfastly. An evil smile curved her lips, . . . a smile of cold menace and derisive scorn, . . . the iris-colored jewel on her breast darted forth vivid flashes of azure, and green and gray, . . . the snakes in her hair seemed to rise and hiss at him, . . . and then,—with an awful unspoken threat written resolvedly on every line of her fair features, . . . she let the gold draperies fall softly,—and so disappeared, . . . leaving him alone with Sah-luma! He stood for a moment half amazed, half perplexed,—then, drawing a deep breath, he pushed the clustering hair off his forehead with an unconscious gesture of relief. She was gone! . . . and he felt as though he had gained a victory over something, though he knew not what. The cold air from the lake blew refreshingly on his heated brow, . . . and a thousand odors from orange-flowers and jessamine floated caressingly about him. The night was very still,—and approaching the opening of the tent, he looked out. There, in the soft sky gloom, moved the majestic procession of the Undiscovered Worlds seeming to be no more than bright dots on the measureless expanse of pure ether, . . . there, low on the horizon, the yellow moon swooned languidly downwards in a bed of fleecy cloud,—the drowsy chirrup of a dreaming bird came softly now and again from the deep-branched shadows of the heavy foliage,—and the lilies on the surface of the lake nodded mysteriously among the slow ripples, like wise, white elves whispering to one another some secret of fairyland. And Sah-luma still slept, . . . and still that puzzled and weary frown darkened the fairness of his broad brow, . . . and, coming back to his side, Theos stood watching him with a yearning and sorrowful wistfulness. Gathering up the jewels that had fallen out of his dress, he replaced them one by one,—and strove to re-arrange the tossed and tumbled garb as best he might. While he was thus occupied his hand happened to touch the tablet that hung by a silver chain from the Laureate's belt,—he glanced at it, . . . it was covered with fine writing, and turning it more toward the light, he soon made out four stanzas, perfectly rhymed and smoothly flowing as a well-modulated harmony. He read them slowly with a faint smile,—he recognized them as HIS OWN!—they were part of a poem he had long ago begun, yet have never finished! And now Sah-luma had the same idea! . . . moreover he had chosen the same rhythm, the same words! . . . well! . . . after all, what did it matter? Nothing, he felt, so far as he was concerned,—he had ceased to care for his own personality or interests,—Sah-luma had become dearer to him than himself!

His immediate anxiety was centered in the question of how to rouse his friend from the torpor in which he lay, and get him out of this voluptuous garden of delights, before any lurking danger could overtake him. Full of this intention, he presently ventured to draw aside the curtain that concealed Lysia's pavilion, . . . and looking in, he saw to his great relief, that she was no longer there. Her couch of crushed roses scented the place with heavy fragrance, and the ruby lamp was still burning, . . . but she herself had departed. Now was the time for escape!—thought Theos—now,—while she was absent,—now, if Sah-luma could be persuaded to come away, he might reach his own palace in safety, and once there, he could be warned of the death that threatened him through the treachery of the woman he loved. But would he believe in, or accept, the warning? At any rate some effort must be made to rescue him, and Theos, without more ado, bent above him and called aloud:

"Sah-luma! . . . Wake! Sah-luma!"

XX

The Passage of the Tombs

Sah-luma stirred uneasily and smiled in his sleep.

"More wine!" he muttered thickly—"More, . . . more I say! What! wilt thou stint the generous juice that warms my soul to song? Pour, . . . pour out lavishly! I will mix the honey of thy luscious lips with the crimson bubbles on this goblet's brim, and the taste thereof shall be as nectar dropped from paradise! Nay, nay! I will drink to none but Myself,—to the immortal bard Sah-luma,—Poet of poets,—named first and greatest on the scroll of Fame! . . . aye, 'tis a worthy toast and merits a deeper draught of mellow vintage! Fill. . . fill again!—the world is but the drunken dream of a God Poet and we but the mad revellers of a shadow day! 'Twill pass—'twill pass, . . . let us enjoy ere all is done,—drown thought in wine, and love, and music, . . . wine and music. . ."

His voice broke in a short, smothered sigh,—Theos surveyed him with mingled impatience, pity, and something of repulsion, and there was a warm touch of indignant remonstrance in his tone when he called again:

"Sah-luma! Rouse thee, man, for very shame's sake! Art thou dead to the honor of thy calling, that thou dost wilfully consent to be the victim of wine-bibbing and debauchery? O thou frail soul! how hast thou quenched the heavenly essence within thee! . . . why wilt thou be thus self-disgraced and all inglorious? Sah-luma! Sah-luma!"—and he shook him violently by the arm—"Up,—up, thou truant to the faith of Art! I will not let thee drowse the hours away in such unseemliness, . . . wake! for the night is almost past,—the morning is at hand, and danger threatens thee,—wouldst thou be found here drunk at sunrise?"

This time Sah-luma was thoroughly disturbed, and with a half uttered oath he sat up, pushed his tumbled hair from his brows, and stared at his companion in blinking, sleepy wonderment.

"Now, by my soul! . . . thou art a most unmannerly ruffian!" he said pettishly, yet with a vacant smile,—"what question didst thou bawl unmusically in mine ear? Will I be drunk at sunrise? Aye! . . . and at sunset too, Sir Malapert, if that will satisfy thee! Hast thou been grudged sufficient wine that thou dost envy me my slumber? What dost thou here? . . . where hast thou been?" . . . and, becoming more conscious of his surroundings he suddenly stood up, and catching hold of Theos to support himself, gazed upon him suspiciously with very dim and bloodshot eyes. . . "Art thou fresh from the arms of the ravishing Nelida? . . . is she not fair? a choice morsel for a lover's banquet? . . . Doth she not dance a madness into the veins? . . . aye, aye!—she was reserved for thee, my jolly roysterer! but thou art not the first nor wilt thou be the last that hath revelled in her store of charms! No matter!"— and he laughed foolishly. . . "Better a wild dancer than a tame prude!" Here he looked about him in confused bewilderment. "Where is Lysia? Was she not here a moment since? . . ." and he staggered toward the neighboring pavilion, and dashed the dividing curtain aside. . . "Lysia! . . . Lysia! . . ." he shouted noisily,—then, receiving no answer, he flung himself down on the vacant couch of roses, and gathering up a handful of the crumpled flowers, kissed them passionately,—"The witch has flown!" he said, laughing again that mirthless, stupid laugh as he spoke—"She doth love to tantalize me thus! . . . Tell me! what dost thou think of her? Is she not a peerless moon of womanhood? . . . doth she not eclipse all known or imaginable beauty? . . . Aye! . . . and I will tell thee a secret,—she is mine!—mine from the dark tresses down to the dainty feet! . . . mine, all mine, so long as I shall please to call her so! . . . —notwithstanding that the foolish people of Al-Kyris think she is impervious to love, self-centered, holy and 'immaculate'! Bah! . . . as if a woman ever was 'immaculate'! But mark you! . . . though she loves me,—me, crowned Laureate of the realm, she loves no other man! And why? Because no other man is found half so worthy of love! All men must love her, . . . Nirjalis loved her, and he is dead because of overmuch presumption, . . . and many there be who shall still die likewise, for love of her, but *I* am her chosen and elected one,—her faith is mine!—her heart is mine,—her very soul is mine!—mine I would swear though all the gods of the past, present, and future denied her constancy!"

Here his uncertain, wandering gaze met the grave, pained, and almost stern regard of Theos. "Why dost thou stare thus owl-like upon me?"—he demanded irritably. "Art thou not my friend and worshipper? Wilt preach? Wilt moralize on the folly of the time,—the vices of the age? Thou lookest it,—but prithee hold thy peace an thou lovest me!— we can but live and die and there's an end, . . . all's over with the best and wisest of us soon,—let us be merry while we may!"

And he tossed a cluster of roses playfully in the air, catching them as they fell again in a soft shower of severed fluttering pink and white petals. Theos listened to his rambling, unguarded words with a sense of acute personal sorrow. Here was a man, young, handsome, and endowed with the rarest gift of nature, a great poetic genius,—a man who had attained in early manhood the highest worldly fame together with the friendship of a king, and the love of a people, . . . yet what was he in himself? A mere petty Egoist, . . . a poor deluded fool, the unresisting prey of his own passions, . . . the besotted slave of a treacherous woman and the voluntary degrader of his own life! What was the use of Genius, then, if it could not aid one to overcome Self, . . . what the worth of Fame, if it were not made to serve as a bright incentive and noble example to others of less renown? As this thought passed across his mind, Theos sighed, . . . he felt curiously conscience-stricken, ashamed, and humiliated, THROUGH Sah-luma, and solely for Sah-luma's sake! At present, however, his chief anxiety was to get his friend safely out of Lysia'a pavilion before she should return to it, and his spirit chafed within him at each moment of enforced delay.

"Come, come, Sah-luma!" he said at last, gently, yet with persuasive earnestness. "Come away from this place, . . . the feast is over,—the fair ones are gone, . . . why should we linger? Thou art half-asleep,— believe me 'tis time thou wert home and at rest. Lean upon me, . . . so! that is well!"—this, as the other rose unsteadily to his feet and lurched heavily against him, . . . "Now let me guide thee,—though of a truth I know not the way through this wondrous woodland maze, . . . canst tell me whither we should turn? . . . or hast thou no remembrance of the nearest road to thine own dwelling?"—

Thus speaking, he managed to lead his stupefied companion out of the tent into the cool, dewy garden, where, feeling somewhat refreshed by the breath of the night wind blowing on his face, Sah-luma straightened himself, and made an absurd attempt to look exceedingly dignified.

"Nay, an thou wilt depart with such scant ceremony"—he grumbled peevishly—"get thee thence and find out the road as best thou mayest! . . . why should I aid thee? For myself I am well contented here to remain and sleep,—no better couch can the Poet have than this violet-scented moss"—and he waved his arm with a grandiloquent gesture,—"no grander canopy than this star-besprinkled heaven! Leave me,—for my eyes are wondrous heavy, and I would fain slumber undisturbed till the break of day! By my soul, thou art a rough companion! . . ." and

MARIE CORELLI

he struggled violently to release himself from Theos's resolute and compelling grasp. "Where wouldst thou drag me?"

"Out of danger and the shadow of death!" replied Theos firmly. "Thy life is threatened, Sah-luma, and I will not see thee slain! If thou canst not guard thyself, then I must guard thee! . . . Come, delay no longer, I beseech thee!—do I not love thee, friend?—and would I urge thee thus without good reason? O thou misguided soul! thou dost most ignorantly court destruction, but if my strength can shield thee, thou shalt not die before thy time!"

And he hurried his pace, half leading, half carrying the reluctant poet, who, however, was too drowsy and lethargic to do more than feebly resent his action,—and thus they went together along a broad path that seemed to extend itself in a direct line straight across the grounds, but which in reality turned and twisted about through all manner of perplexing nooks and corners,—now under trees so closely interwoven that not a glimpse of the sky could be seen through the dense darkness of the crossed boughs,—now by gorgeous banks of roses, pale yellow and white, that looked like frozen foam in the dying glitter of the moon,—now beneath fairy-light trellis work, overgrown with jasmine, and peopled by thousands of dancing fire-flies,—while at every undulating bend or sharp angle in the road, Theos's heart beat quickly in fear lest they should meet some armed retainer or spy of Lysia's, who might interrupt their progress, or perhaps peremptorily forbid their departure. Nothing of the kind happened, or seemed likely to happen,—the splendid gardens were all apparently deserted,—and not a living soul was anywhere to be seen. Presently through an archway of twisted magnolia stems, Theos caught a glimpse of the illuminated pool with the marble nymph in its centre which had so greatly fascinated him on his first arrival,—and he pressed forward eagerly, knowing that now they could not be very far from the gates of exit. All at once the tall figure of a man clad in complete armor came into sudden view between some heavily drooping boughs,—it stood out for a second, and then hurriedly disappeared, muffling its face in a black mantle as it fled. Not, however, before Theos had recognized those dark, haughty features, those relentless brows, and that, stern almost lurid smile! . . . and with a quick convulsive movement he grasped his companion's arm.

"Hist, Sah-luma!" he whispered. . . "Saw you not the King?"

Sah-luma started as though he had received a dagger thrust, . . . his very lips turned pale in the moonlight.

"The KING?" he echoed, with an accent of incredulous amazement. . . "The King? . . . thou art mad! . . . it could not be! Where didst thou see him?"

In silence Theos pointed to the dark shrubbery. Sahluma shook himself free of his friend's hold, and, standing erect, gazed in the direction indicated, with an expression of mingled fear, distrust, bewilderment, and wrath on his features, . . . he was suddenly but effectually sobered, and all the delicate beauty of his face came back like the rich tone of a fine picture restored. His hand fell instinctively toward the jewelled hilt of the poniard at his belt.

"The King?" he muttered under his breath, . . . "The King? . . . Then. . . is Khosrul right after all, and must one learn wisdom from a madman? . . . By my soul! . . . If I thought. . ." Here he checked himself abruptly and turned upon Theos. . . "Nay, thou art deceived!" he said with a forced smile. "'Twas not the King! . . . 'twas some rash, unknown intruder whose worthless life must pay the penalty of trespass!"—and he drew his flashing weapon from his sheath. "THIS shall unmask him! . . . And thou, my friend, get thee away and home, . . . fear nothing for my safety! . . . go hence and quickly; I'll follow thee anon!"

And before Theos could utter a word of warning, he plunged impetuously into the innermost recess of the dense foliage behind which the mysterious armed figure had just vanished, and was instantly lost to sight.

"Sah-luma! . . . Sah-luma!"—called Theos passionately. . . "Come back! Whether wilt thou go? . . . Sah-luma!"

Only silence answered him,—silence rendered even more profound by the subdued, faint rustling of the wind among the leaves,—and agitated by all manner of vague alarms and dreary forebodings, he stood still for a moment hesitating as to whether he should follow his friend or no. Some instinct stronger than himself, however, persuaded him that it would be best to continue his road,—he therefore went on slowly, hoping against hope that Sah-luma might still rejoin him,—but herein he was disappointed. He waited a little while near the illuminated water, dreamily eying the beautiful marble nymph crowned with her wreath of amethystine flame, . . . she resembled Lysia somewhat, he thought,—only this was a frozen fairness, while the peerless charms of the cruel High Priestess were those of living flesh and blood. Yet the remembrance of all the tenderly witching loveliness that might have been his, had he slain Sah-luma at her bidding, now moved him

MARIE CORELLI

neither to regret nor lover's passion, but only touched his spirit with a sense of bitter repulsion, . . . while a strange pity for the Poet Laureate's infatuation awoke in him,—pity that any man could be so reckless, blind, and desperate as to love a woman for her mere perishable beauty of body, and never care to know whether the graces of her mind were equal to the graces of her form.

"We men have yet to learn the true meaning of love,"—he mused rather sadly—"We consider it from the selfish standpoint of our own unbridled passions,—we willingly accept a fair face as the visible reflex of a fair soul, and nine times out of ten, we are utterly mistaken! We begin wrongly, and we therefore end miserably,—we should love a woman for what she Is, and not for what she appears to be. Yet, how are we to fathom her nature? how shall we guess, . . . how can we decide? Are we fooled by an evil fate?—or do we in our loves and marriages deliberately fool ourselves?"

He pondered the question hazily without arriving at any satisfactory answer, . . . and as Sah-luma still did not return, he resumed his slow, unguided, and solitary way. He presently found himself in a close boscage of tall trees straight as pines, and covered with very large, thick leaves that exhaled a peculiarly faint odor,—and here, pausing abruptly, he looked anxiously about him. This was certainly not the avenue through which he had previously come with Sah-luma, . . . and he soon felt uncomfortably convinced that he had somehow taken the wrong path. Perceiving a low iron gate standing open in front of him, he went thither and discovered a steep stone staircase leading down, down into what seemed to be a vast well, black and empty as a starless midnight. Peering doubtfully into this gloomy pit, he fancied he saw a small, blue flame wavering to and fro at the bottom, and, pricked by a sudden impulse of curiosity, he made up his mind to descend.

He went down slowly and cautiously, counting each step as he placed his foot upon it, . . . there were a hundred steps in all, and at the end the light he had seen completely vanished, leaving him in the most profound darkness. Confused and startled, he stretched out his hands instinctively as a blind man might do, and thus came in contact with something sharp, pointed, and icy cold like the frozen talon of a dead bird. Shuddering at the touch, he recoiled,—and was about to try and grope his way up the stairs again, when the light once more appeared, this time casting a thin, slanting, azure blaze through the dense shadows,—and he was able gradually to realize the horrors of the place into which he had unwittingly adventured. One faint cry escaped his lips,—and then he was mute and motionless,—chilled to the very heart. A great awe and speechless dread overwhelmed him, . . . for he—a living man and fully conscious of life—stood alone, surrounded by a ghastly multitude of skeletons, skeletons bleached white as ivory and glistening with a smooth, moist polish as of pearl. Shoulder to shoulder, arm against arm, they stood, placed upright, and as close together as possible,—every bony hand held a rusty spear,—and on every skull gleamed a small metal casque inscribed with hieroglyphic characters. Thousands of eyeless sockets seemed to turn toward him in blank yet questioning wonder, suggesting awfully to his mind that the eyes might still be there, fallen far back into the head from whence they yet Saw, themselves unseen,—thousands of grinning jaws seemed to mock at him, as he leaned half-fainting against the damp, weed-grown portal,—he fancied he could hear the derisive laugh of death echoing horribly through those dimly distant arches! This, . . . this, he thought wildly, was the sequel to his brief and wretched history! . . . for this one end he had wandered out of the ways of his former life, and forgotten almost all he had ever known,—here was the only poor finale an all-wise and all-potent God could contrive for the close of His marvelous symphony of creative Love and Light! . . . Ah, cruel, cruel! Then there was no justice, no pity, no compensation in all the width and breadth of the Universe, if Death indeed was the end of everything!—and God or the great Force called by that name was nothing but a Tyrant and Torturer of His helpless creature, Man! So thinking, dully and feebly, he pressed his hand on his aching eyes, to shut out the sight of that grim crowd of fleshless, rigid Shapes that everywhere confronted him, . . . the darkness of the place seemed to descend upon him crushingly, and, reeling forward, he would have fallen in a swoon, had not a strong hand suddenly grasped his arm and supported him firmly upright.

"How now, my son!"—said a grave, musical voice that had in it a certain touch of compassion, . . . "What ails thee? . . . and why art thou here? Art thou condemned to die! . . . or dost thou seek an escape from death?"

Making an effort to overcome the sick giddiness that confused his brain, he looked up,—a bright lamp flared in his eyes, contrasting so dazzlingly with the surrounding gloom that for a moment he was half-blinded by its brilliancy, but presently steadying his gaze he was able to discern the dark outline of a tall, black-garmented figure standing beside him,—the figure of an old man, whose severe and dignified aspect at first reminded him somewhat of the prophet Khosrul. Only that Khosrul's rugged features had borne the impress of patient, long-endured, bitter suffering, and the personage who now confronted him had a face so calm and seriously impassive that it might have been taken for that of one newly dead, from whose lineaments all traces of earthly passion had forever been smoothed away.

"Art thou condemned to die, or dost thou seek an escape from death?" The question had, or seemed to have, a curious significance,—it reiterated itself almost noisily in his ears,—his mind was troubled by vague surmises and dreary forebodings,—speech was difficult to him, and his lips quivered pathetically, when he at last found force to frame his struggling thoughts into language.

"Escape from death!" he murmured, gazing wildly around as he spoke, on the vast skeleton crowd that encircled him. "Old man, dost thou also talk of dream-like impossibilities? Wilt thou also maintain a creed of hope when naught awaits us but despair? Art thou fooled likewise with the glimmering Soul-mirage of a never-to-be-realized future? . . . Escape from death? . . . How?—and where! Art not these dry and vacant forms sufficiently eloquent of the all-omnipotence of Decay?" . . . and he caught his unknown companion almost fiercely by the long robe, while a sound that was half a sob and half a sigh came from his aching throat. "Lo you, how emptily they stare upon us! . . . how frozen-piteous is their smile! . . . Poor, poor frail shapes! . . . nay!— who would think these hollow shells of bone had once been men! Men with strong hearts, warm-flowing blood, and throbbing pulses, . . . men of thought and action, who maybe did most nobly bear themselves in life upon the earth, and yet are now forgotten, . . . men—ah, great Heaven! can it be that these most rueful, loathly things have loved, and hoped, and labored through all their days for such an end as this! Escape from death! . . . alas, there is no escape, . . . 'tis evident we all must die, . . . die, and with dust-quenched eyes unlearn our knowledge of the sun, the stars, the marvels of the universe,—for us no more shall the flowers bloom or the sweet birds sing; the poem of the world will write itself anew in every roseate flushing of the dawn,—but we,—we who have joyed therein,—we who have sung the praises of the light, the harmonies of wind and sea, the tunefulness of woods and fields,—we whose ambitious thoughts have soared archangel-like through unseen empyreans of space, there to drink in a honeyed hope of Heaven,—we shall be but DEAD! . . . mute, cold, and stirless as deep, undug stones, . . . dead! . . . Ah God, thou Utmost Cruelty!"—and in a sudden access of grief and passion he raised one hand and shook it aloft with a menacing gesture—"Would I might look upon Thee face to face, and rebuke Thee for Thy merciless injustice!"

He spoke wildly as though possessed by a sort of frenzy,—his unknown companion heard him with an air of mild and pitying patience.

"Peace—peace! Blaspheme not the Most High, my son!" he said gently, yet reproachfully. "Distraught as thou dost seem with some strange misery, and sick with fears, forbear thine ignorant fury against Him who hath for love's dear sake alone created thee. Control thy soul in patience!—surely thou art afflicted by thine own vain and false imaginings, which for a time contort and darken the clear light of truth. Why dost thou thus disquiet thyself concerning the end of life, seeing that verily it hath No end? . . . and that what we men call death is not a conclusion but merely a new beginning? Waste not thy pity on these skeleton forms,—the empty dwellings of martial spirits long since fled, . . . as well weep over fallen husks of corn from which the blossoms have sprung right joyously upward! This world is but our roadside hostelry, wherein we heaven-bound sojourners tarry for one brief, restless night,—why regret the loss of the poor refreshment offered thee here, when there are a thousand better feasts awaiting thee elsewhere on thy way? Come,—let me lead thee hence, . . . this place is known as the Passage of the Tombs,—and communicates with the Inner Court of the Sacred Temple,—and if, as I fear, thou art a stray fugitive from the accursed Lysia's band of lovers, thou mayest be tracked hither and quickly slain. Come,—I will show thee a secret labyrinth by which thou canst gain the embankment of the river, and from thence betake thyself speedily home, . . . if thou hast a home. . ." here he paused, and a keen, questioning glance flashed in his dark eyes. "But,—notwithstanding thy fluency of speech and fashion of attire, methinks thou hast the lost and solitary air of one who is a stranger in the city of Al-Kyris?"

Theos sighed.

"A stranger I am indeed!" he said drearily—"A stranger to my very self and all my former belongings! Ask me no questions, good father, for, as I live, I cannot answer them! I am oppressed by a nameless and mysterious suffering, . . . my brain is darkened,—my thoughts but half-formed and never wholly uttered, and I,—I who once deemed human intelligence and reason all-supreme, all-clear, all-absolute, am now compelled to use that reason reasonlessly, and to work with that intelligence in helpless ignorance as to what end my mental toil shall serve! Woeful and strange it is!—yet true; . . . I am as a broken straw in a whirlwind,—or the pale ghost of my own identity groping for things forgotten in a land of shadows; . . . I know not whence I came, nor whither I go! Nay, do not fear me,—I am not mad: I am conscious of my life, my strength, and physical well-being,—and though I may speak wildly, I harbor no ill-intent toward any man—my quarrel is with God alone!"

He paused,—then resumed in calmer accents,—"You judge rightly, reverend sir,—I am a stranger in Al-Kyris. I entered the city-gates this morning when the sun was high,—and ere noon I found courteous welcome and princely shelter,—I am the guest of the poet Sah-luma."

The old man looked at him half compassionately.

"Ah, Sah-luma is thine host?" he said with a touch of melancholy surprise in his tone—"Then wherefore art thou here? . . . here in this dark abode where none may linger and escape with life? . . . how earnest thou within the bounds of Lysid's fatal pleasaunce! . . . Has the Laureate's friendship thus misguided thee?"

Theos hesitated before replying. He was again moved by that curious instinctive dread of hearing Sah-luma's name associated with any sort of reproach,—and his voice had a somewhat defiant ring as he answered:

"Nay, surely I am neither child nor woman that I should weakly yield to guidance or misleading! Some trifling matter of free-will remains to me in spite of mine affliction,—and that I have supped with Sah-luma at the Palace of the High Priestess, has been as much my choice as his example. Who among men would turn aside from high feasting and mirthful company? . . . not I, believe me! . . . and Sah-luma's desires herein were but the reflex of mine own. We came together through the woodland, and parted but a moment since. . ."

He stopped abruptly, startled by a sudden clash as of steel and the tramp-tramp of approaching feet. His aged companion caught him by the arm. . .

"Hush!" he whispered. "Not a word more. . . not a breath! . . . or thy life must pay the penalty! Quick,—follow me close! . . . step softly! . . . there is a hiding-place near at hand where we may couch unseen till these dread visitants pass by."

Moving stealthily and with anxious precaution, he led the way to a niche hollowed deeply out in the thickness of the wall, and turning his lamp aside so that not the faintest glimmer of it could be perceived, he took Theos by the hand, and drew him into what seemed to be a huge cavernous recess, utterly dark and icy cold.

Here, crouching low in the furthest gloom, they both waited silently,—Theos ignorant as to the cause of the sudden alarm, and wondering vaguely what strange new circumstance was about to happen. The measured tramp-tramp of feet came nearer and nearer, and in another moment the flare of smoking torches illumined the vaulted passage, casting many a ruddy flicker and flash on the ivory-gleaming whiteness of the vast skeleton army that stood with such grim and pallid patience as though waiting for a marching signal.

Presently there appeared a number of half-naked men, carrying short axes stained with blood,—coarse, savage, cruel-looking brutes all, whose lowering faces bore the marks of a thousand unrepented crimes,—these were followed by four tall personages clad in flowing white robes and closely masked,—and finally there came a band of black slaves clothed in vivid scarlet, dragging between them two writhing, bleeding creatures,—one a man, the other a girl in her earliest youth, both convulsed by the evident last agonies of death.

Arrived at the centre of that part of the vault where the skeleton crowd was thickest, this horrible cortege halted, while one of the masked personages undid from his girdle a large bunch of keys. And now Theos, watching everything with dreadful interest from the obscure corner where he was, thanks to his unknown friend, successfully concealed, perceived for the first time a low, iron door, heavily barred, and surmounted by sharp spikes as long as drawn daggers. When this dreary portal was, with many a jarring groan and clang, slowly opened, such an awful cry broke from the lips of the tortured man as might have wrung compassion from the most hardened tyrant. Wresting himself fiercely out of the grasp of the slaves who held him, he struggled to his feet, while the blood poured from the cruel wounds that were inflicted all over his body, and raising his manacled hands aloft he cried.

"Mercy! . . . mercy! . . . not for me, but for her! . . . for her, my love, my life, my tenderest little one! . . . What is her crime, ye fiends? . . . why do ye deem love a sin and passion a dishonor? . . . Shall there be no more heart-longings because ye are cold? . . . Spare her! . . . she is so young, so fond, so innocent of all reproach save one, the shame of loving me! Spare her! . . . or, if ye will not spare, slay her at once! . . . now!—now, with swift compassionate sword, . . . but cast her not alive into yon hideous serpent's den! . . . not alive! . . . ah no, no,—ye gods have pity! . . ."

Here his voice broke and a sudden light passed over his agonized countenance. Gazing steadfastly at the girl, whose beautiful, white body now lay motionless on the cold stone, with a cloud of fair hair falling veil-like over it, his eyes seemed to strain themselves out of their sockets in the intensity of his eager regard, when all at once he gave vent to a wild peal of delirious laughter and exclaimed.

"Dead. . . dead! . . . Thanks be to the merciless gods for this one gift of grace at the last! Dead. . . dead! . . . O the blessed favor and freedom of death! . . . Sweetheart, they can torture thee no more. . . no more! . . . Ah, devils that ye are!" and his voice grown frantically loud, pierced the gloomy arches with terrible resonance, as he saw the red-garmented slaves vainly endeavoring to rouse, with ferocious blows and thrusts, new life in the fair, stiffening corpse before them. . . "This time ye are baffled! . . . Baffled!—and I live to see your vanquishment! Give her to me!" and he stretched out his trembling arms. . . "Give her. . . she is dead—and ye cannot offer to Nagaya any lifeless thing! I will weave her a shroud of her own gold hair—I will bury her softly away in the darkness—I will sing to her as I used to sing in the silent summer evenings, when we fancied our secret of forbidden love unknown,— and with my lips on hers, I will pray. . . pray for the pardon of passion grown stronger. . . than. . . life! . . ."

He ceased, and swaying forward, fell, . . . a shiver ran through his limbs. . . one deep, gasping sigh. . . and all was over. The band of torturers gathered round the body, uttering fierce oaths and exclamations of dismay.

"Both dead!" said one of the individuals in white. "'Tis a most fatal augury!"

"Fatal indeed!" said another, and turning to the men with the blood stained axes, he added angrily—"Ye were too swift and lavish of your weapons—ye should have let these criminals suffer slowly inch by inch, and yet have left them life enough wherewith to linger on in anguish many hours."

The wretches thus addressed looked sullen and humiliated, and approaching the two corpses, would have brutally inflicted fresh wounds on them, had not the seeming chief of the party interfered.

"Let be. . . let be!" he said austerely—"Ye cannot cause the dead to feel, . . . would that it were possible! Then might the glorious and god like thirst of vengeance in our great High Priestess be somewhat more appeased in this matter. For the unlawful communion of love between a vestal virgin and an anointed priest cannot be too utterly abhorred and condemned,—and these twain, who thus did foully violate their vows, have perished far too easily. The sanctity of the Temple has been outraged, . . . Lysia will not be satisfied, . . . and how shall we pacify her righteous wrath, concerning this too tranquil death of the undeserving and impure?"

Drawing all together in a close group they held a whispered consultation, and finally, appearing to have come to some sort of decision, they took up the dead bodies one after another, and flung them carelessly into the dark aperture lately unclosed. As they did this, a stealthy, rustling sound was heard, as of some great creature moving to and fro in the far interior, but they soon locked and barred the iron portal once more, and then took their departure rather hurriedly, leaving the vault by the way Theos had entered it—namely, up the stone stairway that led into Lysia's palace-gardens. As the last echo of their retreating steps died away and the last glimmer of their lurid torches vanished, Theos sprang out from his hiding-place,—his venerable companion slowly followed.

"Oh, God! Can such things be!" he cried loudly, reckless of all possible risk for himself as his voice rang penetratingly through the deep silence—"Were these brute-murderers actual men?—or but the wandering, grim shadows of some long past crime? . . . Nay,—surely I do but dream!—and ghouls and demons born out of nightmare-sleep do vex my troubled spirit! Justice! . . . justice for the innocent! . . . Is there none in all Al-Kyris?"

"None!" replied the old man who stood beside him, lamp in hand, fixing his dark, melancholy eyes upon him as he spoke—"None! . . . neither in Al-Kyris nor in any other great city on the peopled earth! Justice? . . . I who am named Zuriel the Mystic, because of my tireless searching into things that are hidden from the unstudious and unthinking,—I know that Justice is an idle name,—an empty braggart-word forever on the mouths of kings and judges, but never in their hearts! Moreover,—what is guilt? . . . What is innocence? Both must be defined according to the law of the realm wherein we dwell,—and from that law there can be no appeal. These men we lately saw were the chief priests and executioners of the Sacred Temple,—they have done no wrong—they have simply fulfilled their duty. The culprits slain deserved their fate,—they loved where loving was forbidden,—

MARIE CORELLI

torture and death was the strictly ordained punishment, and herein was justice,—justice as portioned out by the Penal Code of the High Court of Council."

Theos heard, and gave an expressive gesture of loathing and contempt.

"O narrow jurisdiction! . . . O short-sighted, false equity!" he exclaimed passionately. "Are there different laws for high and low? . . . Must the weak and defenceless be condemned to death for the self-same sin committed openly by their more powerful brethren who yet escape scot-free? What of the High Priestess then? . . . If these poor lover-victims merited their doom, why is not Lysia slain? . . . Is not SHE a willingly violated vestal? . . . doth SHE not count her lovers by the score? . . . are not her vows long since broken? . . . is not her life a life of wanton luxury and open shame? . . . Why doth the Law, beholding these things, remain in her case dumb and ineffectual?"

"Hush, hush, my son!" said the aged Zuriel anxiously—"These stone walls hear thee far too loudly,—who knows but they may echo forth thy words to unsuspected listeners! Peace—peace! . . . Lysia is as much Queen, as Zephoranim is King of Al-Kyris; and surely thou knowest that the sins of tyrants are accounted virtues, so long as they retain their ruling powers? The public voice pronounces Lysia chaste, and Zephoranim faithful; who then shall dare to disprove the verdict?—'Tis the same in all countries, near and far,—the law serves the strong, while professing to defend the weak. The rich man gains his cause,—the beggar loses it,—how can it be otherwise, while lust of gold prevails? Gold is the moving-force of this our era,—without it kings and ministers are impotent, and armies starve, . . . with it, all things can be accomplished even to the concealment of the foulest crimes. Come, come! . . ." and he laid one hand kindly on Theos's arm, "Thou hast a generous and fiery spirit, but thou shouldst never have been born into this planet if thou seekest such a thing as Justice! No man will ever deal true justice to his fellow man on earth, unless perhaps in ages to come, when the old creeds are swept away for a new, and a grander, wider, purer form of faith is accepted by the people. For religion in Al-Kyris to-day is a hollow mockery,—a sham, kept up partly from fear,—partly from motives of policy,—but every thinker is an atheist at heart, . . . our splendid civilization is tottering towards its fall, . . . and should the fore-doomed destruction of this city come to pass, vast ages of progress, discovery, and invention will be swept away as though they had never been!"

He paused and sighed,—then continued sorrowfully—"There is, there must be something wrong in the mechanism of life,—some little hitch that stops the even wheels,—some curious perpetual mischance that crosses us at every turn,—but I doubt not all is for the best, and will prove most truly so hereafter!"

"Hereafter!" echoes Theos bitterly. . . "Thinkest thou that even God, repenting of the evil He hath done, will ever be able to compensate us by any future bliss, for all the needless anguish of the Present?"

Zuriel looked at him with a strange, almost spectral expression of mingled pity, fear, and misgiving, but he offered no reply to this home-thrust of a question. In grave silence and with slow, majestic tread he began to lead the way along through the dismal labyrinth of black, winding arches, holding his blue lamp aloft as he went, the better to lighten the dense gloom.

Theos followed him, silent also, and wrapped in stern, and mournful musings of his own, . . . musings through which faint threads of pale recollection connected with his past glimmered hazily from time to time, perplexing rather than enlightening his bewildered brain.

Presently he found himself in a low, narrow vestibule illumined by the bright yet soft radiance of a suspended Star,—and here, coming close up with his guide and observing his dress and manner more attentively, he suddenly perceived a shining SOMETHING which the old man wore hanging from his neck and which flashed against the sable hue of his garment like a wandering moonbeam.

Stopping abruptly, he examined this ornament with straining, wistful gaze, . . . and slowly, very slowly, recognized its fashion of construction,—it was a plain silver Cross—nothing more. Yet at sight of the sacred, strange, yet familiar Symbol, a chord seemed to snap in his brain,—tears rushed to his tired eyes, and with a sharp cry he fell on his knees, grasping his companion's robe wildly, as a drowning man grasps at a floating spar,—while the venerable Zuriel, startled at his action, stared down upon him in evident amazement and terror.

"Rescue! . . . rescue!" he cried, . . . "O thou blessed among men!—thou dost wear the Sign of Eternal Safety! . . . the Sign of the Way, the Truth, and the Life! . . . 'without the Way, there is no going, without the Truth there is no knowing, without the Life there is no living'! Now do I know thee for a saint in Al-Kyris,—for thou dost openly avow thyself a follower of the Divine Faith that fools despise, and selfish souls repudiate, . . . ah, I do beseech thee, thou good and holy man, absolve me of my sin of Unbelief! Teach me! . . . help me! . . . and I will hear thy counsels with the meekness of a listening child! . . . See you, I kneel! . . . I pray! . . . I, even I, am humiliated to the very dust of shame! I have no pride, . . . I seek no glory, . . . I do entreat, even as I once rejected the blessing of the Cross, whereby I shall regain my lost love,—my despised pardon,—my vanished peace!"

And, with pathetic earnestness, he raised his hands toward the silver emblem, and touched it tenderly, reverently, . . . then as though unworthy, he bent his head low, and waited eagerly for a Name, . . . a Name that he himself could not remember, . . . a Name suggested by the Cross, but not declared. If that Name were once spoken in the form of a benediction, he felt instinctively that he would straightway be released from the mysterious spell of misery that bound his intelligence in such a grievous thrall. But not a word of consolation did his companion utter, . . . on the contrary, he seemed agitated by the strangest surprise and alarm.

"Now may all the gods in Heaven defend thee, thou unhappy, desperate, distracted soul!" he said in trembling, affrighted accents. "Thou dost implore the blessing of a Faith unknown! . . . a Mystery predicted but not yet fulfilled. . . a Creed that shall not be declared to men for full FIVE THOUSAND YEARS!"

XXI

The Crimson River

At these unexpected words Theos sprang wildly to his feet. An awful darkness seemed to close in upon him,—and a chaotic confusion of memories began to whirl and drift through his mind like flotsam and jetsam tossed upon a storm-swept sea. The aged and shadowy-looking Zuriel stood motionless, watching him with something of timid pity and mild patience.

"Five Thousand Years!" he muttered hoarsely, pressing his hands into his aching brows, while his eyes again fixed themselves yearningly on the Cross. "Five thousand years before. . . before What?"

He caught the old man's arm, and in spite of himself, a laugh, wild, discordant, and out of all keeping with his inward emotions, broke from his parched lips,—"Thou doting fool!" he cried almost furiously,—"Why dost thou mock me then with this false image of a hope unrealized? . . . Who gave thee leave to add more fuel to my flame of torment? . . . What means this symbol to thine eyes? Speak. . . speak! What admonition does it hold for thee? . . . what promise? . . . what menace? . . . what warning? . . . what love? . . . Speak. . . speak! O, shall I force confession from thy throat, or must I die unsatisfied and slain by speechless longing! What didst thou say? . . . Five Thousand Years? . . . Nay, by the gods, thou liest!"—and he pointed excitedly to the sacred Emblem,—"I tell thee that Holy Sign is as familiar to my suffering soul as the chiming of bells at sunset! . . . as well known to my sight as the unfolding of flowers in the fields of spring! . . . What shall be done or said of it, in five thousand years, that has not already been said and done?"

Zuriel regarded him more compassionately than ever, with a penetrating, mournful expression in his serious dark eyes.

"Alas, alas, my son! thou art most grievously distraught!" he said in troubled tones. "Thy words but prove the dark disorder of thy wits,— may Heaven soon heal thee of thy mental wound! Restrain thy wild and wandering fancies? . . . for surely thou canst not be familiar, as

thou sayest with this silver Symbol, seeing that it is but the Talisman*
or Badge of the Mystic Brethren of Al-Kyris, and has no signification
whatsoever save for the Elect. It was designed some twenty years ago
by the inspired Chief of our Order, Khosrul, and such as are still
his faithful disciples wear it as a record and constant reminder of his
famous Prophecy."

Theos heard, and a dull apathy stole over him,—his recent excitement
died out under a chilling weight of vague yet bitter disappointment.

"And this Prophecy?" he asked listlessly. "What is its nature and
whom doth it concern?"

"Nay, in very truth it is a strange and marvellous thing!" replied
Zuriel, his calm voice thrilling with a mellow touch of fervor. Khosrul,
'tis said, has heard the angels whispering in Heaven, and his attentive
ears have caught the echo of their distant speech.

"Thus spiritually instructed, he doth powerfully predict Salvation for
the human race,—and doth announce, that in five thousand years or
more, a God shall be moved by wondrous mercy to descend from Heaven,
and take the form of Man, wherein, unknown, despised, rejected, he
will live our life from commencement to finish, teaching, praying, and
sanctifying by His Divine Presence the whole sin-burdened Earth. This
done, He will consent to suffer a most cruel death, . . . and the manner
of His death will be that He shall hang, nailed hands and feet to a Cross,
as though He were a common criminal, . . . His holy brows shall be
bound about with thorns,—and after hours of agony He, innocent of
every sin, shall perish miserably—friendless, unpitied, and alone. But
afterward, . . . and mark you! this is the chiefest glory of all! . . . He will
rise again triumphant from the grave to prove his God-head, and to
convince Mankind beyond all doubt an question, that there is indeed an
immortal Hereafter,—an actual, free Eternity of Life, compared with
which this our transient existence is a mere brief breathing-space of
pause and probation, . . . and then for evermore His sacred Name shall
dominate and civilize the world. . ."

"What Name?" interrupted Theos, with eager abruptness. . . "Canst
thou pronounce it?"

Zuriel shook his head.

---

* The Cross was held in singular veneration in the Temple of Serapis, and by many tribes
in the East, ages before the coming of Christ.

"Not I, my son"—he answered gravely. "Not even Khosrul can penetrate thus far! The Name of Him who is to come, is hidden deep among God's unfathomed silences! It should suffice thee that thou knowest now the sum and substance of the Prophecy. Would I might live to see the days when all shall be fulfilled! . . . but alas, my remaining years are few upon the earth, and Heaven's time is not ours!"

He sighed,—and resumed his slow pacing onwards,—Theos walked beside him as a man may walk in sleep, uncertainly and with unseeing eyes, his heart beating loudly, and a sick sense of suffocation in his throat. What did it all mean? . . . Had his life gone back in some strange way? . . . or had he merely DREAMED of a former existence different to this one? He remembered now what Sah-luma had told him respecting Khosrul's "new" theory of a future religion,—a theory that to him had seemed so old, so old!—so utterly exhausted and worn threadbare! In what a cruel problem was he hopelessly involved!—what a useless, perplexed, confused being he had become! . . . he who would once to have staked his life on the unflinching strength and capabilities of human reason! After a pause, . . .

"Forgive me!" he said in a low tone, and speaking with some effort. . . "forgive me and have patience with my laggard comprehension, . . . I am perplexed at heart and slow of thought; wilt thou assure me faithfully, that this God-Man thou speakest of is not yet born on earth?"

The faintest shadow of a wondering smile flickered over the old man's wrinkled countenance, like the reflection of a passing taper-flame on a faded picture.

"My son, my son!" he murmured with compassionate tolerance— "Have I not told thee that five thousand years and more must pass away ere the prediction be accomplished? . . . I marvel that so plain a truth should thus disquiet thee! Now, by my soul, thou lookest pallid as the dead! . . . Come, let us hasten on more rapidly,—thy fainting spirits will revive in fresher air."

He hurried his pace as he spoke, and glided along with such a curious, stealthy noiselessness that by and by Theos began dubiously to wonder whether after all he were a real personage or a phantom? He noticed that his own figure seemed to possess much more substantiality and distinctness of outline than that of this mysterious Zuriel, whose very garments resembled floating cloud rather than actual, woven fabric. Was his companion then a fitting Spectre? . . .

He smiled at the absurdity of the idea, and to change the drift of his own foolish fancies he asked suddenly,—"Concerning this wondrous city of Al-Kyris. . . is it of very ancient days, and long lineage?"

"The annals of its recorded history reach over a period of twelve thousand years"—replied Zuriel, . . . "But 'tis the present fashion to count from the Deification of Nagaya or the Snake,—and, according to this, we are now in the nine hundred and eighty-ninth year of so-called Grace and Knowledge,—rather say Dishonor and Crime! . . . for a crueler, more bloodthirsty creed than the worship of Nagaya never debased a people! Who shall number up the innocent victims that have been sacrificed in the great Temple of the Sacred Python!—and even on this very day which has just dawned, another holocaust is to be offered on the Veiled Shrine,—or so it hath been publicly proclaimed throughout the city,—and the crowd will flock to see a virgin's blood spilt on the accursed altars where Lysia, in all the potency of triumphant wickedness, presides. But if the auguries of the stars prevail, 'twill be for the last time!" Here he paused and looked fixedly at Theos. "Thou dost return straightway to Sah-luma. . . is it not so?"

Theos bent his head in assent.

"Art thou true friend, or mere flatterer to that spoilt child of fair fame and fortune?"

"Friend!"—cried Theos with eager enthusiasm, . . . "I would give my life to save his!"

"Aye, verily? . . . is it so?" . . . and Zuriel's melancholy eyes dwelt upon him with a strange and sombre wistfulness, . . . "Then, as thou art a man, persuade him out of evil into good! . . . rouse him to noble shame and nobler penitence for all those faults which mar his poet-genus and deprive it of immortal worth! . . . urge him to depart from Al-Kyris while there is yet time ere the bolt of destruction falls! . . . and, . . . mark you well this final warning! . . . bid him to-day avoid the Temple, and beware the King!"—

As he said this he stopped and extinguished the lamp he carried. There was no longer any need of it, for a broad patch of gray light fell through an aperture in the wall, showing a few rough, broken steps that led upwards,—and pointing to these he bade the bewildered Theos a kindly farewell.

"Thou wilt find Sah-luma's palace easily,"—he said—"Not a child in the streets but knows the way thither. Guard thy friend and be thyself also on guard against coming disaster,—and if thou art not yet resolved to die, escape from the city ere to-night's sun-setting. Soothe thy distempered fancies with thoughts of God, and cease not to pray for thy soul's salvation! Peace be with thee!"—

He raised his hands with an expressive gesture of benediction, and turning round abruptly disappeared. Where had he gone? . . . how had he vanished? . . . It was impossible to tell! . . . he seemed to have melted away like a mist into utter nothingness! Profoundly perplexed, Theos ascended the steps before him, his mind anxiously revolving all the strange adventures of the night, while a dim sense of some unspeakable, coming calamity brooded darkly upon him.

The solemn admonitions he had just heard affected him deeply, for the reason that they appeared to apply so specially to Sah-luma,— and the idea that any evil fate was in store for the bright, beautiful creature, whom he had, oddly enough, learned to love more than himself, moved him to an almost womanish apprehension. In case of pressing necessity, could he exercise any authority over the capricious movements of the wilful Laureate, whose egotism was so absolute, whose imperious ways were so charming, whose commands were never questioned?

He doubted it! . . . for Sah-luma was accustomed to follow the lead of his own immediate pleasure, in reckless scorn of consequences,— and it was not likely he would listen to the persuasions or exhortations, however friendly, of any one presuming to run counter to his wishes.

Again and again Theos asked himself—"If Sah-luma of his own accord, and despite all warning, deliberately rushed into deadly peril, could I, even loving him as I do, rescue him?"—And as he pondered on this, a strange answer shaped itself unbidden in his brain—an answer that seemed as though it were spoken aloud by some interior voice. "No,—no!—ten thousand times no! You could not save him any more than you could save yourself from the results of your own misdoing! If you voluntarily choose evil, not all the forces in the world can lift you into good,—if you voluntarily choose danger, not all the gods can bring you into safety! FREE WILL is the divine condition attached to human life, and each man by thought, word, and deed, determines his own fate, and decides his own future!"

He sighed despondingly, . . . a curious, vague contrition stirred within him, . . . he felt as though HE were in some mysterious way to blame for all his poet-friend's short-comings!

In a few minutes he found himself on the broad marble embankment,

MARIE CORELLI

close to the very spot from whence he had first beheld the beautiful High Priestess sailing slowly by in all her golden pomp and splendor, and as he thought of her now, a shudder, half of aversion, half of desire, quivered through him, flushing his brows with the warm uprising blood that yet burned rebelliously at the remembrance of her witching, perfect loveliness!

Here too he had met Sah-luma, . . . ah Heaven!—how many things had happened since then! . . . how much he had seen and heard! . . . Enough, at any rate, to convince him, that the men and women of Al-Kyris were more or less the same as those of other great cities he seemed to have known in far-off, half-forgotten days,—that they plotted against each other, deceived each other, accused each other falsely, murdered each other, and were fools, traitors, and egotists generally, after the customary fashion of human pigmies,—that they set up a Sham to serve as Religion, Gold being their only god,—that the rich wantoned in splendid luxury, and wilfully neglected the poor,— that the King was a showy profligate, ruled by a treacherous courtesan, just like many other famous Kings and Princes, who, because of their stalwart, martial bearing, and a certain surface good-nature, manage to conceal their vices from the too lenient eyes of the subjects they mislead,—and that finally all things were evidently tending toward some great convulsion and upheaval possibly arising from discontent and dissension among the citizens themselves,—or, likelier still, from the sudden invasion of a foreign foe,—for any more terrific termination of events did not just then suggest itself to his imagination.

Absorbed in thought, he walked some paces along the embankment, before he perceived that a number of people were already assembled there,—men, women, and children, who, crowding eagerly together to the very edge of the parapet, appeared to be anxiously watching the waters below.

What unusual sight attracted them? . . . and why were they all so silent as though struck dumb by some unutterable dismay? One or two, raising their heads, turned their pale, alarmed faces toward Theos as he approached, their eyes seeming to mutely inquire his opinion, concerning the alarming phenomenon which held them thus spellbound and fear-stricken.

He made his way quickly to where they stood, and looking where they looked, uttered a sharp, involuntary exclamation, . . . the river, the clear, rippling river was RED As BLOOD. Beneath the slowly breaking light of dawn, that streaked the heavens with delicate lines of silver-gray and daffodil, the whole visible length and breadth of the heaving waters shone with a darkly flickering crimson hue, deeper than the lustre of the deepest ruby, flowing sluggishly the while as though clogged with some thick and weedy slime.

As the sky brightened gradually into a pale, ethereal blue, so the tide became ruddier and more pronounced in color,—and presently, as though seized by a resistless panic, the group of staring, terrified bystanders broke up suddenly, and rushed away in various directions, covering their faces as they fled and uttering loud cries of lamentation and despair.

Theos alone remained behind, . . . resting his folded arms on the sculptured balustrade, he gazed down, down into those crimson depths till their strange tint dazzled and confused his sight,—looking up for relief to the eastern horizon where the sun was just bursting out in full splendor from a pavilion of violet cloud, the red reflection was still before his eyes, so much so, that the very air seemed flushed with spreading fire.

And then like the sound of a tocsin ringing in his ears, the words of the Prophet Khosrul, as pronounced in the presence of the King, recurred to his memory with new and suggestive force. "BLOOD— BLOOD! 'TIS A SCARLET SEA WHEREIN LIKE A BROKEN AND EMPTY SHIP AL-KYRIS FOUNDERS,—FOUNDERS NEVER TO RISE AGAIN!"

Still painfully oppressed by an increasing sense of some swift-approaching disaster, his thoughts once more reverted anxiously to Sah-luma. He must be warned,—yes!—even if he disdained all warning! Yet, . . . warn him against what? "BID HIM AVOID THE TEMPLE AND BEWARE THE KING!"

So had said Zuriel the Mystic,—but to the laurelled favorite of the monarch, and idol of the people, such an admonition would seem more than absurd! It was useless to talk to him about the prophecies of Khosrul,—he had heard them all, and laughed them to scorn.

"How can I"—then mused Theos disconsolately,—"How can I make him believe that some undeclared evil threatens him, when he is at the very pinnacle of fame and fortune with all Al-Kyris at his feet? . . . He would never listen to me, . . . nor would any persuasions of mine induce him to leave the city where his name is so glorious and his renown so firmly established. Of Lysia's treachery I may perhaps convince him, . . . yet even in this attempt I may fail, and incur his hatred for my pains! If I had only myself to consider! . . ."—And here his reflections suddenly took a strange, unbidden turn. If he had only himself to consider! . . . well, what then! Was it not just within the bounds of probability that, under the same circumstances, he might be precisely as self-willed and as haughtily opinionated as the friend whose arrogance he deplored, yet could not alter?

So pointed a suggestion was not exactly suited to his immediate humor, and he felt curiously vexed with himself for indulging in such a foolish association of ideas! The positions were entirely different, he argued, angrily addressing the troublesome inward monitor that every now and then tormented him,—there was no resemblance whatever between himself, the unknown, unfamed wanderer in a strange land, and the brilliant Sah-luma, chosen Poet Laureate of the realm!

No resemblance, . . . none at all! . . . he reiterated over and over again in his own mind, . . . except. . . except, . . . well! . . . except in perhaps a few trifling touches of character and temper that were scarcely worth the noting! At this juncture, his uncomfortable reverie was interrupted by the sound of a harsh, metallic voice close behind him.

"What fools there are in the world!" said the voice in emphatic accents of supreme contempt—"What braying asses!—What earth-snouting swine! Saw you not yon crowd of whimpering idiots flying helter-skelter like chaff before the wind, weeping, wailing, and bemoaning their miserable little sins, scattering dust on their addled pates, and howling on their gods for mercy,—all forsooth! because for once in their unobserving lives they behold the river red instead of green! Ay me! 'tis a thing to laugh at, this crass, and brutish ignorance of the multitude,—no teaching will ever cleanse their minds from the cobwebs of vulgar superstition,—and I, in common with every wise and worthy sage of sound repute and knowledge, must needs waste all my scientific labors on a perpetually ungrateful public!"

Turning hastily round Theos confronted the speaker,—a tall, spare man with a pale, clean-shaven, intellectual face, small, shrewd, speculative eyes, and very straight, neatly parted locks,—a man on whose every lineament was expressed a profound belief in himself, and an equally profound scorn for the opinions of any one who might possibly presume to disagree with him. He smiled condescendingly as he met Theos's half-surprised, half-inquiring look, and saluted him with a gravely pompous air, which however, was not without a saving touch of that indescribable, easy grace which seemed to distinguish the manners of all the inhabitants of Al-Kyris. Theos returned the salutation with equal gravity, whereupon the new-comer waving his hand majestically, continued:

"You sir, I see, are young, . . . and probably you are enrolled among the advanced students of one or other of our great collegiate institutions,— therefore the peculiar, though not at all unnatural tint of the river this morning, is of course no mystery to you, if, as I presume, you follow the Scientific Classes of Instruction in the Physiology of Nature, of Manifestation of Simple and Complex Motive Force, and the Perpetual Evolution of Atoms?"

Theos smiled,—the grandiloquent manner of this self-important individual amused him.

"Most worthy sir," he replied, "you form too favorable an opinion of my scholarly attainments! I am a stranger in Al-Kyris,—and know naught of its educational system, or the interior mechanism of its wondrous civilization! I come from far-off lands, where, if I remember rightly, much is taught and but little retained,—where petty pedagogues persist in dragging new generations of men through old and worn-out ruts of knowledge that future ages shall never have need of, . . . and concerning even the progress of science, I confess to a certain incredulity, seeing that to my mind Science somewhat resembles a straight line drawn clear across country but leading, alas! to an ocean wherein all landmarks are lost and swallowed up in blankness. Over and over again the human race has trodden the same pathway of research,—over and over again has it stood bewildered and baffled on the shores of the same vast sea,— the most marvellous discoveries are after all mere child's play compared to the tremendous secrets that must remain forever unrevealed; and the poor and trifling comprehension of things that we, after a life-time of study, succeed in attaining, is only just sufficient to add to our already burdened existence the undesirable clogs of discontent and disappointed endeavor. We die,—in almost as much ignorance as we were born, . . . and when we come face to face with the Last Dark Mystery, what shall our little wisdom profit us?"

With his arms folded in an attitude of enforced patience and complacent superiority, the other listened.

"Curious, . . . curious!" he murmured in a mild sotto-voce,—"A would-be pessimist!—aye, aye,—'tis very greatly the fashion for young men in these days to assume the manner of elderly and exhausted cynics who have tried everything and approve of nothing! 'Tis a strange

MARIE CORELLI

craze!—but, my good sir, let us keep to the subject at present under discussion. Like all unripe philosophers, you wander from the point. I did not ask you for your opinion concerning the uselessness or the efficiency of learning,—I merely sought to discover whether you, like the silly throng that lately scattered right and left of you, had any foolish forebodings respecting the transformed color of this river,—a color which, however seeming peculiar, arises, as all good scholars know, from causes that are perfectly simple and easily explainable."

Theos hesitated,—his eyes wandered involuntarily to the flowing tide, which now with the fully risen sun seemed more than ever brilliant and lurid in its sanguinary hue.

"Strange things have been said of late concerning Al-Kyris,—" he answered at last, slowly and after a thoughtful pause,—"Things that, though wild and vague, are not without certain dark presages and ominous suggestions. This crimson flood may be, as you say, the natural effect of purely natural causes,—yet, notwithstanding this, it seems to me a singular phenomenon—nay, even a weird and almost fatal augury?"

His companion laughed—a gentle, careless laugh of amused disdain.

"Phenomenon! . . . augury! . . ." he exclaimed shrugging his shoulders lightly. . . "These words, my young friend, are terms that nowadays belong exclusively to the vocabulary of the uneducated masses; we,—and by WE, I mean scientists, and men of the highest culture,—have long ago rejected them as unmeaning and therefore unnecessary. Phenomenon is a particularly vile expression, serving merely to designate anything wonderful and uncommon,—whereas to the scientific eye, there is nothing left in the world that ought to excite so vulgar and barbarous an emotion as wonder, . . . nothing so apparently rare that cannot be reduced at once from the ignorant exaggerations of enthusiasm to the sensible level of the commonplace? The so-called 'marvels' of nature have, thanks to the advancement of practical education, entirely ceased to affect by either surprise or admiration the carefully matured, mathematically adjusted, and technically balanced brain of the finished student or professor of Organic Evolution,—and as for the idea of 'auguries' or portents, nothing could well be more entirely at variance with our present system of progressive learning, whereby Human Reason is trained and taught to pulverize into indistinguishable atoms all supernatural propositions, and to gradually eradicate from the mind the absurd notion of a Deity or deities, whom it is necessary to propitiate in order to live well. Much time is of course required to elevate the multitude above all desire for a Religion,—but the seed has been sown, and the harvest will be reaped, and a glorious Era is fast approaching, when the free-thinking, free-speaking people of all nations shall govern themselves and rejoice in the grand and God-less Light of Universal Liberty?"

Somewhat heated by the fervor of his declamatory utterance, he passed his hand among his straight locks, whether to cool his forehead, or to show off the numerous jewelled rings on his fingers, it was difficult to say, and continued more calmly:

"No, young sir!—the color of this river,—a color which, I willingly admit, resembles the tint of flowing human blood,—has naught to do with foolish omens and forecasts of evil,—'tis simply caused by the influx of some foreign alluvial matter, probably washed down by storm from, the sides of the distant mountains whence these waters have their rising,—see you not how the tide is thick and heavy with an unfloatable cargo of red sand? Some sudden disturbance of the soil,—or a volcanic movement underneath the ocean,—or even a distant earthquake, . . . any of these may be the reason." . . .

"May be?—why not say MUST be," observed Theos half ironically, "since learning makes you sure!"

His companion pressed the tips of his fingers delicately together, as though blandly deprecating this observation.

"Nay, nay!—none of us, however wise, can say 'MUST BE'"—he argued suavely—"It is not,—strictly speaking,—possible in this world to pronounce an incontestable certainty."

"Not even that two and two are four?" suggested Theos, smiling.

"Not even that!" . . . replied the other with perfect gravity—"Inasmuch as in the kingdom of Hypharus, whose borders touch ours, the inhabitants, also highly civilized, do count their quantities by a totally different method; and to them two and two are NOT four, the numbers two and four not being included in their system of figures. Thus,—a Professor from the Colleges of Hypharus could obstinately deny what to us seems the plainest fact known to common-sense,—yet, were I to argue against him I should never persuade him out of his theory,—nor could he move me one jot from mine. And viewed from our differing standpoints, therefore, the first simple multiplication of numbers could never be proved correct beyond all question!"

Theos glanced at him in wonder,—the man must be mad, he thought, since surely any one in his senses could see that two objects placed with other two must necessarily make four!

"I confess you surprise me greatly, sir!"—he said, and, in spite of himself, a little quiver of laughter shook his voice. . . "What I asked was by way of jest,—and I never thought to hear so simple a subject treated with so much profound and almost doubting seriousness! See!"—and he picked up four small stones from the roadway—"Count these one by one, . . . how many have you? Surely even a professor from Hypharus could find no more, and no less than four?"

Very deliberately, and with unruffled equanimity, the other took the pebbles in his hand, turned them over and over, and finally placed them in a row on the edge of the balustrade near which he stood.

"There SEEM to be four, . . ." he then observed placidly—"But I would not swear to it,—nor to anything else of which the actuality is only supported by the testimony of my own eyes and sense of touch."

"Good heavens, man!" cried Theos, in amazement,—"But a moment since, you were praising the excellence of Reason, and the progressive system of learning that was to educate human beings into a contempt for the Supernatural and Spiritual, and yet almost in the same breath you tell me you cannot rely on the evidence of your own senses! Was there ever anything more utterly incoherent and irrational!"

And he flung the pebbles into the redly flowing river with a gesture of irritation and impatience. The scientist,—if scientist he could be called,—gazed at him abstractedly, and stroked his well-shaven chin with a somewhat dejected air. Presently heaving a deep sigh, he said:

"Alas, I have again betrayed myself! . . .'tis my fatal destiny! Always, by some unlooked-for mischance, I am compelled to avow what most I desire to conceal! Can you not understand, sir,"—and he laid his hand persuasively on Theos's arm,—"that a Theory may be one thing and one's own private opinion another? My Theory is my profession,—I live by it! Suppose I resigned it,—well, then I should also have to resign my present position in the Royal Institutional College,—my house, my servants, and my income. I advance the interests of pure Human Reason, because the Age has a tendency to place Reason as the first and highest attribute of Man,—and it would not pay me to pronounce my personal preference for the natural and vastly superior gift of Intellectual Instinct. I advise my scholars to become atheists, because I perceive they have a positive passion for Atheism, and it is not my business, nor would it be to my advantage to interfere with the declared predilections of my wealthiest patrons. Concerning my own ideas on these matters, they are absolutely Nil, . . . I have no fixed principles,—because"—and his brows contracted in a puzzled line—"it is entirely out of my ability to fix anything! The whole world of manners and morals is in a state of perpetual ferment and consequent change,— equally restless and mutable is the world of Nature, for at any moment mountains may become plains, and plains mountains,—the dry land may be converted into oceans, and oceans into dry land, and so on forever. In this incessant shifting of the various particles that make up the Universe, how can you expect a man to hold fast to so unstable a thing as an idea! And, respecting the testimony offered by sight and sense, can You rely upon such slippery evidence?"

Theos moved uneasily,—a slight shiver ran through his veins, and a momentary dizziness seized him, as of one who gazing down from some lofty mountain-peak sees naught below but the white, deceptive blankness of a mist that veils the deeper deathful chasms from his eyes. Could he rely on sight and sense. . . Dared he take oath that these frail guides of his intelligence could never be deceived? . . . Doubtfully he mused on this, while his companion continued:

"For example, I look an arm's length into space, . . . my eyes assure me that I behold nothing save empty air,—my touch corroborates the assertion of my eyes,—and yet, . . . Science proves to me that every inch of that arm's length of supposed blank space is filled with thousands of minute living organisms that no human vision shall ever be able to note or examine! Wonder not, therefore, that I decline to express absolute confidence in any fact, however seemingly obvious, such as that two and two are four, and that I prefer to say the blood-red color of this river May be caused by an earth-tremor or a land-slip, rather than positively assert that it Must be so; though I confess that, as far as my knowledge guides me, I incline to the belief that 'Must be' is in this instance the correct term."

He sighed again, and rubbed his nose perplexedly. Theos glanced at him curiously, uncertain whether to laugh at or pity him.

"Then the upshot of all your learning, sir, . . ." he said, . . . "is that one can never be quite certain of anything?"

"Exactly so!"—replied the pensive sage with a grave shake of his head,—"Judged by the very finest lines of metaphysical argument, you cannot really be sure whether you behold in me a Person or a Phantasm! You Think you see me,—I Think I see you,—but after all it is only an IMPRESSION mutually shared,—an impression which like many another, less distinct, may be entirely erroneous! Ah, my dear young sir!—education is advancing at a very rapid rate, and the art of close analysis is reaching such a pitch of perfection that I believe we shall soon be able logically to prove, not only that we do not actually exist, but moreover that we never have existed! . . . And herein, as I consider, will be the final triumph of philosophy!"

"A poor triumph!"—murmured Theos wearily. "What, in such a case, would become of all the nobler sentiments and passions of man,—love, hope, gratitude, duty, ambition?"

"They would be precisely the same as before"—rejoined the other complacently—"Only we should have learned to accept them merely as the means whereby to sustain the IMPRESSION that we live,—an impression which would always be agreeable, however delusive!"

Theos shrugged his shoulders. "You possess a peculiarly constituted mind, sir!"—he said—"And I congratulate you on the skill you display in following out a somewhat puzzling investigation to almost its last hand's-breadth of a conclusion,—but. . . pardon me,—I should scarcely think the discussion of such debatable theories conducive to happiness!"

"Happiness!" . . . and the scientist smiled scornfully,—"'Tis a fool's term, and designates a state of being that can only pertain to foolishness! Show me a perfectly happy man, and I will show you an ignorant witling, light-headed, hardhearted, and of a most powerfully good digestion! Many such there be now wantoning among us, and the head and chief of them all is perhaps the most popular numskull in Al-Kyris, . . . the Poet,—bah! . . . let us say the braying Jack-ass in office,—the laurelled Sah-luma!"

Theos gave an indignant start,—the hot color flushed his brows, . . . then he restrained himself by an effort.

"Control the fashion of your speech, I pray you, sir!" he said, with excessive haughtiness—"The noble Laureate is my friend and host,—I suffer no man to use his name unworthily in my presence!"

The sage drew back, and spread out his hands in a pacifying manner.

"Oh, I crave your pardon, good stranger!"—he murmured, with a kind of apologetic satire in his acrid voice,—"I crave it most abjectly! Yet to somewhat excuse the hastiness of my words, I would explain that a contempt for poets and poetry is now universal among persons of profound enlightenment and practical knowledge. . ."

"I am aware of it!" interrupted Theos swiftly and with passion—"I am aware that so-called 'wise' men, rooted in narrow prejudice, with a smattering of even narrower logic, presume, out of their immeasurable littleness, to decry and make mock of the truly great, who, thanks to God's unpurchasable gift of inspiration, can do without the study of books or the teaching of pedants,—who flare through the world flame-winged and full of song, like angels passing heavenward,—and whose voices, rich with music, not only sanctify the by-gone ages, but penetrate with echoing, undying sweetness the ages still to come! Contempt for poets!—Aye, 'tis common!—the petty, boastful pedagogues of surface learning ever look askance on these kings in exile, these emperors masked, these gods disguised! . . . but humiliated, condemned, or rejected, they are still the supreme rulers of the human heart,—and a Love-Ode chanted in the Long-Ago by one such fire-lipped minstrel outlasts the history of many kingdoms!"

He spoke with rapid, almost unconscious fervor, and as he ended raised one hand with an enthusiastic gesture toward the now brilliant sapphire sky and glowing sun. The scientist looked at him furtively and smiled,—a bland, expostulatory smile.

"Oh, you are young!—you must be very young!" he said forbearingly. "In a little time you will grow out of all this ill-judged fanaticism for an Art, the pursuance of which is really only wasted labor! Think of the absurdity of it!—what can be more foolish than the writing of verse to express or to encourage emotion in the human subject, when the great aim of education at the present day is to carefully eradicate emotion by degrees, till we succeed in completely suppressing it! An outburst of feeling is always vulgar,—the highest culture consists in being impassively equable of temperament, and absolutely indifferent to the attacks of either joy or sorrow. I should be inclined to ask you to consider this matter more seriously, and from the strictly common-sense point of view, did I not know that for you to undertake a course of useful meditation while you remain is Sah-luma's companionship would be impossible, . . . quite impossible! Nevertheless our discourse has been so far interesting, that I shall be happy to meet you again and give you an opportunity for further converse should you desire it, . . . ask for the Head Professor of Scientific Positivism, any day in the Strangers' Court of the Royal Institutional College, and I will at once receive you! My name is Mira-Khabur,—Professor Mira Khabur. . . at your service!"

And laying one hand on his breast he bowed profoundly.

"A Professor of Positivism who is himself never positive!"—observed Theos with a slight smile.

"Ah pardon!" returned the other gravely—"On the contrary, I am always positive! . . . of the UNpositiveness of Positivism!"

And with this final vindication of his theories he made another stately obeisance and went his way. Theos looked after his tall, retreating figure half in sadness, half in scorn. This proudly incompetent, learned-ignorant Mira-Khabur was no uncommon character—surely there were many like him!

Somewhere in the world,—somewhere in far lands of which the memory was now as indistinct as the outline of receding shores blurred by a falling mist, Theos seemed painfully to call to mind certain cold-blooded casuists he had known, who had attempted to explain away the mysteries of life and death by rule and line calculations, and who for no other reason than their mathematically argued denial of God's existence had gained for themselves a temporary, spurious celebrity. Yes! . . . surely he had met such men, . . . but WHERE? Realizing, with a sort of shock, that he was quite as much in the dark as ever with regard to any real cognizance of his former place of abode and the manner of life he must have led before he entered this bewildering city of Al-Kyris, he roused himself abruptly, and resolutely banishing the heavy thoughts that threatened to oppress his soul, he began without further delay to direct his steps towards Sah-luma's palace.

He glanced once more at the river before leaving the embankment,—it was still blood red, and every now and then, between the sluggish ripples, multitudes of dead fish could be seen drifting along in shoals, and tangled in nets of slimy weed that at a little distance looked like the floating tresses of drowned women.

It was an uncanny sight, and though it might certainly be as the wise Mira Khabur had stated, the purely natural effect of purely natural causes, still those natural causes were not as yet explained satisfactorily. An earthquake or land-slip would perhaps account sufficiently for everything,—but then an inquiring mind would desire to know WHERE the earthquake or land-slip occurred,—and also WHY these supposed far-off disturbances should thus curiously affect the river surrounding Al-Kyris? Answers to such questions as these were not forthcoming either from Professor Mira-Khabur or any other sagacious pundit,—and Theos was therefore still most illogically and unscientifically puzzled as well as superstitiously uneasy.

Turning up a side street, he quickened his pace, in order to overtake a young vendor of wines whom he perceived sauntering along in front of him, balancing a flat tray, loaded with thin crystal flasks, on his head. How gloriously the sunshine quivered through those delicately tinted glass bottles, lighting up the glittering liquid contained within them!— why, they look more like soap-bubbles than anything else! . . . and the boy who carried them moved with such a lazy, noiseless grace that he might have been taken for a dream-sylph rather than a human being!

"Hola, my lad!" called Theos, running after him. "Tell me,—is this the way to the palace of the King's Laureate?"

The youth looked up,—what a beautiful creature he was, with his brilliant, dark eyes and dusky, warm complexion!

"Why ask for the King's Laureate?" he demanded with a pretty scorn,—"The PEOPLE's Sah-luma lives yonder!"—and he pointed to a mass of towering palms from whose close and graceful frondage a white dome rose glistening in the clear air,—"Our Poet's fame is not the outgrowth of a mere king's favor, 'tis the glad and willing tribute of the Nation's love and praise! A truce to monarchs!—they will soon be at a discount in Al-Kyris!"

And with a flashing glance of defiance, and a saucy smile, he passed on, easily sauntering as before.

"A budding republican!" though Theos amusedly, as he pursued his course in the direction indicated. "That is how the 'liberty, equality, fraternity' system always begins—first among street-boys who think they ought to be gentlemen,—then among shopkeepers who persuade themselves that they deserve to be peers,—then comes a time of topsey-turveydom and fierce contention and by and by everything gets shaken together again in the form of a Republic, wherein the street-boys and shopkeepers are not a whit better off than they were under a monarchy—they become neither peers nor gentlemen, but stay exactly in their original places, with the disadvantage of finding their trade decidedly damaged by the change that has occurred in the national economy! Strange that the inhabitants of this world should make such a fuss about resisting tyranny and oppression, when each particular individual man, by custom and usage, tyrannizes over and oppresses his fellow-man to an extent that would be simply impossible to the fiercest kings!"

Thus meditating a few steps more brought him to the entrance of Sah-luma's princely abode,—the gates stood wide open, and a pleasant murmur of laughter and soft singing floated toward him across the splendid court where the great fountains were tossing up to the bright sky their straight, glistening columns of snowy spray. He listened,— and his heart leaped with an intense relief and joy,—Sah-luma, the beloved Sah-luma, was evidently at home and as yet unharmed,—these mirthful sounds betokened that all was well. The vague trouble and depression that had weighed upon his soul for hours now vanished completely, and hastening along, he sprang lightly up the marble stairs, and into the rainbow-colored, spacious hall, where the first person he saw was Zabastes the Critic.

"Ah, good Zabastes!" he cried gayly,—"Where is thy master Sah-luma? Has he returned in safety?"

"In safety?" croaked Zabastes with an accent of ironic surprise. "To be sure! . . . Is he a baby in swaddling-clothes that he cannot be trusted out alone to take care of himself? In safety?—aye! I warrant you he is safe enough, and silly enough, and lazy enough to please any one of his idiot flatterers, . . . moreover my 'master!'"—and he emphasized this word with indescribable bitterness—"hath slept as soundly as a swine, and hath duly bathed with the punctiliousness of a conceited swan, and being suitably combed, perfumed, attired, and throned as becomes his dainty puppetship, is now condescending to partake of vulgar food in the seclusion of his own apartment. Go thither and you shall find his verse-stringing Mightiness nobly enshrined as a god among a worshipping crowd of witless maidens,—he hath inquired for you many times, which is somewhat of a wonder, seeing that as a rule he concerns his mind with naught save himself! Furthermore, he is graciously pleased to be in a manner solicitous on behalf of the maiden Niphrata, who hath suddenly disappeared from the household, leaving no message to explain the cause of her evanishment. Hath seen her? . . . No?"—and the old man thumped his stick petulantly on the floor as Theos shook his head in the negative—"'Tis the only feminine creature I ever had patience to speak with,—a modest wench and a gentle one, and were it not for her idolatrous adoration of Sah-luma, she would be fairly sensible withal. No matter!—she has gone; everything goes, even good women, and nothing lasts save folly, of which there shall surely never be an end!"

Here apparently conscious that he had shown more feeling in speaking of Niphrata than was usual with him, he looked up impatiently and waved his staff toward Sah-luma's study; "In, in, boy! In, to, the

Chief of poets and prince of egotists! He waits your service,—he is all agape and thirsty for more flattery and delicate cajolement, . . . stuff him with praise, good youth! . . . and who knows but a portion of his mantle may descend on You hereafter and make of You as conceited and pretty a bantling bard for the glory of proud posterity!"

And chuckling audibly, he hobbled down a side passage, while Theos, half angry, half amused, crossed the hall quickly, and arrived at the door of the Laureate's private sanctum, where, gently drawing aside the silken draperies, he looked in for a moment without being himself perceived. What a picture he beheld! . . . How perfection every shade of color in every line of detail! Sah-luma, reclining in a quaintly carved ebony chair, was toying with the fruit and wine set out before him on an ivory and gold stand,—his dress, simpler than it had been on the previous evening, was of fine white linen gathered loosely about his classic figure,—he wore neither myrtle-wreath nor jewels,—the expression of his face was serious, even noble, and his attitude was one of languid grace and unstudied ease that became him infinitely well. The maidens of his household waited near him,—some of them held flowers,—one, kneeling at a small lyre, seemed just about to strike a few chords, when Sah-luma silenced her by a light gesture:

"Peace, Zoralin!" he said softly. "I cannot listen: thou hast not my Niphrata's tenderness!"

Zoralin, a beautiful, dark girl, with hair as black as night, and eyes that looked as though they held suppressed yet ever burning fire, let her hands instantly drop from the instrument, and sighing, shrank back a little in abashed silence. At that moment Theos advanced,—and the Laureate sprang up delightedly:

"Ah, at last, my friend!" he cried, enthusiastically clasping him by both hands,—"Where, in the name of all the gods, hast thou been roaming? How did we part?—by my soul I forget!—but no matter!—thou art here once more, and as I live, we will not separate again so easily! My noble Theos!" and he threw one arm affectionately around his neck—"I have missed thee more than I can tell these past few hours,—thou dost seem so sympathetically conjoined with me, that verily I think I am but half myself in thine absence! Come,—sit thee down and break thy fast! . . . I almost feared thou hadst met with some mischance on thy way hither, and that I should have had to sally forth and rescue thee again even as I did yesternoon! Say, hast thou occupied thyself with so much friendly consideration on my behalf, as I have on thine?"

MARIE CORELLI

He laughed gayly as he spoke,—and Theos, looking into his bright, beautiful face, was for a moment too deeply moved by his own strange inward emotions, to utter a word in reply. WHY did he love Sah-luma so ardently, he wondered? WHY was it that every smile on that proud mouth, every glance of those flashing eyes, possessed such singular, overwhelming fascination for him? He could not tell,—but he readily yielded to the magic influence of his friend's extraordinary attractiveness, and sitting down beside him in the azure light and soft fragrance of his regal apartment, he experienced a sudden sense of rest, satisfaction, and completeness, such as may be felt by a man AT ONE WITH HIMSELF, and with all the world!

XXII

WASTED PASSION

The assembled maidens had retired modestly into the background, while the Laureate had thus joyously greeted his returned guest; but now, at a signal from their lord, they again advanced, and taking up the glittering dishes of fruit and the flasks of wine, proffered them in turn to Theos with much deferential grace and courtesy. He was by no means slow in responding to the humble attentions of these fair ones, . . . there was a sort of deliciously dreamy enchantment in being waited upon by such exquisitely lovely creatures! The passing touch of their little white hands that supported the heavy golden salvers seemed to add new savor to the luscious fare,—the timorous fire of their downcast eyes, softly sparkling through the veil of their long lashes, gave extra warmth to the ambrosial wine,—and he could not refrain from occasionally whispering a tender flattery or delicate compliment in the ear of one or other of his sylph-like servitors, though they all appeared curiously unmoved by his choicely worded adulation. Now and then a pale, flickering blush or sudden smile brightened their faces, but for the most part they maintained a demure and serious demeanor, as though possessed by the very spirit of invincible reserve. With Sah-luma it was otherwise,—they hovered about him like butterflies round a rose,—a thousand wistful, passionate glances darted upon him, when he, unconscious or indifferent, apparently saw nothing,—many a deep, involuntary sigh was stifled quickly ere it could escape between the rosy lips whose duty it was to wreathe themselves with smiles, and Theos noticing these things thought:

"Heavens! how this man is loved!—and yet. . . he, out of all men, is perhaps the most ignorant of Love's true meaning!"

Scarcely had this reflection entered his mind than he became bitterly angry with himself for having indulged in it. How recreant, how base an idea! . . . how incompatible with the adoring homage he felt for his friend! What!—Sah-luma,—a Poet, whose songs of Love were so perfect, so wildly sweet and soul-entrancing—HE, to be ignorant of Love's true meaning? . . . Oh, impossible!—and a burning flush of shame rose to Theos's brow,—shame that he could have entertained such a blasphemy against his Idol for a moment! Then that curious, vague, soft contrition he had before experienced stole over him once again—a sudden moisture filled his eyes,—and turning abruptly toward his host he held out his own just filled goblet:

"Drink we the loving-cup together, Sah-luma!" he said, and his voice trembled a little with its own deep tenderness, . . . "Pledge me thy faith as I do pledge thee mine! And for to-day at least let me enjoy thy boon companionship, . . . who knows how soon we may be forced to part. . . forever!" And he breathed the last word softly with a faint sigh.

Sah-luma looked at him with an expressive glance of bright surprise.

"Part?" he exclaimed joyously—"Nay, not we, my friend! . . . Not till we find each other tiresome, . . . not till we prove that our spirits, like over-mettlesome steeds, do chafe and fret one another too rudely in the harness of custom, . . . wherefore then, and then only, 'twill be time to break loose at a gallop, and seek each one a wider pasture-land! Meanwhile, here's to thee!"—and bending his handsome head he readily drank a deep draught of the proffered wine. . . "May all the gods hold fast our bond of friendship!"

And with a graceful salute he returned the jewelled cup half-empty. Theos at once drained off what yet remained within it, and then, leaning more confidentially over the Laureate's chair, he whispered:

"Hast thou in very truth forgotten thy rashness of last night, Sah-luma? Surely thou must guess how unquiet I have been concerning thee! Tell me, . . . was thy hot pursuit in vain? . . . or. . . didst thou discover the King?"

"Peace!" and a quick frown darkened the smooth beauty of Sah-luma's face as he grasped Theos's arm hard to warn him into silence,—then forcing a smile he answered in the same low tone. "'Twas not the King, . . . it could not be! Thou wert mistaken. . ."

"Nay but," persisted Theos gently—"convince me of mine error! Didst thou overtake and steadily confront yon armed and muffled stranger?"

"Not I!"—and Sah-luma shrugged his shoulders petulantly—"Sleep fell upon me suddenly when I left thee,—and methinks I must have wandered home like a shadow in a dream! Was I not drunk last night?—Aye!—and so in all likelihood wert thou! . . . little could we be trusted to recognize either King or clown!"—He laughed,—then added—"Nevertheless I tell thee once again 'twas not the King, . . . His Majesty hath too much at stake, to risk so dangerous a pleasantry!"

Theos heard, but he was dissatisfied and ill at ease, . . . Sah-luma's careless contentment increased his own disquietude. Just then a curious-looking personage entered the apartment,—a gray-haired, dwarfish negro, who carried slung across his back a large bundle, consisting of several neatly rolled-up pieces of linen, one of which he presently detached from the rest and set down before the Laureate, who in return gave him a silver coin, at the same time asking jestingly:

"Is the news worth paying for to-day, Zibya?—or is it the same ill-written, clumsy chronicle of trumpery, common-place events?"

Zibya, slipping the coin he had received into a wide leathern pouch which hung from his girdle, appeared to meditate a moment,—then he replied:

"If the truth must be told, most illustrious, there is nothing whatever to interest the minds of the cultured. The cheap scribes of the Daily Circular cater chiefly for the mob, and do all in their power to foster morbid qualities of disposition and murderous tendencies among the lower orders; hence though there is nothing in the news-sheet pertaining to Literature or the Fine Arts, there is much concerning the sudden death of the young sculptor Nir-jalis, whose body was found flung on the banks of the river this morning."

Theos started, . . . Sah-luma listened with placid indifference. "'Tis a case of self-slaughter"—pursued Zibya chattily. . . "or so say the wise writers who are supposed to know everything, . . . self-slaughter committed during a state of temporary insanity! Well, well! I myself would have had a different opinion."

"And a sagacious one no doubt!" interrupted Sah-luma coldly, and with a dangerous flash as of steel in his eyes. "But. . . be advised, good Zibya! . . . give thine opinion no utterance!"

The old negro shrank back nervously, making numerous apologetic gestures, and waited in abashed silence till the Laureate's features regained their wonted soft serenity. Then he ventured to speak again,— though not without a little hesitation.

"Concerning the topics of the hour. . ." he murmured timorously. "My lord is perhaps not aware that the river itself is a subject of much excited discussion,—the water having changed to a marvellous blood-color during the night, which singular circumstance hath caused a great panic among the populace. Even now, as I passed by the embankment, the crowd there was thick as a hive of swarming bees!"

He paused, but Sah-luma made no remark, and he continued

more glibly, "Also, to-day's 'Circular' contains the full statement of the King's reward for the capture of the Prophet Khosrul, and the formal Programme of the Sacrificial Ceremonial announced to take place this evening in the Temple of Nagaya. All is set forth in the fine words of the petty public scribes, who needs must make as much as possible out of little,—and there is likewise a so-called facsimile of the King's signature, which will naturally be of supreme interest to the vulgar. Furthermore it is proclaimed that a grand Combat of wild beasts in the Royal Arena will follow immediately after the Service in the Temple is concluded,—methinks none will go to bed early, seeing there is so full a list of amusements!"

He paused again, somewhat out of breath,—and Sah-luma meanwhile unrolled the linen scroll he had purchased, which measured about twenty-four inches in length and twenty in width. Carefully ruled black and red lines divided it into nearly the same number of columns as those on the page of an ordinary newspaper, and it was covered with close writing, here and there embellished by bold, profusely ornamented headings. One of these, "Death of the Sculptor, Nir-jalis," seemed to burn into Theos's brain like letters of fire,—how was it, he wondered, that the body of that unfortunate victim had been found on the shore of the river, when he himself had seen it loaded with iron weights, and cast into the lake that formed part of Lysia's fatal garden? Presently Sah-luma passed the scroll to him with a smile, saying lightly:

"There, my friend, is a specimen of the true mob-literature! . . . written to-day, forgotten to-morrow! 'Tis a droll thing to meditate upon, the ephemeral nature of all this pouring-out of unnecessary words and stale stock-phrases!—and, wouldst thou believe it, Theos! each little paid scribe that adds his poor quota to this ill-assorted trash deems himself wiser and greater far than any poet or philosopher dead or living! Why, in this very news-sheet I have seen the immortal works of the divine Hyspiros so hacked by the blunt knives of ignorant and vulgar criticism that, by my faith! . . . were it not for contempt, one would be disposed to nail the hands of such trumpery scribblers to a post, and scourge their bare backs with thorny rods to cure them of their insolence! Nay, even my fool Zabastes hath found place in these narrow columns, to write his carping diatribes against me,—me, the King's Laureate! . . . As I live, his cumbersome diction hath caused me infinite mirth, and I have laughed at his crabbed and feeble wit till my sides have ached most potently! Now get thee gone, fellow!—thou and thy news!"—and he nodded a good-humored dismissal to the deferential Zibya, who with his woolly gray head very much on one side stood listening gravely and approvingly to all that was said,—"Yet stay! . . . has gossip whispered thee the name of the poor virgin self-destined for this evening's sacrifice?"

"No, my lord"—responded Zibya promptly—"'Tis veiled in deeper mystery than usual. I have inquired of many, but in vain,—and even the Chief Flamen of the Outside Court of the Temple, always drunk and garrulous as he is, can tell me naught of the holy victim's title or parentage. 'Tis a passing fair wench!' said he, with a chuckle. 'That is all I know concerning her. . . a passing fair wench!' Ah!" and Zibya rolled up the whites of his eyes and sighed in a comically contemplative manner. "If ever a Flamen deserved expulsion from his office, it is surely yon ancient, crafty, carnal-minded soul! . . . so keen a glance for a woman's beauty is not a needful qualification for a servant of the Snake Divine! Methinks we have fallen upon evil days! . . . maybe the crazed Prophet is right after all, and things are coming to an end!"

"Like thy discourse, I hope, Zibya!" observed Sah-luma, yawning and flinging himself lazily back on his velvet couch,—"Get hence, and serve thy customers with their cheap news, . . . depend upon it, some of them are cursing thee mightily for thy delay! And if thou shouldst chance to meet the singing-maiden of my household, Niphrata, bid her make haste homeward,—she hath been absent since the break of morn,—too long for my contentment. Maybe I did unwisely to give the child her freedom,—as slave she would not have presumed to gad abroad thus wantonly, without her lord's permission. Say, if thou seest her, that I am wrathful,—the thought of mine anger will be as a swift wing to waft her hither like a trembling dove,—afraid, all penitent, and eager for my pardon! Remember! . . . be sure thou tell her of my deep displeasure!"

Zibya bowed profoundly, his outspread hands almost touching the floor in the servility of his obeisance, and backed out of the room as humbly as though he were leaving the presence of royalty. When he had gone, Theos looked up from the news-scroll he was perusing:

"Is it not strange Niphrata should have left thee thus, Sah-luma?" . . . he said with a touch of anxiety in his tone. . . "Maybe" . . . and he hesitated, conscious of a strange, unbidden remorse that suddenly and without any apparent reason overwhelmed his conscience. "Maybe she was not happy?" . . .

"Not happy!" exclaimed Sah-luma amazedly, "Not happy with

ME? . . . not happy in MY house,—protected by MY patronage? Where then, if not here, could she find happiness?"

And his beautiful flashing eyes betokened his entire and naive astonishment at the mere supposition. Theos smiled involuntarily. . . how, charming, after all was Sah-luma's sublime egotism!—how almost child-like was his confidence in himself and his own ability to engender joy! All at once the young girl Zoralin spoke,—her accents were low and timorous:

"May it please my lord Sah-luma to hear me. . ." she said and paused.

"Thy lord Sah-luma hears thee with pleasure, Zoralin," replied the Laureate gently. "Thou dost speak more sweetly than many a bird doth sing!"

A rich, warm blush crimsoned the maiden's cheeks at these dulcet words,—she drew a quick, uneasy breath, and then went on,—

"I love Niphrata!" she murmured in a soft tone of touching tenderness, . . . "And I have watched her often when she deemed herself unseen, . . . she has, methinks, shed many tears for sake of some deep, heart-buried sorrow! We have lived as sisters, sharing the same room, and the same couch of sleep, but alas! in spite of all my lord's most constant kindly favor, Niphrata is not happy, . . . and. . . and I have sometimes thought—" here her mellow voice sank into a nervous indistinctness— "that it may be because she loves my lord Sah-luma far too well!"

And as she said this she looked up with a sudden affright in her dark, lovely eyes, as though she were alarmed at her own presumption. Sah-luma met her troubled gaze calmly and with a bright smile of complacent vanity.

"And dost thou plead for thine absent friend, Zoralin?" . . . he asked with just sufficient satire in his utterance to render it almost cruel. "Am I to blame for the foolish fancies of all the amorous maidens in Al-Kyris? . . . Many there be who love me, . . . well,—what then?—Must I love many in return? Nay! Not so! the Poet is the worshiper of Ideal Beauty, and for him the brief passions of mortal men and women serve as mere pastime to while away an hour! But. . . by my faith, thou hast gained wondrous boldness in thy speech to prate so glibly of the heart's emotion,—what knowest THOU concerning such things. . . thou, who hast counted scarcely fifteen summers! . . . hast thou caught contagion from Niphrata, and art thou too, sick of love?"

Oh, the dazzling smile with which he accompanied this poignant question! . . . the pitiless, burning ardor he managed to convey into the sleeping brilliancy of his soft, poetic eyes! . . . the beautiful languor of his attitude, as leaning his head back easily on one arm, he turned upon the shrinking girl a look that seemed intended to pierce into the very inmost recesses of her soul! The roseate color faded from her cheeks, . . . white as a marble image she stood, her breath coming between her lips in quick, frightened gasps. . .

"My lord! . . ." she stammered. . . "I. . ." Here her voice failed her, and suddenly covering her face with her hands, she broke into a passion of weeping. Sah-luma's delicate brows darkened into a close frown,— and he waved his hand with a petulant gesture of impatience.

"Ye gods! what fools are women!" he said wearily. "Ever hovering uncertainly on a narrow verge between silly smiles and sillier tears! As I live, they are most uncomfortable play-fellows!—and dwelling with them long would drive all the inspiration out of man, no matter how nobly he were gifted! Ye butterflies—ye little fluttering souls!" and beginning to laugh as readily as he had frowned, he addressed the other maidens, who, though they did not dare to move or speak, were evidently affected by the grief of their companion—"Go hence all!-and take this sensitive baby, Zoralin, into your charge, and console her for her fancied troubles—'tis a mere frenzy of feminine weakness, and will pass like an April shower. But, . . . by the Sacred Veil!—if I saw much of woman's weeping, I would discard forever woman's company, and dwell in peaceful hermit fashion alone among the treetops! . . . so heed the warning, pretty ones! . . . Let me witness none of your tears if ye are wise,—or else say farewell to Sah-luma, and seek some less easy and less pleasing service!"

With this injunction he signed to them all to depart,—whereupon the awed and trembling girls noiselessly surrounded the still convulsively sobbing Zoralin, and gently leading her away, they quickly withdrew, each one making a profound obeisance to their imperious master ere leaving his presence. When they had finally disappeared Sah-luma heaved a sigh of relief.

"Can anything equal the perverseness of these frivolous feminine toys!" he murmured pettishly, turning his head round toward Theos as he spoke—"Was ever a more foolish child than Zoralin? . . . Just as I would fain have consoled her for her pricking heartache, she must needs pour out a torrent of tear-drops to change my humor and quench her own delight! 'Tis the most irksome inconsistency!"

Theos glanced at him with a vague emotion of wonder and self-reproachful sadness.

"Nay, wouldst thou indeed have consoled her, Sah-luma?" he inquired gravely, "How?"

"How?" and Sah-luma laughed musically. "My simple friend, dost thou ask me such a babe's question?" . . . He sprang from his couch, and standing erect, pushed his clustering dark hair off his wide, bold brows. "Am I disfigured, aged, lame, or crooked-limbed? . . . Cannot these arms embrace?—these lips engender kisses?—these eyes wax amorous? . . . and shall not one brief hour of love with me console the weariest maid that ever pined for passion? . . . Now, by my faith, how solemn is thy countenance! . . . Art thou an anchorite, good Theos, and wouldst thou have me scourge my flesh and groan, because the gods have given me youth and vigorous manhood?"

He drew himself up with an inimitable gesture of pride,—his attitude was statuesque and noble,—and Theos looked at him as he would have looked at a fine picture, with a sense of critically satisfied admiration.

"Most assuredly I am no anchorite, Sah-luma!" he said smiling slightly, yet with a touch of sorrow in his voice. "But methinks the consolement thou wouldst offer to enamoured maids is far more dangerous than lasting! Thy love to them means ruin,—thy embraces shame,—thy unthinking passion death! What!—wilt thou be a spendthrift of desire?—wilt thou drain the fond souls of women as a bee drains the sweetness of flowers?—wilt thou, being honey-cloyed, behold them droop and wither around thee, and wilt thou leave them utterly destroyed and desolate? Hast thou no vestige of a heart, my friend? a poet-heart, to feel the misery of the world? . . . the patient grief of all-appealing Nature, commingled with the dreadful, yet majestic silence of an unknown God? . . . Oh, surely, thou hast this supremest gift of genius, . . . this loving, enduring, faithful, sympathetic HEART! . . . for without it, how shall thy fame be held long in remembrance? . . . how shall thy muse-grown laurels escape decay? Tell me! . . ." and leaning forward he caught his friend's hand in his eagerness. "Thou art not made of stone, . . . thou art human, . . . thou art not exempt from mortal suffering. . ."

"Not exempt—no!" interposed Sah-luma thoughtfully. . . "But, as yet,—I have never really suffered!"

"Never really suffered!" . . . Theos dropped the hand he held, and an invisible barrier seemed to rise slowly up between him and his beautiful companion. Never really suffered! . . . then he was no true poet after all, if he was ignorant of sorrow! If he could not spiritually enter into the pathos of speechless griefs and unshed tears,—if he could not absorb into his own being the prayers and plaints of all Creation, and utter them aloud in burning and immortal language, his calling was in vain, his election futile! This thought smote Theos with the strength of a sudden blow,—he sat silent, and weighed with a dreary feeling of disappointment to which he was unable to give any fitting expression.

"I have never really suffered. . ." repeated Sah-luma slowly: . . . "But—I have IMAGINED suffering! That is enough for me! The passions, the tortures, the despairs of imagination are greater far than the seeming REAL, petty afflictions with which human beings daily perplex themselves; indeed, I have often wondered. . ." here his eyes grew more earnest and reflective. . . "whether this busy working of the brain called 'Imagination' may not perhaps be a special phase or supreme effort of MEMORY, and that therefore we do not IMAGINE so much as we remember. For instance,—if we have ever lived before, our present recollection may, in certain exalted states of the mind, serve to bring back the shadow-pictures of things long gone by, . . . good or evil deeds, . . . scenes of love and strife, . . . ethereal and divine events, in which we have possibly enacted each our different parts as unwittingly as we enact them here!" He sighed and seemed somewhat troubled, but presently continued in a lighter tone. "Yet, after all, it is not necessary for the poet to personally experience the emotions whereof he writes. The divine Hyspiros depicts murderers, cowards, and slaves in his sublime Tragedies,—but thinkest thou it was essential for him to become a murderer, coward, and slave himself in order to delineate these characters? And I. . . I write of Love,—love spiritual, love eternal,—love fitted for the angels I have dreamt of—but not for such animals as men,—and what matters it that I know naught of such love, . . . unless perchance I knew it years ago in some far-off fairer sphere! . . . For me the only charm of worth in woman is beauty! . . . Beauty! . . . to its entrancing sway my senses all make swift surrender. . ."

"Oh, too swift and too degrading a surrender!" interrupted Theos suddenly with reproachful vehemence. . . "Thy words do madden patience!—Better a thousand times that thou shouldst perish, Sah-lama, now in the full plenitude of thy poet-glory, than thus confess thyself a prey to thine own passions,—a credulous victim of Lysia's treachery!"

For one second the Laureate stood amazed, . . . the next, he sprang upon his guest and grasping him fiercely by the throat.

MARIE CORELLI

"Treachery?" he muttered with white lips. "Treachery? . . . Darest thou speak of treachery and Lysia in the same breath? . . . O thou rash fool! dost thou blaspheme my lady's name and yet not fear to die?"

And his lithe brown fingers tightened their clutch. But Theos cared nothing for his own life,—some inward excitation of feeling kept him resolute and perfectly controlled.

"Kill me, Sah-luma!" he gasped—"Kill me, friend whom I love! . . . death will be easy at thy hands! Deprive me of my sad existence, . . . 'tis better so, than that *I* should have slain THEE last night at Lysia's bidding!"

At this, Sah-luma suddenly released his hold and started backward with a sharp cry of anguish, . . . his face was pale, and his beautiful eyes grew strained and piteous.

"Slain ME! . . . Me! . . . at Lysia's bidding!" he murmured wildly. "O ye gods, the world grows dark! is the sun quenched in heaven? . . . At Lysia's bidding! . . . Nay, . . . by my soul, my sight is dimmed! . . . I see naught but flaring red in the air, . . . Why! . . ." and he laughed discordantly. . . "thou poor Theos, thou shalt use no dagger's point,—for lo! . . . I am dead already! . . . Thy words have killed me! Go, . . . tell her how well her cruel mission hath sped,—my very soul is slain. . . at her bidding! Hasten to her, wilt thou!" . . . and his accents trembled with pathetic plaintiveness! . . . "Say I am gone! . . . lost! drawn into a night of everlasting blackness like a taper blown swiftly out by the wind, . . . tell her that Sah-luma,—the poet Sah-luma, the foolish-credulous Sah-luma who loved her so madly is no more!"

His voice broke, . . . his head drooped, . . . while Theos, whose every nerve throbbed in responsive sympathy with the passion of his despair, strove to think of some word of comfort, that like soothing balm might temper the bitterness of his chafed and wounded spirit, but could find none. For it was a case in which the truth must be told, . . . and truth is always hard to bear if it destroys, or attempts to destroy, any one of our cherished self-delusions!

"My friend, my friend!" he said presently with gentle earnestness,— "Control this fury of thy heart! . . . Why such unmanly sorrow for one who is not worthy of thee?"

Sah-luma looked up,—his black, silky lashes were wet with tears.

"Not worthy! . . . Oh, the old poor consolation!" he exclaimed, quickly dashing the drops from his eyes, . . . "Not worthy?—No! . . . what mortal woman Is ever worthy of a poet's love?—Not one in all the world! Nevertheless, worthy or unworthy, true or treacherous, naught can make Lysia otherwise than fair! Fair beyond all fairness! . . . and I—I was sole possessor of her beauty!—for me her eyes warmed into stars of fire,—for me her kisses ripened in their pearl and ruby nest, . . . all—all for me!—and now! . . ." He flung himself desolately on his couch, and fixed his wistful gaze on his companion's grave, pained countenance,—till all at once a hopeful light flashed across his features, . . . a light that seemed to shine through him like an inwardly kindled flame.

"Ah! what a querulous fool am I!" he cried, joyously,—so joyously that Theos knew not whether to be glad or sorry at his sudden and capricious change of mood. . . "why should I thus bemoan myself for fancied wrong?—Good, noble Theos, thou hast been misled!—My Lysia's words were but to try thy mettle! . . . to test thee to the core, and prove thee truly faithful as Sah-luma's friend! She bade thee slay me! . . . Even so!—but hadst thou rashly undertaken such a deed, thine own life would have paid the forfeit! Now I begin to understand it all—'tis plain!"—and his face grew brighter and brighter, as he cheated himself into the pleasing idea his own fancy had suggested. "She tried thee,—she tempted thee, . . . she found thee true and incorruptible. Ah! 'twas a jest, my friend!"—and entirely recovering from his depression, he clapped his hand heartily on Theos's shoulder— "'Twas all a jest!—and she the fair inquisitor will herself prove it so ere long, and make merry with our ill-omened fears! Why, I can laugh now at mine own despondency!— come, look thou also more cheerily, gentle Theos,—and pardon these uncivil fingers that so nearly gripped thee into silence!"—and he laughed—"Thou art the best and kindest of loyal comrades, and I will so assure Lysia of thy merit, that she shall institute no more torture-trials upon thy frank and trusting nature. Heigho!"—and stretching out his arms lazily, he heaved a sigh of tranquil satisfaction—"Methought I was wounded into death! but 'twas the mere fancied prick of an arrow after all, and I am well again! What, art thou still melancholy! . . . still sombre! . . . Nay, surely thou wilt not be a veritable kill-joy!"

Theos stood mute and sorely perplexed. He saw at once how useless it was now to try and convince Sah luma of any danger threatening him through the instigation of the woman he loved,—he would never believe it! And yet. . . something must be done to put him on his guard. Taking up the scroll of the public news, where the account of the finding of the body of Nir-jalis was written with all that exaggerated attention to repulsive details which seems to be a special gift of the cheap reporters, Theos pointed to it.

"His was a cruel end!"—he said in a low, uncertain voice,—"Sah-luma, canst thou expect mercy from a woman who has once been so merciless?"

"Bah!" returned the Laureate lightly. "Who and what was Nir-jalis? A hewer of stone images—a no-body!—he will not be missed! Besides, he is only one of many who have perished thus."

"Only one of many!" exclaimed Theos with a shudder of aversion. "And yet, ... O thou most reckless and misguided soul! . . . thou dost love this wanton murderess!"

A warm flush tinted Sah-luma's olive skin,—his hands clenched and unclenched slowly as though he held some struggling, prisoned thing, and raising his head he looked at his companion full and steady with a singularly solemn and reproving expression in his luminous eyes.

"Hast THOU not loved her also?" he demanded, a faint, serious smile curving his lips as he spoke, . . . "If only for the space of some few passing moments, was not thy soul ravished, thy heart enslaved, thy manhood conquered by her spell? . . . Aye! . . . Thou dost shrink at that!" And his smile deepened as Theos, suddenly conscience-stricken, avoided his friend's too-scrutinizing gaze. "Blame ME not, therefore, for THINE OWN weakness!"

He paused. . . then went on slowly with a meditative air. "I love her, . . . yes!—as a man must always love the woman that baffles him, . . . the woman whose moods are complex and fluctuating as the winds on the sea,—and whose humor sways between the softness of the dove and the fierceness of the tiger. Nothing is more fatally fascinating to the masculine sense than such a creature,—more especially if to this temperament is united rare physical grace, combined with keen intellectual power. 'Tis vain to struggle against the irresistible witchery exercised over us by the commingling of beauty and ferocity,—we see it in the wild animals of the forest and the high-soaring birds of the air,—and we like nothing better than to hunt it, capture it, tame it. . . or. . . kill it—as suits our pleasure!"

He paused again,—and again smiled, . . . a grave, reluctant, doubting smile such as seemed to Theos oddly familiar, suggesting to his bewildered fancy that he must have seen it before, ON HIS OWN FACE, reflected in a mirror!

"Even thus do I love Lysia!" continued Sah-luma—"She perplexes me, . . . she opposes her will to mine, . . . the very irritation and ferment into which I am thrown by her presence adds fire to my genius, . . . and but for the spur of this never-satiated passion, who knows whether I should sing so well!"

He was silent for a little space—then he resumed in a more ordinary tone:

"The wretched Nir-jalis, whose fate thou dost so persistently deplore, deserved his end for his presumption, . . . didst thou not hear his insolent insinuation concerning the King?"

"I heard it—yes!" replied Theos—"And I saw no harm in the manner of his utterance."

"No harm!" exclaimed Sah-luma excitedly—"No harm! Nay, but I forget! . . . thou art a stranger in Al-Kyris, and therefore thou art ignorant of the last words spoken by the Sacred Oracle some hundred years or more ago. They are these:

> *"When the High Priestess*
> *Is the King's mistress*
> *Then fall Al-Kyris!'*

'Tis absolute doggerel, and senseless withal,—nevertheless, it has caused the enactment of a Law, which is to the effect that the reigning monarch of Al-Kyris shall never, under any sort of pretext, confer with the High Priestess of the Temple on any business whatsoever,—and that, furthermore, he shall never be permitted to look upon her face except at times of public service and state ceremonials. Now dost thou not at once perceive how vile were the suggestions of Nir-jalis, . . . and also how foolish was thy fancy last night with regard to the armed masquerader thou didst see in Lysia's garden?"

Theos made no reply, but sat absorbed in his own reflections. He began now to understand much that had before seemed doubtful and mysterious,—no wonder, he thought, that Zephoranim's fury against the audacious Khosrul had been so excessive! For had not the crazed Prophet called Lysia an "unvirgined virgin and Queen-Courtesan"? . . . and, according to Sah-luma's present explanation, nothing more dire and offensive in the way of open blasphemy could be uttered! Yet the question still remained—, was Khosrul right or wrong? This was a problem which Theos longed to investigate and yet recoiled from,— instinctively he felt that upon its answer hung the fate of Al-Kyris,— and also, what just then seemed more precious than anything else,—the life of Sah-luma. He could not decide with himself WHY this was so,—he simply accepted his own inward assurance that so it was. Presently he inquired:

"How comes it, Sah-luma, that the corpse of Nir-jalis was found on the shores of the river? Did we not see it weighted with iron and laid elsewhere. . . ?"

"O simpleton!" laughed Sah-luma—"Thinkest thou Lysia's lake of lilies is a common grave for criminals? The body of Nir-jalis sank therein, 'tis true, . . . but was there no after-means of lifting it from thence, and placing it where best such carrion should be found? Hath not the High Priestess of Nagaya slaves enough to work her will? . . . Verily thou dost trouble thyself overmuch concerning these trivial every-day occurences,—I marvel at thee!—Hundreds have drained the Silver Nectar gladly for so fair a woman's sake,—hundreds will drain it gladly still for the mere privilege of living some brief days in the presence of such peerless beauty! . . . But,—speaking of the river—didst thou remark it on thy way hither?"

"Aye!" responded Theos dreamily—"'Twas red as blood"!"

"Strange!" and Sah-luma looked thoughtful for an instant, then rousing himself, said lightly, "'Tis from some simple cause, no doubt—yet 'twill create a silly panic in the city—and all the fanatics for Khosrul's new creed will creep forth, shouting afresh their prognostications of death and doom. By my faith, 'twill be a most desperate howling! . . . and I'll not walk abroad till the terror hath abated. Moreover, I have work to do,—some lately budded thoughts of mine have ripened into glorious conclusion,—and Zabastes hath orders presently to attend me that he may take my lines down from mine own dictation. Thou shalt hear a most choice legend of love an thou wilt listen—" here he laid his hand affectionately on Theos's shoulder—"a legend set about, methinks, with wondrous jewels of poetic splendor! . . .'tis a rare privilege I offer thee, my friend, for as a rule Zabastes is my only auditor,—but I would swear thou art no plagiarist, and wouldst not dishonor thine own intelligence so far as to filch pearls of fancy from another minstrel! As well steal my garments as my thoughts!—for verily the thoughts are the garments of the poet's soul,—and the common thief of things petty and material is no whit more contemptible than he who robs an author of ideas wherein to deck the bareness of his own poor wit! Come, place thyself at ease upon this cushioned couch, and give me thy attention, . . . I feel the fervor rising within me, . . . I will summon

Zabastes, . . ." Here he pulled a small silken cord which at once set a clanging bell echoing loudly through the palace, . . . "And thou shalt freely hear, and freely judge, the last offspring of my fertile genius,—my lyrical romance 'Nourhalma!'" Theos started violently, . . . he had the greatest difficulty to restrain the anguished cry that arose to his lips. "Nourhalma!" O memory! . . . slow-filtering, reluctant memory! . . . why, why was his brain thus tortured with these conflicting pang, of piteous recollection! Little by little, like sharp deep stabs of nervous suffering, there came back to him a few faint, fragmentary suggestions which gradually formed themselves into a distinct and comprehensive certainty, . . . "Nourhalma" was the title of His Own Poem,—the poem He had written, surely not so very long ago, among the mountains of the Pass of Dariel!

XXIII

"Nourhalma"

His first emotion on making this new mental rediscovery was, as it had been before in the King's audience-hall, one of absolute TERROR, . . . feverish, mad terror which for a few moments possessed him so utterly that, turning away, he buried his aching head among the cushion where he reclined, in order to hide from his companion's eyes any outward sign that might betray his desperate misery. Clenching his hands convulsively, he silently, and with all his strength, combated the awful horror of himself that grew up spectrally within him,—the dreadful, distracting uncertainty of his own identity that again confused his brain and paralyzed his reason.

At last, he thought wildly, at last he knew the meaning of Hell! . . . the frightful spiritual torment of a baffled intelligence set adrift among the wrecks and shadows of things that had formerly been its pride and glory! What was any physical suffering compared to such a frenzy of mind-agony? Nothing! . . . less than nothing! This was the everlasting thirst and fire spoken of so vaguely by prophets and preachers,—the thirst and fire of the Soul's unquenchable longing to unravel the dismal tangle of its own bygone deeds, . . . the striving forever in vain to steadfastly establish the wavering mystery of its own existence!

"O God! . . . God!—what hast Thou made of me!" he groaned inwardly, as he endeavored to calm the tempest of his unutterable despair,—"Who am I? . . . Who WAS I in that far Past which, like the pale spirit of a murdered friend, haunts me so indistinctly yet so threateningly! Surely the gift of Poesy was mine! . . . surely I too could weave the harmony of words and thoughts into a sweet and fitting music, . . . how comes it then that all Sah-luma's work is but the reflex of my own? O woeful, strange, and bitter enigma! . . . when shall it be unraveled? 'Nourhalma!' 'Twas the name of what I deemed my masterpiece! . . . O silly masterpiece, if it prove thus easy of imitation! . . . Yet stay. . . let me be patient! . . . titles are often copied unconsciously by different authors in different lands, . . . and it may chance that Sah-luma's poem is after all his own,—not mine. Not mine, as were the ballads and the love-ode he chanted to the King last night! . . . O Destiny! . . . inscrutable, pitiless Destiny! . . . rescue my tortured soul from chaos! . . . declare unto me who,—WHO is the plagiarist and thief of Song. . . MYSELF or SAH-LUMA?"

The more he perplexed his mind with such questions, the deeper grew the darkness of the inexplicable dilemma, to which a fresh obscurity was now added in his suddenly distinct and distressful remembrance of the "Pass of Dariel." Where was this place, he wondered wearily?—When had he seen it? whom had he met there?—and how had he come to Al-Kyris from thence? No answer could his vexed brain shape to these demands, . . . he recollected the "Pass of Dariel" just as he recollected the "Field of Ardath"—without the least idea as to what connection existed between them and his own personal adventures. Presently controlling himself, he raised his head and ventured to look up,—Sah-luma stood beside him, his fine face expressive of an amiable solicitude.

"Was the sunshine too strong, my friend, that thou didst thus bury thine eyes in thy pillow?" he inquired. . . "Pardon my discourteous lack of consideration for thy comfort! . . . I love the sun myself so well that methinks I could meet his burning rays at full noon-day and yet take pleasure in the warmth of such a golden smile! But thou perchance art unaccustomed to the light of Eastern lands,—wherefore thy brows must not be permitted to ache on, uncared for. See!—I have lowered the awnings, . . . they give a pleasant shade,—and in very truth, the heat to-day is greater far than ordinary; one would think the gods had kindled some new fire in heaven!"

And as he spoke he took up a long palm-leaf fan and waved it to and fro with an exquisitely graceful movement of wrist and arm, while Theos gazing at him in mute admiration, forgot his own griefs for the time in the subtle, strange, and absorbing spell exercised upon him by his host's irresistible influence. Just then, too, Sah-luma appeared handsomer than ever in the half-subdued tints of radiance that flickered through the lowered pale-blue silken awnings: the effect of the room thus shadowed was as of a soft azure mountain mist lit sideways by the sun,—a mist through which the white-garmented, symmetrical figure of the Laureate stood forth in curiously brilliant outlines, as though every curve of supple shoulder and proud throat was traced with a pencil of pure light. Scarcely a breath of air made its way through the wide-open casements—the gentle dashing noise of the fountains in the court alone disturbed the deep, warm stillness of the morning, or the occasional sweeping rustle of peacocks' plumes as these stately birds

MARIE CORELLI

strutted majestically up and down, up and down, on the marble terrace outside.

Soothed by the luxurious peace of his surroundings, the delirium of Theos's bewildering affliction gradually abated,—his tempest-tossed mind regained to a certain extent its equilibrium,—and falling into easy converse with his fascinating companion, he was soon himself again,—that is, as much himself as his peculiar condition permitted him to be. Yet he was not altogether free from a certain eager and decidedly painful suspense with regard to the "Nourhalma" problem,—and he was conscious of what he in his own opinion considered an absurd and unnecessary degree of excitement, when the door of the apartment presently opened to admit Zabastes, who entered, carrying several sheets of papyrus and other material for writing.

The old Critic's countenance was expressively glum and ironical,—he, however, was compelled, like all the other paid servants of the household, to make a low and respectful obeisance as soon as he found himself in Sah-luma's presence,—an act of homage which, he performed awkwardly, and with evident ill-will. His master nodded condescendingly in response to his reluctant salute, and signed to him to take his place at a richly carved writing-table adorned with the climbing figures of winged cupids exquisitely wrought in ivory. He obeyed, shuffling thither uneasily, and sniffing the rose-fragrant air as he went like an ill-conditioned cur scenting a foe,—and seating himself in a high-backed chair, he arranged his garments fussily about him, rolled up his long embroidered sleeves to the elbow, and spread his writing implements all over the desk in front of him with much mock-solemn ostentation. Then, rubbing his lean hands together, he gave a stealthy glance of covert derision round at Sah-luma and Theos,—a glance which Theos saw and in his heart resented, but which Sah-luma, absorbed in his own reflections, apparently failed to notice.

"All is in readiness, my lord!" he announced in his disagreeable croaking tones,—"Here are the clean and harmless slips of river-reed waiting to be soiled and spotted with my lord's indelible thoughts,—here also are the innocent quills of the white heron, as yet unstained by colored writing-fluid whether black, red, gold, silver, or purple! Mark you, most illustrious bard, the touching helplessness and purity of these meek servants of a scribbler's fancy! . . . Blank papyrus and empty quills! Bethink you seriously whether it were not better to leave them thus unblemished, the simple products of unfaulty Nature, than use them to indite the wondrous things of my lord's imagination, whereof, all wondrous though they seem, no man shall ever be the wiser!"

And he chuckled, stroking his stubbly gray beard the while with a blandly suggestive, yet malign look directed at Sah-luma, who met it with a slight, cold smile of faintly amused contempt.

"Peace, fool!" he said,—"That barbarous tongue of thine is like the imperfect clapper of a broken bell that strikes forth harsh and undesired sounds suggesting nothing! Thy present duty is to hear, and not to speak,—therefore listen discerningly and write with exactitude, so shall thy poor blank scrolls of reed grow rich with gems, . . . gems of high poesy that the whole world shall hoard and cherish miser-like when the poet who created their bright splendor is no more!"

He sighed—a short, troubled sigh,—and stood for a moment silent in an attitude of pensive thought. Theos watched him yearningly,—waiting in almost breathless suspense till he should dictate aloud the first line of his poem. Zabastes meanwhile settled himself more comfortably in his chair, and taking up one of the long quills with which he was provided, dipped it in a reddish-purple liquid which at once stained its point to a deep roseate hue, so that when the light flickered upon it from time to time, it appeared as though it were tipped with fire. How intense the heat was, thought Theos!—as with one hand he pushed his clustering hair from his brow, not without noticing that his action was imitated almost at once by Sah-luma, who also seemed to feel the oppressiveness of the atmosphere. And what a blaze of blue pervaded the room! . . . delicate ethereal blue as of shimmering lakes and summer skies melted together into one luminous radiance, . . . radiance that, while filmy, was yet perfectly transparent, and in which the Laureate's classic form appeared to be gloriously enveloped like that of some new descended god!

Theos rubbed his eyes to cure them of their dazzled ache, . . . what a marvellous scene it was to look upon, he mused! . . . would he,—could he ever forget it? Ah no!—never, never! not till his dying day would he be able to obliterate it from his memory,—and who could tell whether even after death he might not still recall it! Just then Sah-luma raised his hand by way of signal to Zabastes, . . . his face became earnest, pathetic, even grand in the fervent concentration of his thoughts, . . . he was about to begin his dictation, . . . now. . . now! . . . and Theos leaned forward nervously, his heart beating with apprehensive expectation. . . Hush! . . . the delicious, suave melody of his friend's voice penetrated the silence like the sweet harmonic of a harp-string.

　　　　　　　　　　　　　　　　MARIE CORELLI

"Write—" said he slowly. . . "write first the title of my poem thus: 'Nourhalma: A Love-Legend of the Past.'"

There was a pause, during which the pen of Zabastes traveled quickly over the papyrus for a moment, then stopped. Theos, almost suffocated with anxiety, could hardly maintain even the appearance of calmness,— the title proclaimed, with its second appendage, was precisely the same as that of his own work—but this did not now affect him so much. What he waited for with such painfully strained attention was the first line of the poem. If it was his line he knew it already!—it ran thus:

"A central sorrow dwells in perfect joy!—"

Scarcely had he repeated this to himself inwardly, than Sah-luma, with majestic grace and sweetness of utterance, dictated aloud:

"A central sorrow dwells in perfect joy!"

"Ah GOD!"

The sharp cry, half fierce, half despairing, broke from Theos's quivering lips in spite of all the efforts he made to control his agitation, and the Laureate turned toward him with a surprised and somewhat irritated movement that plainly evinced annoyance at the interruption.

"Pardon, Sah-luma!" he murmured hastily. "'Twas a slight pang at the heart troubled me,—a mere nothing!—I take shame to myself to have cried out for such a pin's prick! Speak on!—thy first line is as soft as honey dew,—as suggestive as the light of dawn on sleeping flowers!"

And, leaning dizzily back on his couch, he closed his eyes to shut in the hot and bitter tears that welled up rebelliously and threatened to fall, notwithstanding his endeavor to restrain them. His head throbbed and burned as though a chaplet of fiery thorns encircled it, instead of the once desired crown of Fame he had so fondly dreamed of winning!

Fame? . . . Alas! that bright, delusive vision had fled forever,—there were no glory-laurels left growing for him in the fields of poetic art and aspiration,—Sah-luma, the fortunate Sah-luma, had gathered and possessed them all! Taking everything into serious consideration, he came at last to the deeply mortifying conclusion that it must be himself who was the plagiarist,—the unconscious imitator of Sah-luma's ideas and methods, . . . and the worst of it was that his imitation was so terribly EXACT!

Oh, how heartily he despised himself for his poor and pitiful lack of originality! Down to the very depths of humiliation he sternly abased his complaining, struggling, wounded, and sorely resentful spirit, . . . he then and there became the merciless executioner of his own claims to literary honor,—and deliberately crushing all his past ambition, mutinous discontent and uncompliant desires with a strong master-hand he lay quiet. . . as patiently unmoved as is a dead man to the wrongs inflicted on his memory. . . and forced himself to listen resignedly to every glowing line of his, . . . no, not his, but Sah-luma's poem, . . . the lovely, gracious, delicate, entrancing poem he remembered so well! And by and by, as each mellifluous stanza sounded softly on his ears, a strangely solemn tranquillity swept over him,—a most soothing halcyon calm, as though some passing angel's hand had touched his brow in benediction.

He looked at Sah-luma, not enviously now but all admiringly,—it seemed to him that he had never heard a sweeter, tenderer music than the story of "Nourhalma" as recited by his friend. And so to that friend he silently awarded his own wished-for glory, praise, and everlasting fame!—that glory, praise, and fame which had formerly allured his fancy as being the best of all the world could offer, but which he now entirely and willingly relinquished in favor of this more deserving and dear comrade, whose superior genius he submissively acknowledged!

There was a great quietness everywhere,—the rising and falling inflections of Sah-luma's soft, rich voice rather, deepened than disturbed the stillness,—the pen of Zabastes glided noiselessly over the slips of papyrus,—and the small sounds of the outer air, such as the monotonous hum of bees among the masses of lily-bloom that towered in white clusters between the festooned awnings, the thirsty twitterimg of birds hiding under the long palm leaves to shelter themselves from the heat, and the incessant splash of the fountains, . . . all seemed to be, as it were, mere appendages to enhance the breathless hush of nature. Presently Sah-luma paused,—and Zabastes, heaving a sigh of relief, looked up from his writing, and laid down his pen.

'The work is finished, most illustrious?" he demanded, a curious smile playing on his thin, satirical lips.

"Finished?" echoed Sah-luma disdainfully—"Nay,—'tis but the end of the First Canto"

The scribe gave vent to a dismal groan.

"Ye gods!" he exclaimed—"Is there more to come of this bombastic ranting and vile torturing of phrases unheard of and altogether unnatural! O Sah-luma!—marvellous Sah-luma! twaddler Sah-luma! what a brain box is thine! . . . How full of dislocated word-puzzles and similes gone mad! Now, as I live, expect no mercy from me this time!" . . . and he shook his head threateningly,—"For if the public news sheet will serve me as mine anvil, I will so pound thee in pieces with the sledge-hammer of my criticism, that, by the Ship of the Sun! . . . for once Al-Kyns shall be moved to laughter at thee! Mark me, good tuner-up of tinkling foolishness! . . . I will so choose out and handle thy feeblest lines that they shall seem but the doggerel of a street ballad monger! I will give so bald an epitome of this sickly love-tale that it shall appeal to all who read my commentary the veriest trash that ever poet penned! . . . Moreover, I can most admirably misquote thee, and distort thy meanings with such excellent bitter jesting, that thou thyself shall scarcely recognize thine own production! By Nagaya's Shrine! what a feast 'twill be for my delectation!"—and he rubbed his hands gleefully—"With what a weight of withering analysis I can pulverize this idol of 'Nourhalma' into the dust and ashes of a common sense contempt!"

While Zabastes thus spoke, Sah-luma had helped himself, by way of refreshment, to two ripe figs, in whose luscious crimson pulp his white teeth met, with all the enjoying zest of a child's healthy appetite. He now held up the rind and stalks of these devoured delicacies, and smiled.

'Thus wilt thou swallow up my poem in thy glib clumsiness, Zabastes!" he said lightly—"And thus wilt them hold up the most tasteless portions of the whole for the judgment of the public! 'Tis the manner of thy craft,—yet see!"—and with a dexterous movement of his arm he threw the fruit-peel through the window far out into the garden beyond—"There goes thy famous criticism!" and he laughed. "And those that taste the fruit itself at first hand will not soon forget its flavor! Nevertheless I hope indeed that thou wilt strive to slaughter me with thy blunt paper sword! I do most mirthfully relish the one-sided combat, in which I stand in silence to receive thy blows, myself unhurt and tranquil as a marble god whom ruffians rail upon! Do I not pay thee to abuse me? . . . here, thou crusty soul!—drink and be content!"— And with a charming condescension he handed a full goblet of wine to his cantankerous Critic, who accepted it ungraciously, muttering in his beard the necessary words of thanks for his master's consideration,— then, turning to Theos, the Laureate continued:

"And thou, my friend, what dost thou think of 'Nourhalma' so far? Hath it not a certain exquisite smoothness of rhythm like the ripple of a woodland stream clear-winding through the reeds? . . . and is there not a tender witchery in the delineation of my maiden-heroine, so warmly fair, so wildly passionate? Methinks she doth resemble some rich flower of our tropic fields, blooming at sunset and dead at moonrise!"

Theos waited a moment before replying. Truth to tell, he was inwardly overcome with shame to remember how wantonly he had copied the description of this same Nourhalma! . . . and plaintively he wondered how he could have unconsciously committed so flagrant a theft! Summoning up all his self-possession, however, he answered bravely.

"Thy work, Sah-luma, is worthy of thyself! . . . need I say more? . . . Thou hast most aptly proved thy claim upon, the whole world's gratitude, . . . such lofty thoughts, . . . such noble discourse upon love,—such high philosophy, wherein the deepest, dearest dreams of life are grandly pictured in enduring colors,—these things are gifts to poor humanity whereby it Must become enriched and proud! Thy name, bright soul, shall be as a quenchless star on the dark brows of melancholy Time, . . . men gazing thereat shall wonder and adore,— and even I, the least among thy friends, may also win from thee a share of glory! For, simply to know thee,—to listen to thy heaven-inspired utterance, might bring the most renownless student some reflex of thine honor! Yes, thou art great, Sah-luma! . . . great as the greatest of earth's gifted sons of song!—and with all my heart I offer thee my homage, and pride myself upon the splendor of thy fame!"

And as the eager, enthusiastic words came from his lips, he beheld Sah-luma's beautiful countenance brighten more and more, till it appeared mysteriously transfigured into a majestic Angel-face that for one brief moment startled him by the divine tenderness of its compassionate smile! This expression, however, was transitory,—it passed, and the dark eyes of the Laureate gleamed with a merely serene and affectionate complacency as he said:

"I thank thee for thy praise, good Theos!—thou art indeed the friendliest of critics! Hadst thou THYSELF been the author of 'Nourhalma' thou couldst not have spoken with more ardent feeling! Were Zabastes like thee, discerningly just and reasonable, he would be all unfit for his vocation,—for 'tis an odd circumstance that praise in the public news-sheet does a writer more harm than good, while ill-conditioned and malicious abuse doth very materially increase and strengthen his reputation. Yet, after all, there is a certain sense in the argument,—for if much eulogy be penned by the cheap scribes, the reading populace at once imagine these fellows have been bribed to give their over-zealous approval, or that they are close friends and banquet-comrades of the author whom they arduously uphold, ... whereas, on the contrary, if they indulge in bitter invective, flippant gibing, or clumsy satire, like my amiable Zabsastes here. . ." and he made an airy gesture toward the silent yet evidently chafing Critic, . . ." (and, mark you!-HE is not bribed, but merely paid fair wages to fulfil his chosen and professed calling)—why, thereupon the multitude exclaim—What! this poet hath such enemies?—nay, then, how great a genius he must be!"—and forthwith they clamor for his work, which, if it speak not for itself, is then and only then to be deemed faulty, and meriting oblivion. 'Tis the People's verdict which alone gives fame."

"And yet the people are often ignorant of what is noblest and best in literature!" observed Theos musingly.

"Ignorant in some ways, yes!" agreed Sah-luma—"But in many others, no! They may be ignorant as to WHY they admire a certain thing, yet they admire it all the same, because their natural instinct leads them so to do. And this is the special gift which endows the uncultured masses with an occasional sweeping advantage over the cultured few,—the superiority of their INSTINCT. As in cases of political revolution for example,—while the finely educated orator is endeavoring by all the force of artful rhetoric to prove that all is in order and as it should be, the mob, moved by one tremendous impulse, discover for themselves that everything is wrong, and moreover that nothing will come right, unless they rise up and take authority, . . . accordingly, down go the thrones and the colleges, the palaces, the temples, and the law-assemblies, all like so many toys before the resistless instinct of the people, who revolt at injustice, and who feel and know when they are injured, though they are not clever enough to explain WHERE their injury lies. And so, as they cannot talk about it coherently, any more than a lion struck by an arrow can give a learned dissertation on his wound, they act, . . . and the heat and fury of their action upheaves dynasties! Again,—reverting to the question of taste and literature,—the mob, untaught and untrained in the subtilties of art, will applaud to the echo certain grand and convincing home-truths set forth in the plays of the divine Hyspiros,—simply because they instinctively FEEL them to be truths, no matter how far they themselves may be from acting up to the standard of morality therein contained. The more highly cultured will hear the same passages unmoved, because they, in the excess of artificially gained wisdom, have deadened their instincts so far, that while they listen to a truth pronounced, they already consider how best they can confute it, and prove the same a lie! Honest enthusiasm is impossible to the over-punctilious and pedantic scholar,—but on the other hand, I would have it plainly understood that a mere brief local popularity is not Fame, . . . No! for the author who wins the first never secures the last. What I mean is, that a book or poem to be great, and keep its greatness hereafter, must be judged worthy by the natural instinct of PEOPLES. Their decision, I own, may be tardy,—their hesitation may be prolonged through a hundred or more years,—but their acceptance, whether it be declared in the author's life-time or ages after his death, must be considered final. I would add, moreover, that this world-wide decision has never yet been, and never will be, hastened by any amount of written criticism,—it is the responsive beat of the enormous Pulse of Life that thrills through all mankind, high and low, gentle and simple,— its great throbs are slow and solemnly measured,—yet if once it answers to a Poet's touch, that Poet's name is made glorious forever!"

He spoke with a rush of earnestness and eloquence that was both persuasive and powerful, and he now stood silent and absorbed, his dreamy eyes resting meditatively on the massive bust of the immortal personage he called Hyspiros, which smiled out in serene, cold whiteness from the velvet-shadowed shrine it occupied. Theos watched him with fascinated and fraternal fondness, . . . did ever man possess so dulcet a voice, he thought? . . . so grave and rich and marvellously musical, yet thrilling with such heart-moving suggestions of mingled pride and plaintiveness?

"Thou art a most alluring orator, Sah-luma!" he said suddenly— "Methinks I could listen to thee all day and never tire!"

"I' faith, so could not I!" interposed Zabastes grimly. "For when a bard begins to gabble goose-like platitudes which merely concern his own vocation, the gods only know when he can be persuaded to stop! Nay, 'tis more irksome far than the recitation of his professional jingle—for to that there must in time come a merciful fitting end, but, as I live, if 'twas my custom to say prayers, I would pray to be delivered from the accursed volubility of a versifier's tongue! And perchance it will not be considered out of my line of duty if I venture to remind my most illustrious and renowned MASTER—" this with a withering sneer,— "that if he has any more remarkable nothings to dictate concerning this particularly inane creation of his fancy 'Nourhalma,' 'twill be well that we should proceed therewith, for the hours wax late and the sun veereth toward his House of Noon."

And he spread out fresh slips of papyrus and again prepared his long quill.

Sah-luma smiled, as one who is tolerant of the whims of a hired buffoon,—and, this time seating himself in his ebony chair, was about to commence dictating his Second Canto when Theos, yielding to his desire to speak aloud the idea that had just flashed across his brain said abruptly:

"Has it ever seemed to thee, Sah-luma, as it now does to me, that there is a strange resemblance between thy imaginative description of the ideal 'Nourhalma,' and the actual charms and virtues of thy strayed singing-maid Niphrata?"

Sah-luma looked up, thoroughly astonished, and laughed.

"No!—Verily I have not traced, nor can I trace the smallest vestige of a similarity! Why, good Theos, there is none!—not the least in the world,—for this heroine of mine, Nourhalma, loves in vain, and sacrifices all, even her innocent and radiant life, for love, as thou wilt hear in the second half of the poem,—moreover she loves one who is utterly unworthy of her faithful tenderness. Now Niphrata is a child of delicate caprice. . . she loves ME,—me, her lord,—and methinks I am not negligent or undeserving of her devotion! . . . again, she has no strength of spirit,—her timorous blood would freeze at the mere thought of death,—she is more prone to play with flowers and sing for pure delight of heart than perish for the sake of love! 'Tis an unequal simile, my friend!—as well compare a fiery planet with a twinkling dewdrop, as draw a parallel between the heroic ideal maid 'Nourhalma'—and my fluttering singing-bird, Niphrata!"

Theos sighed involuntarily,—but forcing a smile, let the subject drop and held his peace, while Sah-luma, taking up the thread of his poetical narrative, went on reciting. When the story began to ripen toward its conclusion he grew more animated, . . . rising, he paced the room as he declaimed the splendid lines that now rolled gloriously one upon another like deep-mouthed billows thundering on the shore,— his gestures were all indicative of the fervor of his inward ecstasy,— his eyes flashed,—his features glowed with that serene, proud light of conscious power and triumph that rests on the calm, wide brows of the sculptured Apollo,—and Theos, leaning one arm in a half-sitting posture, contemplated him with a curious sensation of wistful eagerness and passionate pain, such as might be felt by some forgotten artist mysteriously permitted to come out of his grave and wander back to earth, there to see his once-rejected pictures hung in places of honor among the world's chief treasures.

A strange throb of melancholy satisfaction stirred his pulses as he reflected that he might now, without any self-conceit, at least ADMIRE the poem!—since he had decided that was no longer his, but another's, he was free to bestow on it as much as he would of unstinting praise! For it was very fine,—there could be no doubt of that, whatever Zabastes might say to the contrary,—and it was not only fine, but intensely, humanly pathetic, seeming to strike a chord of passion such as had never before been sounded,—a chord to which the world would be COMPELLED to listen,—yes,—COMPELLED! thought Theos exultingly,— as Sah-luma drew nearer and nearer the close of his dictation. . . The deep quiet all around was so heavy as to be almost uncomfortable in its oppressiveness,—it exercised a sort of strain upon the nerves. . .

Hark! what was that? Through the hot and silent air swept a sullen surging noise as of the angry shouting of a vast multitude,—then came the fast and furious gallop of many horses,—and again that fierce, resentful roar of indignation, swelling up as it seemed from thousands of throats. Moved, all three at once, by the same instinctive desire to know what was going on, Theos, Sah-luma, and Zabastes sprang from their different places in the room, and hurried out on the marble terrace, dashing aside the silken awnings as they went in order the better to see the open glimpses of the city thoroughfares that lay below. Theos, leaning far out over the western half of the balustrade, was able to command a distant view of the great Square in which the huge white granite Obelisk occupied so prominent a position, and, fixing his eyes attentively on this spot, saw that it was filled to overflowing with a dense mass of people, whose white-raimented forms, pressed together in countless numbers, swayed restlessly to and fro like the rising waves of a stormy sea.

Lifted above this troubled throng, one tall, dark figure was distinctly outlined against the dazzling face of the Obelisk—a figure that appeared to be standing on the back of the colossal Lion that lay couchant beneath. And as Theos strained his sight to distinguish the details of the scene

MARIE CORELLI

more accurately, he suddenly beheld a glittering regiment of mounted men in armor, charging straightly and with cruelly determined speed, right into the centre of the crowd, apparently regardless of all havoc to life and limb that might ensue. Involuntarily he uttered an exclamation of horror at what seemed to him so wanton and brutal an act, when just then Sah-luma caught him eagerly by the arm,—Sah-luma, whose soft, oval countenance was brilliant with excitement, and in whose eyes gleamed a mingled expression of mirth and ferocity.

"Come, come, my friend!" he said hastily—"Yonder is a sight worth seeing! 'Tis the mad Khosrul who is thus entrenched and fortified by the mob,—as I live, that sweeping gallop of His Majesty's Royal Guards is magnificent! They will seize the Prophet this time without fail! Aye, if they slay a thousand of the populace in the performance of their duty! Come!—let us hasten to the scene of action—'twill be a struggle I would not miss for all the world!"

He sprang down the steps of the loggia, accompanied by Theos, who was equally excited,—when all at once Zabastes, thrusting out his head through a screen of vine-leaves, cried after them:

"Sah-luma!—Most illustrious! What of the poem? It is not finished!"

"No matter!" returned Sah-luma—"'Twill be finished hereafter!"

And he hastened on, Theos treading close in his footsteps and thinking as he went of the new enigma thus proposed to puzzle afresh the weary workings of his mind. His poem of Nourhalma—or rather the poem he had fancied was his—had been entirely completed down to the last line; now Sah-luma's was left "To Be Finished Hereafter."

Strange that he should find a pale glimmering of consolation in this!—a feeble hope that perhaps after all, at some future time, he might be able to produce a few, a very few lines of noble verse that should be deemed purely original! . . . enough perchance, to endow him with a faint, far halo of diminished glory such as plodding students occasionally win, by following humbly yet ardently. . . even as he now followed Sah-luma. . . in the paths of excellence marked out by greater men!

XXIV

The Fall of the Obelisk

In less time than he could have imagined possible, he found himself in the densely crowded Square, buffeting and struggling against an angry and rebellious mob, who half resentful and half terrified, had evidently set themselves to resist the determined charge made by the mounted soldiery into their midst. For once Sah-luma's appearance created no diversion,—he was pushed and knocked about as unceremoniously as if he were the commonest citizen of them all, He seemed carelessly surprised at this, but nevertheless took his hustling very good humoredly, and, keeping his shoulders well squared forced his way with Theos by slow degrees through the serried ranks of people, many of whom, roused to a sort of frenzy threw themselves in front of the advancing horses of the guard, and seizing the reins held on to these like grim death, reckless of all danger.

As yet no weapons were used either by the soldiers or the populace,—the former seemed for the present contented to simply ride down those who impeded their progress,—and that they had done so in terrible earnest was plainly evident from the numbers of wounded creatures that lay scattered about on every side in an apparently half dying condition. Yet there was surely a strange insensibility to suffering among them all, inasmuch as in spite of the contention and confusion there were no violent shrieks of either pain or fury,—no exclamations of rage or despair,—no sound whatever indeed, save a steady, sullen, monotonous snarl of opposition, above which the resonant voice of the Prophet Khosrul rang out like a silver clarion.

"O people doomed and made desolate!" he cried. "O nation once mighty, brought low to the dust of destruction! Hear me, ye strong men and fair women!—and you, ye poor little children who never again shall see the sun rise on the thousand domes of Al-Kyris! Lift up the burden of bitter lamentation!—lift it up to the Heaven of Heavens, the Throne of the All-Seeing Glory, the Giver of Law, the Destroyer of Evil! Weep! . . . weep for your sins and the sins of your sons and your daughters—cast off the jewels of pride,—rend the fine raiment, . . . let your tears be abundant as the rain and dew! Kneel down and cry aloud on the great and terrible Unknown God—the God ye have denied and wronged,—the Founder of worlds, who doth hold in His Hand the Sun as a torch, and scattereth stars with the fire of His breath! Mourn and bend ye all beneath the iron stroke of Destiny!—for know ye not how fierce a thing has come upon Al-Kyris? . . . a thing that lips cannot utter nor words define,—a thing more horrible than strange sounds in thick darkness,—more deadly than the lightning when it leaps from Heaven with intent to slay! O City stately beyond all cities! Thy marble palaces are already ringed round with a river of blood!—the temples of thy knowledge wherein thy wise men have studied to exceed all wisdom, begin to totter to their fall,—thou shalt be swept away even as a light heap of ashes, and what shall all thy learning avail thee in that brief and fearful end! Hear me, O people of Al-Kyris!—Hear me and cease to strive among yourselves, . . . resist not thus desperately the King's armed minions, for to them I also speak and say,—Lo! the time approaches when a stronger hand than that of the mighty Zephoranim shall take me prisoner and bear me hence where most I long to go! Peace, I command you! . . . in the Name of that God whose truth I do proclaim. . . Peace!"

As he uttered the last word an instantaneous hush fell upon the crowd,—every head was turned toward his grand, gaunt, almost spectral figure; and even the mounted soldiery reined up their plunging, chafing steeds and remained motionless as though suddenly fixed to the ground by some powerful magnetic spell. Theos and Sah-luma took immediate advantage of this lull in the conflict, to try and secure for themselves a better point of vantage, though there was much difficulty in pressing through the closely packed throng, inasmuch as not a man moved to give them passage-room.

Presently, however, Sah-luma managed to reach the nearest one of the two great fountains, which adorned either side of the Obelisk, and, springing as lightly as a bird on its marble edge, he stood erect there, his picturesque form presenting itself to the view like a fine statue set against the background of sun-tinted foaming water that dashed high above him and sprinkled his garments with drops of sparkling spray. Theos at once joined him, and the two friends, holding each other fast by the arm, gazed down on the silent, mighty multitude around them,—a huge concourse of the citizens of Al-Kyris, who, strange as this part of their behavior seemed, still paid no heed to the presence of their Laureate, but with pale, rapt faces and anxious, frightened eyes, riveted their attention entirely on the sombre, black-garmented Prophet whose thin ghostly arms, outstretched above them, appeared to mutely invoke in their behalf some special miracle of mercy.

"See you not" . . . whispered Sah-luma to his companion,—"how yon aged fool wears upon his breast the Symbol of his own Prophecy? 'Tis the maddest freak to thus display his death-warrant!—Only a month ago the King issued a decree, warning all those whom it might concern, that any one of his born subjects presuming to carry the sign of Khosrul's newly invented Faith should surely die! And that the crazed reprobate carries it himself makes no exemption from the rule!"

Theos shuddered. His eyes were misty, but he could very well see the Emblem to which Sah-luma alluded,—it was the Cross again! . . . the same sacred Prefiguration of things "to come," according to the perplexing explanation given by the Mystic Zuriel whom he had met in the Passage of the Tombs, though to his own mind it conveyed no such meaning. What was it then? . . . if not a Prototype of the future, was it a Record of the Past? He dared not pursue this question,—it seemed to send his brain reeling on the verge of madness! He made no answer to Sah-luma's remark,—but fixed his gaze wistfully on the tall, melancholy Shape that like a black shadow darkened the whiteness of the Obelisk,—and his sense of hearing became acute almost to painfulness when once more Khosrul's deep vibrating tones peeled solemnly through the heavy air.

"God speaks to Al-Kyris!" and as the Prophet enunciated these words with majestic emphasis a visible thrill ran through the hushed assemblage. "God saith: Get thee up, O thou City of Pleasure, from thy couch of sweet wantonness,—get thee up, gird thee with fire, and flee into the desert of forgotten things! For thou art become a blot on the fairness of My world, and a shame to the brightness of My Heaven!—thy rulers are corrupt,—thy teachers are proud of heart and narrow in judgment,—thy young men and maidens go astray and follow each after their own vain opinions,—in thy great temples and holy places Falsehood abides, and Vice holds court in thy glorious palaces. Wherefore because thou hast neither sought nor served Me, and because thou hast set up gold as thy god, and a multitude of riches as thy chief good, lo! now mine eyes have grown weary of beholding thee, and I will descend upon thee suddenly and destroy thee, even as a hill of sand is destroyed by the whirlwind,—and thou shalt be known in the land of My creatures no more! Woe to thee that thou hast taken pride in thy wisdom and learning, for therein lies thy much wickedness! If thou wert truly wise thou wouldst have found Me,—if thou wert nobly learned thou wouldst have understood My laws,—but thou art proved altogether gross, foolish, and incapable,—and the studies whereof thou hast boasted, the writings of thy wise men, the charts of sea and land, the maps of thy chief astronomers, the engraved tablets of learning, in gold, in silver, in ivory, in stone, thy chronicles of battle and conquest, the documents of thine explorers in far countries, the engines of thine invention whereby thou dost press the lightning into thy service, and make the air respond to the messages of thy kings and councillors,—all these shall be thrust away into an everlasting silence, and no man hereafter shall be able to declare that such things have ever been!"

Here the speaker paused,—and Theos, surveying the vast listening crowds, fancied they looked like an audience of moveless ghosts rather than human beings,—so still, so pallid, so grave were they, one and all. Khosrul continued in softer, more melancholy accents, that, while plaintive, were still singularly impressive.

"O my ill-fated, my beloved fellow-countrymen!" he exclaimed, extending his arms with a vehemently pleading gesture as though in the excess of emotion he would have drawn all the people to his heart.—"Ye unhappy ones? . . . have I not given ye warning? Have I not bidden ye beware of this great evil which should come to pass?—Evil for which there is no remedy,—none,—neither in the earth, nor the sea, nor the invisible comforts of the air! . . . for God hath spoken, and who shall contradict the thunder of His voice! Behold the end is at hand of all the pleasant things of Al-Kyris,—the feasting and the musical assemblies, the cymbal-symphonies and the choir-dances, the labors of students and the triumphs of sages,—all these shall seem but the mockery of madness in the swift-descending night of overwhelming destruction! Woe is me that ye would not listen when I called, but turned every man to his own devices and the following after idols? Nay now, what will ye do in extremity?—Will ye chant hymns to the Sun? Lo, he is deaf and blind for all his golden glory, and is but a taper set in the window of the sky, to be extinguished at God's good pleasure! Will ye supplicate Nagaya? O fools and desperate!—how shall a brute beast answer prayer!—Vain, vain is all beseeching,—shut forever are the doors of escape,—therefore cover yourselves with the garments of burial,—prepare each one his grave and rich funeral things,—gather together the rosemary and myrrh, the precious ointments and essences, the strings of gold and the jewelled talismans whereby ye think to fight against corruption,—and fall down, every man in his own wrought hollow in the ground, face turned to earth and die—for Death hath broken through the strong gates of Al-Kyris, and hath taken the City Magnificent captive unknowingly! Alas, alas! that ye would not follow whither I led,—that ye would not hearken to the Vision of the Future, dimly yet gloriously revealed! . . . the Future! . . . the Future!" . . .

He broke off suddenly, and raising his eyes to the deep blue sky above him, seemed for a moment as though he were caught up in the cloud of some wondrous dream. Still the enormous throng of people stood hushed and motionless,—not a word, not a sound escaped them,—there was something positively appalling in such absolute immobility,—at least it appeared so to Theos, who could not understand this dispassionate behavior on the part of so large and lately excited a multitude. All at once a voice marvellously tender, clear, and pathetic trembled on the silence,—was it, could it be the voice of Khosrul? Yes! but so changed, so solemn, so infinitely sweet, that it might have been some gentle angel speaking:

"Like a fountain of sweet water in the desert, or the rising of the moon in a gloomy midnight," he said slowly,—"Even so is the hope and promise of the Supremely Beloved! Through the veiling darkness of the coming ages His Light already shines upon my soul! O blessed Advent! . . . O happy Future! . . . O days when privileged Humanity shall bridge by Love the gulf between this world and Heaven! What shall be said of Him who cometh to redeem us, O my foreseeing spirit! What shall be told concerning His most marvellous Beauty? Even as a dove that for pity of its helpless younglings doth battle soft-breasted with a storm, even so shall He descend from out His glory sempiternal, and teach us how to conquer Sin and Death,—aye, even with the meekness of a little child He shall approach, and choose His dwelling here among us. O heavenly Child! O wisdom of God contained in innocence! . . . happy the learning that shall learn from Thee!—noble the pride that shall humble itself before Thy gentleness!* O Prince of Manhood and

---

* The idea of a Saviour who should be born as Man to redeem the world was prevalent among all nations and dates from the remotest ages. Coming down to what must be termed quite a modern period compared to that in which the city of Al-Kyris had its existence, we find that the Romans under Octavius Caesar were wont to exclaim at their sacred meetings, "The times FORETOLD BY THE SYBIL are arrived; may a new age soon

MARIE CORELLI

Divinity entwined! Thou shalt acquaint Thyself with human griefs, and patiently unravel the perplexities of human longings!—to prove Thy sacred sympathy with suffering, Thou shalt be content to suffer,—to explain the mystery of Death, Thou shalt even be content to die. O people of Al-Kyris, hear ye all the words that tell of this Wonderful, Inestimable King of Peace,—mine aged eyes do see Him now, far, far off in the rising mist of unformed future things!—the Cross—the Cross, on which His Man's pure Life dissolves itself in glory, stretches above me in spreading beams of light! . . . Ah! 'tis a glittering pathway in the skies whereon men and the angels meet and know each other! He is the strong and perfect Spirit, that shall break loose from Death and declare the insignificance of the Grave,—He is the lingering Star in the East that shall rise and lighten all spiritual darkness—the unknown, unnamed Redeemer of the World, . . . the Man-God Saviour that Shall Come?"

"Shall come?" cried Theos, suddenly roused to the utmost pitch of frenzied excitement, and pronouncing each word with loud and involuntary vehemence. . . "Nay! . . . for He Has come! He Died For Us, And Rose Again From The Dead More Than Eighteen Hundred Years Ago!"

A frightful silence followed,—a breathless cessation of even the faintest quiver of sound. The mighty mass of people, apparently moved by one accord, turned with swift, stealthy noiselessness toward the audacious speaker, . . . thousands of glittering eyes were fixed upon him in solemnly inquiring wonderment, while he himself, now altogether dismayed at the effect of his own rash utterance, thought he had never experienced a more awful moment! For it was as though all the skeletons he had lately seen in the Passage of the Tombs had suddenly clothed themselves with spectral flesh and hair and the shadowy garments of men, and had advanced into broad daylight to surround him in their terrible lifeless ranks, and wrench from him the secret of an after-existence concerning which They were ignorant!

How ghostly and drear seemed that dense crowd in this new light of his delirious fancy! A clammy dew broke out on his forehead,—he

restore that Saturn? Soon May The Child Be Born Who Shall Banish The Age Of Iron?" Tacitus and Suetonius both mention the prophecies "in the sacred books of the priests" which declare that the "East shall be in commotion," and that "Men From Judea" shall subject "everything to their dominion."

saw the blue skies, the huge buildings in the Square, the Obelisk, the fountains, the trees, all whirling round him in a wild dance of the dizziest distraction, . . . when Sah-luma's rich voice close to his ear recalled his wandering senses:

"Why, man, art thou drunk or mad?" and the Laureate's face expressed a kind of sarcastic astonishment,—"What a fool thou hast made of thyself, good comrade! . . . By my soul, how shall thy condition be explained to these open-mouthed starers below! See how they gape upon thee! . . . thou art most assuredly a noticeable spectacle! . . . and yon maniac Prophet doth evidently judge thee as one of his craft, a fellow professional howler of marvels, else he would scarcely deign to fix his eyes so obstinately on thy countenance! Nay, verily thou dost outrival him in the strangeness of thy language! . . . What moved thee to such frenzied utterance? Surely thou hast a stroke of the sun!—thy words were most absolutely devoid of reason! . . . as senseless as the jabber of an idiot to his own shadow on the wall!"

Theos was mute,—he had no defense to offer. The crowd still stared upon him,—and his heart beat fast with a mingled sense of fear and pride—fear of his present surroundings,—pride that he had spoken out his conviction boldly, reckless of all consequences. And this pride was a most curious thing to analyze, because it did not so much consist in the fact of his having openly confessed his inward thought, as that he felt he had gained some special victory in thus ACKNOWLEDGING HIS BELIEF IN THE POSITIVE EXISTENCE OF THE "Saviour" who formed the subject of Khosrul's prophecy. Full of a singular sort of self-congratulation which yet had nothing to do with selfishness, he became so absorbed in his own reflections that he started like a man brusquely aroused from sleep when the Prophet's strong grave voice apostrophized him personally over the heads of the throng:

"Who and what art thou, that dost speak of the FUTURE as though it were the PAST? Hast thou held converse with the Angels, and is Past and Future ONE with thee in the dream of the departing Present? Answer me, thou stranger to the city of Al-Kyris! . . . Has God taught THEE the way to Everlasting Life?"

Again that awful silence made itself felt like a deadly chill on the sunlit air,—the quiet, patient crowds seemed waiting in hushed suspense for some reply which should be as a flash of spiritual enlightenment to leap from one to the other with kindling heat and radiance, and vivify them all into a new and happier existence. But now, when Theos most strongly desired to speak, he remained dumb as stone! . . . vainly he struggled against and contended with the invisible, mysterious, and relentless despotism that smote him on the mouth as it were, and deprived him of all power of utterance, . . . his tongue was stiff and frozen, . . . his very lips were sealed! Trembling violently, he gazed beseechingly at Sah-luma, who held his arm in a firm and friendly grasp, and who, apparently quickly perceiving that he was distressed and embarrassed, undertook himself to furnish forth what he evidently considered a fitting response to Khosrul's adjuration.

"Most venerable Seer!" he cried mockingly, his bright face radiant with mirth and his dark eyes flashing a careless contempt as he spoke— "Thou art as short-sighted as thine own auguries if thou canst not at once comprehend the drift of my friend's humor! He hath caught the infection of thy fanatic eloquence, and, like thee, knows naught of what he says: moreover he hath good wine and sunlight mingled in his blood, whereby he hath been doubtless moved to play a jest upon thee. I pray thee heed him not! He is as free to declare thy Prophecy is of the PAST, as thou art to insist on its being of the FUTURE,—in both ways 'tis a most foolish fallacy! Nevertheless, continue thy entertaining discourse, Sir Graybeard! . . . and if thou must needs address thyself to any one soul in particular, why let it be me,—for though, thanks to mine own excellent good sense, I have no faith in angels nor crosses, nor everlasting life, nor any of the strange riddles wherewith thou seekest to perplex and bewilder the brains of the ignorant, still am I Laureate of the realm, and ready to hold argument with thee,—yea!—until such time as these dumfounded soldiers and citizens of Al-Kyris shall remember their duty sufficiently to seize and take thee captive in the King's great name!"

As he ceased a deep sigh ran, like the first sound of a rising wind among trees, through the heretofore motionless multitude,—a faint, dawning, yet doubtful smile reflected itself on their faces,—and the old familiar shout broke feebly from their lips:

"Hail, Sah-luma! Let us hear Sah-luma!"

Sah-luma looked down upon them all in airy derision.

"O fickle, terror-stricken fools!" he exclaimed—"O thankless and disloyal people! What!—ye WILL see me now? . . . ye WILL hear me? . . . Aye! but who shall answer for your obedience to my words! Nay, is it possible that I, your country's chosen Chief Minstrel, should have stood so long among ye disregarded! How comes it your dull eyes and ears were fixed so fast upon yon dotard miscreant whose days are numbered? Methought t'was but Sah-luma's voice that could persuade ye to assemble thus in such locust-like swarms. . . since when have the Poet and the People of Al-Kyris ceased to be as one?"

A vague, muttering sound answered him, whether of shame or dissatisfaction it was difficult to tell. Khosrul's vibrating accent struck sharply across that muffled murmur.

"The Poet and the People of Al-Kyris are further asunder than light and darkness!" he cried vehemently—"For the Poet has been false to his high vocation, and the People trust in him no more!"

There was an instant's hush, . . . a hush as it seemed of grieved acquiescence on the part of the populace,—and during that brief pause Theos's heart gave a fierce bound against his ribs as though some one had suddenly shot at him with a poisoned arrow. He glanced quickly at Sah-luma,—but Sah-luma stood calmly unmoved, his handsome head thrown back, a cynical smile on his lips and his eyes darker than ever with an intensity of unutterable scorn.

"Sah-luma! . . . Sah-luma!" and the piercing, reproachful voice of the Prophet penetrated every part of the spacious square like a sonorous bell ringing over a still landscape: "O divine Spirit of Song pent up in gross clay, was ever mortal more gifted than thou! In thee was kindled the white fire of Heaven,—to thee were confided the memories of vanished worlds, . . . for thee God bade His Nature wear a thousand shapes of varied meaning,—the sun, the moon, the stars were appointed as thy servants,—for thou wert born POET, the mystically chosen Teacher and Consoler of Mankind! What hast thou done, Sah-luma, . . . what hast thou done with the treasures bestowed upon thee by the all-endowing Angels? . . . How hast thou used the talisman of thy genius? To comfort the afflicted? . . . to dethrone and destroy the oppressor? . . . to uphold the cause of Justice? . . . to rouse the noblest instincts of thy race? . . . to elevate and purify the world? . . . Alas, alas!—thou hast made Thyself the idol of thy muse, and thou being but perishable, thy fame shall perish with thee! Thou hast drowsed away thy manhood in the lap of vice, . . . thou hast slept and dreamed when thou should have been awake and vigilant! Not I, but THOU shouldst have warned the people of their coming doom! . . . not I, but THOU shouldst have marked the threatening signs of the pregnant hour,—not I, but THOU shouldst have perceived the first faint glimmer of God's future scheme of glad salvation,—not I, but THOU shouldst have taught and pleaded, and swayed by thy matchless sceptre of sweet song, the passions of thy countrymen! Hadst thou been true to that first flame of Thought within thee, O Sah-luma, how thy glory would have dwarfed the power of kings! Empires might have fallen, cities decayed, and nations been absorbed in ruin,—and yet thy clear-convincing voice, rendered imperishable by its faithfulness should have sounded forth in triumph above the foundering wrecks of Time! O Poet unworthy of thy calling! . . . How thou hast wantoned with the sacred Muse! . . . how thou hast led her stainless feet into the mire of sensual hypocrisies, and decked her with the trumpery gew-gaws of a meaningless fair speech!— How thou hast caught her by the virginal hair and made her chastity the screen for all thine own licentiousness! . . . Thou shouldst have humbly sought her benediction,—thou shouldst have handled her with gentle reverence and patient ardor,—from her wise lips thou shouldst have learned how best to Practice those virtues whose praise thou didst evasively proclaim, . . . thou shouldst have shrined her, throned her, worshiped her, and served her, . . . yea! . . . even as a sinful man may serve an Angel who loves him!"

Ah, what a strange, cold thrill ran through Theos as he heard these last words! 'As a sinful man may serve an Angel who loves him!' How happy the man thus loved! . . . how fortunate the sinner thus permitted to serve! . . . Who Was He? . . . Could there be any one so marvellously privileged? He wondered dimly,—and a dull, aching pain throbbed heavily in his brows. It was a very singular thing too, that he should find himself strongly and personally affected by Khosrul's address to Sah-luma, yet such was the case, . . . so much so, indeed, that he accepted all the Prophet's reproaches as though they applied solely To His Own Past Life! He could not understand his emotion, . . . nevertheless he kept on dreamily regretting that things Were as Khosrul had said, . . . that he had Not fulfilled his vocation,—and that he had neither been humble enough nor devout enough nor unselfish enough to deserve the high and imperial name of Poet.

Round and round like a flying mote this troublesome idea circled in his brain, . . . he must do better in future, he resolved, supposing that any future remained to Him in which to work, . . . He Must Redeem The Past! . . . Here he roused his mental faculties with a start and forced himself to realize that it was Sah-Luma to whom the Prophet spoke, . . . Sah-luma, Only Sah-luma,—not himself!

Then straightway he became indignant on his friend's behalf,—why should Sah-luma be blamed? . . . Sah-luma was a glorious poet!—a master-singer of singers! . . . his fume must and should endure forever! . . . Thus thinking, he regained his composure by degrees, and strove to assume the same air of easy indifference as that exhibited by his companion, when again Khosrul's declamatory tones thundered forth with an absoluteness of emphasis that was both startling and convincing:

"Hear me, Sah-luma, Chief Minstrel of Al-Kyris!—hear me, thou who hast willfully wasted the golden moments of never-returning time! THOU ART MARKED OUT FOR DEATH!—death sudden and fierce as the leap of the desert panther on its prey! . . . death that shall come to thee through the traitorous speech of the evil woman whose beauty has sapped thy strength and rendered thy glory inglorious! . . . death that for thee, alas! shall be mournful and utter oblivion! Naught shall it avail to thee that thy musical weaving of words hath been graven seven times over, on tablets of stone and agate and ivory, of gold and white silex and porphyry, and the unbreakable rose-adamant,—none of these shall suffice to keep thy name in remembrance,—for what cannot be broken shall be melted with flame, and what cannot be erased shall be buried miles deep in the bosom of earth, whence it never again shall be lifted into the light of day! Aye! thou shalt be FORGOTTEN!— forgotten as though thou hadst never sung,—other poets shall chant in the world, yet maybe none so well as thou!—other laurel and myrtle wreaths shall be given by countries and kings to bards unworthy, of whom none perchance shall have thy sweetness! . . . but thou,—thou the most grandly gifted, gift-squandering Poet the world has ever known, shalt be cast among the dust of unremembered nothings, and the name of Sah-luma shall carry no meaning to any man born in the coming here-after! For thou hast cherished within Thyself the poison that withers thee, . . . the deadly poison of Doubt, the Denial of God's existence, . . . the accursed blankness of Disbelief in the things of the Life Eternal! . . . wherefore, thy spirit is that of one lost and rebellious,—whose best works are futile,—whose days are void of example,—and whose carelessly grasped torch of song shall be suddenly snatched from thy hand and extinguished in darkness! God pardon thee, dying Poet! . . . God give thy parting soul a chance of penance and of sweet redemption! . . . God comfort thee in that drear Land of Shadow whither thou art bound! . . . God bring thee forth again from Chaos to a nobler Future! . . . Sin-burdened as thou art, my blessing follows thee in thy last agony! Sah-luma! . . . FALLEN ANGEL, SELF-EXILED FROM THY PEERS! . . . FAREWELL!"

The effect of these strange words was so extraordinarily impressive, that for one instant the astonished and evidently affrighted crowds pressed round Sah-luma eagerly, staring at him in morbid fear and wonder, as though they expected him to drop dead before them in immediate fulfillment of the Prophet's solemn valediction. Theos, oppressed by an inward sickening sense of terror, also regarded him with close and anxious solicitude, but was almost reassured at the first glance.

Never was a greater opposition offered to Khosrul's gloomy prognostications, than that contained in the handsome Laureate's aspect at that moment,—his supple, graceful figure alert with life, . . . his glowing face flushed by the sun, and touched with that faintly amused look of serene scorn, . . . his glorious eyes, brilliant as jewels under their drooping amorous lids, and the regal poise of his splendid shoulders and throat, as he lifted his head a little more haughtily than usual, and glanced indifferently down from his foothold on the edge of the fountain at the upturned, questioning faces of the throng, . . . all even to the careless balance and ease of his attitude, betokened his perfect condition of health, and the entire satisfaction he had in the consciousness of his own strength and beauty.

He seemed about to speak, and raised his hand with the graceful yet commanding gesture of one accustomed to the art of elegant rhetoric, . . . when suddenly his expression changed, . . . shrugging his shoulders lightly as who should say. . . "Here comes the conclusion of the matter,—no time for further argument"—he silently pointed across the Square, while a smile dazzling yet cruel played on his delicately parted lips, . . . a smile, the covert meaning of which was soon explained. For all at once a brazen roar of trumpets split the silence into torn and discordant echoes,—the crowd turned swiftly, and seeing who it was that approached, rushed hither and thither in the wildest confusion, making as though they would have fled, . . . and in less than a minute, a gleaming cohort of mounted and armed spearmen galloped furiously into the thick of the melee.

Following these came a superb car drawn by six jet-black horses that plunged and pranced through the multitude with no more heed than if these groups of living beings had been mere sheafs of corn, . . . a car flashing from end to end with gold and precious stones, in which towered the erect, massive form of Zephoranim, the King. His dark face was ablaze with wrath, . . . tightly grasping the reins of his reckless steeds, he drew himself haughtily upright and turned his rolling, fierce black eyes indignantly from side to side on the scared people, as he drove through their retreating ranks, smiting down and mangling with the sharp spikes of his tall chariot-wheels men, women, and children without care or remorse, till he forced his terrible passage straight to the foot of the Obelisk. There he came to an abrupt standstill, and, lifting high his strong hand and brawny arm glittering with jewels, he cried:

"Soldiers! Seize yon traitorous rebel! Ten thousand pieces of gold for the capture of Khosrul!"

There was an instant of hesitation, . . . not one of the populace stirred to obey the order. Then suddenly, as though released by their monarch's command from some mesmeric spell, the before inactive mounted guards started into action, cantered sharply forward and surrounded the Obelisk, while the armed spearsmen closed together and made a swift advance upon the venerable figure that stood alone and defenseless, tranquilly awaiting their approach. But there was evidently some unknown and mysterious force pent up within the Prophet's feeble frame, for when the soldiers were just about an arm's length from him, they seemed all at once troubled and irresolute, and turned their looks away, as though fearing to gaze too steadfastly upon that grand, thought-furrowed countenance in which the eyes, made young by inward fervor, blazed forth with unearthly lustre beneath a silvery halo of tossed white hair. Zephoranim perceived this touch of indecision on the part of his men, and his black brows contracted in an ominous frown.

"Halt!" he shouted fiercely, apparently to make it seem to the mob that the pause in the action of the soldiery was in compliance with his own behest, . . . "Halt! . . . Bind him, and bring him hither, . . . I myself will slay him!"

"Halt!" echoed a voice, discordantly sharp and wild. "Halt thou also, great Zephoranim! for Death bars thy further progress!"

And Khosrul, manifestly possessed by some superhuman access of frenzy, leaped from his position on the back of the stone Lion, and slipping agilely through the ranks of the startled spearsmen and guards, who were all unprepared for the suddenness and rapidity of his movements, he sprang boldly on the edge of the Royal chariot, and there clung to the jewelled wheel, looking like a gaunt aerial spectre, an ambassador of coming ruin. The King, speechless with amazement and fury, dragged at his huge sword till he wrenched it out of its sheath, . . .

raising it, he whirled it round his head so that it gave a murderous hiss in the air, . . . and yet. . . was his strong arm paralyzed that he forbore to strike!

"Zephoranim!" Khosrul, in terms that were piercing and dolorous as the whistling of the wind among hollow reeds,—"Zephoranim, Thou Shalt Die To-night! Art Thou Ready? Art thou ready, proud King? . . . ready to be made less than the lowest of the low? Hush! . . . Hush!" and his aged face took upon itself a ghastly greenish pallor— "Hear you not the muttering of the thunder underground? There are strange powers at work! . . . powers of the undug earth and unfathomed sea! . . . hark how they tear at the stately foundations of Al-Kyris! . . . Flame! flame! it is already kindled!—it shall enwrap thee with more closeness than thy coronation robe, O mighty Sovereign! . . . with more gloating fondness than the serpent-twining arms of thy beloved! Listen, Zephoranim, listen!"

Here he stretched out his skinny hand and pointed upwards,—his eyes grew fixed and glassy,—his throat rattled convulsively. At that moment the monarch, recovering his self-possession, once more lifted his sword with direct and deadly aim, but the Prophet, uttering a wild shriek, caught at his descending wrist and gripped it fast.

"See. . . See!" he exclaimed. "Put up thy weapon! . . . Thou shalt never need it where thou art summoned! . . . Lo! how yon blood-red letters blaze against the blue of heaven! . . . There! . . . there it comes!—Read. . . read!'tis written plain. . . 'Al-Kyris Shall Fall, And The King Shall Die!' . . . Hist. . . hist! . . . Dumb oracles speak and dead voices find tongue! . . . hark how they chant together the old forgotten warning:

'When the High Priestess
Is the King's mistress
Then fall Al-Kyris!'

Fall Al-Kyris! . . . Aye! . . . the City of a thousand palaces shall fall to-night! . . . To-night! . . . O night of desperate horror! . . . and thou, O King, Shalt Die!"

And as he shrilled the last word on the air with terrific emphasis, he threw up his arms like a man suddenly shot, and reeling backward fell heavily on the ground,—a corpse.

A great cry went up from the crowd, . . . the King leaned eagerly out of his car.

"Is the fool dead, or feigning death?" he demanded, addressing one of a group of soldiers standing near.

The officer stooped and felt the motionless body.

"O great King, live forever! He is dead!"

Zephoranim hesitated. Cruelty and clemency struggled for the mastery in the varying expression of his frowning face, but cruelty conquered. Grasping his sword firmly, he bent still further forward out of his chariot, and with one swift, keen stroke, severed the lifeless Prophet's head from its trunk, and taking it up on, the point of his weapon, showed it to the multitude. A smothered, shuddering sigh that was half a groan rippled through the dense throng—a sound that evidently added fresh irritation to the already heated temper of the haughty sovereign. With a savage laugh, he tossed his piteous trophy on the pavement, where it lay in a pool of its own blood, the white hair about it stained ruddily, and the still open eyes upturned as though in dumb appeal to heaven. Then, without deigning to utter another word, or to bestow another look upon the surrounding crowd of his disconcerted subjects, he gathered up his coursers' reins and prepared to depart.

Just then the sun went behind a cloud, and only a side-beam of radiance shot forth, pouring itself straight down on the royally attired figure of the monarch and the headless body of Khosrul, and at the same time bringing into sudden and prominent relief the silver Cross that glittered on the breast of the bleeding corpse, and that seemed to mysteriously offer itself as the Key to some unsolved Enigma. As if drawn by one strangely mutual attraction, all eyes, even those of Zephoranim himself, turned instinctively toward the flashing Emblem, which appeared to burn like living fire on that perished mass of stiffening clay, . . . and there was a brief silence,—a pause, during which Theos, who had watched everything with curiously calm interest, such as may be felt by a spectator watching the progress of a finely acted tragedy, became conscious of the same singular sensation he had already several times experienced,—namely, THAT HE HAD WITNESSED THE WHOLE OF THIS SCENE BEFORE!

he remembered it quite well,—particularly that apparently trifling incident of the sunlight happening to shine so brilliantly on the dead man and his cross while the rest of the vast assemblage were in comparative shadow. It was very odd! . . . his memory was like a wonderful art-gallery in which some pictures were fresh of tint, while others were dim and faded, . . . but this special "tableau" in the Square of Al-Kyris was very distinctly painted in brilliant and vivid colors on the sombre background of his past recollections, and he found the circumstance so remarkable that he was on the point of saying something to Sah-luma about it,—when the sun came out again in full splendor, and Zephoranim's spirited steeds started forward at a canter.

The King, controlling them easily with one hand, extended the other majestically by way of formal salutation to his people, . . . his tall, muscular form was displayed to the best advantage,—the narrow jewelled fillet that bound his rough dark locks emitted a myriad scintillations of light, . . . his close-fitting coat-of-mail, woven from thousands of small links of gold, set off his massive chest and shoulders to perfection,— and as he moved along royally in his sumptuous car, the effect of his striking presence was such, that a complete change took place in the before sullen humor of the populace. For seeing him thus alive and well in direct opposition to Khosrul's ominous prediction,—even as Sah-luma also stood unharmed in spite of his having been apostrophized as a "dying" Poet,—the mob, always fickle and always dazzled by outward show, suddenly set up a deafening roar of cheering. The pallid hue of terror vanished from faces that had but lately looked spectrally thin with speechless dread, and crowds of servile petitioners and place-hunters began to press eagerly round their monarch's chariot, . . . when all at once a woman in the throng gave a wild scream and rushed away shrieking "THE OBELISK! . . . THE OBELISK!"

Every eye was instantly turned toward the stately pillar of white granite that sparkled in the sunlight like an immense carven jewel, . . . great Heaven! . . . It was tottering to and fro like the unsteadied mast of a ship at sea! . . . One look sufficed,—and a frightful panic ensued—a horrible, brutish stampede of creatures without faith in anything human or divine save their own wretched personalities,—the King, infected by the general scare, urged his horses into furious gallop, and dashed through the cursing, swearing, howling throng like an embodied whirlwind,—and for a few seconds nothing seemed distinctly visible But a surging mass of infuriated humanity, fighting with itself for life.

Theos alone remained singularly calm,—his sole consideration was for his friend Sah-luma, whom he entwined with one arm as he sprang down from the position they had hitherto occupied on the brink of the fountain, and made straight for the nearest of the six broad avenues that opened directly into the Square. Sah-luma looked pale, but was apparently unafraid,—he said nothing, and passively allowed himself to be piloted by Theos through the madly raging multitude, which, oddly enough, parted before them like mist before the wind, so that in a magically short interval they successfully reached a place of safety.

And they reached it not a moment too soon. For the Obelisk was now plainly to be seen lurching forward at an angle of several degrees, . . . strange muffled, roaring sounds were heard at its base, as though demons were digging up its foundations, . . . then, seemingly shaken by underground tremors, it began to oscillate violently,—a terrific explosion was heard as of the bursting of a giant bomb,—and immediately afterward the majestic monolith toppled over and fell!—with the crash of a colossal cannonade that sent its thunderous reverberations through and through the length and breadth of the city! Hundreds of persons were killed and wounded,—many of the mounted guards and spearmen, who were striving to force a way of escape through the crowd, were struck down and crushed pell-mell with their horses as they rode,—the desperate people trampled each other to death in their frenzied efforts to reach the nearest outlet to the river embankment, . . . but when once the Obelisk had actually fallen, all this turmoil was for an instant checked, and the gasping, torn, and bleeding survivors of the struggle stopped, as it were to take breath, and stared in blank dismay upon the strange ruin before them.

Theos, still holding Sah-luma by the arm, with the protecting fondness of an elder brother guarding a younger, gazed also at the scene with quiet, sorrowfully wondering eyes. For it meant something to him he was sure, because it was so familiar,—yet he found it impossible to grasp the comprehension of that meaning! It was a singular spectacle enough; the lofty four-sided white pillar, that had so lately been a monumental glory of Al-Kyris, had split itself with the violence of its fall into two huge desolate-looking fragments, which now lay one on each side of the square, as though flung thither by a Titan's hand,—the great lion had been hurled from its position and overturned like a toy, while the shield it had supported between its paws had entirely disappeared in minutely scattered atoms, . . . the fountains had altogether ceased playing. Now and then a thin, vaporous stream of smoke appeared to issue between the crannies of the pavement,—otherwise there was no visible sign of the mysterious force that had wrought so swift and sudden a work of destruction,—the sun shone brilliantly, and over all the havoc beamed the placid brightness of a cloudless summer sky!

The most prominent object of all amid the general devastation, and the one that fascinated Theos more than the view of the destroyed monolith and the debased Lion, was the uninjured head of the Prophet Khosrul. There it lay, exactly between the sundered halves of the Obelisk, . . . pale rays of light glimmered on its bloodstained silvery hair and open glazed eyes,—a solemn smile seemed graven on its waxen-pallid features. And at a little distance off, on the breast of the black-robed headless corpse that remained totally uncrushed in an open space by itself, among the surrounding heaps of slain and wounded, glistened the Cross like a fiery gem, . . . an all-significant talisman that, as he beheld it, filled Theos's heart with a feverish craving,—an inexplicable desire mingled with remorse far greater than any fear!

Instinctively he drew Sah-luma away. . . away! . . . still keeping his wistful gaze fixed on that uncomprehended, yet soul-recognized Symbol, till gradually the drooping branches of trees interrupted and shadowed the vista, and, as he moved further and further backward, closed their soft network of green foliage like the closing curtain on the strange but awfully remembered scene, shutting it out from his bewildered sight. . . forever!

XXV

A Golden Tress

Once clear of the Square the two friends apparently became mutually conscious of the peril they had just escaped, . . . and coming to a sudden standstill they looked at each other in blank, stupefied silence. Crowds of people streamed past them, wandering hither and thither in confused, cloudy masses,—some with groans and dire lamentations bearing away their dead and wounded,—others rushing frantically about, beating their breasts, tearing their hair, calling on the gods and lamenting Khosrul, while not a few muttered curses on the King. And ever and anon the name of "Lysia," coupled with heavy execrations, was hissed from mouth to mouth, which Theos, overhearing, began to foresee might serve as a likely cause for Sah-luma's taking offence and possibly resenting in his own person this public disparagement of the woman he loved,—therefore, without more ado he roused himself from his momentarily dazed condition, and urged his comrade on at a quick pace toward the safe shelter of his own palace, where at any rate he could be kept out of the reach of immediate harm.

The twain walked side by side, exchanging scarcely a word,—Sah-luma seemed in a manner stunned by the violence of the late catastrophe, and Theos was too busy with his own thoughts to speak. On their way they were overtaken by the King's chariot,—it flew by with a glittering whirl and clatter, amid sweeping clouds of dust, through which the dark face of Zephoranim loomed out upon them like an almost palpable shadow. As it vanished Sah-luma stopped short, and stared at his companion in utter amazement.

"By my soul!" he exclaimed indignantly. "The whole world must be going mad! 'Tis the first time in all my days of Laureateship that Zephoranim hath failed to reverently salute me as he passed!"

And he looked far more perturbed than when the falling Obelisk had threatened him with imminent destruction.

Theos caught his arm with a quick movement of vexed impatience.

"Tush, man, no matter!" he said hastily—"What are Kings to thee? . . . thou who art an Emperor of Song? These little potentates that wield earth's sceptres are as fickle in their moods as the very mob they are supposed to govern, . . . moreover, thou knowest Zephoranim hath had enough to-day to startle him out of all accustomed rules of courtesy. Be assured of it, his mind is like a ship at sea, storm-tossed and at the mercy of the winds,—thou canst not surely blame him, that for once after so strange a turbulence, and unwonted a disaster, he hath no eyes for thee whose sole sweet mission, is to minister to pleasure."

"To minister to pleasure!" echoed Sah-luma petulantly. "Nay, have I done nothing more than this? Art thou already grown so disloyal a friend that thou wilt half repeat the jargon of yon dead fanatic Khosrul who dared to tell me I had served my Art unfittingly? Have I not ministered to grief as well as joy? To hours of pain and bitterness, as well as to long days of ease and amorous dreaming? . . . Have I not. . ." here he paused and a warm flush crept through the olive pallor of his skin,—his eyes grew plaintive and wistful and he threw one arm round Theos's neck as he continued: "No I. . . after all 'tis vain to deny it. . . I have hated grief,—I have loathed the very suggestion of care,—I have thrust sorrow out of my sight as a thing vile and unwelcome,—and I have chosen to sing to the world of rapture more than pain,—inasmuch as methinks Humanity suffers enough, without having its cureless anguish set to the music of a poet's rhythm to incessantly haunt and torture its already breaking heart."

"Say rather to soothe and tranquillize"—murmured Theos, more to himself than to his friend—"For suppressed sorrow is hardest to endure, and when grief once finds apt utterance 'tis already half consoled! So should the world's great singers tenderly proclaim the world's most speechless miseries, and who knows but vexed Creation being thus relieved of pent-up woe may not take new heart of grace and comfort?"

The words were spoken in a soft Sotto-Voce, and Sah-luma seemed not to hear. He leaned, however, very confidingly and affectionately against Theos's shoulder as he walked along, and appeared to have speedily forgotten his annoyance at the recent slighting conduct of the King.

"I marvel at the downfall of the Obelisk!" he said presently. . . "'Twas rooted full ten feet deep in solid earth, . . . maybe the foundations were ill-fitted,—nevertheless, if history speaks truly, it hath stood unshaken for two thousand years! Strange that it should be now hurled forth thus desperately! . . . I would I knew the hidden cause! Many, alas! have met their death to-day, . . . pushed out of life in haste, . . . all unprepared. . . One wonders where such souls have fled! Something there is that troubles me, . . . methinks I am more than half disposed to leave Al-Kyris for a time, and wander forth into a world of unknown things—"

"With me!" cried Theos impetuously—"Come with me, Sah-luma! . . . Come now, this very day! I too have been warned of evil. . . evil undeclared, yet close at hand, . . . let us escape from danger while time remains! . . . Let us depart!"

"Whither should we go?" . . . and Sah-luma, pausing in his walk, fixed his large, soft eyes full on his companion as he put the question.

Theos was mute. Covered with confusion, he asked himself the same thing. "Whither should we go?" He had no knowledge of the country that lay outside Al-Kyris, . . . he had no distinct remembrance of any other place than this in which he was. All his past existence was as blotted and blurred as a child's spoiled and discarded copybook, . . . true, he retained two names in his thoughts,—namely "ARDATH" and "THE PASS OF DARIEL" but he was hopelessly ignorant as to what these meant or how he had become connected with them! He was roused from his distressful cogitation by Sah-luma's voice speaking again half gayly, half sadly:

"Nay, nay, my friend! . . . we cannot leave the City, we two alone and unguided, for beyond the gates is the desert wide and bare, with scarce a spring of cool water in many weary miles,—and beyond the desert is a forest, gloomy and tiger haunted, wherein the footsteps of man have seldom penetrated. To travel thus far we should need much preparation, . . . many servants, many beasts of burden, and many months' provision. . . moreover, 'tis a foolish, fancy crossed my mind at best,—for what should I, the Laureate of Al-Kyris, do in other lands? Besides, my departure would indeed be the desolation of the city,—well may Al-Kyris fall when Sah-luma no longer abides within it! Seawards the way lies open,—maybe, in days to come, we twain may take ship and sail hence for a brief sojourn to those distant western shores, whence thou, though thou sayest naught of them, must assuredly have come; I have often dreamed idly of a gray coast washed with dull rain and swathed in sweeping mists, where ever and anon the sun shines through,—a country cheerless, where a poet's fame like mine might ring the darkness of the skies with light, and stir the sleepy silence into song!"

Still Theos said nothing,—there were hot tears in his throat that choked his utterance. He gazed up at the glowing sky above him,—it was a burning vault of cloudless blue in which the sun glared forth witheringly like a scorching mass of flame, . . . Oh for the freshness of a "gray coast washed with dull rain and swathed in sweeping mists" . . .

MARIE CORELLI

such as Sah-luma spoke of! . . . and what a strange sickening yearning suddenly filled his soul for the unforgotten sonorous dash of the sea! He drew a quick breath and pressed his friend's arm with unconscious fervor, . . . why, why could he not take this dear companion away out of possible peril? . . . away to those far lands dimly remembered, yet now so completely lost sight of, that they seemed to him but as a delusive mirage faintly discerned above the rising waters of Lethe! Sighing deeply, he controlled his emotion and forced himself to speak calmly though his voice trembled.

"Not now then, but hereafter, thou'lt be my fellow-traveller, Sah-luma? . . .'twill be a joyous time when we, set free of present hindrance, may journey through a myriad glorious scenes together, sharing such new and mutual gladness that perchance we scarce shall miss the splendor of Al-Kyris left behind! Meanwhile I would that thou couldst promise me one thing," . . . here he paused, but, seeing Sah-luma's inquiring look, went on in a low, eager tone! "Go not to the Temple to-night!—absent thyself from this Sacrifice, which, though it be the law of the realm, is nevertheless mere murderous barbarity,—and—inasmuch as the King is wrathful—I pray thee avoid his presence!"

Sah-luma broke into a laugh. "Now by my faith, good comrade, as well ask me for my head as demand such impossibilities! Absent myself from the temple to-night of all nights in the world, when owing to these late phenomenal occurrences in the city, every one who is of repute and personal distinction will be present to assist at the Service and offer petitions to the fabulous gods that haply their supposititious indignation may be averted? My friend, if only for the sake of custom I must be there, . . . moreover, I should be liable to banishment from the realm for so specially marked a breach of religious discipline! And as for the King, he is my puppet; were he savage as a starving bear my voice could tame him,—and concerning his late churlishness 'twas no doubt mere heat of humor, and thou shalt see him sue to me for pardon as only monarchs can sue to the bards who keep them in their thrones! Knowest thou not that were I to string three stanzas of a fiery republican ditty, and set it floating on the lips of the people, that song would sing down Zephoranim from his royal estate more surely than the fury of an armed conqueror! Believe it!—We, the poets, rule the nation, . . . A rhyme has oft had power to kill a king!"

Theos smiled at the proud boast, but made no reply, as by this time they had reached the Laureate's palace, and were ascending the steps that led into the entrance-hall. A young page advanced to meet them, and, dropping on one knee before his master, held out a small scroll tied across and across with what appeared to be a thick strand of amber-colored floss silk.

"For the most illustrious Chief of Poets, Sah-luma" . . . said the little lad, keeping his head bent humbly as he spoke. . . "It was brought lately by one masked, who rode in haste and fear, and, ere he could be questioned, swift departed."

Sah-luma took the missive carelessly, scarcely glancing at it, and crossed the hall toward his own apartment, Theos following him. On his way, however, he paused and turned round:

"Has Niphrata yet come home?" he demanded of the page who still lingered.

"No, my lord! . . . naught hath been seen or heard concerning her."

Sah-luma gave a petulant gesture of annoyance and passed on. Arrived in his study he seated himself, and allowed his eyes to rest more attentively on the packet just given him. As he looked he uttered a slight exclamation, . . . Theos hastened to his side. "What has happened, Sah-luma? . . . hast thou ill news?"

"Ill news?—nay, of a truth I know not" . . . and the Laureate gazed up blankly into his friend's face. "But this" . . . and he touched the fair silken substance that tied the scroll he held, "this is Niphrata's hair!"

"Niphrata's hair!" . . . Theos was too much surprised to do more than repeat the words mechanically, while a strange pang shot through his heart as of inward shame or sorrow.

"Naught can deceive me in the color of that gold!" went on Sah-luma dreamily, as with careful, somewhat tremulous fingers, he gently loosened the twisted shining threads that were so delicately knotted together, and smoothing them out to their full length, displayed what was indeed a lovely tress of hair bright as woven sunlight with a rippling wave in it that, like the tendril of a vine caught and wound about his hand as though it were a fond and feeling thing.

"See you not, Theos, how warm and soft and shuddering a curl it is? . . . It clings to me as if it knew my touch!—as if it half remembered how many and many a time it had been drawn with its companions to my lips and kissed full tenderly! . . . How sad and desolate it seems thus severed and alone!"

He spoke gently, yet not without a touch of passion, and twined the fair tresses lingeringly round his fingers, . . . then, with the air of one

　　　　　　　　　　　　　　　　　　　MARIE CORELLI

who is instinctively prepared for some unpleasing tidings, he opened the scroll and perused its contents in silence. As he read on, his face grew very grave, and full of pained and wondering regret. . . quietly he passed the missive to Theos, who took it from his hand with a tremor of something like fear. The delicately traced characters with which it was covered floated for a moment in a faint blur before his eyes,—then they resolved themselves into legible shape and meaning, as follows:

To the ever-worshiped and immortally renowned

Sah-luma.
Poet-Laureate of the Kingdom of Al-Kyris.

"Blame me not, O my beloved Lord, that I have left thy
dearest presence thus unwarnedly forever, staying no time
to weary thee with my too fond and foolish tears and kisses
of farewell! I owe to thee the gift of freedom, and while I
thank thee for that gift, I do employ it now to serve me as a
sacrifice to Love,—an immolation of myself upon the altars
of my own desire! For thou knowest I have loved thee, O
Sah-luma—not too well but most unwisely,—for what am I
that thou shouldst stoop to cover my unworthiness with the
royal purple of thy poet-passion? . . . what could I ever be
save the poor trembling slave-idolater, of whose endearments
thou must needs most speedily tire! Nevertheless I cannot
still this hunger of my heart,—this love that stings me
more than it consoles,—and out of the very transport of
my burning thoughts I have learned many and strange
things,—things whereby I, a woman feebled and unlessoned,
have grasped the glimmering foreknowledge of events to
come,—events wherein I do perceive for thee, thou Chiefest
among men, some dark and threatening disaster. When fore I
have prayed unto the most high gods, that they will deign to
accept me as thy hostage to misfortune, and set me as a bar
between thy life and dawning peril, so that I, long valueless,
may serve at least awhile to avert doom from thee who art
unparagoned throughout the world!
    "Thus I go forth alone to brave and pacify the wrath of the
Immortals,—call me not back nor weep for my departure, . . .

thou wilt not miss me long! To die for thee, Sah-luma, is better than to live for thee, . . . for living I must needs be conquered by my sin of love and lose myself and thee,—but in the quiet Afterwards of Death, no passion shall have strength to mar the peaceful, patient waiting of my soul on thine! Farewell thou utmost heart of my weak heart! . . . thou only life of my frail life! . . . think of me sometimes if thou will, but only as of a flower thou didst gather once in some past half-forgotten spring-time. . . a flower that, as it slowly withered, blessed the dear hand in whose warm clasp it died!

NIPHRATA

Tears rose to Theos's eyes as he finished reading these evidently unpremeditated pathetic words that suggested so much more than they actually declared. He silently returned the scroll to Sah-luma, who sat very still, thoughtfully stroking the long, bright curl that was twisted round his fingers like a glittering strand of spun glass,—and he felt all at once so unreasonably irritated with his friend, that he was even inclined to find fault with the very grace and beauty of his person, . . . the mere indolence of his attitude was, for the moment, provoking.

"Why art thou so unmoved?" he demanded almost sternly.

"What hast thou done to Niphrata, to thus grieve her gentle spirit beyond remedy?"

Sah-luma looked up, like a surprised child.

"Done? . . . Nay, what should I do? . . . I have let her love me!"

O sublime permission! . . . he had "LET HER LOVE" him! . . . He had condescendingly allowed her, as it were, to waste all the treasures of her soul upon him! Theos stared at him in vague amazement,—while he, apparently tired of his own reflections, continued with some impatience:

"What more could she desire? . . . I never barred her from my presence, . . . nor checked the fervor of her greetings! I wore the flowers she chose,—I listened to the songs she sang, and when she looked more fair than ordinary I stinted not the warmth of my caresses. She was too meek and loving for my fancy. . . no will save mine—no happiness save in my company,—no thought beyond my pleasure—one wearies of such a fond excess of sweetness! Nevertheless her sole delight was still to serve me,—could I debar her from that joy because I saw therein some danger for her peace? Slave as she was, I made her free—and lo! how capriciously she plays with her late-given liberty! 'Tis always the way with women,—no man shall ever learn how best to please them! She knew I loved her not as lovers love,—she knew my heart was elsewhere fixed and fated. . . and if, notwithstanding this knowledge, she still chose to love me, then assuredly her grief is of her own creating! Methinks 'tis I who am most injured in this matter! . . . all the day long I have tormented myself concerning the silly maiden's absence, while she, seized by some crazed idea of new adventure, has gone forth heedlessly, scarce knowing whither. Her letter is the exalted utterance of an overwrought, excited brain,—she has in all likelihood caught the contagion of superstitious alarm that seems just now to possess the whole city, and she knows naught of what she writes or what she means to do. To leave me forever, as she says, is out of her power,—for I will demand her back at the hands of Lysia or the King,—and no demand of mine has ever been refused. Moreover, with Lysia's aid, her hiding-place is soon and easily discovered!"

"How?" asked Theos mechanically, still surveying the beautiful, calm features of the charming egotist whose nature seemed such a curious mixture of loftiness and littleness. "She may have left the city!"

"No one can leave the city without express permission,"—rejoined Sah-luma tranquilly—"Besides, . . . didst thou not see the Black Disc last night in Lysia's palace?"

Theos nodded assent. He at once remembered the strange revolving thing that had covered itself with brilliant letters at the approach of the High Priestess, and he waited somewhat eagerly to hear the meaning of so singular an object explained.

"The Priest of the Temple of Nagaya,"—went on Sah-luma—"are the greatest scientists in the world, with the exception of the lately formed Circle of Mystics, who it must be confessed exceed them in certain new lines of discovery. But setting aside the Mystic School, which it behoves us not to speak of, seeing it is condemned by law,—there are no men living more subtly wise in matters pertaining to aerial force and light-phenomena, than the Servants of the Secret Doctrine of the Temple. All seeming-marvellous things are to them mere child's play,—and the miracles by which they keep the multitude in awe are not by any means vulgar, but most exquisitely scientific. As, for instance, at the great New Year Festival, called by us 'The Sailing-Forth of the Ship of the Sun,'— which takes place at the commencement of the Spring solstice, a fire is kindled on the summit of the highest tower, and a Ship of gold rises from the centre of the flames, carrying the body of a slain virgin eastwards, . . .

'tis wondrously performed! . . . and I, like others, have gaped upon the splendor of the scene half-credulous, and wholly dazzled! For the Ship doth rise aloft with excellent stateliness, plowing the air with as much celerity as sailing-vessels plow the seas; departing straightway from the watching eyes of thousands of spectators, it plunges deep, or so it seems, into the very heart of the rising Sun, which doth apparently absorb it in devouring flames of glory, for never again doth it return to earth, . . . and none can solve the mystery of its vanishing! 'Tis a graceful piece of jugglery and perfectly accomplished, . . . while as for Oracles* that command and repeat their commands in every shade of tone, from mild to wrathful, there are only too many of these, . . . moreover the secret of their manufacture is well known to all students of acoustic science. But concerning the Black Disc in Lysia's hall, it is a curiously elaborate piece of workmanship. It corresponds with an electric wheel in the Interior Chamber of the Temple, where all the priests and flamens meet and sum up the entire events of the day, both public and private, condensing the same into brief hieroglyphs. Setting their wheel in motion, they start a similar motion in the Disc, and the bright characters that flash upon it and disappear like quicksilver, are the reflection of the working electric wires which write what only Lysia is skilled to read. From sunset to midnight these messages keep coming without intermission,—and all the most carefully concealed affairs of Al-Kyris are discovered by the Temple Spies and conveyed to Lysia by this means. Whatever the news, it is repeated again and again on the Disc, till she, by rapidly turning it with a peculiar movement of her own, causes a small bell to ring in the Temple, which signifies to her informers that she has understood all their communications, and knows everything. Her inquisitorial system is searching and elaborate, . . . there is no secret so carefully guarded that the Black Disc will not in time reveal!"

Theos listened wonderingly and with a sense of repugnance and fear, . . . he felt as though the beautiful Priestess, with her glittering robes and the dreadful jewelled Eye upon her breast, were just then entering the room stealthily and rustling hither and thither like a snake beneath covering leaves. She was an ever-present Temptation,—a bewildering snare and distracting evil,—was it not possible to shake her trail off the life of his friend-and also to pluck from out his own heart

---

* The Phonograph was known and used for the utterance of Oracles by one Savan the Asmounian, a Priest-King of ancient Egypt.

MARIE CORELLI

the poison-sting of her fatal, terrible fascination? A red mist swam before his eyes—his lips were dry and feverish,—his voice sounded hoarse and faint in his own ears when he forced himself to speak again.

"So thou dost think that, wheresoever Niphrata hath strayed, Lysia can find her?" he said.

"Assuredly!" returned Sah-luma with easy complacency—"I would swear that, even at this very moment, Lysia could restore her to my arms in safety."

"Then why" . . . suggested Theos anxiously—"why not go forth and seek her now?"

"Nay, there is time!" . . . and Sah-luma half closed his languid lids and stretched himself lazily. "I would not have the child imagine I vexed myself too greatly for her unkind departure, . . . she must have space wherein to weep and repent her of her folly. She is the strangest maiden!" . . . and he brushed his lips lightly against the golden curl he held,—"She loves me, . . . and yet repulses all attempted passion,—I remember" . . . here his face grew more serious—"I remember one night in the beginning of summer,—the moon was round and high in heaven,—we were alone together in this room,—the lamps burned low,—and she. . . Niphrata, . . . sang to me. Her voice was full, and withal tremulous,—her form, bent to her ebony harp was soft and yielding as an iris stem, her eyes turned upon mine seemed wonderingly to question me as to the worth of love! . . . or so I fancied. The worth of love! . . . I would have taught it to her then in the rapture of an hour!— but seized with sudden foolish fear she fled, leaving me dissatisfied, indifferent, and weary! No matter! when she returns again her mood will alter, . . . and though I love her not as she would fain be loved, I shall find means to make her happy."

"Nay, but she speaks of dying" . . . said Theos quickly. . . "Wilt thou constrain her back from death?"

"My friend, all women speak of dying when they are love-wearied" . . . replied Sah-luma with a slight smile. . . "Niphrata will not die, . . . she is too young and fond of life, . . . the world is as a garden wherein she has but lately entered, all ignorant of the pleasures that await her there. 'Tis an odd notion that she has of danger threatening me,—thou also, good Theos, art become full of omens,—and yet, . . . there is naught of visible ill to trouble the fairness of the day."

He stepped out as he spoke on the terrace and looked up at the intense calm of the lovely sky. Theos followed him, and stood leaning on the balustrade among the clambering vines, watching him with earnest, half-regretful half-adoring eyes. He, meanwhile, gathered a scarcely opened white rosebud and loosening the tress of Niphrata's hair from his fingers, allowed it to hang to its full rippling length,—then laying the flower against it, he appeared dreamily to admire the contrast between the snowy blossom and shining curl.

"Many strange men there are in the world," he said softly—"lovers and fools who set priceless store on a rose and a lock of woman's hair! I have heard of some who, dying, have held such trifles as chiefest of all their worldly goods, and have implored that whereas their gold and household stuff can be bestowed freely on him who first comes to claim it, the faded flower and senseless tress may be laid on their hearts to comfort them in the cold and dreamless sleep from which they shall not wake again!" He sighed and his eyes darkened into deep and musing tenderness. "Poets there have been too and are, who would string many a canticle on this soft severed lock and gathered blossom,—and many a quaint conceit could I myself contrive concerning it, did I not feel more prone to tears to-day than minstrelsy. Canst thou believe it, Theos"— and he forced a laugh, though his lashes were wet, . . . "I, the joyous Sah-luma, am for once most truly sad! . . . this tress of hair doth seem to catch my spirit in a chain that binds me fast and draws me onward. . . onward. . . to some mournful end I may not dare to see!"

And as he spoke he mechanically wound the golden curl round and about the stem of the rosebud in the fashion of a ribbon, and placed the two entwined together in his breast. Theos looked at him wistfully, but was silent, . . . he himself was too full of dull and melancholy misgivings to be otherwise than sad also. Instinctively he drew closer to his friend's side, and thus they remained for some minutes, exchanging no words, and gazing dreamily out on the luxurious foliage of the trees and the wealth of bright blossoms that adorned the landscape before them.

"Thou art confident Niphrata will return?" questioned Theos presently in a low tone.

"She will return," . . . rejoined Sah-luma quietly—"because she will do anything for love of me."

"For love's sake she may die!" said Theos. Sah-luma smiled.

"Not so, my friend! . . . for love's sake she will live!"

XXVI

THE PRIEST ZEL

As he uttered the last word the sound of an approaching light step disturbed the silence. It was one of the young girls of the household, . . . a dark, haughty-looking beauty whom Theos remembered to have seen in the palace-hall when he first arrived, lying indolently among cushions, and playing with a tame bird which flew to and fro at her beckoning. She advanced now with an almost imperial stateliness,— her salute to Sah-luma was grateful, yet scarcely submissive,—while he, turning eagerly toward her, seemed gladdened and relieved at her appearance, his face assuming a gratified expression like that of a child who, having broken one toy, is easily consoled with another.

"Welcome, Irenya!" he exclaimed gayly—"Thou art the very bitter-sweetness I desire. Thy naughty pout and coldly mutinous eyes are pleasing contrasts to the overlanguid heat and brightness of the day! What news hast thou, my sweet? . . . Is there fresh havoc in the city? . . . more deaths? . . . more troublous tidings? . . . nay, then hold thy peace, for thou art not a fit messenger of woe—thou'rt much too fair!"

Irenya's red lips curled disdainfully, . . . the "naughty pout" was plainly visible.

"My lord is pleased to flatter his slave!" she said with a touch of scorn in her musical accents, . . . "Certes, of ill news there is more than enough,— and evil rumors have never been lacking these many months, as my lord would have known, had he deigned to listen to the common talk of those who are not poets but merely sad and suffering men. Nevertheless, though I may think, I speak not at all of matters such as these,—and for my present errand 'tis but to say that a Priest of the Inner Temple waits without, desirous of instant speech with the most illustrious Sah-luma."

"A Priest of the Inner Temple!" echoed the Laureate wonderingly, . . . "By my faith, a most unwelcome visitor! . . . What business can he have with me?"

"Nay, that I know not"—responded Irenya calmly—"He hath come hither, so he bade me say, by command of The Absolute Authority."

Sah-luma's face flushed and he looked annoyed. Then taking Theos by the arm he turned away from the terrace, and re-entered his apartment, where he flung himself full length on his couch, pillowing his handsome head against a fold of glossy leopard skin which formed a most becoming background for the soft, dark oval beauty of his features.

"Sit thee down, my friend!" he said glancing smilingly at Theos, and signing to him to take possession of a luxurious lounge-chair near him. "If we must needs receive this sanctified professor of many hypocrisies, we will do it with suitable indifference and ease. Wilt thou stay here with us, Irenya," he added, stretching out one arm and catching the maiden round the waist in spite of her attempted resistance. "Or art thou in a froward mood, and wilt thou go thine own proud way without so much as a consoling kiss from Sah-luma?"

Irenya looked full at him, a repressed anger blazing in her large black eyes.

"Let my lord save his kisses for those who value them!" she said contemptuously, "'Twere pity he should waste them upon me, to whom they are unmeaning and therefore all unwelcome!"

He laughed heartily, and instantly loosened her from his embrace.

"Off, off with thee, sweet virtue! . . . fairest prude!" he cried, still laughing. . . "Live out thy life an thou wilt, empty of love or passion— count the years as they slip by, leaving thee each day less lovely and less fit for pleasure, . . . grow old,—and on the brink of death, look back, poor child, and see the glory thou hast missed and left behind thee! . . . the light of love and youth that, once departed, can dawn again no more!"

And lifting himself slightly from his cushions he kissed his hand playfully to the girl, who, as though suddenly overcome by a sort of vague regret, still lingered, gazing at him, while a faint color crept through her cheeks like the deepening hue on the leaves of an opening rose. Sah-luma saw her hesitation, and his face grew yet more radiant with malicious mirth.

"Hence. . . hence, Irenya!" he exclaimed—"Escape temptation quickly while thou mayest! Support thy virgin pride in peace! . . . thou shalt never say again Sah-luma's kisses are unwelcome! The Poet's touch shall never wrong or sanctify thy name!—thou art safe from me as pillared icicles in everlasting snow! Dear little one, be happy without love if that be possible! . . . nevertheless take heed thou do not weakly clamor in the after-years for once rejected joy!—Now bid yon waiting Priest attend me,—tell him I can but spare a few brief moments audience."

Irenya's head drooped,—Theos saw tears in her eyes,—but she managed to restrain them, and with something of a defiant air she made her formal obeisance and withdrew. She did not return again, but a page appeared instead, ushering in with ceremonious civility a tall personage, clad in flowing white robes and muffled up to the eyes in a mantle of silver tissue,—a majestic, mysterious, solemn-looking individual, who, pausing on the threshold of the apartment, described a circle in the air with a small staff he carried, and said in monotonous accents:

"By the going-in and passing-out of the Sun through the Gates of the East and the Gates of the West,—by the Vulture of Gold and White Lotus and the countless virtues of Nagaya, may peace dwell in this house forever!"

"Agreed to with all my heart!" responded Sah-luma, carelessly looking up from his couch but making no attempt to rise, . . . "Peace is an excellent thing, most holy father!"

"Excellent!" returned the Priest slowly advancing and undoing his mantle so that his face became fully visible,—"So truly excellent indeed, that at times it is needful to make war in order to insure it."

He sat down, as he spoke, in a chair which was placed for him at Sah-luma's bidding by the page who had ushered him in, and he maintained a grave silence till that youthful servitor had departed. Theos meanwhile studied his countenance with some curiosity,—it was so strangely impassive, yet at the same time so full of distinctly marked intellectual power. The features were handsome but also singularly repulsive,—they were rendered in a certain degree dignified by a full, dark beard which, however, failed entirely to conceal the receding chin, and compressed, cruel mouth,—the eyes were keen and crafty and very clear,—the forehead was high and intelligent, and deeply furrowed with lines that seemed to be the result of much pondering over close and cunning calculation, rather than the marks of profound, unselfish, and ennobling thought. The page having left the room, Sah-luma began the conversation:

"To what unexpected cause, most righteous sir, am I indebted for the honor of this present visit? Methinks I recognize the countenance of the famous Zel, the High-Priest of the Sacrificial Altar—if so, 'tis marvellous so great a man should venture forth alone and unattended, to the house of one who loves not priestly company, and who hath at best for all professors of religion a somewhat indifferent welcome!"

The Priest smiled coldly.

"Most rightly dost thou speak, Sah-luma"—he answered, his measured, metallic voice seeming to strike a wave of chilling discord through the air, "and most frankly hast thou thus declared one of thy many deficiencies! Atheist as thou art and to that manner born, thou art in very deed outside the pale of all religious teaching and consolement, . . . nevertheless there is much gentle mercy shown thee by the Virgin Priestess of Nagaya" . . . here he solemnly bent his head and made the rapid sign of a Circle on his breast, . . . "who, knowing thy great genius, doth ever strive with thoughtful zeal to draw thee closely within the saving Silver Veil! Yet it is possible that even her patience with thy sins may tire at last,—wherefore while there is time, offer due penance to the offended gods and humble thy stiff heart before the Holy Maid, lest she expel thee from her sight forever." He paused, . . . a satirical, half-amused smile hovered round Sah-luma's delicate mouth—his eyes flashed.

"All this is the mere common rhetoric of the Temple Craft"—he said indolently. "Why not, good Zel, give plainer utterance to thine errand?—we know each other's follies well enough to spare formalities! Lysia has sent thee hither, . . . what then? . . . what says the beauteous Virgin to her willing slave?"

An undertone of mockery rang through the languid silvery sweetness of his accents, and the Priest's dark brows knitted in an irritated frown.

"Thou art over-flippant of speech, Sah-luma!" he observed austerely. "Take heed thou be not snared into misfortune by the glibness of thy tongue! Thou dost speak of the chaste Lysia with unseemly lightness.— learn to be reverent, and so shalt thou be wiser!"

Sah-luma laughed and settled himself more easily on his couch, turning in such a manner as to look the stately Zel full in the face. They exchanged one glance, expressive as it seemed of some mutual secret understanding,—for the Priest coughed as though he were embarrassed, and stroked his beard deliberately with one hand in an endeavor to hide the strange smile that, despite his efforts to conceal it, visibly lightened his cold eyes to a sudden tigerish brilliancy.

"The mission with which I am charged," he resumed presently,—"is to thee, Chief Laureate of the realm, and runs as followeth: Whereas thou hast of late avoided many days of public service in the Temple, so that those among the people who admire thee follow thine ill example, and absent themselves also with equal readiness,—the Priestess

MARIE CORELLI

Undefiled, the noble Lysia, doth to-night command thy presence as a duty not to be foregone. Therefore come thou and take thy part in the Great Sacrifice, for these late tumults and disaster in the city, notably the perplexing downfall of the Obelisk, have caused all hearts to fail and sink for very fear. The river darkens in its crimson hue each hour by passing hour,—strange noises have been heard athwart the sky and in the deeper underground, . . . and all these drear unwonted things are so many cogent reasons why we should in solemn unison implore the favor of Nagaya and the gods whereby further catastrophes may be perchance averted. Moreover for motives of most urgent state-policy it is advisable that all who hold place, dignity, and renown within the city should this night be seen as fervent suppliants before the Sacred Shrine,—so may much threatening rebellion be appeased, and order be restored out of impending confusion. Such is the message I am bidden to convey to thee,—furthermore I am required to bear back again to the High Priestess thy faithful promise that her orders shall be surely and entirely obeyed. Thou art not wont" . . . and a pale sneer flitted over his features. . . "to set her mandate at defiance."

Sah-luma bit his lips angrily, and folded his arms above his head with a lazy yet impatient movement.

"Assuredly I shall be present at the Service," he said curtly. "There needed no such weighty summoning! 'Twas my intention to join the ranks of worshippers to-night, though for myself I have no faith in worship, . . . the gods I ween are deaf, and care not a jot whether we mortals weep or sing. Nevertheless I shall look on with fitting gravity, and deport myself with due decorum throughout the ceremonious Ritual, though verily I tell thee, reverend Zel, 'tis tedious and monotonous at best, . . . and concerning the poor maiden-sacrifice, it is a shuddering horror we could well dispense with."

"I think not so," . . . replied the Priest calmly. "Thou, who art well instructed in the capricious humors of men, must surely know how dearly the majority of them love the shedding of blood,—'tis a clamorous brute-instinct in them which must be satisfied. Better therefore that we, the anointed Priests, should slay one willing victim for the purposes of religion, than that they, the ignorant mob, should kill a thousand to gratify their lust of murder. An unresentful, all-loving Deity would be impossible of comprehension to a mutually hating and malignant race of beings,—all creeds must be accommodated to the dispositions of the million."

"Pardon me. . ." suddenly interrupted Theos, "I am a stranger, and in a great measure ignorant of this city's customs, . . . but I confess I am amazed to hear a Priest uphold so specious an argument! What! . . . must divine Religion be dragged down from its pure throne to pander to the selfish passions of the multitude? . . . because men are vile, must a vile god be invented to suit their savage caprices? . . . because men are so cruel, must the unseen Creator of things be delineated as even more barbarous than they, in order to give them some pietistical excuse for wickedness?—I ask these questions not out of wanton curiosity, but for the sake of instruction!"

The haughty Zel turned upon him in severe astonishment.

"Sir," he said—"Stranger undoubtedly thou art,—and so bold a manner of speech most truly savors of the utterly uneducated western barbarian! All wise and prudent governments have learned that a god fit for the adoration of men must be depicted as much like men as possible,—any absolutely superhuman attributes are unnecessary to the character of a useful deity, inasmuch as no man ever will, or ever can, understand the worth of superhuman qualities. Humanity is only capable of worshipping Self—thus, it is necessary, that when people are persuaded to pay honor to an elected Divinity, they should be well and comfortably assured in their own minds that they are but offering homage to an Image of Self placed before them in a deified or heroic form. This satisfies the natural idolatrous cravings of Egotism, and this is all that priests or teachers desire. Now in the worship of Nagaya, we have the natures of Man and Woman conjoined, . . . the Snake is the emblem of male wisdom united with female subtilty—and the two essences, mingled in one, make as near an approach to what we may imagine the positive Divine capacity as can be devised on earth by earthly intelligences. If, on the other hand, such an absurd doctrine as that formulated in the fanatic madman Khosrul's 'Prophecy' could be imagined as actually admitted, and proclaimed to the nations, it would have very few followers, and the sincerity of those few might well be open to doubt. For the Deity it speaks of is supposed to be an immortal God disguised as Man,—a God who voluntarily rejects and sets aside His own glory to serve and save His perishable creatures,—thus the root of that religion would consist in Self-abnegation, and Self-abnegation is, as experience proves, utterly impossible to the human being."

"Why is it impossible?" asked Theos with a quiver of passionate earnestness in his voice,—"Are there none in all the world who would sacrifice their own interests to further another's welfare and happiness?"

The Priest smiled,—a delicately derisive smile.

"Certainly not!" he replied blandly. "The very question strikes me as singularly foolish, inasmuch as we live in a planet where, if we do not serve ourselves and look after our own personal advantage, we may as well die the minute we are born, or, better still, never be born at all. There is no one living, . . . at least not in the wide realm of Al-Kyris,—who would put himself to the smallest inconvenience for the sake of another, were that other his nearest and dearest blood-relation. And in matters of love and friendship, 'tis the same as in business,—each man eagerly pursues his own chance of enjoyment,—even when he loves, or fancies he loves, a woman, it is solely because her beauty or attractiveness gives HIM temporary pleasure, not because he has any tenderness or after-regard for the nature of HER feelings. How can it be otherwise? . . . We elect friends that are useful to Us personally,—we care little for THEIR intrinsic merit, and we only tolerate them as long as they happen to suit OUR taste. For generally, on the first occasion of a disagreement or difference of opinion, we shake ourselves free of them without either regret or remorse, and seek others who will be meek enough not to offer us any open contradiction. It is, and it must be always so: Self is the first person we are bound to consider, and all religions, if they are intended to last, must prudently recognize and silently acquiesce in this, the chief dogma of Man's constitution."

Sah-luma laughed. "Excellently argued, most politic Zel!" he exclaimed. "Yet methinks it is easy to worship Self without either consecrated altars or priestly assistance!"

"Thou shouldst know better than any one with what facility such devotion can be practiced!" returned Zel ironically, rising as he spoke, and beginning to wrap his mantle round him preparatory to departure—"Thou hast a wider range of perpetual adoration than most men, seeing thou dost so fully estimate the value of thine own genius! Some heretics there are in the city, who say thy merit is but a trick of song shared by thee in common with the birds, . . . who truly seem to take no pride in the particular sweetness of their unsyllabled language, . . . but thou thyself art better instructed, and who shall blame thee for the veneration with which thou dost daily contemplate thine own intellectual powers? Not I, believe me!" . . . and his crafty eyes glittered mockingly, as he arranged his silver gauze muffler so that it entirely veiled the lower part of his features, . . . "And though I do somewhat regret to learn that thou, among other noblemen of fashion, hast of late taken part in the atheistic discussions encouraged by the Positivist School of Thought, still, as a priest, my duty is not so much to reproach as to call thee to repentance. Therefore I inwardly rejoice to know thou wilt present thyself before the Shrine to-night, if only for the sake of custom. . ."

"'Only' for the sake of custom!" repeated Sah-luma amusedly—"Nay, good Zel, custom should be surely classified as an exceeding powerful god, inasmuch as it rules all things, from the cut of our clothes to the form of our creeds!"

"True!" replied Zel imperturbably. "And he who despises custom becomes an alien from his kind,—a moral leper among the pure and clean."

"Oh, say rather a lion among sheep, a giant among pigmies!" laughed the Laureate,—"For by my soul, a man who had the courage to scorn custom, and set the small hypocrisies of society at defiance, would be a glorious hero! a warrior of strange integrity whom it would be well worth travelling miles to see!"

"Khosrul was such an one!" interposed Theos suddenly.

"Tush, man! Khosrul was mad!" retorted Sah-luma.

"Are not all men thought mad who speak the truth?" queried Theos gently.

The priest Zel looked at him with proud and supercilious eyes.

"Thou hast strange notions for one still young," he said. . . "What art thou? . . . a new disciple of the Mystics? . . . or a student of the Positive Doctrines?"

Theos met his gaze unflinchingly. "What am I?" he murmured sadly, and his voice trembled, . . . "Reverend Priest, I am nothing! . . . Great are the sufferings of men who have lost their wealth, their home, their friends, . . . but I. . . I have lost Myself! Were I anything. . . could I ever hope to be anything, I would pray to be accepted a servant of the Cross, . . . that far-off unknown Faith to which my tired spirit clings!"

As he uttered these words, he raised his eyes, . . . how dim and misty at the moment seemed the tall white figure of the majestic Zel! and in contrast to it, how brilliantly distinct Sah-luma's radiant face appeared, turned toward him in inquiring wonderment! . . . He felt a swooning dizziness upon him, but the sensation swiftly passed, and he saw the haughty Priest's dark brows bent upon him in a frown of ominous disapproval.

"'Tis well thou art not a citizen of Al-Kyris"—he said scornfully—"To strangers we accord a certain license of opinion,—but if thou wert a native of these realms, thy speech would cost thee dear! As it is, I warn thee! . . . dare not to make public mention of the Cross, the accursed Emblem of the dead Khosrul's idolatry, . . . guard thy tongue heedfully!—and thou, Sah-luma if thou dost bring this rashling with thee to the Temple, thou must take upon thyself all measures for his safety. For in these days, some words are like firebrands, and he who casts them forth incautiously may kindle flames that only the forfeit of his life can quench."

There was a quiver of suppressed fury in his tone, and Sah-luma lifted his lazy lids, and looked at him with an air of tranquil indifference.

"Prithee, trouble not thyself, most eminent Zel!" he answered nonchalantly. . . "I will answer for my friend's discretion! Thou dost mistake his temperament,—he is a budding poet, and utters many a disconnected thought which hath no meaning save to his own fancy-swarming brain,—he saw the frantic Khosrul die, and the picture hath impressed him for the moment—nothing more! I pledge my word for his demurest prudence at the Service to-night—I would not have him absent for the world, . . .'twere pity he should miss the splendor of a scene which doubtless hath been admirably contrived, by priestly art and skill, to play upon the passions of the multitude. Tell me, good Zel, what is the name of the self-offered Victim?"

The Priest flashed a strangely malevolent glance at him.

"'Tis not to be divulged," he replied curtly—"The virgin is no longer counted among the living. . . she is as one already departed—the name she bore hath been erased from the city registers, and she wears instead the prouder title of 'Bride of the Sun and Nagaya.' Restrain thy curiosity until night hath fallen,—it may be that thou, who hast a wide acquaintance among fair maidens, wilt recognize her countenance."

"Nay, I trust I know her not"—said Sah-luma carelessly—"For, though all women die for me when once their beauty fades, still am I loth to see them perish ere their prime."

"Yet many are doomed to perish so"—rejoined the Priest impassively—"Men as well as women,—and methinks those who are best beloved of the gods are chosen first to die. Death is not difficult, . . . but to live long enough for life to lose all savor, and love all charm, . . . this is a bitterness that comes with years and cannot be consoled."

And retreating slowly toward the door, he paused as he had previously done on the threshold.

"Farewell, Sah-luma!" he said. . . "Beware that nothing hinders thee from the fulfillment of thy promise! . . . and let thy homage to the Holy Maid be reverent at the parting of the Silver Veil!"

He waited, but Sah-luma made no answer—he therefore raised his staff and described a circle with it in the same solemn fashion that had distinguished his entrance.

"By the coming-forth of the Moon through the ways of Darkness, . . . by the shining of Stars, . . . by the Sleeping Sun and the silence of Night, . . . by the All-Seeing Eye of Raphon and the Wisdom of Nagaya may the protection of the gods abide in this house forever!"

As he pronounced these words he noiselessly departed, without any salutation whatever to Sah-luma, who heaved a sigh of relief when he had gone, and, rising from his couch came and placed one hand affectionately on Theos's shoulder.

"Thou foolish, yet dear comrade!" he murmured. "What moves thee to blurt forth such strange and unwarrantable sayings? . . . Why wouldst thou pray to be a servant of the Cross? . . . or why, at any rate, if thou hast taken a fancy for the dead Khosrul's new doctrine, wert thou so rash as to proclaim thy sentiment to yon unprincipled, bloodthirsty Zel, who would not scruple to poison the King himself, if his Majesty gave sufficient cause of offence! Dost thou desire to be straightway slain?—Nay, I will not have thee run thus furiously into danger,—thou wilt be offered the Silver Nectar like Nir-jahs, and not even the intercession of my friendship would avail to save thee then!"

Theos smiled rather sadly.

"And thus would end for ever my mistakes and follies, . . ." he answered softly. "And I should perchance discover the small hidden secret of things—the little, simple unguessed clue, that would unravel the mystery and meaning of Existence! For can it be that the majestic marvel of created Nature is purposeless in its design?—that we are doomed to think thoughts which can never be realized?—to dream dreams that perish in the dreaming? . . . to build up hopes without foundation? . . . to call upon God when there is no God? . . . to long for Heaven when there is no Heaven? . . . Ah no, Sah-luma!—surely we are not the mere fools and dupes of Time, . . . surely there is some Eternal Beyond which is not Annihilation, . . . some greater, vaster sphere of soul-development where we shall find all that we have missed on earth!"

Sah-luma's face clouded, and a sigh escaped him.

"I would my thoughts were similar to thine!" he said sorrowfully. "I would I could believe in an immortal destiny, . . . but alas, my friend! there is no shadow of ground for such a happy faith,—none neither in sense nor science. I have reflected on it many a time till I have wearied myself with mournful musing, and the end of all my meditation has been a useless protest against the Great Inevitable, . . . a clamor of disdain hurled at the huge, blind, indifferent Force that poisons the deep sea of Space with an ever-productive spawn of wasted Life! Anon I have flouted my own despair, and have consoled myself with the old wise maxim that was found inscribed on the statue of a smiling god some centuries ago. . . 'Enjoy your lives, ye passing tribes of men. . . take pleasure in folly, for this is the only wisdom that avails! Happy is he whose days are filled with the delight of love and laughter, for there is nothing better found on earth, and whatsoever ye do, whether wise or foolish, the same End comes to all!' . . . Is not this true philosophy, my Theos? . . . what can a man do better than enjoy?"

"Much depends on the particular form of enjoyment. . ." responded Theos thoughtfully. "Some there are, for example, who might find their greatest satisfaction in the pleasures of the table,—others in the gratification of sensual desires and gross appetites,—are these to be left to follow their own devices, without any effort being made to raise them from the brute-level where they lie?"

"Why, in the name of all the gods, SHOULD they be raised?" demanded Sah-luma impatiently—"If their choice is to grovel in mire, why ask them to dwell in a palace?—They would not appreciate the change!"

"Again," went on Theos—"there are others who are only happy in the pursuit of wisdom, and the more they learn, the more they seek to know. One wonders, . . . one cannot help wondering. . . are their aspirations all in vain? . . . and will the grave seal down their hopes forever?"

Sah-luma paused a moment before replying.

"It seems so. . ." he said at last slowly and hesitatingly. . . "And herein I find the injustice of the matter,—because however great may be the imagination and fervor of a poet for instance, he never is able WHOLLY to utter his thoughts. Half of them remain in embryo, like buds of flowers that never come to bloom, . . . yet they are THERE, burning in the brain and seeming too vast of conception to syllable themselves into the common speech of mortals! I have often marvelled why such ideas suggest themselves at all, as they can neither be written nor spoken, unless. . ." and here his voice sank into a dreamy softness, "unless indeed they are to be received as hints, . . . foreshadowings. . . of greater works destined for our accomplishment, hereafter!"

He was silent a minute's space, and Theos, watching him wistfully, suddenly asked:

"Wouldst thou be willing to live again, Sah-luma, if such a thing could be?"

"Friend, I would rather never die!"—responded the Laureate, half playfully, half seriously. "But. . . if I were certain that death was no more than a sleep, from which I should assuredly awaken to another phase of existence, . . . I know well enough what I would do!"

"What?" questioned Theos, his heart beginning to beat with an almost insufferable anxiety.

"I would live a different life Now!" answered Sah-luma steadily, looking his companion full in the eyes as he spoke, while a grave smile shadowed rather than lightened his features. "I would begin at once, . . . so that when the new Future dawned for me, I might not be haunted or tortured by the remembrance of a misspent Past! For if we are to believe in any everlasting things at all, we cannot shut out the fatal everlastingness of Memory!" His words sounded unlike himself. . . his voice was as the voice of some reproving angel speaking,—and Theos, listening, shuddered, he knew not why, and held his peace.

"Never to be able to FORGET!" continued Sah-luma in the same grave, sweet tone. . . "Never to lose sight of one's own bygone wilful sins, . . . this would be an immortal destiny too terrible to endure! For then, inexorable Retrospection would forever show us where we had missed the way, and how we had failed to use the chances given us, . . . moreover, we might haply find ourselves surrounded. . ." and his accents grew slower and more emphatic. . . "by strange phantoms of our own creating, who would act anew the drama of our obstinate past follies, perplexing us thereby into an anguish greater than mortal fancy can depict. Thus if we indeed possessed the positive foreknowledge of the eternal regeneration of our lives, 'twould be well to free them from all hindrance to perfection HERE,—here, while we are still conscious of Time and opportunity." He paused, then went on in his customary gay manner: "But fortunately we are not positive, nothing is certain, no truth is so satisfactorily demonstrated that some wiseacre cannot be found to disprove it, . . . hence it happens my friend. . ." and his face assumed its wonted careless expression. . . "that we men whose

MARIE CORELLI

common-sense is offended by priestly hypocrisy and occult necromantic jugglery,—we, who perhaps in our innermost heart of hearts ardently desire to believe in a supreme Divinity and the grandly progressive Sublime Intention of the Universe, but who, discovering naught but ignoble Cant and Imposture everywhere, are incontinently thrown back on our own resources, . . . hence it comes, I say, that we are satisfied to accept ourselves, each man in his own personality, as the Beginning and End of Existence, and to minister to that Absolute Self which after all concerns us most, and which will continue to engage our best service until. . . well!—until History can show us a perfectly Selfless Example, which, if human nature remains consistent with its own traditions, will assuredly never be!"

This was almost more than Theos could bear, . . . there was a tightening agony at his heart that made him long to cry out, to weep, or, better still, to fling himself on his knees and pray, . . . pray to that far-removed mild Presence, that "Selfless Example" who he KNEW had hallowed and dignified the world, and yet whose Holy and Beloved Name, he, miserable sinner, was unworthy to even remember! His suffering at the moment was so intense that he fancied some reflection of it must be visible in his face. Sah-luma, however, apparently saw nothing,—he stepped across the room, and out to the vine-shaded loggia, where he turned and beckoned his companion to his side.

"Come!" he said, pushing his hair off his brows with a languid gesture, . . . "The afternoon wears onward, and the very heavens seem to smoke with heat,—let us seek cooler air beneath the shade of yonder cypresses, whose dark-green boughs shut out the glaring sky. We'll talk of love and poesy and tender things till sunset, . . . I will recite to thee a ballad of mine that Niphrata loved,—'tis called 'An Idyl of Roses,' . . . and it will lighten this hot and heavy silence, when even birds sleep, and butterflies drowse in the hollowed shelter of the arum-leaves. Come, wilt thou? . . . To-night perchance we shall have little time for pleasant discourse!"

As he spoke, Theos obediently went toward him with the dazed sensations of one under the influence of mesmerism, . . . the dazzling face and luminous eyes of the Laureate exercised over him an indescribable yet resistless authority,—and it was certain that, wherever Sah-luma led the way, he was bound to follow. Only, as he mechanically descended from the terrace into the garden, and linked his arm within that of his companion, he was conscious of a vague feeling of pity for himself. . . pity that he should have dwindled into such a nonentity, when Sah-luma was so renowned a celebrity, . . . pity too that he should have somehow never been able to devise anything original in the Art of Poetry!

This last was evident, . . . for he knew already that the "Idyl of Roses" Sah-luma purposed reciting could be no other than what he had fancied was His "Idyl of Roses" . . . a poem he had composed, or rather had plagiarized in some mysterious fashion before he had even dreamt of the design of "Nourhalma" . . . However he had become in part resigned to the peculiar position he occupied,—he was just a little sorry for himself, and that was all. Even as the parted spirit of a dead man might hover ruthfully above the grave of its perished mortal body, so he compassionated his own forlorn estate, and heaved a passing sigh of regret, not only for all He Once Had Been, but also for all He Could Never Be!

XXVII

In the Temple of Nagaya

The hours wore on with stealthy rapidity,—but the two friends, reclining together under a deep-branched canopy of cypress-boughs, paid little or no heed to the flight of time. The heat in the garden was intense—the grass was dry and brittle as though it had been scorched by passing flames,—and a singularly profound stillness reigned everywhere, there being no wind to stir the faintest rustle among the foliage. Lying lazily upon his back, with his arms clasped above his head, Theos looked dreamily up at the patches of blue sky seen between the dark-green gnarled stems and listened to the measured cadence of the Laureate's mellow voice as he recited with much tenderness the promised poem.

Of course it was perfectly familiar,—the lines were precisely the same as those which he, Theos, remembered to have written out, thinking them his own, in an old manuscript book he had left at home. "At-home!" . . . Where was that? It must be a very long way off! . . . He half-closed his eyes,—a sense of delightful drowsiness was upon him, . . . the rise and fall of his friend's rhythmic utterance soothed him into a languid peace, . . . the "Idyl of Roses" was very sweet and musical, and, though he knew it of old, he heard it now with special satisfaction, inasmuch as, it being no longer his, he was at liberty to bestow upon it that full measure of admiration which he felt it deserved!

Yet every now and then his thoughts wandered,—and though he anxiously strove to concentrate his attention on the lovely stanzas that murmured past his ears like the gentle sound of waves flowing beneath the mesmerism of the moon, his brain was in a continual state of ferment, and busied itself with all manner of vague suggestions to which he could give no name.

A great weariness weighed down his spirit—a dim consciousness of the futility of all ambition and all endeavor—he was haunted, too, by the sharp hiss of Lysia's voice when she had said, "Kill Sah-Luma!" . . . Her look, her attitude, her murderous smile, troubled his memory and made him ill at ease,—the thing she had thus demanded at his hands seemed more monstrous than if she had bidden him kill himself!

For there had been one moment, when, mastered by her beauty and the force of his own passion, he WOULD have killed himself had she requested it. . . but to kill his adored, his beloved friend! . . . ah no! not for a thousand sorceress-queens as fair as she!

He drew a long breath, . . . an irresistible desire for rest came over him, . . . the air was heavy and warm and fragrant,—his companion's dulcet accents served as a lullaby to his tired mind,—it seemed a long time since he had enjoyed a pleasant slumber, for the previous night he had not slept at all. Lower and lower drooped his aching lids, . . . he was almost beginning to slip away slowly into a blissful unconsciousness, . . . when all at once Sah-luma ceased reciting, and a harsh, brazen clang of bells echoed through the silence, storming to and fro with a violent, hurried uproar suggestive of some sudden alarm. He sprang to his feet, rubbing his eyes,—Sah-luma rose also, a slightly petulant expression on his face.

"Canst thou do no better than sleep"—he queried complainingly, "when thou art privileged to listen to an immortal poem?"

Impulsively Theos caught his hand and pressed it fervently.

"Nay, dost thou deem me so indifferent, my noble friend?" he cried. . . "Thou art mistaken, for though perchance mine eyes were closed, my ears were open; I heard thy every word,—I loved thy every line! What dost thou need of praise? . . . thou, who canst do naught but work which, being perfect, is beyond all criticism!"

Sah-luma smiled, well satisfied, and the little lines of threatening ill-humor vanished from his countenance.

"Enough!" he said. "I know that thou dost truly honor me above all poets, and that thou wouldst not willingly offend. Hearest thou how great a clamor the ringers of the Temple make to-night?—'tis but the sunset chime, . . . yet one would think they were pealing forth an angry summons to battle."

"Already sunset!" exclaimed Theos, surprised. "Why, it seems scarce a minute since, that we came hither!"

"Aye!—such is the magic charm of poesy!" rejoined Sah-luma complacently. "It makes the hours flit like moments, and long days seemed but short hours! . . . Nevertheless 'tis time we were within doors and at supper,—for if we start not soon for the Temple, 'twill be difficult to gain an entrance, and I, at any rate, must be early in my place beside the King."

He heaved a short, impatient sigh,—and as he spoke, all Theos's old misgivings came rushing back upon him and in full force, filling him with vague sorrow, uneasiness, fear. But he knew how useless it was to try and impart any of his inward forebodings to Sah-luma,—Sah-luma, who had so lightly explained Lysia's treacherous conduct to his own entire satisfaction, . . . Sah-luma, on whom neither the prophecies of Khosrul nor the various disastrous events of the day had taken any permanent effect, . . . while no attempt could now be made to deter him from attending the Sacrificial Service in the Temple, seeing he had been so positively commanded thither by Lysia, through the medium of the priest Zel.

Feeling bitterly his own incompetency to exercise any protective influence on the fate of his companion, Theos said nothing, but silently followed him, as he thrust aside the drooping cypress boughs and made his way out to more open ground, his lithe, graceful figure looking even more brilliant and phantom-like than ever, contrasted with the deep green gloom spread about him by the hoary moss-covered trees that were as twisted and grotesque in shape as a group of fetich idols. As he bent back the last branchy barrier however, and stepped into the full light, he stopped short,—and, uttering a loud exclamation, lifted his hand and pointed westward, his dark eyes dilating with amazement and awe.

Theos at once came swiftly up beside him, and looked where he looked, . . . what a scene of terrific splendor he beheld! . . . Right across the horizon, that glistened with a pale green hue like newly frozen water, a cloud, black as the blackest midnight, lay heavy and motionless, in form resembling an enormous leaf, fringed at the edges with tremulous lines of gold.

This nebulous mass was absolutely stirless, . . . it appeared as though it had been thrown, a ponderous weight, into the vault of heaven, and having fallen, there purposed to remain. Ever and anon beamy threads of lightning played through it luridly, veining it with long, arrowy flashes of orange and silver,—while poised immediately above it was the sun, looking like a dull scarlet seal, . . . a ball of dim fire destitute of rays.

On all sides the sky was crossed by wavy flecks of pearl and sudden glimpses as of burning topaz,—and down toward the earth drooped a thin azure fog,—filmy curtain, through which the landscape took the strangest tints and unearthly flushes of color. A moment,—and the spectral sun dropped suddenly into the lower darkness, leaving behind it a glare of gold and green,—lowering purple shadows crept over across the heavens, darkening them as smoke darkens flame,—but the huge cloud, palpitating with lightning, moved not at all nor changed its shape by so much as a hair's breadth, . . . it appeared like a vast pall spread out in readiness for the solemn state-burial of the world.

Fascinated by the aspect of the weird sky-phenomenon, Theos was at the same time curiously impressed by a sense of its UNREALITY, . . . indeed he found himself considering it with the calm attentiveness of one who is brought face to face with a remarkable picture effectively painted. This peculiar sensation, however, was, like many others of his experience, very transitory, . . . it passed, and he watched the lightnings come and go with a certain hesitating fear mingled with wonder. Sah-luma was the first to speak.

"Storm at last!" . . . he said, forcing a smile though his face was unusually pale,—"It has threatened us all day. . .'twill break before the night is over. How sullenly yonder heavens frown! . . . they have quenched the sun in their sable darkness as though it were a beaten foe! This will seem an ill sign to those who worship him as a god,—for truly he doth appear to have withdrawn himself in haste and anger. By my soul! 'Tis a dull and ominous eve!" . . . and a slight shudder ran through his delicate frame, as he turned toward the white-pillared loggia garlanded with its climbing vines, roses, and passion-flowers, through which there now floated a dim golden, suffused radiance reflected from lamps lit within, . . . "I would the night were past and that the new day had come!"

With these words, he entered the house, Theos accompanying him, and together they went at once to the banqueting-hall. There they supped royally, served by silent and attentive slaves,—they themselves, feeling mutually depressed, yet apparently not wishing to communicate their depression one to the other, conversed but little. After the repast was finished, they set forth on foot to the Temple, Sah-luma informing his companion, as they went, that it was against the law to use any chariot or other sort of conveyance to go to the place of worship, the King himself being obliged to dispense with his sumptuous car on such occasions, and to walk thither as unostentatiously as any one of his poorest subjects.

"An excellent rule!" . . . observed Theos reflectively,—"For the pomp and glitter of an earthly potentate's display assorts ill with the homage he intends to offer to the Immortals,—and Kings are no more than commoners in the sight of an all-supreme Divinity."

"True, if there WERE an all-supreme Divinity!" rejoined Sah-luma dryly,—"But in the present state of well-founded doubt regarding the existence of any such omnipotent personage, thinkest thou there is a monarch living, who is sincerely willing to admit the possibility of any power superior to himself? Not Zephoranim, believe me! . . . his enforced humility on all occasions of public religious observance serves him merely as a new channel wherein to proclaim his pride. Certes, in obedience to the Priests, or rather let us say in obedience to the High Priestess, he paces the common foot-path in company with the common folk, uncrowned and simply clad,—but what avails this affectation of meekness? All know him for the King—all make servile way for him,—all flatter him! . . . and his progress to the Temple resembles as much a triumphal procession as though he were mounted in his chariot and returning from some wondrous victory. Besides, humility in my opinion is more a weakness than a virtue, . . . and even granting it were a virtue, it is not possible to Kings,—not as long as people continue to fawn on royalty like grovelling curs, and lick the sceptred hand that often loathes their abject touch."

He spoke with a certain bitterness and impatience as though he were suffering from some inward nervous irritation, and Theos, observing this, prudently made no attempt to continue the conversation. They were just then passing down a narrow, rather dark street, lined on both sides by lofty buildings of quaint and elaborate architecture. Long, gloomy shadows had gathered in this particular spot, where for a short space the silence was so intense that one could almost hear one's own heart beat. Suddenly a yellowish-green ray of light flashed across the pavement, and lo! the upper rim of the moon peered above the house-tops, looking strangely large and rosily brilliant, . . . the air seemed all at once to grow suffocating and sulphurous, and between whiles there came the faint plashing sound of water lapping against stone with a monotonous murmur as of continuous soft whispers.

The vast silence, the vast night, were full of a solemn weirdness,—the moon, curiously magnified to twice her ordinary size, soared higher and higher, firing the lofty solitudes of heaven with long, shooting radiations of rose and green, while still in the purple hollow of the horizon lay that immense, immovable Cloud, nerved as it were with living lightning which leaped incessantly from its centre like a thousand swords drawn and re-drawn from as many scabbards.

Presently the deep booming noise of a great bell smote heavily on the stillness, . . . a sound that Theos, oppressed by the weight of unutterable forebodings, welcomed with a vague sense of relief, while Sah-luma, hearing it, quickened his pace. They soon reached the end of the street, which terminated in a spacious quadrangular court guarded on all sides by gigantic black statues, and quickly crossing this place, which was entirely deserted, they came out at once into a dazzling blaze of light, . . . the Temple of Nagaya in all its stately magnificence towered before them, a stupendous pile of marvellously delicate architecture so fine as to seem like lace-work rather than stone.

It was lit up from base to summit with glittering lamps of all colors, . . . the twelve revolving stars on its twelve tall turrets cast forth wide beams of penetrating radiance into the deepening darkness of the night, . . . aloft in its topmost crown of pinnacles swung the prayer-commanding bell, . . . while the enormous crowds swarming thick about it gave it the appearance of a brilliant Pharos set in the midst of a surging sea. The steps leading up to it were strewn ankle-deep with flowers, . . . the doors stood open, and a thunderous hum of solemn music vibrated in wave-like pulsations through the heavy, heated air.

Half blinded by the extreme effulgence, and confused by the jostling to and fro of a multitude immeasurably greater than any he had ever seen or imagined, Theos instinctively stretched out his hand in the helpless fashion of one not knowing whither next to turn, . . . Sah-luma immediately caught it in his own, and hurried him along without saying a word.

How they managed to glide through the close ranks of pushing, pressing people, and effect an entrance he never knew,—but when he recovered from his momentary dazed bewilderment, he found himself inside the Temple, standing near a pillar of finely fluted white marble that shot up like the stem of a palm-tree and lost its final point in the dim yet sparkling splendor of the immense dome above. Lights twinkled everywhere,—there was the odor of faint perfumes mingled with the fresher fragrance of flowers,—there were distant glimpses of jewelled shrines, and the leering faces of grotesque idols clothed in draperies of amber, purple, and green,—and between the multitudinous columns that ringed the superb fane with snowy circles, one within the other, hung glittering lamps, set with rare gems and swinging by long chains of gold.

But the crowning splendor of the whole was concentrated on the place of the secret Inner Shrine. There an Arch of pale-blue fire spanned the dome from left to right, . . . there, from huge bronze vessels mounted on tall tripods the smoke of burning incense arose in thick and odorous clouds,—there children clad in white, and wearing garlands of vivid scarlet blossoms, stood about in little groups as still as exquisitely modelled statuettes, their small hands folded, and their eyes downcast, . . . there, the steps were strewn with branches of palm, flowering oleander, rose-laurel, and olive-sprays,—but the Sanctuary itself was not visible.

Before that Holy of Holies hung the dazzling folds of the "Silver Veil," a curtain of the most wonderfully woven silver tissue, that seen in the flashing azure light of the luminous arch above it, resembled nothing so much as a suddenly frozen sheet of foam. Across it was emblazoned in large characters:

I Am The Past, The Present, The Future,
The Might-Have-Been, And The Shall-Not-Be,
The Ever, And The Never,
No Mortal Knoweth My Name.

As Theos with some difficulty, owing to the intense brilliancy of the Veil, managed to decipher these words, he heard a solitary trumpet sounded,—a clear-blown note that echoed itself many times among the lofty arches before it finally floated into silence. Recognizing this as an evident signal for some new and important phase in the proceedings, he turned his eyes away from the place of the Shrine, and looking round the building was surprised to see how completely the vast area was filled with crowds upon crowds of silent and expectant people. It seemed as though not the smallest wedge could have been inserted between the shoulders of one man and another, yet where he stood with Sah-luma there was plenty of room. The reason of this however was soon apparent,—they were in the place reserved for the King and the immediate officers of the Royal Household,—and scarcely had the sweet vibration of that clear trumpet-blast died away, when Zephoranim himself appeared, walking slowly and majestically in the midst of a select company of his nobles and courtiers.

He wore the simple white garb of an ordinary citizen of Al-Kyris, together with a silver belt and plain-sheathed dagger, . . . not a jewel relieved the classic severity of his costume, and not even the merest fillet of gold in his rough dark hair denoted his royal rank. But the pride of precedence spoke in his flashing eyes,—the arrogance of authority in the self-conscious poise of his figure and haughtiness of his step,—his brows were knitted in something of a frown, and his face looked pale and slightly careworn. He spied out Sah-luma at once and smiled kindly,—there was not a trace of coldness in his manner toward his favored minstrel, and Theos noted this with a curious sense of sudden consolation and encouragement. "Why should I have feared Zephoranim?" he thought. "Sah-luma has no greater friend, . . . except myself! The King would be the last person in the world to do him any injury!"

Just then a magnificent burst of triumphal music rolled through the Temple,—the music of some mighty instrument, organ-like in sound, but several tones deeper than the grandest organ ever made, mingled with children's voices singing. The King seated himself on a cushioned chair directly in front of the Silver Veil, . . . Sah-luma took a place at his right hand, giving Theos a low bench close beside him, while the various distinguished personages who had attended Zephoranim disposed themselves indifferently wherever they could find standing-room, only keeping as near to their monarch as they were able to do in the extreme pressure of so vast a congregation.

For now every available inch of space was occupied,—as far as eye could see there were rows upon rows of men and white-veiled women, . . . Theos imagined there must have been more then five thousand people present. On went the huge pulsations of melody, surging through the incense-laden air like waves thudding incessantly on a rocky shore, and presently out of a side archway near the Sanctuary-steps came with slow and gliding noiselessness a band of priests, walking two by two, and carrying branches of palm. These were all clad in purple and crowned with ivy-wreaths,—they marched sedately, keeping their eyes lowered, while their lips moved constantly, as though they muttered inaudible incantations. Waving their palm-boughs to and fro, they paced along past the King and down the centre aisle of the Temple,—then turning, they came back again to the lowest step of the Shrine and there they all prostrated themselves, while the children who stood near the incense-burners flung fresh perfumes on the glowing embers and chanted the following recitative:

"*O Nagaya, great, everlasting and terrible!*
Thou who dost wind thy coils of wisdom into the heart!
Thou, whose eyes, waking and sleeping, do behold all things!
Thou who art the joy of the Sun and the Master of Virgins!
Hear us, we beseech thee, when we call upon thy name!"

MARIE CORELLI

Their young treble voices were clear and piercing, and pealed up to the dome to fall again like the drops of distinct round melody from a lark's singing-throat,—and when they ceased there came a short impressive pause. The Silver Veil quivered from end to end as though swayed by a faint wind, and the flaming Arch above turned from pale blue to a strange shimmering green. Then, in mellow unison, the kneeling priests intoned:

"O thou who givest words of power to the dumb mouth of the soul in Hades; hear us, Nagaya!
O thou who openest the grave and givest peace to the heart; plead for us, Nagaya!
O thou who art companion of the Sun and controller of the East and of the West; comfort us, Nagaya!"

Here they ended, and the children began again, not to chant but to sing. . . a strange and tristful tune, wilder than any that vragrant winds could play on the strings of an aeolian lyre:

"O Virgin of Virgins, Holy Maid, to what shall we resemble thee?
Chaste Daughter of the Sun, how shall we praise thy peerless beauty!
Thou art the Gate of the House of Stars!—thou art the first of the Seven Jewels of Nagaya!
Thou dost wield the sceptre of ebony, and the Eye of Raphon beholds thee with love and contentment!
Thou art the Chiefest of Women, . . . thou hast the secrets of earth and heaven, thou knowest the dark mysteries!
Hail, Lysia! Queen of the Hall of Judgment!
Hail, pure Pearl in the Sea of the Sun's glory!
Declare unto us, we beseech thee, the Will of Nagaya!"

They closed this canticle softly and slowly, . . . then flinging themselves prone, they pressed their faces to the earth, . . . and again the glittering Veil waved to and fro suggestively, while Theos, his heart beating fast, watched its shining woof with straining eyes and a sense of suffocation in his throat, . . . what ignorant fools, what mad barbarians, what blind blasphemers were these people, he indignantly thought, who could thus patiently hear the praise of an evil woman like Lysia publicly proclaimed with almost divine honors!

Did they actually intend to worship her, he wondered? If so, he at any rate would never bend the knee to one so vile! He might have done so once, perhaps, . . . but now. . . ! At that instant a flute like murmur of melody crept upward as it seemed from the ground, with a plaintive whispering sweetness like the lament of some exiled fairy,—so exquisitely tender and pathetic, and yet withal so heart-stirring and passionate, that, despite himself, he listened with a strange, swooning sense of languor stealing insidiously over him,—a dreamy lassitude, that while it made him feel enervated and deprived of strength, was still not altogether unpleasing, . . . a faint sigh escaped his lips,—and he kept his gaze fixed on the Silver Veil as pertinaciously as though behind it lay the mystery of his soul's ruin or salvation.

How the light flashed on its shimmering folds like the rippling phosphorescence on southern seas! . . . as green and clear and brilliant as rays reflected from thousands and thousands of glistening emeralds! . . . And that haunting, sorrowful, weird music! . . . How it seemed to eat into his heart and there waken a bitter remorse combined with an equally bitter despair!

Once more the Veil moved, and this time it appeared to inflate itself in the fashion of a sail caught by a sudden breeze,—then it began to part in the middle very slowly and without sound. Further and further back on each side it gradually receded, and. . . like a lily disclosed between folding leaves—a Figure, white, wonderful and angelically fair, shone out, the centre jewel of the stately shrine,—a shrine whose immense carven pillars, grotesque idols, bronze and gold ornaments, jewelled lamps and dazzling embroideries, only served as a sort of neutral-tinted background to intensify with a more lustrous charm the statuesque loveliness revealed! O Lysia, Unvirgined Priestess of the Sun and Nagaya, how gloriously art thou arrayed in sin! . . . O singular Sweetness whose end must needs be destruction, was ever woman fairer than thou! . . . O love, love, lost in the dead Long-Ago, and drowned in the uttermost darkness of things evil, wilt thou drag my soul with thee again into everlasting night!

Thus Theos inwardly raved, without any real comprehension of his own thoughts, but only stricken anew by a feverish passion of mingled love and hatred as he stared on the witching sorceress whose marvellous beauty was such wonder and torture to his eyes, . . . what mattered it to him that King, Laureate, and people had all prostrated themselves

MARIE CORELLI

before her in reverent humility? . . . HE knew her nature, . . . he had fathomed her inborn wickedness, . . . and though his senses were attracted by her, his spirit loathingly repelled her, . . . he therefore remained seated stiffly upright, watching her with a sort of passive, immovable intentness. As she now appeared before him, her loveliness was absolutely and ideally perfect,—she looked the embodiment of all grace,—the model of all chastity.

She stood quite still, . . . her hands folded on her breast, . . . her head slightly lifted, her dark eyes upturned, . . . her unbound black hair streamed over her shoulders in loose glossy waves, and above her brows her diadem of serpents' heads sparkled like a coronal of flame. Her robe was white, made of some silky shining stuff that glistened with soft pearly hues; it was gathered about her waist by a twisted golden girdle. Her arms were bare, decked as before with the small jewelled snakes that coiled upward from wrist to shoulder,—and when after a brief pause she unfolded her hands and raised them with a slow, majestic movement above her head, the great Symbolic Eye flared from her bosom like a darting coal, seeming to turn sinister glances on all sides as though on the search for some suspected foe.

Fortunately no one appeared to notice Theos's deliberate non-observance of the homage due to her,—no one except. . . Lysia, herself. She met the open defiance, scorn, and reluctant admiration of his glance, . . . and a cold smile dawned on her features, . . . a smile more dreadful in its very sweetness than any frown, . . . then, turning away her beautiful, fathomless, slumberous eyes and still keeping her arms raised, she lifted up her voice, a voice mellow as a golden flute, that pierced the silence with a straight arrow of pure sound, and chanted:

"Give glory to the Sun, O ye people! for his Light doth illumine your darkness!"

And the murmur of the mighty crowd surged back in answer:

"We give him glory!"

Here came a brief clash of brazen bells, and when the clamor ceased, Lysia continued:

"Give glory to the Moon, O ye people! . . . for she is the servant of the Sun and the Ruler of the House of Sleep!"

Again the people responded;

"We give her glory!" . . . and again the bells jangled tempestuously.

"Give glory to Nagaya, O ye people! for he alone can turn aside the wrath of the Immortals!"

"We give him glory!" . . . rejoined the multitude,—and "We give him glory! seemed to be shouted high among the arches of the Temple with a strange sound as of the mocking laughter of devils."

This preliminary over, there came out of unseen doors on both sides of the Sanctuary twenty priests in companies of ten each; ten advancing from the left, ten from the right. These were clad in flowing garments of carnation-colored silk, heavily bordered with gold, and the leader of the right-hand group was the priest Zel. His demeanor was austere and dignified, . . . he carried a square cushion covered in black, on which lay a long, thin cruel-looking knife with a jewelled hilt. The chief of the priests, who stood on the left, bore a very tall and massive staff of polished ebony, which he solemnly presented to the High Priestess, who grasped it firmly in one slight hand and allowed it to rest steadily on the ground, while its uppermost point reached far above her head.

Then followed the strangest, weirdest scene that even the pen of poets or brush of painter devised, . . . a march round and round the Temple of all the priests, bearing lighted flambeaux and singing in chorus a wild Litany,—a confused medley of supplications to the Sun and Nagaya, which, accompanied as it was by the discordant beating drums and the clanging of bells, had an evidently powerful effect on the minds of the assembled populace, for presently they also joined in the maddening chant, and growing more and more possessed by the contagious fever of fanaticism, began to howl and shriek and clap their hands furiously, creating a frightful din suggestive of some fiendish clamor in hell.

Theos, half deafened by the horrible uproar, as well as roused to an abnormal pitch of restless excitement, looked round to see how Sah-luma comported himself. He was sitting quite still, in a perfectly composed attitude,—a faint, derisive smile played on his lips, . . . his profile, as it just then appeared, had the firmness and the pure soft outline of a delicately finished cameo, . . . his splendid eyes now darkened, now lightened with passion, as he gazed at Lysia, who, all alone in the centre of the Shrine, held her ebony staff as perpendicularly erect as though it were a tree rooted fathoms deep in earth, keeping herself too as motionless as a figure of frozen snow.

And the King? . . . what of him? . . . Glancing at that bronze-like brooding countenance, Theos was startled and at the same time half fascinated by its expression. Such a mixture of tigerish tenderness, servile idolatry, intemperate desire, and craven fear he had never seen delineated on the face of any human being. In the black thirsty eyes there was a look that spoke volumes,—a look that betrayed what the heart concealed,—and reading that featured emblazonment of hidden guilt, Theos knew beyond all doubt that the rumors concerning the High Priestess and the King were true, . . . that the dead Khosrul had spoken rightly, . . . that Zephoranim loved Lysia! . . . Love? . . . it seemed too tame a word for the pent-up fury of passion that visibly and violently consumed the man! What would be the result? . . .

"When the High Priestess Is the King's mistress Then fall Al-Kyris!"

These foolish doggerel lines! . . . why did they suggest themselves? . . . they meant nothing. The question did not concern Al-Kyris at all,—let the city stand or fall as it list, who cared, so long as Sah-luma escaped injury! Such, at least, was the tenor of Theos's thoughts, as he rapidly began to calculate certain contingencies that now seemed likely to occur. If, for instance, the King were made aware of Sah-luma's intrigue with Lysia, would not his rage and jealousy exceed all bounds? . . . and if, on the other hand, Sah-luma were convinced of the King's passion for the same fatally fair traitress, would not his wrath and injured self-love overbear all loyalty and prudence?

And between the two powerful rivals who thus by stealth enjoyed her capricious favors, what would Lysia's own decision be?—Like a loud hissing in his ears, he heard again the murderous command,—a command which was half a menace: "KILL SAH-LUMA!"

Faint shudders as of icy cold ran through him,—he nerved himself to meet some deadly evil, though he could not guess what that evil might be,—he was willing to throw away all the past that haunted him, and cut off all hope of a future, provided he could only baffle the snares of the pitiless beauty to whom the torture of men was an evident joy, and rescue his beloved and gifted friend from her perilous attraction! Making a strong effort to master the inward conflict of fear and pain that tormented him, he turned his attention anew to the gorgeous ceremony that was going on, . . . the march of the priests had come to an abrupt end. They stood now on each side of the Shrine, divided in groups of equal numbers, tossing their flambeaux around and above them to the measured ringing of bells. At every upward wave of these flaring torches, a tongue of fire leaped aloft, to instantly break and descend in a sparkling shower of gold,—the effect of this was wonderful in the extreme, as by the dexterous way in which the flames were flung forth, it appeared to the spectator's eyes as though a luminous Snake were twisting and coiling itself to and fro in mid-air.

All loud music ceased, . . . the multitude calmed down by degrees and left off their delirious cries of frenzy or rapture, . . . there was nothing heard but a monotonous chanting in undertone, of which not a syllable was distinctly intelligible. Then from out a dark portal unperceived in the shadowed gloom of a curtained niche, there advanced a procession of young girls,—fifty in all, clad in pure white and closely veiled.

They carried small citherns, and arriving in front of the shrine, they knelt down in a semicircle, and very gently began to strike the short, responsive strings. The murmur of a lazy rivulet among whispering reeds, . . . the sighing suggestions of leaves ready to fall in autumn,— the low, languid trilling of nightingales just learning to sing,—any or all these might be said to resemble the dulcet melody they played; while every delicate arpeggio, every rippling chord was muffled with a soft pressure of their hands ere the sound had time to become vehement. This elf-like harping continued for a short interval, during which the priests, gathering in a ring round a huge bronze font-shaped vessel hard by, dipped their flambeaux therein and suddenly extinguished them.

At the same moment the lights in the body of the Temple were all lowered, . . . only the Arch spanning the Shrine blazed in undiminished brilliancy, its green tint appearing more intense in contrast with the surrounding deepening shadow. And now with a harsh clanging noise as of the turning of heavy bolts and keys, the back of the Sanctuary parted asunder in the fashion of a revolving double doorway,—and a golden grating was disclosed, its strong glistening bars welded together like knotted ropes and wrought with marvellous finish and solidity. Turning toward this semblance of a prison-cell Lysia spoke aloud—her clear tones floating with mellifluous slowness above the half-hushed quiverings of the cithern-choir:

"Come forth, O Nagaya, thou who didst slumber in the bosom of
Space ere ever the world was made!
"Come forth, O Nagaya, thou who didst behold the Sun born out of
Chaos, and the Earth enriched with ever-producing life!
"Come forth, O Nagaya, Friend of the gods and the people, and
comfort us with the Divine Silence of thy Wisdom supernal!"

While she pronounced these words, the golden grating ascended gradually inch by inch, with the steady clank as of the upward winding of a chain,—and when she ceased, there came a mysterious, rustling,

MARIE CORELLI

slippery sound, suggestive of some creeping thing forcing its way through wet and tangled grass, or over dead leaves, . . . one instant more, and a huge Serpent—a species of python some ten feet in length— glided through the round aperture made by the lifted bars, and writhed itself slowly along the marble pavement straight to where Lysia stood.

Once it stopped, curving back its glistening body in a strange loop as though in readiness to spring—but it soon resumed its course, and arrived at the High Priestess's feet. There, its whole frame trembled and glowed with extraordinary radiance, . . . the prevailing color of its skin was creamy white, marked with countless rings and scaly bright spots of silver, purple, and a peculiar livid blue,—and all these tints came into brilliant prominence, as it crouched before Lysia and twisted its sinuous neck to and fro with an evidently fawning and supplicatory gesture; while she, keeping her sombre dark eyes fixed full upon it, moved not an inch from her position, but, majestically serene, continued to hold the tall staff of ebony straight and erect as a growing palm.

The cithern-playing had now the soothing softness of a mother's lullaby to a tired child, and as the liquid notes quavered delicately on the otherwise deep stillness, the formidable reptile began to coil itself ascendingly round and round the ebony rod, . . . higher and higher,— one glistening ring after another,—higher still, till its eyes were on a level with the "Eye of Raphon" that flamed on Lysia's breast, . . . there it paused in apparent reflectiveness, and seemed to listen to the slumberous strains that floated toward it in wind-like breaths of sound, . . . then, starting afresh on its upward way, it carefully, and with almost human tenderness, avoided touching Lysia's hand, which now rested on the staff between two thick twists of its body, . . . and finally it reached the top, where fully raising its crested head, it displayed the prismatic tints of its soft, restless, wavy throat, which was adorned furthermore by a flexible circlet of magnificent diamonds.

Nothing more striking or more singular could Theos imagine than the scene now before him, . . . the beautiful woman, still as sculptured marble, and the palpitating Snake coiled on that mast-like rod and uplifted above her,—while round the twain knelt the Priests, their faces covered in their robes, and from all parts of the Temple the loud shout arose:

"ALL HAIL, NAGAYA!"
"Praise, Honor, and Glory be unto thee forever and ever!"

Then it was that the proud King flung himself to earth and kissed the dust in abject submission,—then Sah-luma, carelessly complaisant, bent the knee and smiled to himself mockingly as he performed the act of veneration, . . . then the enormous multitude with clasped hands and beseeching looks fell down and worshipped the glittering beast of the field, whose shining, emerald-like, curiously sad eyes roved hither and thither with a darting yet melancholy eagerness over all the people who called it Lord!

To Theos's imagination it looked a creature more sorrowful than fierce,—a poor charmed brute, that while netted in the drowsy woofs of its mistress Lysia's magnetic spell, seemed as though it dimly wondered why it should thus be raised aloft for the adoration of infatuated humankind. Its brilliant crest quivered and emitted little arrowy scintillations of lustre—the "god" was ill at ease in the midst of all his splendor, and two or three times bent back his gleaming neck as though desirous of descending to the level ground.

But when these hints of rebellion declared themselves in the tremors running through the scaly twists of his body, Lysia looked up, and at once, compelled as it were by involuntary attraction, "Nagaya the Divine" looked down. The strange, subtle, mesmeric, sleepy eyes of the woman met the glittering green, mournful eyes of the snake,—and thus the two beautiful creatures regarded each other steadfastly and with an apparent vague sympathy, till the "deity," evidently overcome by a stronger will than his own, and resigning himself to the inevitable, twisted his radiant head back again to the top of the ebony staff, and again surveyed the kneeling crowds of worshippers.

Presently his glistening jaws opened,—his tongue darted forth vibratingly,—and he gave vent to a low hissing sound, erecting and depressing his crest with extraordinary rapidity, so that it flashed like an aigrette of rare gems. Then, with slow and solemn step, the Priest Zel advanced to the front of the Shrine, and spreading out his hands in the manner of one pronouncing a benediction, said loudly and with emphasis:

> "Nagaya the Divine doth hear the prayers of his people!
> "Nagaya the Supreme doth accept the offered Sacrifice!
> "BRING FORTH THE VICTIM!"

The last words were spoken with stern authoritativeness, and scarcely had they been uttered when the great entrance doors of the Temple flew open, and a procession of children appeared, strewing flowers and singing:

> *"O happy Bride, we bring thee unto joy and peace!*
> *"To thee are opened the Palaces of the Air,*
> *"The beautiful silent Palaces where the bright stars dwell*
> *"O happy Bride of Nagaya! how fair a fate is thine!"*

Pausing, they flung wreaths and garlands among the people, and continued:

> *"O happy Bride! for thee are past all Sorrows and Sin,*
> *"Thou shalt never know shame, or pain or grief or the weariness of tears;*
> *"For thee no husband shall prove false, no children prove ungrateful;*
> *"O happy Bride of Nagaya! how glad a fate is thine.*
> *"O happy Bride! when thou art wedded to the beautiful god, the god of Rest,—*
> *"Thou shalt forget all trouble and dwell among sweet dreams for ever!*
> *"Thou art the blessed one, chosen for the love-embraces of Nagaya!*
> *"O happy Bride! . . . how glorious a fate is thine!"*

Thus they sang in the soft, strange vowel-language of Al-Kyris, and tripped along with that innocent, unthinking gayety usual to such young creatures, up to the centre aisle toward the Sanctuary. They were followed by four priests in scarlet robes and closely masked, . . . and walking steadfastly between these, came a slim girl clad in white, veiled from head to foot and crowned with a wreath of lotus lilies. All the congregation, as though moved by an impulse, turned to look at her as she passed,—but her features were not as yet discernible through the mist-like draperies that enfolded her.

The singing children, always preceding her and scattering flowers, having arrived at the steps of the Shrine, grouped themselves on either side,—and the red garmented Priests, after having made several genuflections to the glittering Python that now, with reared neck and quivering fangs, seemed to watch everything that was going on with absorbed and crafty vigilance, proceeded to unveil the maiden martyr, and also to tie her slight hands behind her back by means of a knotted silver cord. Then in a firm voice the Priest Zel proclaimed:

"Behold the elected Bride of the Sun and the Divine Nagaya!

"She bears away from the city the burden of your sins, O ye people, and by her death the gods are satisfied!

"Rejoice greatly, for ye are absolved,—and by the Silver Veil and the Eye of Raphon we pronounce upon all here present the blessing of pardon and peace!"

As he spoke the girl turned round as though in obedience to some mechanical impulse, and fully confronted the multitude, . . . her pale, pure face, framed in a shining aureole of rippling fair hair, floated before Theos's bewildered eyes like a vision seen indistinctly in a magic crystal, and he was for a moment uncertain of her identity; but quick as a flash Sah-luma's glance lighted upon her, and, with a cry of horror that sent desolate echoes through and through the arches of the Temple, he started from his seat, his arms outstretched, his whole frame convulsed and quivering.

"Niphrata! . . . Niphrata! . . ." and his rich voice shook with a passion of appeal, "O ye gods! . . . what mad, blind, murderous cruelty! Zephoranim!" . . . and he turned impetuously on the astonished monarch: "As thou livest crowned King I say this maid is MINE! . . . and in the very presence of Nagaya, I swear she shall NOT die!"

XXVIII

The Sacrifice

A solemn silence ensued. Consternation and wrath were depicted on every countenance. The Sacred Service was interrupted! . . . a defiance had been hurled as it were in the very teeth of the god Nagaya! . . . and this horrible outrage to Religion and Law had been actually committed by the Laureate of the realm! It was preposterous, . . . incredible! . . . and the gaping crowds reached over each other's shoulders to stare at the offender, pressing forward eager, wondering, startled faces, which to Theos looked far more spectral than real, seen in the shimmering green radiance that was thrown flickering upon them from the luminous Arch above the Altar. The priests stood still in speechless indignation, . . . Lysia moved not at all, nor raised her eyes; only her lips parted in a very slight cold smile.

Seized with mortal dread, Theos gazed helplessly at his reckless, beautiful poet friend, who with head erect and visage white as a waning moon, haughtily confronted his Sovereign and audaciously asserted his right to be heard, even in the Holy place of worship! The King was the first to break the breathless stillness: his words came harshly from his throat, . . . and the great muscles in his neck seemed to swell visibly with his hardly controlled anger.

"Peace! . . . Thou art suddenly distraught, Sah-luma! . . ." he said, in half-smothered, fierce accents—"How darest thou uplift thy clamorous tongue thus wantonly before Nagaya, and interrupt the progress of his Sacred Ritual? . . . check thy mad speech! . . . if ever yonder maid were thine, 'tis certain she is thine no longer; . . . she hath offered herself, a voluntary sacrifice, and the gods are pleased to claim what thou perchance hast failed to value!"

For all answer, Sah-luma flung himself desperately at the monarch's feet. "Zephoranim!" he cried again. . . "I tell thee she is mine! . . . mine, as truly mine as Love can make her! Oh, she is chaster than lily-buds in her sweet body! . . . but in her spirit she is wedded—wedded to me, Sah-luma, whom thou, O King, hast ever delighted to honor! And now must I kneel to thee in vain?—thou whose victories I have sung, whose praises I have chanted in burning words that shall carry thy name forever with triumph, down to unborn generations? . . . Wilt thou become inglorious? . . . a warrior stricken strengthless by the mummeries of priestcraft,—the juggleries of a perishing creed? Thou art the ruler of Al-Kyris,—thou and thou only! Restore to me this innocent virgin-life that has scarcely yet begun to bloom! . . . speak but the word and she is saved! . . . and her timely rescue shall add lustre to the record of thy noblest deeds!"

His matchless voice, full of passionate pulsations, exercised for a moment a resistless influence and magnetic charm. The King's lowering brows relaxed,—and a gleam of pity passed like light across his countenance. Instinctively he extended his hand to raise Sah-luma from his humble attitude, as though, even in his wrath, he were conscious of the immense intellectual superiority of a great Poet to ever so great a King; and a thrill of involuntary compassion seemed at the same time to run sympathetically through the vast congregation. Theos drew a quick breath of relief, and glanced at Niphrata, . . . how cold and unconcerned was her demeanor! . . . Did she not hear Sah-luma's pleading in her behalf? . . . No matter!—she would be saved, he thought, and all would yet be well!

And truly it now appeared as if mercy, and not cruelty, were to be the order of the hour, . . . for just then the Priest Zel, after having exchanged a few inaudible words with Lysia, advanced again to the front of the Shrine and spoke in distinct tones of forced gentleness and bland forbearance:

"Hear me, O King, Princes and People! . . . Whereas it has unhappily occurred, to the wonder and sorrow of many, that the holy Spouse of the divine Nagaya is delayed in her desired departure, by the unforeseen opposition and unedifying contumacy of Sah-luma, Poet Laureate of this realm; and lest it may be perchance imagined by the uninitiated, that the maiden is in any way unwilling to fulfil her glorious destiny, the High and Immaculate Priestess of the Shrine doth bid me here pronounce a respite; a brief interval wherein, if the King and the People be willing, he who is named Sah-luma shall, by virtue of his high renown, be permitted to address the Virgin-victim and ascertain her own wishes from her own lips. Injustice cannot dwell within this Sacred Temple,—and if, on trial, the maiden chooses the transitory joys of Earth in preference to the everlasting joys of the Palaces of the Sun, then in Nagaya's name shall she go free!—inasmuch as the god loves not a reluctant bride, and better no Sacrifice at all, than one that is grudgingly consummated!"

He ceased,—and Sah-luma sprang erect, his eyes sparkling, his whole demeanor that of a man unexpectedly disburdened from some crushing grief.

"Thanks be unto the benevolent destinies!" he exclaimed, flashing a quick glance of gratitude toward Lysia, . . . the statuesque Lysia, on whose delicately curved lips the faintly derisive smile still lingered. . . "And in return for the life of my Niphrata I will give a thousand jewels rare beyond all price to deck Nagaya's tabernacle!—and I will pour libations to the Sun for twenty days and nights, in token of my heart's requital for mercy well bestowed!"

Stooping he kissed the King's hand,—whereupon at a sign from Zel, one of the priests attired in scarlet unfastened Niphrata's bound hands, and led her, as one leads a blind child, straight up to where Sah-luma and Theos stood, close beside the King, who, together with many others, stared curiously upon her. How fixed and feverishly brilliant were her large dark-blue eyes! . . . how set were the sensitive lines of her mouth!—how indifferent she seemed, how totally unaware of the Laureate's presence! The priest who brought her retired into the background, and she remained where he left her, quite mute and motionless. Oh, how every nerve in Theos's body throbbed with inexpressible agony as he beheld her thus! The wildest remorse possessed him, . . . it was as though he looked on the dim picture of a ruin which he himself had recklessly wrought, . . . and he could have groaned aloud in the horrible vagueness of his incomprehensible despair! Sah-luma caught the girl's hand, and peered into her white, still face.

"Niphrata! . . . Niphrata!" he said in a tremulous half-whisper, "I am here,—Sah-luma! . . . Dost thou not know me!"

She sighed, . . . a long, shivering sigh,—and smiled, . . . what a strange, wistful, dying smile it was! . . . but she made no answer.

"Niphrata!"—continued the Laureate, passionately pressing the little, cold fingers that lay so passively in his grasp. . . "Look at me! . . . I have come to save thee! . . . to take thee home again, . . . home to thy flowers, thy birds, thy harp, . . . thy pretty chamber with its curtained nook, where thy friend Zoralin waits and weeps all day for thee! . . . O ye gods!—how weak am I!" . . . and he fiercely dashed away the drops that glistened on his black silky lashes, . . . "Come with me, sweet one! . . ." he resumed tenderly—"Come!—Why art thou thus silent? . . . thou whose voice hath many a time outrivalled the music of the nightingales! Hast thou no word for me, thy lord?—Come!" . . .

and Theos, struggling to repress his own rising tears, heard his friend's accents sink into a still lower, more caressing cadence. . . "Thou shalt never again have cause for grief, my Niphrata, never! . . . We will never part! . . . Listen! . . . am I not he whom thou lovest?"

The poor child's set mouth trembled,—her beautiful sad eyes gazed at him uncomprehendingly.

"He whom I love is not here!" . . . she said in tired, soft tones; "I left him, but he followed me; and now, he waits for me. . . yonder!" . . . And she turned resolutely toward the Sanctuary, as though compelled to do so by some powerful mesmeric attraction, . . . "See you not how fair he is!" . . . and she pointed with her disengaged hand to the formidable python, through whose huge coils ran the tremors of impatient and eager breathing, . . . "How tenderly his eyes behold me! . . . those eyes that I have worshipped so patiently, so faithfully, and yet that never lightened into love for me till now! O thou more than beloved!— How beautiful thou art, my adored one, my heart's idol!" and a look of pale exaltation lightened her features, as she fixed her wistful gaze, like a fascinated bird, on the shadowy recess whence the Serpent had emerged—"There,—there thou dost rest on a couch of fadeless roses!— how softly the moonlight enfolds thee with a radiance as of outspread wings!—I hear thy voice charming the silence! . . . thou dost call me by my name, . . . O once poor name made rich by thy sweet utterance! Yes, my beloved, I am ready! . . . I come! I shall die in thy embraces, . . . nay, I shall not die but sleep! . . . and dream a dream of love that shall last forever and ever! No more sorrow. . . no more tears, . . . no more heartsick longings. . ."

Here she stopped in her incoherent speech, and strove to release her hand from Sah-luma's, her blue eyes filling with infinite anxiety and distress.

"I pray thee, good stranger," she entreated with touching mildness,— "whosoever thou art, delay me not, but let me go! . . . I am but a poor love-sorrowful maid on whom Love hath at last taken pity!—be gentle therefore, and hinder me not on my way to Sah-luma. I have waited for happiness so long! . . . so long!"

Her young, plaintive voice quavered into a half sob,—and again she endeavored to break away from the Laureate's hold. But he, overcome by the excess of his own grief and agitation, seized her other hand, and drew her close up to him.

"Niphrata, Niphrata!" he cried despairingly. "What evil hath befallen thee? Where is thy sight. . . thy memory? . . . Look! . . . Look straight in these eyes of mine, and read there my truth and tenderness! . . . *I* am Sah-luma, thine own Sah-luma! . . . thy poet, thy lover, thy master, thy slave, . . . all that thou wouldst have me be, I am! Whither wouldst thou wander in search of me? Thou hast no further to go, dear heart, than these arms, . . . thou art safe with me, my singing bird, . . . come! . . . Let me lead thee hence, and home!"

She watched him while he spoke, with a strange expression of distrust and uneasiness. Then, by a violent effort, she wrenched her hands from his clasp, and stood aloof, waving him back with an eloquent gesture of amazed reproach.

"Away!" she said, in firm accents of sweet severity,—"Thou art a demon that dost seek to tempt my soul to ruin! Thou Sah-luma!" . . . and she lifted her lily-crowned head with a movement of proud rejection. "Nay! . . . thou mayst wear his look, his smile, . . . thou mayst even borrow the clear heaven-lustre of his eyes,—but I tell thee thou art fiend, not angel, and I will not follow thee into the tangled ways of sin! Oh, thou knowest not the meaning of true love, thou! . . . There is treachery on thy lips, and thy tongue is trained to utter honeyed falsehood! Methinks thou hast wantonly broken many a faithful heart!—and made light jest of many a betrayed virgin's sorrow! And thou darest to call thyself My Poet, . . . My Sah-luma, in whom there is no guile, and who would die a thousand deaths rather than wound the frailest soul that trusted him! . . . Depart from me, thou hypocrite in Poet's guise! . . . thou cruel phantom of my love! . . . Back to that darkness where thou dost belong, and trouble not my peace!"

Sah-luma recoiled from her, amazed and stupefied. Theos clenched his hands together in a sort of physical effort to keep down the storm of emotions working within him,—for Niphrata's words burnt into his brain like fire, . . . too well, too well he understood their full intensity of meaning! She loved the IDEAL Sah-luma, . . . the Sah-luma of her own pure fancies and desires, . . . NOT the REAL man as he was, with all his haughty egotism, vainglory, and vice,—vice in which he took more pride than shame. Perhaps she had never known him in his actual character,—she, like other women of her lofty and ardent type, had no doubt set up the hero of her life as a god in the shrine of her own holy and enthusiastic imagination, and had there endowed him with resplendent virtues, which he had never once deemed it worth his while to practise. Oh the loving hearts of women!—How much men have to answer for, when they voluntarily break these clear mirrors of affection, wherein they, all unworthy, have been for a time reflected angel-wise, with all the warmth and color of an innocently adoring passion shining about them like the prismatic rays in a vase of polished crystal! To Niphrata, Sah-luma remained as a sort of splendid divinity, for whom no devotion was too vast, too high, or too complete, . . . better, oh surely far better that she should die in her beautiful self-deception, than live to see her elected idol descend to his true level, and openly display all the weaknesses of his volatile, flippant, godless, sensual, yet, alas! most fascinating and genius-gifted nature, . . . a nature, which, overflowing as it was with potentialities of noble deeds, yet lacked sufficient intrinsic faith and force to accomplish them! This thought stung Theos like a sharp arrow-prick, and filled him with a strange, indescribable penitence; and he stood in dumb misery, remorsefully eyeing his friend's consternation, disappointment, and pained bewilderment, without being able to offer him the slightest consolation.

Sah-luma was indeed the very picture of dismay, . . . if he had never suffered in his life before, surely he suffered now! Niphrata, the tender, the humbly adoring Niphrata, positively rejected him!—refused to recognize his actual presence, and turned insanely away from him toward some dream-ideal Sah-luma whom she fancied could only be found in that unexplored country bordered by the cold river of Death! Meanwhile, the silence in the Temple was intense,—the Priests were like so many wax figures fastened in fixed positions; the King, leaning slightly forward in his chair, had the appearance of a massively moulded image of bronze,—and to Theos's overwrought condition of mind, the only actually living things present seemed to be the monster Serpent whose scaly folds palpitated visibly in the strong light, . . . and the hideous "Eye of Raphon," that blazed on Lysia's breast with a menacing stare, as of a wrathful ghoul. All at once a flash of comprehension lightened the Laureate's sternly perplexed face,—a bitter laugh broke from his lips.

"She has been drugged!" he cried fiercely, pointing to Niphrata's white and rigid form, . . . "Poisoned by some deadly potion devised of devils, to twist and torture the quivering centres of the brain! Accursed work!—Will none undo it?" and springing forward nearer the Shrine, he raised his angry, impassioned eyes to the dark, inscrutable ones of the High Priestess, who met his troubled look with serene and irresponsive gravity. . . "Is there no touch of human pity in things divine? . . . no mercy in the icy fate that rules our destinies? . . . This child knows naught of what she does; she hath been led astray in a moment of excitement and religious exaltation, . . . her mind hath lost its balance,—her thoughts float disconnectedly on a sea of vague illusions, . . . Ah! . . . by the gods! . . . I understand it all now!" and he suddenly threw himself on his knees, his appealing gaze resting, not on the Snake-Deity, but on the lovely countenance of Lysia, fair and brilliant as a summer morn, with a certain waving light of triumph about it, like the reflected radiance of sunbeams, . . . "She is under the influence of Raphon! . . . O withering madness! . . . O cureless misery. . . She is ruled by that most horrible secret force, unknown as yet to the outer world of men! . . . and she hears things that are not, and sees what has no existence! O Lysia, Daughter of the Sun! . . . I do beseech thee, by all the inborn gentleness of womanhood, unwind the Mystic Spell!"

A serious smile of feigned, sorrowful compassion parted the beautiful lips of the Priestess; but she gave no word or sign in answer,—and the weird Jewel on her breast at that moment shot forth a myriad scintillations as of pointed sharp steel. Some extraordinary power in it, or in Lysia herself, was manifestly at work,—for with a violent start Sah-luma rose from his knees, and staggered helplessly backward, . . . one hand pressed to his eyes as though to shut out some blinding blaze of lightning! He seemed to be vaguely groping his way to his former place beside the King, and Theos, seeing this, quickly caught him by the arm and drew him thither, whispering anxiously the while:

"Sah-luma!-Sah-luma! . . . What ails thee?"

The Laureate turned upon him a bewildered, piteous face, white with an intensity of speechless anguish.

"Nothing!" . . . he faltered,—"Nothing! . . .'tis over, . . . the child must die!" . . . Then all suddenly the hard, drawn lines of his countenance relaxed,—great tears gathered in his eyes, and fell slowly one by one, . . . and moving aside, he shrank away as far as possible into the shadow cast by a huge column close by. . . "O Niphrata! . . . Niphrata!" . . . Theos heard him say in a voice broken by despair. "Why do I love thee only now, . . . Now, when thou art lost to me forever!"

The King looked after him half-compassionately, half-sullenly; but presently paid no further heed to his distress. Theos, however, kept near him, whispering whatever poor suggestions of comfort he could, in the extremity of his own grief, devise, . . . a hopeless task,—for to all his offered solace Sah-luma made but the one reply:

"Oh let me weep! . . . Let me weep for the untimely death of Innocence!"

And now the cithern-playing, which had ceased, commenced again, accompanied by the mysterious thrilling bass notes of the invisible organ-like instrument, whose sound resembled the roll and rush of huge billows breaking into foam. As the rich and solemn strains swept grandly through the spacious Temple, Niphrata stretched out her hands toward the High Priestess, a smile of wonderful beauty lighting up her fair child-face.

"Take me, O ye immortal gods!" she cried, her voice ringing in clear tune above all the other music. "Take me and bear me away on your strong, swift wings to the Everlasting Palaces of Air, wherein all sorrows have end, and patient love meets at last its long-delayed reward! Take me. . . for lo! I am ready to depart! My soul is wounded and weary of its prison,—it struggles to be free! O Destiny, I thank thee for thy mercy! . . . I praise thee for the glory thou dost here unveil before mine eyes! Pardon my sins! . . . accept my life! . . . sanctify my love!"

A murmur of relief and rejoicing ran rippling through the listening crowds,—a weight seemed lifted from their minds, . . . the victim was willing to die after all! . . . the Sacrifice would be proceeded with. There was a slight pause,—during which the priests crossed and re-crossed the Sanctuary many times, one of them descending the steps to tie Niphrata's hands behind her back as before. In the immediate interest of the moment, Sah-luma and his hot interference seemed to be almost forgotten, . . . a few people, indeed, cast injured and indignant looks toward the corner where he dejectedly leaned, and once the wrinkled, malicious head of old Zabastes peered at him, with an expression of incredulous amazement,—but otherwise no sympathy was manifested by any one for the popular Laureate's suffering and discomfiture. He was the nation's puppet, . . . its tame bird, whose business was to sing when bidden, . . . but he was not expected to have any voice in matters of religion or policy,—and still less was he supposed to intrude any of his own personal griefs on the public notice. Let him sing!—and sing well,—that was enough; but let him dare to be afflicted, and annoy others with his wants and troubles, why then he at once became uninteresting! . . . he might even die for all anybody cared! This was the unspoken sullen thought that Theos, sensitive to the core on his friend's behalf, instinctively felt to be smouldering in the heart of the mighty multitude,—and he resented the half-implied, latent ungratefulness of the people with all his soul.

"Fools!" . . . he muttered under his breath,—"For you, and such as you, the wisest sages toil in vain! . . . on you Art wastes her treasures of suggestive loveliness! . . . low grovellers in earth, ye have no eyes for heaven! O ignorant, ungenerous, fickle hypocrites, whose ruling passion is the greed of gold!—Why should great men perish, that Yᴇ may live! . . . And yet. . . your acclamations make up the thing called Fame! Fame? . . . Good God!—'tis a brief shout in the universal clamor, scarce heard and soon forgotten!"

And filled with strange bitterness, he gazed disconsolately at Niphrata, who stood like one in a trance of ecstasy, patiently awaiting her doom, her lovely, innocent blue eyes gladly upturned to the long, jewel-like head of Nagaya, which twined round the summit of the ebony staff, seemed to peer down at her in a sort of drowsy reflectiveness. Then, all suddenly, Lysia spoke, . . . how enchanting was the exquisite modulation of that slow, languid, silvery voice!

> *"Come hither, O Maiden fair, pure, and faithful!*
> *The desire of thy soul is granted!*
> *Before thee are the Gates of the Unknown World!*
> *Already they open to admit thee;*
> *Through their golden bars gleams the glory of thy future!*
> *Speak! . . . What seest thou?"*

A moment of breathless silence ensued,—all present seemed to be straining their ears to catch the victim's answer. It came,—soft and clear as a bell:

"I see a wondrous land o'er-canopied with skies of gold and azure: . . . white flowers grow in the fragrant fields, . . . there are many trees, . . . I hear the warbling of many birds; . . . I see fair faces that smile upon me and gentle hands that beckon! . . . Figures that wear glistening robes, and carry garlands of roses and myrtle, pass slowly, singing as they go! . . . How beautiful they are! How strange! . . . how sweet!"

And as she uttered these words, in accents of dreamy delight, she ascended the first step of the Shrine. Theos, looking, held his breath in wonder and fear, while Sah-luma with a groan turned himself resolutely away, and, pressing his forehead against the great column where he stood, hid his eyes in his clasped hands.

The High Priestess continued:

"Come hither, O Maiden of chaste and patient life!
Rejoice greatly, for thy virtue hath pleased the gods:
The undiscovered marvels of the Stars are thine,
Earth has no more control over thee:
Heaven is thine absolute Heritage! . . .
Behold! the Ship of the Sun awaits thee!
Speak! . . . What seest thou?"

A soft cry of rapture came from the girl's lips.

"Oh, I see glory everywhere!" . . . she exclaimed. "Light everywhere! . . . Peace everywhere! . . . O joy, joy! . . . The face of my beloved shines upon me,—he calls, . . . he bids me come to him! . . . Ah! we shall be together at last, . . . we twain shall be as one never to part, never to doubt, never to suffer more! O let me hasten to him! . . . Why should I linger thus, when I would fain, be gone!"

And she sprang eagerly up the second and third steps of the Sanctuary, and faced Lysia,—her head thrown back, her blue eyes ablaze with excitement, her bosom heaving, and her delicate features transfigured and illumined by unspeakable inward delirious bliss. Just then the Priest Zel lifted the long, jewel-hilted knife from the black cushion where it had lain till now, and, crouching stealthily in the shadow behind Lysia, held it in both bands, pointed straight forward in a level line with Niphrata's breast. Thus armed, he waited, silent and immovable.

A slight shudder of morbid expectancy seemed to quiver through the vast congregation, . . . but Theos's nerves were strung up to such a high pitch of frenzied horror that he could neither speak nor sigh,— motionless as a statue, he could only watch, with freezing blood, each detail of the extraordinary scene. Once more the High Priestess spoke:

"Come hither, O happy Maiden whose griefs are ended:
The day of thy triumph and reward has dawned!
For thee the Immortals unveiled the mysteries of being,—
To thee, they openly declare all secrets. . .
To thee the hidden things of Wisdom are made manifest:
For the last time ere thou leavest us, hear, and answer, . . .
Speak!—What seest thou?"

"Love!" replied Niphrata in a tone of thrilling and solemn tenderness. "Love, the Eternal All, in which dark things are made light!—Love, that is never served in vain! . . . Love wherein lost happiness is rediscovered and perfected! . . . O Divine Love, by whom the passion of my heart is sanctified! Absorb me in the quenchless glory of thine Immortality! . . . Draw me to Thyself, and let me find in Thee my Soul's completion!"

Her voice sank to a low prayerful emphasis, . . . her look was as of a rapt angel waiting for wings. Lysia's gaze dwelt upon her with slow-dilating wonder and contempt. . . such a devout and earnest supplication was evidently not commonly heard from the lips of Nagaya's victims. At that instant, too, Nagaya himself seemed curiously excited and disturbed,—his great glittering coils quivered so violently, as to shake the rod on which he was twined, . . . and when his Priestess raised her mesmeric reproving eyes toward him, he bent back his head rebelliously, and sent a vehement hiss through the silence, like the noise made by the whirl of a scimitar.

Suddenly, and with deafening abruptness, a clap of thunder, short and sharp as a quick volley of musketry, crashed overhead,— accompanied by a strange circular sweep of lightning that blazed through the windows of the Temple, illumining it from end to end with a brilliant blue glare. The superstitious crowd exchanged startled looks of terror, . . . the King moved uneasily and glanced frowningly about him,—it was plainly manifest that no one had forgotten the disastrous downfall of the Obelisk, . . . and there seemed to be a contagion of alarm in the very air. But Lysia was perfectly self-possessed, . . . in fact she appeared to accept the threat of a storm as an imposing, and by no means undesirable, adjunct to the mysteries of the Sacrificial Rite, for riveting her basilisk eyes on Niphrata, she said in firm, clear, decisive accents:

"The gods grow impatient! . . . Wherefore, O Princess and People of Al-Kyris, let us hasten to appease their anger! Depart, O stainless Maid! . . . depart hence, and betake thee to the Golden Throne of the Sun, our Lord and Ruler, . . . and in the Name of Nagaya, may the shedding of thy virginal blood avert from us and ours the wrath of the Immortals! Linger no longer, . . . Nagaya accepts thee! . . . and the Hour strikes Death!"

With the last word a sullen bell boomed heavily through and through the Temple. . . and, at once, . . . like a frenzied bird or butterfly winging its way into scorching flame, . . . Niphrata rushed forward with swift, unhesitating, dreadful precision straight on the knife outheld by the untrembling ruthless hands of the Priest Zel! One second,—and Theos sick with horror, saw her speeding thus, . . . the next,—and the whole place was enveloped in dense darkness!

XXIX

The Cup of Wrath and Trembling

A flash of time, . . . an instant of black, horrid eclipse, too brief for the utterance of even a word or cry, . . . and then,—with an appalling roar, as of the splitting of huge rocks and the tearing asunder of mighty mountains, the murky gloom was lifted, rent, devoured, and swept away on all sides by a sudden bursting forth of Fire! . . . Fire leaped up alive in twenty different parts of the building, springing aloft in spiral coils from the marble pavement that yawned crashingly open to give the impetuous flames their rapid egress, . . . fire climbed lithely round and round the immense carven columns, and ran, nimbly dancing and crackling its way among the painted and begemmed decorations of the dome, . . . fire enwrapped the side-altars, and shrivelled the jewelled idols at a breath, . . . fire unfastened and shook down the swinging-lamps, the garlands, the splendid draperies of silk and cloth-of-gold. . . fire—fire everywhere! . . . and the madly affrighted multitude, stunned by the abrupt shock of terror, stood for a moment paralyzed and inert, . . . then, with one desperate yell of wild brute fear and ferocity, they rushed headlong in a struggling, shrieking, cursing, sweltering swarm toward the great closed portals of the central aisle. As they did so, a tremendous weight of thunder seemed to descend solidly on the roof with a thudding burst as though a thousand walls had been battered down at one blow, . . . the whole edifice rocked and trembled in the terrific reverberation, and almost simultaneously, the doors were violently jerked open, wrenched from their hinges, and hurled, all burning and split with flame, against the forward-fighting crowds! Several hundred fell under the fiery mass, a charred heap of corpses,—the raging remainder pressed on in frenzied haste, clambering over piles of burning dead,—trampling on scorched, disfigured faces that perhaps but a moment since had been dear to them,—each and all bent on forcing a way out to the open air. In the midst of the overwhelming awfulness of the scene, Theos still retained sufficient presence of mind to remember that, whatever happened, his first care must be for Sah-luma, . . . always for Sah-luma, no matter who else perished! . . . and he now held that beloved comrade closely clasped by the arm, while he eagerly glanced about him on every side for some outlet through which to make a good and swift escape.

The most immediate place of safety seemed to be the Inner Sanctuary of Nagaya, . . . it was untouched by the flames, and its Titanic pillars of brass and bronze suggested, in their very massiveness, a nearly impregnable harbor of refuge. The King had fled thither, and now stood, like a statue of undaunted gloomy amazement, beside Lysia, who on her part appeared literally frozen with terror. Her large, startled eyes, roving here and there in helpless anxiety, alone gave any animation to the deathly, rigid whiteness of her face, and she still mechanically supported the Sacred Ebony Staff, without apparently being aware of the fact that the Snake Deity, convulsed through all his coils with fright, had begun to make there-from his rapid DESCENT. The priests, the virgins,—the poor, unhappy little singing children,—flocked hurriedly together, and darted to the back of the great Shrine, in the manifest intention of reaching some private way of egress known only to themselves,—but their attempts were evidently frustrated, for no sooner had they gone than they sped back again, their faces scorched and blackened, and uttering cries and woeful lamentations they flung themselves wildly among the struggling crowds in the main body of the Temple, and fought for life in the jaws of death, every one for Self, and no one for another! Volumes of smoke rolled up from the ground, in thick and suffocating clouds, accompanied by incessant sharp reports like the close firing of guns, . . . jets of flame and showers of cinders broke forth fountain-like, scattering hot destruction on every hand, . . . while a few flying sparks caught the end of the "Silver Veil"—and withered it into nothingness with one bright resolute flare!

Half maddened by the shrieks and dying groans that resounded everywhere about him, and yet all the time feeling as though he were some spectator set apart, and condemned to watch the progress of a ghastly phantasmagoria in Hell, Theos was just revolving in his mind whether it would or would not be possible to make a determined climb for escape through one of the tall painted windows, some of which were not yet reached by the fire, when, with a sudden passionate exclamation, Sah-luma broke from his hold and rushed to the Sanctuary. Quick as lightning, Theos followed him, . . . followed him close, as he sprang up the steps and confronted Lysia with eager, outstretched arms. The dead Niphrita lay near him, . . . fair as a sculptured saint, with the cruel wound of sacrifice in her breast,—but he seemed not to see that piteous corpse of Faithfulness! His grief for her death had been a mere transient emotion, . . . his stronger earthly passions re-asserted their tempestuous sway,—and for sweet things perished and gone to heaven he had no further care. On Lysia, and on Lysia's living beauty alone, his eyes flamed their ardent glory.

"Come! . . . Come!" he cried. "Come, my love—my life! . . . Let me save thee! . . . Or if I cannot save thee, let us die together!"

Scarcely had the words left his lips, when the King, with a swift forward movement like the pounce of some desert-panther, turned fiercely upon him, . . . amazement, jealousy, distrust, revenge, all gathering stormily in the black frown of his bent vindictive brows. His great chest heaved pantingly—his teeth glittered wolfishly through his jetty beard, . . . and in the terrible nerve-tension of the moment, the fury of the spreading conflagration was forgotten, at any rate, by Theos, who, stricken numb and rigid by a shock of alarm too poignant for expression, stared aghast at the three figures before him. . . Sah-luma, Lysia, Zephoranim, . . . especially Zephoranim, whose bursting wrath threatened to choke his utterance.

"What sayest thou, Sah-luma?" he demanded in a sort of ferocious gasping whisper. . . "Repeat thy words! . . . Repeat them!" . . . and his hand clutched at his dagger-hilt, while his restless, lowering glance flashed from Lysia to the Laureate and from the Laureate back to Lysia again. "Death encompasses us, . . . this is no time for trifling! . . . Speak!" . . . and his voice suddenly rose to a frantic shout of rage, "Speak! What is this woman to thee?"

"Everything!" . . . returned Sah-luma with prompt and passionate fearlessness, his glorious eyes blazing a proud defiance as he spoke. . . "Everything that woman can be, or ever shall be, unto man! Call her by whatsoever name a foolish creed enjoins, . . . Virgin-Daughter of the Sun, or High-Priestess of Nagaya,—she is nevertheless MINE!—and mine only! I am her lover!"

"THOU!" and with a hoarse cry, Zephoranim sprang upon, and seized him by the throat. "Thou liest! I,—I, crowned King of Al-Kyris, I am her lover!—chosen by her out of all men! . . . and dost thou dare to pretend that she hath preferred THEE, a mere singer of mad songs, to ME? . . . Thou unscrupulous knave! . . . I tell thee she is MINE! . . . Dost hear me?—Mine. . . mine. . . MINE!" and he shrieked the last word out in a perfect hurricane of passion,—"My Queen. . . my mistress!—heart of my heart!—soul of my soul! . . . Let the city burn to ashes, and the whole land be utterly consumed, in death as in life Lysia is mine! . . . and the gods themselves shall never part her from me!"

And suddenly releasing his grasp he hurled Sah-luma away as he might have hurled aside a toy figure,—and a peal of reckless musical laughter echoed mockingly through the vaulted shrine. It was Lysia's laughter! . . . and Theos's blood grew cold as he heard its cruel, silvery ring. . . even so had she laughed when Nir-jalis died!

Sah-luma reeled backward from the King's thrust, but did not fall,—white and trembling, with his sad and splendid features, frozen as it were into a sculptured mask of agonized beauty, he turned upon the treacherous woman he loved the silent challenge of his eloquent eyes. Oh, that look of piteous pain and wonder! a whole lifetime's wasted opportunities seemed concentrated in its unspeakable reproach! She met it with a sort of triumphant, tranquil indifference, . . . an uncontrollable wicked smile curved the corners of her red lips, . . . the sacred Ebony Staff had somehow slipped from her hands, and it now lay on the ground, the half-uncoiled Serpent still clinging to it, in glittering lengths that appeared to be quite motionless.

"Ah, Lysia, hast thou played me false?" . . . cried the unhappy Laureate at last, as with a quick, impulsive movement, he caught her round jewelled arm in a resolute grip. "After all thy vows, thy endearments, thy embraces, hast thou betrayed me? Speak truly! . . . Art thou not all in all to me? . . . hast thou not given thyself body and soul into my keeping? To this braggart King I deign no answer—one word of thine will suffice! . . . Be brave. . . be faithful! . . . Declare thy love for me, even as thou hast oft declared it a thousand remembered times!"

Over the face of the beautiful Priestess swept a strange expression of mingled fear, antagonism, loathing, and exultation. Her eyes wandered to the red tongued leaping flames that tossed in eddying rings round the Temple, running every second nearer to the place where she stood, and in that one glance she seemed to recognize the hopelessness of rescue and certainty of death. A careless, haughty acceptance of her fate manifested itself in the pallid resolve of her drawn features, . . . but as she allowed her gaze to return and dwell on Sah-luma, the old, malicious mirth flushed and gave lustre to her loveliness, and she laughed again. . . a laugh of uttermost bitter scorn.

"Declare my love for thee!" she said in thrilling accents. "Thou boaster! Let the gods, who have kindled this fiery end for us, bear witness to my hatred! I hate thee! . . . Aye, even THEE!" . . . and she pointed at him jeeringly, as he recoiled from her in wide eyed anguish and amazement:—"No man have I ever loved, but thee have I hated most of all! All men have I despised for their folly, greed and vain-glory,—I have fought them with their own weapons of avarice, cunning, cruelty, and falsehood,—but THOU hast been even beneath MY contempt! 'Twas scarcely worth my while to fool thee, thou wert so easily fooled! . . .'Twas idle sport to rouse thy passions, they were so easily roused! Poet and Perjurer, . . . Singer and Sophist! Thou to whom the Genius of Poesy was as a pearl set in a swine's snout! . . . thou wert not worthy to be my dupe, seeing that thou camest to me already in bonds, the dupe of thine own Self! Niphrata loved thee,—and thou didst play with and torture her more unmercifully than wild beasts play with and torture their prey; . . . but thou couldst never trifle with ME! O thou who hast taken so much pride in the breaking of many women's hearts, learn that thou hast never stirred one throb of passion in MINE! . . . that I have loathed thy beauty while caressing thee, and longed to slay thee while embracing thee! . . . and that even now I would I saw thee dead before me, ere I myself am forced to die!"

Pausing in the swift torrent of her words, her white breast heaved violently with the rise and fall of her panting breath,—her dark, brilliant eyes dilated, while the symbolic Jewel she wore, and the crown of serpents' heads in her streaming hair, seemed to glitter about her like so many points of lightning. At that instant one side of the Sanctuary split asunder, giving way to a bursting wreath of flames. Seeing this, she uttered a piercing cry, and stretched out her arms.

"Zephoranim! . . . Save me!"

In a second, the King sprang toward her, but not before Sah-luma, wild with wrath, had interposed himself between them.

"Back!" he exclaimed passionately, addressing the infuriated monarch. "While I live, Lysia is mine!—let her hate and deny me as she will!—and sooner than see her in thine arms, O King, I will slay her where she stands!"

His bold attitude was magnificent,—his countenance more than beautiful in its love betrayed despair, . . . and for a moment the savage Zephoranim paused irresolute, his scowling brows bent on his erstwhile favorite Minstrel with an expression that hovered curiously between bitterest enmity and reluctant reverence. There seemed to be a struggling consciousness in his mind of the immortality of a Poet as compared with the evanescent power of a King,—and also a quick realization of the truth that, let his anger be what it would, they twain were partakers in the same evil, and were mutually deceived by the same false woman! But ere his saving sense of justice could prevail, a ripple of discordant, delirious laughter broke once more from Lysia's lips,—her eye shone vindictively,—her whole face became animated with a sudden glow of fiendish triumph.

"Zephoranim!" she cried, "Hero! . . . Warrior! . . . King! . . . Thou who hast risked thy crown and throne and life for my sake and the love of me! . . . Wilt lose me now? . . . Wilt let me perish in these raging flames, to satisfy this wanton liar and unbeliever in the gods, to whose disturbance of the Holy Ritual we surely owe this present fiery disaster! Save me, O strong and noble Zephoranim! . . . Save me, and with me save the city and the people! KILL SAH-LUMA!"

O barbarous, inexorable words!—they rang like a desolating knell in the ears of the bewildered, fear-stricken Theos, and startled him from his rigid trance of speechless misery. Uttering an inarticulate dull groan, he made a violent effort to rush forward—to serve as a living shield of defence to his adored friend, . . . to ward off the imminent blow! Too late! too late! . . . Zephoranim's dagger glittered in the air, and rapidly descended. . . One gasping cry! . . . and Sah-luma lay prone,—beautiful as a slain Adonis, . . . the rich red blood pouring from his heart, and a faint, stern smile frozen on the proud lips whose dulcet singing-speech was now struck dumb forever! With a shriek of agony, Theos threw himself beside his murdered comrade, . . . heedless of King, Priestess, flames, and all the out-breaking fury of earth and heaven, he bent above that motionless form, and gazed yearningly into the fair colorless face.

"Sah-luma! . . . Sah-luma!"

No sign! . . . No tremulous stir of breath! Dead—dead,—dead in his prime of years—dead in the zenith of his glory!—all the delicate, dreaming genius turned to dust and ashes! . . . all the ardent light of inspiration quenched in the never-lifting darkness of the grave! . . . and in the first delirious paroxysm of his grief Theos felt as though life, time, and the world were ended for him also, with this one suddenly destroyed existence!

"O thou mad King!" he cried fiercely, "Thou hast slain the chief wonder of thy realm and reign! Die now when thou wilt, thou shalt only he remembered as the murderer of Sah-luma! . . . Sah-luma, whose name shall live when thine is covered in shameful oblivion!"

Zephoranim frowned,—and threw the blood-stained dagger from him.

"Peace, clamorous fool!" he said, "Sah-luma hath gone but a moment before me, . . . as Poet he hath received precedence even in death! When the last hour comes for all of us, it matters not how we die, . . . and whether I am hereafter remembered or forgotten I care not! I have lived as a man should live,—fearing nothing and conquered by none,—except perchance by Love, that hath brought many kings ere now to untimely ruin!" Here his moody eyes lighted on Lysia. "How many lovers hast thou had, fair soul?" . . . he demanded in a stern yet tremulous voice. . . "A thousand? . . . I would swear this dead Minstrel of mine was one,—for though I slew him at thy bidding I saw the truth in his dying eyes! . . . No matter!—We shall meet in Hades,— and there we shall have ample time to urge our rival claims upon thy favor! Ah!" . . . and he suddenly laid his two strong hands on her white uncovered shoulders, and gazed at her reproachfully as she shrank a little beneath his close scrutiny, . . . "Thou divine Traitress! Have I not challenged the very heavens for thy sake? . . . and lo! the prophecy is fulfilled and Al-Kyris must fall! How many men would have loved thee as I have loved? . . . None! not even this dead Sah-luma, slain like a dog to give thee pleasure! Come! . . . Let me kiss thee once again ere death makes cold our lips! False or true, thou art nevertheless fair!—and the wrathful gods know best how I worship thy fairness!"

And folding his arms about her, he kissed her passionately. She clung to him like a lithe serpentine thing,—her eyes ablaze, her mouth quivering with suppressed hysterical laughter. Pointing to Sah-luma's body, she said in a strange excited whisper:

"Nay, hast thou slain him in very truth, Zephoranim! . . . slain him utterly? For I have heard that poets cannot die,—they live when the whole world deems them dead,—they rise from their shut graves and re-invest the earth with all the secrets of past time, . . . Oh! my brain reels! . . . I talk mere madness! . . . there is no afterwards of death!— No, no! No gods, no anything but blankness. . . forgetfulness. . . and silence! . . . for us, and for all men! . . . How good it is!—how excellently devised a jest! . . . that the whole wide Universe should be but a cheat of time! . . . a bubble blown into Space, to float, break, and perish,—all for the idle sport of some unknown and shapeless Devil-Mystery!"

Shuddering, half-laughing, half-weeping, she clasped her hands round the monarch's throat, and hid her wild eyes in his breast, while he, unnerved by her distraction and his own inward torture, glared about him on all sides for some glimmering chance of rescue, but could see none. The flames were now attacking the Shrine on every side like a besieging army,—their leaping darts of blue and crimson gleaming here and there with indescribable velocity, . . . and still Theos knelt by Sah-luma's corpse in dry-eyed despair, endeavoring with feverish zeal to stanch the oozing blood with a strip torn from his own garments, and listening anxiously for the feeblest heart-throb, or smaller pulsation of smouldering life in the senseless stiffening clay.

All at once a hideous scream assailed his ears,—another, and yet another rang above the crackling roar of the gradually conquering fire, . . . and half-lifting Sah-luma's body in his arms, he looked up. . . O horror, horror! his nerves contracted,—his blood seemed to turn to ice in his veins, . . . his head swam giddily, . . . and he thought the moment of his own death had come, for surely no man could behold the sight he saw and yet continue to live on! Lysia the captor was made captive at last! . . . bound, helpless, imprisoned, and hopelessly doomed, . . . Nagaya had claimed his own! The huge Snake, terrified beyond all control at the bursting breadth of fire environing the shrine, had turned in its brute fear to the mistress it had for years been accustomed to obey, and had now, with one stealthy noiseless spring, twisted its uppermost coil close about her waist, where its restless head, alarmed eyes, and darting fangs all glistened together like a blazing cluster of gems! the more she struggled to release herself from its deathful embrace, the tighter its body contracted and the more maddened with fright it became. Shriek upon shriek broke from her lips and pierced the suffocating air, . . . while with all his great muscular force Zephoranim the King strove in desperate agony to tear her from the awful clutch of the monster he had but lately knelt to as divine! In vain, . . . in vain! . . . the strongest efforts were useless, . . . the cruel, beautiful, pitiless Priestess of Nagaya was condemned to suffer the same frightful death she had so often mercilessly decreed for others! Closer and closer grew the fearful Python's constricting clasp, . . . nearer and nearer swept the dancing battalion of destroying flames! . . . For one fleeting breath of time Theos stared aghast at the horrid scene, . . . then making a superhuman effort he raised Sah-luma's corpse entirely from the ground and staggered with his burden away, . . . away from the burning Shrine, . . . the funeral pyre, as it vaguely seemed to him, of a wasted Love and a dead passion!

WHITHER SHOULD HE GO! . . . Down into the blazing area of the fast-perishing Temple? Surely no safety could be found there, where the fire was raging at its utmost height! . . . yet he went on mechanically, as though urged forward by some force superior to his own, . . . always clinging to the idea that his friend still lived and that if he could only reach some place of temporary shelter he might yet be able to restore him. It was possible the wound was not fatal, . . . far more possible to his mind than that so gloriously famed a Poet should be dead!

So he dimly thought, while he stumbled dizzily along, . . . his forehead wet with clammy dews, . . . his limbs trembling under the weight he bore, . . . his eyes half-blinded by the hot flying sparks and drifting smoke, . . . and his soul shaken and appalled by the ghastly sights that met his view wheresoever he turned. Crushed and writhing bodies of men, women, and children, half-living, half-dead, . . . heaps of corpses, fast blazing to ashes,—broken and falling columns, . . . yawning gaps in the ground, from which were cast forth volleys of red cinders and streams of lava, . . . all these multitudinous horrors surrounded him, as with uncertain, faltering steps he moved on like a sick man walking in sleep, carrying his precious burden! He knew nothing of where he was bound,—he saw no outlet anywhere—no corner wherein the Fire-fiend had not set up devouring dominion, . . . but nevertheless he steadily continued his difficult progress, clasping Sah-luma's corpse with a strange tenacity, and concentrating all his attention on protecting it from the withering touch of the ravenous flames. All at once,—as he strove to force his way over a fallen altar from which the hideous presiding stone idol had toppled headlong, killing in its descent some twenty or thirty people whose bodies lay crushed beneath it,—a face horribly disfigured and tortured into a mere burnt sketch of its former likeness twisted itself up and peered at him, the face of Zabastes, the Critic. His protruding eyes glistened with something of their old malign expression as he perceived whose helpless form it was that was being carried by.

"What! . . . is the famous Sah-luma gone?" he gasped, his words half choking him in their utterance as he stretched out a skinny hand and caught at Theos's garments. . . "Good youth, stay! . . . Stay! . . . Why burden thyself with a corpse when thou mightest rescue a living man? Save ME! . . . Save ME! . . . I was the Poet's adverse Critic, and who but I should write his Eulogy now that he is no more! . . . Pity! . . . Pity, most courteous, gentle sir! . . . Save me if only for the sake of Sah-luma's future honor! Thou knowest not how warmly, how generously, how nobly, I can praise the dead!"

Theos gazed down upon him in unspeakable, melancholy scorn, . . . was it only through time-serving creatures such as this miserable Zabastes, that the after-glory of perished poets was proclaimed to the world? . . . What then was the actual worth of Fame?

Shuddering, he wrenched himself away, and passed on silently, heedless of the savage curses the despairing scribe yelled after him as he went, and he involuntarily pressed the dead corpse of his beloved friend closer to his heart, as though he thought he could re-animate it by this mute expression of tenderness! Meanwhile the fire raged continuously,—the Temple was fast becoming a pillared mass of flames, . . . and presently,—choked and giddy with the sulphurous vapors—he stopped abruptly, struggling for breath. His time had come at last, he thought, . . . he with Sah-luma must die!

Just then a loud muttering and rolling of thunder swept in eddying vibrations round him, followed by a sharp, splitting noise, . . . raising his aching eyes, he saw straight before him, a yawning gloomy archway, like the solemn portal of a funeral vault. . . dark, yet with a white glimmer of steps leading outward, and a dim sparkle as of stars in heaven. A rush of new vigor inspired him at this sight, and he resumed his way, stumbling over countless corpses strewn among fallen blocks of marble,—and every now and then looking back in awful fascination to the fiery furnace of the body of the Temple, where of all the vast numbers that had lately crowded it from end to end, there were only a hundred or so remaining alive,—and these were fast perishing in frightful agony. The Shrine of Nagaya was enveloped in thick black smoke, crossed here and there by flashes of flame,—the bare outline of its Titanic architecture was scarcely discernible! Yet the thought of the dreadful end of Lysia, the loveliest woman he had ever seen, moved him now to no emotion whatever—save. . . gladness! Some deadly evil seemed burnt out of his life, . . . moreover her command had slain Sah-luma! . . . Enough! . . . no fate however horrible, could be more so than she in her wanton wickedness deserved! . . . But alas! her beauty! . . . He dared not think of its subtle, slumberous charm! . . . and stung to a new sense of desperation, he plunged recklessly toward the dusky aperture he had seen, which appeared to enlarge itself mysteriously as he approached, like the opening gateway of some magic cavern.

Suddenly a faint groan at his feet startled him,—and, looking down hastily, he perceived an unfortunate man lying half crushed under the ponderous fragment of a split column, which had fallen across his body in such manner that any attempt to extricate him would have been worse than useless. By the bright light of the leaping flames, Theos had no difficulty in recognizing the pallid countenance of his late acquaintance, the learned Professor of Positivism, Mira-Khabur, who was evidently very near his woeful and most positive end! Struck by an impulse of compassion he paused, . . . yet what could he say? . . . In such a case, where rescue was impossible, all comfort seemed mockery,—and while he stood silent and irresolute, he fancied the Professor smiled! It was a very ghastly smile,—nevertheless it hid in it a curious touch of bland and scrupulous inquiry.

"Is not this. . . a very. . . remarkable occurrence?" . . . asked a voice so feeble and far away that it was difficult to believe it came from the lips of the suffering sage. "Of course. . . it arises from. . . a volcanic eruption! . . . and the mystery of the red river. . . is. . . solved!" Here an irrepressible moan of anguish broke through his heroic effort at equanimity;—"It is NOT a phenomenon!" . . . and a gleam of obstinate self-assertion lit up his poor glazing eyes, "Nothing is phenonmenal! . . . only I am not able. . . to explain. . . I have no time. . . no time. . . to analyze. . . my very. . . singular. . . sensations!"

A rush of blood choked his utterance—his throat rattled, . . . he was dead! . . . and the dreary speculative smile froze on his mouth in the likeness of a solemn sneer. At that moment, a terrific swirling, surging noise, like the furious boiling of an underground whirlpool, rumbled heavily through the air, . . . and lo! with a sudden, swift shock that sent Theos reeling forward and almost falling, under the burdensome weight he carried, the earth opened, . . . disclosing a huge pit of black nothingness,—an enormous chasm,—into which, with an appalling clamor as of a hundred incessant peals of thunder, the whole main area of the Temple, together with its mass of dead and dying human beings, sank in less than five seconds!—the ground closing instantaneously over its prey with a sullen roar, as though it were some gigantic beast devouring food too long denied. And instead of the vanished fane arose a mighty Pillar of Fire! . . . a vast increasing volume of scarlet and gold flame that spread outward and upward,—higher and higher, in tapering lines and dome-like curves of living light, . . . while Theos, being hurled along resistlessly by the force of the convulsion, had reached, though he knew not how, the dark and quiet cell-like portal with its out-leading steps, . . . the only visible last hope and chance of safety, . . . and he now leaned against its cold stone arch, trembling in every limb, clasping the dead Sah-luma close, and looking back in affrighted awe at the tossing vortex of fury from which he had miraculously escaped. And,— as he looked,—a host of spectral faces seemed to rise whitely out of the flames and wonder at him! . . . faces that were solemn, wistful, warning, and beseeching by turns! . . . they drifted through the fire and smiled, and wept, and vanished, to reappear again and yet again! . . . and as, with painfully beating heart, he strove to combat the terror that seized him at this strange spectacular delusion, all suddenly the heavy wreaths of smoke that had till now hung over the Inner Shrine of Nagaya parted like drapery drawn aside from a picture. . . and for a brief breathing space of direst agony he saw Lysia once more,—Lysia, in a torture as horrible as any ever depicted in a bigot's idea of his enemy's Hell! Round and round her writhing form the sacred Serpent was twined in all his many coils,—with both hands she had grasped the creature's throat in her frenzy, striving to thrust back its quivering fangs from her breast, whereon the evil "Eye of Raphon" still gleamed distinctly with its adamantine chilly stare, . . . at her feet lay the body of the King her lover, dead and wrapped in a ring of flames! . . . Alone—all, all alone, she confronted Death in its most appalling shape. . . her countenance was distorted, yet beautiful still with the beauty of a maddened Medusa, . . . white and glittering as a fair ghost invoked from some deadly gulf of pain, she stood, a phantom-figure of mingled loveliness and horror, circled on every side by fire!

With wild, straining eyes Theos gazed upon her thus, . . . for the last time! . . . For with a crash that seemed to rend the very heavens, the great bronze columns surrounding her, which had, up to the present, resisted the repeated onslaughts of the flames, bent together all at once and fell in a melting ruin. . . and the victorious fire roared loudly above them, enveloping the whole Shrine anew in dense clouds of smoke and jets of flame,—Lysia had perished! All that proud loveliness, that dazzling supremacy, that superb voluptuousness, that triumphant dominion, . . . swept away into a heap of undiscoverable ashes! And Zephoranim's haughty spirit too had fled,—fled, stained with guilt and most unroyal dishonor, all for the sake of one woman's fairness—the fairness of body only—the brilliant mask of flesh that too often hides the hideousness of a devil's nature!

For one moment Theos remained stupefied by the sheer horror of the catastrophe,—then, recalling his bewildered wits to his aid, he peered anxiously through the archway where he rested, . . . there seemed to be a dim red glow at the end of the downward-leading steps, as well as a dusky azure tint, like a patch of midnight sky. The Temple was now nothing but a hissing shrieking pyramid of flames,—the hot and blinding glare was almost too intense for his eyes to endure,—yet so fascinated was he by the sublime terror and grandeur of the spectacle, that he could scarcely make up his mind to turn away from it! The thought of Sah-luma, however, gave the needful spur to his flagging energies, and without pausing to consider where he might be going, he slowly and hesitatingly descended the steps before him, and presently reached a sort of small open court paved with black marble. Here he tenderly laid his burden down,—a burden grown weightier with each moment of its bearing,—and letting his aching arms drop listlessly at his sides, he looked up dreamily,—not all at once comprehending the cause of the vast lurid light that crimsoned the air like a wide aurora borealis everywhere about him, . . . then,—as the truth suddenly flashed on his mind, he uttered a loud, irrepressible cry of amazement and awe!

Far as his gaze could see,—east, west, north, south, the whole city of Al-Kyris was in flames!—and the burning Temple of Nagaya was but a mere spark in the enormous breadth of the general conflagration! Palaces, domes, towers, and spires were tottering to red destruction, . . . fire. . . fire everywhere! . . . nothing but fire,—save when a furious gust of scorching wind blew aside the masses of cindery smoke, and showed glimpses of sky and the changeless shining of a few cold quiet stars. He cast one desperate glance from earth to heaven, . . . how was it possible to escape from this kindling furnace of utter annihilation! . . . Where all were manifestly doomed, how could He expect to be saved! And moreover, if Sah-luma was indeed dead, what remained for him but to die also!

CALMING THE FRENZY OF HIS thoughts by a strong effort, he began to vaguely wonder why and how it happened that the place where he now was, . . . this small and insignificant court,—had so far escaped the fire, and was as cool and sombre as a sacred tomb set apart for some hero, . . . or Poet? Poet!—The word acted as a stimulant to his tired struggling brain, and he all at once remembered what Sah-luma had said to him at their first meeting: "There is but one Poet in Al-Kyris, and I am he!"

O true, true! Only one Poet! . . . Only one glory of the great city, that now served him as funeral pyre!—only one name worth remembering in all its perishing history. . . the name of SAH-LUMA! Sah-luma, the beautiful, the gifted, the famous, the beloved, . . . he was dead! This thought, in its absorbing painfulness, straightway drove out all others,—and Theos, who had carried his comrade's corpse bravely and unshrinkingly through a fiery vortex of imminent peril, now sank on his knees all desolate and unnerved, his hot tears dropping fast on that fair, still, white face that he knew would never flush to the warmth of life again!

"Sah-luma! Sah-luma!" he whispered, "My friend. . . My more than brother! Would I could have died for thee! . . . Would thou couldst have lived to fulfil the nobler promise of thy genius! . . . Better far thou hadst been spared to the world than I! . . . for I am Nothing, . . . but thou wert Everything!"

And taking the clay-cold hands in his own, he kissed them reverently, and, with an unconscious memory not born of his recent adventures, folded them on the dead Laureate's breast in the fashion of a Cross.

As he did this an icy spasm seemed to contract his heart, . . . seized by a sudden insufferable anxiety, he stared like one spell-bound into Sah-luma's wide-open, fixed, and glassy eyes. Dead eyes! . . . yet how full of mysterious significance! . . . What—WHAT was their weird secret, their imminent meaning! . . . Why did their dark and frozen depths appear to retain a strange, living undergleam of melting, sorrowful, beseeching sweetness? . . . like the eyes of one who prays to be remembered, though changed after long absence! What hot and terrible delirium was this that snatched at his whirling brain as he bent closer and closer over the marble quiet countenance, and studied with a sort of fierce intentness every line of those delicate, classic features, on which high thought had left so marked an impress of dignity and power! What a marvellous, half-reproachful, half-appealing smile lingered on the finely-curved set lips! . . . How wonderful, how beautiful, how beloved beyond all words was this fair dead god of poesy on whom he gazed with such a passion of yearning!

Stooping more and more, he threw his arms round the senseless form, and partly lifting it from the ground, brought the wax-pallid face nearer to his own. . . so near that the cold mouth almost touched his, . . . then filled with an awful, unnamable misgiving, he scanned his murdered comrade's perished beauty in puzzled, vague bewilderment, much as an ignorant dullard might perplexedly scan the incomprehensible characters of some hieroglyphic scroll. And, as he looked, a sharp pang shot through him like a whizzing ball of fire, . . . a convulsion of mental agony shook his limbs,—he could have shrieked aloud in the extremity of his torture, but the struggling cry died gasping in his throat. Still as stone he kept his strained, steadfast gaze fixed on Sah-luma's corpse, slowly absorbing the full horror of a tremendous Suggestion, that like a scorching lava-flood swept into every subtle channel of his brain. For the dead Sah-luma's eyes grew into the semblance of his own eyes! . . . the dead Sah-luma's face smiled spectrally back at him in the image of his own face! . . . it was as though he beheld the Picture of himself, slain and reflected in a magician's mirror! Round him the very heavens seemed given up to fire,—but he heeded it not,—the world might be at an end and the day of Judgment, proclaimed,—nothing would have stirred him from where he knelt, in that dreadful stillness of mystic martyrdom, drinking in the gradual, glimmering consciousness of a terrific Truth, . . . the amazing, yet scarcely graspable solution of a supernatural Enigma, . . . an enigma through which, like a man lost in the depths of a dark forest, he had wandered up and down, seeking light, yet finding none!

"O God!" he dumbly prayed. "Thou, with whom all things are possible, give eyes to this blind trouble of my heart! I am but as a grain of dust before thee, . . . a poor perishable atom, devoid of simplest comprehension! . . . Do Thou of Thy supernal pity teach me what I must know!"

As he thought out this unuttered petition, a tense cord seemed to snap suddenly in his brain, . . . a rush of tears came to his relief, and through their salt and bitter haze the face of Sah-luma appeared to melt into a thin and spiritual brightness,—a mere aerial outline of what it had once been, . . . the glazed dark eyes seemed to flash living lightning into his, . . . the whole lost Personality of the dead Poet seemed to environ him with a mysterious, potent, incorporeal influence. . . an influence that he felt he must now or never repel, reject, and utterly Resist! . . . With a shuddering cry, he tore his reluctant arms away from the beloved corpse, . . . with trembling, tender fingers he closed and pressed down the white eyelids of those love-expressive eyes, and kissed the broad poetic brow!

"Whatever thou Wert or Art to me, Sah-luma," he murmured in sobbing haste,—"thou knowest that I loved thee, though now I leave thee! Farewell!"—and his voice broke in its strong agony—"O how much easier to divide body from soul than part myself from thee!

Sah-luma, beloved Sah-luma! God give thee rest! . . . God pardon thy sins,—and mine!"

And he pressed his lips once more on the folded rigid hands; . . . as he did so, he inadvertently touched the writing-tablet that hung from the dead Laureate's girdle. The red glow of the fire around him enabled him to see distinctly what was written on it, . . . there were about twenty lines of verse, in exquisitely clear and fine caligraphy, . . . and, as he read, he knew them well, . . . they were the last lines of the poem "Nourhalma"!

He dared trust his own strength no longer, . . . one wild, adoring, lingering, parting look at his dead rival in song, whom he had loved better than himself,—and then,—full of a nameless fear, he fled! . . . fled recklessly, and with swift, mad fury as though demons followed in pursuit, . . . fled through the burning city, as a lost and frenzied spirit might speed through the deserts of Hell! Everywhere about him resounded the crackling hiss of the flames, and the crash of falling buildings, . . . mighty pinnacles and lofty domes melted and vanished before is eyes in a blaze of brilliant destruction! . . . on—on he went, meeting confused, scattered crowds of people, whose rushing, white-garmented figures looked like ghosts flying before a storm, . . . the cries and shrieks of women and children, and the groans of men were mingled with the restless roaring of lions and other wild beasts burnt out of their dens in the Royal Arena, the distant circle of which could be dimly seen, surrounded by fountain-like jets of fire. Some of these maddened animals ran against him, as he sped along the blazing thoroughfares,—but he made no attempt to avoid them, nor was he sensible of any other terror than that which was WITHIN HIMSELF and was purely mental. On! . . . On!—Still on he went,—a desperate, lonely man, lost in a hideous nightmare of flame and fury, . . . seeing nothing but one vast flying rout of molten red and gold, . . . speaking to none, . . . utterly reckless as to his own fate, . . . only impelled on and on, but whither he knew not, nor cared to know!

All at once his, strength gave way. . . his nerves seemed to break asunder like so many over-wound harp-strings, . . . a sudden silvery clanging of bells rang in his ears, and with them came a sound of multitudinous soft, small voices: "Kyrie Eleison! Kyrie Eleison!"

Hush! . . . What was that? . . . What did it mean? . . . Halting abruptly, he gave a wild glance round him,—up to the sky, where the flaring flames spread in tangled lengths and webs of light, . . . then, straight before him to the City of Al-Kyris, now a wondrous vision of redly luminous columns and cupolas, with the wet gleam of the river enfolding its blazing streets and towers: . . . and while he yet beheld it, lo! It Receded From His View! Further, . . . further!—further away, till it seemed nothing but the toppling and smoldering of heavy clouds after the conflagration of the sunset!

Hark, hark again! . . . "Kyrie, Eleison! . . . Kyrie, Eleison!" With a sense of reeling rapture and awe he listened, . . . he understood! . . . he found the Name he had so long forgotten! "Christ, have mercy upon me!" . . . he cried, and in that one urgent supplication he uttered all the pent-up anguish of his soul! Blind and dizzy with the fevered whirl of his own emotions, he stumbled forward and fell! . . . fell heavily over a block of stone, . . . stunned by the shock, he lost consciousness, but only for a moment; . . . a dull aching in his temples roused him,—and making a faint effort to rise, he turned slowly and languidly on his arm, . . . and with a long, deep, shuddering sigh. . . Awoke!

He was on the Field of Ardath. Dawn had just broken. The east was one wide, shimmering stretch of warm gold, and over it lay strips of blue and gray, like fragments of torn battle-banners. Above him sparkled the morning star, white and glittering as a silver lamp, among the delicate spreading tints of saffron and green, . . . and beside him,—her clear, pure features flushed by the roseate splendor of the sky, her hands clasped on her breast, and her sweet eyes full of an infinite tenderness and yearning, knelt Edris!—Edris, his flower-crowned Angel, whom last he had seen drifting upward and away like a dove through the glory of the Cross in Heaven!

XXX

SUNRISE

Entranced in amazed ecstasy he lay quite quiet, . . . afraid to speak or stir! This gentle Presence,—this fair, beseeching face, might vanish if he moved! So he dimly fancied, as he gazed up at her in mute wonder and worship, his devout eyes drinking in her saintly loveliness, from the deep burnished gold of her hair to the soft, white slimness of her prayerfully folded hands. And while he looked, old thoughts like home-returning birds began to hover round his soul,—sweet and dear remembrances, like the sunset lighting up the windows of an empty house, began to shine on the before semi-darkened nooks and crannies of his brain. Clearer and clearer grew the reflecting mirror of his consciousness,—trouble and perplexity seemed passing away forever from his mind, . . . a great and solemn peace environed him, . . . and he began to believe he had crossed the boundary of death and had entered at last into the Kingdom of Heaven! O let him not break this holy silence! . . . Let him rest so, with all the glory of that Angel-visage shed like summer sunbeams over him! . . . Let him absorb into his innermost being the exquisite tenderness of those innocent, hopeful, watchful, starry eyes whose radiance seemed to steal into the golden morning and give it a sacred poetry and infinite marvel of meaning! So he mused, gravely contented, . . . while all through the brightening skies overhead, came the pale, pink flushing of the dawn, like a far fluttering and scattering of rose-leaves. Everything was so still that he could hear his own heart beating forth healthful and regular pulsations, . . . but he was scarcely conscious of his own existence,—he was only aware of the vast, beautiful, halcyon calm that encircled him shelteringly and soothed all care away.

Gradually, however, this deep and delicious tranquillity began to yield to a sweeping rush of memory and comprehension, . . . he knew WHO he was and WHERE he was,—though he did not as yet feel absolutely certain of life and life's so-called realities. For if the City of Al-Kyris, with all its vivid wonders, its distinct experiences, its brilliant pageantry, had been indeed a DREAM, then sorely it was possible he might be dreaming still! . . . Nevertheless he was able to gather up the

MARIE CORELLI

fragments of lost recollection consecutively enough to realize, by gentle degrees, his actual identity and position in the world, . . . he was Theos Alwyn, . . . a man of the nineteenth century after Christ. Ah! thank God for that! . . . AFTER Christ! . . . not one who had lived five thousand years BEFORE Christ's birth! . . . And this quiet, patient Maiden at his side, . . . who was she? A vision? . . . or an actually existent Being? Unable to resist the craving desire of his heart, he spoke her name as he now remembered it, . . . spoke it in a faint, awed whisper.

"Edris!"

"Theos, my Beloved!"

O sweet and thrilling voice! more musical than the singing of birds in a sun-filled Spring!

He raised himself a little, and looked at her more intently:—she smiled,—and that smile, so marvellous in its pensive peace and lofty devotion, was as though all the light of an unguessed paradise had suddenly flashed upon his soul!

"Edris!" he said again, trembling in the excess of mingled hope and fear. . . "Hast thou then returned again from heaven, to lift me out of darkness? . . . Tell me, fair Angel, do I wake or sleep? . . . Are my senses deceived? Is this land a dream? . . . Am I myself a dream, and thou the only manifest sweet Truth in a world of drifting shadows! . . . Speak to me, gentle Saint! . . . In what vast mystery have I been engulfed? . . . in what timeless trance of soul-bewilderment? . . . in what blind uncertainty and pain? . . . O Sweet! . . . resolve my wordless wonder! Where have I strayed? . . . what have I seen? . . . Ah, let not my rough speech fright thee back to Paradise! . . . Stay with me! . . . comfort me! . . . I have lost thee so long! let me not lose thee now!"

Smiling still, she bent over him, and pressed her warm, delicate ringers lightly on his brow and lips. Then softly she rose and stood erect.

"Fear nothing, my beloved!" she answered, her silvery accents sending a throb of holy triumph through the air. "Let no trouble disquiet thee, and no shadow of misgiving dim the brightness of thy waking moments! Thou hast slept ONE night on the Field of Ardath, in the Valley of Vision!—but lo! the Night is past!" . . . and she pointed toward the eastern horizon now breaking into waves of rosy gold, "Rise! and behold the dawning of thy new Day!"

Roused by her touch, and fired by her tone and the grand, unworldly dignity of her look and bearing, he sprang up, . . . but as he met the full, pure splendor of her divine eyes, and saw, wavering round her hair, a shining aureole of amber radiance like a wreath of woven sunbeams, his spirit quailed within him, . . . he remembered all his doubts of her,—his disbelief, . . . and falling at her feet, he hid his face in a shame that was better than all glory,—a humiliation that was sweeter than all pride.

"Edris! Immortal Edris!" . . . he passionately prayed, "As thou art a crowned saint in Heaven, shed light on the chaos of my soul! From the depths of a penitence past thought and speech I plead with thee! Hear me, my Edris, thou who art so maiden-meek, so tender-patient! . . . hear me, help me, guide me. . . I am all thine! Say, didst thou not summon me to meet thee here upon this wondrous Field of Ardath?—did I not come hither according to thy words?—and have I not seen things that I am not able to express or understand? Teach me, wise and beloved one! . . . I doubt no more! I know Myself and Thee:—thou art an angel,—but I! . . . alas, what am I? A grain of sand in thy sight and in God's, . . . a mere Nothing, comprehending nothing,—unable even to realize the extent of my own nothingness! Edris, O Edris! . . . Thou canst not love me! . . . thou mayst pity me perchance, and pardon, and bless me gently in Christ's dear Name! . . . but love! . . . Thy love! . . . Oh let me not aspire to such heights of joy, where I have no place, no right, no worthiness!"

"No worthiness!" echoed Edris! . . . what a rapture trembled through her sweet caressing voice!—"My Theos, who is so worthy to win back what is thine own, as thou? All Heaven has wondered at thy voluntary exile,—thy place in God's supernal Sphere has long been vacant, . . . thy right to dwell there, none have questioned, . . . thy throne is empty—thy crown unclaimed! Thou art an Angel even as I! . . . but thou art in bonds while I am free! Ah, how sad and strange it is to me to see thee here thus fettered to the Sorrowful Star, when, countless aeons since, thou mightest have enjoyed full liberty in the Eternal Light of the everlasting Paradise!"

He listened, . . . a strong, sweet hope began to kindle in him like flame, . . . but he made no answer. Only he caught and kissed the edge of her garment, . . . its soft gray cloudy texture brushed his lips with the odorous coolness of a furled roseleaf. She seemed to tremble at his action, . . . but he dared not look up. Presently he felt the pulsing pressure of her hands upon his head! and a rush of strange, warm vigor thrilled through his veins like an electric flash of new and never-ending life.

"Thou wouldst seek after and know the truth!" she said, "Truth

Celestial,—Truth Unchangeable, . . . Truth that permeates and underlies all the mystic inward workings of the Universe, . . . workings and secret laws unguessed by Man! Vast as Eternity is this Truth,—ungraspable in all its manifestations by the merely mortal intelligence, . . . nevertheless thy spirit, being chastened to noble humility and repentance, hath risen to new heights of comprehension, whence thou canst partly penetrate into the wonders of worlds unseen. Did I not tell thee to 'LEARN FROM THE PERILS OF THE PAST, THE PERILS OF THE FUTURE'—and understandest thou not the lesson of the Vision of Al-Kyris? Thou hast seen the Dream-reflection of thy former Poet-fame and glory in old time,—THOU WERT SAH-LUMA!"

An agony of shame possessed him as he heard. His soul at once seized the solution of the mystery, . . . his quickened thought plunged plummet-like straight through the depths of the bewildering phantasmagoria, in which mere reason had been of no practical avail, and straightway sounded its whole seemingly complex, but actually simple meaning! HE WAS SAH-LUMA! . . . or rather, he HAD BEEN Sah-luma in some far stretch of long-receded time, . . . and in his Dream of a single night, he had loved the brilliant Phantom of his Former Self more than his own present Identity! Not less remarkable was the fact that, in this strange Sleep-Mirage, he had imagined himself to be perfectly UNselfish, whereas all the while he had honored, flattered, and admired the more Appearance of Himself more than anything or everything in the world! Ay!—even his occasional reluctant reproaches to Himself in the ghostly impersonation of Sah-luma had been far more tender than severe!

O deep and bitter ingloriousness! . . . O speechless degradation of all the higher capabilities of Man! to love one's own ephemeral Shadow-Existence so utterly as to exclude from thought and sympathy all other things whether human or divine! And was it not possible that this Spectre of Self might still be clinging to him? Was it dead with the Dream of Sah-luma? . . . or had Sah-luma never truly died at all? . . . and was the fine, fire-spun Essence that had formed the Spirit of the Laureate of Al-Kyris yet part of the living Substance of his present nature, . . . he, a world-unrecognized English poet of the nineteenth century? Did all Sah-luma's light follies, idle passions, and careless cruelties remain inherent in him? Had he the same pride of intellect, the same vain-glory, the same indifference to God and Man? Oh, no, no! . . . he shuddered at the thought! . . . and his head sank lower and lower beneath the benediction touch of Her whose tenderness revived his noblest energies, and lit anew in his heart the pure, bright fire of heaven-encompassing Aspiration.

"THOU WERT SAH-LUMA!" went on the mildly earnest voice, "And all the wide, ungrudging fame given to Earth's great poets in ancient days, was thine! Thy name was on all men's mouths, . . . thou wert honored by kings, . . . thou wert the chief glory of a great people, . . . great though misled by their own false opinions, . . . and the City of Al-Kyris, of which thou wert the enshrined jewel, was mightier far than any now built upon the earth! Christ had not come to thee, save by dim types and vague prefigurements which only praying prophets could discern, . . . but God had spoken to thy soul in quiet moments, and thou wouldst neither hear Him nor believe in Him! I had called thee, but thou wouldst not listen, . . . thou didst foolishly prefer to hearken to the clamorous tempting of thine own beguiling human passions, and wert altogether deaf to an Angel's whisper! Things of the earth earthly gained dominion over thee. . . by them thou wert led astray, deceived, and at last forsaken, . . . the genius God gave thee thou didst misuse and indolently waste, . . . thy brief life came, as thou hast seen, to sudden-piteous end,—and the proud City of thy dwelling was destroyed by fire! Not a trace of it was left to mark the spot where once it stood. The foundations of Babylon were laid above it, and no man guessed that it had ever been. And thy poems, . . . the fruit of thy heaven-sent but carelessly accepted inspiration,—who is there that remembers them? . . . No one! . . . save THOU! THOU hast recovered them like sunken pearls from the profound ocean of limitless Memory, . . . and to the world of To-day thou dost repeat the SELF-SAME MUSIC to which Al-Kyris listened entranced so many thousands of generations ago!"

A deep sigh, that was half a groan, broke from his lips, . . . he could now take the measurement of his own utter littleness and incompetency! HE COULD CREATE NOTHING NEW! Everything he had written, as he fancied only just lately, had been written by himself before! The problem of the poem "Nourhalma" . . . was explained, . . . he had designed it when he had played his part on the stage of life as Sah-luma,—and perhaps not even then for the first time! In this pride-crushing knowledge there was only one consolation, . . . namely, that if his Dream was a true reflection of his Past, and exact in details as he felt it must be, then "Nourhalma," had not been given to Al-Kyris, . . . it had been composed, but not made public. Hence, so far, it was new to the world, though not new to himself. Yet he had considered it wondrously new! a "perfectly original" idea! . . . Ah! who dares to boast of any idea as humanly "original" . . . seeing that all ideas whatsoever must be referred back to God and admitted as His and His only! What is the wisest man that ever lived, but a small, pale, ill-reflecting mirror of the Eternal Thought that controls and dominates all things! . . . He remembered with conscience-stricken confusion what pleasure he had felt, what placid satisfaction, what unqualified admiration, when listening to his own works recited by the ghost-presentment of his Former Self! . . . pleasure that had certainly exceeded whatever pain he had suffered by the then enigmatical and perplexing nature of the incident. O what a foolish Atom he now seemed, viewed by the standard of his newly aroused higher consciousness! . . . how poor and passive a slave to the glittering, beckoning Phantasm of his own perishable Fame!

Thus on the Field of Ardath he drained the cup of humility to the dregs,—the cup which like that offered to the Prophet of Holy Writ was "full as it were with water, but the color of it was like fire"—the water of tears. . . the fire of faith, . . . and with that prophet he might have said. . . "When I had drunk of it, my heart uttered understanding, and wisdom grew in my breast, for my spirit strengthened my memory."

Meanwhile Edris, still keeping her gentle hands on his bent head, went on:

"In such wise didst thou, my Beloved, as the famous Sah-luma, mournfully perish. . . and the nations remembered thee no more! But thy spiritual, indestructible Essence lived on, and wandered dismayed and forlorn through a myriad forms of existence in the depths of Perpetual Darkness which MUST be, even as the Everlasting Light Is. Thy immortal but perverted Will bore thee always further from God, . . . further from Him, and so far from me, that thou wert at times beyond even an Angel's ken! Ages upon ages rolled away, . . . the centuries between Earth and Earths purposed redemption passed, . . . and, . . . though in Heaven these measured spaces of time that appear so great to men are as a mere world's month of summer, . . . still, to me, for once God's golden days seemed long! I had lost THEE! Thou wert my soul's other soul, my king!—my immortality's completion! . . . and though thou wert, alas! a fallen brightness, yet I held fast to my one hope, . . . the hope in thy diviner nature, which, though sorely overcome, WAS NOT, and COULD NOT BE wholly destroyed. I knew the fate in store for thee, . . . I knew that thou with other erring spirits wert bound to live again on earth when Christ had built His Holy Way therefrom to Heaven,—and never did I cease for thy dear sake to wait and watch and pray! At last I found thee, . . . but ah! how I trembled for thy destiny! To thee had been delivered, as to all the children of men, the final message of salvation. . . the Message of Love and Pardon which made all the angels wonder! . . . but thou didst utterly reject it—and with the same willful arrogance of thy former self, Sahluma, thou wert blindly and desperately turning anew into darkness! O my Beloved, that darkness might have been eternal! . . . and crowded with memories dating from the very beginning of life! . . . Nay, let me not speak of that Supernal Agony, since Christ hath died to quench its terrors! . . . Enough!—by happy chance, through my desire, thine own roused better will, and the strength of one who hath many friends in Heaven, thy spirit was released to temporary liberty, . . . and in thy vision at Dariel, which was No vision, but a Truth, I bade thee meet me here. And why? . . . SOLELY TO TEST THY POWER OF OBEDIENCE TO A DIVINE IMPULSE UNEXPLAINABLE BY HUMAN REASON,—and I rejoiced as only angels can rejoice, when of thine own Free-Will thou didst keep the tryst I made with thee! Yet thou knewest me not! . . . or rather thou WOULDST NOT KNOW ME, . . . till I left thee! . . .'Tis ever the way of mortals, to doubt their angels in disguise!"

Her sweet accents shook with a liquid thrill suggestive of tears,—but he was silent. It seemed to him that he would be well content to hold his place forever, if forever he might hear her thus melodiously speak on! Had she not called him her "other soul, her king, her immortality's completion!"—and on those wondrous words of hers his spirit hung, impassioned, dazzled, and entranced beyond all Time and Space and Nature and Experience!

After a brief pause, during which his ravished mind floated among the thousand images and vague feelings of a whole Past and Future merged in one splendid and celestial Present, she resumed, always softly and with the same exquisite tenderness of tone:

"I left thee, Dearest, but a moment, . . . and in that moment, He who hath himself shared in human sorrows and sympathies,—He who is the embodiment of the Essence of God's Love,—came to my aid. Plunging thy senses in deep sleep, as hath been done before to many a saint and prophet of old time here on this very field of Ardath,—he summoned up before thee the phantoms of a PORTION of thy Past, . . . phantoms which, to thee, seemed far more real than the living presence of thy faithful Edris! . . . alas, my Beloved! . . . thou art not the only one on the Sorrowful Star who accepts a Dream for Reality and rejects Reality as a Dream!"

She paused again,—and again continued: "Nevertheless, in some degree thy Vision of Al-Kyris was true, inasmuch as thou wert shown therein as in a mirror, ONE phase, ONE only of thy former existence upon earth. The final episode was chosen,—as by the end of a man's days alone shall he be judged! As much as thy dreaming-sight was able to see,—as much as thy brain was able to bear, appeared before thee, . . . but that thou, slumbering, wert yet a conscious Personality among Phantoms, and that these phantoms spoke to thee, charmed thee, bewildered thee, tempted thee, and swayed thee, . . . this was the Divine Master's work upon thine own retrospective Thought and Memory. He gave the shadows of thy bygone life, seeming color, sense, motion, and speech,—He blotted out from thy remembrance His own Most Holy Name, . . . and, shutting up the Present from thy gaze, He sent thy spirit back into the Past. There, thou, perplexed and sorrowful, didst painfully re-weave the last fragments of thy former history, . . . and not till thou hadst abandoned the Shadow of Thyself, didst thou escape from the fear of destruction! Then, when apparently all alone, and utterly forsaken, a cloud of angels circled round thee, . . . THEN, at thy first repentant cry for help, He who has never left an earnest prayer unanswered bade me descend hither, to waken and comfort thee! . . . Oh, never was His bidding more joyously obeyed! Now I have plainly shown thee the interpretation of thy Dream, . . . and dost thou not comprehend the intention of the Highest in manifesting it unto thee? Remember the words of God's Prophet of old:

"Behold the Field thou thoughtest barren, how great a glory hath the moon unveiled!
"And I beheld and was sore amazed, for I was no longer Myself, but Another
"And the sword of death was in that Other's soul,—and yet that Other was but Myself in pain
"And I knew not the things which were once familiar, and my heart failed within me for very fear!"

She spoke the quaint and mystic lines with a grave, pure, rhythmic utterance that was like the far-off singing of sweet psalmody;—and when she ceased, the stillness that followed seemed quivering with the rich vibrations of her voice, . . . the very air was surely rendered softer and more delicate by such soul-moving sound!

But Theos, who had listened dumbly until now, began to feel a sudden sorrowful aching at his heart, a sense of coming desolation, . . . a consciousness that she would soon depart again, and leave him and, with a mingled reverence and passion, he ventured to draw one of the fair hands that rested on his brows, down into his own clasp. He met with no resistance, and half-happy, half-agonized, he pressed his lips upon its soft and dazzling whiteness, while the longing of his soul broke forth in words of fervid, irrepressible appeal.

"Edris!" he implored. "If thou dost love me give me my death! Here,— now, at thy feet where I kneel! . . . of what avail is it for me to struggle in this dark and difficult world? . . . O deprive me of this fluctuating breath called Life and let me live indeed! I understand. . . I know all thou hast said,—I have learned my own sins as in a glass darkly,—I have lived on earth before, and as it seems, made no good use of life, . . . and now: now I have found THEE! Then why must I lose thee? . . . thou who camest to me so sweetly at the first? . . . Nay, I cannot part from thee—I will not! . . . If thou leavest me, I have no strength to follow thee; I shall but miss the way to thine abode!"

"Thou canst not miss the way!"—responded Edris softly, . . . "Look up, my Theos,—be of good cheer, thou Poet to whom Heaven's greatest gifts of Song are now accorded! Look up and tell me, . . . is not the way made plain?"

Slowly and in reverential fear, he obeyed, and raised his eyes, still holding her by the hand,—and saw behind her a distinctly marked shadow that seemed flung downward by the reflection of some brilliant light above, . . . the shadow of a Cross, against which her delicate figure stood forth in shining outlines. Seeing, he understood,—but nevertheless his mind grew more and more disquieted. A thousand misgivings crowded upon him,—he thought of the world, . . . he remembered what it was, . . . he was living in an age of heresy and wanton unbelief, where not only Christ's Divinity was made blasphemous mock of, but where even God's existence was itself called in question. . . and as for ANGELS! . . . a sort of shock ran through his nerves as he reflected that though preachers preached concerning these supernatural beings,— though the very birth of Christ rested on Angels' testimony,—though poets wrote of them, and painters strove to delineate them on their most famous canvases, each and all thus PRACTICALLY DEMONSTRATING

THE SECRET INSTINCTIVE INTUITION OF HUMANITY that such celestial Forms ARE,—yet it was most absolutely certain that not a man in the prosaic nineteenth century would, if asked, admit, to any actual belief in their existence! Inconsistent? . . . yes!—but are not men more inconsistent than the very beasts of the field their tyranny controls? What, as a rule, Do men believe in? . . . Themselves! . . . only themselves! They are, in their own opinion, the Be-All and the End-All of everything! . . . as if the Supreme Creative Force called God were incapable of designing any Higher Form of Thinking-Life than their pigmy bodies which strut on two legs and, with two eyes and a small, quickly staggered brain, profess to understand and weigh the whole foundation and plan of the Universe!

Growing swiftly conscious of all that in the Purgatory of the Present awaited him, Theos felt as though the earth-chasm that had swallowed up Al-Kyris in his dream had opened again before him, affrighting him with its black depth of nothingness and annihilation,—and in a sudden agony of self-distrust he gazed yearningly at the fair, wistful face above him, . . . the divine beauty that was HIS after all, if he only knew how to claim it!—Something, he knew not what, filled him with a fiery restlessness,—a passion of protest and aspiration, which for a moment was so strong that it seemed to him he must, with one fierce effort, wrench himself free from the trammels of mortality, and straightway take upon him the majesty of immortal nature, and so bear his Angel love company whithersoever she went! Never had the fetters of flesh weighed upon him with such-heaviness! . . . but, in spite of his feverish longing to escape, some authoritative yet gentle Force held him prisoner.

"God!" he muttered. . . "Why am I thus bound?—why can I not be free?"

"Because thy time for freedom has not come!" said Edris, quickly answering his thought. . . "Because thou hast work to do that is not yet done! Thy poet labors have, up till now, been merely REPETITION, . . . the repetition of thy Former Self, . . . Go! the tired world waits for a new Gospel of Poesy, . . . a new song that shall rouse it from its apathy, and bring it closer unto God and all things high and fair! Write!—for the nations wait for a trumpet-voice of Truth! . . . the great poets are dead, . . . their spirits are in Heaven, . . . and there is none to replace them on the Sorrowful Star save THOU! Not for Fame do thy work— nor for Wealth, . . . but for Love and the Glory of God!—for Love of Humanity, for Love of the Beautiful, the Pure, the Holy! . . . let the race of men hear one more faithful Apostle of the Divine Unseen, ere Earth is lost in the withering light of a larger Creation! Go! . . . perform thy long-neglected mission,—that mission of all poets worthy the name. . . To Raise The World! Thou shalt not lack strength nor fervor, so long as thou dost write for the benefit of others. Serve God and live!—serve Self and die! Such is the Eternal Law of Spheres Invisible, . . . the less thou seest of Self, the more thou seest of Heaven! . . . thrust Self away, and lo! God invests thee with His Presence! Go forth into the world, . . . a King uncrowned, . . . a Master of Song, . . . and fear not that I, Edris, will forsake thee,—I, who have loved thee since the birth of Time!"

He met her beautiful, luminous, inspired eyes, with a sad interrogativeness in his own. What a hard fate was meted out to him! . . . To teach the world that scoffed at teaching!—to rouse the gold-thirsting mass of men to a new sense of things divine! O vain task!—O dreary impossibility! . . . Enough surely, to guide his own Will aright, without making any attempt to guide the wills of others!

Her mandate seemed to him almost cruel,—it was like driving him into a howling wilderness, when with one touch, one kiss, she might transport him into Paradise! If She were in the world, . . . if She were always with him. . . ah! then how different, how easy life would be! Again he thought of those strange entrancing words of hers. . . "My other soul, . . . my king. . . my immortality's completion!"—and a sudden wild idea took swift possession of his brain.

"Edris!" he cried. "If I may not yet come to thee, then come Thou to me! . . . Dwell thou with me! . . . O by the force of my love, which God knoweth, let me draw thee, thou fair Light, into my heart's gloom! Hear me while I swear my faith to thee as at some holy shrine! . . . As I live, with all my soul I do accept thy Master Christ, as mine utmost good, and His Cross as my proudest glory! . . . but yet, bethink thee, Edris, bethink thee of this world,—its wilful sin, its scorn of God, and all the evil that like a spreading thunder-cloud darkens it day by day! Oh, wilt thou leave me desolate and alone? . . . Fight as I will, I shall often sink under blows, . . . conquer as I may, I shall suffer the solitude of conquest, unless Thou art with me! Oh, speak!—is there no deeper divine intention in the marvellous destiny that has brought us together?—thou, pure Spirit, and I, weak Mortal? Has love, the primal mover of all things, no hold upon thee? . . . If I am, as thou sayest, thy Beloved, loved by thee so long, even while forgetful of and unworthy of thy love, can I not Now,—now when I am all thine,—

persuade thee to compassionate the rest of my brief life on earth? . . . Thou art in woman's shape here on this Field of Ardath,—and yet thou art not woman! Oh, could my love constrain thee in God's Name, to wear the mask of mortal body for my sake, would not our union even now make the Sorrowful Star seem fair? . . . Love, love, love! Come to mine aid, and teach me how to shut the wings of this sweet bird of paradise in mine own breast! . . . God! Spare her to me for one of Thy sweet moments which are our mortal years! . . . Christ, who became a mere child for pity of us, let me learn from Thee the mystic spell that makes Thine angel mine!"

Carried away by his own forceful emotion he hardly knew what he said, . . . but an unspeakable, dizzy joy flooded his soul, as he caught the look she gave him! . . . a wild, sweet, amazed, half-tender, half-agonized, wholly HUMAN look, suggestive of the most marvellous possibilities! One effort and she released her hand from his, and moved a little apart, her eyes kindling with celestial sympathy in which there was the very faintest touch of self-surrender. Self-surrender? . . . what! from an Angel to a mortal? . . . Ah no! . . . it could not be,—yet he felt filled all at once with a terrible sense of power that at the same time was mingled with the deepest humility and fear.

"Hush!"—she said, and her lovely, low voice was tremulous,— "Hush!—Thou dost speak as if we were already in God's World! I love thee, Theos! . . . and truly, because thou art prisoned here, I love the sad Earth also! . . . but dost thou think to what thou wouldst so eagerly persuade me? To live a mortal life? . . . to die? . . . to pass through the darkest phase of world-existence known in all the teeming spheres? Nay!" . . . and a look of pathetic sorrow came over her face. "How could I, even for thee, my Theos, forsake my home in Heaven?"

Her last words were half-questioning, half-hesitating, . . . her manner was as of one in doubt. . . and Theos, kneeling still, surveyed her in worshipping silence. Then he suddenly remembered what the Monk and Mystic, Heliobas, had said to him at Dariel on the morning after his trance of soul-liberty: . . . "If, as I conjecture, you have seen one of the fair inhabitants of higher spheres than ours, you would not drag her spiritual and death-unconscious brightness down to the level of the 'reality' of a mere human life? . . . Nay, if you would you could not!" And now, strange to say, he felt that he COULD but WOULD NOT; and he was overcome with remorse and penitence for the egotistical nature of his own appeal.

"My love—my life!" he said brokenly,—"Forgive me,—forgive my selfish prayer! . . . Self spoke,—not I, . . . yet I had thought Self dead, and buried forever!" A faint sigh escaped him. . . "Believe me, Sweet, I would not have thee lose one hour of Heaven's ecstasies, . . . I would not have thee saddened by Earth's wilful miseries, . . . no! not even for that lightning-moment which numbers up man's mortal days! Speed back to Angel-land, my Edris!—I will love thee till I die, and leave the Afterward to Christ. Be glad, thou fairest, dearest One! . . . unfurl thy rainbow wings and fly from me! . . . and wander singing through the groves of Heaven, making all Heaven musical, . . . perchance in the silence of the night I may catch the echo of thy voice and fancy thou art near! And trust me, Edris! . . . trust me! . . . for my faith will not falter, . . . my hope shall not waver, . . . and though in the world I may, I Must have tribulation, yet will I believe in Him who hath by simple love overcome the world!"

He ceased, . . . a great quiet seemed to fall upon him,—the quiet of a deep and passive resignation.

Edris drew nearer to him,—timidly as a shy bird, yet with a wonderful smile quivering on her lips, and in the clear depths of her starry eyes. Very gently she placed her arms about his neck and looked down at him with divinely compassionate tenderness.

"Thou beloved one!" she said, "Thou whose spirit was formerly equal to mine, and to all angels, in God's sight though through pride it fell! Learn that thou art nearer to me now than thou hast been for a myriad ages! . . . between us are renewed the strong, sweet ties that shall nevermore be broken, unless. . ." and her voice faltered,— "Unless thou, of thine own Free Will, break them again in spite of all my prayers! For, Because thou art immortal even as I, though thou art pent up in mortality, even so must thy Will remain immortally unfettered, and what thou dost firmly elect to do, God will not prevent. The Dream of thy Past was a lesson, not a command,—thou art free to forget or remember it as thou wilt while on earth, since it is only After Death that Memory is ineffaceable, and, with its companion Remorse, constitutes Hell. Obey God, or disobey Him,—He will not force thee either way, . . . constrained love hath no value! Only this is the Universal Law,—that whosoever disobeys, his disobedience recoils on his own head as of Necessity it Must,—whereas obedience is the working in perfect harmony with all Nature, and of equal Necessity brings its own reward. Cling to the Cross for one moment. . . the moment called by mortals, Life, . . . and it shall lift thee straightway into highest Heaven! There will I wait for thee,—and there thou shalt make me thine own forever!"

He sighed and gazed at her wistfully.

"Alas, my Edris! . . . Not till then?" he murmured.

She bent over him and kissed his forehead,—a caress as brief and light as the passing flutter of a bird's wing.

"Not till then!"—she whispered—"Unless the longing of thy love compels!"

He started. What did she mean? . . . His eyes flashed eager inquiry into hers, so soft and brilliantly clear, with the light of an eternal peace dwelling in their liquid, mysterious loveliness,—and meeting his questioning look, the angelic smile brightened more gloriously round her lips. But there was now something altogether unearthly in her beauty, . . . a wondrous inward luminousness began to transfigure her face and form, . . . he saw her garments whiten to a sparkling radiance as of sunbeams on snow, . . . the halo round her bright hair deepened into flame-like glory—her stature grew loftier, and became as it were endowed with supreme and splendid majesty, . . . and the exquisite fairness of her countenance waxed warmly transparent, with the delicate hue of a white rose, through which the pink color faintly flushes soft suggestions of ruddier life. His gaze dwelt upon her in unspeakable wondering adoration, mingled with a sense of irrepressible sorrow and heaviness of heart, . . . he felt she was about to leave him, . . . and was it not a parting of soul from soul?

Just then the Sun stepped royally forth from between the red and gold curtains of the east,—and in that blaze of earth's life-radiance her figure became resplendently invested with vivid rays of roseate lustre that far surpassed the amber shining of the Orb of day! Awed, dazzled, and utterly overcome, he yet strove to keep his straining eyes steadily upon her,—conscious that her smile still blessed him with its tenderness, . . . he made a wild effort to drag himself nearer to her, . . . to touch once more the glittering edge of her robe. . . to detain her one little, little moment longer! Ah! how wistfully, how fondly she looked upon him! . . . Almost it seemed as if she might, after all, consent to stay! . . . He stretched out his arms with a pathetic gesture of love, fear, and soul-passionate supplication.

"Edris! . . . Edris!" . . . he cried half despairingly. "Oh, by the strength of thine Angelhood have pity on the weakness of my Manhood!"

Surely she heard, or seemed to hear! . . . and yet she gave no answer! . . . No sign! . . . No promise!—no gesture of farewell! . . . only a look of divine, compassionating, perfect love, . . . a look so pure, so penetrating, so true, so rapturous, that flesh and blood could bear the glory of her transfigured Presence no longer,—and blind with the burning effulgence of her beauty, he shut his eyes and covered his face. He knew now, if he had never known it before, what was meant by "an Angel standing in the sun!"* Moreover, he also knew that what Humanity calls "miracles" ARE possible, and Do happen,—and that instead of being violations of the Law of Nature as we understand it, they are but confirmations of that Law in its DEEPER DEPTHS,— depths which, controlled by Spiritual Force alone, have not as yet been sounded by the most searching scientists. And what is Material Force but the visible manifestation of the Spiritual behind it? . . . He who accepts the Material and denies the Spiritual, is in the untenable position of one who admits an Effect and denies a Cause! And if both Spiritual and Material BE accepted, then how can we reasonably dare to set a limit to the manifestations of either the one or the other?

WHEN HE AT LAST LOOKED up, Edris had vanished! He was alone, . . . alone on the Field of Ardath, . . . the field that was "barren" in very truth, now she, his Angel, had been drawn away, as it seemed, into the sunlight, . . . absorbed like a paradise-pearl into those rays of life-giving gold that lit and warmed the reddening earth and heaven!

Slowly and dizzily he rose to his feet, and gazed about him in vague bewilderment. He had passed ONE NIGHT on the field! One night only! . . . and he felt as though he had lived through years of experience! Now, the VISION was ended, . . . Edris, the REALITY, had fled, . . . and the World was before him, . . . the World, with all the unsatisfying things it grudgingly offers, . . . the World in which Al-Kyris had been a "City Magnificent" in the centuries gone,—and in which he, too, had played his part before, and had won fame, to be forgotten as soon as dead! Fame! . . . how he had longed and thirsted for it! . . . and what a foolish, undesirable distinction it seemed to him now!

Steadying his thoughts by a few moments of calm reflection, he remembered what he had in charge to do, . . . To REDEEM HIS PAST. To use and expend whatever force was in him for the good, the help, the

---

* Revelation, chap, xix., 17.

consolement, and the love of others, . . . Not to benefit himself! This was his task, . . . and the very comprehension of it gave him a rush of vigor and virile energy that at once lifted the cloud of love-loneliness from his soul.

"My Edris!" he whispered. "Thou shalt have no cause to weep for me in Heaven again! . . . with God's help I will win back my lost heritage!"

As he spoke the words his eyes caught a glimpse of something white on the turf where, but a moment since, his Angel-love had stood,—he stooped toward it, . . . it was one half-opened bud of the wonderful "Ardath-flowers" that had covered the field in such singular profusion on the previous night when she first appeared. One only! . . . might he not gather it?

He hesitated, . . . then very gently and reverently broke it off, and tenderly bore it to his lips. What a beautiful blossom it was! . . . its fragrance was unlike that of any other flower,—its whiteness was more pure and soft than that of the rarest edelweiss on Alpine snows, and its partially disclosed golden centre had an almost luminous brightness. As he held it in his hand, all sorts of vague, delicious thoughts came sweeping across his brain, . . . thoughts that seemed to set themselves to music wild and strange and New, and suggestive of the sweetest, noblest influences! A thrill of expectation stirred in him, as of great and good things to be done,—grand changes to be wrought in the complex web of human destiny, brought about by the quickening and development of a pure, unselfish, spiritual force, that might with saving benefit flow into the perplexed and weary intelligence of man; . . . and cheered, invigorated, and conscious of a circling, widening, ever-present Supreme Power that with all-surrounding love was ever on the side of work done for love's sake, he gently shut the flower within his breast, resolving to carry it with him wheresoever he went as a token and proof of the "signs and wonders" of the Prophet's Field.

And now he prepared to quit the scene of his mystic Vision, in which he had followed with prescient pain the brief, bright career, the useless fame, the evil love-passion, and final fate of his Former Self,— and crossing the field with lingering tread, he looked back many times to the fallen block of stone where he had sat when he had first perceived God's maiden Edris, stepping softly through the bloom. When should he again meet her? Alas! . . . not till Death, the beautiful and beneficent Herald of true Liberty, summoned him to those lofty heights of Paradise where she had habitation. Not till then, unless, . . . unless, . . . and his

heart beat with a sudden tumult as he recollected her last words, . . .
"UNLESS THE LONGING OF THY LOVE COMPELS!"

Could love COMPEL her, he wondered, to come to him once more
while yet he lived on earth? Perhaps! . . . and yet if he indeed had such
power of love, would it be generous or just to exert it? No! . . . for to
draw her down from Heaven to Earth seemed to him now a sort of
sacrilege,—dearer to him was HER joy than his own! But suppose the
possibility of her being actually HAPPY with him in mortal existence, . . .
suppose that Love, when absolutely pure, unselfishly mutual, helpful,
and steadfast, had it in its gift to make even the Sorrowful Star a
Heaven in miniature, what then?

He would not trust himself to think of this! . . . the mere shadowy
suggestion of such supreme delight filled him with a strong passion of
yearning, to which in his accepted creed of Self-abnegation he dared
not yield! Firmly restraining, resisting, and renouncing his own desires,
he mentally raised a holy shrine for her in his soul, . . . a shrine of pure
faith, warm with eternal aspirations and bright with truth, wherein
he hallowed the memory of her beauty with a sense of devout, love-like
gladness. She was safe. . . she was content, . . . she blossomed flower-
like in the highest gardens of God where all things fared well;—enough
for him to worship her at a distance, . . . to keep the clear reflection
of her loveliness in his mind, . . . and to live, so that he might deserve
to follow and find her when his work on earth was done. Moreover,
Heaven to him was no longer a vague, mythical realm, ill-defined by
the prosy descriptions of church-preachers,—it was an actual WORLD
to which HE was linked,—in which HE had possessions, of which
HE was a native, and for the perpetuation and enlargement of whose
splendor ALL worlds existed!

Arrived at the boundary of the field, the spot marked by the broken
half-buried pillar of red granite Heliobas had mentioned, he paused—
thinking dreamily of the words of Esdras, who in answer to his Angel-
visitant's inquiry: "Why art thou disquieted?" had replied: "Because
thou hast forsaken me, and yet I did according to thy words, and I
went into the field, and lo! I have seen and yet see, that I am not able
to express." Whereupon the Angel had said, "Stand up manfully and I
will advise thee!"

"Stand up manfully!" Yes! . . . this is what he, Theos Alwyn, meant
to do. He would "stand up manfully" against the howling iconoclasm
and atheism of the Age,—he would be Poet henceforth in the true

meaning of the word, namely Maker, . . . he would MAKE not BREAK the grand ideal hopes and heaven-climbing ambitions of Humanity! . . . he would endeavor his utmost best to be that "Hierarch and Pontiff of the world"—as a modern rugged Apostle of Truth has nobly said,— "who Prometheus-like can shape new Symbols and bring new fire from heaven to fix them into the deep, infinite faculties of Man."

With a brief silent prayer, he turned away at last, and walked slowly, in the lovely silence of the early Eastern morning, back to the place from whence he had last night wandered,—the Hermitage of Elzear, near the Ruins of Babylon. He soon came in sight of it, and also perceived Elzear himself, stooping over a small plot of ground in front of his dwelling, apparently gathering herbs. When he approached, the old man looked up and smiled, giving him a silent, expressively courteous morning greeting,—by his manner it was evident that he thought his guest had merely been out for an early stroll ere the heat of the day set in. And yet Al-Kyris! . . . How real had seemed that dream-existence in that dream-city! The figure of Elzear looked scarcely more substantial than the phantom-forms of Sah-luma, Zephoranim, Khosrul, Zuriel, or Zabastes,—while Lysia's exquisite face and seductive form, Niphrata's pensive beauty, and all the local characteristics of the place, were stamped on the dreamer's memory as faithfully as scenes flashed by the sun on the plates of photography! True, the pictures were perhaps now slightly fading into the similitude of pale negatives, . . . but still, would not everything that happened in the ACTUAL world merge into that same undecided dimness with the lapse of time?

He thought so, . . . and smiled at the thought, . . . the transitory nature of earthly things was a subject for joy to him now,—not regret. With a kindly word or two to his venerable host, he went through the open door of the Hermitage, and entered the little room he had left only a few hours previously. It appeared to him as familiar and UNfamiliar as Al-Kyris itself! . . . till raising his eyes he saw the great Crucifix against the wall,—the sacred Symbol whose meaning he had forgotten and hopelessly longed for in his Dream,—and from which, before his visit to the field of Ardath, he had turned with a sense of bitter scorn and proud rejection. But Now! . . . Now he gazed upon it in unspeakable remorse,—in tenderest desire to atone, . . . the sweet, grave, patient Eyes of the holy Figure seemed to meet his with a wondrous challenge of love, longing, and most fraternal, sympathetic comprehension of his nature. . . he paused, looking, . . . and the pre-eminently false words of George Herbert suddenly occurred to him, "Thy Saviour sentenced joy!" O blasphemy! . . . SENTENCED joy? Nay!—rather re-created it, and invested it with divine certainties, beyond all temporal change or evanishment! . . . Yielding to a swift impulse, he threw himself on his knees, and with clasped hands, leaned his brows against the feet of the sculptured Christ. There he rested in wordless peace,—his whole soul entranced in a divine passion of faith, hope, and love. . . there with the "Ardath flower" in his breast, he consecrated his life to the Highest Good,—and there in absolute humility, and pure, child-like devotion, he crucified SELF forever!

PART III
POET AND ANGEL

"O Golden Hair! . . . O Gladness of an Hour
Made flesh and blood!"

*   *   *   *   *

"Who speaks of glory and the force of love
And thou not near, my maiden-minded dove!
With all the coyness, all the beauty sheen
Of thy rapt face? A fearless virgin-queen,
A queen of peace art thou,—and on thy head
The golden light of all thy hair is shed
Most nimbus-like, and most suggestive too
Of youthful saints enshrined and garlanded."

*   *   *   *   *

"Our thoughts are free,—and mine have found at last
Their apt solution; and from out the Past
There seems to shine as 'twere a beacon-fire:
And all the land is lit with large desire
Of lambent glory; all the quivering sea

Is big with waves that wait the Morn's decree
As I, thy vassal, wait thy beckoning smile
Athwart the splendors of my dreams of thee!"

—"A Lover's Litanies"—ERIC MACKAY

XXXI

FRESH LAURELS

It was a dismal March evening. London lay swathed in a melancholy fog,—a fog too dense to be more than temporarily disturbed even by the sudden gusts of the bitter east wind. Rain fell steadily, sometimes changing to sleet, that drove in sharp showers on the slippery roads and pavements, bewildering the tired horses, and stirring up much irritation in the minds of those ill-fated foot-passengers whom business, certainly not pleasure, forced to encounter the inconveniences of the weather. Against one house in particular—an old-fashioned, irregular building situated in a somewhat out-of-the-way but picturesque part of Kensington—the cold, wet blast blew with specially keen ferocity, as though it were angered by the sounds within,—sounds that in truth rather resembled its own cross groaning. Curious short grunts and plaintive cries, interspersed with an occasional pathetic long-drawn whine, suggested dimly the idea that somebody was playing, or trying to play, on a refractory stringed instrument, the well-worn composition known as Raff's "Cavatina." And, in fact, had the vexed wind been able to break through the wall and embody itself into a substantial being, it would have discovered the producer of the half-fierce, half-mournful noise, in the person of the Honorable Frank Villiers, who, with that amazingly serious ardor so often displayed by amateur lovers of music, was persistently endeavoring to combat the difficulties of the violoncello. He adored his big instrument,—the more unmanageable it became in his hands, the more he loved it. Its grumbling complaints at his unskilful touch delighted him,—when he could succeed in awakening a peevish dull sob from its troubled depths, he felt a positive thrill of almost professional triumph,—and he refused to be daunted in his efforts by the frequently barbaric clamor his awkward bowing wrung from the tortured strings. He tried every sort of music, easy and intricate—and his happiest hours were those when, with glass in eye and brow knitted in anxious scrutiny, he could peer his way through the labyrinth of a sonata or fantasia much too complex for any one but a trained artist, enjoying to the full the mental excitement of the discordant struggle, and comfortably conscious that as his residence was "detached," no obtrusive neighbor could either warn him to desist, or set up an opposition nuisance next door by constant practice on the distressingly over-popular piano. One thing very much in his favor was, that he never manifested any desire to perform in public. No one had ever heard him play, . . . he pursued his favorite amusement in solitude, and was amply satisfied, if when questioned on the subject of music, he could find an opportunity to say with a conscious-modest air, "My instrument is the 'cello." That was quite enough self-assertion for him, . . . and if any one ever urged him to display his talent, he would elude the request with such charming grace and diffidence, that many people imagined he must really be a great musical genius who only lacked the necessary insolence and aplomb to make that genius known.

The 'cello apart, Villiers was very generally recognized as a discerning dilettante in most matters artistic. He was an excellent judge of literature, painting, and sculpture, . . . his house, though small, was a perfect model of taste in design and adornment, . . . he knew where to pick up choice bits of antique furniture, dainty porcelain, bronzes, and wood-carvings, while in the acquisition of rare books he was justly considered a notable connoisseur. His delicate and fastidious instincts were displayed in the very arrangement of his numerous volumes, . . . none were placed on such high shelves as to be out of hand reach, . . . all were within close touch and ready to command, ranged in low, carved oak cases or on revolving stands, . . . while a few particularly rare editions and first folios were shut in curious little side niches with locked glass-doors, somewhat resembling small shrines such as are used for the reception of sacred relics. The apartment he called his "den"—where he now sat practising the "Cavatina" for about the two-hundredth time— was perhaps the most fascinating nook in the whole house, inasmuch as it contained a little bit of everything, arranged with that perfect attention to detail which makes each object, small and great, appear not only ornamental, but positively necessary. In one corner a quaint old jar overflowed with the brightness of fresh yellow daffodils; in another a long, tapering Venetian vase held feathery clusters of African grass and fern, . . . here the medallion of a Greek philosopher or Roman Emperor gleamed whitely against the sombrely painted wall; there a Rembrandt portrait flashed out from the semi-obscure background of some rich, carefully disposed fold of drapery,—while a few admirable casts from the antique lit up the deeper shadows of the room, such as the immortally youthful head of the Apollo Belvedere, the wisely serene countenance of the Pallas Athene that Goethe loved, and the Cupid of Praxiteles.

Judging from his outward appearance only, few would have given Villiers credit for being the man of penetrative and almost classic refinement he really was,—he looked far more athletic than aesthetic. Broad-shouldered and deep-chested, with a round, blunt head firmly set on a full, strong throat, he had, on the whole, a somewhat obstinate and pugilistic air which totally belied his nature. His features, open and ruddy, were, without being handsome, decidedly attractive—the mouth was rather large, yet good-tempered; the eyes bright, blue, and sparklingly suggestive of a native inborn love of humor. There was something fresh and piquant in the very expression of naive bewilderment with which he now adjusted his eyeglass—a wholly unnecessary appendage—and set himself strenuously to examine anew the chords of that extraordinary piece of music which others thought so easy and which he found so puzzling, . . . he could manage the simple melody fairly well, but the chords!

"They are the very devil!" . . . he murmured plaintively, staring at the score, and hitching up his unruly instrument more securely against his knee, . . . "Perhaps the bow wants a little rosin."

This was one of his minor weaknesses,—he would never quite admit that false notes were his own fault. "They COULDN'T be, you know!" he mildly argued, addressing the obtrusive neck of the 'cello, which had a curious, stubborn way of poking itself into his chin, and causing him to wonder how it got there, . . . surely the manner in which he held it had nothing to do with this awkward occurrence! "I'm not such a fool as not to understand how to find the right notes, after all my practice! There's something wrong with the strings,—or the bridge has gone awry,—or"—and this was his last resource—"the bow wants more rosin!"

Thus he hugged himself in deliciously wilful ignorance of his own shortcomings, and shut his ears to the whispered reproaches of musical conscience. Had he been married his wife would no doubt have lost no time in enlightening him,—she would have told him he was a wretched player, that his scrapings on the 'cello were enough to drive one mad, and sundry other assurances of the perfectly conjugal type of frankness,— but as it chanced he was a happy bachelor, a free and independent man with more than sufficient means to gratify his particular tastes and whims. He was partner in a steadily prosperous banking concern, and had just enough to do to keep him pleasantly and profitably occupied.

Asked why he did not marry, he replied with blunt and almost brutal honesty, that he had never yet met a woman whose conversation he could stand for more than an hour.

"Silly or clever," he said, "they are all possessed of the same infinite tedium. Either they say nothing, or they say everything; they are always at the two extremes, and announce themselves as dunces or blue-stockings. One wants the just medium,—the dainty commingling of simplicity and wisdom that shall yet be pure womanly,—and this is precisely the jewel 'far above rubies' that one cannot find. I've given up the search long ago, and am entirely resigned to my lot. I like women very well—I may say very much—as friends, but to take one on chance as a comrade for life! . . . No, thank you!"

Such was his fixed opinion and consequent rejection of matrimony; and for the rest, he studied art and literature and became an authority on both; so much so that on one occasion he kept a goodly number of people away from visiting the Royal Academy Exhibition, he having voted it a "disgrace to Art."

"English artists occupy the last grade in the whole school of painting," he had said indignantly, with that decisive manner of his which somehow or other carried conviction, . . . "The very Dutch surpass them; and instead of trying to raise their standard, each year sees them grovelling in lower depths. The Academy is becoming a mere gallery of portraits, painted to please the caprices of vain men and women, at a thousand or two thousand guineas apiece; ugly portraits, too, woodeny portraits, utterly uninteresting portraits of prosaic nobodies. Who cares to see 'No. 154. Mrs. Flummery in her presentation-dress' . . . except Mrs. Flummery's own particular friends? . . . or '283. Miss Smox, eldest daughter of Professor A. T. Smox,' or '516. Baines Bryce, Esq.'? . . . Who Is Baines Bryce? . . . Nobody ever heard of him before. He may be a retired pork-butcher for all any one knows! Portraits, even of celebrities, are a mistake. Take Algernon Charles Swinburne, for instance, the man who, when left to himself, writes some of the grandest lines in the English language, He had his portrait in the Academy, and everybody ran away from it, it was such an unutterable hideous disappointment. It was a positive libel of course, . . . Swinburne has fine eyes and a still finer brow, but instead of idealizing the Poet in him, the silly artist painted him as if he had no more intellectual distinction than a bill-sticker! . . . English art! . . . pooh! . . . don't speak to me about it! Go to Spain, Italy, Bavaria—see what They can do, and then say a Miserere for the sins of the R A's!"

Thus he would talk, and his criticisms carried weight with a tolerably large circle of influential and wealthy persons, who when they called upon him, and saw the perfection of his house and the rarity of his art collections, came at once to the conclusion that it would be wise, as well as advantageous to themselves, to consult him before purchasing pictures, books, statues, or china, so that he occupied the powerful position of being able with a word to start an artist's reputation or depreciate it, as he chose,—a distinction he had not desired, and which was often a source of trouble to him, because there were so few, so very few, whose work he felt he could conscientiously approve and encourage. He was eminently good-natured and sympathetic; he would not give pain to others without being infinitely more pained himself; and yet, for all his amiability, there was a stubborn instinct in him which forbade him to promote, by word or look, the fatal nineteenth century spread of mediocrity. Either a thing must be truly great and capable of being measured by the highest standards, or for him it had no value. This rule he carried out in all branches of art,—except his own 'cello-playing. That was NOT great,—that would never be great,—but it was his pet pastime; he chose it in preference to the billiards, betting, and bar-lounging that make up the amusements of the majority of the hopeful manhood of London, and, as has already been said, he never inflicted it upon others.

He rubbed the rosin now thoughtfully up and down his bow, and glanced at the quaint old clock—an importation from Nurnberg— that ticked solemnly in one corner near the deep bay-window, across which the heavy olive green plush curtains were drawn, to shut out the penetrating chill of the wind. It wanted ten minutes to nine. He had given orders to his man servant that he was on no account to be disturbed that evening, . . . no matter what visitors called for him, none were to be admitted. He had made up his mind to have a long and energetic practice, and he felt a secret satisfaction as he heard the steady patter of the rain outside, . . . the very weather favored his desire for solitude,—no one was likely to venture forth on such a night.

Still gravely rubbing his brow, his eyes travelled from the clock in the corner to a photograph on the mantel-shelf—the photograph of a man's face, dark, haughty, beautiful, yet repellent in its beauty, and with a certain hard sternness in its outline—the face of Theos Alwyn. From this portrait his glance wandered to the table, where, amid a picturesque litter of books and papers, lay a square, simply bound volume, with an ivory leaf-cutter thrust in it to mark the place where the reader left off, and its title plainly lettered in gold at the back—"Nourhalma."

"I wonder where he is!" . . . he mused, his thoughts naturally reverting to the author of the book. "He cannot know what all London knows, or surely he would be back here like a shot! It is six months ago now since I received his letter and that poem in manuscript from Tiflis in Armenia,—and not another line has he sent to tell me of his whereabouts! Curious fellow he is! . . . but, by Jove, what a genius! No wonder he has besieged Fame and taken it by storm! I don't remember any similar instance, except that of Byron, in which such an unprecedented reputation was made so suddenly! And in Byron's case it was more the domestic scandal about him than his actual merit that made him the rage, . . . now the world knows literally nothing about Alwyn's private life or character—there's no woman in his history that I know of—no vice, . . . he hasn't outraged the law, upset morals, flouted at decency, or done anything that according to modern fashions Ought to have made him famous—no! . . . he has simply produced a perfect poem, stately, grand, pure, and pathetic,—and all of a sudden some secret spring in the human heart is touched, some long-closed valve opened, and lo and behold, all intellectual society is raving about him,— his name is in everybody's mouth, his book in every one's hands. I don't altogether like his being made the subject of a 'craze';—experience shows me it's a kind of thing that doesn't last. In fact, it Can't last. . . the reaction invariably sets in. And the English public is, of all publics, the most insane in its periodical frenzies, and the most capricious. Now, it is all agog for a 'shilling sensational'—then it discusses itself hoarse over a one-sided theological novel made up out of theories long ago propounded and exhaustively set forth by Voltaire, and others of his school,—anon it revels in the gross descriptions of shameless vice depicted in an 'accurately translated' romance of the Paris slums,— now it writes thousands of letters to a black man, to sympathize With him because he has been Called black!—could anything be more absurd! . . . it has even followed the departure of an elephant from the Zoo in weeping crowds! However, I wish all the crazes to which it is subject were as harmless and wholesome as the one that has seized it for Alwyn's book,—for if true poetry were brought to the front, instead of being, as it often is, sneered at and kept in the background, we should have a chance of regaining the lost Divine Art, that, wherever it has been worthily followed, has proved the glory of the greatest nations.

MARIE CORELLI

And then we should not have to put up with such detestable inanities as are produced every day by persons calling themselves poets, who are scarcely fit to write mottoes for dessert crackers, . . . and we might escape for good and all from the infliction of 'magazine-verse,' which is emphatically a positive affront to the human intelligence. Ah me! what wretched upholders we are of Shakespeare's standard! . . . Keats was our last splendor,—then there is an unfilled gap, bridged in part by Tennyson. . . and now comes Alwyn blazing abroad like a veritable meteor,—only I believe he will do more than merely flare across the heavens,—he promises to become a notable fixed star."

Here he smiled, somewhat pleased with his own skill in metaphor, and having rubbed his bow enough, he drew it lingeringly across the 'cello strings. A long, sweet, shuddering sound rewarded him, like the upward wave of a wind among high trees, and he heard it with much gratification. He would try the Cavatina again now, he decided, and bringing his music-stand closer, he settled himself in readiness to begin. Just then the Nurnberg clock commenced striking the hour, accompanying each stroke with a very soft and mellow little chime of bells that sent fairy-like echoes through the quiet room. A bright flame started up from the glowing fire in the grate, flinging ruddy flashes along the walls,—a rattling gust of rain dashed once at the windows,—the tuneful clock ceased, and all was still. Villiers waited a moment; then with heedful earnestness, started the first bar of Raff's oft-murdered composition, when a knock at the door disturbed him and considerably ruffled his equanimity.

"Come in!" he called testily.

His man-servant appeared, a half-pleased, half-guilty look on his staid countenance.

"Please, sir, a gentleman called—"

"Well!—you said I was out?"

"No, sir! leastways I thought you might be at home to him, sir!"

"Confound you!" exclaimed Villiers petulantly, throwing down his bow in disgust,—"What business had you to think anything about it? . . . Didn't I tell you I wasn't at home to ANYBODY?"

"Come, come, Villiers!" . . . said a mellow voice outside, with a ripple of suppressed laughter in its tone, . . . "Don't be inhospitable! I'm sure you are at home to ME!"

And passing by the servant, who at once retired, the speaker entered the apartment, lifted his hat, and smiled. Villiers sprang from his chair in delighted astonishment.

"Alwyn!" he cried; and the two friends—whose friendship dated from boyhood—clasped each other's hands heartily, and were for a moment both silent,—half-ashamed of those affectionate emotions to which impulsive women may freely give vent, but to which men may not yield without being supposed to lose somewhat of the dignity of manhood.

"By Jove!" said Villiers at last, drawing a deep breath. "This Is a surprise! Only a few minutes ago I was considering whether we should not have to note you down in the newspaper as one of the 'mysterious disappearances' grown common of late! Where do you come from, old fellow?"

"From Paris just directly," responded Alwyn, divesting himself of his overcoat, and stepping outside the door to hang it on an evidently familiar nail in the passage, and then re-entering,—"But from Bagdad in the first instance. I visited that city, sacred to fairy-lore, and from thence journeyed to Damascus like one of our favorite merchants in the Arabian Nights,—then I went to Beyrout, and Alexandria, from which latter place I took ship homeward, stopping at delicious Venice while on my way."

"Then you did the Holy Land, I suppose?" queried Villiers, regarding him with sudden and growing inquisitiveness.

"My dear fellow, certainly Not! The Holy Land, invested by touts, and overrun by tourists, would neither appeal to my imagination nor my sentiments—and in its present state of vulgar abuse and unchristian sacrilege, it is better left unseen by those who wish to revere its associations, . . . don't you think so?"

He smiled as he put the question, and drawing up an old-fashioned oak chair to the fire, seated himself. Villiers meanwhile stared at him in unmitigated amazement, . . . what had come to the fellow, he wondered? How had he managed to invest himself with such an overpowering distinction of look and grace of bearing? He had always been a handsome man,—yes, but there was certainly something more than handsome about him now. There was a singular magnetism in the flash of the fine soft eyes, a marvellous sweetness in the firm lines of the perfect mouth, a royal grandeur and freedom in the very poise of his well-knit figure and noble head, that certainly had not before been apparent in him. Moreover, that was an odd remark for him to make about "wishing to revere" the associations of the Holy Land,—very odd, considering his formerly skeptical theories!

MARIE CORELLI

Rousing himself from his momentary bewilderment, Villiers remembered the duties of hospitality.

"Have you dined, Alwyn?" he asked, with his hand on the bell.

"Excellently!" was the response, accompanied by a bright upward glance; "I went to that big hotel opposite the Park, had dinner, left the surplus of my luggage in charge, selected one small portmanteau, took a hansom and came on here, resolved to pass one night at least under your roof. . ."

"One night!" interrupted Villiers; "You're very much mistaken, if you think you are going to get off so easily! You'll not escape from me for a month, I tell you! Consider yourself a prisoner!"

"Good! Send for the luggage to-morrow!" laughed Alwyn, flinging himself back in his chair in an attitude of lazy comfort, "I give in!—I resign myself to my fate! But what of the 'cello?"

And he pointed to the bulgy-looking casket of sweet sleeping sounds—sleeping generally so far as Villiers was concerned, but ready to wake at the first touch of the master-hand. Villiers glanced at it with a comical air of admiring vanquishment.

"Oh, never mind the 'cello!" he said indifferently, "that can bear being put by for a while. It's a most curious instrument,—sometimes it seems to sound better when I have let it rest a little. Just like a human thing, you know—it gets occasionally tired of me, I suppose! But I say, why didn't you come straight here, bag, baggage, and all? . . . What business had you to stop on the way at any hotel? . . . Do you call that friendship?"

Alwyn laughed at his mock injured tone.

"I apologize, Villiers! . . . I really do! But I felt it would be scarcely civil of me to come down upon you for bed, board, and lodging, without giving you previous notice, and at the same time I wanted to take you by surprise, as I Did. Besides I wasn't sure whether I should find you in town—of course I knew I should be welcome if you were!"

"Rather!" assented Villiers shortly and with affected gruffness. "If you were sure of nothing else in this world, you might be sure of that!" He paused squared his shoulders, and put up his eyeglass, through which he scanned his friend with such a persistently scrutinizing air, that Alwyn was somewhat amused.

"What are you staring at me for?" he demanded gayly,—"Am I so bronzed?"

"Well—you Are rather brown," admitted Villiers slowly. . . "But that doesn't surprise me. The fact is, it's very odd and I can't altogether explain it, but somehow I find you changed, . . . positively very much changed too!"

"Changed? In appearance, do you mean? How?"

"'Look here upon this picture and on this,'" quoted Villiers dramatically, taking down Alwyn's portrait from the mantleshelf, and mentally comparing it with the smiling original. "No two heads were ever more alike, and yet more distinctly UNlike. Here"—and he tapped the photograph—"you have the appearance of a modern Timon or Orestes. . . but now, as you actually ARE, I see more resemblance in your face to THAT"—and he pointed to the serene and splendid bust of the "Apollo"—"than to this 'counterfeit presentment,' of your former self."

Alwyn flushed,—not so much at the implied compliment, as at the words "FORMER SELF." But quickly shaking off his embarrassment, he glanced round at the "Apollo" and lifted his eyebrows incredulously.

"Then all I can say, my dear boy, is, that that eyeglass of yours represents objects to your own view in a classic light which is entirely deceptive, for I fail to trace the faintest similitude between my own features and that of the sunborn Lord of Laurels."

"Oh, YOU may not trace it," said Villiers calmly, "but nevertheless others will. Some people say that no man knows what he really is like, and that even his own reflection in the glass deceives him. Besides, it is not so much the actual contour for the features that impresses one, it is the LOOK,—you have the LOOK of the Greek god, the look of conscious power and inward happiness."

He spoke seriously, thoughtfully,—surveying his friend with a vague feeling of admiration akin to reverence.

Alwyn stooped, and stirred the fire into a brighter blaze. "Well, so far, my looks do not belie me," he said gently, after a pause. "I AM conscious of both power and joy!"

"Why, naturally!" and Villiers laid one hand affectionately on his shoulder. "Of course the face of the whole world has changed for you, now that you have won such tremendous fame!"

"FAME!"—Alwyn sprang upright so suddenly that Villiers was quite startled,—"Fame! Who says I am famous?" And his eyes flashed forth an amazed, almost haughty resentment.

His friend stared—then laughed outright.

"Who says it? . . . Why, all London says it. Do you mean to tell me, Alwyn, that you've not seen the English papers and magazines, containing all the critical reviews and discussions on your poem of Nourhalma?"

Alwyn winced at the title,—what a host of strange memories it recalled!

"I have seen nothing," he replied hurriedly, "I have made it a point to look at no papers, lest I should chance on my own name coupled, as it has been before, with the languid abuse common to criticism in this country. Not that I should have cared,—Now! . . ." and a slight smile played on his lips. "In fact I have ceased to care. Moreover, as I know modern success in literature is chiefly commanded by the praise of a 'clique,' or the services of 'log-rollers,' and as I am not included in any of the journalistic rings, I have neither hoped nor expected any particular favor or recognition from the public."

"Then," said Villiers excitedly, seizing him by the hand, "let me be the first to congratulate you! It is often the way that when we no longer specially crave a thing, that thing is suddenly thrust upon us whether we will or no,—and so it has happened in YOUR case. Learn, therefore, my dear fellow, that your poem, which you sent to me from Tiflis, and which was published under my supervision about four months ago, has already run through six editions, and is now in its seventh. Seven editions of a poem,—a POEM, mark you!—in four months, isn't bad, . . . moreover, the demand continues, and the long and the short of it is, that your name is actually at the present moment the most celebrated in all London,—in fact, you are very generally acknowledged the greatest poet of the day! And," continued Villiers, wringing his friend's hand with uncommon fervor. "I say, God bless you, old boy! If ever a man deserved success, YOU do! 'Nourhalma' is magnificent!—such a genius as yours will raise the literature of the age to a higher standard than it has known since the death of Adonais* You can't imagine how sincerely I rejoice at your triumph!"

Alwyn was silent,—he returned his companion's cordial hand-pressure almost unconsciously. He stood, leaning against the mantelpiece, and looking gravely down into the fire. His first emotion was one of repugnance,—of rejection, . . . what did he need of this will-o'-the-wisp called Fame, dancing again across his path,—this transitory torch of world-approval! Fame in London! . . . What was it, what COULD it be, compared to the brilliancy of the fame he had once enjoyed as Laureate of Al-Kyris! As this thought passed across his mind, he gave a quick interrogative glance at Villiers, who was observing him

---

* Keats.

with much wondering intentness, and his handsome face lighted with sudden laughter.

"Dear old boy!" he said, with a very tender inflection in his mellow, mirthful voice—"You are the best of good fellows, and I thank you heartily for your news, which, if it seems satisfactory to you, ought certainly to be satisfactory to me! But tell me frankly, if I am as famous as you say, how did I become so? . . . how was it worked up?"

"Worked up!" Villiers was completely taken back by the oddity of this question.

"Come!" continued Alwyn persuasively, his fine eyes sparkling with mischievous good-humor. "You can't make me believe that 'All England' took to me suddenly of its own accord,—it is not so romantic, so poetry-loving, so independent, or so generous as THAT! How was my 'celebrity' first started? If my book,—which has all the disadvantage of being a poem instead of a novel,—has so suddenly leaped into high favor and renown, why, then, some leading critic or other must have thought that I myself was dead!"

The whimsical merriment of his face seemed to reflect itself on that of Villiers.

"You're too quick-witted, Alwyn, positively you are!" he remonstrated with a frankly humorous smile. "But as it happens, you're perfectly right! Not ONE critic, but THREE,—three of our most influential men, too—thought you WERE dead!—and that 'Nourhalma' was a posthumous work of PERISHED GENIUS!"

XXXII

Zabastesism and Paulism

The delighted air of triumphant conviction with which Alwyn received this candid statement was irresistible, and Villiers's attempt at equanimity entirely gave way before it. He broke into a roar of laughter,—laughter in which his friend joined,—and for a minute or two the room rang with the echoes of their mutual mirth.

"It wasn't MY doing," said Villiers at last, when he could control himself a little,—"and even now I don't in the least know how the misconception arose! 'Nourhalma' was published, according to your instructions, as rapidly as it could be got through the press, and I had no preliminary 'puffs' or announcements of any kind circulated in the papers. I merely advertised it with a notable simplicity, thus: 'Nourhalma. A Love-Legend of the Past. A Poem. By Theos Alwyn.' That was all. Well, when it came out, copies of it were sent, according to custom, round to all the leading newspaper offices, and for about three weeks after its publication I saw not a word concerning it anywhere. Meanwhile I went on advertising. One day at the Constitutional Club, while glancing over the Parthenon, I suddenly spied in it a long review, occupying four columns, and headed 'A Wonder-Poem'; and just out of curiosity, I began to read it. I remember—in fact I shall never forget,—its opening sentence, . . . it was so original!" and he laughed again. "It commenced thus: 'It has been truly said that those whom the gods love die young!' and then on it went, dragging in memories of Chatterton and Shelley and Keats, till I found myself yawning and wondering what the deuce the writer was driving at. Presently, about the end of the second column, I came to the assertion that 'the posthumous poem of "Nourhalma" must be admitted as one of the most glorious productions in the English language.' This woke me up considerably, and I read on, groping my way through all sorts of wordy phrases and used-up arguments, till my mind gradually grasped the fact that the critic of the Parthenon had evidently never heard of Theos Alwyn before, and being astonished, and perhaps perplexed, by the original beauty and glowing style of 'Nourhalma,' had jumped, without warrant, to the conclusion that its author must be dead. The wind-up of his lengthy dissertation was, as far as I can recollect, as follows:

"'It is a thousand pities this gifted poet is no more. Splendid as the work of his youthful genius is, there is no doubt but that, had he lived, he would have endowed the world anew with an inheritance of thought worthy of the grandest master-minds.' Well, when I had fully realized the situation, I began to think to myself, Shall I enlighten this Sir Oracle of the Press, and tell him the 'DEAD' author he so enthusiastically eulogizes, is alive and well, or was so, at any rate, the last time I heard from him? I debated the question seriously, and, after much cogitation, decided to leave him, for the present, in ignorance. First of all, because critics like to consider themselves the wisest men in the world, and hate to be told anything,—secondly, because I rather enjoyed the fun. The publisher of 'Nourhalma'—a very excellent fellow—sent me the critique, and wrote asking me whether it was true that the author of the poem was really dead, and if not, whether he should contradict the report. I waited a bit before answering that letter, and while I waited two more critiques appeared in two of the most assertively pompous and dictatorial journals of the day, echoing the eulogies of the Parthenon, declaring 'this dead poet' worthy 'to rank with the highest of the Immortals,' and a number of other similar grandiose declarations. One reviewer took an infinite deal of pains to prove 'that if the genius of Theos Alwyn had only been spared to England, he must have infallibly been elected Poet Laureate as soon as the post became vacant, and that too, without a single dissentient voice, save such as were raised in envy or malice. But, being dead'—continued this estimable scribe—'all we can say is that he yet speaketh, and that "Nourhalma" is a poem of which the literary world cannot be otherwise than justly proud. Let the tears that we shed for this gifted singer's untimely decease be mingled with gratitude for the priceless value of the work his creative genius has bequeathed to us!'"

Here Villiers paused, his blue eyes sparkling with inward amusement, and looked at Alwyn, whose face, though perfectly serene, had now the faintest, softest shadow of a grave pathos hovering about it.

"By this time," he continued. "I thought we had had about enough sport, so I wrote off to the publisher to at once contradict the erroneous rumor. But now that publisher had HIS story to tell. He called upon me, and with a blandly persuasive air, said, that as 'Nourhalma' was having an extraordinary sale, was it worth while to deny the statement of your death just yet? . . . He was very anxious, . . . but I was firm, . . . and lest he should waver, I wrote several letters myself to the leading journals, to establish the certainty, so far as I was aware, of your being in the land of the living. And then what do you think happened?"

Alwyn met his bright, satirical glance with a look that was half-questioning, half-wistful, but said nothing.

"It was the most laughable, and at the same time the most beautifully instructive, lesson ever taught by the whole annals of journalism! The Press turned round like a weathercock with the wind, and exhausted every epithet of abuse they could find in the dictionaries. 'Nourhalma' was a 'poor, ill-conceived work,'—'an outrage to intellectual perception,'—'a good idea, spoilt in the treatment; an amazingly obscure attempt at sublimity'—et cetera, . . . but there! you can yourself peruse all the criticisms, both favorable and adverse, for I have acted the part of the fond granny to you in the careful cutting out and pasting of everything I could find written concerning you and your work in a book devoted to the purpose, . . . and I believe I've missed nothing. Mark you, however, the Parthenon never reversed its judgment, nor did the other two leading journals of literary opinion,—it wouldn't do for such bigwigs to confess they had blundered, you know! . . . and the vituperation of the smaller fry was just the other weight in the balance which made the thing equal. The sale of 'Nourhalma' grew fast and furious; all expenses were cleared three times over, and at the present moment the publisher is getting conscientiously anxious (for some publishers are more conscientious than some authors will admit!) to hand you over a nice little check for an amount which is not to be despised in this workaday world, I assure you!"

"I did not write for money,"—interrupted Alwyn quietly. "Nor shall I ever do so."

"Of course not," assented Villiers promptly. "No poet, and indeed no author whatsoever, who lays claim to a fraction of conscience, writes for money ONLY. Those with whom money is the first consideration debase their Art into a coarse huckstering trade, and are no better than contentious bakers and cheesemongers, who jostle each other in a vulgar struggle as to which shall sell perishable goods at the highest profit. None of the lasting works of the world were written so. Nevertheless, if the public voluntarily choose to lavish what they can of their best on the author who imparts to them inspired thoughts and noble teachings, then that author must not be churlish, or slow to accept the gratitude implied. I think the most appropriate maxim for a poet to address to his readers is, 'Freely ye have received, freely give.'"

There was a moment's silence. Alwyn resumed his seat in the chair near the fire, and Villiers, leaning one arm on the mantelpiece, still stood, looking down upon him.

"Such, my dear fellow," he went on complacently. . . "is the history of the success of 'Nourhalma.' It certainly began with the belief that you were no longer able to benefit by the eulogy received.—but all the same that eulogy has been uttered and cannot be UNuttered. It has led all the lovers of the highest literature to get the book for themselves, and to prove your actual worth, independently of press opinions,—and the result is an immense and steadily widening verdict in your favor. Speaking personally, I have never read anything that gave me quite so much artistic pleasure as this poem of yours except 'Hyperion,'—only 'Hyperion' is distinctly classical, while 'Nourhalma' takes us back into some hitherto unexplored world of antique paganism, which, though essentially pagan, is wonderfully full of pure and lofty sentiment. When did the idea first strike you?"

"A long time ago!" returned Alwyn with a slight, serious smile—"I assure you it is by no means original!"

Villiers gave him a quick, surprised glance.

"No? Well, it seems to me singularly original!" he said. "In fact, one of your critics says you are Too original! Mind you, Alwyn, that is a very serious fault in this imitative age!"

Alwyn laughed a little. His thoughts were very busy. Again in imagination he beheld the burning "Temple of Nagaya" in his Dream of Al-Kyris,—again he saw himself carrying the corpse of his FORMER Self through fire and flame,—and again he heard the last words of the dying Zabastes—"I was the Poet's adverse Critic, and who but I should write his Eulogy? Save me, if only for the sake of Sah-luma's future honor!—thou knowest not how warmly, how generously, how nobly, I can praise the dead!"

True! . . . How easy to praise the poor, deaf, stirless clay when sense and spirit have fled from it forever! No fear to spoil a corpse by flattery,— the heavily sealed-up eyes can never more unclose to lighten with glad hope or fond ambition; the quiet heart cannot leap with gratitude or joy at that "word spoken in due season" which aids its noblest aspirations to become realized! The DEAD poet?—Press the cold clods of earth over him, and then rant above his grave,—tell him how great he was,

MARIE CORELLI

what infinite possibilities were displayed in his work, what excellence, what merit, what subtlety of thought, what grace of style! Rant and rave!—print reams of acclaiming verbosity, pronounce orations, raise up statues, mark the house he lived and starved in, with a laudatory medallion, and print his once-rejected stanzas in every sort of type and fashion, from the cheap to the costly,—teach the multitude how worthy he was to be loved, and honored,—and never fear that he will move from his rigid and chill repose to be happy for once in his life, and to learn with amazement that the world he toiled so patiently for is actually learning to be grateful for his existence! Once dead and buried he can be safely made glorious,—he cannot affront us either with his superior intelligence, or make us envy the splendors of his fame!

Some such thoughts as these passed through Alwyn's mind as he dreamily gazed into the red hollows of the fire, and reconsidered all that his friend had told him. He had no personal acquaintances on the press,—no literary club or clique to haul him up into the top-gallant mast of renown by persistent puffery; he was not related, even distantly, to any great personage, either statesman, professor, or divine—he had not the mysterious recommendation of being a "university man"; none of the many "wheels" within wheels which are nowadays so frequently set in motion to make up a momentary literary furore, were his to command,—and yet—the Parthenon had praised him! . . . Wonder of wonders! The Parthenon was a singularly obtuse journal, which glanced at the whole world of letters merely through the eyes of three or four men of distinctly narrow and egotistical opinions, and these three or four men kept it as much as possible to themselves, using its columns chiefly for the purpose of admiring one another. As a consequence of this restricted arrangement, very few outsiders could expect to be noticed for their work, unless they were in the "set," or at least had occasionally dined with one of the mystic Three or Four, . . . and so it had chanced that Alwyn's first venture into literature had been totally disregarded by the Parthenon. In fact, that first venture, being a small and unobtrusive book, had, most probably, been thrown into the waste-paper basket, or sold for a few pence to the second-hand dealer. And now,—now because he had been imagined DEAD,—the Parthenon's leading critic had singled him out and held him up for universal admiration!

Well, well! . . . after all, Nourhalma WAS a posthumous work,—it had been written before, ages since, when he, as Sah-luma, had perished ere he had had time to give it to the world! He had merely REMEMBERED it. . . drawn it forth again, as it were, from the dim, deep vistas of past deeds;—so those who had reviewed it as the production of one dead in youth, were right in their judgment, though they did not know it! . . . It was old,—nothing but repetition,—but now he had something new and true and passionate to say, . . . something that, if God pleased, it should be his to utter with the clearness and forcibleness common to the Greek thunderers of yore, who spoke out what was in them, grandly, simply, and with the fearless majesty of thought that reeked nothing of opinions. Oh, he would rouse the hearts of men from paltry greed and covetousness, . . . from lust, and hatred, and all things evil,—no matter if he lost his own life in the effort, he would still do his utmost best to lift, if only in a small degree, the deepening weight of self-wrought agony from self-blinded mankind! Yes! . . . he must work to fulfil the commands and deserve the blessings of Edris!

Edris! . . . ah, the memory of her pure angel-loveliness rushed upon him like a flood of invigorating warmth and light, and when he looked up from his brief reverie, his countenance, beautiful, and kindling with inward ardor, affected Villiers strangely,—almost as a very grand and perfect strain of music might affect and unsteady one's nerves. The attraction he had always felt for his poet-friend deepened to quite a fervent intensity of admiration, but he was not the man to betray his feelings outwardly, and to shake off his emotion he rushed into speech again.

"By the by, Alwyn, your old acquaintance, Professor Moxall, is very much 'down' on your book. You know he doesn't write reviews, except on matters connected with evolutionary phenomena, but I met him the other day, and he was quite upset about you. 'Too transcendental'! he said, dismally shaking his bald pate to and fro—'The whole poem is a vaporous tissue of absurd impossibilities! Ah dear, dear me! what a terrible falling-off in a young man of such hopeful ability! I thought he had done with poetry forever!—I took the greatest pains to prove to him what a ridiculous pastime it was, and how unworthy to be considered for a moment seriously as an ART,—and he seemed to understand my reasoning thoroughly. Indeed he promised to be one of our most powerful adherents, . . . he had an excellent grasp of the material sciences, and a fine contempt for religion. Why, with such a quick, analytical brain as his, he might have carried on Darwin's researches to an extremer point of the origination of species than has yet been reached! All a ruin, sir! a positive ruin,—a man who will in cold blood write such lines as these. . .

"'Grander is Death than Life, and sweeter far The splendors of the Infinite Future, than our eyes, Weary with tearful watching, yet can see"—

condemns himself as a positive lunatic! And young Alwyn too!— he who had so completely recognized the foolishness and futility of expecting any other life than this one! Good heavens! . . . "Nourhalma," as I understand it, is a sort of pagan poem—but with such incredible ideas and sentiments as are expressed in it, the author might as well go and be a Christian at once!' And with that he hobbled off, for it was Sunday afternoon, and he was on his way to St. George's Hall to delight the assembled skeptics, by telling them in an elaborate lecture what absurd animalculae they all were!"

Alwyn smiled. There was a soft light in his eyes, an expression of serene contentment on his face.

"Poor old Moxall!" he said gently—"I am sorry for him! He makes life very desolate, both for himself and others who accept his theories. I'm afraid his disappointment in me will have to continue, . . . for as it happens I Am a Christian,—that is, so far as I can, in my unworthiness, be a follower of a faith so grand, and pure, and True!"

Villiers started, . . . his month opened in sheer astonishment, . . . he could scarcely believe his own ears, and he uttered some sound between a gasp and an exclamation of incredulity. Alwyn met his widely wondering gaze with a most sweet and unembarrassed calm.

"How amazed you look!" he observed, half playfully,—"Religion must be at a very low ebb, if in a so-called Christian country you are surprised to hear a man openly acknowledge himself a disciple of the Christian creed!"

There was a brief pause, during which the chiming clock rang out the hour musically on the stillness. Then Villiers, still in a state of most profound bewilderment, sat down deliberately in a chair opposite Alwyn's, and placed one hand familiarly on his knee.

"Look here, old fellow," he said impressively, "do you really Mean it! . . . Are you 'going over' to some Church or other?"

Alwyn laughed—his friend's anxiety was so genuine.

"Not I!"—he responded promptly. "Don't be alarmed, Villiers,—I am not a 'convert' to any particular set Form of faith,—what I care for is the faith itself. One can follow and serve Christ without any church dogma.

He has Himself told us plainly, in words simple enough for a child to understand, what He would have us to do, . . . and though I, like many others, must regret the absence of a true Universal Church where the servants of Christ may meet altogether without a shadow of difference in opinion, and worship Him as He should be worshipped, still that is no reason why I should refrain from endeavoring to fulfil, as far as in me lies, my personal duty toward Him. The fact is, Christianity has never yet been rightly taught, grasped or comprehended,—moreover, as long as men seek through it their own worldly advantage, it never will be,— so that the majority of the people are really as yet ignorant of its true spiritual meaning, thanks to the quarrels and differences of sects and preachers. But, notwithstanding the unhappy position of religion at the present day, I repeat, I am a Christian, if love for Christ, and implicit belief in Him, can make me so."

He spoke simply, and without the slightest affectation of reserve. Villiers was still puzzled.

"I thought, Alwyn," he ventured to say presently with some little diffidence,—"that you entirely rejected the idea of Christ's Divinity, as a mere superstition?"

"In dense ignorance of the extent of God's possibilities, I certainly did so," returned Alwyn quietly,—"But I have had good reason to see that my own inability to comprehend supernatural causes was entirely to blame for that rejection. Are we able to explain all the numerous and complex variations and manifestations of Matter? No. Then why do we dare to doubt the certainly conceivable variations and manifestations of Spirit? . . . The doctrine of a purely HUMAN Christ is untenable,—a Creed founded on that idea alone would make no way with the immortal aspirations of the soul, . . . what link could there be between a mere man like ourselves and heaven? None whatever,—it needs the DIVINE in Christ to overleap the darkness of the grave, . . . to serve us as the Symbol of certain Resurrection, to teach us that this life is not the ALL, but only ONE loop in the chain of existence, . . . only ONE of the 'many mansions' in the Father's House. Human teachers of high morals there have always been in the world,—Confucius, Buddha, Zoroaster, Socrates, Plato, . . . there is no end to them, and their teachings have been valuable so far as they went, but even Plato's majestic arguments in favor of the Immortality of the Soul fall short of anything sure and graspable. There were so many prefigurements of what WAS to come, . . . just as the sign of the Cross was used in the Temple of Serapis, and was held in singular mystic veneration by various tribes of Egyptians, Arabians, and Indians, ages before Christ came. And now that these prefigurements have resolved themselves into an actual Divine Symbol, the doubting world still hesitates, and by this hesitation paralyzes both its Will and Instinct—so that it fails to cut out the core of Christianity's true solution, or to learn what Christ really meant when He said 'I am the Way, the Truth, and the Life,—no man cometh to the Father but by Me.' Have you ever considered the particular weight of that word 'MAN' in that text? It is rightly specified that 'no MAN cometh'—for there are hosts of other beings, in other universes, who are not of our puny race, and who do not need to be taught either the way, truth, or life, as they know all three, and have never lost their knowledge from the beginning."

His voice quivered a little, and he paused,—Villiers watched him with a strange sense of ever-deepening fascination and wonder.

"I have lately studied the whole thing carefully," . . . he resumed presently, . . . "and I see no reason why we, who call ourselves a progressive generation, should revert back to the old theory of Corinthus, who, as early as sixty-seven years after Christ, denied His Divinity. There is nothing new in the hypothesis—it is no more original than the doctrine of evolution, which was skilfully enough handled by Democritus, and probably by many another before him. Voltaire certainly threshed out the subject exhaustively, . . . and I think Carlyle's address to him on the uselessness of his work is one of the finest of its kind. Do you remember it?"

Villiers shook his head in the negative, whereupon Alwyn rose, and glancing along an evidently well-remembered book-shelf, took from thence "Sartor Resartus"—and turned over the pages quickly.

"Here it is,"—and he read out the following passage. "'Cease, my much-respected Herr von Voltaire, . . . shut thy sweet voice; for the task appointed thee seems finished. Sufficiently hast thou demonstrated this proposition, considerable or otherwise: That the Mythus of the Christian Religion looks not in the eighteenth century as it did in the eighth. Alas, were thy six-and-thirty quartos, and the six-and-thirty thousand other quartos and folios and flying sheets or reams, printed before and since on the same subject, all needed to convince us of so little! But what next? Wilt thou help us to embody the Divine Spirit of that Religion in a new Mythus, in a new vehicle and vesture, that our Souls, otherwise too like perishing, may live? What! thou hast no faculty in that kind? Only a torch for burning and no hammer for building? Take our thanks then—and thyself away!'"

Villiers smiled, and straightened himself in military fashion, as was his habit when particularly gratified.

"Excellent old Teufelsdrockh!" he murmured sotto-voce—"He had a rugged method of explaining himself, but it was decisive enough, in all conscience!"

"Decisive, and to the point," . . . assented Alwyn, putting the book back in its place, and then confronting his friend.—"And he states precisely what is wanted by the world to-day,—wanted pressingly, eagerly, . . . namely that the 'Divine Spirit' of the Christian Religion should be set forth in a 'new vehicle and vesture' to keep pace with the advancing inquiry and scientific research of man. And truly for this, it need only be expounded according to its old, pure, primal, spiritual intention, and then, the more science progresses the more true will it be proved. Christ distinctly claimed His Divinity, and everywhere gave manifestations of it. Of course it can be said that these manifestations rest on Testimony,—and that the 'testimony' was drawn up afterward and is a spurious invention—but we have no more proof that it Is spurious than we have of* Homer's Iliad being a compilation of several writers and not the work of a Homer at all. Nothing—not even the events of the past week—can be safely rested on absolute, undiffering testimony, inasmuch as no two narrators tell the same story alike. But all the same we Have the Iliad,—it cannot be taken from us by any amount of argument, . . . and we have the Fruits of Christ's gospel, half obscured as it is, visible among us. Everywhere civilization of a high and aspiring order has followed Christianity even at the cost of blood and tears, . . . slavery has been abolished, and women lifted from unspeakable degradation to honor and reverence,—and had men been more reasonable and self-controlled, the purifying work would have been done peacefully and without persecution. It was St. Paul's preaching that upset all the beautiful, pristine simplicity of the faith,—it is very evident he had no 'calling or election' such as he pretended, . . . I wonder Jeremy Bentham's conclusive book on the subject is not more universally known. Paul's sermonizing gave rise to a thousand different shades of opinion and argument,—and for a mere hair's-breadth of needless discussion, nation has fought against nation, and man against

---

* See Chapter XIII. "In Al-Kyris"—the allusion to "Oruzel."

MARIE CORELLI

man, till the very name of religion has been made a ghastly mockery. That, however, is not the fault of Christianity, but the fault of those who PROFESS to follow it, like Paul, while merely following a scheme of their own personal advantage or convenience, . . . and the result of it all is that at this very moment, there is not a church in Christendom where Christ's actual commands are really and to the letter fulfilled."

"Strong!" exclaimed Villiers with a slight smile. "Mustn't say that before a clergyman!"

"Why not?" demanded Alwyn. "Why should not clerics be told, once and for all, how ill they perform their sacred mission? Look at the wilderness of spreading Atheism to-day! . . . and look at the multitudes of men and women who are hungering and thirsting for a greater comprehension of spiritual things than they have hitherto had!—and yet the preachers trudge drowsily on in the old ruts they have made for themselves, and give neither sympathy nor heed to the increasing pain, feverish bewilderment, and positive WANT of those they profess to guide. Concerning science, too, what is the good of telling a toiling, more or less suffering race, that there are eighteen millions of suns in the Milky Way, and that viewed by the immensity of the Universe, man is nothing but a small, mean, and perishable insect? Humanity hears the statement with dull, perplexed brain, and its weight of sorrow is doubled,—it demands at once, why, if an insect, its insect life should BE at all, if nothing is to come of it but weariness and woe? The marvels of scientific discovery offer no solace to the huge Majority of the Afflicted, unless we point the lesson that the Soul of Man is destined to live through more than these wonders; and that the millions of planetary systems in the Milky Way are but the ALPHA BETA of the sublime Hereafter which is our natural heritage, if we will but set ourselves earnestly to win it. Moreover, we should not foolishly imagine that we are to lead good lives MERELY for the sake of some suggested reward or wages,—no,—but simply because in practising progressive good we are equalizing ourselves and placing ourselves in active working harmony with the whole progressive good of the Creator's plan. We have no more right to do a deliberately evil thing, than a musician has a right to spoil a melody by a false note on his instrument. Why should we willfully JAR God's music, of which we are a part? I tell you that religion, as taught to-day, is rather one of custom and fear than love and confidence,—men cower and propitiate, when they should be full of thankfulness and praise,—and as for any reserve on these matters, I have none,—in fact, I fail to see why truth, . . . spiritual truth, . . . should not be openly proclaimed now, even as it is sure to be proclaimed hereafter."

His manner had warmed with his words, and he lifted his head with an involuntary gesture of eloquent resolve, his eyes flashing splendid scorn for all things hypocritical and mean. Villiers looked at him, feeling curiously moved and impressed by his fervent earnestness.

"Well, I was right in one thing, at any rate, Alwyn"—he said softly. . . "you ARE changed,—there's not a doubt about it! But it seems to me the change is distinctly for the better. It does my heart good to hear you speak with such distinct and manly emphasis on a subject, which, though it is one of the burning questions of the day, is too often treated irreverently, or altogether dismissed with a few sentences of languid banter or cheap sarcasm."

"As regards myself personally, I must say that a man without faith in anything but himself, has always seemed to me exactly in keeping with the description given of an atheist by Lady Ashburton to Carlyle,— namely 'a person who robs himself, not only of clothes, but of flesh as well, and walks about the world in his bones.' And, oddly enough in spite of all the controversies going on about Christianity, I have always really worshipped Christ in my heart of hearts, . . . and yet. . . I CAN'T go to church! I seem to lose the idea of Him altogether there: . . . but" . . . and his frank face took upon itself a dreamy light of deep feeling—"there are times when, walking alone in the fields, or through a very quiet grove of trees, or on the sea-shore, I begin to think of His majestic life and death, and the immense, unfailing sympathy He showed for every sort of human suffering, and then I can really believe in him as Divine friend, comrade, Teacher, and King, and I am scarcely able to decide which is the deepest emotion in my mind toward Him— love, or reverence."

He paused,—Alwyn's eyes rested upon him with a quick, comprehensive friendliness,—in one exchange of looks the two men became mutually aware of the strong undercurrents of thought that lay beneath each other's individual surface history, and that perhaps had never been so clearly recognized before,—and a kind of swift, speechless, satisfactory agreement between their two separate natures seemed suddenly drawn up, ratified, and sealed in a glance.

"I have often thought," continued Villiers more lightly, and smiling as he spoke—"that we are all angels or devils,—angels in our best moments, devils in our worst. If we could only keep the best moments always uppermost! 'Ah, poor deluded human nature!' as old Moxall says,—while in the same breath he contradicts himself by asserting that human Reason is the only infallible means of ascertaining anything! How it can be 'deluded' and 'infallible' at the same time, I can't quite understand! But, Alwyn, you haven't told me how you like the 'get-up' of your book?"

And he handed the volume in question to its author, who turned it over with the most curious air of careless recognition—in his fancy he again saw Zabastes writing each line of it down to Sah-luma's dictation!

"It's very well printed"—he said at last,—"and very tastefully bound. You have superintended the work con amore, Villiers, . . . and I am as obliged to you as friendship will let me be. You know what that means?"

"It means no obligation at all"—declared Villiers gayly. . . "because friends who are the least worthy the name take delight in furthering each other's interests and have no need to be thanked for doing what is particularly agreeable to them. You really like the appearance of it, then? But you've got the sixth edition. This is the first."

And he took up from a side-table a quaint small quarto, bound is a very superb imitation of old embossed leather, which Alwyn, beholding, was at once struck by the resemblance it bore to the elaborate designs that had adorned the covers of the papyrus volumes possessed by his Shadow-Self, Sahluma!

"This is very sumptuous!" he said with a dreamy smile—"It looks quite antique!"

"Doesn't it!" exclaimed Villiers, delighted—"I had it copied from a first edition of Petrarca which happens to be in my collection. This specimen of 'Nourhalma' has become valuable and unique. It was published at ten-and-six, and can't be got anywhere under five or six guineas, if for that. Of course a copy of each edition has been set aside for You."

Alwyn laid down the book with a gentle indifference.

"My dear fellow, I've had enough of 'Nourhalma,'" . . . he said. . ."I'll keep a copy of the first edition, if only as a souvenir of your good-will and energy in bringing it out so admirably—but for the rest! . . . the book belongs to me no more, but to the public,—and so let the public do with it what they will!"

Villiers raised his eyebrows perplexedly.

"I believe, after all, Alwyn, you don't really care for your fame!"

"Not in the least!" replied Alwyn, laughing. "Why should I?"

"You longed for it once as the utmost good!"

"True!—but there are other utmost goods, my friend, that I desire more keenly."

"But are they attainable?"—queried Villiers. "Men, and specially poets, often hanker after what is not possible to secure."

"Granted!" responded Alwyn cheerfully—"But I do not crave for the impossible. I only seek to recover what I have lost."

"And that is?"

"What most men have lost, or are insanely doing their best to lose"—said Alwyn meditatively. "A grasp of things eternal, through the veil of things temporal."

There was a short silence, during which Villiers eyed his friend wistfully.

"What was that 'adventure' you spoke about in your letter from the Monastery on the Pass of Dariel?" he asked after a while—"You said you were on the search for a new sensation-did you experience it?"

Alwyn smiled. "I certainly Dɪᴅ!"

"Did it arise from a contemplation of the site of the Ruins of Babylon?"

"Not exactly. Babylon,—or rather the earth-mounds which are now called Babylon,—had very little to do with it."

"Don't you want to tell me about it?" demanded Tilliers abruptly.

"Not just yet"—answered Alwyn, with good-humored frankness,—"Not to-night, at any rate! But I Wɪʟʟ tell you, never fear! For the present we've talked enough, . . . don't you think bed suggests itself as a fitting conclusion to our converse?"

Villiers laughed and acquiesced, and after pressing his friend to partake of something in the way of supper, which refreshment was declined, he preceded him to a small, pleasantly cosy room,—his "guest-chamber" as he called it, but which was really almost exclusively set apart for Alwyn's use alone, and was always in readiness for him whenever he chose to occupy it. Turning on the pretty electric lamp that lit the whole apartment with a soft and shaded lustre, Villiers shook hands heartily with his old school-fellow and favorite comrade, and bidding him a brief but cordial good-night left him to repose.

As soon as he was alone Alwyn took out from his breast pocket a small velvet letter-case, from which he gently drew forth a slightly pressed but unfaded white flower. Setting this in a glass of water he placed it near his bed, and watched it for a moment. Delicately and gradually its pressed petals expanded, . . . its golden corolla brightened in hue, . . . a subtle, sweet odor permeated the air, . . . and soon the angelic "immortelle" of the Field of Ardath shone wondrously as a white star in the quiet room. And when the lamp was extinguished and the poet slept, that strange, fair blossom seemed to watch him like a soft, luminous eye in the darkness,—a symbol of things divine and lasting,—a token of far and brilliant worlds where even flowers cannot fade!

XXXIII

Realism

At the end of about a week or so, it became very generally known among the mystic "Upper Ten" of artistic and literary circles, that Theos Alwyn, the famous author of "Nourhalma" was, to put it fashionably, "in town." According to the classic phrasing of a leading society journal, "Mr. Theos Alwyn, the poet, whom some of our contemporaries erroneously reported as dead, has arrived in London from his tour in the East. He is for the present a guest of the Honorable Francis Villiers." The consequence of this and other similar announcements was, that the postman seemed never to be away from Villiers's door; and every time he came he was laden with letters and cards of invitation, addressed, for the most part, to Villiers himself, who, with something of dismay, saw his study table getting gradually covered with accumulating piles of society litter, such as is comprised in the various formal notifications of dinners, dances, balls, soirees, "at homes," and all the divers sorts of entertainment with which the English "s'amusent moult tristement." Some of these invitations, less ceremonious, were in form of pretty little notes from great ladies, who entreated their "Dear Mr. Villiers" to give them the "Extreme honor and pleasure" of his company at certain select and extra brilliant receptions where Royalty itself would be represented, adding, as an earnest postscript—"and Do bring the Lion, you know, your Very interesting friend, Mr. Alwyn, with you!"—A good many such billets-doux were addressed to Alwyn personally, and as he opened and read them he was somewhat amused to see how many who had formerly been mere bowing acquaintances were now suddenly, almost magically, transformed into apparently eager, admiring, and devoted friends.

"One would think these people really liked me for myself,"—he said one morning, tossing aside a particularly gushing, pressing note from a lady who was celebrated for the motley crowds she managed to squeeze into her rooms, regardless of any one's comfort or convenience,—"And yet, as the matter stands, they actually know nothing of me. I might be a villain of the deepest dye, a kickable cad, or a coarse ruffian, but so long as I have written a 'successful' book and am a 'somebody'—a literary 'notable'—what matter my tastes, my morals, or my disposition! If this sort of thing is Fame, all I can say is, that it savors of very detestable vulgarity!"

"Of course it does!"—assented Villiers-"But what else do you expect from modern society? . . . What CAN you expect from a community which is chiefly ruled by moneyed parvenus, BUT vulgarity? If you go to this woman's place, for instance"—and he glanced at the note Alwyn had thrown on the table,—"you will share the honors of the evening with the famous man-milliner of Bond Street, an 'artist' in gowns, the female upholsterer and house decorator, likewise an 'artist,'—the ladies who 'compose' sonnets in Regent Street, also 'artists,—' and chiefest among the motley crowd, perhaps, the so-called new 'Apostle' of aestheticism, a ponderous gentleman who says nothing and does nothing, and who, by reason of his stupendous inertia and taciturnity, is considered the greatest 'gun' of all! . . . it's no use YOUR going among such people,—in fact, no one who has any reverence left in him for the TRUTH of Art CAN mix with those whose profession of it is a mere trade and hypocritical sham. Such dunderheads would see no artistic difference between Phidias and the man of to-day who hews out and sets up a common marble mantel-piece! I'm not a fellow to moan over the 'good old times,'—no, not a bit of it, for those good old times had much in them that was decidedly bad,—but I wish progress would not rob us altogether of refinement."

"But society professes to be growing more and more cultured every day," observed Alwyn.

"Oh, it PROFESSES! . . . yes, that's just the mischief of it. Its professions are not worth a groat. It PROFESSES to be one thing while anybody with eyes can see that it actually is another! The old style of aristocrat and gentleman is dying out,—the new style is the horsey lord, the betting Duke, the coal-dealing Earl, the stock-broking Viscount! Trade is a very excellent thing,—a very necessary and important thing,— but its influence is distinctly NOT refining. I have the greatest respect for my cheesemonger, for instance (and he has an equal respect for me, since he has found that I know the difference between real butter and butterine), but all the same I don't want to see him in Parliament. I am arrogant enough to believe that I, even I, having studied somewhat, know more about the country's interest than he does. I view it by the light of ancient and modern historical evidence,—he views it according to the demand it makes on his cheese. We may both be narrow and limited in judgment,—nevertheless, I think, with all due modesty, that His judgment is likely to be more limited than mine. But it's no good talking about it,—this dear old land is given up to a sort of ignorant democracy, which only needs time to become anarchy, . . . and we haven't got a strong man among us who dares speak out the truth of the inevitable disasters looming above us all. And society is not only vulgar, but demoralized,—moreover, what is worse is, that, aided by its preachers and teachers, it is sinking into deeper depths of demoralization with every passing month and year of time."

Alwyn leaned hack in his chair thoughtfully, a sorrowful expression clouding his face.

"Surely things are not so bad as they seem, Villiers,"—he said gently—"Are you not taking a pessimistic view of affairs?"

"Not at all!" and Villiers, warming with his subject, walked up and down the room excitedly. . . "Nor am I judging by the narrow observation of any particular 'set' or circle. I look at the expressive visible outcome of the whole,—the plainly manifest signs of the threatening future. Of course there are ever so many good people,—earnest people,—thinking people,—but they are a mere handful compared to the overpowering millions opposed to them, and whose motto is 'Evil, be thou my good.' Now you, for instance, are full of splendid ideas, and lucid plans of check and reform,—you are seized with a passionate desire to do something great for the world, and you are ready to speak the truth fearlessly on all occasions. But just think of the enormous task it would be to stir to even half an inch of aspiring nobleness, the frightful mass of corruption in London to-day! In all trades and professions it is the same story,— everything is a question of Gain. To begin with, look at the Church, the 'Pillar of the State!' There, all sorts of worthless, incompetent men are hastily thrust into livings by wealthy patrons who care not a jot as to whether they are morally or intellectually fit for their sacred mission,— and a disgraceful universal muddle is the result. From this muddle, which resembles a sort of stagnant pool, emerge the strangest fungus-growths,—clergymen who take to acting a 'miracle-play,' ostensibly for the purposes of charity, but really to gratify their own tastes and leanings toward the mummer's art,—all the time utterly regardless of the effect their behavior is likely to have on the minds of the unthinking populace, who are led by the newspapers, and who read therein bantering inquiries as to whether the Church is coquetting with the Stage? whether the two are likely to become one? and whether Religion will in the future

MARIE CORELLI

occupy no more serious consideration than the Drama? What is one to think, when one sees clerical notabilities seated in the stalls of a theatre complacently looking on at the representation of a 'society play' degrading in plot, repulsive in detail, and in nearly every case having to do with a married woman who indulges in a lover as a matter of course,—a play full of ambiguous side hits and equivocal jests, which, if the men of the Church were staunch to their vocation, they would be the first to condemn. Why, I saw the other day, in a fairly reliable journal, that some of these excellent 'divines' were going to start 'smoking sermons'—a sort of imitation of smoking concerts, I suppose, which are vile enough, in all conscience,—but to mix up religious matters with the selfish 'smoke mania' is viler still. I say that any clergyman who will allow men to smoke in his presence, while he is preaching sacred doctrine, is a coarse cad, and ought to be hounded out of the Church!"

He paused, his face flushing with vigorous, righteous wrath. Alwyn's eyes grew dark with an infinite pain. His thoughts always fled back to his Dream of Al-Kyris, with a tendency to draw comparisons between the Past and the Present. The religion of that long-buried city had been mere mummery and splendid outward show,—what was the religion of London? He moved restlessly.

"How all the warnings of history repeat themselves!" he said suddenly. "An age of mockery, sham sentiment, and irreverence has always preceded a downfall,—can it be possible that we are already receiving hints of the downfall of England?"

"Aye, not only of England, but of a good many other nations besides," said Villiers—"or if not actual downfall, change and terrific upheaval. France and England particularly are the prey of the Demon of Realism,—and all the writers who SHOULD use their pens to inspire and elevate the people, assist in degrading them. When their books are not obscene, they are blasphemous. Russia, too, joins in the cry of Realism!— Realism! . . . Let us have the filth of the gutters, the scourgings of dustholes, the corruption of graves, the odors of malaria, the howlings of drunkards, the revellings of sensualists, . . . the worst side of the world in its vilest aspect, which is the only REAL aspect of those who are voluntarily vile! Let us see to what a reeking depth of unutterable shameless brutality man can fall if he chooses—not as formerly, when it was shown to what glorious heights of noble supremacy he could rise! For in this age, the heights are called 'transcendental folly'—and the reeking depths are called Realism!"

"And yet what Is Realism really?" queried Alwyn.—"Does anybody know? . . . It is supposed to be the actuality of everyday existence, without any touch of romance or pathos to soften its frequently hideous Commonplace; but the fact is, the Commonplace is not the Real. The highest flights of imagination in the human being fail to grasp the Reality of the splendors everywhere surrounding him,—and, viewed rightly, Realism would become Romance and Romance Realism. We see a ragged woman in the streets picking up scraps for her daily food, . . . that is what we may call realistic,—but we are not looking at the ACTUAL woman, after all! We cannot see her Inner Self, or form any certain comprehension of the possible romance or tragedy which that Inner Self HAS experienced, or Is experiencing. We see the outer Appearance of the woman, but what of that? . . . The REALISM of the suffering creature's hidden history lies beyond us,—so far beyond us that it is called ROMANCE, because it seems so impossible to fathom or understand."

"True, most absolutely true!" said Villiers emphatically—"But it is a truth you will get very few to admit! . . . Everything to-day is in a state of substantiality and sham;—we have even sham Realism, as well as sham sentiment, sham religion, sham art, sham morality. We have a Parliament that sits and jabbers lengthy platitudes that lead to nothing, while Army and Navy are slowly slipping into a state of helpless desuetude, and the mutterings of discontented millions are almost unregarded; the spectre of Revolution, assuming somewhat of the shape in which it appalled the French in 1789, is dimly approaching in the distance, . . . even our London County Council hears the far-off, faint shadow of a very prosaic resemblance to the National Assembly of that era, . . . and our weak efforts to cure cureless grievances, and to deafen our ears to crying evils, are very similar to the clumsy attempts made by Louis XVI and his partisans to botch up a terribly bad business. Oh, the people, the people! . . . They are unquestionably the flesh, blood, bone, and sinew of the country,—and the English people, say what sneerers will to the contrary, are a GOOD people,—patient, plodding, forbearing, strong, and, on the whole, most equable-tempered,—but their teachers teach them wrongly, and confuse their brains instead of clearing them, and throw a weight of Compulsory Education at their heads, without caring how they may use it, or how such a blow from the clenched fist of Knowledge may stupefy and bewilder them, . . . and the consequence is that now, were a strong man to arise, with a lucid

MARIE CORELLI

brain, an eloquent power of expressing truth, a great sympathy with his kind, and an immense indifference to his own fate in the contest, he could lead this vast, waiting, wandering, growling, hydra-headed London wheresoever he would!"

"What an orator you are, Villiers!" . . . said Alwyn, with a half-smile. "I never heard you come out so strongly before!"

"My dear fellow," replied Villiers, in a calmer tone—"it's enough to make any man with warm blood in his veins FEEL! Everywhere signs of weakness, cowardice, compromise, hesitation, vacillation, incompetency, and everywhere, in thoughtful minds, the keen sense of a Fate advancing like the giant in the seven-leagued boots, at huge strides every day. The ponderous Law and the solid Police hem us in on each side, as though the nation were a helpless infant, toddling between two portly nurses,— we dare not denounce a scoundrel and liar, but must needs put up with him, lest we should be involved in an action for libel; and we dare not knock down a vulgar bully, lest we should be given in charge for assault. Hence, liars, and scoundrels, and vulgar bullies abound, and men skulk and grin, and play the double-face, till they lose all manfulness. Society sits smirking foolishly on the top of a smouldering volcano,—and the chief Symbols of greatness among us, Religion, Poesy, Art, are burning as feebly as tapers in the catacombs, . . . the Church resembles a drudge, who, tired of routine, is gradually sinking into laziness and inertia, . . . and the Press! . . . ye gods! . . . the Press!"

Here speech seemed to fail him,—he threw himself into a chair, and, to relieve his mind, kicked away the advertisement sheet of the morning's newspaper with so much angry vehemence that Alwyn laughed outright.

"What ails you now, Villiers?" he demanded mirthfully. "You are a regular fire-eater—a would-be Crusader against a modern Saracen host! Why are you choked with such seemingly unutterable wrath! . . . what of the Press? . . . it is at any rate free."

"Free!" cried Villiers, sitting bolt upright and shooting out the word like a bullet from a gun,—"Free? . . . the Press? It is the veriest bound slave that was ever hampered by the chains of party prejudice,—and the only attempt at freedom it ever makes in its lower grades is an occasional outbreak into scurrility! And yet think what a majestic power for good the true, REAL Liberty of the Press might wield over the destinies of nations! Broadly viewed, the Press should be the strong, practical, helping right hand of civilization, dealing out equal justice, equal sympathy, equal instruction,—it should be the fosterer of the arts and sciences,—the everyday guide of the morals and culture of the people,—it should not specially advocate any cause save Honor,—it should be as far as possible the unanimous voice of the Nation. It Should be,—but what Is it? Look round and judge for yourself. Every daily paper panders more or less to the lowest tastes of the mob,—while if the higher sentiments of man are not actually sneered at, they are made a subject for feeble surprise, or vapid 'gush.' An act of heroic unselfishness meets with such a cackling chorus of amazed, half-bantering approval from the leading-article writers, that one is forced to accept the suggestion implied,— namely that to Be heroic or unselfish is evidently an outbreak of noble instinct that is entirely unexpected and remarkable,—nay, even eccentric and inexplicable! The spirit of mockery pervades everything,—and while the story of a murder is allowed to occupy three and four columns of print, the account of some great scientific discovery, or the report of some famous literary or artistic achievement is squeezed into a few lukewarm and unsatisfactory lines. I have seen a female paragraphist's idiotic description of an actress's gown allowed to take more space in a journal than the review of a first-class book! Moreover, if an honest man, desirous of giving vent to an honest opinion on some crying abuse of the day, were to set forth that opinion in letter form and try to get it published in a leading and important newspaper, the chances are ten to one that it would never he inserted, unless he happened to know the editor, or one of the staff, and perhaps not even then, because, mark you! his opinion Must be in accordance with the literary editor's opinion, or it will be considered of no value to the world! Consider That gigantic absurdity! . . . consider, that when we read our newspapers we are not learning the views of Europe on a certain point,—we are absorbing the ideas of the Editor, to whom everything must be submitted before insertion in the oracular columns we pin our faith on! Thus it is that criticism,—literary criticism, at any rate,—is a lost art,—You know that. A man must either be dead (or considered dead) or in a 'clique' to receive any open encouragement at all from the so-called 'crack' critics. And the cliquey men are generally such stupendous bigots for their own particular and restricted form of 'style.' Anything new they hate,—anything daring they treat with ridicule. Some of them have no hesitation in saying they prefer Matthew Arnold (remember he's dead!) to Tennyson and Swinburne (as yet living) . . . while, as a fact, if we are to go by the high standards of poetical art left us by Shakespeare, Keats,

Shelley, and Byron, Matthew Arnold is about the very tamest, most unimaginative, bald bard that ever kindled a lucifer match of verse and fancied it the fire of Apollo! It's utterly impossible to get either a just or broad view of literature out of cliques,—and the Press, like many of our other 'magnificent' institutions, is working entirely on a wrong system. But who is going to be wise, or strong, or diplomatic enough to reform it? . . . No one, at present,—and we shall jog along, and read up the details of vice in our dailies and weeklies, till we almost lose the savor of virtue, and till the last degraded end comes of it all, and blatant young America thrones herself on the shores of Britain and sends her eagle screech of conquest echoing over Old World and New."

"Don't think it, Villiers!" exclaimed Alwyn impetuously. "There is a mettle in the English that will never be conquered!"

Villiers shrugged his shoulders. "We will hope so, my dear boy!" he said resignedly. "But the 'mettle' under bad government, with bad weapons, and more or less untried ships, can scarcely be blamed if it should not be able to resist a tremendous force majeure. Besides, all the Parliaments in the world cannot upset the laws of the universe. If things are false and corrupt, they MUST be swept away,—Nature will not have them,—she will transmute and transform them somehow, no matter at what cost. It is the cry of the old Prophets over again,—'Because ye have not obeyed God's Law, therefore shall ye meet with destruction.' Egoism is certainly NOT God's Law, and we shall have to return on our imagined progressive steps, and be beaten with rods of affliction, till we understand what His Law Is. It is, for one thing, the wheel that keeps this Universe going—OUR laws are no use whatever in the management of His sublime cosmos! Nations, like individuals, are punished for their own wilful misdeeds—the punishment may be tardy, but sure as death it comes. And I fancy America will be our 'scourge in the Lord's hand'— as the Bible hath it. That pretty, dollar-crusted young Republican wants an aristocracy, . . . she will engraft it on the old roots here,—in fact, she has already begun to engraft it. It is even on the cards that she may need a Monarchy—if she does, she will plant it. . . HERE! Then it will be time for Englishmen to adopt another country, and forget, if they can, their own disgraced nationality. And yet, if, as Shakespeare says, England were to herself but true,—if she had great statesmen as of yore,—intellectual, earnest, self-abnegating, fearless, unhesitating workers, who would devote themselves heart and soul to her welfare, she might gather, not only her Colonies, but America also, to her knee, as a mother gathers children, and the most magnificent Christian Empire the world has ever seen might rise up, a supreme marvel of civilization and union that would make all other nations wonder and revere. But the selfishness of the day, and the ruling passion of gain, are the fatal obstructions in the path of such a desirable millennium."

He ended abruptly—he had unburdened his mind to one who he knew understood him and sympathized with him, and he turned to the perusal of some letters just received.

The two friends were sitting that morning in the breakfast-room,—a charming little octagonal apartment, looking out on a small, very small garden, which, despite the London atmosphere, looked just now very bright with tastefully arranged parterres of white and yellow crocuses, mingled with the soft blue of the dainty hepatica,—that frank-faced little blossom which seems to express such an honest confidence in the goodness of God's sky. A few sparrows of dissipated appearance were bathing their sooty plumes in a pool of equally sooty water left in the garden as a token of last night's rain, and they splashed and twittered and debated and fussed with each other concerning their ablutions, with almost as much importance as could have been displayed by the effeminate Romans of the Augustan era when disporting themselves in their sumptuous Thermae. Alwyn's eyes rested on them unseeingly,— his thoughts were very far away from all his surroundings. Before his imagination rose a Gehenna-like picture of the world in which he had to live,—the world of fashion and form and usage,—the world he was to try and rouse to a sense of better things. A Promethean task indeed! to fill human life with new symbols of hope,—to set up a white standard of faith amid the swift rushing on and reckless tramping down of desperate battle,—to pour out on all, rich or poor, worthy or unworthy, the divine-born balm of Sympathy, which, when given freely and sincerely from man to man, serves often as a check to vice—a silent, yet all eloquent, rebuke to crime,—and can more easily instill into refractory intelligences things of God and desires for good, than any preacher's argument, no matter how finely worded. To touch the big, wayward, BETTER heart of Humanity! . . . could he in very truth do it? . . . Or was the work too vast for his ability? Tormented by various cross-currents of feeling, he gave vent to a troubled sigh and looked dubiously at his friend.

"In such a state of things as you describe, Villiers," he aid, "what a useless unit *I* am! A Poet!—who wants me in this age of Sale and

Barter? . . . Is not a producer of poems always considered more or less of a fool nowadays, no matter how much his works may be in fashion for the moment? I am sure, in spite of the success of 'Nourhalma,' that the era of poetry has passed; and, moreover, it certainly seems to have given place to the very baldest and most unbeauteous forms of prose! As, for instance, if a book is written which contains what is called 'poetic prose' the critics are all ready to denounce it as 'turgid,' 'overladen,' 'strained for effect,' and 'hysterical sublime.' Heine's Reisebilder, which is one of the most exquisite poems in prose ever given to the world, is nearly incomprehensible to the majority of English minds; so much so, indeed, that the English translators in their rendering of it have not only lost the delicate glamour of its fairy-like fancifulness, but have also blunted all the fine points of its dazzling sarcasm and wealth of imagery. It is evident enough that the larger mass of people prefer mediocrity to high excellence, else such a number of merely mediocre works of art would not, and could not, be tolerated. And as long as mediocrity is permitted to hold ground, it is almost an impossibility to do much toward raising the standard of literature. The few who love the best authors are as a mere drop in the ocean of those who not only choose the worst, but who also fail to see any difference between good and bad."

"True enough!" assented Villiers,—"Still the 'few' you speak of are worth all the rest. For the 'few' Homer wrote,—Plato, Marcus Aurelius, Epictetus,—and the 'few' are capable of teaching the majority, if they will only set about it rightly. But at present they are setting about it wrongly. All children are taught to read, but no child is guided in WHAT to read. This is like giving a loaded gun to a boy and saying, 'Shoot away! . . . No matter in which direction you point your aim, . . . shoot yourself if you like, and others too,—anyhow, you've GOT the gun!' Of course there are a few fellows who have occasionally drawn up a list of books as suitable for everybody's perusal,—but then these lists cannot be taken as true criterions, as they all differ from one another as much as church sects. One would-be instructor in the art of reading says we ought all to study 'Tom Jones'—now I don't see the necessity of THAT! And, oddly enough, these lists scarcely ever include the name of a poet,—which is the absurdest mistake ever made. A liberal education in the highest works of poesy is absolutely necessary to the thinking abilities of man. But, Alwyn, You need not trouble yourself about what is good for the million and what isn't, . . . whatever you write is sure to be read Now—you've got the ear of the public,—the 'fair, large ear' of the ass's head which disguises Bottom the Weaver, who frankly says of himself, 'I am such a tender ass, if my hair do but tickle me, I must scratch!'"

Alwyn smiled. He was thinking of what his Shadow-Self had said on this very subject—"A book or poem, to be great, and keep its greatness hereafter, must be judged by the natural instinct of PEOPLES. This world-wide decision has never yet been, and never will be, hastened by any amount of written criticism,—it is the responsive beat of the enormous Pulse of Life that thrills through all mankind, high and low, gentle and simple,—its great throbs are slow and solemnly measured, yet if once it answers to a Poet's touch, that Poet's name is made glorious forever!" He. . . in the character of Sah-luma. . . had seemed to utter these sentiments many ages ago,—and now the words repeated themselves in his thoughts with a new and deep intensity of meaning.

"Of course," added Villiers suddenly—"you must expect plenty of adverse criticism now, as it is known beyond all doubt that you are alive and able to read what is written concerning you,—but if you once pay attention to critics, you may as well put aside pen altogether, as it is the business of these worthies never to be entirely satisfied with anything. Even Shelley and Byron, in the critical capacity, abused Keats, till the poor, suffering youth, who promised to be greater then either of them, died of a broken heart as much as disease. This sort of injustice will go on to the end of time, or till men become more Christianized than Paul's version of Christianity has ever yet made them."

Here a knock at the door interrupted the conversation. The servant entered, bringing a note gorgeously crested and coroneted in gold. Villiers, to whom it was addressed, opened and read it.

"What shall we do about this?" he asked, when his man had retired. "It is an invitation from the Duchess de la Santoisie. She asks us to go and dine with her next week,—a party of twenty—reception afterward. I think we'd better accept,—what do you say?"

Alwyn roused himself from his reverie. "Anything to please you, my dear boy!" he answered cheerfully—"But I haven't the faintest idea who the Duchess de la Santoisie is!"

"No? . . . Well, she's an Englishwoman who has married a French Duke. He is a delightful old fellow, the pink of courtesy, and the model of perfect egotism. A true Parisian, and of course an atheist,—a very polished atheist, too, with a most charming reliance on his own infallibility. His wife writes novels which have a SLIGHT leaning toward

Zolaism,—she is an extremely witty woman sarcastic, and cold-blooded enough to be a female Robespierre, yet, on the whole, amusing as a study of what curious nondescript forms the feminine nature can adopt unto itself, if it chooses. She has an immense respect for GENIUS,— mind, I say genius advisedly, because she really is one of those rare few who cannot endure mediocrity. Everything at her house is the best of its kind, and the people she entertains are the best of theirs. Her welcome of you will be at any rate a sincerely admiring one,—and as I think, in spite of your desire for quiet, you will have to show yourself somewhere, it may as well be there."

Alwyn looked dubious, and not at all resigned to the prospect of "showing himself."

"Your description of her does not strike me as particularly attractive,"— he said—"I cannot endure that nineteenth-century hermaphroditic production, a mannish woman."

"Oh but she isn't altogether mannish,"—declared Villiers, . . . "Besides, I mustn't forget to add, that she is extremely beautiful."

Alwyn shrugged his shoulders indifferently. His friend noticed the gesture and laughed.

"Still impervious to beauty, old boy?"—he said gayly—"You always were, I remember!"

Alwyn flushed a little, and rose from his chair.

"Not always,"—he answered steadily,—"There have been times in my life when the beauty of women,—mere physical beauty—has exercised great influence over me. But I have lately learned how a fair face may sometimes mask a foul mind,—and unless I can see the SUBSTANCE of Soul looking through the SEMBLANCE of Body, then I know that the beauty I SEEM to behold is mere Appearance, and not Reality. Hence, unless your beautiful Duchess be like the 'King's daughter' of David's psalm, 'all glorious WITHIN'—her APPARENT loveliness will have no charm for me!—Now"—and he smiled, and spoke in a less serious tone. . . "if you have no objection, I am off to my room to scribble for an hour or so. Come for me if you want me—you know I don't in the least mind being disturbed."

But Villiers detained him a moment, and looked inquisitively at him full in the eyes.

"You've got some singular new attraction about you, Alwyn,"— he said, with a strange sense of keen inward excitement as he met his friend's calm yet flashing glance,—"Something mysterious, . . .

something that COMPELS! What is it? . . . I believe that visit of yours to the Ruins of Babylon had a more important motive than you will admit, . . . moreover. . . I believe you are in love!"

"IN love!"—Alwyn laughed a little as he repeated the words. "What a foolish term that is when you come to think of it! For to be IN love suggests the possibility of getting OUT again,—which, if love be true, can never happen. Say that I LOVE!—and you will be nearer the mark! Now don't look so mystified, and don't ask me any more questions just now—to-night, when we are sitting together in the library, I'll tell you the whole story of my Babylonian adventure!"

And with a light parting wave of the hand he left the room, and Villiers heard him humming a tune softly to himself as he ascended the stairs to his own apartments, where, ever since he arrived, he had made it his custom to do two or three hours' steady writing every morning. For a moment or so after he had gone Villiers stood lost in thought, with knitted brows and meditative eyes, then, rousing himself, he went on to his study, and sitting down at his desk wrote an answer to the Duchess de la Santoisie accepting her invitation.

XXXIV

Rewards of Fame

An habitual resident in London who is gifted with a keen faculty of hearing and observation, will soon learn to know instinctively the various characteristics of the people who call upon him, by the particular manner in which each one handles his door-bell or knocker. He will recognize the timid from the bold, the modest from the arrogant, the meditative thinker from the bustling man of fashion, the familiar friend from the formal acquaintance. Every individual's method of announcing his or her arrival to the household is distinctly different,—and Villiers, who studied a little of everything, had not failed to take note of the curiously diversified degrees of single and double rapping by means of which his visitors sought admittance to his abode. In fact, he rather prided himself on being able to guess with almost invariable correctness what special type of man or woman was at his door, provided he could hear the whole diapason of their knock from beginning to end. When he was shut in his "den," however, the sounds were muffled by distance, and he could form no just judgment,—sometimes, indeed, he did not hear them at all, especially if he happened to be playing his 'cello at the time. So that this morning he was considerably startled, when, having finished his letter to the Duchess de la Santoisie, a long and persistent rat-tat-tatting echoed noisily through the house, like the smart, quick blows of a carpenter's hammer—a species of knock that was entirely unfamiliar to him, and that, while so emphatic in character, suggested to his mind neither friend nor foe. He laid down his pen, listened and waited. In a minute or two his servant entered the room.

"If you please, sir, a lady to see Mr. Alwyn. Shall I show her up?"

Villiers rose slowly out of his chair, and stood eyeing his man in blank bewilderment.

"A Lady! . . . To see Mr. Alwyn!"—he repeated, his thoughts instantly reverting to his friend's vaguely hinted love-affair,—"What name?"

"She gives no name, sir. She says it isn't needed,—Mr. Alwyn will know who she is."

"Mr. Alwyn will know who she is, will he?" murmured Villiers dubiously.—"What is she like? Young and pretty?"

Over the man-servant's staid countenance came the glimmer of a demure, respectful smile.

"Oh no, sir,—not young, sir! A person about fifty, I should say."

This was mystifying. A person about fifty! Who could she be? Villiers hastily considered,—there must be some mistake, he thought,— at any rate, he would see the unknown intruder himself first, and find out what her business was, before breaking in upon Alwyn's peaceful studies upstairs.

"Show the lady in here"—he said—"I can't disturb Mr. Alwyn just now."

The servant retired, and soon re-appeared, ushering in a tall, gaunt, black-robed female, who walked with the stride of a dragoon and the demeanor of a police-inspector, and who, merely nodding briskly in response to Villiers's amazed bow, selected with one comprehensive glance the most comfortable chair in the room, and seated herself at ease therein. She then put up her veil, displaying a long, narrow face, cold, pale, arrogant eyes, a nose inclined to redness at the tip, and a thin, close-set mouth lined with little sarcastic wrinkles, which came into prominent and unbecoming play as soon as she began to speak, which she did almost immediately.

"I suppose I had better introduce myself to you, Mr. Alwyn"—she said with a condescending and confident air—"Though really we know each other so well by reputation that there seems scarcely any necessity for it! Of course you have heard of 'Tiger-Lily!'"

Villiers gazed at her helplessly,—he had never felt so uncomfortable in all his life. Here was a strange woman, who had actually taken bodily possession of his apartment as though it were her own,—who had settled herself down in his particular pet Louis Quatorze chair,— who stared at him with the scrutinizing complacency of a professional physiognomist,—and who seemed to think no explanation of her extraordinary conduct was necessary, inasmuch as "of course" he, Villiers, had heard of "Tiger-Lily!" It was very singular! . . . almost like madness! . . . Perhaps she Was mad! How could he tell? She had a remarkably high, knobby brow,—a brow with an unpleasantly bald appearance, owing to the uncompromising way in which her hair was brushed well off it—he had seen such brows before in certain "spiritualists" who believed, or pretended to believe, in the suddenly willed dematerialization of matter, and They were mad, he knew, or else very foolishly feigning madness!

Endeavoring to compose his bewildered mind, he fixed glass in eye, and regarded her through it with an inquiring solemnity,—he would have spoken, but before he could utter a word, she went on rapidly:

"You are not in the least like the person I imagined you to be! . . . However, that doesn't matter. Literary celebrities are always so different to what we expect!"

"Pardon me, madam,"—began Villiers politely. "You are making a slight error,—my servant probably did not explain. I am not Mr. Alwyn, . . . my name is Villiers. Mr. Alwyn is my guest,—but he is at present very much occupied,—and unless your business is extremely urgent. . ."

"Certainly it is urgent"—said the lady decisively. . . "otherwise I should not have come. And so you are NOT Mr. Alwyn! Well, I thought you couldn't be! Now then, will you have the kindness to tell Mr. Alwyn I am here?"

By this time Villiers had recovered his customary self-possession, and he met her commanding glance with a somewhat defiant coolness.

"I am not aware to whom I have the honor of speaking," he said frigidly. "Perhaps you will oblige me with your name?"

"My name doesn't in the least matter," she replied calmly—"though I will tell you afterward if you wish. But you don't seem to understand I. . . I am 'Tiger-Lily'!"

The situation was becoming ludicrous. Villiers felt strongly disposed to laugh.

"I'm afraid I am very ignorant!"—he said, with a humorous sparkle in his blue eyes,—"But really I am quite in the dark as to your meaning. Will you explain?"

The lady's nose grew deeper of tint, and the look she shot at him had quite a killing vindictiveness. With evident difficulty she forced a smile.

"Oh, you MUST have heard of me!"—she declared, with a ponderous attempt at playfulness—"You read the papers, don't you?"

"Some of them," returned Villiers cautiously—"Not all. Not the Sunday ones, for instance."

"Still, you can't possibly have helped seeing my descriptions of famous people 'At Home,' you know! I write for ever so many journals. I think"—and she became complacently reflective—"I think I may say with perfect truth that I have interviewed everybody who has ever done anything worth noting, from our biggest provision dealer to our latest sensational novelist! And all my articles are signed 'Tiger-Lily.' Now do you remember? Oh, you MUST remember? . . . I am so VERY well known!"

There was a touch of genuine anxiety in her voice that was almost pathetic, but Villiers made no attempt to soothe her wounded vanity.

"I have no recollection whatever of the name," he said bluntly—"But that is easily accounted for, as I never read newspaper descriptions of celebrities. So you are an 'interviewer' for the Press?"

"Exactly!" and the lady leaned back more comfortably in the Louis Quatorze fauteuil—"And of course I want to interview Mr. Alwyn. I want. . ." here drawing out a business looking note-book from her pocket she opened it and glanced at the different headings therein enumerated,—"I want to describe his personal appearance,—to know when he was born, and where he was educated,—whether his father or mother had literary tastes,—whether he had, or has, brothers or sisters, or both,—whether he is married, or likely to be, and how much money he has made by his book." She paused and gave an upward glance at Villiers, who returned it with a blank and stony stare.

"Then,"—she resumed energetically—"I wish to know what are his methods of work;—WHERE he gets his ideas and How he elaborates them,—how many hours he writes at a time, and whether he is an early riser,—also what he usually takes for dinner,—whether he drinks wine or is a total abstainer, and at what hour he retires to rest. All this is so INTENSELY interesting to the public! Perhaps he might be inclined to give me a few notes of his recent tour in the East, and of course I should be very glad if he will state his opinions on the climate, customs, and governments of the countries through which he has passed. It's a great pity this is not his own house,—it is a pretty place and a description of it would read well. Let me see!"—and she meditated,—"I think I could manage to insert a few lines about this apartment, . . . it would be easy to say 'the picturesque library in the house of the Honble. Francis Villiers, where Mr. Alwyn received me,' etc.,—Yes! that would do very well!—very well indeed! I should like to know whether he has a residence of his own anywhere, and if not, whether he intends to take one in London, because in the latter case it would be as well to ascertain by whom he intends to have it furnished. A little discussion on upholstery is so specially fascinating to my readers! Then, naturally, I am desirous to learn how the erroneous rumor of his death was first started, . . . whether in the course of his travels he met with some serious accident, or illness, which gave rise to the report. Now,"—and she shut her note-book and folded her hands,—"I don't mind waiting an hour or more if necessary,—but I am sure if you will tell Mr. Alwyn who I am, and what I have come for, he will be only too delighted to see me with as little delay as possible."

She ceased. Villiers drew a long breath,—his compressed lips parted in a slightly sarcastic smile. Squaring his shoulders with that peculiar pugnacious gesture of his which always indicated to those who knew him well that his mind was made up, and that nothing would induce him to alter it, he said in a tone of stiff civility:

"I am sorry, madam, . . . very sorry! . . . but I am compelled to inform you that your visit here is entirely useless! Were I to tell my friend of the purpose you have in view concerning him, he would not feel so much flattered as you seem to imagine, but rather insulted! Excuse my frankness,—you have spoken plainly,—I must speak plainly too. Provision dealers and sensational story writers may find that it serves their purpose to be interviewed, if only as a means of gaining extra advertisement, but a truly great and conscientious author like Theos Alwyn is quite above all that sort of thing."

The lady raised her pale eyebrows with an expression of interrogative scorn.

"Above all that sort of thing!" she echoed incredulously—"Dear me! How very extraordinary! I have always found all our celebrities so exceedingly pleased to be given a little additional notoriety! . . . and I should have thought a POET," this with much depreciative emphasis— "would have been particularly glad of the chance! Because, of course you know that unless a very astonishing success is made, as in the case of Mr. Alwyn's 'Nourhalma,' people really take such slight interest in writers of verse, that it is hardly ever worth while interviewing them!"

"Precisely!" agreed Villiers ironically,—"The private history of a prize-fighter would naturally be much more thrilling!" He paused,— his temper was fast rising, but, quickly reflecting that, after all, the indignation he felt was not so much against his visitor as against the system she represented, he resumed quietly, "May I ask you, madam, whether you have ever 'interviewed' Her Majesty the Queen?"

Her glance swept slightingly over him.

"Certainly not! Such a thing would be impossible!"

"Then you have never thought," went on Villiers, with a thrill of earnestness in his manly, vibrating voice—"that it might be quite as impossible to 'interview' a great Poet?—who, if great indeed, is in every way as royal as any Sovereign that ever adorned a throne! I do not speak of petty verse-writers,—I say a great Poet, by which term I imply a great creative genius who is honestly faithful to his high vocation. Such an one could no more tell you his methods of work than a rainbow could prattle about the way it shines,—and as for his personal history, I should like to know by what right society is entitled to pry into the sacred matters of a man's private life, simply because he happens to be famous? I consider the modern love of prying and probing into other people's affairs a most degrading and abominable sign of the times,—it is morbid, unwholesome, and utterly contemptible. Moreover, I think that writers who consent to be 'interviewed' condemn themselves as literary charlatans, unworthy of the profession they have wrongfully adopted. You see I have the courage of my opinions on this matter,—in fact, I believe, if every one were to speak their honest mind openly, a better state of things might be the result, and 'interviewing' would gradually come to be considered in its true light, namely, as a vulgar and illegitimate method of advertisement. I mean no disrespect to you, madam,"—this, as the lady suddenly put down her veil, thrust her note-book in her pocket, and rose somewhat bouncingly from her chair—"I am only sorry you should find such an occupation as that of the 'interviewer' open to you. I can scarcely imagine such work to be congenial to a lady's feelings, as, in the case of really distinguished personages, she must assuredly meet with many a rebuff! I hope I have not offended you by my bluntness, . . ."—here he trailed off into inaudible polite murmurs, while the "Tiger-Lily" marched steadily toward the door.

"Oh dear, no, I am not in the least offended!" she retorted contemptuously,—"On the contrary, this has been a most amusing experience!—most amusing, I assure you! and quite unique! Why—" and suddenly stopping short, she turned smartly round and gesticulated with one hand. . . "I have interviewed all the favorite actors and actresses in London! The biggest brewers in Great Britain have received me at their country mansions, and have given me all the particulars of their lives from earliest childhood! The author of 'Hugger Mugger's Curse' took the greatest pains to explain to me how he first collected the materials for his design. The author of that most popular story, 'Darling's Twins,' gave me a description of all the houses he has ever lived in,—he even told me where he purchased his writing-paper, pens, and ink! And to think that a POET should be too grand to be interrogated! Oh, the idea is really very funny! . . . quite too funny for anything! "She gave a short laugh,—then relapsing into severity, she added. . ." You will, I hope, tell Mr. Alwyn I called?"

Villiers bowed. "Assuredly!"

"Thank you! Because it is possible he may have different opinions to yours,—in that case, if he writes me a line, fixing an appointment, I shall be very pleased to call again. I will leave my card,—and if Mr. Alwyn is a sensible man, he will certainly hold broader ideas on the subject of 'interviewing' than You appear to entertain. You are QUITE sure I cannot see him?"

"Quite!"—There was no mistake about the firm emphasis of this reply.

"Oh, very well!"—here she opened the door, rattling the handle with rather an unnecessary violence,—"I'm sorry to have taken up any of your time, Mr. Villiers. Good-morning!"

"Good-morning!" . . . returned Villiers calmly, touching the bell that his servant might be in readiness to show her out. But the baffled "Tiger-Lily" was not altogether gone. She looked back, her face wrinkling into one of those strangely unbecoming expressions of grim playfulness.

"I've half a mind to make an 'At Home' out of You!" she said, nodding at him energetically. "Only you're not important enough!"

Villiers burst out laughing. He was not proof against this touch of humor, and on a sudden good-natured impulse, sprang to the door and shook hands with her.

"No, indeed, I am not!" he said, with a charming smile—"Think of it!—I haven't even invented a new biscuit! Come, let me see you into the hall,—I'm really sorry if I've spoken roughly, but I assure you Alwyn's not at all the sort of man you want for interviewing,—he's far too modest and noble-hearted. Believe me!—I'm not romancing a bit—I'm in earnest. There ARE some few fine, manly, gifted fellows left in the world, who do their work for the love of the work alone, and not for the sake of notoriety, and he is one of them. Now I'm not certain, if you were quite candid with me, you'd admit that you yourself don't think much of the people who actually LIKE to be interviewed?"

His amiable glance, his kindly manner, took the gaunt female by surprise, and threw her quite off her guard. She laughed,—a natural, unforced laugh in which there was not a trace of bitterness. He was really a delightful young man, she thought, in spite of his old-fashioned, out-of-the-way notions!

"Well, perhaps I don't!" she replied frankly—"But you see it is not my business to think about them at all. I simply 'interview' them,—and I generally find they are very willing, and often eager, to tell me all about themselves, even to quite trifling and unnecessary details. And, of course, each one thinks himself or herself the ONLY or the chief 'celebrity' in London, or, for that matter, in the world. I have always to tone down the egotistical part of it a little, especially with authors, for if I were to write out exactly what THEY separately say of their contemporaries, it would be simply frightful! They would be all at daggers drawn in no time! I assure you 'interviewing' is often a most delicate and difficult business!"

"Would it were altogether impossible!" said Villiers heartily—"But as long as there is a plethora of little authors, and a scarcity of great ones, so long, I suppose, must it continue—for little men love notoriety, and great ones shrink from it, just in the same way that good women like flattery, while bad ones court it. I hope you don't bear me any grudge because I consider my friend Alwyn both good and great, and resent the idea of his being placed, no matter with what excellent intention soever, on the level of the small and mean?"

The lady surveyed him with a twinkle of latent approval in her pale-colored eyes.

"Not in the least!" she replied in a tone of perfect good-humor. "On the contrary, I rather admire your frankness! Still, I think, that as matters stand nowadays, you are very odd,—and I suppose your friend is odd too,—but, of course, there must be exceptions to every rule. At the same time, you should recollect that, in many people's opinion, to be 'interviewed' is one of the chiefest rewards of fame!—" Villiers shrugged his shoulders expressively. "Oh, yes, it seems a poor reward to you, no doubt,"—she continued smilingly,—"but there are no end of authors who would do anything to secure the notoriety of it! Now, suppose that, after all, Mr. Alwyn DOES care to submit to the operation, you will let me know, won't you?"

"Certainly I will!"—and Villiers, accepting her card, on which was inscribed her own private name and address, shook hands once more, and bowed her courteously out. No sooner had the door closed upon her than he sprang upstairs, three steps at a time, and broke impetuously in upon Alwyn, who, seated at a table covered with papers, looked up with a surprised smile at the abrupt fashion of his entrance. In a few minutes he had disburdened himself of the whole story of the "Tiger-Lily's" visit,

MARIE CORELLI

telling it in a whimsical way of his own, much to the amusement of his friend, who listened, pen in hand, with a half-laughing, half-perplexed light in his fine, poetic eyes.

"Now did I express the proper opinion?" he demanded in conclusion. "Was I not right in thinking you would never consent to be interviewed?"

"Right? Why of course you were!"—responded Alwyn quickly. "Can you imagine me calmly stating the details of my personal life and history to a strange woman, and allowing her to turn it into a half-guinea article for some society journal! But, Villiers, what an extraordinary state of things we are coming to, if the Press can actually condescend to employ a sort of spy, or literary detective, to inquire into the private experience of each man or woman who comes honorably to the front!"

"Honorably or Dishonorably,—it doesn't matter which,"—said Villiers, "That is just the worst of it. One day it is an author who is 'interviewed,' the next it is a murderer,—now a statesman,—then a ballet dancer,—the same honor is paid to all who have won any distinct notoriety. And what is so absurd is, that the reading million don't seem able to distinguish between 'notoriety' and 'fame.' The two things are so widely, utterly apart! Byron's reputation, for instance, was much more notoriety during his life than fame—while Keats had actually laid hold on fame while as yet deeming himself unfamous. It's curious, but true, nevertheless, that very often the writers who thought least of themselves during their lifetime have become the most universally renowned after their deaths. Shakespeare, I dare say, had no very exaggerated idea of the beauty of his own plays,—he seems to have written just the best that was in him, without caring what anybody thought of it. And I believe that is the only way to succeed in the end."

"In the end!" repeated Alwyn dreamily—"In the end, no worldly success is worth attaining,—a few thousand years and the greatest are forgotten!"

"Not the GREATEST,"—said Villiers warmly—"The greatest must always be remembered."

"No, my friend!—Not even the greatest! Do you not think there must have been great and wise and gifted men in Tyre, in Sidon, in Carthage, in Babylon?—There are five men mentioned in Scripture, as being 'ready to write swiftly'—Sarea, Dabria, Selemia, Ecanus, and Ariel—where is the no doubt admirable work done by these? Perhaps. . . who knows? . . . one of them was as great as Homer in genius,—we cannot tell!"

"True,—we cannot tell!" responded Villiers meditatively—"But, Alwyn, if you persist in viewing things through such tremendous vistas of time, and in measuring the Future by the Past, then one may ask what is the use of anything?"

"There Is no use in anything, except in the making of a strong, persistent, steady effort after good," said Alwyn earnestly. . . "We men are cast, as it were, between two swift currents, Wrong and Right,—Self and God,—and it seems more easy to shut our eyes and drift into Self and Wrong, than to strike out brave arms, and swim, despite all difficulty, toward God and Right, yet if we once take the latter course, we shall find it the most natural and the least fatiguing. And with every separate stroke of high endeavor we carry others with us,—we raise our race,—we bear it onward,—upward! And the true reward, or best result of fame, is, that having succeeded in winning brief attention from the multitude, a man may be able to pronounce one of God's lightning messages of inspired Truth plainly to them, while they are yet willing to stand and listen. This momentary hearing from the people is, as I take it, the sole reward any writer can dare to hope for,—and when he obtains it, he should remember that his audience remains with him but a very short while,—so that it is his duty to see that he employ his chance WELL, not to win applause for himself, but to cheer and lift others to noble thought, and still more noble fulfilment."

Villiers regarded him wistfully.

"Alwyn, my dear fellow, do you want to be the Sisyphus of this era?— You will find the stone of Evil heavy to roll upward,—moreover, it will exhibit the usually painful tendency to slip back and crush you!"

"How can it crush me?" asked his friend with a serene smile. "My heart cannot be broken, or my spirit dismayed, and as for my body, it can but die,—and death comes to every man! I would rather try to roll up the stone, however fruitless the task, than sit idly looking at it, and doing nothing!"

"Your heart cannot be broken? Ah! how do you know" . . . and Villiers shook his head dubiously—"What man can be certain of his own destiny?"

"Everyman can WILL his own destiny,"—returned Alwyn firmly. "That is just it. But here we are getting into a serious discussion, and I had determined to talk no more on such subjects till to-night."

"And to-night we are to go in for them thoroughly, I suppose?"— inquired Villiers with a quick look. "To-night, my dear boy, you will have to decide whether you consider me mad or sane," said Alwyn cheerfully—"I shall tell you truths that seem like romances—and facts that sound like fables,—moreover, I shall have to assure you that miracles Do happen whenever God chooses, in spite of all human denial of their possibility. Do you remember Whately's clever skit—'Historical Doubts of Napoleon I'?—showing how easy it was to logically prove that Napoleon never existed?—That ought to enlighten people as to the very precise and convincing manner in which we can, if we choose, argue away what is nevertheless an incontestible FACT. Thus do skeptics deny miracles—yet we live surrounded by miracles! . . . do you think me crazed for saying so?"

Villiers laughed. "Crazed! No, indeed!—I wish every man in London were as sane and sound as you are!"

"Ah, but wait till to-night!" and Alwyn's eyes sparkled mirthfully—"Perhaps you will alter your opinion then!"—Here, collecting his scattered manuscripts, he put them by—"I've done work for the present,"—he said—"Shall we go for a walk somewhere?"

Villiers assented, and they left the room together.

XXXV

ONE AGAINST MANY

The beautiful and socially popular Duchess de la Santoisie sat her at brilliantly appointed dinner-table, and flashed her bright eyes comprehensively round the board,—her party was complete. She had secured twenty of the best-known men and women of letters in all London, and yet she was not quite satisfied with the result attained. One dark, splendid face on her right hand had taken the lustre out of all the rest,—one quiet, courteous smile on a mouth haughty, yet sweet, had somehow or other made the entertainment of little worth in her own estimation. She was very fair to look upon, very witty, very worldly-wise,—but for once her beauty seemed to herself defective and powerless to charm, while the graceful cloak of social hypocrisy she was always accustomed to wear would not adapt itself to her manner tonight so well as usual. The author of "Nourhalma" the successful poet whose acquaintance she had very eagerly sought to make, was not at all the kind of man she had expected,—and now, when he was beside her as her guest, she did not quite know what to do with him.

She had met plenty of poets, so called, before,—and had, for the most part, found them insignificant looking men with an enormous opinion of themselves, and a suave, condescending contempt for all others of their craft; but this being,—this stately, kingly creature with the noble head, and far-gazing, luminous eyes,—this man, whose every gesture was graceful, whose demeanor was more royal than that of many a crowned monarch,—whose voice had such a singular soft thrill of music in its tone,—he was a personage for whom she had not been prepared,—and in whose presence she felt curiously embarrassed and almost ill at ease. And she was not the only one present who experienced these odd sensations. Alwyn's appearance, when, with his friend Villiers, he had first entered the Duchess's drawing-room that evening, and had there been introduced to his hostess, had been a sort of revelation to the languid, fashionable guests assembled; sudden quick whispers were exchanged—surprised glances,—how unlike he was to the general type of the nervous, fagged, dyspeptic "literary" man!

And now that every one was seated at dinner, the same impression remained on all,—an impression that was to some disagreeable and humiliating, and that yet could not be got over,—namely, that this "poet," whom, in a way, the Duchess and her friends had intended to patronize, was distinctly superior to them all. Nature, as though proud of her handiwork, proclaimed him as such,—while he, quite unconscious of the effect he produced, wondered why this bevy of human beings, most of whom were more or less distinguished in the world of art and literature, had so little to say for themselves. Their conversation was BANAL,—tame,—ordinary; they might have been well-behaved, elegantly dressed peasants for aught they said of wise, cheerful, or witty. The weather,—the parks,—the theatres,—the newest actress, and the newest remedies for indigestion,—these sort of subjects were bandied about from one to the other with a vaguely tame persistence that was really irritating,—the question of remedies for indigestion seemed to hold ground longest, owing to the variety of opinions expressed thereon.

The Duchess grew more and more inwardly vexed, and her little foot beat an impatient tattoo under the table, as she replied with careless brevity to a few of the commonplace observations addressed to her, and cast an occasional annoyed glance at her lord, M le Duc, a thin, military-looking individual, with a well waxed and pointed mustache, whose countenance suggested an admirably executed mask. It was a face that said absolutely nothing,—yet beneath its cold impassiveness linked the satyr-like, complex, half civilized, half brutish mind of the born and bred Parisian,—the goblin-creature with whom pure virtues, whether in man or woman, are no more sacred than nuts to a monkey. The suave charm of a polished civility sat on M le Due's smooth brow, and beamed in his urbane smile,—his manners were exquisite, his courtesy irreproachable, his whole demeanor that of a very precise and elegant master of deportment. Yet, notwithstanding his calm and perfectly self-possessed exterior, he was, oddly enough, the frequent prey of certain extraordinary and ungovernable passions; there were times when he became impossible to himself,—and when, to escape from his own horrible thoughts, he would plunge headlong into an orgie of wild riot and debauchery, such as might have made the hair of his respectable English acquaintances stand on end, had they known to what an extent he carried his excesses. But at these seasons of moral attack, he "went abroad for his health," as he said, delicately touching his chest in order to suggest some interesting latent weakness there, and in these migratory excursions his wife never accompanied him, nor did she complain of his absence. When he returned, after two or three months, he looked more the "chevalier sans peur et sans reproche" than ever; and neither he, nor the fair partner of his joys and sorrows, even committed such a breach of politeness as to inquire into each other's doings during the time of their separation. So they jogged on together, presenting the most delightful outward show of wedded harmony to the world,—and only a few were found to hazard the remark, that the "racy" novels Madame la Duchesse wrote to wile away her duller hours were singularly "bitter" in tone, for a woman whose lot in life was so extremely enviable!

On this particular evening, the Duke affected to be utterly unconscious of the meaning looks his beautiful spouse shot at him every now and then,—looks which plainly said—"Why don't you start some interesting subject of conversation, and stop these people from talking such every-day twaddle?" He was a clever man in his way, and his present mood was malign and mischievous; therefore he went on eating daintily, and discussing mild platitudes in the most languidly amiable manner imaginable, enjoying to the full the mental confusion and discomfort of his guests,—confusion and discomfort which, as he very well knew, was the psychological result of their having one in their midst whose life and character were totally opposite to, and distinctly separate from, their own. As Emerson truly says, "Let the world beware when a Thinker comes into it!" . . . and here WAS this Thinker,—this type of the Godlike in Man,—this uncomfortably sincere personage, whose eyes were clear of falsehood, whose genius was incontestable, whose fame had taken society by assault, and who, therefore, was entitled to receive every attention and consideration.

Everybody had desired to see him, and here he was,—the great man, the new "celebrity"—and now that he was actually present, no one knew what to say to him; moreover, there was a very general tendency in the company to avoid his direct gaze. People fidgeted on their chairs and looked aside or downward, whenever his glance accidentally fell on them,—and to the analytical Voltairean mind of M. le Duc there was something grimly humorous in the whole situation. He was a great admirer of physical strength and beauty, and Alwyn's noble face and fine figure had won his respect, though of the genius of the poet he knew nothing, and cared less. It was enough for all the purposes of social usage that the author of "Nourhalma" was CONSIDERED illustrious,— no matter whether he deserved the appellation or not. And so the

Duke, satirically amused at the obvious embarrassment of the other "notabilities" assembled, did nothing whatsoever to relieve or to lighten the conversation, which remained so utterly dull and inane that Alwyn, who had been compelled, for politeness' sake, to appear interested in the account of a bicycle race detailed to him by a very masculine looking lady-doctor whose seat at table was next his own, began to feel a little weary, and to wonder dismally how long this "feast of reason and flow of soul" was going to last.

Villiers, too, whose easy, good-natured, and clever talk generally gave some sparkle and animation to the dreariest social gathering, was to-night unusually taciturn:—he was bored by his partner, a middle-aged woman with a mania for philology, and, moreover, his thoughts, like those of most of the persons present, were centered on Alwyn, whom every now and then he regarded with a certain wistful wonder and reverence. He had heard the whole story of the Field of Ardath; and he knew not how much to accept of it as true, or how much to set down to his friend's ardent imagination. He had come to a fairly logical explanation of the whole matter,—namely, that as the City of Al-Kyris had been proved a dream, so surely the visit of the Angel-maiden Edris must have been a dream likewise,—that the trance at the Monastery of Dariel, followed by the constant reading of the passages from Esdras, and the treatise of Algazzali, had produced a vivid impression on Alwyn's susceptible brain, which had resolved itself into the visionary result narrated.

He found in this the most practical and probable view of what must otherwise be deemed by mortal minds incredible; and, being a frank and honest fellow, he had not scrupled to openly tell his friend what he thought. Alwyn had received his remarks with the most perfect sweetness and equanimity,—but, all the same, had remained unchanged in his opinion as to the REALITY of his betrothal to his Angel-love in Heaven. And one or two points had certainly baffled Villiers, and perplexed him in his would-be precise analysis of the circumstances: first, there was the remarkable change in Alwyn's own nature. From an embittered, sarcastic, disappointed, violently ambitious man, he had become softened, gracious, kindly,—showing the greatest tenderness and forethought for others, even in small, every-day trifles; while for himself he took no care. He wore his fame as lightly as a child might wear a flower, just plucked and soon to fade,—his intelligence seemed to expand itself into a broad, loving, sympathetic comprehension of the wants and afflictions of human-kind; and he was writing a new poem, of which Villiers had seen some lines that had fairly amazed him by their grandeur of conception and clear passion of utterance. Thus it was evident there was no morbidness in him,—no obscurity,—nothing eccentric,—nothing that removed him in any way from his fellows, except that royal personality of his,—that strong, beautiful, well-balanced Spirit in him, which exercised such a bewildering spell on all who came within its influence, He believed himself loved by an Angel! Well,—if there WERE angels, why not? Villiers argued the proposition thus:

"Whether we are Christians, Jews, Buddhists, or Mahometans, we are supposed to accept angels as forming part of the system of our Faith. If we are nothing,—then, of course, we believe in nothing. But granted we are SOMETHING, then we are bound in honor, if consistent, to acknowledge that angels help to guide our destinies. And if, as we are assured by Holy Writ, such loftier beings Do exist, why should they not communicate with, and even love, human creatures, provided those human creatures are worthy of their tenderness? Certainly, viewed by all the chief religions of the world, there is nothing new or outrageous in the idea of an angel descending to the help of man."

Such thoughts as these were in his mind now, as he ever and anon glanced across the glittering table, with its profusion of lights and flowers, to where his poet-friend sat, slightly leaning back in his chair, with a certain half-perplexed, half-disappointed expression on his handsome features, though his eyes brightened into a smile as he caught Villiers's look, and he gave the smallest, scarcely perceptible shrug, as who should say, "Is this your brilliant Duchess?—your witty and cultured society?"

Villiers flashed back an amused, responsive glance, and then conscientiously strove to pay more attention to the irrepressible feminine philologist beside him, determining to take her, as he said to himself, by way of penance for his unremembered sins. After a while there came one of those extraordinary, sudden rushes of gabble that often occur at even the stiffest dinner-party,—a galloping race of tongues, in which nothing really distinct is heard, but in which each talks to the other as though moved by an impulse of sheer desperation. This burst of noise was a relief after the strained murmurs of trite commonplaces that had hitherto been the order of the hour, and the fair Duchess, somewhat easier in her mind, turned anew to Alwyn, with greater grace and gentleness of manner than she had yet shown.

"I am afraid," she said smilingly, "you must find us all very stupid after your travels abroad? In England we ARE dull,—our tristesse cannot be denied. But, really, the climate is responsible,—we want more sunshine. I suppose in the East, where the sun is so warm and bright, the people are always cheerful?"

"On the contrary, I have found them rather serious and contemplative than otherwise," returned Alwyn,—"yet their gravity is certainly of a pleasant, and not of a forbidding type. I don't myself think the sun has much to do with the disposition of man, after all,—I fancy his temperament is chiefly moulded by the life he leads. In the East, for instance, men accept their existence as a sort of divine command, which they obey cheerfully, yet with a consciousness of high responsibility:—on the Continent they take it as a bagatelle, lightly won, lightly lost, hence their indifferent, almost childish, gayety;—but in Great Britain"—and he smiled,—"it looks nowadays as if it were viewed very generally as a personal injury and bore,—a kind of title bestowed without the necessary money to keep it up! And this money people set themselves steadily to obtain, with many a weary grunt and groan, while they are, for the most part, forgetful of anything else life may have to offer."

"But what Is life without plenty of money?" inquired the Duchess carelessly—"Surely, not worth the trouble of living!"

Alwyn looked at her steadily, and a swift flush colored her smooth cheek. She toyed with the magnificent diamond spray at her breast, and wondered what strange spell was in this man's brilliant gray-black eyes!—did he guess that she—even she—had sold herself to the Duc de la Santoisie for the sake of his money and title as easily and unresistingly as though she were a mere purchasable animal?

"That is an argument I would rather not enter into," he said gently—"It would lead us too far. But I am convinced, that whether dire poverty or great riches be our portion, life, considered apart from its worldly appendages, is always worth living, if lived WELL."

"Pray, how can you separate life from its worldly appendages?"— inquired a satirical-looking gentleman opposite—"Life Is the world, and the things of the world; when we lose sight of the world, we lose ourselves,—in short, we die,—and the world is at an end, and we with it. That's plain practical philosophy."

"Possibly it may be called philosophy"—returned Alwyn—"It is not Christianity."

"Oh, Christianity!"—and the gentleman gave a portentous sniff of contempt—"That is a system of faith that is rapidly dying out; fast falling into contempt!—In fact, with the scientific and cultured classes, it is already an exploded doctrine."

"Indeed!"—Alwyn's glance swept over him with a faint, cold scorn—"And what religion do the scientific and cultured classes propose to invent as a substitute?"

"There's no necessity for any substitute,"—said the gentleman rather impatiently. "For those who want to believe in something supernatural, there are plenty of different ideas afloat, Esoteric Buddhism for example,—and what is called Scientific Religion and Natural Religion,—any, or all, of these are sufficient to gratify the imaginative cravings of the majority, till they have been educated out of imagination altogether:—but, for advanced thinkers, religion is really not required at all."*

"Nay, I think we must worship SOMETHING!" retorted Alwyn, a fine satire in his rich voice, "if it be only SELF!—Self is an excellent deity!—accommodating, and always ready to excuse sin,—why should we not build temples, raise altars, and institute services to the glory and honor of SELF?—Perhaps the time is ripe for a public proclamation of this creed?—It will be easily propagated, for the beginnings of it are in the heart of every man, and need very little fostering!"

His thrilling tone, together with the calm, half-ironical persuasiveness of his manner, sent a sudden hush down the table. Every one turned eagerly toward him,—some amused, some wondering, some admiring, while Villiers felt his heart beating with uncomfortable quickness,—he hated religious discussions, and always avoided them, and now here was Alwyn beginning one, and he the centre of a company of persons who were for the most part avowed agnostics, to whose opinions his must necessarily be in direct and absolute opposition! At the same time, he remembered that those who were sure of their faith never lost their temper about it,—and as he glanced at his friend's perfectly serene and coldly smiling countenance, he saw there was no danger of his letting slip, even for a moment, his admirable power of self-command. The Duc de la Santoisie, meanwhile, settling his mustache, and gracefully

---

* The world is indebted to Mr. Andrew Lang for the newest "logical" explanation of the Religious Instinct in Man:—namely, that the very idea of God first arose from the terror and amazement of an ape at the sound of the thunder! So choice and soul-moving a definition of Deity needs no comment!

MARIE CORELLI

waving one hand, on which sparkled a large diamond ring, bent forward a little with a courteous, deprecatory gesture.

"I think"—he said, in soft, purring accents,—"that my friend, Dr. Mudley"—here he bowed toward the saturnine looking individual who had entered into conversation with Alwyn—"takes a very proper, and indeed a very lofty, view of the whole question. The moral sense"— and he laid a severely weighty emphasis on these words,—"the moral sense of each man, if properly trained, is quite sufficient to guide him through existence, without any such weakness as reliance on a merely supposititious Deity."

The Duke's French way of speaking English was charming; he gave an expressive roll to his r's, especially when he said "the moral sense," that of itself almost carried conviction. His wife smiled as she heard him, and her smile was not altogether pleasant. Perhaps she wondered by what criterion of excellence he measured his own "moral sense," or whether, despite his education and culture, he had any "moral sense" at all, higher than that of the pig, who eats to be eaten! But Alwyn spoke, and she listened intently, finding a singular fascination in the soft and quiet modulation of his voice, which gave a vaguely delicious suggestion of music underlying speech.

"To guide people by their moral sense alone"—he said—"you must first prove plainly to them that the moral sense exists, together with moral responsibility. You will find this difficult,—as the virtue implied is intangible, unseeable;—one cannot say of it, lo here!—or lo there!— it is as complicated and subtle as any other of the manifestations of pure Spirit. Then you must decide on one universal standard, or reasonable conception of what 'morality' is. Again, you are met by a crowd of perplexities,—as every nation, and every tribe, has a totally different idea of the same thing. In some countries it is 'moral' to have many wives; in others, to drown female children; in others, to solemnly roast one's grandparents for dinner! Supposing, however, that you succeed, with the aid of all the philosophers, teachers, and scientists, in drawing up a practical Code of Morality—do you not think an enormous majority will be found to ask you by whose authority you set forth this Code?—and by what right you deem it necessary to enforce it? You may say, 'By the authority of Knowledge and by the right of Morality'—but since you admit to there being no spiritual or divine inspiration for your law, you will be confronted by a legion of opponents who will assure you, and probably with perfect justice, that their idea of morality is as good as yours, and their knowledge as excellent,—that your Code appears to them faulty in many respects, and that, therefore, they purpose making another one, more suited to their liking. Thus, out of your one famous Moral System would spring thousands of others, formed to gratify the various tastes of different individuals, precisely in the same manner as sects have sprung out of the wholly unnecessary and foolish human arguments on Christianity;—only that there would lack the one indestructible, pure Selfless Example that even the most quarrelsome bigot must inwardly respect,—namely, Christ Himself. And 'morality' would remain exactly where it is:—neither better nor worse for all the trouble taken concerning it. It needs something more than the 'moral' sense to rightly ennoble man,—it needs the SPIRITUAL sense;—the fostering of the INSTINCTIVE IMMORTAL ASPIRATION OF THE CREATURE, to make him comprehend the responsibility of his present life, as a preparation for his higher and better destiny. The cultured, the scholarly, the ultra-refined, may live well and uprightly by their 'moral sense,'—if they so choose, provided they have some great ideal to measure themselves by,—but even these, without faith in God, may sometimes slip, and fall into deeper depths of ruin than they dreamed of, when self-centred on those heights of virtue where they fancied themselves exempt from danger."

He paused,—there was a curious stillness in the room,—many eyes were lowered, and M. le Duc's composure was evidently not quite so absolute as usual.

"Taken at its best"—he continued—"the world alone is certainly not worth fighting for;—we see the fact exemplified every day in the cases of those who, surrounded by all that a fair fortune can bestow upon them, deliberately hurl themselves out of existence by their own free will and act,—indeed, suicide is a very general accompaniment of Agnosticism. And self-slaughter, though it may be called madness, is far more often the result of intellectual misery."

"Of course, too much learning breeds brain disease"—remarked Dr. Mudley sententiously—"but only in weak subjects,—and in my opinion the weak are better out of the world. We've no room for them nowadays."

"You say truly, sir,"—replied Alwyn—"we have no room for them, and no patience! They show themselves feeble, and forthwith the strong oppress them;—they can hope for little comfort here, and less help. It is well, therefore, that some of these 'weak' should still believe in God,

MARIE CORELLI

since they can certainly pin no faith on the justice of their fellow-man! But I cannot agree with you that much learning breeds brain disease. Provided the learning be accompanied by a belief in the Supreme Wisdom,—provided every step of study be taken upward toward that Source of all Knowledge,—one cannot learn too much, since hope increases with discernment, and on such food the brain grows stronger, healthier, and more capable of high effort. But dispense with the Spirit of the Whole, and every movement, though it SEEM forward, is in truth BACKWARD;—study involves bewilderment,—science becomes a reeling infinitude of atoms, madly whirling together for no purpose save death, or, at the best, incessant Change, in which mortal life is counted as nothing:—and Nature frowns at us, a vast Question, to which there is no Answer,—an incomprehensible Force, against which wretched Man, gifted with all manner of splendid and Godlike capacities, battles forever and forever in vain! This is the terrible material lesson you would have us learn to-day, the lesson that maddens pupil and teacher alike, and has not a glimmer of consolation to offer to any living soul! What a howling wilderness this world would be if given over entirely to Materialism!—Scarce a line of division could be drawn between men and the brute beasts of the field! I consider,—though possibly I am only one among many of widely differing opinion,—that if you take the hope of an after-joy and blessedness away from the weary, perpetually toiling Million, you destroy at one wanton blow their best, purest, and noblest aspirations. As for the Christian Religion, I cannot believe that so grand and holy a Symbol is perishing among us,—we have a monarch whose title is 'Defender of the Faith,'—we live in an age of civilization which is primarily the result of that faith,—and if, as this gentleman assures me,"—and he made a slight, courteous inclination toward his opposite neighbor—"Christianity is exploded,— then certainly the greatness of this hitherto great nation is exploding with it! But I do not think that because a few skeptics uplift their wailing 'All is vanity' from their self-created desert of Agnosticism, THEREFORE the majority of men and women are turning renegades from the simplest, most humane, most unselfish Creed that ever the world has known. It may be so,—but, at present, I prefer to trust in the higher spiritual instincts of man at his best, rather than accept the testimony of the lesser Unbelieving against the greater Many, whose strength, comfort, patience, and endurance, if these virtues come not from God, come not at all."

His forcible, incisive manner of speaking, together with his perfect equanimity and concise clearness of argument, had an evident effect on those who listened. Here was no rampant fanatic for particular forms of doctrine or pietism,—here was a man who stated his opinions calmly, frankly, and with an absolute setting-forth of facts which could scarcely be denied,—a man, who firmly grounded himself, made no attempt to force any one's belief, but who simply took a large view of the whole, and saw, as it were in a glance, what the world might become without faith in a Divine Cause and Principle of Creation. And once GRANT this Divine Cause and Principle to be actually existent, then all other divine and spiritual things become possible, no matter how IMPOSSIBLE they seem to dull mortal comprehension.

A brief pause followed his words,—a pause of vague embarrassment. The Duchess was the first to break it.

"You have very noble ideas, Mr. Alwyn,"—she said with a faint, wavering smile—"But I am afraid your conception of things, both human and divine, is too exalted, and poetically imaginative, to be applied to our every-day life. We cannot close our ears to the thunders of science,—we cannot fail to perceive that we mortals are of as small account in the plan of the Universe as grains of sand on the seashore. It is very sad that so it should be, and yet so it is! And concerning Christianity, the poor system has been so belabored of late with hard blows, that it is almost a wonder it still breathes. There is no end to the books that have been written disproving and denouncing it,—moreover, we have had the subject recently treated in a novel which excites our sympathies in behalf of a clergyman, who, overwhelmed by scholarship, finds he can no longer believe in the religion he is required to teach, and who renounces his living in consequence. The story is in parts pathetic,—it has had a large circulation,—and numbers of people who never doubted their Creed before, certainly doubt it now."

Alwyn shrugged his shoulders. "Faith uprooted by a novel!" he said—"Alas, poor faith! It could never have been well established at any time, to be so easy of destruction! No book in the world, whether of fact or fiction, could persuade me either To or FROM the consciousness of what my own individual Spirit instinctively KNOWS. Faith cannot be taught or forced,—neither, if TRUE, can it be really destroyed,—it is a God-born, God-fostered INTUITION, immortal as God Himself. The ephemeral theories set forth in books should not be able to influence it by so much as a hair's breadth."

"Truth is, however, often conveyed through the medium of fiction,"—observed Dr. Mudley—"and the novel alluded to was calculated to disturb the mind, and arouse trouble in the heart of many an ardent believer. It was written by a woman."

"Nay, then"—said Alwyn quickly, with a darkening flash in his eyes,—"if women give up faith, let the world prepare for strange disaster! Good, God-loving women,—women who pray,—women who hope,—women who inspire men to do the best that is in them,—these are the safety and glory of nations! When women forget to kneel,—when women cease to teach their children the 'Our Father,' by whose grandly simple plea Humanity claims Divinity as its origin,—then shall we learn what is meant by 'men's hearts failing them for fear and for looking after those things which are coming on the earth.' A woman who denies Christ repudiates Him, who, above all others, made her sex as free and honored as everywhere in Christendom it Is. He never refused woman's prayer,—He had patience for her weakness,—pardon for her sins,—and any book written by woman's hand that does Him the smallest shadow of wrong is to me as gross an act, as that of one who, loaded with benefits, scruples not to murder his benefactor!"

The Duchess de la Santoisie moved uneasily,—there was a vibration in Alwyn's voice that went to her very heart. Strange thoughts swept cloud-like across her mind,—again she saw in fancy a little fair, dead child that she had loved,—her only one, on whom she had spent all the tenderness of which her nature was capable. It had died at the prettiest age of children,—the age of lisping speech and softly tottering feet, when a journey from the protecting background of a wall to outstretched maternal arms seems fraught with dire peril to the tiny adventurer, and is only undertaken with the help of much coaxing, sweet laughter, and still sweeter kisses. She remembered how, in spite of her "free" opinions, she had found it impossible not to teach her little one a prayer;—and a sudden mist of tears blurred her sight, as she recollected the child's last words,—words uttered plaintively in the death grasp of a cruel fever, "Suffer me. . . to come to Thee!"—A quick sigh escaped her lips,—the diamonds on her breast heaved restlessly,—lifting her eyes, grown soft with gentle memory, she encountered those of Alwyn, and again she asked herself, could he read her thoughts? His steadfast gaze seemed to encompass her, and absorb in a grave, compassionate earnestness the entire comprehension of her life. Her husband's polite, mellifluous accents roused her from this half-reverie.

"I confess I am surprised, Mr. Alwyn,"—he was saying—"that you, a man of such genius and ability, should be still in the leading strings of the Church!"

"There is No Church"—returned Alwyn quietly,—"The world is waiting for one! The Alpha Beta of Christianity has been learned and recited more or less badly by the children of men for nearly two thousand years,—the actual grammar and meaning of the whole Language has yet to be deciphered. There have been, and are, what are CALLED Churches,—one especially, which, if it would bravely discard mere vulgar superstition, and accept, absorb, and use the discoveries of Science instead, might, and possibly WILL, blossom into the true, universal, and pure Christian Fabric. Meanwhile, in the shaking to and fro of things,—the troublous sifting of the wheat from the chaff,—we must be content to follow by the Way of the Cross as best we can. Christianity has fallen into disrepute, probably because of the Self-Renunciation it demands,—for, in this age, the primal object of each individual is manifestly to serve Self only. It is a wrong road,—a side-lane that leads nowhere,—and we shall inevitably have to turn back upon it and recover the right path—if not now, why then hereafter!"

His voice had a tremor of pain within it;—he was thinking of the millions of men and women who were voluntarily wandering astray into a darkness they did not dream of,—and his heart, the great, true heart of the Poet, became filled with an indescribable passion of yearning.

"No wonder," he mused—"no wonder that Christ came hither for the sake of Love! To rescue, to redeem, to save, to bless! . . . O Divine sympathy for sorrow! If I—a man—can feel such aching pity for the woes of others, how vast, how limitless, how tender, must be the pity of God!"

And his eyes softened,—he almost forgot his surroundings. He was entirely unaware of the various deep and wistful emotions he had wakened in the hearts of his hearers. There was a great attractiveness in him that he was not conscious of,—and while all present certainly felt that he, though among them, was not of them, they were at the same time curiously moved by an impression that notwithstanding his being, as it were, set apart from their ways of existence, his sympathetic influence surrounded them as resistlessly as a pure atmosphere in which they drew long refreshing breaths of healthier life.

"I should like,"—suddenly said a bearded individual who was seated half-way down the table, and who had listened attentively to everything—"I should like to tell you a few things about Esoteric Buddhism!—I am sure it is a faith that would suit you admirably!"

Alwyn smiled, courteously enough. "I shall be happy to hear your views on the subject, sir," he answered gently—"But I must tell you that before I left England for the East, I had studied that theory, together with many others that were offered as substitutes for Christianity, and I found it totally inadequate to meet the highest demands of the spiritual intelligence. I may also add, that I have read carefully all the principal works against Religion,—from the treatises of the earliest skeptics down to Voltaire and others of our own day. Moreover, I had, not so very long ago, rejected the Christian Faith; that I now accept and adhere to it, is not the result of my merit or attainment,—but simply the outcome of an undeserved blessing and singularly happy fortune."

"Pardon me, Mr. Alwyn"—said Madame de la Santoisie with a sweet smile—"By all the laws of nature I must contradict you there! Your fame and fortune must needs be the reward of merit,—since true happiness never comes to the undeserving."

Alwyn made no reply,—inasmuch as to repudiate the idea of personal merit too warmly is, as such matters are judged nowadays, suggestive of more conceit than modesty. He skilfully changed the conversation, and it glided off by degrees into various other channels,—music, art, science, and the political situation of the hour. The men and women assembled, as though stimulated and inspired by some new interest, now strove to appear at their very best—and the friction of intellect with intellect resulted in more or less brilliancy of talk, which, for once, was totally free from the flippant and mocking spirit which usually pervaded the Santoisie social circle. On all the subjects that came up for discussion Alwyn proved himself thoroughly at home—and M. le Duc, sitting in a silence that was most unwonted with him, became filled with amazement to think that this man, so full of fine qualities and intellectual abilities, should be actually a CHRISTIAN!—The thing was quite incongruous, or seemed so to the ironical wit of the born and bred Parisian,—he tried to consider it absurd,—even laughable,—but his efforts merely resulted in a sense of uneasy personal shame. This poet was, at any rate, a MAN,—he might have posed for a Coriolanus or Marc Antony;—and there was something supreme about him that could not be SNEERED DOWN.

The dinner, meanwhile, reached its dessert climax, and the Duchess rose, giving the customary departing signal to her lady-guests. Alwyn hastened to open the door for her, and she passed out, followed by a train of women in rich and rustling costumes, all of whom, as they swept past the kingly figure that with slightly bent head and courteous mien thus paid silent homage to their sex, were conscious of very unusual emotions of respect and reverence. How would it be, some of them thought, if they were more frequently brought into contact with such royal and gracious manhood? Would not love then become indeed a hallowed glory, and marriage a true sacrament! Was it not possible for men to be the gods of this world, rather than the devils they so often are? Such were a few of the questions that flitted dimly through the minds of the society-fagged fair ones that clustered round the Duchess de la Santoisie, and eagerly discussed Alwyn's personal beauty and extraordinary charm of manner.

The gentlemen did not absent themselves long, and with their appearance from the dining-room the reception of the evening began. Crowds of people arrived and crammed up the stairs, filling every corridor and corner, and Alwyn, growing tired of the various introductions and shaking of hands to which he was submitted, managed presently to slip away into a conservatory adjoining the great drawing-room,—a cool, softly lighted place full of flowering azaleas and rare palms. Here he sat for a while among the red and white blossoms, listening to the incessant hum of voices, and wondering what enjoyment human beings could find in thus herding together en masse, and chattering all at once as though life depended on chatter, when the rustling of a woman's dress disturbed his brief solitude. He rose directly, as he saw his fair hostess approaching him.

"Ah, you have fled away from us, Mr. Alwyn!" she said with a slight smile—"I do not wonder at it. These receptions are the bane of one's social existence."

"Then why do you give them?"—asked Alwyn, half laughingly.

"Why? Oh, because it is the fashion, I suppose!" she answered languidly, leaning against a marble column that supported the towering frondage of a tropical fern, and toying with her fan,—"And I, like others, am a slave to fashion. I have escaped for one moment, but I must go back directly. Mr. Alwyn. . ." She hesitated,—then came straight up to him, and laid her hand upon his arm—"I want to thank you!"

"To thank me?" he repeated in surprised accents.

"Yes!"—she said steadily—"To thank you for what you have said to-night. We live in a dreary age, when no one has much faith or hope, and still less charity,—death is set before us as the final end of all,—and life as lived by most, people is not only not worth living, but utterly contemptible! Your clearly expressed opinions have made me think it is possible to do better,"—her lips quivered a little, and her breath came and went quickly,—"and I shall begin to try and find out how this 'better' can be consummated! Pray do not think me foolish—"

"*I* think you foolish!" and with gravest courtesy Alwyn raised her hand, and touched it gently with his lips, then as gently released it. His action was full of grace,—it implied reverence, trust, honor,—and the Duchess looked at him with soft, wet eyes in which a smile still lingered.

"If there were more men like you,"—she said suddenly—"what a difference it would make to us women! We should be proud to share the burdens of life with those on whose absolute integrity and strength we could rely,—but, in these days, we do not rely, so much as we despise,— we cannot love, so much as we condemn! You are a Poet,—and for you the world takes ideal colors,—for you perchance the very heavens have opened;—but remember that the millions, who, in the present era, are ground down under the heels of the grimmest necessity, have no such glimpses of God as are vouchsafed to You! They are truly in the darkness and shadow of death,—they hear no angel music,—they sit in dungeons, howled at by preachers and teachers who make no actual attempt to lead them into light and liberty,—while we, the so-called 'upper' classes, are imprisoned as closely as they, and crushed by intolerable weights of learning, such as many of us are not fitted to bear. Those who aspire heavenwards are hurled to earth,—those who of their own choice cling to death, become so fastened to it, that even if they wished, they could not rise. Believe me, you will be sorely disheartened in your efforts toward the highest good,—you will find most people callous, careless, ignorant, and forever scoffing at what they do not, and will not, understand,—you had better leave us to our dust and ashes,"— and a little mirthless laugh escaped her lips,—"for to pluck us from thence now will almost need a second visitation of Christ, in whom, if He came, we should probably not believe! Moreover, you must not forget that we have read Darwin,—and we are so charmed with our monkey ancestors, that we are doing our best to imitate them in every possible way,—in the hope that, with time and patience, we may resolve ourselves back into the original species!"

With which bitter sarcasm, uttered half mockingly, half in good earnest, she left him and returned to her guests. Not very long afterward, he having sought and found Villiers, and suggested to him that it was time to make a move homeward, approached her in company with his friend, and bade her farewell.

"I don't think we shall see you often in society, Mr. Alwyn"—she said, rather wistfully, as she gave him her hand,—"You are too much of a Titan among pigmies!"

He flushed and waved aside the remark with a few playful words; unlike his Former Self, if there was anything in the world he shrank from, it was flattery, or what seemed like flattery. Once outside the house he drew a long breath of relief, and glanced gratefully up at the sky, bright with the glistening multitude of stars. Thank God, there were worlds in that glorious expanse of ether peopled with loftier types of being than what is called Humanity! Villiers looked at him questioningly:

"Tired of your own celebrity, Alwyn?" he asked, taking him by the arm,—"Are the pleasures of Fame already exhausted?"

Alwyn smiled,—he thought of the fame of Sah-luma, Laureate bard of Al-kyris!

"Nay, if the dream that I told you of had any meaning at all"—he replied—"then I enjoyed and exhausted those pleasures long ago! Perhaps that is the reason why my 'celebrity' seems such a poor and tame circumstance now. But I was not thinking of myself,—I was wondering whether, after all, the slight power I have attained can be of much use to others. I am only one against many."

"Nevertheless, there is an old maxim which says that one hero makes a thousand"—said Villiers quietly—"And it is an undeniable fact that the vastest number ever counted, begins at the very beginning with ONE!"

Alwyn met his smiling, earnest eyes with a quick, responsive light in his own, and the two friends walked the rest of the way home in silence.

XXXVI

HELIOBAS

Some few days after the Duchess's dinner-party, Alwyn was strolling one morning through the Park, enjoying to the full the keen, fresh odors of the Spring,—odors that even in London cannot altogether lose their sweetness, so long as hyacinths and violets consent to bloom, and almond-trees to flower, beneath the too often unpropitious murkiness of city skies. It had been raining, but now the clouds had rolled off, and the sun shone as brightly as it ever CAN shine on the English capital, sending sparkles of gold among the still wet foliage, and reviving the little crocuses, that had lately tumbled down in heaps on the grass, like a frightened fairy army put to rout by the onslaught of the recent shower. A blackbird, whose cheery note suggested melodious memories drawn from the heart of the quiet country, was whistling a lively improvisation on the bough of a chestnut-tree, whereof the brown shining buds were just bursting into leaf,—and Alwyn, whose every sense was pleasantly attuned to the small, as well as great, harmonies of nature, paused for a moment to listen to the luscious piping of the feathered minstrel, that in its own wild woodland way had as excellent an idea of musical variation as any Mozart or Chopin. Leaning against one of the park benches, with his back turned to the main thoroughfare, he did not observe the approach of a man's tall, stately figure, that, with something of his own light, easy, swinging step, had followed him rapidly along for some little distance, and that now halted abruptly within a pace or two of where he stood,—a man whose fine face and singular distinction of bearing had caused many a passer-by to stare at him in vague admiration, and to wonder who such a regal-looking personage might possibly be. Alwyn, however, absorbed in thought, saw no one, and was about to resume his onward walk, when suddenly, as though moved by some instinctive impulse, he turned sharply around, and in so doing confronted the stranger, who straightway advanced, lifting his hat and smiling. One amazed glance,—and then with an exclamation of wonder, recognition, and delight, Alwyn sprang forward and grasped his extended hand.

"HELIOBAS!" he exclaimed. "Is it possible YOU are in London!—YOU, of all men in the world!"

"Even so!"—replied Heliobas gayly—"And why not? Am I incongruous, and out of keeping with the march of modern civilization?"

Alwyn looked at him half-bewildered, half-incredulous,—he could hardly believe his own eyes. It seemed such an altogether amazing thing to meet this devout and grave Chaldean philosopher, this mystic monk of the Caucasus, here in the very centre, as it were, of the world's business, traffic, and pleasure; one might as well have expected to find a haloed saint in the whirl of a carnival masquerade! Incongruous? Out of keeping?—Yes, certainly he was,—for though clad in the plain, conventional garb to which the men of the present day are doomed by the fiat of commerce and custom, the splendid dignity and picturesqueness of his fine personal appearance was by no means abated, and it was just this that marked him out, and made of him as wonderful a figure in London as though some god or evangelist should suddenly pass through a wilderness of chattering apes and screaming vultures.

"But how and when did you come?"—asked Alwyn presently, recovering from his first glad shock of surprise—"You see how genuine is my astonishment,—why, I thought you were a perpetually vowed recluse,—that you never went into the world at all, . . ."

"Neither I do"—rejoined Heliobas—"save when strong necessity demands. But our Order is not so 'inclosed' that, if Duty calls, we cannot advance to its beckoning, and there are certain times when both I and those of my fraternity mingle with men in common, undistinguished from the ordinary inhabitants of cities either by dress, customs, or manners,—as you see!"—and he laughingly touched his overcoat, the dark rough cloth of which was relieved by a broad collar and revers of rich sealskin,—"Would you not take me for a highly respectable brewer, par example, conscious that his prowess in the making of beer has entitled him, not only to an immediate seat in Parliament, but also to a Dukedom in prospective?"

Alwyn, smiled at the droll inapplicability of this comparison,—and Heliobas cheerfully continued—"I am on the wing just now,—bound for Mexico. I had business in London, and arrived here two days since,—two days more will see me again en voyage. I am glad to have met you thus by chance, for I did not know your address, and though I might have obtained that through your publishers, I hesitated about it, not being quite certain as to whether a letter or visit from me might be welcome."

"Surely,"—began Alwyn, and then he paused, a flush rising to his brow as he remembered how obstinately he had doubted and suspected this man's good faith and intention toward him, and how he had even received his farewell benediction at Dariel with more resentment than gratitude.

"Everywhere I hear great things of you, Mr. Alwyn,"—went on Heliobas gently, taking no notice of his embarrassment—"Your fame is now indeed unquestionable! With all my heart I congratulate you, and wish you long life and health to enjoy the triumph of your genius!"

Alwyn smiled, and turning, fixed his clear, soft eyes full on the speaker.

"I thank you!" he said simply,—"But, . . . you, who have such a quick instinctive comprehension of the minds and characters of men,—judge for yourself whether I attach any value to the poor renown I have won,—renown that I once would have given my very life to possess!"

As he spoke, he stopped,—they were walking down a quiet side-path under the wavering shadow of newly bourgeoning beeches, and a bright shaft of sunshine struck through the delicate foliage straight on his serene and handsome countenance. Heliobas gave him a swift, keen, observant glance,—in a moment he noticed what a marvellous change had been wrought in the man who, but a few months before, had come to him, a wreck of wasted life,—a wreck that was not only ready, but willing, to drift into downward currents and whirlpools of desperate, godless, blank, and hopeless misery. And now, how completely he was transformed!—Health colored his cheeks and sparkled in his eyes; health, both of body and mind, gave that quick brilliancy to his smile, and that easy, yet powerful poise to his whole figure,—while the supreme consciousness of the Immortal Spirit within him surrounded him with the same indescribable fascination and magnetic attractiveness that distinguished Heliobas himself, even as it distinguishes all who have in good earnest discovered and accepted the only true explanation of their individual mystery of being. One steady, flashing look,—and then Heliobas silently held out his hand. As silently Alwyn clasped it,—and the two men understood each other. All constraint was at an end,—and when they resumed their slow sauntering under the glistening green branches, they were mutually aware that they now held an almost equal rank in the hierarchy of spiritual knowledge, strength, and sympathy.

"Evidently your adventure to the Ruins of Babylon was not altogether without results!" said Heliobas softly—"Your appearance indicates happiness,—is your life at last complete?"

"Complete?—No!"—and Alwyn sighed somewhat impatiently—"It cannot be complete, so long as its best and purest half is elsewhere! My fame is, as you can guess, a mere ephemera,—a small vanishing point, in comparison with the higher ambition I have now in view. Listen,—you know nothing of what happened to me on the Field of Ardath,—I should have written to you perhaps, but it is better to speak—I will tell you all as briefly as I can."

And talking in an undertone, with his arm linked through that of his companion, he related the whole strange story of the visitation of Edris, the Dream of Al-Kyris, his awakening on the Prophet's Field at sunrise, and his final renunciation of Self at the Cross of Christ. Heliobas listened to him in perfect silence, his eyes alone expressing with what eager interest and attention he followed every incident of the narrative.

"And now," said Alwyn in conclusion,—"I always try to remember for my own comfort that I LEFT my dead Self in the burning ruin of that dream built city of the past,—or SEEMED to leave it, . . . and yet I feel sometimes as if its shadow presence clung to me still! I look in the mirror and see strange, faint reflections of the actual personal attributes of the slain Sah-luma,—occasionally these are so strong and distinctly marked that I turn away in anger from my own image! Why, I loved that Phantasm of a Poet in my dream as I must for ages have loved myself to my own utter undoing!—I admired his work with such extravagant fondness, that, thinking of it, I blush for shame at my own thus manifest conceit!—In truth there is only one thing in that pictured character of his, I can for the present judge myself free from,—namely, the careless rejection of true love for false,—the wanton misprisal of a faithful heart, such as Niphrata's, whose fair child-face even now often flits before my remorseful memory,—and the evil, sensual passion for a woman whose wickedness was as evident as her beauty was paramount! I could never understand or explain this wilful, headstrong weakness in my Shadow-Self—it was the one circumstance in my vision that seemed to have little to do with the positive Me in its application,—but now I thoroughly grasp the meaning of the lesson conveyed, which is that No MAN EVER REALLY KNOWS HIMSELF, OR FATHOMS THE DEPTHS OF HIS OWN POSSIBLE INCONSISTENCIES. And as matters stand with me at the present time, I am hemmed in on all sides by difficulties,—for since the modern success of that very anciently composed poem, 'Nourhalma'"—and he smiled—"my friends and acquaintances are doing their best to make me think as much of myself as if I were,—well!

all that I am NOT. Do what I will, I believe am still an egoist,—nay, I am sure of it,—for even as regards my heavenly saint, Edris, I am selfish!"

"How so?" asked Heliobas, with a grave side-glance of admiration at the thoughtful face and meditative earnest eyes of this poet, this once bitter and blasphemous skeptic, grown up now to a majesty of faith that not all the scorn of men or devils could ever shake again.

"I want her!"—he replied, and there was a thrill of pathetic yearning in his voice—"I long for her every moment of the day and night! It seems, too, as if everything combined to encourage this craving in me,—this fond, mad desire to draw her down from her own bright sphere of joy,—down to my arms, my heart, my life! See!"—and he stopped by a bed of white hyacinths, nodding softly in the faint breeze—"Even those flowers remind me of her! When I look up at the blue sky I think of the radiance of her eyes,—they were the heaven's own color,—when I see light clouds floating together half gray, half tinted by the sun, they seem to me to resemble the soft and noiseless garb she wore,—the birds sing, only to recall to me the lute-like sweetness of her voice,—and at night, when I behold the millions upon millions of stars that are worlds, peopled as they must be with thousands of wonderful living creatures, perhaps as spiritually composed as she, I sometimes find it hard, that out of all the exhaustless types of being that love, serve, and praise God in Heaven, this one fair Spirit,—only this one angel-maiden should not be spared to help and comfort me! Yes!—I am selfish to the heart's core, my friend!"—and his eyes darkened with a vague wistfulness and trouble,—"Moreover, I have weakly striven to excuse my selfishness to my own conscience thus:—I have thought that if SHE were vouchsafed to me for the remainder of my days, I might then indeed do lasting good, and leave lasting consolation to the world,—such work might be performed as would stir the most callous souls to life and energy and aspiration,—with HER sweet Presence near me, visibly close and constant, there is no task so difficult that I would not essay and conquer in, for her sake, her service, her greater glory! But ALONE!"—and he gave a slight, hopeless gesture—"Nay,—Christ knows I will do the utmost best I can, but the solitary ways of life are hard!"

Heliobas regarded him fixedly.

"You SEEM to be alone"—he said presently, after a pause,—"but truly you are not so. You think you are set apart to do your work in solitude,—nevertheless, she whom you love may be near you even while you speak!

Still I understand what you mean,—you long to SEE her again,—to realize her tangible form and presence,—well!—this cannot be until you pass from this earth and adopt HER nature, . . . unless,—unless SHE descends hither, and adopts YOURS!"

The last words were uttered slowly and impressively, and Alwyn's countenance brightened with a sudden irresistible rapture.

"That would be impossible!" he said, but his voice trembled, and there was more interrogativeness than assertion in his tone.

"Impossible in most cases,—yes"—agreed Heliobas—"but in your specially chosen and privileged estate, I cannot positively say that such a thing might not be."

For one moment a strange, eager brilliancy shone in Alwyn's eyes,— the next, he set his lips hard, and made a firm gesture of denial.

"Do not tempt me, good Heliobas," he said, with a faint smile—"Or, rather, do not let me tempt myself! I bear in constant mind what she, my Edris, told me when she left me,—that we should not meet again till after death, unless the longing of my love COMPELLED. Now, if it be true, as I have often thought, that I COULD compel,—by what right dare I use such power, if power I have upon her? She loves me,—I love her,— and by the force of love, such love as ours, . . . who knows!—I might perchance persuade her to adopt a while this mean, uneasy vesture of mere mortal life,—and the very innate perception that I MIGHT do so, is the sharpest trial I have to endure. Because if I would thoroughly conquer myself, I must resist this feeling;—nay, I WILL resist it,—for let it cost me what it may, I have sworn that the selfishness of my own personal desire shall never cross or cloud the radiance of her perfect happiness!"

"But suppose"—suggested Heliobas quietly, "suppose she were to find an even more complete happiness in making YOU happy?"

Alwyn shook his head. "My friend do not let us talk of it!"—he answered—"No joy can be more complete than the joy of Heaven,— and that in its full blessedness is hers."

"That in its full blessedness is NOT hers,"—declared Heliobas with emphasis—"And, moreover, it can never be hers, while YOU are still an exile and a wanderer! Friend Poet, do you think that even Heaven is wholly happy to one who loves, and whose Beloved is absent?"

A tremor shook Alwyn's nerves,—his eyes glowed as though the inward fire of his soul had lightened them, but his face grew very pale.

"No more of this, for God's sake!" he said passionately. "I must not dream of it,—I dare not! I become the slave of my own imagined rapture,—the coward who falls conquered and trembling before his own desire of delight! Rather let me strive to be glad that she, my angel-love, is so far removed from my unworthiness,—let her, if she be near me now, read my thoughts, and see in them how dear, how sacred is her fair and glorious memory,—how I would rather endure an eternity of anguish, than make her sad for one brief hour of mortal-counted time!"

He was greatly moved,—his voice trembled with the fervor of its own music, and Heliobas looked at him with a grave and very tender smile.

"Enough!"—he said gently—"I will speak no further on this subject, which I see affects you deeply. Nevertheless, I would have you remember how, when the Master whom we serve passed through His Agony at Gethsemane, and with all the knowledge of His own power and glory strong upon Him, still in His vast self-abnegation said, 'Not My will, but Thine be done!' that then 'there appeared an Angel unto Him from heaven strengthening Him!' Think of this,—for every incident in that Divine-Human Life is a hint for ours,—and often it chances that when we reject happiness for the sake of goodness, happiness is suddenly bestowed upon us. God's miracles are endless,—God's blessings exhaustless, . . . and the marvels of this wondrous Universe are as nothing, compared to the working of His Sovereign Will for good on the lives of those who serve Him faithfully."

Alwyn flashed upon him a quick, half-questioning glance, but was silent,—and they walked on together for some minutes without exchanging a word. A few people passed and repassed them,—some little children were playing hide-and-seek behind the trunks of the largest trees,—the air was fresh and invigorating, and the incessant roar of busy traffic outside the Park palings offered a perpetual noisy reminder of the great world that surged around them,—the world of petty aims and transitory pleasures, with which they, filled full of the knowledge of higher and eternal things, had so little in common save sympathy,—sympathy for the wilful wrong-doing of man, and pity for his self-imposed blindness. Presently Heliobas spoke again in his customary light and cheerful tone:

"Are you writing anything new just now?" he asked. "Or are you resting from literary labor?"

"Well, rest and work are with me very nearly one and the same"— replied Alwyn,—"I think the most absolutely tiring and exhausting thing in the world would be to have nothing to do. Then I can imagine life becoming indeed a weighty burden! Yes, I am engaged on a new poem, . . . it gives me intense pleasure to write it—but whether it will give any one equal pleasure to read it is quite another question."

"Does 'Zabastes' still loom on your horizon?" inquired his companion mirthfully—"Or are you still inclined—as in the Past—to treat him, whether he comes singly or in numbers, as the Poet's court-jester, and paid fool?"

Alwyn laughed lightly. "Perhaps!" he answered, with a sparkle of amusement in his eyes,—"But, really, so far as the wind of criticism goes, I don't think any author nowadays particularly cares whether it blows fair weather or foul. You see, we all know how it is done,—we can name the clubs and cliques from whence it emanates, and we are fully aware that if one leading man of a 'set' gives the starting signal of praise or blame, the rest follow like sheep, without either thought or personal discrimination. Moreover, some of us have met and talked with certain of these magazine and newspaper oracles, and have tested for ourselves the limited extent of their knowledge and the shallowness of their wit. I assure you it often happens that a great author is tried, judged, and condemned by a little casual press-man who, in his very criticism, proves himself ignorant of grammar. Of course, if the public choose to accept such a verdict, why, then, all the worse for the public,— but luckily the majority of men are beginning to learn the ins and outs of the modern critic's business,—they see his or HER methods (it is a notable fact that women do a great deal of criticism now, they being willing to scribble oracular commonplaces at a cheaper rate of pay than men), so that if a book is condemned, people are dubious, and straight way read it for themselves to see what is in it that excites aversion,—if it is praised, they are still dubious, and generally decide that the critical eulogist must have some personal interest in its sale. It is difficult for an author to WIN his public,—but WHEN won, the critics may applaud or deride as suits their humor, it makes no appreciable difference to his popularity. Now I consider my own present fame was won by chance,—a misconception that, as I know, had its ancient foundation in truth, but that, as far as everybody else is concerned, remains a misconception,— so that I estimate my success at its right value, or rather, let me say, at its proper worthlessness."

And in a few words he related how the leaders of English journalism had judged him dead, and had praised his work chiefly because it was posthumous. "I believe"—he added good-humoredly—"that if this mistake had not arisen, I should scarcely have been heard of, since I advocate no particular 'cult' and belong to no Mutual Admiration Alliance, offensive or defensive. But my supposed untimely decease served me better than the Browning Society serves Browning!"

Again he laughed,—Heliobas had listened with a keen and sarcastic enjoyment of the whole story.

"Undoubtedly your 'Zabastes' was no phantom!"—he observed emphatically—"His was evidently a very real existence, and he must have divided himself from one into several, to sit in judgment again upon you in this present day! History repeats itself,—and unhappily all the injustice, hypocrisy, and inconsistency of man is repeated too,—and out of the multitudes that inhabit the earth, how few will succeed in fulfilling their highest destinies! This is the one bitter drop in the cup of our knowledge,—we can, if we choose, save ourselves,—but we can seldom, if ever, save others!"

Alwyn stopped short, his eyes darkening with a swift intensity of feeling.

"Why not?"—he asked earnestly—"Must we look on, and see men rushing toward certain misery, without making an effort to turn them hack?—to warn them of the darkness whither they are bound?—to rescue them before it is too late?"

"My friend, we can make the effort, certainly,—and we are bound to make it, because it is our duty,—but in ninety-nine cases out of a hundred we shall fail of our persuasion. What can I, or you, or any one, do against the iron force of Free-Will? God Himself will not constrain it,—how then shall we? In the Books of Esdras, which have already been of such use to you, you will find the following significant words: 'The Most High hath made this world for many, but the world to come for few. As when thou askest the earth, it shall say unto thee that it giveth much mold wherein earthen vessels are made, and but little dust that gold cometh of, even so is the course of this present world. There be many created but Few shall be saved.'—God elects to be served by Choice—and Not by compulsion; it is His Law that Man shall work out his own immortal destiny,—and nothing can alter this overwhelming Fact. The sublime Example of Christ was given us as a means to assist us in forming our own conclusions,—but there is no coercion in it,—only a Divine Love. You, for instance, were, and are, still perfectly free to reject the whole of your experience on the

Field of Ardath as a delusion,—nothing would be easier, and, from the world's point of view, nothing more natural. Faith and Doubt are equally voluntary acts,—the one is the instinct of the immortal Soul, the other the tendency of the perishable Body,—and the Will decides which of the two shall conquer in the end. I know that you are firm in your high and true conviction,—I know also what thoughts are at work in your brain,—you are bending all your energies on the task of trying to instil into the minds of your fellow-men some comprehension of the enlightenment and hope you yourself possess. Ah, you must prepare for disappointment!—for though the times are tending toward strange upheavals and terrors, when the trumpet-voice of an inspired Poet may do enormous good,—still the name of the wilfully ignorant is Legion,—the age is one of the grossest Mammon worship, and coarsest Atheism,—and the noblest teachings of the noblest teacher, were he even another Shakespeare, must of necessity be but a casting of pearls before swine. Still"—and his rare sweet smile brightened the serene dignity of his features—"fling out the pearls freely all the same,—the swine may grunt at, but cannot rend you,—and a poet's genius should be like the sunlight, that falls on rich and poor, good and bad, with glorious impartiality! If you can comfort one sorrow, check one sin, or rescue one soul from the widening quicksand of the Atheist world, you have sufficient reason to be devoutly thankful."

By this time their walk had led them imperceptibly to one of the gates of egress from the Park, and Heliobas, pointing to a huge square building opposite, said:

"There is the hotel at which I am staying—one of the Americanized monster fabrics in which tired travellers find much splendid show, and little rest! Will you lunch with me?—I am quite alone."

Alwyn gladly assented,—he was most unwilling to part at once from this man, to whom in a measure he felt he owed his present happy and tranquil condition of body and mind; besides, he was curious to find out more about him—to obtain from him, if possible, an entire explanation of the actual tenets and chief characteristics of the system of religious worship he himself practiced and followed. Heliobas seemed to guess his thoughts, for suddenly turning upon him with a quick glance, he observed:

"You want to 'pluck out the heart of my mystery,' as Hamlet says, do you not, my friend?"—and he smiled—"Well, so you shall, if you can discover aught in me that is not already in yourself! I assure you there is nothing preternatural about me,—my peculiar 'eccentricity' consists in steadily adapting myself to the scientific spiritual, as well as scientific material, laws of the Universe. The two sets of laws united make harmony,—hence I find my life harmonious and satisfactory,— this is my 'abnormal' condition of mind,—and you are now fully as 'abnormal' as I am. Come, we will discuss our mutual strange non-conformity to the wild world's custom or caprice over a glass of good wine,—observe, please, that I am neither a 'total abstainer' nor a 'vegetarian,' and that I have a curious fashion of being TEMPERATE, and of using all the gifts of beneficent Nature equally, and without prejudice! While he spoke, they had crossed the road, and they now entered the vestibule of the hotel, where, declining the hall-porter's offer of the "lift," Heliobas ascended the stairs leisurely to the second floor, and ushered his companion into a comfortable private sitting-room.

"Fancy men consenting to be drawn up to their apartments like babes in a basket!" he said laughingly, alluding to the "lift" process—"Upon my word, when I think of the strong people of a past age and compare them with the enervated race of to-day, I feel not only pity, but shame, for the visible degeneration of mankind. Frail nerves, weak hearts, uncertain limbs,—these are common characteristics of the young, nowadays, instead of being as formerly the natural failings of the old. Wear and tear and worry of modern existence?—Oh yes, I know!— but why the wear tear and worry at all? What is it for? Simply for the OVER-GETTING of money. One must live? . . . certainly,—but one is not bound to live in foolish luxury for the sake of out-flaunting one's neighbors. Better to live simply and preserve health, than gain a fortune and be a moping dyspeptic for life. But unless one toils and moils like a beast of burden, one cannot even live simply, some will say! I don't believe that assertion. The peasants of France live simply, and save,—the peasants of England live wretchedly, and waste! Voila la différence! As with nations, so with individuals,—it is all a question of Will. 'Where there's a will there's a way,' is a dreadfully trite copybook maxim, but it's amazingly true all the same. Now let us to the acceptation of these good things,"—this, as a pallid, boyish-looking waiter just then entered the room with the luncheon, and in his bustling to and fro manifested unusual eagerness to make himself agreeable—"I have made excellent friends with this young Ganymede,—he has sworn never to palm off raisin-wine upon me for Chambertin!"

The waiter blushed and chuckled as though he were conscious of having gained special new dignity and importance,—and having laid the table, and set the chairs, he departed with a flourishing bow worthy of a prince's maitre-d'hotel.

"Your name must seem a curious one to these fellows"—observed Alwyn, when he had gone,—"Unusual and even mysterious?"

"Why, yes!"—returned Heliobas with a laugh—"It would be judged so, I suppose, if I ever gave it,—but I don't. It was only in England, and by an Englishman, that I was once, to my utter amazement, addressed as 'He-ly-oh-bas'—and I was quite alarmed at the sound of it! One would think that most people in these educational days knew the Greek word helios,—and one would also imagine it as easy to say Heliobas as heliograph. But now to avoid mistakes, whenever I touch British territory and come into contact with British tongues, I give my Christian name only, Cassimir—the result of which arrangement is, that I am known in this hotel as Mr. Kasmer! Oh, I don't mind in the least—why should I?—neither the English nor the Americans ever pronounce foreign names properly. Why I met a newly established young publisher yesterday, who assured me that most of his authors, the female ones especially, are so ignorant of foreign literature that he doubts whether any of them know whether Cervantes was a writer or an ointment!"

Alwyn laughed. "I dare say the young publisher may be perfectly right,"—he said—"But all the same he has no business to publish the literary emanations of such ignorance."

"Perhaps not!—but what is he to do, if nothing else is offered to him? He has to keep his occupation going somehow,—from bad he must select the best. He cannot create a great genius—he has to wait till Nature, in the course of events, evolves one from the elements. And in the present general dearth of high ability the publishers are really more sinned against than sinning. They spend large sums, and incur large risks, in launching new ventures on the fickle sea of popular favor, and often their trouble is taken all in vain. It is really the stupid egotism of authors that is the stumbling-block in the way of true literature,—each little scribbler that produces a shilling sensational thinks his or her own work a marvel of genius, and nothing can shake them from their obstinate conviction. If every man or woman, before putting pen to paper, would be sure they had something new, suggestive, symbolical, or beautiful to say, how greatly Art might gain by their labors! Authors who take up arms against publishers en masse, and in every transaction expect to be cheated, are doing themselves irreparable injury—they betray the cloven hoof,—namely a greed for money—and when once that passion dominates them, down goes their reputation and they with it. It is the old story over again—'ye cannot serve God and Mammon,'—and all Art is a portion of God,—a descending of the Divine into Humanity."

Alwyn sat for a minute silent and thoughtful. "A descending of the Divine into Humanity!" he repeated slowly—"It seems to me that 'miracle' is forever being enacted—and yet. . . we doubt!"

"We do not doubt—" said Heliobas—"We know,—we have touched Reality! But see yonder!"—and he pointed through the window to the crowded thoroughfare below—"There are the flying phantoms of life,—the men and women who are God-oblivious, and who are therefore no more actually Living than the shadows of Al-Kyris! They shall pass as a breath and be no more,—and this roaring, trafficking metropolis, this immediate centre of civilization, shall ere long disappear off the surface of the earth, and leave not a stone to mark the spot where once it stood! So have thousands of such cities fallen since this planet was flung into space,—and even so shall thousands still fall. Learning, civilization, science, progress,—these things exist merely for the training and education of a chosen few—and out of many earth centuries and generations of men, shall be won only a very small company of angels! Be glad that you have fathomed the mystery of your own life's purpose,—for you are now as much a Positive Identity among vanishing spectres, as you were when, on the Field of Ardath, you witnessed and took part in the Mirage of your Past."

XXXVII

A Missing Record

He spoke the last words with deep feeling and earnestness, and Alwyn, meeting his clear, grave, brilliant eyes, was more than ever impressed by the singular dignity and overpowering magnetism of his presence. Remembering how insufficiently he had realized this man's true worth, when he had first sought him out in his monastic retreat, he was struck by a sudden sense of remorse, and leaning across the table, gently touched his hand.

"How greatly I wronged you once, Heliobas!" he said penitently, with a tremor of appeal in his voice—"Forgive me, will you?—though I shall never forgive myself!"

Heliobas smiled, and cordially pressed the extended hand in his own.

"Nay, there is nothing to forgive, my friend," he answered cheerfully—"and nothing to regret. Your doubts of me were very natural,—indeed, viewed by the world's standard of opinion, much more natural than your present faith, for faith is always a Super-natural instinct. Would you be practically sensible according to modern social theories?—then learn to suspect everybody and everything, even your best friend's good intentions!"

He laughed, and the luncheon being concluded, he rose from the table, and taking an easy-chair nearer the window, motioned Alwyn to do the same.

"I want to talk to you"—he continued, "We may not meet again for years,—you are entering on a difficult career, and a few hints from one who knows and thoroughly understands your position may possibly be of use to you. In the first place, then, let me ask you, have you told any one, save me, the story of your Ardath adventure?"

"One friend only,—my old school comrade, Frank Villiers"—replied Alwyn.

"And what does he say about it?"

"Oh, he thinks it was a dream from beginning to end,"—and Alwyn smiled a little,—"He believes that I set out on my journey with my brain already heated to an imaginative excess, and that the whole thing, even my Angel's presence, was a pure delusion of my

MARIE CORELLI

own overwrought fancy,—a curious and wonderful delusion, but always a delusion."

"He is a very excellent fellow to judge you so leniently"—observed Heliobas composedly, "Most people would call you mad."

"Mad!" exclaimed Alwyn hotly—"Why, I am as sane as any man in London!"

"Saner, I should say,"—replied Heliobas, smiling,—"Compared with some of the eminently 'practical' speculating maniacs that howl and struggle among the fluctuating currents of the Stock Exchange, for instance, you are indeed a marvel of sound and wholesome mental capability! But let us view the matter coolly. You must not expect such an exceptional experience as yours to be believed in by ordinary persons. Because the majority of people, being utterly Unspiritual and worldly, have No such experiences, and they therefore deem them impossible;—they are the gold-fish born in a bowl, who have no consciousness of the existence of an ocean. Moreover, you have no proofs of the truth of your narrative, beyond the change in your own life and disposition,—and that can be easily referred to various other causes. You spoke of having gathered one of the miracle-flowers on the Prophet's field,—may I see it?"

Silently Alwyn drew from his breast-pocket the velvet case in which he always kept the cherished blossom, and taking it tenderly out, placed it in his companion's hand.

"An immortelle"—said Heliobas softly, while the flower, uncurling its silvery petals in the warmth of his palm, opened star-like and white as snow. "An immortelle, rare and possibly unique!—that is all the world would say of it! It cannot be matched,—it will not fade,—true! but you will get no one to believe that! Frown not, good Poet!—I want you to consider me for the moment a practical worldling, bent on driving you from the spiritual position yon have taken up,—and you will see how necessary it is for you to keep the secret of your own enlightenment to yourself, or at least only hint at it through the parables of poesy."

He gave back the Ardath blossom to its owner with reverent care,—and when Alwyn had as reverently put it by, he resumed:

"Your friend Villiers has offered you a perfectly logical and common-sense solution of the mystery of Ardath,—one which, if you chose to accept it, would drive you back into skepticism as easily as a strong wind blows a straw. Only see how simple the intricate problem is unravelled by this means! You, a man of ardent and imaginative temperament, made more or less unhappy by the doctrines of materialism, come to me, Heliobas, a Chaldean student of the Higher Philosophies, an individual whose supposed mysterious power and inexplicably studious way of life entitle him to be considered by the world at large an IMPOSTER!—Now don't look so indignant!"—and he laughed,—"I am merely discussing the question from the point of view that would be sure to be adopted by 'wise' modern society! Thus—I, Heliobas, the impostor, take advantage of your state of mind to throw you into a trance, in which, by occult means, you see the vision of an Angel, who bids you meet her at a place called Ardath,—and you, also, in your hypnotized condition, write a poem which you entitle 'Nourhalma.' Then I,—always playing my own little underhand game!—read you portions of 'Esdras,' and prove to you that 'Ardath' exists, while I delicately SUGGEST, if I do not absolutely COMMAND, your going thither. You go,—but I, still by magnetic power, retain my influence over you. You visit Elzear, a hermit, whom we will, for the sake of the present argument, call my accomplice,—he reads between the lines of the letter you deliver to him from me, and he understands its secret import. He continues, no matter how, your delusion. You broke your fast with him,—and surely it was easy for him to place some potent drug in the wine he gave you, which made you DREAM the rest;—nay, viewed from this standpoint, it is open to question whether you ever went to the Field of Ardath at all, but merely DREAMED you did! You see how admirably I can, with little trouble, disprove the whole story, and make myself out to be the veriest charlatan and trickster that ever duped his credulous fellow-man! How do you like my practical dissection of your new-found joys?"

Alwyn was gazing at him with puzzled and anxious eyes.

"I do not like it at all"—he murmured, in a pained tone—"It is an insidious SEMBLANCE of truth;—but I know it is not the Truth itself!"

"Why, how obstinate you are!" said Heliobas, good-humoredly, with a quick, flashing glance at him. "You insist on seeing things in a directly reverse way to that in which the world sees them! How can you be so foolish! To the world your Ardath adventure is the SEMBLANCE of truth,—and only man's opinion thereon is worth trusting as the Truth itself!"

Over the wistful, brooding thoughtfulness of Alwyn's countenance swept a sudden light of magnificent resolution.

"Heliobas, do not jest with me!" he cried passionately—"I know, better perhaps than most men, how divine things can be argued away

MARIE CORELLI

by the jargon of tongues, till heart and brain grow weary,—I know, God help me!—how the noblest ideals of the soul can be swept down and dispersed into blank ruin, by the specious arguments of cold-blooded casuists,—but I also know, by a supreme INNER knowledge beyond all human proving, that GOD EXISTS, and with His Being exist likewise all splendors, great and small, spiritual and material,—splendors vaster than our intelligence can reach,—ideals loftier than imagination can depict! I want no proof of this save those that burn in my own individual consciousness,—I do not need a miserable taper of human reason to help me to discern the Sun! I, OF MY OWN CHOICE, PRAYER, AND HOPE, voluntarily believe in God, in Christ, in angels, in all things beautiful and pure and grand!—let the world and its ephemeral opinions wither, I will NOT be shaken down from the first step of the ladder whereon one climbs to Heaven!"

His features were radiant with fervor and feeling,—his eyes brilliant with the kindling inward light of noblest aspiration,—and Heliobas, who had watched him intently, now bent toward him with a grave gesture of the gentlest homage.

"How strong is he whom an Angel's love makes glorious!" he said— "We are partners in the same destiny, my friend,—and I have but spoken to you as the world might speak, to prepare you for opposition. The specious arguments of men confront us at every turn, in every book, in every society,—and it is not always that we are ready to meet them. As a rule, silence on all matters of personal faith is best,—let your life bear witness for you;—it shall thunder loud oracles when your mortal limbs are dumb."

He paused a moment—then went on: "You have desired to know the secret of the active and often miraculous power of the special form of religion I and my brethren follow; well, it is all contained in Christ, and Christ only. His is the only true Spiritualism in the world—there was never any before He came. We obey Christ in the simple rules he preached,—Christ according to His own enunciated wish and will. Moreover, we,—that is, our Fraternity,—received our commission from Christ Himself in person."

Alwyn started,—his eyes dilated with amazement and awe.

"From Christ Himself in person?"—he echoed incredulously.

"Even so"—returned Heliobas calmly. "What do you suppose our Divine Master was about during the years between His appearance among the Rabbis of the Temple and the commencement of His public preaching? Do you, can you, imagine with the rest of the purblind world, that he would have left His marvellous Gospel in the charge of a few fishermen and common folk Only."

"I never thought,—I never inquired—" began Alwyn hurriedly.

"No!"—and Heliobas smiled rather sadly, "Few men do think or inquire very far on sacred subjects! Listen,—for what I have to say to you will but strengthen you in your faith,—and you will need more than all the strength of the Four Evangelists to bear you stiffly up against the suicidal Negation of this present disastrous epoch. Ages ago,—ay, more than six or seven thousand years ago, there were certain communities of men in the East,—scholars, sages, poets, astronomers, and scientists, who, desiring to give themselves up entirely to study and research, withdrew from the world, and formed themselves into Fraternities, dividing whatever goods they had in common, and living together under one roof as the brotherhoods of the Catholic Church do to this day. The primal object of these men's investigations was a search after the Divine Cause of Creation; and as it was undertaken with prayer, penance, humility, and reverence, much enlightenment was vouchsafed to them, and secrets of science, both spiritual and material, were discovered by them,—secrets which the wisest of modern sages know nothing of as yet. Out of these Fraternities came many of the prophets and preachers of the Old Testament,—Esdras for one,— Isaiah for another. They were the chroniclers of many now forgotten events,—they kept the history of the times, as far is it was possible,— and in their ancient records your city of Al-Kyris is mentioned as a great and populous place, which was suddenly destroyed by the bursting out of a volcano beneath its foundations—Yes!"—this as Alwyn uttered an eager exclamation,—"Your vision was a perfectly faithful reflection of the manner in which it perished. I must tell you, however, that nothing concerning its kings or great men has been preserved,—only a few allusions to one Hyspiros, a writer of tragedies, whose genius seems to have corresponded to that of our Shakespeare of to-day. The name of Sah-luma is nowhere extant."

A burning wave of color flushed Alwyn's face, but he was silent. Heliobas went on gently:

"At a very early period of their formation, these Fraternities I tell you of were in possession of most of the Material scientific facts of the present day,—such things as the electric wire and battery, the phonograph, the telephone, and other 'new' discoveries, being perfectly familiar to them. The SPIRITUAL manifestations of Nature were more intricate and difficult to penetrate,—and though they knew that material effects could only be produced by spiritual causes, they worked in the dark, as it were, only groping toward the light. However, the wisdom and purity of the lives they led was not without its effect,—emperors and kings sought their advice, and gave them great stores of wealth, which they divided, according to rule, into equal portions, and used for the benefit of those in need, willing the remainder to their successors; so that, at the present time, the few brotherhoods that are left hold immense treasures accumulated through many centuries,—treasures which are theirs to share with one another in prosecution of discoveries and the carrying on of good works in secret. Ages before the coming of Christ, one Aselzion, a man of austere and strict life, belonging to a Fraternity stationed in Syria, was engaged in working out a calculation of the average quantity of heat and light provided per minute by the sun's rays, when, glancing upward at the sky, the hour being clear noonday, he beheld a Cross of crimson hue suspended in the sky, whereon hung the cloudy semblance of a human figure. Believing himself to be the victim of some optical delusion, he hastened to fetch some of his brethren, who at a glance perceived the self-same marvel,—which presently was viewed with reverent wonder by the whole assembled community. For one entire hour the Symbol stayed—then vanished suddenly, a noise like thunder accompanying its departure. Within a few months of its appearance, messages came from all the other Fraternities stationed in Egypt, in Spain, in Greece, in Etruria, stating that they also had seen this singular sight, and suggesting that from henceforth the Cross should be adopted by the united Brotherhoods as a holy sign of some Deity unrevealed,—a proposition that was at once agreed to. This happened some five thousand years before Christ,—and hence the Sign of the Cross became known in all, or nearly all, the ancient rites of worship, the multitude considering that because it was the emblem of the Philosophical Fraternities, it must have some sacred meaning. So it was used in the service of Serapis and the adoration of the Nile-god,—it has been found carved on Egyptian disks and obelisks, and it was included among the numerous symbols of Saturn."

He paused. Alwyn was listening with eager, almost breathless, attention.

"After this"—went on Heliobas—"came a long period of prefigurements; types and suggestions, that, running through all the various religions that sprang up swiftly and as swiftly decayed, hinted vaguely at the birth of a child,—offspring of a pure Virgin—a miraculously generated God-in-Man—an absolutely Sinless One, who should be sent to remind Humanity of its intended final high destiny, and who should, by precept and example, draw the Earth nearer to Heaven. I would here ask you to note what most people seem to forget,—namely, that since Christ came, all these shadowy types and prefigurements have CEASED; a notable fact, even to skeptical minds. The world waited dimly for something, it knew not what,—the various Fraternities of the Cross waited also, feeling conscious that some great era of hope and happiness was about to dawn for all men. When the Star in the East arose announcing the Redeemer's birth, there were some forty or fifty of these Fraternities existing, three in the ancient province of Chaldea, from whence a company of the wisest seers and sages were sent to acknowledge by their immediate homage the Divinity born in Bethlehem. These were the 'wise men out of the East' mentioned in the Gospel. We knew—I say WE, because I am descended directly from one of these men, and have always belonged to their Brotherhood—we knew it was DIVINITY that had come amongst us,—and in our parchment chronicles there is a long account of how the deserts of Arabia rang with music that holy night— what wealth of flowers sprang up in places that had hither to lain waste and dry—how the sky blazed with rings of roseate radiance,—how fair and wondrous shapes were seen flitting across the heavens,—the road of communication between men and Angels being opened at a touch by the Saviour's advent."

Again he paused,—and after a little silence resumed:

"Then we added the Star to our existing Symbol, the Cross, and became the Brotherhood of the Cross and Star. As such, after the Redeemer's birth, we put all other matters from us, and set ourselves to chronicle His life and actions, to pray and wait, unknowing what might be the course of His work or will. One Day He came to us,—ah! happy those whom He found watching, and whose privilege it was to receive their Divine Guest!"

His voice had a passionate thrill within it, as of tears,—and Alwyn's heart beat fast,—what a wonderful new chapter was here revealed of the old, old story of the Only Perfect Life on earth!

"One of the Fraternities," went on Heliobas, "had its habitation in the wilderness where, some years later, the Master wandered fasting forty days and forty nights. To that solitary abode of prayerful men He came, when He was about twenty-three earthly years of age; the record of His visit has been reverently penned and preserved, and from it we know how fair and strong He was,—how stately and like a King—how gracious and noble in bearing—how far exceeding in beauty all the sons of men! His speech was music that thrilled to the heart,—the wondrous glory of His eyes gave life to those who knelt and worshipped Him— His touch was pardon—His smile was peace! From His own lips a store of wisdom was set down,—and prophecies concerning the fate of His own teaching, which then He uttered, are only now, at this very day, being fulfilled. Therefore we know the time has come—" he broke off, and sighed deeply.

"The time has come for what?" demanded Alwyn eagerly.

"For certain secrets to be made known to the world which till now have been kept sacred," returned Heliobas,—"You must understand that the chief vow of the Fraternity of the Cross and Star is SECRECY,—a promise never to divulge the mysteries of God and Nature to those who are unfitted to receive such high instruction. It is Christ's own saying— 'A faithless and perverse generation asketh for a sign, and no sign shall be given.' You surely are aware how, even in the simplest discoveries of material science, the world's attitude is at first one of jeering incredulity,—how much more so, then, in things which pertain solely to the spiritual side of existence! But God will not be mocked,—and it behooves us to think long, and pray much, before we unveil even one of the lesser mysteries to the eyes of the vulgar. Christ knew the immutable condition of Free-Will,—He knew that faith, humility, and obedience are the hardest of all hard virtues to the self-sufficient arrogance of man; and we learned from Him that His Gospel, simple though it is, would be denied, disputed, quarrelled over, shamefully distorted, and almost lost sight of in a multitude of 'free' opinions,—that His life-giving Truth would be obscured and rendered incomprehensible by the WILFUL obstinacy of human arguments concerning it. Christ has no part whatever in the distinctly human atrocities that have been perpetrated under cover of His Name,—such as the Inquisition, the Wars of the Crusades, the slaughter of martyrs, and the degrading bitterness of SECTS; in all these things Christ's teaching is entirely set aside and lost. He knew how the proud of this world would misread His words—that is why He came to men who for thousands of years in succession had steadily practised the qualities He most desired,— namely, faith, humility, and obedience,—and finding them ready to carry out His will, He left with them the mystic secrets of His doctrine, which He forbade them to give to the multitude till men's quarrels and disputations had called His very existence into doubt. Then,—through pure channels and by slow degrees—we were to proclaim to the world His last message."

Alwyn's eyes rested on the speaker in reverent yet anxious inquiry.

"Surely"—he said—"you will begin to proclaim it now?"

"Yes, we shall begin," answered Heliobas, his brow darkening as with a cloud of troubled thought—"But we are in a certain difficulty,—for we may not speak in public ourselves, nor write for publication,—our ancient vow binds us to this, and may not be broken. Moreover, the Master gave us a strange command,—namely, that when the hour came for the gradual declaration of the Secret of His Doctrine, we should intrust it, in the first place, to the hands of one who should be young,—IN the world, yet not OF it,—simple as a child, yet wise with the wisdom of faith,—of little or no estimation among men,—and who should have the distinctive quality of loving NOTHING in earth or Heaven more dearly than His Name and Honor. For this unique being we have searched, and are searching still,—we can find many who are young and both wise and innocent, but, alas! one who loves the unseen Christ actually more than all things,—this is indeed a perplexity! I have fancied of late that I have discovered in my own circle,—that is, among those who have been DRAWN to study God and Nature according to my views,—one who makes swift and steady progress in the higher sciences, and who, so far as I have been able to trace, really loves our Master with singular adoration above all joys on earth and hopes of Heaven; but I cannot be sure—and there are many tests and trials to be gone through before we dare bid this little human lamp of love shine forth upon the raging storm."

He was silent a moment,—then went on in a low tone, as though speaking to himself:

"WHEN THE MECHANISM OF THIS UNIVERSE IS EXPLAINED IN SUCH WISE THAT NO DISCOVERY OF SCIENCE CAN EVER DISPROVE, BUT MUST RATHER SUPPORT IT, . . . WHEN THE ESSENCE OF THE IMMORTAL SOUL IN MAN IS DESCRIBED IN CLEAR AND CONCISE LANGUAGE,—AND WHEN THE MARVELLOUS ACTION OF SPIRIT ON MATTER IS SHOWN TO BE ACTUALLY EXISTENT AND NEVER IDLE,— then, if the world still doubts and denies God, it will only have itself to blame!—But to you"—and he resumed his ordinary tone—"all things, through your Angel's love, are made more or less plain,—and I have told you the history of our Fraternity merely that you may understand how it is we know so much that the outer world is ignorant of. There are very few of us left nowadays,—only a dozen Brotherhoods scattered far apart on different portions of the earth,—but, such as we are, we are all UNITED, and have never, through these eighteen hundred years, had a shade of difference in opinion concerning the Divinity of Christ. Through Him we have learned TRUE Spiritualism, and all the miraculous power which is the result of it; and as there is a great deal of FALSE spiritualism rampant just now, I may as well give you a few hints whereby you may distinguish it at once,—Imprimis: if a so-called Spiritualist tells you that he can summon spirits who will remove tables and chairs, write letters, play the piano, and rap on the walls, he is a CHARLATAN. FOR SPIRITS CAN TOUCH NOTHING CORPOREAL UNLESS THEY TAKE CORPOREAL SHAPE FOR THE MOMENT, as in the case of your angelic Edris. But in this condition, they are only seen by the one person whom they visit,—never by several persons at once—remember that! Nor can they keep their corporeal state long,—except, by their express wish and will, they should seek to enter absolutely into the life of humanity, which, I must tell you, HAS BEEN DONE, but so seldom, that in all the history of Christian Spirituality there are only about four examples. Here are six tests for all the 'spiritualists' you may chance to meet:

"First. Do they serve themselves more than others? If so, they are entirely lacking in spiritual attributes.

"Secondly. Will they take money for their professed knowledge? If so, they condemn themselves as paid tricksters.

"Thirdly. Are they men and women of commonplace and thoroughly material life? Then, it is plain they cannot influence others to strive for a higher existence.

"Fourthly. Do they love notoriety? If they do, the gates of the unseen world are shut upon them.

"Fifthly. Do they disagree among themselves, and speak against one another? If so, they contradict by their own behavior all the laws of spiritual force and harmony.

"Sixthly and lastly.—Do they reject Christ! If they do, they know nothing whatever about Spiritualism, there being NONE without Him. Again, when you observe professing psychists living in any eccentric way, so as to cause their trifling every-day actions to be remarked and commented upon, you may be sure the real power is not in them,—as, for instance, people who become vegetarians because they imagine that by so doing they will see spirits—people who adopt a singular mode of dress in order to appear different from their fellow-creatures—people who are lachrymose, dissatisfied, or in any way morbid. Never forget that TRUE Spiritualism engenders HEALTH OF BODY AND MIND, serenity and brightness of aspect, cheerfulness and perfect contentment,—and that its influence on those who are brought within its radius is distinctly MARKED and BENEFICIAL. The chief characteristic of a true, that is, CHRISTIAN, spiritualist is, that he or she CANNOT be shaken from faith, or thrown into despair by any earthly misfortune whatsoever. And while on this subject, I will show you where the existing forms of Christianity depart from the teachings of Christ: first, in LACK OF SELF ABNEGATION,—secondly, in LACK OF UNITY,—thirdly, in failing to prove to the multitude that Death is is not DESTRUCTION, but simply CHANGE. Nothing really DIES; and the priests should make use of Science to illustrate this fact to the people. Each of these virtues has its Miracle Effect: Unity is strength; Self abnegation attracts the Divine Influences, and Death, viewed as a glorious transformation, which it Is, inspires the soul with a sense of larger life. Sects are UNchristian,—there should be only ONE vast, UNITED Church for all the Christian world—a Church, whose pure doctrines should include all the hints received from Nature and the scientific working of the Universe,—the marvels of the stars and the planetary systems,—the wonders of plants and minerals,—the magic of light and color and music; and the TRUE MIRACLES of Spirit and Matter should be inquired into reverently, prayerfully, and always with the deepest HUMILITY;—while the first act of worship performed every holy Morn and Eve should be Gratitude! Gratitude—gratitude! Ay, even for a sorrow we should be thankful,—it may conceal a blessing we wot not of! For sight, for sense, for touch, for the natural beauty of this present world,—for the smile on a face we love—for the dignity and responsibility of our lives, and the immortality with which we are endowed,—

Oh my friend! would that every breath we drew could in some way express to the All Loving Creator our adoring recognition of His countless benefits!"

Carried away by his inward fervor, his eyes flashed with extraordinary brilliancy,—his countenance was grand, inspired, and beautiful, and Alwyn gazed at him in wondering, fascinated silence. Here was a man who had indeed made the best of his manhood!—what a life was his! how satisfying and serene! Master of himself, he was, as it were, master of the world,—all Nature ministered to him, and the pageant of passing history was as a mere brilliant picture painted for his instruction,—a picture on which he, looking, learned all that it was needful for him to know. And concerning this mystic Brotherhood of the Cross and Star, what treasures of wisdom they must have secreted in their chronicles through so many thousands of years! What a privilege it would be to explore such world-forgotten tracks of time! Yielding to a sudden impulse, Alwyn spoke his thought aloud:

"Heliobas," he said, "tell me, could not I, too, become a member of your Fraternity?"

Heliobas smiled kindly. "You could, assuredly"—he replied—"if you chose to submit to fifteen years' severe trial and study. But I think a different sphere of duty is designed for you. Wait and see! The rules of our Order forbid the disclosure of knowledge attained, save through the medium of others not connected with us; and we may not write out our discoveries for open publication. Such a vow would be the death-blow to your poetical labors,—and the command your Angel gave you points distinctly to a life lived In the world of men,—not out of it."

"But you yourself are in the world of men at this moment"—argued Alwyn—"And you are free; did you not tell me you were bound for Mexico?"

"Does going to Mexico constitute liberty?" laughed Heliobas. "I assure you I am closely constrained by my vows wherever I am,—as closely as though I were shut in our turret among the heights of Caucasus! I am going to Mexico solely to receive some manuscripts from one of our brethren, who is dying there. He has lived as a recluse, like Elzear of Melyana, and to him have been confided certain important chronicles, which must be taken into trustworthy hands for preservation. Such is the object of my journey. But now, tell me, have you thoroughly understood all I have said to you?"

"Perfectly!" rejoined Alwyn. "My way seems very clear before me,—a happy way enough, too, if it were not quite so lonely!" And he sighed a little.

Heliobas rose and laid one hand kindly on his shoulder. "Courage!" . . . he said softly. "Bear with the loneliness a while, IT MAY NOT LAST LONG!"

A slight thrill ran through Alwyn's nerves,—he felt as though he were on the giddy verge of some great and unexpected joy,—his heart beat quickly and his eyes grew dim. Mastering the strange emotion with an effort, he was reluctantly beginning to think it was time to take his leave, when Heliobas, who had been watching him intently, spoke in a cheerful, friendly tone:

"Now that we have had our serious talk out, Mr. Alwyn, suppose you come with me and hear the Ange-Demon of music at St. James's Hall? Will you? He can bestow upon you a perfect benediction of sweet sound,—a benediction not to be despised in this workaday world of clamor,—and out of all the exquisite symbols of Heaven offered to us on earth, Music, I think, is the grandest and best."

"I will go with you wherever you please," replied Alwyn, glad of any excuse that gave him more of the attractive Chaldean's company,—"But what Ange-Demon are you speaking of?"

"Sarasate,—or 'Sarah Sayty,' as some of the clear Britishers call him—" laughed Heliobas, putting on his overcoat as he spoke; "the 'Spanish fiddler,' as the crabbed musical critics define him when they want to be contemptuous, which they do pretty often. These, together with the literary 'oracles,' have their special cliques,—their little chalked out circles, in which they, like tranced geese, stand cackling, unable to move beyond the marked narrow limit. As there are fools to be found who have the ignorance, as well as the effrontery, to declare that the obfuscated, ill-expressed, and ephemeral productions of Browning are equal, if not superior, to the clear, majestic, matchless, and immortal utterances of Shakespeare,—ye gods! the force of asinine braying can no further go than this! . . . even so there are similar fools who say that the cold, correct, student-like playing of Joachim is superior to that of Sarasate. But come and judge for yourself,—if you have never heard him, it will be a sort of musical revelation to you,—he is not so much a violinist, as a human violin played by some invisible sprite of song. London listens to him, but doesn't know quite what to make of him,—he is a riddle that only poets can read. If we start now, we shall be just in time,—I have two stalls. Shall we go?"

Alwyn needed no second invitation,—he was passionately fond of music,—his interest was aroused, his curiosity excited,—moreover, whatever the fine taste of Heliobas pronounced as good must, he felt sure, be super-excellent. In a few minutes they had left the hotel together, and were walking briskly toward Piccadilly, their singularly handsome faces and stately figures causing many a passer-by to glance after them admiringly, and murmur sotto voce, "Splendid-looking fellows! . . . not English!" For though Englishmen are second to none in mere muscular strength and symmetry of form, it is a fact worth noting, that if any one possessing poetic distinction of look, or picturesque and animated grace of bearing, be seen suddenly among the more or less monotonously uniform crowd in the streets of London, he or she is pretty sure to be set down, rightly or wrongly, as "NOT English." Is not this rather a pity?—for England!

XXXVIII

The Wizard of the Bow

W hen they entered the concert-hall, the orchestra had already begun the programme of the day with Mendelssohn's "Italian" Symphony. The house was crowded to excess; numbers of people were standing, apparently willing to endure a whole afternoon's fatigue, rather than miss hearing the Orpheus of Andalusia,—the "Endymion out of Spain," as one of our latest and best poets has aptly called him. Only a languidly tolerant interest was shown in the orchestral performance,— the "Italian" Symphony is not a really great or suggestive work, and this is probably the reason why it so often fails to arouse popular enthusiasm. For, be it understood by the critical elect, that the heart-whole appreciation of the million is by no means so "vulgar" as it is frequently considered,—it is the impulsive response of those who, not being bound hand and foot by any special fetters of thought or prejudice, express what they instinctively Feel to be true. You cannot force these "vulgar," by any amount of "societies," to adopt Browning as a household god,— but they will appropriate Shakespeare, and glory in him, too, without any one's compulsion. If authors, painters, and musicians would probe more earnestly than they do to the core of this Instinctive Higher Aspiration Of Peoples, it would be all the better for their future fame. For each human unit in a nation has its great, as well as base passions,—and it is the clear duty of all the votaries of art to appeal to and support the noblest side of nature only—moreover, to do so with a simple, unforced, yet graphic eloquence of meaning that can be grasped equally and at once by both the humble and exalted.

"It is not in the least Italian"—said Heliobas, alluding to the Symphony, when it was concluded, and the buzz of conversation surged through the hall like the noise that might be made by thousands of swarming bees,—"There is not a breath of Italian air or a glimpse of Italian light about it. The dreamy warmth of the South,—the radiant color that lies all day and all night on the lakes and mountains of Dante's land,—the fragrance of flowers—the snatches of peasants' and fishermen's songs—the tunefulness of nightingales in the moonlight,— the tinkle of passing mandolins,—all these things should be hinted at in an 'Italian' Symphony—and all these are lacking. Mendelssohn tried to do what was not in him,—I do not believe the half-phlegmatic, half-philosophical nature of a German could ever understand the impetuously passionate soul of Italy."

As he spoke, a fair girl, with gray eyes that were almost black, glanced round at him inquiringly,—a faint blush flitted over her cheeks, and she seemed about to speak, but, as though restrained by timidity, she looked away again and said nothing. Heliobas smiled.

"That pretty child is Italian," he whispered to Alwyn. "Patriotism sparkled in those bright eyes of hers—love for the land of lilies, from which she is at present one transplanted!"

Alwyn smiled also, assentingly, and thought how gracious, kindly, and gentle were the look and voice of the speaker. He found it difficult to realize that this man, who now sat beside him in the stalls of a fashionable London concert-room, was precisely the same one who, clad in the long flowing white robes of his Order, had stood before the Altar in the chapel at Dariel, a stately embodiment of evangelical authority, intoning the Seven Glorias! It seemed strange, and yet not strange, for Heliobas was a personage who might be imagined anywhere,—by the bedside of a dying child, among the parliaments of the learned, in the most brilliant social assemblies, at the head of a church,—anything he chose to do would equally become him, inasmuch as it was utterly impossible to depict him engaged in otherwise than good and noble deeds. At that moment a tumultuous clamor of applause broke out on all sides,—applause that was joined in by the members of the orchestra as well as the audience,—a figure emerged from a side door on the left and ascended the platform—a slight, agile creature, with rough, dark hair and eager, passionate eyes—no other than the hero of the occasion, Sarasate himself. Sarasate e il suo Violino!—there they were, the two companions; master and servant—king and subject. The one, a lithe, active looking man of handsome, somewhat serious countenance and absorbed expression,—the other, a mere frame of wood with four strings deftly knotted across it, in which cunningly contrived little bit of mechanism was imprisoned the intangible, yet living Spirit of Sound. A miracle in its way!—that out of such common and even vile materials as wood, catgut, and horsehair, the divinest music can be drawn forth by the hand of the master who knows how to use these rough implements! Suggestive, too, is it not, my friends?—for if man can by his own poor skill and limited intelligence so invoke spiritual melody by material means,—shall not God contrive some wondrous tunefulness for Himself even out of our common earthly discord? . . . Hush!—A sound sweet and far as the chime of angelic bells in some vast sky-tower, rang clearly through the hall over the heads of the now hushed and attentive audience—and Alwyn, hearing the penetrating silveriness of those first notes that fell from Sarasate's bow, gave a quick sigh of amazement and ecstasy,—such marvellous purity of tone was intoxicating to his senses, and set his nerves quivering for sheer delight in sympathetic tune. He glanced at the programme,—"Concerto—Beethoven"—and swift as a flash there came to his mind some lines he had lately read and learned to love:

> *"It was the Kaiser of the Land of Song,*
> *The giant singer who did storm the gates*
> *Of Heaven and Hell—a man to whom the Fates*
> *Were fierce as furies,—and who suffered wrong,*
> *And ached and bore it, and was brave and strong*
> *And grand as ocean when its rage abates."*

Beethoven! . . . Musical fullness of divine light! how the glorious nightingale notes of his unworded poesy came dropping through the air like pearls, rolling off the magic wand of the Violin Wizard, whose delicate dark face, now slightly flushed with the glow of inspiration, seemed to reflect by its very expression the various phases of the mighty composer's thought! Alwyn half closed his eyes and listened entranced, allowing his soul to drift like an oarless boat on the sweeping waves of the music's will. He was under the supreme sway of two Emperors of Art,—Beethoven and Sarasate,—and he was content to follow such leaders through whatever sweet tangles and tall growths of melody they might devise for his wandering. At one mad passage of dancing semitones he started,—it was as though a sudden wind, dreaming an enraged dream, had leaped up to shake tall trees to and fro,—and the Pass of Dariel, with its frozen mountain-peaks, its tottering pines, and howling hurricanes, loomed back upon his imagination as he had seen it first on the night he had arrived at the Monastery—but soon these wild notes sank and slept again in the dulcet harmony of an Adagio softer than a lover's song at midnight. Many strange suggestions began to glimmer ghost-like through this same Adagio,—the fair, dead face of Niphrata flitted past him, as a wandering moonbeam flits athwart a cloud,—then came flashing reflections of light and color,—the bewildering dazzlement of Lysia's beauty shone before the eyes of his memory with a blinding lustre as of flame, . . . the phantasmagoria of the city of Al-Kyris seemed to float in the air like a faintly discovered mirage ascending from the sea,—again he saw its picturesque streets, its domes and bell-towers, its courts and gardens. . . again he heard the dreamy melody of the dance that had followed the death of Nir-jalis, and saw the cruel Lysia's wondrous garden lying white in the radiance of the moon; anon he beheld the great Square, with its fallen Obelisk and the prostrate, lifeless form of the Prophet Khosrul. . . and. . . Oh, most sad and dear remembrance of all! . . . the cherished Shadow of Himself, the brilliant, the joyous Sah-luma appeared to beckon him from the other side of some vast gulf of mist and darkness, with a smile that was sorrowful, yet persuasive; a smile that seemed to say—"O friend, why hast thou left me as though I were a dead thing and unworthy of regard?—Lo, I have never died,—*I am* here, an abandoned part of THEE, ready to become thine inseparable comrade once more if thou make but the slightest sign!"—Then it seemed as though voices whispered in his ear—"Sah-luma! beloved Sah-luma!"—and "Theos! Theos, my beloved!"—till, moved by a vague tremor of anxiety, he lifted his drooping eyelids and gazed full in a sort of half-incredulous, half-reproachful amaze at the musical necromancer who had conjured up all these apparitions,—what did this wonderful Sarasate know of his Past?

Nothing, indeed,—he had ceased, and was gravely bowing to the audience in response to the thunder of applause, that, like a sudden whirlwind, seemed to shake the building. But he had not quite finished his incantations,—the last part of the Concerto was yet to come,—and as soon as the hubbub of excitement had calmed down, he dashed into it with the delicious speed and joy of a lark soaring into the springtide air. And now on all sides what clear showers and sparkling coruscations of melody!—what a broad, blue sky above!—what a fair, green earth below!—how warm and odorous this radiating space, made resonant with the ring of sweet bird-harmonies!—wild thrills of ecstasy and lover-like tenderness—snatches of song caught up from the flower-filled meadows and set to float in echoing liberty through the azure dome of heaven!—and in all and above all, the light and heat and lustre of the unclouded sun!—Here there was no dreaming possible, . . . nothing but glad life, glad youth, glad love! With an ambrosial rush of tune, like the lark descending, the dancing bow cast forth the final chord from the violin as though it were a diamond flung from the hand of a king, a flawless jewel of pure sound,—and the Minstrel monarch of Andalusia, serenely saluting the now wildly enthusiastic audience, left the platform. But he was not allowed to escape so soon,—again and again, and yet again, the enormous crowd summoned him before them, for the mere satisfaction of looking at his slight figure, his dark, poetic face, and soft, half-passionate, half-melancholy eyes, as though anxious to convince themselves that he was indeed human, and not a supernatural being, as his marvellous genius seemed to indicate. When at last he had retired for a breathing-while, Heliobas turned to Alwyn with the question:

"What do you think of him?"

"Think of him!" echoed Alwyn—"Why, what CAN one think,—what CAN one say of such an artist!—He is like a grand sunrise,—baffling all description and all criticism!"

Heliobas smiled,—there was a little touch of satire in his smile.

"Do you see that gentleman?" he said, in a low tone, pointing out by a gesture a pale, flabby-looking young man who was lounging languidly in a stall not very far from where they themselves sat,—"He is the musical critic for one of the leading London daily papers. He has not stirred an inch, or moved an eyelash, during Sarasate's performance,—and the violent applause of the audience was manifestly distasteful to him! He has merely written one line down in his note-book,—it is most probably to the effect that the 'Spanish fiddler met with his usual success at the hands of the undiscriminating public!'"

Alwyn laughed. "Not possible!"—and he eyed the impassive individual in question with a certain compassionate amusement,— "Why, if he cannot admire such a magnificent artist as Sarasate, what is there in the world that WILL rouse his admiration!"

"Nothing!" rejoined Heliobas, his eyes twinkling humorously as he spoke—"Nothing,—unless it is his own perspicuity! Nil admirari is the critic's motto. The modern 'Zabastes' must always be careful to impress his readers in the first place with his personal superiority to all men and all things,—and the musical Oracle yonder will no doubt be clever enough to make his report of Sarasate in such a manner as to suggest the idea that he could play the violin much better himself, if he only cared to try!"

"Ass!" said Alwyn under his breath—"One would like to shake him out of his absurd self-complacency!"

Heliobas shrugged his shoulders expressively:

"My dear fellow, he would only bray!—and the braying of an ass is not euphonious! No!—you might as well shake a dry clothes-prop and expect it to blossom into fruit and flower, as argue with a musical critic, and expect him to be enthusiastic! The worst of it is, these men are not REALLY musical,—they perhaps know a little of the grammar and technique of the thing, but they cannot understand its full eloquence. In the presence of a genius like Pablo de Sarasate they are more or less perplexed,—it is as though you ask them to describe in set, cold terms the counterpoint and thoroughbass of the wind's symphony to the trees,—the great ocean's sonata to the shore, or the delicate madrigals sung almost inaudibly by little bell-blossoms to the tinkling fall of April rain. The man is too great for them—he is a blazing star that dazzles and confounds their sight—and, after the manner of their craft, they abuse what they can't understand. Music is distinctly the language of the emotions,—and they have no emotion. They therefore generally prefer Joachim,—the good, stolid Joachim, who so delights all the dreary old spinsters and dowagers who nod over their knitting-needles at the 'Monday Popular' concerts, and fancy themselves lovers of the 'classical' in music. Sarasate appeals to those who have loved, and thought, and suffered—those who have climbed the heights of passion and wrung out the depths of pain,—and therefore the PEOPLE, taken en masse, as, for instance, in this crowded hall, instinctively respond to his magic touch. And why?—Because the greater majority of human beings are full of the deepest and most passionate feelings, not as yet having been 'educated' OUT of them!"

Here the orchestra commenced Liszt's "Preludes"—and all conversation ceased. Afterwards Sarasate came again to bestow upon his eager admirers another saving grace of sound, in the shape of the famous Mendelssohn Concerto, which he performed with such fiery ardor, tenderness, purity of tone, and marvellous execution that many listeners held their breath for sheer amazement and delighted awe. Anything approaching the beauty of his rendering of the final "Allegro" Alwyn had never heard,—and indeed it is probable none WILL ever hear a more poetical, more exquisite SINGING OF THOUGHT than this matchless example of Sarasate's genius and power. Who would not warm to the brightness and delicacy of those delicious rippling tones, that seemed to leap from the strings alive like sparks of fire—the dainty, tripping ease of the arpeggi, that float from the bow with the grace of rainbow bubbles blown forth upon the air,—the brilliant runs, that glide and glitter up and down like chattering brooks sparkling among violets and meadow-sweet,—the lovely softer notes, that here and there sigh between the varied harmonies with the dreamy passion of lovers who part, only to meet again in a rush of eager joy!—Alwyn sat absorbed and spellbound; he forgot the passing of time,—he forgot even the presence of Heliobas,—he could only listen, and gratefully drink in every drop of sweetness that was so lavishly poured upon him from such a glorious sky of sunlit sound.

Presently, toward the end of the performance, a curious thing happened. Sarasate had appeared to play the last piece set down for him,—a composition of his own, entitled "Zigeunerweisen." A gypsy song, or medley of gypsy songs, it would be, thought Alwyn, glancing at his programme,—then, looking towards the artist, who stood with lifted bow like another Prospero, prepared to summon forth the Ariel of music at a touch, he saw that the dark Spanish eyes of the maestro were fixed full upon him, with, as he then fancied, a strange, penetrating smile in their fiery depths. One instant. . . and a weird lament came sobbing from the smitten violin,—a wildly beautiful despair was wordlessly proclaimed, . . . a melody that went straight to the heart and made it ache, and burn, and throb with a rising tumult of unlanguaged passion and desire! The solemn, yet unfettered, grace of its rhythmic respiration suggested to Alwyn, first darkness,—then twilight—then the gradual far-glimmering of a silvery dawn,—till out of the shuddering notes there seemed to grow up a vague, vast, and cool whiteness, splendid and mystical,—a whiteness that from shapeless, fleecy mist took gradual form and substance, . . . the great concert-hall, with its closely packed throng of people, appeared to fade away like vanishing smoke,—and lo!—before the poet's entranced gaze there rose up a wondrous vision of stately architectural grandeur,—a vision of snowy columns and lofty arches, upon which fell a shimmering play of radiant color flung by the beams of the sun through stained glass windows glistening jewel-wise,—a tremulous sound of voices floated aloft, singing, "Kyrie Eleison!—Kyrie Eleison!"—and the murmuring undertone of the organ shook the still air with deep vibrations of holy tune. Everywhere peace,—everywhere purity! everywhere that spacious whiteness, flecked with side-gleams of royal purple, gold, and ardent crimson,—and in the midst of all,—O dearest tenderness!—O fairest glory!—a face, shining forth like a star in a cloud!—a face dazzlingly beautiful and sweet,—a golden head, above which the pale halo of a light ethereal hovered lovingly in a radiant ring!

"Edris!"—The chaste name breathed itself silently in Alwyn's thoughts,—silently and yet with all the passion of a lover's prayer! How was it, he wondered dimly, that he saw her thus distinctly Now,—now, when the violin-music wept its wildest tears—now when love, love, love, seemed to clamor in a tempestuous agony of appeal from the low, pulsating melody of the marvellous "Zigeunerweisen," a melody which, despite its name, had revealed to one listener, at any rate, nothing concerning the wanderings of gypsies over forest and moorland,—but on the contrary had built up all these sublime cathedral arches, this lustrous light, this exquisite face, whose loveliness was his life! How had he found his way into such a dream sanctuary of frozen snow?— what was his mission there?—and why, when the picture slowly faded, did it still haunt his memory invitingly,—persuasively,—nay, almost commandingly?

He could not tell,—but his mind was entirely ravished and possessed by an absorbing impression of white, sculptured calm,—and he was as startled as though he had been brusquely awakened from a deep sleep, when the loud plaudits of the people made him aware that Sarasate had finished his programme, and was departing from the scene of his triumphs. The frenzied shouts and encores, however brought him once more before the excited public, to play a set of Spanish dances, fanciful and delicate as the gamboling of a light breeze over rose-gardens and dashing fountains,—and when this wonder-music ceased, Alwyn woke from tranced rapture into enthusiasm, and joined in the thunders of applause with fervent warmth and zeal. Eight several times did the wearied, but ever affable, maestro ascend the platform to bow and smile his graceful acknowledgments, till the audience, satisfied with having thoroughly emphasized their hearty appreciation of his genius, permitted him to finally retire. Then the people flocked out of the hall in crowds, talking, laughing, and delightedly commenting upon the afternoon's enjoyment, the brief remarks exchanged by two Americans who were sauntering on immediately in front of Heliobas and Alwyn being perhaps the very pith and essence of the universal opinion concerning the great artist they had just heard.

"I tell you what he is," said one, "he's a demi-god!"

"Oh, don't halve it!" rejoined the other wittily, "he's the whole thing anyway!"

Once outside the hall and in the busy street, now rendered doubly brilliant by the deep saffron light of a gloriously setting sun, Heliobas prepared to take leave of his somewhat silent and preoccupied companion.

"I see you are still under the sway of the Ange-Demon," he remarked cheerfully, as he shook hands, "Is he not an amazing fellow? That bow of his is a veritable divining-rod, it finds out the fountain of Elusidis* in each human heart,—it has but to pronounce a note, and straightway the hidden waters begin to bubble. But don't forget to read the newspaper accounts of this concert! You will see that the critics will make no allusion whatever to the enthusiasm of the audience, and that the numerous encores will not even be mentioned!"

"That is unfair," said Alwyn quickly. "The expression of the people's appreciation should always be chronicled."

"Of course!—but it never is, unless it suits the immediate taste of the cliques. Clique-Art, clique-Literature, clique-Criticism, keep all three things on a low ground that slopes daily more and more toward decadence. And the pity of it is, that the English get judged abroad chiefly by what their own journalists say of them,—thus, if Sarasate is coldly criticised, foreigners laugh at the 'Unmusical English,' whereas, the fact is that the nation itself is Not unmusical, but its musical critics mostly are. They are very often picked out of the rank and file of the dullest Academy students and contrapuntists, who are incapable of understanding anything original, and therefore are the persons most unfitted to form a correct estimate of genius. However, it has always been so, and I suppose it always will be so,—don't you remember that when Beethoven began his grand innovations, a certain critic-ass-ter wrote of him, 'The absurdity of his effort is only equalled by the hideousness of its result'."

He laughed lightly, and once more shook hands, while Alwyn, looking at him wistfully, said:

"I wonder when we shall meet again?"

"Oh, very soon, I dare say," he rejoined. "The world is a wonderfully small place, after all, as men find when they jostle up against each other unexpectedly in the most unlikely corners of far countries. You may, if you choose, correspond with me, and that is a privilege I accord to few,

---

* A miraculous fountain spoken of in old chronicles, whose waters rose to the sound of music, and, the music ceasing, sank again.

I assure you!" He smiled, and then went on in a more serious tone, "You are, of course, welcome at our monastery whenever you wish to come, but, take my advice, do not wilfully step out of the sphere in which you are placed. Live IN society, it needs men of your stamp and intellectual calibre; show it a high and consistent example—let no eccentricity mar your daily actions—work at your destiny steadily, cheerfully, serenely, and leave the rest to God, and—the angels!"

There was a slight, tender inflection in his voice as he spoke the last words,—and Alwyn gave him a quick, searching glance. But his blue, penetrating eyes were calm and steadfast, full of their usual luminous softness and pathos, and there was nothing expressed in them but the gentlest friendliness.

"Well! I'm glad I may write to you, at any rate," said Alwyn at last, reluctantly releasing his hand. "It is possible I may not remain long in London; I want to finish my poem, and it gets on too slowly in the tumult of daily life in town."

"Then will you go abroad again?" inquired Heliobas.

"Perhaps. I may. Bonn, where I was once a student for a time. It is a peaceful, sleepy little place,—I shall probably complete my work easily there. Moreover, it will be like going back to a bit of my youth. I remember I first began to entertain all my dreams of poesy at Bonn."

"Inspired by the Seven Mountains and the Drachenfels!" laughed Heliobas. "No wonder you recalled the lost 'Sah-luma' period in the sight of the entrancing Rhine! Ah, Sir Poet, you have had your fill of fame! and I fear the plaudits of London will never be like those of Al-Kyris! No monarchs will honor you now, but rather despise! for the kings and queens of this age prefer financiers to Laureates! Now, wherever you wander, let me hear of your well-being and progress in contentment; when you write, address to our Dariel retreat, for though on my return from Mexico I shall probably visit Lemnos, my letters will always be forwarded. Adieu!"

"Adieu!" and their eyes met. A grave sweet smile brightened the Chaldean's handsome features.

"God remain with you, my friend!" he said, in a low, thrillingly earnest tone. "Believe me, you are elected to a strangely happy fate!—far happier than you at present know!"

With these words he turned and was gone,—lost to sight in the surging throng of passers-by. Alwyn looked eagerly after him, but saw him no more. His tall figure had vanished as utterly as any of the phantom shapes in Al-Kyris, only that, far from being spectre-like, he had seemed more actually a living personality than any of the people in the streets who were hurrying to and fro on their various errands of business or pleasure.

That same night when Alwyn related his day's adventure to Villiers, who heard it with the most absorbed interest, he was describing the effect of Sarasate's violin-playing, when all at once he was seized by the same curious, overpowering impression of white, lofty arches, stained windows, and jewel-like glimmerings of color, and he suddenly stopped short in the midst of his narrative.

"What's the matter?" asked Villiers, astonished. "Go on!—you were saying,—"

"That Sarasate is one of the divinest of God's wandering melodies," went on Alwyn, slowly and with a faint smile. "And that though, as a rule, musicians are forgotten when their music ceases, this Andalusian Orpheus in Thrace will be remembered long after his violin is laid aside, and he himself has journeyed to a sunnier land than Spain! But I am not master of my thoughts to-night, Villiers; my Chaldean friend has perhaps mesmerized me—who knows! and I have an odd fancy upon me. I should like to spend an hour in some great and beautiful cathedral, and see the light of the rising sun flashing through the stained windows across the altar!"

"Poet and dreamer!" laughed Villiers. "You can't gratify that whim in London; there's no 'great and beautiful' edifice of the kind here,—only the unfinished Oratory, Westminster Abbey, broken up into ugly pews and vile monuments, and the repellently grimy St. Paul's—so go to bed, old boy, and indulge yourself in some more 'visions,' for I assure you you'll never find any reality come up to your ideal of things in general."

"No?" and Alwyn smiled. "Strange that I see it in quite the reverse way! It seems to me, no ideal will ever come up to the splendor of reality!"

"But remember," said Villiers quickly, "Your reality is heaven,—a 'reality' that is every one else's myth!"

"True! terribly true!" . . . and Alwyn's eyes darkened sorrowfully. "Yet the world's myth is the only Eternal Real, and for the shadows of this present Seeming we barter our immortal Substance!"

XXXIX

By the Rhine

In the two or three weeks that followed his meeting with Heliobas, Alwyn made up his mind to leave London for a while. He was tired and restless,—tired of the routine society more or less imposed upon him,—restless because he had come to a standstill in his work—an invisible barrier, over which his creative fancy was unable to take its usual sweeping flight. He had an idea of seeking some quiet spot among mountains, as far remote as possible from the travelling world of men,—a peaceful place, where, with the majestic silence of Nature all about him, he might plead in lover-like retirement with his refractory Muse, and strive to coax her into a sweeter and more indulgent humor. It was not that thoughts were lacking to him,—what he complained of was the monotony of language and the difficulty of finding new, true, and choice forms of expression. A great thought leaps into the brain like a lightning flash; there it is, an indescribable mystery, warming the soul and pervading the intellect, but the proper expression of that thought is a matter of the deepest anxiety to the true poet, who, if he be worthy of his vocation, is bound not only to proclaim it to the world CLEARLY, but also clad in such a perfection of wording that it shall chime on men's ears with a musical sound as of purest golden bells. There are very few faultless examples of this felicitous utterance in English or in any literature, so few, indeed, that they could almost all be included in one newspaper column of ordinary print. Keats's exquisite line:

> *"Æea's Isle was wondering at the moon"* . . .

in which the word "wondering" paints a whole landscape of dreamy enchantment, and the couplet in the "Ode to a Nightingale," that speaks with a delicious vagueness of

> *"Magic casements opening on the foam*
> *Of perilous seas in faery lands forlorn,"*—

are absolutely unique and unrivalled, as is the exquisite alliteration taken from a poet of our own day:

> "The holy lark,
> With fire from heaven and sunlight on his wing,
> Who wakes the world with witcheries of the dark,
> Renewed in rapture in the reddening air!"

Again from the same:

> "The chords of the lute are entranced
> With the weight of the wonder of things";

and

> "his skyward notes
> Have drenched the summer with the dews of song! . . ."

this last line being certainly one of the most suggestive and beautiful in all poetical literature. Such expressions have the intrinsic quality of COMPLETENESS,—once said, we feel that they can never be said again;—they belong to the centuries, rather than the seasons, and any imitation of them we immediately and instinctively resent as an outrage.

And Theos Alwyn was essentially, and above all things, faithful to the lofty purpose of his calling,—he dealt with his art reverently, and not in rough haste and scrambling carelessness,—if he worked out any idea in rhyme, the idea was distinct and the rhyme was perfect,— he was not content, like Browning, to jumble together such hideous and ludicrous combinations as "high;—Humph!" and "triumph,"— moreover, he knew that what he had to tell his public must be told comprehensively, yet grandly, with all the authority and persuasiveness of incisive rhetoric, yet also with all the sweetness and fascination of a passioned love-song. Occupied with such work as this, London, with its myriad mad noises and vulgar distractions, became impossible to him,—and Villiers, his fidus Achates, who had read portions of his great poem and was impatient to see it finished, knowing, as he did, what an enormous sensation it would create when published, warmly seconded his own desire to gain a couple of months complete seclusion and tranquillity.

He left town, therefore, about the middle of May and started across the Channel, resolving to make for Switzerland by the leisurely and delightful way of the Rhine, in order to visit Bonn, the scene of his old student days. What days they had been!—days of dreaming, more than action, for he had always regarded learning as a pastime rather than a drudgery, and so had easily distanced his comrades in the race for knowledge. While they were flirting with the Lischen or Gretchen of the hour, he had willingly absorbed himself in study—thus he had attained the head of his classes with scarce an effort, and, in fact, had often found time hanging heavily on his hands for want of something more to do. He had astonished the university professors— but he had not astonished himself, inasmuch as no special branch of learning presented any difficulties to him, and the more he mastered the more dissatisfied he became. It had seemed such a little thing to win the honors of scholarship! for at that time his ambition was always climbing up the apparently inaccessible heights of fame,—fame, that he then imagined was the greatest glory any human being could aspire to. He smiled as he recollected this, and thought how changed he was since then! What a difference between the former discontented mutability of his nature, and the deep, unswerving calm of patience that characterized it now! Learning and scholarship? these were the mere child's alphabet of things,—and fame was a passing breath that ruffled for one brief moment the on-rushing flood of time—a bubble blown in the air to break into nothingness. Thus much wisdom he had acquired,—and what more? A great deal more! he had won the difficult comprehension of HIMSELF; he had grasped the priceless knowledge that man has no enemy save THAT WHICH IS WITHIN HIM, and that the pride of a rebellious Will is the parent Sin from which all others are generated. The old Scriptural saying is true for all time, that through pride the angels fell; and it is only through humility that they will ever rise again. Pride! the proud Will that is left FREE by Divine Law, to work for itself and answer for itself, and wreak upon its own head the punishment of its own errors,—the Will that once voluntarily crushed down, in the dust at the Cross of Christ, with these words truly drawn from the depths of penitence, "Lord, not as I will, but as Thou wilt!" is straightway lifted up from its humiliation, a supreme, stately Force, resistless, miraculous, world-commanding;—smoothing the way for all greatness and all goodness, and guiding the happy Soul from joy to joy, from glory to glory, till Heaven itself is reached and the perfection of all love and life begins. For true humility is not slavish, as some people imagine, but rather royal, since, while acknowledging the supremacy of God, it claims close kindred with Him, and is at once invested with all the diviner virtues. Fame and wealth, the two perishable prizes for which men struggle with one another in ceaseless and cruel combat, bring no absolute satisfaction in the end—they are toys that please for a time and then grow wearisome. But the conquering of Self is a battle in which each fresh victory bestows a deeper content, a larger happiness, a more perfect peace,—and neither poverty, sickness, nor misfortune can quench the courage, or abate the ardor, of the warrior who is absorbed in a crusade against his own worser passions. Egotism is the vice of this age,—the maxim of modern society is "each man for himself, and no one for his neighbor"—and in such a state of things, when personal interest or advantage is the chief boon desired, we cannot look for honesty in either religion, politics, or commerce. Nor can we expect any grand work to be done in art or literature. When pictures are painted and books are written for money only,—when laborers take no pleasure in labor save for the wage it brings,—when no real enthusiasm is shown in anything except the accumulation of wealth,—and when all the finer sentiments and nobler instincts of men are made subject to Mammon worship, is any one so mad and blind as to think that good can come of it? Nothing but evil upon evil can accrue from such a system,—and those who have prophetic eyes to see through the veil of events can perceive, even now, the not far distant end—namely, the ruin of the country that has permitted itself to degenerate into a mere nation of shopkeepers,—and something worse than ruin,—degradation!

It was past eight in the evening when Alwyn, after having spent a couple of days in bright little Brussels, arrived at Cologne. Most travelers know to their cost how noisy, narrow, and unattractive are the streets of this ancient Colonia Agrippina of the Romans,—how persistent and wearying is the rattle of the vehicles over the rough, cobbly stones— how irritating to the nerves is the incessant shrieking whistle and clank of the Rhine steamboats as they glide in, or glide out, from the cheerless and dirty pier. But at night, when these unpleasant sounds have partially subsided, and the lights twinkle in the shop-windows, and the majestic mass of the Cathedral casts its broad shadow on the moonlit Dom-Platz, and a few soldiers, with clanking swords and glittering spurs, come marching out from some dark stone archway, and the green gleam of the river sparkles along in luminous ripples,—then it is that a something weird and mystical creeps over the town, and the glamour of ancient historical memories begins to cling about its irregular buildings,—one thinks of the legendary Three Kings, and believes in them, too,—of St. Ursula and her company of virgins; of Marie de Medicis dying alone in that tumbled-down house in the Stern-gasse,—of Rubens, who, it is said, here first saw the light of this world,—of an angry Satan flinging his Teufelstein from the Seven Mountains in an impotent attempt to destroy the Dom; and gradually, the indestructible romantic spell of the Rhine steals into the spirit of common things that were unlovely by day, and makes the old city beautiful under the sacred glory of the stars.

Alwyn dined at his hotel, and then, finding it still too early to retire to rest, strolled slowly across the Platz, looking up at the sublime God's Temple above him, the stately Cathedral, with its wondrously delicate carvings and flying buttresses, on which the moonlight glittered like little points of pale flame. He knew it of old; many and many a time had he taken train from Bonn, for the sole pleasure of spending an hour in gazing on that splendid "sermon in stone,"—one of the grandest testimonies in the world of man's instinctive desire to acknowledge and honor, by his noblest design and work, the unseen but felt majesty of the Creator. He had a great longing to enter it now, and ascended the steps with that intention; but, much to his vexation, the doors were shut. He walked from the side to the principal entrance; that superb western frontage which is so cruelly blocked in by a dwarfish street of the commonest shops and meanest houses,—and found that also closed against him. Disappointed and sorry, he went back again to the side of the colossal structure, and stood on the top of the steps, close to the central barred doors, studying the sculptured saints in the niches, and feeling a sudden, singular impression of extreme LONELINESS,—a sense of being shut out, as it were, from some high festival in which he would gladly have taken part.

Not a cloud was in the sky, . . . the evening was one of the most absolute calm, and a delicious warmth pervaded the air,—the warmth of a fully declared and balmy spring. The Platz was almost deserted,— only a few persons crossed it now and then, like flitting shadows,—and somewhere down in one of the opposite streets a long way off, there was a sound of men's voices singing a part-song. Presently, however, this distant music ceased, and a deep silence followed. Alwyn still remained in the sombre shade of the cathedral archway, arguing with himself against the foolish and unaccountable depression that had seized him, and watching the brilliant May moon soar up higher and higher in the heavens; when,—all at once, the throbbing murmur of the great organ inside the Dom startled him from pensive dreaminess into swift attention. He listened,—the rich, round notes thundered through the stillness with forceful and majestic harmony; anon, wierd tones, like the passionate lament of Sarasate's "Zigeunerweisen" floated around and above him: then, a silvery chorus of young voices broke forth in solemn unison:

"Kyrie Eleison! Christe Eleison! Kyrie Eleison!"

A faint cold tremor crept through his veins,—his heart beat violently,—again he vainly strove to open the great door. Was there a choir practising inside at this hour of the night? Surely not! Then,—from whence had this music its origin? Stooping, he bent his ear to the crevice of the closed portal,—but, as suddenly as they had begun, the harmonies ceased; and all was once more profoundly still.

Drawing a long, deep breath, he stood for a moment amazed and lost in thought—these sounds, he felt sure, were not of earth but of heaven! they had the same ringing sweetness as those he had heard on the Field of Ardath! What might they mean to him, here and now? Quick as a flash the answer came—DEATH! God had taken pity upon his solitary earth wanderings,—and the prayers of Edris had shortened his world-exile and probation! He was to die! and that solemn singing was the warning,—or the promise,—of his approaching end!

Yes! it must be so, he decided, as, with a strange, half-sad peace at his heart, he quietly descended the steps of the Dom,-he would perhaps be permitted to finish the work he was at present doing,—and then,—then, the poet-pen would be laid aside forever, chains would be undone, and he would be set at liberty! Such was his fixed idea. Was he glad of the prospect, he asked himself? Yes, and No! For himself he was glad; but in these latter days he had come to understand the thousand wordless wants and aspirations of mankind,—wants and aspirations to which only the Poet can give fitting speech; he had begun to see how much can be done to cheer and raise and ennoble the world by even ONE true, brave, earnest, and unselfish worker,—and he had attained to such a height in sympathetic comprehension of the difficulties and drawbacks of others, that he had ceased to consider himself at all in the question, either with regard to the Present or the immortal Future,—he was, without knowing it, in the simple, unconsciously perfect attitude of a Soul that is absolutely at one with God, and that thus, in involuntary

God-likeness, is only happy in the engendering of happiness. He believed that, with the Divine help, he could do a lasting good for his fellow-men,—and to this cause he was willing to sacrifice everything that pertained to his own mere personal advantage. But now,—now,—or so he imagined,—he was not to be allowed to pursue his labors of love,—his trial was to end suddenly,—and he, so long banished from his higher heritage, was to be restored to it without delay,—restored and drawn back to the land of perfect loveliness where Edris, his Angel, waited for him, his saint, his queen, his bride!

A thrill of ecstatic joy rushed through him,—joy intermingled with an almost supernal pain. For he had not as yet said enough to the world,—the world of many afflictions,—the little Sorrowful Star covered with toiling, anxious, deluded God-forgetting millions, in every unit of which was a spark of Heavenly flame, a germ of the spiritual essence that makes the angel, if only fostered aright.

Lost in a deep reverie, his footsteps had led him unconsciously to the Rhine bridge,—paying the customary fee, he walked about half-way across it, and stood for a while listening to the incessant swift rush of the river beneath him. Lights twinkled from the boats moored on either side,—the moon poured down a wide shower of white beams on the rapid flood,—the city, dusky and dream-like, crowned with the majestic towers of the Dom, looked picturesquely calm and grand—it was a night of perfect beauty and wondrous peace. And he was to die!—to die and leave all this, the present fairness of the world,—he was to depart, with, as he felt, his message half unspoken,—he was to be made eternally happy, while many of the thousands he left behind were, through ignorance, wilfully electing to be eternally miserable! A great, almost divine longing to save ONE,—only ONE downward drifting soul, possessed him,—and the comprehension of Christ's Sacrifice was no longer a mystery! Yet he was so certain that death, sudden and speedy closely, awaited him that he seemed to feel it in the very air,—not like a coming chill of dread, but like the soft approach of some holy seraph bringing benediction. It mattered little to him that he was actually in the very plenitude of health and strength,—that perhaps in all his life he had never felt such a keen delight in the physical perfection of his manhood as now,—death, without warning and at a touch, could smite down the most vigorous, and to be so smitten, he believed, was his imminent destiny. And while he lingered on the bridge, fancy-perplexed between grief and joy, a small window opened in a quaint house that bent its bulging gables crookedly over the gleaming water, and a girl, holding a small lamp, looked out for a moment. Her face, fresh and smiling, was fair to see against the background of dense shadow,—the light she carried flashed like a star,—and leaning down from the lattice she sang half-timidly, half mischievously, the first two or three bars of the old song. "Du, du, liegst in mein Herzen. . . !" "Ah! Gute Nacht, Liebchen!" said a man's voice below.

"Gute Nacht! Schlafen sie wohl!"

A light laugh, and the window closed, "Good-night! Sleep well!" Love's best wish!—and for some sad souls life's last hope,—a "good-night and sleep well!" Poor tired World, for whose weary inhabitants oftentimes the greatest blessing is sleep! Good-night! sleep well! but the sleep implies waking.—waking to a morning of pleasure or sorrow,— or labor that is only lightened by,—Love! Love!—love divine,—love human,—and, sweetest love of all for us, as Christ has taught when both divine and human are mingled in one!

Alwyn, glancing up at the clustering stars, hanging like pendent fire-jewels above him, thought of this marvel-glory of Love,—this celestial visitant who, on noiseless pinions, comes flying divinely into the poorest homes, transfiguring common life with ethereal radiance, making toil easy, giving beauty to the plainest faces and poetry to the dullest brains. Love! its tremulous hand-clasp,—its rapturous kiss,—the speechless eloquence it gives to gentle eyes!— the grace it bestows on even the smallest gift from lover to beloved, were such gift but a handful of meadow blossoms tied with some silken threads of hair!

Not for the poet creator of "Nourhulma" such love any more,—had he not drained the cup of Passion to the dregs in the far Past, and tasted its mixed sweetness and bitterness to no purpose save self-indulgence? All that was over;—and yet, as he walked away from the bridge, back to his hotel in the quiet moonlight, he thought what a transcendent thing Love might be, even on earth, between two whose spirits were SPIRITUALLY AKIN,—whose lives were like two notes played in tuneful concord,—whose hearts beat echoing faith and tenderness to one another,—and who held their love as a sacred bond of union—a gift from God, not to be despoiled by that rough familiarity which surely brings contempt. And then before his fancy appeared to float the radiant visage of Edris, half-child, half-angel,—he seemed to see her beautiful eyes, so pure, so clear, so unshadowed by any knowledge of sin,—and the exquisite lines of a poet-contemporary, whose work he specially admired, occurred to him with singular suggestiveness:

> "Oh, thou'lt confess that love from man to maid
> Is more than kingdoms,—more than light and shade
> In sky-built gardens where the minstrels dwell,
> And more than ransom from the bonds of Hell.
> Thou wilt, I say, admit the truth of this,
> And half relent that, shrinking from a kiss,
> Thou didst consign me to mine own disdain,
> Athwart the raptures of a vision'd bliss.
>
> "I'll seek no joy that is not linked with thine,
> No touch of hope, no taste of holy wine,
> And after death, no home in any star,
> That is not shared by thee, supreme, afar
>
> As here thou'rt first and foremost of all things!
> Glory is thine, and gladness, and the wings
> That wait on thought, when, in thy spirit-sway,
> Thou dost invest a realm unknown to kings!"

Had not she, Edris, consigned him to his "own disdain, Athwart the raptures of a visioned bliss?" Ay! truly and deservedly!—and this disdain of himself had now reached its culminating point,—namely, that he did not consider himself worthy of her love,—or worthy to do aught than sink again into far spaces of darkness and perpetually retrospective Memory, there to explore the uttermost depths of anguish, and count up his errors one by one from the very beginning of life, in every separate phase he had passed through, till he had penitently striven his best to atone for them all! Christ had atoned! yes,—but was it not almost base on his part to shield himself with that Divine Light and do nothing further? He could not yet thoroughly grasp the amazing truth that ONE ABSOLUTELY PURE act of faith in Christ, blots out Past Sin forever,—it seemed too marvellous and great a boon!

When he retired to rest that night he was fully and firmly PREPARED TO DIE. With this expectation upon him he was nevertheless happy and tranquil. The line—"Glory is thine, and gladness, and the wings" haunted him, and he repeated it over and over again without knowing why. Wings! the brilliant shafts of radiance that part angels from mortals,—wings, that, after all, are not really wings, but lambent rays of living lightning, of which neither painter nor poet has any true conception, . . . long, dazzling rays such as encircled God's maiden, Edris, with an arch of roseate effulgence, so that the very air was sunset-colored in the splendor of her presence! How if she were a wingless angel,—made woman?

"Glory is thine, and gladness, and the wings!" And with the name of his angel-love upon his lips he closed his eyes and sank into a deep and dreamless slumber.

XL

In the Cathedral

A booming, thunderous, yet mellow sound! a grand, solemn, sonorous swing of full and weighty rhythm, striking the air with deep, slowly measured resonance like the rolling of close cannon! Awake, all ye people!—Awake to prayer and praise! for the Night is past and sweet Morning reddens in the east, . . . another Day is born,—a day in which to win God's grace and pardon,—another wonder of Light, Movement, Creation, Beauty, Love! Awake, awake! Be glad and grateful for the present joy of life,—this life, dear harbinger of life to come! open your eyes, ye drowsy mortals, to the divine blue of the beneficent sky, the golden beams of the sun, the color of flowers, the foliage of trees, the flash of sparkling waters!—open your ears to the singing of birds, the whispering of winds, the gay ripple of children's laughter, the soft murmurs of home affection,—for all these things are freely bestowed upon you with each breaking dawn, and will you offer unto God No thanksgiving?—Awake! Awake! the Voice you have yourselves set in your high Cathedral towers reproaches your lack of love with its iron tongue, and summons you all to worship Him the Ever-Glorious, through whose mercy alone you live!

To and fro,—to and fro,—gravely persistent, sublimely eloquent, the huge, sustained, and heavy monotone went thudding through the stillness,—till, startled from his profound sleep by such loud, lofty, and incessant clangor, Alwyn turned on his pillow and listened, half-aroused, half-bewildered,—then, remembering where he was, he understood; it was the great Bell of the Dom pealing forth its first summons to the earliest Mass. He lay quiet for a little while, dreamily counting the number of reverberations each separate stroke sent quivering on the air,—but presently, finding it impossible to sleep again, he got up, and drawing aside the curtain looked out of the window of his room, which fronted on the Platz. Though it was not yet six o'clock, the city was all astir,—the Rhinelanders are an early working people, and to see the sun rise is not with them a mere fiction of poesy, but a daily fact. It was one of the loveliest of lovely spring mornings—the sky was clear as a pale, polished sapphire, and every little bib of delicate carving and sculpture on the Dom stood out from its groundwork with microscopically beautiful distinctness. And as his gaze rested on the perfect fairness of the day, a strange and sudden sense of rapturous anticipation possessed his mind,—he felt as one prepared for some high and exquisite happiness,—some great and wondrous celebration or feast of joy! The thoughts of death, on which he had brooded so persistently during the past yester-eve, had fled, leaving no trace behind,—only a keen and vigorous delight in life absorbed him now. It was good to be alive, even on this present earth! it was good to see, to feel, to know! and there was much to be thankful for in the mere capability of easy and healthful breathing!

Full of a singular light-heartedness, he hummed a soft tune to himself as he moved about his room,—his desire to view the interior of the Cathedral had not abated with sleep, but had rather augmented,— and he resolved to visit it now, while he had the chance of beholding it in all the impressive splendor of uncrowded tranquillity. For he knew that by the time he was dressed, the first Mass would be over,—the priests and people would be gone,—and he would be alone to enjoy the magnificence of the place in full poet-luxury,—the luxury of silence and solitude. He attired himself quickly, and with a vaguely nervous eagerness,—he was in almost as great a hurry to enter the Dom as he had been to arrive at the Field of Ardath! The same feverish impatience was upon him—impatience that he was conscious of, yet could not account for,—his fancy busied itself with a whole host of memories, and fragments of half-forgotten love-songs he had written in his youth, came back to him without his wish or will,—songs that he instinctively felt belonged to his Past, when as "Sah-luma" he had won golden opinions in Al-Kyris. And though they were but echoes, they seemed this morning to touch him with half-pleasing, half-tender suggestiveness,—two lines especially from the Idyl of Roses he had penned so long,—ah! so very long ago,—came floating through his brain like a message sent from some other world,—

> *"By the pureness of love shall our glory in loving increase,*
> *And the roses of passion for us are the lilies of peace."*

The "lilies of peace" and the flowers of Ardath,—the "roses of passion" and the love of Edris, these were all mingled almost unconsciously in his thoughts, as with an inexplicable, happy sense of tremulous expectation,—expectation of he knew not what-he went, walking as one in haste, across the broad Platz and ascended the steps of the Cathedral. But the side-entrance was fast shut, as on the previous night,—he therefore made his rapid way round to the great western door. That stood open,—the bell had long ago ceased,—Mass was over,—and all was profoundly still.

Out of the warm sunlit air he stepped into the vast, cool, clear-obscure, white glory of the stately shrine,—with bared head and noiseless, reverent feet, he advanced a little way up the nave, and then stood motionless, every artistic perception in him satisfied, soothed, and entranced anew, as in his student-days, by the tranquil grandeur of the scene. What majestic silence! What hallowed peace! How jewel-like the radiance of the sun pouring through the rich stained glass on those superb carved pillars, that, like petrified stems of forest-trees, bear lightly up the lofty, vaulted roof to that vast height suggestive of a white sky rather than stone!

Moving on slowly further toward the altar, he was suddenly seized by an overpowering impression,—a memory that rushed upon him with a sort of shock, albeit it was only the memory of a tune!—a wild melody, haunting and passionate, rang in his eras,—the melody that Sarasate, the Orpheus of Spain, had evoked from the heart of his speaking violin,—the sobbing love-lament of the "Zigeunerweisen"—the weird minor-music that had so forcibly suggested—What? THIS VERY PLACE!—these snowy columns,—this sculptured sanctity—this flashing light of rose and blue and amber,—this wondrous hush of consecrated calm! What next? Dear God! Sweet Christ! what next? The face of Edris?—Would that heavenly countenance shine suddenly though those rainbow-colored beams that struck slantwise down toward him?—and should he presently hear her dulcet voice charming the silence into deeper ecstasy?

Overcome by a sensation that was something like fear, he stopped abruptly, and leaning against one of the quaint old oaken benches, strove to control the quick, excited throbbing of his heart,—then gradually, very gradually he become conscious that HE WAS NOT ALONE,—another besides himself was in the church,—another, whom it was necessary for him to see!

He could not tell how he first grew to be certain of this,—but he was soon so completely possessed by the idea, that for a moment he dared not raise his eyes, or move! Some invincible force held him there spell-bound, yet trembling in every limb,—and while he thus waited hesitatingly, the great organ woke up in a glory of tuneful utterance,—wave after wave of richest harmony rolled through the stately aisles and. . . "Kyrie eleison! Kyrie eleison!" rang forth in loud, full, and golden-toned chorus!

Lifting his head, he stared wonderingly around him; not a living creature was visible in all the spacious width and length of the cathedral! His lips parted,—he felt as though he could scarcely breathe,—strong shudders ran through him, and he was penetrated by a pleasing terror that was almost a physical pang,—an agonized entrancement, like death or the desire of love! Presently, mastering himself by a determined effort, he advanced steadily with the absorbed air of one who is drawn along by magnetic power. . . steadily and slowly up the nave, . . . and as he went, the music surged more tumultuously among the vaulted arches,—there was a faint echo afar off, as of tinkling crystal bells; and at each onward step he gained a new access of courage, strength, firmness, and untrammelled ease, till every timorous doubt and fear had fled away, and he stood directly in front of the altar railing, gazing at the enshrined Cross, and seeing for the moment nothing save that Divine Symbol alone. And still the organ played, and still the voices sang,—he knew these sounds were not of earth, and he also knew that they were intended to convey a meaning to him,—but WHAT meaning?

All at once, moved by a sudden impulse, he turned toward the right hand side of the altar, where the great statue of St. Christopher stands, and where one of the loveliest windows in the world gleams like a great carven gem aloft, filtering the light through a myriad marvellous shades of color, and there he beheld, kneeling on the stone pavement, one solitary worshipper,—a girl. Her hands were clasped, and her face was bent upon them so that her features were not visible,—but the radiance from the window fell on her uncovered golden hair, encircling it with the glistening splendor of a heavenly nimbus,—and round her slight, devotional figure, rays of azure and rose jasper and emerald, flickered in wide and lustrous patterns, like the glow of the setting sun on a translucent sea. How very still she was! . . . how fervently absorbed in prayer!

Vaguely startled, and thrilled by an electric, indefinable instinct, Alwyn went toward her with hushed and reverential tread, his eyes dwelling upon the drooping, delicate outline of her form with fascinated and eager attention. She was clad in gray,—a soft, silken, dove-like gray, that clung about her in picturesque, daintily draped folds,—he approached her still more nearly, and then could scarcely refrain from a loud cry of amazement! What flowers were those she wore at her breast!—so white, so star-like, so suggestive of paradise lilies new-gathered? Were they not the flowers of ARDATH? Dizzy with the sudden tumult of his own emotions, he dropped on his knees beside her,—she did not stir! Was she REAL?—or a phantom? Trembling violently, he touched her garment—it was of tangible, smooth texture, actual enough, if the sense of touch could be relied upon. In an agony of excitement and suspense he lost all remembrance of time, place, or custom,—her bewildering presence must be explained,—he must know who she was,—he must speak to her,—speak, if he died for it!

"Pardon me!" he whispered faintly, scarcely conscious of his own words; "I fancy,—I think,—we have met,—before! May I, . . . dare I, . . . ask your name?"

Slowly she unclasped her gently folded hands; slowly, very slowly, she lifted her bent head, and smiled at him! Oh, the lovely light upon her face! Oh, the angel glory of those strange, sweet eyes!

"My name is EDRIS!"—she said, and as the pure bell-like tone of her voice smote the air with its silvery sound, the mysterious music of the organ and the invisible singers throbbed away,—away,—away,—into softer and softer echoes, that died at last tremulously and with a sigh, as of farewell, into the deepest silence.

"EDRIS!"—In a trance of passionate awe and rapture he caught her hand,—the warm, delicate hand that yielded to his strong clasp in submissive tenderness,—pulsations of terror, pain, and wild joy, all commingled, rushed through him,—with adoring, wistful gaze he scanned every feature of that love-smiling countenance,—a countenance no longer lustrous with Heaven's blinding glory, but only most maiden-like and innocently fair,—dazzled, perplexed, and half afraid, he could not at once grasp the true comprehension of his ineffable delight! He had no doubt of her identity—he knew her well! she was his own heartworshipped Angel,—but on what errand had she wandered out of paradise? Had she come once more, as on the Field of Ardath, to comfort him for a brief space with the beauty of her visible existence, or did she bring from Heaven the warrant for his death?

"Edris!" he said, as softly as one may murmur a prayer, "Edris, my life, my love! Speak to me again! make me sure that I am not dreaming!

Tell me where I have failed in my sworn faith since we parted; teach me how I must still further atone! Is this the hour appointed for my spirit's ransom?—has this dear and sacred hand I hold, brought me my quittance of earth?—and have I so soon won the privilege to die?"

As he spoke, she rose and stood erect, with all the glistening light of the stained window falling royally about her,—and he obeying her mute gesture, rose also and faced her in wondering ecstasy, half expecting to see her vanish suddenly in the sun-rays that poured through the Cathedral, even as she had vanished before like a white cloud absorbed in clear space. But no! She remained quiet as a tame bird,—her eyes met his with beautiful trust and tenderness,—and when she answered him, her low, sweet accents thrilled to his heart with a pathetic note of HUMAN affection, as well as of angelic sympathy!

"Theos, my Beloved, I am ALL THINE!" she said, a holy rapture vibrating through her exquisite voice.—"Thine now, in mortal life as in immortal!—one with thee in nature and condition,—pent up in perishable clay, even as thou art,—subject to sorrow, and pain, and weariness,—willing to share with thee thine earthly lot,—ready to take my part in thy grief or joy! By mine own choice have I come hither,—sinless, yet not exempt from sin, but safe in Christ! Every time thou hast renounced the desire of thine own happiness, so much the nearer hast thou drawn me to thee; every time thou hast prayed God for my peace, rather than thine own, so much the closer has my existence been linked with thine! And now, O my Poet, my lord, my king!—we are together forever more,—together in the brief Present, as in the eternal Future!—the solitary heaven-days of Edris are past, and her mission is not Death, but Love!"

Oh, the transcendent beauty of that warm flush upon her face!—the splendid hope, faith, and triumph of her attitude! What strange miracle was here accomplished!—an Angel had become human for the sake of love, even as light substantiates itself in the colors of flowers!—the Eden lily had consented to be gathered,—the paradise dove had fluttered down to earth! Breathless, bewildered, lifted to a height of transport beyond all words, Alwyn gazed upon her in entranced, devout silence,—the vast cathedral seemed to swing round and round in great glittering circles, and nothing was real, nothing steadfast, but that slight, sweet maiden in her soft gray robes, with the Ardath-blossoms gleaming white against her breast! Angel she was,—angel she ever would be,—and yet—what did she SEEM? Naught but:

"A child-like woman, wise and very fair,
Crowned with the garland of her golden hair!"

This, and no more,—and yet in this was all earth and all heaven comprised!—He gazed and gazed, overwhelmed by the amazement of his own bliss,—he could have gazed upon her so in speechless ravishment for hours, when, with a gesture of infinite grace and appeal, she stretched out her hands toward him:

"Speak to me, dearest one!" she murmured wistfully—"Tell me,— am I welcome?"

"O exquisite humility!—O beautiful maiden-timid hesitation! Was she,—even she, God's Angel, so far removed from pride, as to be uncertain of her lover's reception of such a gift of love? Roused from his half-swooning sense of wonder, he caught those gentle hands, and laid them tenderly against his breast,—tremblingly, and all devoutly, he drew the lovely, yielding form into his arms, close to his heart,—with dazzled sight he gazed down into that pure, perfect face, those clear and holy eyes shining like new-created stars beneath the soft cloud of clustering fair hair!

"Welcome!" he echoed, in a tone that thrilled with passionate awe and ecstasy;—"My Edris! My Saint! My Queen! Welcome, more welcome than the first flowers seen after winter snows!—welcome, more welcome than swift rescue to one in dire peril!—welcome, my Angel, into the darkness of mortal things, which haply so sweet a Presence shall make bright! O sacred innocence that I am not worthy to shield! . . . O sinless beauty that I am all unfitted to claim or possess! Welcome to my life, my heart, my soul! Welcome, sweet Trust, sweet Hope, sweet Love, that as Christ lives, I will never wrong, betray, or resign again through all the glory spaces of far Eternity!"

As he spoke, his arms closed more surely about her,—his lips met hers,—and in the mingled human and divine rapture of that moment, there came a rushing noise, as of thousands of wings beating the air, followed by a mighty wave of music that rolled approachingly and then departingly through and through the Cathedral arches—and a Voice, clear and resonant as a silver clarion, proclaimed aloud:

"Those whom GOD hath joined together, let no MAN put asunder!"

Then, with a surging, jubilant sound, like the sea in a storm, the music seemed to tread past in a measured march of stately harmony,— and presently there was silence once more,—the silence and sunshine of the morning pouring through the rose windows of the church and sparkling on the Cross above the Altar,—the silence of a love made perfect,—of twin souls made One!

And then Edris drew herself gently from her lover's embrace and raised her head,—putting her hand confidingly in his, a lovely smile played on her sweetly parted lips:

"Take me, Theos," she said softly, "Lead me,—into the World!"

Slowly the great side-doors of the Cathedral swung back on their hinges,—and out on the steps in a glorious blaze of sunlight came Poet and Angel together. The one, a man in the full prime of splendid and vigorous manhood,—the other, a maiden, timid and sweet, robed in gray attire with a posy of white flowers at her throat. A simple girl, and most distinctly human,—the fresh, pure color reddened in her cheeks,—the soft springtide wind fanned her gold hair, and the sunbeams seemed to dance about her in a bright revel of amaze and curiosity. Her lustrous eyes dwelt on the busy Platz below with a vaguely compassionate wonder—a look that suggested some far foreknowledge of things, that at the same time were strangely unfamiliar. Hand in hand with her companion she stood,—while he, holding her fast, drunk in the pureness of her beauty, the love-light of her glance, the holy radiance of her smile, till every sense in him was spiritualized anew by the passionate faith and reverence in his heart, the marvellous glory that had fallen upon his life, the nameless rapture that possessed his soul!—To have knelt at her feet, and bowed his head before her in worshipping silence, would have been to follow the strongest impulse in him,—but she had given him a higher duty than this. He was to "Lead Her,"—lead her "into the world!"—the dreary, dark world, so unfitted to receive such brightness,—she had come to him clad in all the sacred weakness of womanhood; and it was his proud privilege to guard and shelter her from evil,—from the evil in others, but chiefly from the evil in himself. No taint must touch that spotless life with which God had entrusted him!—sorrow might come—nay, Must come, since, so long as humanity errs, so long must angels grieve,—sorrow, but not sin! A grand, awed sense of responsibility filled him,—a responsibility that he accepted with passionate gratitude and joy. . . he had attained a vaster dignity than any king on any throne, . . . and all the visible Universe was transfigured into a golden pageant of loveliness and light, fairer than the fabled Valley of Avilion!

Yet still he kept her close beside him on the steps of the mighty Dom, half-longing, half-hesitating to take her further, and ever and anon assailed by a dreamy doubt as to whether she might not even now pass away from him suddenly and swiftly, as a mist fading into heaven,—when all at once the sound of beating drums and martial trumpets struck loudly on the quiet morning air. A brilliant regiment of mounted Uhlans emerged from an opposite street, and cantered sharply across the Platz and over the Rhine-bridge, with streaming pennons, burnished helmets and accoutrements glistening in a long compact line of silvery white, that vanished as speedily as it had appeared, like a winding flash of meteor flame. Alwyn drew a deep, quick breath; the sight of those armed soldiers roused him to the fact that he was actually in the turmoil of present daily events,—that his supernal happiness was no vision, but REALITY,—that Edris, his Spirit-love, was with him in tangible human guise of flesh and blood,—though how such a mysterious marvel had been accomplished, he knew no more than scientists know how the lovely life of green leaf and perfect flower can still be existent in seeds that have lain dormant and dry in old tombs for thousands of years! And as he looked at her proudly,—adoringly,—she raised her beautiful, innocent, questioning eyes to his.

"This is a city?" she asked—"a city of men who labor for good, and serve each other?"

"Alas, not so, my sweet!" he answered, his voice trembling with its own infinite tenderness; "there is no city on the sad Earth where men do not labor for mere vanity's sake, and oppose each other!"

Her inquiring gaze softened into a celestial compassion.

"Come,—let us go!" she said gently. "We twain, made one in love and faith, must hasten to begin our work!—darkness gathers and deepens over the Sorrowful Star,—but we, perchance, with Christ's most holy Blessing, may help to lift the Shadows into Light!"

AWAY IN A SHELTERED MOUNTAINOUS retreat, apart from the louder clamor of the world, the Poet and his heavenly companion dwell in peace together. Their love, their wondrous happiness, no mortal language can define,—for spiritual love perfected as far exceeds material passion as the steadfast glory of the sun outshines the nickering of an earthly taper. Few, very few, there are who recognize, or who attain, such joy,—for men chiefly occupy themselves with the SEMBLANCES of things, and therefore fail to grasp all high realities. Perishable beauty,—perishable fame,—these are mere appearances; imperishable Worth is the only positive and lasting good, and in the search for imperishable Worth alone, the seeker must needs encounter Angels unawares!

But for those whose pleasure it is to doubt and deny all spiritual life and being, the history of Theos Alwyn can be disposed of with much languid ease and cold logic, as a foolish chimera scarce worth narrating. Practically viewed, there is nothing wonderful in it, since it can all be traced to a powerful exertion of magnetic skill. Tranced into a dream bewilderment by the arts of the mystic Chaldean, Heliobas,—tricked into visiting the Field of Ardath, what more likely than that a real earth-born maiden, trained to her part, should have met the dreamer there, and, with the secret aid of the hermit Elezar, continued his strange delusion? What more fitting as a sequel to the whole, than that the same maiden should have been sent to him again in the great Rhine Cathedral, to complete the deception and satisfy his imagination by linking her life finally with his?—It is a perfectly simple explanation of what some credulous souls might be inclined to consider a mystery,—and let the dear, wise, oracular people who cannot admit any mystery in anything, and who love to trace all seeming miracles to clever imposture, accept this elucidation by all means,—they will be able to fit every incident of the story into such an hypothesis, with most admirable and consecutive neatness! Al-Kyris was truly a Vision,—the rest was,—What? Merely the working of a poetic imagination under mesmeric influence!

So be it! The Poet knows the truth,—but what are Poets? Only the Prophets and Seers! Only the Eyes of Time, which clearly behold Heaven's Fact beyond this world's Fable. Let them sing if they choose, and we will hear them in our idle hours,—we will give them a little of our gold,—a little of our grudging praise, together with much of our private practical contempt and misprisal! So say the unthinking and foolish—so will they ever say,—and hence it is, that though the fame of Theos Alwyn widens year by year, and his sweet clarion harp of Song rings loud warning, promise, hope, and consolation above the noisy tumult of the whirling age, people listen to him merely in vague wonderment and awe, doubting his prophet utterance, and loth to put away their sin. But he, never weary in well-doing, works on, . . . ever regardless of Self, caring nothing for Fame, but giving all the riches of his thought for Love. Clear, grand, pure, and musical, his writings fill the time with hope and passionate faith and courage,—his inspiration fails not, and can never fail, since Edris is his fount of ecstasy,—his name, made glorious by God's blessing, shall never, as in his perished Past, be again forgotten!

And what of Edris? What of the "Flower-crowned Wonder" of the Field of Ardath, strayed for a while out of her native Heaven? Does the world know her marvellous origin? Perhaps the mystic Heliobas knows,—perhaps even good Frank Villiers has hazarded a reverent guess at his friend's great secret—but to the uninstructed, what does she seem?

Nothing but a Woman, Most Pure Womanly; a woman whose influence on all is strangely sweet and lasting,—whose spirit overflows with tenderest sympathy for the many wants and sorrows of mankind,—whose voice charms away care,—whose smile engenders peace,—whose eyes, lustrous and thoughtful, are unclouded by any shadow of sin,—and on whose serene beauty the passing of years leaves no visible trace. That she is fair and wise, joyous, radiant, and holy is apparent to all,—but only the Poet, her lover and lord, her subject and servant, can tell how truly his Edris is not so much sweet woman as most perfect Angel! A Dream of Heaven made human! . . . Let some of us hesitate ere we doubt the Miracle; for we are sleepers and dreamers all,—and the hour is close at hand when—we shall Wake.

The End

A Note About the Author

Marie Corelli (1855–1924) was an English novelist. Born Mary Mackay in London, she was sent to a Parisian convent to be educated in 1866. Returning to England in 1870, Corelli worked as a pianist and began her literary career with the novel *A Romance of Two Worlds* (1886). A favorite writer of Winston Churchill and the British Royal Family, Corelli was the most popular author of her generation. Known for her interest in mysticism and the occult, she earned a reputation through works of fantasy, Gothic, and science fiction. From 1901 to 1924, she lived in Stratford-upon-Avon, where she continued to write novels, short story collections, and works of non-fiction. Corelli, whose works have been regularly adapted for film and the theater, was largely rejected by the male-dominated literary establishment of her time. Despite this, she is remembered today as a pioneering author who wrote for the public, not for the critics who sought to deny her talent.

A Note from the Publisher

Spanning many genres, from non-fiction essays to literature classics to children's books and lyric poetry, Mint Edition books showcase the master works of our time in a modern new package. The text is freshly typeset, is clean and easy to read, and features a new note about the author in each volume. Many books also include exclusive new introductory material. Every book boasts a striking new cover, which makes it as appropriate for collecting as it is for gift giving. Mint Edition books are only printed when a reader orders them, so natural resources are not wasted. We're proud that our books are never manufactured in excess and exist only in the exact quantity they need to be read and enjoyed.

Discover more of your favorite classics with Bookfinity™.

- Track your reading with custom book lists.
- Get great book recommendations for your personalized Reader Type.
- Add reviews for your favorite books.
- AND MUCH MORE!

Visit **bookfinity.com** and take the fun Reader Type quiz to get started.

Enjoy our classic and modern companion pairings!